The Complete Saga

COPPINS BRIDGE

The Complete Saga

Elizabeth Daish

Gainsborough Press

This edition published in 1996
by Gainsborough Press

First published in Great Britain in 1991 by Century

This edition published in 1992 by Arrow Books

1 3 5 7 9 10 8 6 4 2

Printed and bound in Great Britain by
Cox & Wyman Ltd, Reading, Berkshire

ISBN 0 752 90353 5

Contents

Dedication

For Derek, Simon and Sally

PART ONE

The Shop

Chapter 1

From the back of the newspaper office of the *County Press*, shadows glanced off the windows, receded and took shape as the clerk walked slowly to the main window at the front and fixed the oil-lamp on the shelf by the bulletin board. The shadows paused, trembled and grew thin as the clerk turned up the wick of the lamp with maddening deliberation and trimmed it with scissors before replacing the large glass globe over the flame.

Satisfied at last, and making the most of his fleeting power, he fastened a sheet of paper to the board which hung in the window, covering the last bulletin and making it lie true to each corner and then he stood back, as if awaiting applause.

Outside, the waiting crowd shifted and tried to get closer, craning their necks to read the latest news that had threatened for so long. 'What's it say?' A man at the back pushed through, fighting to glimpse the clear copperplate writing and a way opened for him as men heard his voice.

'It's war!' said a voice from the front.

'Another bloody war?' The thickset man in a well-cut light overcoat pushed him aside. 'Let me see. Another false alarm, more like! We've had enough of them to know they'll never fight when it comes to it. It's one thing to shout but another to fire the first shot when the whole of the Empire is against them.' He looked more closely at the board, the words of the bulletin making a lie of all his hopes.

'What is it? Read it out! We can't see.'

The man who had been pushed aside turned. 'I'll tell you what it says – *A state of war exists.*' He snorted with derision. 'And there are some fine words about us fighting for Queen and Country and doing our duty, but all it comes to is our boys fighting Kruger and being killed.' He shouldered a way out of the crowd. 'Read it yourselves. It's all there, even the date and the time it started: ten past three on the afternoon of October the eleventh in the year of 1899.'

Bert Cooper watched the men line up to read the news; the thin spiral of smoke from his cigar hung on the damp air. 'Another bloody war,' he muttered and spat into the gutter.

'It's right, then?' Walter Darwen stared at the window, now misted with the hot breath of those determined to wring the last vestige of drama from the announcement.

One of the local hotheads shouted but most of the men drifted away and ignored him. 'It's about time we taught the Boers a thing or two,' he bawled. 'They've asked for it long enough. Did you know they arrested one of our journalists? It's true. They know him on the *County Press*. The Boers said he spread lies about them moving troops.'

'What do you think?' asked Walter Darwen.

Bert took his cigar from his mouth and threw it away. 'It's true enough, I reckon, and bad for trade. All business in Johannesburg has stopped and hundreds of families are fleeing to the Cape.'

'That's right, Mr Darwen,' a man called Fred Cantor said eagerly, and Walter wondered if there was anything that Fred didn't hear when he sidled up so quietly. 'They've nothing left – no food nor clothes and no money. Driven out of their lawful homes.'

'I never thought the Boers would fight. I knew they'd push hard but not that hard.'

'We couldn't let them get away with it, Mr Cooper,' Fred said as if he had signed the Declaration himself. 'They stole the gold from the train to the Cape and they mean to take over the mines.'

'They're nothing but brigands,' said Bert. His face reddened.

'Do you have much tied up in gold?' Walter smiled. 'I bet that really hurt!'

'Gold is safe in the long run,' said Bert uneasily. 'Our troops will guard the mines as soon as they get there.'

'Thought you was against war, Bert?' said Walter.

'When it comes to protecting property, any man would fight,' stated Bert, with the same determined expression that he assumed when trying to convince the local council of something.

'Even you, Bert?' Walter turned up the collar of his overcoat and looked at the dark and starless sky. It was common knowledge that Bert had not been well enough to fight in the Irish Troubles and he had made a packet by it instead while widows and orphans were left by better men than he.

'They need professionals over there,' Bert said firmly.

A man in a black jacket and cloth cap waved unsteady arms as he tried to read the board. 'They think they can fight? I'll take them on, one at a time. I'll be on the first boat! Who will come and fight for our Queen? Who'll volunteer?'

Someone laughed. 'Go home before your missus catches you and gives you a box on the ear!' Others avoided his glassy stare as if he labelled them cowards. 'He's had one over the eight,' they said, but gave the enlistment booth a wide berth.

Rain fell in earnest now, as it can do after a sultry day on the Isle of Wight; men pulled down hats and turned up the collars of their jackets; or moved to shelter under the arches of the Town Hall on the other side of the road. The streets grew slimy with horse manure and newly-laid dust and the air hardly stirred. Bert muttered that the least they could do was to quote share prices to put his mind at rest, but Walter stood in the doorway and thought of his wife, Jane.

A woman, standing apart under the broad archway of the Town Hall, held a child wrapped in a shawl. The child coughed with dreary regularity, but even her mother took no notice.

Bert laughed grimly. 'So it's come to this. I don't know what Annie will say. She was against me putting my money outside the country and what she'd say if I joined up, I hate to think.' He walked with Walter to the sheltered side of the arches where Maudie Dove stood with the child. 'I should never have touched Transvaal Gold and I've a tidy sum there that Annie doesn't know of.'

Walter Darwen smiled. 'Too greedy, that's your trouble, Bert. Never could leave well alone, not even at school. Always wanted that bit more and devil take the loser.'

'You'll have something to worry *you* if it gets any worse,' Bert retorted.

Walter shrugged. His tone was still good-humoured, his smile without malice. 'That's one worry I don't have, too much money.'

'What of your business? Who'll look after it if you went? Who could you expect to look after your shop, your other business interests and that wife and family of yourn? Not to speak of the animals. Think about that and then tell me how to mind my own affairs.' He squinted up at the sky. 'Mark my words, Walt, there's a lot to think about. I'm off home before it pours down.'

The woman plucked at Walter's sleeve. 'What are they saying, Mr Darwen?' she asked timidly.

'War, Maudie!' he said brusquely, moving away. Something about Maudie Dove repelled him. It could be the whiff of dirty linen and the sour smell of the child in her arms, but whatever it was that made him turn away, now made him stop and look at the pale but pretty face, as if unwillingly attracted to her poverty.

'Wait a minute! Your Ben's in the army, isn't he? You poor little soul, he'll be one of the first to go.' Maudie sobbed and Walter shifted uneasily, pulling at his moustache and trying to look stern. 'You get off home and try not to worry. The little one should be inside in the dry.' He half-smiled as she stopped crying. 'That's right. Home for you and I'll ask my wife to look in on you tomorrow. It's come as a shock, but it might blow over and you'll have no cause to worry.'

'Thank you, Mr Darwen.' Maudie seemed to accept his clumsy reassurance as gospel truth and she hitched her shawl closer before stepping out into the rain. Walter stared after her, seeing the natural grace that shabby clothes and slovenly shoes couldn't hide completely. Maudie had been a pretty child, even if her mother was one for hanging round the barges when men came ashore with money in their pockets. Some said that the man who fathered Maudie was Dutch or Scandinavian, and it could be true if the fair hair and clear skin were anything to go by.

Jane would listen to no gossip about the girl, but then Jane didn't gossip like many of the women in the town. He looked down the road past the yellow lights reflected in the black wetness of the street, towards his shop, hidden beyond the bend and rise of the hill. He tried to make up his mind to go home. Would Jane weep for him if he went away? Would she want him as Maudie wanted her Ben? A twinge of anger mixed with sadness made him envy Ben. Not for Maudie, dirty little slut, but for having his woman waiting, ready and able to lie with him and give him the comfort a man needed.

It was near on four years, he thought, with wonder. How long could a man give up the pleasures of the bed? He glanced towards the Square and the lights of the Wheatsheaf spilling over the cobbles. Was that the only alternative?

The vision of Jane, his beautiful Jane, faded as he walked towards the lights. If he went home, what was the use? The doctor had been convincing. Eight babies in as many years and the last one dead, nearly taking Jane with her, were too much. Fred Cantor watched from a distance, sensing that Walt was in no mood for him, and recalling the time when Walt went mad and gave him a black eye because he tried to sell him some new-fangled sheaths they said stopped pregnancies. Hurt pride had made Walter lash out. Did all Newport know that Walter Darwen no longer slept with his wife? Fred knew from a snippet of gossip brought by his daughter who cleaned at the doctor's house. 'It's true, Dad. With seven children living she can't afford to risk dying to have another.'

A wave of beery warm air with promised comfort escaped thankfully from the stuffy snug bar. Walter hung his coat and hat on the bentwood stand and sat in his usual corner. 'Still wet out?' Olive Grace, the landlord's widowed sister, smiled and wiped the table top with an ale-damp rag and hoped that one day, the best-looking man in Newport would see her as a woman without a man. 'Quite a bit of excitement up at the *Press* window,' she remarked.

'I was there,' he grunted. 'The usual.' She brought a carefully full tankard of the best ale and Walter relaxed, viewing the room quizzically and listening. He made a place for Peter Fry and Olive brought more ale.

'What now, Walt? Not worried, are you? You haven't money tied up like Bert, so this won't hit you. Your shop does well enough and you get bits of local business.' He saw Walter's frown. 'Stands to reason, they couldn't take *you*. You did your duty and more in Ireland.'

'Might not be a case of being called back,' said Walter slowly.

'You'd be mad to volunteer! You couldn't leave Jane with all that lot, seven children and the shop!'

'So everyone tells me,' Walter said dryly, 'but as I see it, Kruger has been a nuisance in South Africa for thirty years and there's a lot of injustice. By the time he's finished, all out assets will have gone. He needs to be stopped before he does more harm and he needs to know we mean business.'

'So you want to run off to defend foreigners just to put money into Bert's pockets?' Peter laughed. 'You won't catch me on that lark. Leave that to the Regulars. There are plenty of single men to take the Queen's Shilling.'

Walter drained his ale and called for more. 'It's not all foreigners. There are some as British as you and me but they pay high taxes and have no say in the running of the country. I couldn't live like that. They have no vote and are harassed at every turn.'

'If they choose to live like that, they must sort out their own salvation and any country with gold can't be poor.'

'That Paul Kruger is as sly as a fox. Not educated, but clever. He knows that the Outlanders want the vote but would vote him out of power, so he stirs up trouble. The Dutch Church preaches independence and the Dutch farmers think the Outlanders want all the power, and he's told them they can treat the Kaffirs just as they like.' He saw Peter's surprise. 'The Kaffirs are the natives there who once had their own country. They are black but surely have some rights? They are treated like slaves and it's only just been said that they are now allowed to marry.'

'We can't tell another country what to do. It's all thousands of miles away and it's different there.'

'Have you seen pictures of Kruger?' Walter stuck out his jaw. 'As awkward a cuss as ever I saw. He'll never give rights to anyone or give an inch to disarm his forts until he's pushed.' Walter lit a small cheroot and sensed a kind of excitement as the evening wore on. Even Olive Grace looked quite a tasty bit with that purple flower pinned to her dress where the more than generous curves pushed up over her stays.

Peter ordered more ale. 'Be honest, Walt. Would your heart be in it? There are many in this country think that this war is wrong – the Irish are for Kruger and so are the Germans, or so I hear. The Americans keep quiet but wouldn't be sorry to see us beaten out there.'

'Does that mean you're for Kruger too, Peter?'

'Of course not! But he has as much reason to hate us as we to hate him and he'll be fighting for his own. He does need checking, but the papers say one thing one minute and change their minds the next until I don't know what to believe.' He reddened. 'I'd fight if I had to. I'm as patriotic as the next, but I pray it doesn't come to that.'

The door swung open to admit the drunk in the black jacket. A bottle stuck out from his pocket and he reeled around the room calling for people to volunteer 'for our dear Queen and Country'. He began to sing the National Anthem in a hoarse and quavering voice.

'Quieten down,' Walter said. 'Let peaceful folk sup their beer without that row and sit down before you fall down.'

The man's eyes focused on the local businessman whom every other person in the inn respected as honest and hard-working and yet good for a drink and a song. 'It's Walter Darwen,' the man said thickly. 'Mr Darwen who fought in the other wars. Come on, Walt, they need men like you. They want all the good horsemen they can get.' He sat at the piano and tried to play a tune until someone shut the lid hard on his knuckles. The burst of laughter suddenly faded and Walter looked towards the doors to see who had just come in.

Three non-commissioned officers from Albany Barracks grinned at the sudden rush to buy them drinks, and Walter smiled wryly. He had been fêted like that when in uniform, when his country needed him, but he also recalled the indifference of the public once there was no threat to life or liberty. The sergeant held up a hand in greeting and went over to join him. Walter knew him from his visits to the Barracks to deliver fish and vegetables and when he renewed the contract for fish and fruit for the officers' mess. Peter moved over to make room. 'What's this, then?' Walter nodded towards the drunk who was sucking his bruised knuckles. 'Not enlisting already?'

'We set up a booth by the Town Hall and there are quite a few takers. Some were too young so we sent them home again, and some were half seas over like him, but tomorrow it will be too late to turn back. Interested?'

'I've done my duty and more,' Walter said, wiping the beer froth from his moustache. 'I've far too much doing here to go overseas.'

The sergeant watched him. 'Pity. It's men like you we need. You were in the Royal Horse Artillery, I believe? Did well, or so I hear. Better than most.' Walter nodded. 'I may be mistaken but you *are* the Walter Darwen who earned silver spurs for the best horsemanship in the regiment?' Walter reddened and waved a deprecating hand but the sergeant went on, 'That's darned good. I can sit on anything with four legs but I'm not of that standard. Do you still ride – get any real practice? You look fit and sturdy.'

'I've got a horse that drags the cart,' Walter said cautiously.

The sergeant laughed. 'I don't want your nag. We do need horses but that's none of my business. I want men – men like you who are experienced and can set the right example to recruits. They need licking into shape.' Mrs Grace brought beer for the sergeant and he gave her a squeeze that made her laugh. Men in uniform could take such liberties and it meant nothing more than a lift to a woman's pride.

Walter tried to refuse the offer of more ale but found himself drinking another full tankard. 'There's too much at stake here,' he told the soldier in a kind of desperation. 'I've a wife and seven children and the days aren't long enough to get everything done. I'm tied.'

'You could be safe, training recruits and still be proud to serve the Queen.' Walter shook his head. 'Not you, then,' said the sergeant, and loosened the top button of his tunic. 'Don't tell me you never miss the company, though, or think of the good old days? They've fine horses now, bred for the Artillery from good stock. Not a wrong 'un amongst them.'

'If I went now, it wouldn't be with the Horse – I might end up in the infantry.' And Walter frowned as he imagined the ultimate indignity.

'That's only if you wait. If you do enlist now of your own free will, you have a choice: you can go back to your old regiment with your old rank and full pay.'

The sergeant said no more and the atmosphere became hot and charged with fumes and patriotic fervour. Mrs Grace sat at the piano and sang old sentimental songs and the drunk wept. The sergeant waited and Walter wished that he had gone home. A terrible force plucked at his loyalties and the whole fabric of his life. Memories flooded back evoked by the uniforms and softened by the ale. 'I'm on my way,' announced the sergeant finally and some men went home, but others including Walter Darwen followed him to the booth by the Town Hall. Peter Fry sat huddled over his beer, thinking that Walter was every kind of a fool, but wishing with all his heart that he had the courage to join him.

Chapter 2

One yellow gaslight irradiated the bend in the High Street and misty rain swept over the low stone parapet of Coppins Bridge. Jane Darwen looked out of the second-floor window of the house above the shop and craned her neck to see what was going on up the road, but the worsening weather kept most people at home.

It was nearly ten o'clock after a leaden evening and unlikely that anyone would want fish or vegetables now. 'Edward?' she called to her eldest son. 'Time to fix the shutters.' Edward and Jack lifted the heavy wooden shutters and placed them over the windows of the shop front, sliding the bolts to secure them for the night and blocking out the thin light from the street.

Jane came down the twisting staircase and closed the door at the bottom behind her. She put another lighted candle on the counter and two spare candles in holders by the first. What was the point of wasting gas? If someone came to buy, a knock on the door would bring one of the girls. All Newport knew that the Darwens were there behind the closed shutters, willing to serve.

Hurrying feet and muffled voices from the street brought an air of disquiet and urgency but Jane tried to ignore them, moving the candles to cast a better light over the fruit she was sorting. Rumours, she thought. There had been rumours for weeks and every tongue in the town told a different story. The shop had its share of idle gossips ready to fancy the worst and Jane was sick at heart, even now when the dark night was shut out and the boys were laughing in the back room. The dim candlelight did little to relieve the gloom.

'Edward?' she called. 'Have the girls gone up yet?'

'Yes, Mother.' Edward stood against the light escaping from the main living room of the old shop but she stayed in the dim light, hoping that the fruit sorting would have a tranquillizing effect after her busy day.

'It's time you all went up,' she said.

'Father not home?'

'Not yet.' She smiled to soothe the anxiety in the eyes so like his father's, blue and deepset and with a manliness too old for his twelve years. 'I expect he's on his way back from the *Press* windows. I hear some coming back now. Go to bed – you'll hear enough in the morning. You have to go to school, and your father may want you to get Bess from the arches early. Tell Jack to stop teasing Sidney and go to bed.'

Edward grinned. His mother might be out of sight but she knew to a T what Jack was up to. 'I'll see them upstairs,' he promised. 'Sidney is covered in chalk dust. Can I take some hot water into the scullery for him?'

'The tank is full but make sure you fill it again for the morning. You must all wash well. It's clean underwear tomorrow and clean socks, so leave the dirty in the basket.' She turned back to sorting. Edward was born when she had time to play with a child and love him in a special way because he was so like Walter; there would be no need to check that he'd filled the water tank beside the big kitchen range that was banked up at night and never went out, winter or summer, except for twice a year when the chimney was swept.

She tossed a rotten orange into a box under the counter. Some people had time to waste, standing in the rain to hear bad news. As if it didn't come soon enough in the newspapers. South Africa was hundreds of miles away and could be on the moon for all she cared, so how could a quarrel there affect her or her family?

The three boys came in with candles in broad-based brass holders. 'Father in the Wheatsheaf?' asked Jack.

'He is not.' Jane sounded slightly more Irish, a sign that she was upset. 'He's trying to make sense of the bulletins and will need a bit of peace when he comes in.'

Sidney, the youngest son, kissed his mother's cheek and she wanted to hug him fiercely as the still-damp skin reminded her of baby bathing and cuddles that would be rejected now by her growing family. How they grew. She sighed. Jack was still harum-scarum and might be so all his life, Sidney, no longer the youngest child since Emily was born and Caroline after her, living and dying in one short month, was quiet and dreamy, drawing and making models from cardboard and the soft wood from the orange boxes.

'Goodnight, boys. Remember to say your prayers.' She touched Edward on the arm. 'Thank you, Edward. I don't know what I'd do without my big son when your father's out.' She watched his rather stolid face light up with pleasure and when they had closed the door to the stairs behind them, Jane opened it again as she did every night. 'Quiet, girls!' she called. 'Not another word or I'll come up with the hairbrush.'

'Goodnight,' sang out Emily, trying to stifle giggles. As usual, it was Clare who had made her laugh and now kept silent as if she was good. Clare and Janey seemed more grown up than the boys, and yet Lizzie, Clare's twin, was young for her age – a thin and whining child who longed for attention.

Jane listened. The children were asleep for sure, and sounds from the road were magnified by the stillness of the wet street. Rain ran down the gutter into a deep drain that took it into the River Medina and threatened to overflow onto the road again, leaving a blockage of sodden leaves. She recognized Walter's steps as he crossed Sea Street; she looked up alertly as he came in, but still held a specky apple in her hand. 'Any news from the mainland?' she asked.

Walter tapped the scarred wood of the front door. 'Everyone in?'

'At this hour, I hope they are all in their beds,' she replied shortly. Walter bolted the door. 'Well, then? You look as if you lost sixpence and found a ha'penny.'

'It's war, Jane. It's come and it's serious.'

'Holy Mother,' whispered Jane. 'I've heard all sorts today, enough tales to make my head spin until I didn't know what to believe.'

'Well, we know the worst now but it's still a shock. Fred

says he'll sell his horses privately rather than let the army have them, but he'll not do that. The military can commandeer any animal they like at their prices if they need them. I'm glad I have only Bess and Blackie.'

He stood by his wife. The candlelight softened the hurt in her eyes but there were creases of strain he had never noticed, little lines round her eyes and a tight look to her mouth. It was a long time since he had really looked at her. There was always so much to do. The contract for the Barracks took time, and he was out of the shop for hours getting supplies of fish from Aaron Sheath and goods from the fruit warehouse. Still, he couldn't grumble. The wives of other ranks at the Barracks made sure he left with an empty cart after the mess kitchens had taken what they wanted.

He was tired and full of ale. Jane's deft hands continued to sort the fruit, putting the unblemished ones in the window. The slightly bruised went for horses and pigs and the children, who could cut out the rot and eat the better ones. She was overworked already. What would she do if he had to go away? He pulled at the ends of his moustache. The children were good with the horses and the pigs and ducks in the pens under the railway arches, but now, there would be more to do. He shifted uneasily and dreaded her reaction when she heard he'd bought a share in Bert Cooper's brickyard. Jane looked gentle enough but he knew the violence of her Irish temper and how scathing she could be, when upset.

Jane felt cold. She knew about war from the Troubles in Ireland, when Irish fought Irish and the British soldiers had come. Walter in full uniform had been a dashing figure and she had been helpless. What if he had to go to war? He was still young and healthy. She threw away a good orange and he leaned over and removed it from the rubbish, and she felt reproved. He would make up his own mind about the war, as he did about everything. He'd wanted her as soon as they met, all that time ago. 'Well,' he'd said. 'Are you coming to England with me? I've no time to argue the toss. I've a shop, a home that needs a mistress and enough for two.' He'd never said he loved her even after eight children, but he was often loving, with moments of great tenderness and Jane respected his inability with words even when his need for her was intense.

'What will I do if they take you away?' She looked at him directly, her brown eyes sad. 'What will I do if you go over the water? What about the ducks and pigs and horses and who will take the fish to the Barracks?' Her voice broke. 'And *who* will manage the brickyard?'

Walter fiddled with the door bolt until Jane wanted to scream. 'I was going to tell you,' he muttered. Trust Bert Cooper's wife Annie to tell everyone before Jane knew. She sorted oranges as if each one was a personal treasure. The set of her head was proud and stiff and close to tears. Walter lifted the box of bad fruit onto the counter. 'Any tea?' he said.

Jane pushed the dark hair from her face. 'Yes, it's ready. We'll have a cup.' She left him to snuff out the candle and went into the living room where the flat iron was heating and the kettle sent up spirals of steam from the hob where it had been for most of the evening. Half-finished ironing lay over the big table and the scent of warm ironed linen filled the room. Jane riddled the fire and made tea. The steam rose and Walter cleared his throat. It was going to be even more difficult than he'd imagined. His heart ached with unaccustomed emotion as he saw the familiar room. Jane's hair escaped into tendrils round her face and her whole being spoke of homely comfort, strength and a great beauty. Inside, a cold nucleus of fear caught him. I must have been mad, he decided without hope.

'What was on the board?' she asked. She handed him the big moustache cup filled with strong sweet tea and watched his face.

'Just the Declaration of War. I saw Maudie Dove up by the Town Hall. She's upset because her Ben is in the army – really upset, gal. The child looks rough, too. Take her some specks in the morning and a nice bit of skate.'

'Walter!' Jane felt him slipping away, avoiding something

important. 'What is it? There is something more than the brickyard, isn't there, though that's bad enough.'

'Same as I said, Maudie was in a state.' He buried his face over the cup.

'What have you done?' Jane put her cup down and pushed the linen aside. There was silence as their individual fears became one. He hardly heard her words but saw her lips quiver. 'You volunteered,' she said. 'Walter Darwen, you have volunteered and I doubt if you know the half of what that means.'

In the Wheatsheaf it had been a matter of pride. The songs had done it, too, and the sergeant raising his tankard to Queen Victoria, 'the little lady up at Osborne'. The atmosphere had been charged with patriotism and it was important that he could choose to go back to his old regiment and have the respect of people who saw him in uniform. Jane saw the flash of anger under the shame. 'If I go I must go with the Horse,' he explained sullenly, 'so I volunteered.'

Jane took the flat iron from the range and spat on the heel to test for heat. She folded a sheet so vigorously that a wave of warm clean scent made the lamp flicker. As Walter made to go, Jane stayed him with a withering glance. 'We're quiet now, and there are matters to settle.'

Long after midnight, Jane packed away the irons and Walter filled the huge kettles to put on the hob ready for the next day. He placed kindling and wood ready in the outhouse for the next crab boiling and stumbled up the unlit stairway to the bedroom, where Jane lay in her shift on the edge of the feather bed, heavy with misery. It was as if someone had died, but she could find no tears. Walter groped for her in the darkness but she stiffened and turned away. Not that! Dear God, not another baby or, if the doctor was right, something far worse while Walter was away. She wanted to turn to him and take him in her arms and have the joy of a child kicking inside her again. Dear Mother of God let this pass, she prayed.

Since Caroline, she had lived in fear. 'No more children if you value your life, Mrs Darwen,' Dr Barnes had said.

He coughed. 'You must resist your husband and I shall talk to him. He must choose between total abstinence and losing the mother of his seven live children.' He had frowned over the two varicose ulcers on her legs and bound them up with padded half-crown coins.

'Go down, Jack,' she said, hating a young child to see his mother so, and being frightened.

'No, stay, Jack.' Dr Barnes handed him the smelly discarded dressings with the old half-crowns still in them. 'Put these under the tap and get the coins. Wash them in hot water and share them among your sisters and brothers.' He laughed. 'You don't know your own son, Mrs Darwen. He isn't moved by a bit of dirt, but tell him that half-crowns don't grow on trees or he'll expect more when I come again.' When she was well enough to go downstairs, he had patted her hand and said, 'I've talked to your husband. He's a sensible man and you'll have no trouble with him. You are too good to lose.'

Walter turned away and fell asleep. This was the first time that he had wavered although abstinence had been a bitter blow, but Jane heard the clock in St Thomas' church strike four and she had only dozed briefly, remembering that Caroline would have been nearly four if she had lived. At six, she filled the heavy ewer with warm water and washed in the bedroom. Walter watched her twist her dark hair into a shining black bun and try to tame the curling tendrils. He stifled the lust that rose in him and wished that she was less beautiful. In the queenly way of the dark-haired Irish, her breasts were high even after feeding her babies and she moved with grace and a lack of self-consciousness that made her stand out among other women.

She buttoned her bodice and saw him watching her. 'Don't worry,' she said softly. 'We'll manage somehow.' She went down and opened the damper and stirred the fire, then made the first tea of the day. Walter gulped his and called the boys to go with him to the stables before breakfast. The girls made the beds and Jane sat with her cup in her hands until a cold bronze skin formed on the tea.

'Is breakfast ready?' asked Janey.

'Holy Mother, it's late! Go up and get your clean pinafores on then hurry down.' Jane flung knives and forks on the table and cut bread. She sliced bacon and made fresh tea.

'Why did the boys go with Father?' asked Emily, pinching the stiffly gophered frill on her pinafore.

'Don't ask questions and eat up your bacon.'

'Is it true that we are going to fight the Boers?' persisted Emily. 'I don't want Father to leave us.' Jane was conscious of all eyes watching her.

'It's true, but even if your father was called up, he would stay in Portsmouth to train recruits and you'd see him often.'

Emily sat still, breakfast forgotten and large tears welling up, while Clare tossed her head angrily and soon would blame someone else for her own anger. Lizzie just sniffed. It wasn't going to be easy. Janey smiled sympathetically, sensing her mother's feelings.

The shop door burst open suddenly and the boys rushed in, bringing the smell of the stables with them. Sidney kicked a lump of dung from his boot and was rushed out to the back yard to be cleaned up under the cold tap. 'And don't come back until you all smell sweet,' Jane shouted. Outside, Walter gave Bess a nosebag of hay and hitched the reins over the cart.

Jane raised her eyebrows and Walter nodded, all buoyancy gone. 'More news?' she asked with a calm that surprised her.

'Yes, all enlisted men have to report to the Barracks this afternoon.' Walter went into the kitchen and sat heavily, reaching for his cup. 'I'll get this down and go to the warehouse, but first I must see Aaron.'

'Not until you've eaten.' Jane put a piled-up plate before him and re-filled his cup. Now it was certain that he was leaving, she was calm and clear-thinking. She cleared dishes and chivvied the children off to school early, calling Sidney from the privy where he had escaped to read a book. 'Once you get out there with a book you lose all sense of time. Now off you go; your father needs a bit of peace this morning.' Sidney ran across the bridge after the girls thinking that Walter had drunk too much the night before and was bad-tempered.

Walter asked for his pipe and Jane dusted off a scallop shell to put with it. The last time he had smoked a pipe was on the day that Emily had been taken in the hospital cart up to Fairlee Isolation Hospital with scarlet fever. He watched his wife wash the dishes in a bowl on the table, dry them and put them on the long dresser with the other blue and white plates, then tip the greasy water out into the yard drain. She covered the table with the bobble-edged chenille cloth that matched the festoon over the mantelpiece and poured more tea.

'I'm sorry, Jane.' She felt her hands trembling. She could bear it when he was brusque and demanding but now he was abject, and her heart ached. He saw her discomfiture and knocked the ashes from his pipe. 'I've thought it out,' he said. 'Sam Walmsley at the warehouse will help you if you need advice. I've put a good bit of business his way and he's a friend you can trust. Aaron is too old to be called up so he can bring the boat up to the bridge and fill the cart from there. He might do a turn with deliveries but I wouldn't like to bank on it.'

'There's no call for him to do it – the boys must take things round in the evenings. They should do more. I might have a girl to help in the house while the girls stay in the shop. What of the brickyard?'

'Bert Cooper will look after the pigs if he can have two from each litter. Don't look like that! I know he'll do nothing without a return but he'll do it right and look after the workmen too.' Walter grinned. 'I told him you'd look at the books at the yard each week to see they are straight. That'll keep him on his toes as I think he's a bit afraid of you, Jane.' He saw her doubt. 'If he was ill or called up, you'd have to be in the know.'

Jane nodded reluctantly. 'I suppose so, but he's too fly to be called up. Bert is very good at looking after number one. He's a gambler and drinks more than is good for him, and the only reason he's not a womaniser, too, is that he's scared of Annie in one of her moods. She'd ferret it out of him in five minutes!'

'Come now, Jane, I've had some good times with Bert.' It was a relief to talk of something other than their own fears.

'The only times I've seen you drunk were after being with Bert. I've no time for him or his family, except Dan, and Annie is the meanest woman in Newport as well as the biggest troublemaker. She thinks a black satin afternoon apron and a gold pendant watch makes her a lady.'

'I'm not over-fond of Annie myself.' Walter smiled at Jane's bright colour and flashing eyes, loving her when she was on the verge of a paddy. 'I know the Coopers rile you, but they are important in this town and if the war goes on we'll need all the friends with influence we can get.'

'Well, Annie needn't think she can have something for nothing here. She feeds her family on stale cabbage and specky fruit – says it's for the rabbits but I know better.'

'Think what you like but be careful. If the shippers stop bringing fruit and the farmers grow less when the men are taken away, you'll have to build up the brickyard and the livestock.'

The shop-bell jangled. 'I'll go,' said Jane. 'You get over to the warehouse.'

Chapter 3

Walter turned the horse towards Quay Street across the swing bridge and stopped by the fruit warehouse. Bess stood patiently and was given some apple cut from a pile of bruised fruit on the cart. Sam Walmsley looked up from his office chair and put down the newspaper. 'It's bad, Walt,' he said by way of a greeting. 'Don't know what we're coming to. Her Majesty has given her consent to war, so I suppose we fight in a just cause, but after the ructions we've had everywhere that is under the Crown, I would have thought we'd had enough. I suppose all the silly young 'uns will flock to enlist.'

'Some of the married men, too.' Walter blew his nose hard.

Sam stared in disbelief. 'Not you, Walt? Now stop chewing your moustache – it *is* true! I can see it in your face. Good God Almighty!'

'I must have been out of my mind!' Walter moved restlessly under the gaze of the older man. 'I want to serve my country as I did before, but now there's Jane and the children. I never thought they'd want me so soon but I have to report up at Albany today.' His voice trailed to a whisper. 'So soon, Sam. What will become of my family if I'm away for months or even years?'

Sam spoke briskly. 'You were a bit of a fool, but you'd have been called up sooner or later. They can't afford to miss out on good horsemen like you. If you go quickly it cuts down the anguish, that's all. As for the family, well . . . Jane has a good head on her and they ain't babies any more.'

'Will you keep an eye on them for me, Sam?'

'Bless you, Walt, I'll be a father to that pretty wife of yourn. Tell Jane, if she suffers any rudeness or abuse from anyone – and that means *anyone* – to send one of the young 'uns running to Sam. Mind you tell her, as she's a proud one who asks no favours.' He gave Walter a penetrating look. 'News gets around when a pretty woman is alone and she might be glad of a man behind her. I wonder if you know just how much she is admired? And it isn't always by them who treat her with respect.'

'If I thought that any man would . . .' Walter stood up.

'You should have thought of that afore, Walt. You know your Jane and I know men. Jane can look after herself as far as most things go, but if she needs me she knows where to run. Now, you'll be wanting to stock up.'

Along an inner passage a strong smell of fruit in different stages of ripening was gassy and pungent. Sam pulled aside a muslin screen and examined stems of bananas in the semi-darkness. Walter was conscious of a mild claustrophobia. He took two stems and Sam put labels on them and on two as yet unripe. The small speckled Canary bananas were ready too and Walter took twelve hands of the deep yellow fruit. 'Jane will like them,' he said.

Sam gave the next stem a sharp tap. 'This batch seems clear. Last time we found a black 'un.'

'A snake?'

'They come on the barges. We found two ourselves and none of my men was bitten, thank God, but one over in Portsmouth killed a man. Dead in five minutes.' They added oranges and lemons and a huge crate of compressed dates to the cart, along with dried peas and packets of herbs. Bess shook her head, asking for more apple before she started again, needing only a touch on the reins to send her along to the arches under the railway bridge, where ducks and pigs were penned and the ducks could forage in the river. Walter went through the chores mechanically, scattering pigswill and fruit and grain, wondering if this would be the last time. He caught two ducks and wrung their necks, tossing them on the cart as a surprise for Jane.

Jane. All the morning he thought of her, and for the first time wondered if she had any feelings left for him apart from habit and duty. Did she really wish that they could be close again in bed? It was small consolation to know that even if men lusted after her when he was away, she dared not give herself to anyone for fear she might die. He thought with overwhelming guilt of the times he had left her alone with the children while he went off to Ashey Races or spent hours in the Wheatsheaf.

He backed the cart and eased Bess along Sea Street. He couldn't erase the picture of Jane from his mind, this time with Caroline, their two faces waxen against an even whiter counterpane; Jane was exhausted from loss of blood and the baby dead before many days. He needed Jane too much to risk her life, even during the emotion of leaving. He glanced up at two windows in Sea Street. The local whores were no solution – how could he share the same bed with Jane, even at a distance, after going with a slut who might give him more than he bargained for?

The problem remained. Bert could slide over to Portsmouth to his fancy piece with Annie none the wiser, since a lot of business was done over the Solent. Anyway, Annie, with her buttoned-up mouth and skinny arms might welcome the respite! Was it bad for Jane? Cold women like Annie and Jane's cousin at Wootton might not care, but Jane had been a warm and active partner in love. He grinned. Even a clean widow like Mrs Grace wouldn't do: Jane had a name for faded women who wore artificial flowers on their bosoms.

At the bridge, Aaron put down his yard broom and wiped the sweat from his beard with a tattered shred of butter muslin. A strong smell of fish came from his clothes and the flagstones of the cellar glistened with fish scales. Huge rush baskets full of stiff blue and silver fish sat on slate shelves and Walter nodded appreciatively. Aaron sluiced the last of the fish guts into the river. 'Heard you'd volunteered,' he said. 'What, I said – Walt Darwen? *Never*. Not Walt. He'd never do anything so daft.' He looked sideways and grinned.

'I'd like to know who told you so fast, but you're right. If you'd been in the Wheatsheaf you'd have seen how it was.' Walter reddened. 'I had to do it, Aaron. If I held back now they might have called me up later and put me in a foot regiment, but now I can go with my old unit. I need to be with animals,' he added defensively.

Aaron glanced at the flushed face of the man he had known since childhood. 'You'll suit the uniform, Walt. Have all the girls after you again, like last time.' He gave a high-pitched giggle, guaranteed to annoy with his genius for finding a raw spot. 'Might be a good thing for you, a bit more female company.' Walter smiled grimly. No new baby for four years – people drew their own conclusions.

'Anything worth eating today, Aaron?'

'All prime. When did I ever sell fish that you wouldn't take?' Aaron had his raw spots, too. During the last heat-wave he had forgotten to put fish in the cool cellar where the walls were thick and the cold river lapped the floor at high tide. When he came back with the next catch, the whole town stank of rotting fish that had to be dumped in the Medina.

'Any oysters?'

'What do you need them for? A fine set-up man like you don't need oysters.'

Walter gritted his teeth. 'I need a barrel for the Mess, and I want some special for Jane.' Aaron flicked open a shell with a thin blade and Walter sucked the fish down. 'Good,' he conceded. 'Jane will like them.'

'Are you so tired of England that you have to go and fight the Boers? Jane must have been angry when she heard. She's like me, minds her own business and lets others mind theirs.'

'She was at first, but we talked and now she's with me. She hates people being put upon. I told her what Reverend Moffat said about the way the Boers treat the blacks. Did you know, Aaron, that although they are free men, they are still treated as slaves? They have to step off the pavement if white people pass and they carry a bit of paper saying where they live so police can check that they stay in their own districts. The Outlanders who are as white as you and me are treated almost as badly.'

'Carrying a bit of paper isn't enough to make you go to war.'

'It's Kruger's whole attitude. He's gathering arms and the farmers are prepared for trouble. If we don't get fair deals for all parties under the law there, we'll lose the Cape. Kruger tries to convince people that we want the land and the mines but he only says it to make the Boers rise against us.'

'The Cape? We can't lose the Cape! That's part of our Empire. It's as British as Portsmouth Harbour, solid as a rock! He can't take that away. He'd better watch out!'

'You see!' Walter laughed at the man's anger. 'Even you get hot under the collar when you hear a bit of truth. More people should read the papers and learn what's happening overseas. If we ignore our Empire and look no further than Southampton, we're blinkered and could lose the lot.' He watched Aaron hang his sack apron on the wall to dry. 'It wasn't just the ale talking, Aaron – I believe in the Empire. This afternoon, I have to report to the barracks.'

Aaron covered the fish baskets with clean cheesecloth and filled a skip with freshly-boiled shrimps. He added a cage of crabs and one of lobsters and handed them up to Walter on the cart. Jane was waiting with blocks of ice from the ice factory over the bridge and she quickly arranged the fish on the well-scrubbed marble slab in the shop window. The basket of shrimps was put on the counter with a pint measure for scooping them out and meanwhile, Walter took the ducks to the outhouse and plucked and drew them, scalding the insides and stuffing them with sage and onion and fresh breadcrumbs. He knew that Jane usually ate bread and cheese for her mid-morning break while she worked when the children were back in school, but today he made her sit down with a dozen opened oysters, some crusty bread and a glass of stout. He served in the shop and left her in peace, eating her favourite food and wondering if it would choke her.

Walter tried to remain good-tempered even when every customer asked him if it was true he'd enlisted; some who didn't really want to buy hovered near the door hoping to hear something new. Peter Fry came in for a bit of skate and some catfish. 'You did it, then?' he asked.

At any other time, Walter would have taken Peter into the back room and talked over a glass of cider, but he wanted Jane to have a few minutes to herself so he endured the prying eyes in the shop. 'I volunteered,' he admitted. 'Most men will have to go whether it suits them or not and at least this way, I can go back with my old rank.' His announcement made the waiting housewives look thoughtful.

'At least it's good for trade,' Peter said later when the shop finally emptied.

'Oh, it's a nine days' wonder, but I do feel like a freak at a fair. They've seen me often enough but now they think I must have grown two heads. You can't sneeze in this town without someone saying they saw you use your sleeve.' For that reason it might be a relief to go away. Maybe even if the war hadn't come, there would have had to be changes.

'I nearly did it too, Walt, but my mother is getting on a bit and Mary would have her in the workhouse as soon as she got helpless.'

'No call for you to go, Pete. You've always had a bad chest and you don't ride. We'll need a few honest men left when we go.'

'Anything I can do when you're away, Walt – anything at all?'

'I'll tell Jane you offered.' But Walter knew that Peter's wife wouldn't let him within ten yards of a pretty woman.

In the back room, he waved aside the oysters Jane had left for him and took his usual bread and cheese. Jane picked up another oyster. 'Be sure to have some when I'm away,' he said. 'Aaron will see you get the best – they're strengthening.'

'I'm strong enough,' she replied sadly.

Walter fumbled for words. 'You will take care – look after yourself? Let the others do more and don't get too tired.' He took her hand and there was agony in his eyes. 'What would any of us do without you?' He drew her towards him, about to take her in his arms, when the shop-bell jangled and the moment was lost.

'I'll go,' she said, blinking back her tears. He *does* care, she thought. Poor Walter.

'Oh, it's you, Maudie. I was coming to see you later when I'm not so busy.' She forced a smile. 'What can I get you?'

'Oh, Mrs Darwen, I'm frightened out of my wits.'

'I know, Maudie. Your Ben will be in the war, but so will many.'

'It's not that – it's the child. I don't know what to make of her. I left her in bed and came to you. Could you look at her for me?'

'What about Dr Barnes? He'll be back from his visits by now.'

'I don't want to bother him. If it's nothing, he'd be cross with me and besides, I can't . . . I have no money.'

'You have your army allowance.'

'It's late coming and I had to pay the rent or the landlady said she'll turn us out.'

Jane regarded Maudie steadily. 'When did you last have something to eat? Come into the back room. If you make yourself ill you'll be no use to the child or Ben or anyone.'

Walter took one look at the girl's heaving shoulders and runny nose and disappeared into the outhouse, muttering that he'd boil the crabs. Jane stood over the girl while she ate oysters and drank strong sweet tea until her colour returned.

'Go back now,' ordered Jane. 'You've left your daughter long enough. I'll tell my husband where I am and follow you.' The outhouse door was shut fast, which meant that Walter was trying to get the kindling to light without too much draught, so Jane scribbled a note and left it in a jar on the table. She locked the front door after putting the Closed sign round, clutched her shawl and hurried back over the bridge to Sea Street. It took more than an hour to get the boiler right for crabs and she'd be back before they were done, so there was plenty of time to say goodbye to Walter – and Maudie really did seem to need help.

Chapter 4

Jane hurried through Sea Street to the tall narrow house where Maudie had two rooms. The wailing grew louder and gasping breaths between frightened cries made Jane run up the stairs. She pushed open the door and caught her breath at the foetid atmosphere. 'No wonder she can't breathe. She'll stifle if you don't open the window,' she exclaimed.

'The window won't open and I can't leave the door ajar or the woman complains about the noise.'

Jane set her lips and propped the door wide open. She pulled back the curtains to let in some light and looked at the small child on the bed. The terrified eyes were dilated with the effort of breathing, and with each harsh labouring spasm the small chest heaved desperately to drag air into the lungs.

'I think it's serious enough to fetch Dr Barnes,' Jane said. 'I'll go.' She held up a restraining hand when Maudie tried to stop her. 'Maudie, now listen to me: she must have the doctor. Don't worry, he'll get his money. In the meantime, keep her face cool with a damp cloth but don't try to give her anything to drink. She can't breathe and swallow, so you'd only choke her.'

She hurried down to the street and the blessed fresh air and saw a door close quietly as she passed the bottom floor. Too busy spying to do a good turn to anyone, she decided. The doctor's house looked shining and cared for behind the neat laurel hedge and the trim maid took her message. Dr Barnes came at once from his dining room, pulling on his coat. 'What's wrong?' he said.

'Oh, Dr Barnes, it's Maudie Dove's child. I think she has diphtheria and she's very ill.'

He looked at her sharply. 'You've seen this before?' She nodded. 'Run back with these and get them boiled up,' he said, handing her a packet. 'Take these candles too. They never have enough light in these places. I'll bring the rest.'

Maudie was in tears. The child was a bad colour and her breathing painful to hear. Jane put the clothes and everything else cluttering the table into the other room and told Maudie to fill the kettle and the saucepan with water, and to put the extra candles on saucers. A face appeared in the open doorway and a whining voice asked what the noise was about. 'You can either come and help or get out,' Jane said crisply. 'If you're the landlady, I'll have a few words to say when we're finished. This place isn't fit for a dog!' The face vanished and a door banged below just in time to avoid meeting the doctor.

Dr Barnes opened his bag and immediately put a clean towel on the bare table. Jane picked up the bowl of boiling water into which she had put the scalpel, some forceps and a tracheotomy set of silver. She drained off the water and tipped the instruments onto the towel to cool. The doctor opened the child's mouth gently and placed a metal spatula on her tongue: a grey membrane nearly closed the pulsating throat and the child's breath came in ugly, shuddering sighs. Her terror mounted and her face was livid as she gagged on the spatula.

Jane ripped some old linen into strips then stood back as the doctor arranged his tools. She was torn between her desire to stay and help and the dread that Walter would have left for the Barracks before she could say goodbye.

'I'll need cotton tape tied to the outer tube of the set,' Dr Barnes said. 'Maudie? Do you hear me? Come on, girl, tape!'

'Don't,' said Jane gently. 'I'll stay. She's too young and too frightened to do anything.' She opened a sewing box and stirred a mass of tangled cottons and tape until she found a hank of white tape half an inch wide. 'How much do you want, Doctor?'

'Enough to tie at the back of the neck, or better still, make them long enough to tie to one side so that she doesn't lie on a knot. It looks strong enough. If the mother can't help me, you'll have to do so, Mrs Darwen. The child must be held still.'

Jane blanched. 'She'll see you. She'll see the knife in your hand and she's old enough to know what you mean to do. Holy Mary, she'll know it will hurt!'

Dr Barnes turned away and took off his jacket, folding it with fastidious care before hanging it on the brass bedrail where it couldn't touch the grubby bedclothes. 'If we don't insert this tube into her throat *now*, she will die.' His eyes were hard. 'Yes, she will be frightened and yes, she will be hurt. I have no way of deadening the pain as she can't swallow laudanum. We have very little time left.' He tried to smile, and Jane rolled up her sleeves and nodded. She was no longer trembling but her face was tense with fear.

'Put a pillow under her neck and a towel on her chest,' he ordered. 'Take her hands in one of yours and use the other to keep her head still. If she struggles, keep her hands away and leave the head to me.' Jane was unable to reply as she fought for self-control but he seemed satisfied. He turned to the table and took the bright blade, keeping it out of the child's range of vision. Jane was somehow comforted to see beads of sweat appearing on the doctor's brow.

The small body went rigid under her hands as if suspended without life. There was a rushing intake of air, then another and a convulsive sigh, and the child struggled to free her hands. A strangled scream died and gave way to a hissing, bubbling sound, as if air was released from a balloon. Jane's fingernails dug into the soft flesh of the wrists but she dared not let go. She saw the bleeding gash in the tiny throat and the shining silver tube sliding in through the gap. She raised the now relaxed head while the doctor tied the tapes to make sure the tube was firmly in place, then watched as he inserted clean strips of linen under the silver plate, to cover the cut skin edges.

Only then did he pause and close his eyes for a second, and his hands quivered. Maudie suddenly came to life. 'You've killed her! She's too quiet, doctor. She's dead!'

'Silence, woman! Killed her? If it hadn't been for me and for your good neighbour she would certainly have been dead within the hour! The child is breathing through this tube and she must go up the hill to the isolation hospital as soon as it can be arranged.' Maudie sobbed and protested, but he insisted. 'It's diphtheria and very infectious.'

He touched Maudie on the arm gently. 'You must do as I say, Mrs Dove, but try not to worry. I think she may do now.' He peered into the dingy corners of the room. 'Even if the disease wasn't infectious you couldn't nurse her here. This room is dirty and damp. It needs a good scrub: do you hear? As soon as they come for your daughter, you must get that window open and put the mattress over the sill. Scrub the floor and wash all the bedding and clothes – anything you can't wash must be burned. I shall come tomorrow to see that this has been done and I shall bring a sulphur candle to burn. You will not see that lass of yours here again until this place is clean and wholesome.'

Dr Barnes washed his instruments in the bucket of hot water and dried them carefully before packing them in the leather case with the spare tracheotomy tubes in a baize roll. Maudie tried to speak through tears of gratitude. 'Oh, doctor, I can't pay you.'

The elderly man looked at the distraught face and then at the sleeping two year old child. 'Just keep this place clean,' he grunted. 'I don't want any money. If you make a proper home for this little one, if God spares her, you will have repaid me but if you carry on as you have done, living in a pigsty, then I'll see you end up in the workhouse. You have to make a home for your man, too, Mrs Dove. He'll want a bonny child and a healthy wife when he comes back from the army.' He turned to Jane. 'Thank you, my dear. I could use you as my permanent assistant.'

He clattered down the wooden stairs and Jane forced the window open wide. Maudie fetched a kettle of water from the tap downstairs and Jane noticed with distaste the grey metal of the stove, mottled with rust. 'I'm going home now, Maudie,' she said. 'When the little one has gone and you've hung out the mattress, come over to the shop and I'll give you some carbolic soap and some blacklead for the grate.

Bring a basket and I'll find a cabbage and some fish for you.'

'What do I do if she stops breathing?' Maudie asked, as if frightened to be left alone with her daughter.

'The hospital cart will be here soon, but if the tube gets blocked you must clean it out like this, with one of these duck feathers that the doctor left.' Jane brought the soiled end of the feather out of the tube and tossed it into the fire. 'Make sure you burn each feather you use, because of the germs.'

'I don't know how you know these things,' Maudie said.

'By using my eyes and ears as you must do if you want to be happy. I know it's been hard, but you must make an effort.' Jane looked at the now peaceful child. 'I've never heard you call her by name.'

'She hasn't been christened. I wanted to call her Lucy but Ben doesn't hold with church and since he went away, I haven't got round to it.' Tears fell again.

'When the cart comes, tell them that the hospital chaplain must be informed that she hasn't been christened. He'll do it at once, just in case . . . I mean, to be safe and have her in the Christian church,' Jane added hastily. 'You can call her by name now, you know. I had names for all of mine long before they were christened.' She tried not to think of the minister coming to baptize Caroline the day before she died.

Jane hurried home as if she carried the plague. It was good to see her own gleaming stove and the whitewashed surround to the hearth. The house was empty so she stripped off her clothes, washed at the bedroom washstand and dressed in clean garments. She hung her red stuff dress on the clothes-line to air and felt more normal. Then she looked out old clothes for Maudie and the child, and eventually heard the hospital cart creaking past the door.

When she finally unbolted the shop door, she found two women waiting, their eyes glinting with curiosity. 'I said to Mrs Ralph here, I said, what's wrong? Mrs Darwen always has the shop open by now.' Jane ignored the implied question and smiled. It would be common knowledge soon enough that Maudie Dove's child had diphtheria.

'My husband had to go up to the Barracks,' she said, and was conscious of the empty back room and the fact that Walter had gone without saying goodbye. She served customers in a dream. Her heart was heavy with dread and misery, but what could she have done? Lucy Dove might have died . . . but was she to let Walter go without touching him again?

Jane wished now that she had given him all the tiny gifts that the children had wrapped in such haste in case he went away. He might never see the grubby handmade penwiper from Janey or the carved wooden spoon that Sidney had worked on for weeks and now wanted Walter to have. She went to the outhouse. The crabs were boiled and the copper still hot. The cage of lobsters had gone and the baskets of fish for the officers' mess. She laughed with relief. They'd have to let him bring the cart back – unless they commandeered that, and poor old Bess with her ambling walk would make any soldier unlucky enough to ride her wish he was in the infantry. She went to clear the fish slab and worked hard, and soon heard Walter's familiar whistle.

She rushed out, her face glowing. 'I thought you'd gone for good,' she said shakily and he gave her a quick hug.

'Not for a little while yet. When I took the fish they told me to report in uniform in three days' time. They're having trouble with the victualling and horses.' He laughed. 'I told them they could have Bess to serve her country but they jibbed at that. They didn't ask if I had any other horses, but I met Bert and he's sweating in case they take his new stallion.'

'Serve him right if they did! That black beast is wicked. Best place for him, the army.'

'I wouldn't mind him under me, but I told Bert to keep him in the stables until the barges have left and I shall do the same with Blackie. They are offering next to nothing for mounts, and I want to keep Blackie. If they come sniffing around, say the army have already rejected the horse that drags our cart.'

Jane added water to the tea that had been stewing on the hob for hours. She spooned in sugar and Walter gulped noisily, taking his creature comforts for granted. Janey and Clare pushed back the bead curtain separating the shop from the passage to the living room when the wooden door wasn't closed, and the smell of fresh bread came from under the white cloth covering their basket. Jane put the three large loaves into the crock, then changed her mind and took out a fresh loaf, ignoring the piece of yesterday's bread that should be eaten first. The bread was still warm and she sliced it while Clare fetched butter from the larder. Walter scooped a quart of shrimps into a blue Delft dish and put them before the children.

'Wash first,' said Jane, slapping Sidney on the wrist as he reached for his share. 'You can stop chattering and tell your father what you did today.'

Sidney came back first and sat looking too good to be true. 'All right, what did he do this time?' Walter asked, knowing the signs.

Sidney stuffed his mouth with shrimps, making speech impossible. 'He poked his tongue out at Miss Martin,' Lizzie said with an air of self-importance. Edward tried to kick her under the table for being a telltale and the others sniggered.

'Your father doesn't like rude boys,' said Jane, and Lizzie smirked under Walter's approval. 'And he doesn't like tell-tales, either,' she added sternly. Lizzie peeled a small shrimp with care and looked down at her plate. 'Why did you do it, Sidney?' Jane asked. Sidney swallowed violently and coughed. '*Sidney*! If you bolt your food, I shall be up all night giving you medicine for stomach-ache.'

'Miss Martin said I smelled of manure, so I put out my tongue at her.'

Walter got out of his chair and went round the table and sniffed. 'You've been down at Bert Cooper's again. Did you ride his new horse?' he asked sternly.

'I stroked him over the door and he licked my hand, but I didn't get on his back.'

'You know what I think about that horse, Sidney. I forbid

you to get on his back even in the stableyard. He's a brute and it will take a man to handle him. Whoever broke him ruined his mouth and his temper, which is why Bert got him cheap. If he bolted with anyone less than twelve stone on his back, he'd kill him. Can't think why Bert bought him.' Jane gave her husband a grateful glance.

'Now give me your word that while I'm away you will not ride that horse, and no fancy tricks with other horses. You must understand,' Walter went on firmly, 'that all of you are to help your mother in every way.' He saw the anxious faces. 'I hope to go no further than Portsmouth but you must still be extra good.'

Emily began to cry. She opened her mouth and shut her eyes, treating the family to the sight of her mouth full of half-chewed shrimps. 'Miss Martin says that soldiers are going far across the sea and will get killed.'

Walter took his daughter on his lap. 'Listen – I'm going up to the Barracks and then away for a while. The war may be over before I reach South Africa, but we can't know for certain. I want you all to look after your mother and to help as much as you can. The boys must do the deliveries.'

'Up at the Barracks?' asked Edward.

'Yes, you must do a man's work now. Make sure the beasts lack for nothing and ask Bert Cooper or Sam Walmsley if you need advice. Dan will help if you ask him.' He put Emily down. 'You girls must do your part, too.' He saw Clare toss her head. 'Clare must serve in the shop when she comes home from school and spend less time with Ethel Sheath in the river fields.' He wiped Emily's nose on a large handkerchief. 'Lizzie, you must help in the kitchen and not have sulks and tantrums when asked to wash up. Your mother will need a rest.'

Jane cut wedges of bread pudding that had been cooking slowly in the side oven. The crusted sides were glossy and raisins clustered dark and rich inside. After pudding, Walter took his accounts book to the other side of the room, and the girls helped to serve in the shop while Jane washed up and returned the uneaten shrimps to the basket on the counter. Everyone glanced anxiously at Walter as if he would disappear in a puff of smoke. Lizzie was on the verge of tears and Sidney and Jack were being difficult. They all waited for an inevitable calamity, the realization of which might be a relief. Jane recalled how Walter would chuckle when she said, 'It's always better when you know the worst has happened.' She smiled to herself and Walter saw the smile and was glad. His books were balancing nicely and he had more money than he had supposed.

Jack was teasing the cats and whistling in a way that irritated Walter. 'Go up to the *Press* window and see what the news is, Jack,' he said. Jane looked up sharply. 'I thought I'd stay in tonight,' Walter told her casually. 'Send Edward round to the Jug and Bottle and we'll have a drink here and a bit of music.'

Jane cleared the top of the harmonium of an accumulation of books and oddments and the tapestry runner. The lid was stiff as it hadn't been lifted for nearly a year. She lit two lamps so that one circle of warm light fell over the sheet-music stand, and Walter leafed through a pile of music kept in the seat of the music stool. He selected a few music hall songs and ballads, a hymn with a rousing tune and lastly, *The Lost Chord*. He loosened his collar and tried a few notes, avoiding the one that stuck.

Edward put good coal on the fire instead of the everyday coke and the room soon absorbed the heat. Janey spread newspaper over the chenille cloth before giving Sidney a pile of cards and a bottle of ink. He sharpened a wooden meat skewer into a wedge at the thick end. 'What prices shall I write, Mother?'

'Just two for *1d* and one *2d* and one for the date box. The last one fell in and is too sticky to use. Nice thick numbers now, that everyone can read.'

Sidney dipped the wedge end into the ink and carefully wrote *1d*. He examined the result, underlined the figure and enclosed it in a frame of black – like a mourning card, Janey thought. He propped it up against the sugar bowl and quickly did the others, but left the big one that might have more artistic scope until last.

'Can you spell "Dates"?' asked Janey.

'Of course I can and I've seen a picture of a date tree.'

'They don't grow on trees, they grow on palms,' Clare sniggered.

'Take no notice of her,' Janey said. 'Draw me a date tree.' Sidney frowned with concentration. He wrote *Dates* in the middle of the card and licked the inky end of the skewer. If he got it wrong, Clare would laugh at him. The edges of the leaves were feathery, he remembered and so turned the skewer round to use the pointed end to make light strokes. The ink ran down and settled in a dark stain at the base of his thumb, but he finished the palm and added squiggles at the bottom for sand. 'You've got ink all over your face,' said Janey, smiling and looking as Jane must have done years ago. 'Come into the scullery and let me clean you up before Father sees you.'

'Why do I get dirty when I'm enjoying myself?' Sidney asked. Janey hugged him. 'One day I'll paint proper pictures,' he told her solemnly.

'One day,' she said soothingly, 'but you'll have to earn money to buy paints as Father doesn't think much of artists. I like pictures, though.' She took him back into the warm room.

Jane turned the pages while Walter played. She let the music flow over her while the girls knitted and Edward and Sidney played Halma. She was happy. It was strange that Walter could love music so much. As soon as he tried the old tunes he became softer, gentler. Perhaps that was why he hadn't played for so long, she thought. He had to harden his heart and do without sentiment and love and to concentrate on the company of men, playing the harmonium only at Christmas when there were visitors. It was almost like the old days, when they could go to bed after the singing to love and be loved, naturally. Jane leaned against her husband as she turned the page and his shoulder was firm against her breast.

Emily lay on the hearth rug, her knitting forgotten, watching the fire with its dark caves and dragons and men with flaming swords and beautiful ladies in red robes that undulated against the black rocks. The warmth comforted her and she forgot that her father was going away. This was home, with complete security that could never change and which she would never, ever leave.

A wreath of dark smoke from the lamp made Jane trim the wick. She poured ale and brought out a seedy cake. The wooden clock in the corner came up to the hour and struck nine times. Clare mixed a jug of cocoa and added hot milk and water. 'It's time you all went up,' said Walter.

'We can't – Jack isn't in yet,' said Clare. 'I want to hear the news.'

'You go up with the others, young lady.' Jane was annoyed. 'Where do you think he is all this time?'

Walter took a large slice of cake. 'You worry too much,' he said easily. 'He's waiting for a bulletin.'

'Up to no good under the Town Hall arches, more like, with all the Sea Street riff-raff.'

'He'll come to no harm with the streets full of people,' Walter said. Nothing was going to upset him tonight. He wanted to store this away to fill his mind in Africa.

Emily tore herself away from her fantasies and showed Jane Sidney's cards, now dry. The palm tree had come out nicely with no blots. 'I don't know where he gets his talent from,' marvelled Jane. 'Put them in the shop on your way to bed.' The girls brushed their hair in the warm room and began to squabble over a hair ribbon until Jane gave them a withering glance that sent them up the stairs meekly. Walter checked the shutters and suddenly they were alone.

Jane sat on the stool by the fire and Walter tried a few chords. He looked quizzical and played the notes of one of her favourite pieces. Jane stared into the fire but saw no princesses. She crooned softly, then as her confidence grew, sang in a sweet contralto, lending depth to the old Irish love song. Firelight on her hair brought out the blue-black glints . . . like the wing of a raven, Walter thought. She removed a hairpin that dug into her scalp and shook one side of her hair free. Absentmindedly, she removed the other pins until her hair was a loose silk veil below the shoulders of her dress.

They went from song to song, with Jane singing alone or

joining Walter's low baritone; half-recalled Gaelic songs and snatches of popular ones. The war was a bad dream. Jane sipped her ale and Walter looked for more songsheets then folded them and put them back in the seat. He stirred the fire and sat on the rug at Jane's feet. The firelight was less bright now and he couldn't see the depths of her eyes. He took her chin in his hand and turned her face towards him.

'You're happy,' he said.

'And why would you be thinking that?' Her smile was tender.

'When you are truly happy, your eyes have a greeny tinge in the brown like shamrock trying to grow.' He was teasing her as he used to long ago, knowing that her eyes were dark brown. She looked at the shamrock growing in the pot on the dresser. The plant had been there for years and flourished, although her family in Ireland had told her that neither the shamrock nor she could thrive in England.

He bent his head and kissed her mouth. She trembled with love and a desperate fear. Half of her mind wanted to scream, 'Get away! Leave me alone! Do you want to kill me?' and the rest of her wanted to take him in her arms and murmur that it was all right, to cradle his head and tell him that they could make love whatever happened to her.

He unpinned the cameo brooch at her neckband and unbuttoned the lace at her throat. He pushed all thoughts and conscience away and allowed his desire to grow while Jane sat beside him, hypnotized. This had nothing to do with her. This was another Jane Darwen with no powers of resistance. He kissed her again with increasing passion and her last vestiges of will dissolved. 'No,' she whispered, but his arms tightened, his hands fumbling with her skirt. Jane gave a sob and sank back just as the shop door banged.

Walter sat up as if recovering from a dream. He shook his head violently then buried his face in his hands. Jane buttoned up her bodice and stuck pins in her hair at random, regaining her poise. 'Who is it?' she called and was answered by a sob. She took a candle, holding it high in the dark shop and saw a figure bent double by the counter.

'Dear Mary, what now? Come into the light.' Jack limped into the living room, holding a handkerchief to his face. His shirt was torn and there was road filth on his trousers.

Walter regarded him with amusement. 'So you took on someone bigger than yourself?'

Jane filled a bowl with warm water and found an old rag, ignoring Jack's moans for sympathy. 'Praise be,' she said briskly, 'there's more mess than damage. You'll have a black eye tomorrow and a few bruises, but it's no worse than the last time.'

'Was it Percy Cantor again?' said Walter. Jack nodded. 'And now you can't recall what was important enough to fight over?'

Jack grinned through swollen lips. 'I think it was about the war, but it's never one thing with Percy. He riles me and it starts. We go for each other, hammer and tongs until one of us gives up.' He wiped his nose on his sleeve. 'It was him who had to give in tonight.'

Walter went out to fetch the coke for banking up the fire. 'Why don't you keep away from Percy?' Jane asked despairingly. 'Your brothers don't fight and I'm sure your father never did at your age.'

Jack shrugged away from her. 'He's going to fight now, and it isn't just fists they'll be using on the Boers,' he said defiantly.

Jane shook him. 'That's quite enough from you, young man. Don't you ever say such a thing to your father or he'd . . .'

'Strike me?'

Jane took a deep breath. 'Slip out of those trousers and I'll sponge them. Meanwhile, off upstairs and take your cocoa with you. You'd better be out of sight before your father decides that it's not amusing after all.'

Jack opened the door to the stairs and turned to kiss his mother. 'It's all your fault. I have your temper,' he said cheekily.

'You never see me fighting Percy Cantor! Get along with you.'

Walter took the cold crabs into the shop and shut the

door. 'The cats know there is cooked fish about, and the catch is broken on the outhouse window. I'll fix it tomorrow,' he said.

He stayed downstairs until Jane was in bed and made no further attempt to touch her. She stuffed her hand in her mouth under the bedclothes and dared not cry until he was asleep but when she woke, her face was stiff with dried tears.

Chapter 5

Jane Darwen caught up her basket and hurried along to the grocer's shop a few doors away, after leaving a card on the door to say *Back in 5 minutes*.

'Good morning, Mrs Darwen,' said George Foster, wiping his hands on the coarse apron he wore over his dark trousers. He swept aside spilled sugar from the counter. 'And what can I do for you?' She handed him her list and went from one open sack to another, savouring the smells that never failed to delight her.

'I wish our shop smelled as sweet as this one, Mr Foster,' she said. She sniffed at the cloves and coffee and admired the gleaming black and gold tea chests on the shelves. A handful of lentils running between her fingers was like sand on the seashore at Cowes, rough and clean. She cut a sliver from the cream cheese on the tasting board.

'I knew you'd like that one.'

'Folley Glebe Farm?' she queried.

'That's right, me dear. I could sell twice as many again. Mrs Attril makes them nice and close with a good flavour. Can't think why she doesn't go in for the agricultural show, but then there'd be still more customers after it and I can't get enough as it is.'

Jane nodded. 'I'll make sure of that one for Walter.'

'Will he be here to eat it?' he asked, then wished he had bitten his tongue.

'Why? Has there been another bulletin?' She looked anxious, knowing that George went up to the *County Press* window early each day while his assistant cleaned the shop, so that he could pass on any fresh news to his customers.

'They haven't wasted much time,' he said. 'They've wrecked a train taking supplies to a place called Mafeking. I wrote down all the names as you know I do, in case someone has missed a bulletin that's off the board.' He looked embarrassed. 'I doubt if it will affect you, as the war will be over before your husband goes, but there are families in Little London and Sea Street with regular soldiers who have gone already, and Newport being a garrison town makes people want to know.' He brought out a school exercise book. 'There are six families on Hunney Hill alone.' He turned a page. 'They took the train in a place called Kraaipan. What names, Mrs Darwen! They call the people Outlanders, I call them outlandish!' He laughed at his own standing joke. 'They're an ugly band of ruffians, in my opinion. They fired on a Red Cross train that went to help the people in the wreck. Fired on the Red Cross! If that isn't the work of animals, I'd like to know what is.'

Jane gasped in horror. 'But the Red Cross helps all sides! Their flag is sacred and so is the white flag of truce.'

The grocer smiled. It would be a good day when people heard the news. Even the people from Hunney Hill who usually shopped at Parkhurst would have to patronise his shop. 'You'll take the cheese?'

'Yes.' Everything must go on as usual, she decided. 'I'll take it, and a piece from the block.'

George Foster made a stiff cone of blue paper and emptied the contents of the brass bowl from the scales inside. He tucked in the ends. 'One pound of Greek currants. I don't know that we'll get them if the war goes on. You'd better give me your order for Christmas early to be sure of it.' He weighed up brown sugar, loaf sugar and tea and coffee. 'I'll weigh up the flour later if you're not in a hurry for it and send it down.'

'I'll take the saltpetre and salt as I have a pig's head ready for brawn, and the tea and brown sugar and a bag of broken biscuits.' Jane put a hand into the tin open on the counter. A piece of biscuit broke without sound. Baggy, she thought. George saw the look and reached under the counter. 'Not for you,' he said. 'I give them to the children.' He ripped the paper sealing a fresh tin and the brass scales tipped as he piled broken biscuits into the scoop.

The shop-bell rang and Jane turned to see Annie Cooper watching her. 'I'll pay for these and perhaps you will send the bill with the other things,' said Jane hastily. 'By the way, I need some more carbolic soap.'

'You must be washing your house away, Jane. I was here last week and you bought three bars then.' Annie's beady eyes searched Jane's pile of groceries and she stacked her basket with them quickly. 'I suppose it was that Maudie Dove again,' Annie went on. 'You'll be lucky to see anything back. You are very foolish to go into that house. For one thing it isn't respectable – and think of the diseases they've had in Sea Street!' It suddenly occurred to her that Jane had been in contact with diphtheria and she drew back.

'If everyone felt as you do, there'd be little human charity in the world,' Jane said sharply.

Annie went red. 'It's disgusting! Giving away things and feeding your own on broken biscuits!'

Jane felt her temper flaring. 'Put it all on the same bill, Mr Foster, I haven't time to waste here.' The shop-bell jangled with rage and Annie looked smug. George saw that Annie, too, wanted broken biscuits and he carefully weighed out exactly a bare pound of the soft stale ones on the counter.

Jane was still ruffled but there was a lot to do. She took the two ducks and laid them in the roasting tin with potatoes, carrots and slices of swede and turnip, added rock salt and coarse pepper and topped the dish with lumps of dripping. The bakery was close by and had agreed to take the ducks and have them ready for dinner-time when Walter would be back from the country and the children in from school. The shop filled with women out to hear the latest news, and Jane heard snippets of truth and half-truths: that a gold mine had been taken, that the Boers were showing the white flag and that women would be called up to nurse the wounded in Africa.

'Mr Foster hasn't entered everything in his book yet,' one woman said. 'I asked him to let us know if the Queen is coming to talk to the people by the *County Press* window, as I heard.'

'The Queen isn't even at Osborne now,' said Jane. 'Whatever next!' There was news that she didn't want to believe, of a troopship sunk off the coast of Africa and thousands of refugees flooding into Cape Town; she wished that the women would go away to gossip, but at least if they stayed in the shop they had to buy something.

'I'll have a packet of herbs and a pound of dried peas,' said Peter Fry's wife for the second time in two days, and Jane wondered if he'd have herby dumplings and peas for the next fortnight. Between serving, she made batches of pancakes and stacked them in layers in a closed dish in the side oven. As dinner-time approached and the women had to go home for when their children came out of school, she washed cabbage and finished the pancakes. She laid the table and cut bread and when Walter hitched the horse outside, he took a hessian cloth from her and went to the bakery while Jane fed the horse with bits of broken biscuit.

The children came running down the hill from the Barton, Sidney arriving first and leaning panting against Bess. 'Can I take her back after dinner?' he asked.

'You'll have to ask your father. He may want her again.' She gave him an affectionate slap. 'Get washed or you'll eat bread and cheese.'

'What is there?' Clare looked in the oven. There was no stew in the pot, no pickles and cheese on the table and only pancakes in the side oven. Walter came back and put the hot dish on the table, tossing the hessian to the side of the range.

'It's like Christmas,' breathed Emily. Walter tried to sound as festive as the children and Jane filled plates, put jam on pancakes and made tea but ate very little herself, glad that the children kept up a continual chatter. Walter lit his pipe and nodded when Sidney asked if he could take the horse and cart back to the stable, and nodded again when Clare demanded to go too. Sidney let her climb up beside him on the driver's seat and she spread her skirts and put her nose in the air when she passed Ethel Sheath's house. Then Sidney jerked the reins and made Bess trot. Clare lost her balance and fell backwards into the cart, her legs threshing the air and her drawers on view to the children sitting on the parapet of the bridge. Ethel Sheath nearly fell in the water with mirth and Clare was speechless with fury. She pummelled Sidney's back with her fists.

'You know Mother doesn't like you to be stuck-up,' he said, but found a piece of fluff-covered toffee in his pocket which pacified her. They stabled Bess and dragged the cart under the shed. Blackie was restless and trampled his straw, badly in need of exercise. Sidney slipped a halter on him and led him along the river bank. As he grew quiet, Sidney mounted him and helped Clare up behind him. 'Come on, we've time to go as far as the gypsies.' Clare forgot her bad temper as soon as she saw the gypsy encampment across the river. 'One day, I'm going over to see them,' her brother announced.

Clare gasped. 'Oo-er! You know what Father says about them!'

'He only said we mustn't buy from them before asking him.'

'Granny says they run off with children who are never seen again. They sell them on the mainland and make them work in the mines.'

'That's silly. All they do is make pegs and baskets and tell fortunes. They come in the shop and Mother gives them old clothes and bits of fish, too. I think she likes them.'

'I go and hide when old Mrs Lee comes. She has funny eyes and seems to know what I'm thinking,' said Clare. She clung tighter, knowing that Jack and Edward never let her ride behind them like this. 'I hope they don't run off with you, Sidney,' she said. They got back to school in time for the bell, laughing at the idea that the gypsies might run off with Miss Martin.

Walter hammered in the last nail and put the tools away when Jane called him. He had mended the catch on the window in the boiler-room and put up two shelves that had been needed for months. Jane brought him tea in a mug and he sat on the edge of the boiler to drink it while she surveyed his handiwork. 'It's grand, just grand,' she said.

'Is there anything more I can do?'

'Nothing. You're a dear man and you've done wonders.'

She smiled. 'We'll manage, and tomorrow when you get into uniform, you'll be very handsome.' She forced her tone to be light but her eyes showed her pain and they shared the suffering.

'Last night . . .' he began.

'It didn't happen so there's no harm done,' she said briskly. 'You have no cause to be blaming yourself now.' Her voice deserted her. 'I'm glad,' she whispered, 'that you still want me, that I'm not ugly yet.' He gathered her into an embrace that was comforting rather than passionate, and wiped away her tears. 'For all that, maybe you'd better go to the Wheatsheaf tonight to say goodbye to your friends.' They heard the bugles call from across the river, pure and cold as silver, and Jane shivered.

'I don't think it will be today,' he said. 'They weren't ready when I took the last load up to the Mess. The troop-ship from Liverpool is late and it isn't even standing off Cowes yet. They can't load the horses on the barges until the last minute, but the men are ready to muster by the mill and I have to be ready, too.'

'You'll go with the men?'

'No, I stay with the horses.' He went into the back room and found the old kitbag that had been in the cupboard since his former army days. Jane checked his hussif, the waxed thread and needles, beeswax and an awl, while Walter honed his pocket-knife and packed bootcleaning materials. He wrapped a button stick and polish in old rags and Jane polished the leather case containing the cut-throat razors, strop and scissors and a pair of silver-rimmed hairbrushes. She made him up a parcel of fruit and pies.

'Cheer up,' he said. 'I'm like a bad penny. I'll be back with Bess after taking the fish up. They ordered it so they must let me bring the cart back.'

It was nearly two o'clock when Jane heard the cart return, and she stared. Walter seemed bigger and taller, but slim and fit in the full uniform of the Royal Horse Artillery. The cockade at the side of the fur hat gave a dashing finish to the uniform and the frogging on the tunic was smart and fresh. Walter Darwen, local businessman, had become a handsome non-commissioned officer in Her Majesty's Army.

Jane smiled. Her husband had said nothing about taking his spurs won for horsemanship but the silver mounts were gleaming. He flushed. 'How do I look?'

'Like the man I married,' she said proudly. 'You're like a warhorse – you can smell battle and can't wait to see it settled.' He shook his head but didn't deny it.

'I have to be back there by four,' he said. 'I've had more time at home than most.'

'Oh, Walter, you'll miss the children!'

'I have to take Bess back to the stable,' he said, and frowned.

'Take her back now and ride Blackie up to the school,' Jane suggested impulsively. 'Tell Miss Martin you're off to the war and she *can't* refuse you permission to say goodbye.' Jane's colour deepened and her eyes flashed. 'She should be pleased! You are going to protect people like her!'

Walter kissed her. 'I'll go, but I won't take you! Poor Miss Martin would be in real trouble if she refused to let me see the children.' Jane buried her face in the rough tunic. 'I thought I was fighting for you and my family. If I'd known it was for Miss Martin, I'd never have volunteered!'

He strode out with a slight swagger, and when she saw him later with Blackie she was very proud. The dark brown horse was eager to go and Walter rode him slowly along by the withy beds before putting him to the hill leading to the school. As the hooves crunched on the gravel, the school-bell rang for a change of lessons, and the boy with the bell stopped ringing and stared.

'Tell Miss Martin I want to see her,' Walter said. The bell dropped with a dull clang and the boy ran in through the porch. A minute later the headmistress appeared, flustered and pink, smoothing down her mousy hair.

Walter dismounted and advanced, smiling with considerable charm. 'I'm sorry to disturb you, Miss Martin,' he said, 'but I'm leaving for South Africa and would like to say goodbye to my children.' He went on to explain that he didn't know when he'd see them again and she must surely understand a father's feelings.

'Yes, of course I understand,' she said. 'How brave . . . and yes, the children!' She sent the boy with the bell to fetch all the Darwen children and ordered him to tell every teacher to assemble their classes in the main hall.

Emily came first and flung herself on her father. He kissed her and told her again that she must be a good girl and help her mother. She gazed at him in awe. Was there anyone in the world as handsome as her father? Janey and Lizzie were close to tears but Clare made the most of the situation and posed, head in air, next to him. She was delightfully aware of her friends, and more important her enemies, looking green with envy.

Sidney smoothed the soft flank of the horse and regarded his father, wide-eyed. I must draw him like that, he thought. It was the first time he had seen him in uniform. Edward and Jack tried to appear nonchalant, as if their father came to the school every day wearing silver spurs and a cockade. They shook hands with him after he had kissed the girls, feeling very manly as he put out a hand to each boy in turn. The family waved goodbye to him and then followed Miss Martin rather apprehensively as she lined them up in front of the whole school. Her face was red as it was when she was either very angry or deeply moved, and her eyes gleamed with importance.

'You have seen a brave man about to leave to fight for his Queen and Country and for *us*!' She paused for effect. 'He is leaving his dear wife and children for what may be a long time.' She considered the rapt, upturned faces. 'Because of that, I intend to allow the Darwen children to come to school an hour later each morning so that they can help their mother.'

A buzz that could have been approval but was probably envy, filled the room. Miss Martin secretly wished that the Darwen children would look more impressed and grateful, but she decided that they were too overcome by her generosity. Only Clare looked delighted: that would show them! She saw Ethel's red hair and freckles in the crowd. *Her* father never went further than the Hamble or Portsmouth Harbour.

After school, the other children clustered around the Darwens. 'We have to do all the deliveries,' Edward said casually. 'Even up the hill to the Barracks.'

Percy Cantor put a hand on Edward's shoulder. 'Let's have a ride sometimes, Edward.'

Jack pushed him away. 'Not you, Percy. Only we are allowed to ride in *our* cart. Us and our friends – and you're not a friend, not by a long chalk!'

'If Edward says I can then I can!' Percy clenched his fists. 'He's in charge and older than you.'

Jack spat on the ground. 'That's what I think of you, Percy Cantor, and if I catch you on our cart, you'll get something!'

Edward was suddenly like Walter. 'If you fight while Father is away, neither of you gets a ride.'

Jack shrugged and ran down the hill and when the others arrived, he was sitting on the counter of the shop eating a date as if nothing had disturbed him. 'Come on, Mother wants tea over,' he said. 'There's a rumour that the barges will take the horses and mules out to the troopship. It's arrived at Cowes and they will come up the river close to the lane by the Barracks. Aaron says the barges are drawn up by the mill, so Mother will see the men leave from Hunney Hill.'

Jane ate little. She watched the steam rise from the kettle and wondered if life would ever be the same again. She spread a piece of bread and butter with jam and watched Sidney pick out the caraway seeds from his cake and arrange them in a pattern on the plate. 'Eat it up,' she said, but when she looked away, Sidney lowered the plate to Nero, the black labrador.

'I'll take Jack with me to do the horses,' Edward said. 'We can feed the ducks and clean some harness, too. It will save time in the morning.'

'That's a grand idea. Janey and Lizzie can take the pig-swill to the brickyard and Clare can mind shop. Come along, Sidney and Emily, I want to see if the men are leaving and you'll only get into mischief if you stay here.'

They cut across the two main roads of the town, over the cobbles of the quay. It was still light so Jane didn't mind walking past the cranes and warehouses when they held no menace of darkness. Others were hurrying along there too and the snaking rise of Hunney Hill was swarming with people, all going to Albany. A pedlar sold liquorice sticks and brandy balls from a pitch under the porch of the Cock and Hen, dogs barked, children shouted and bugles called. Jane had heard bugles all her married life and now there was an added sense of urgency, like the gathering call of birds waiting for winter migration. She could hear no hint of return with the spring.

Dark leaves touched with gold marked the forest along to Gunville, and the Barracks appeared through the trees, scrubbed and austere in the evening sun. Sentries prevented people from entering the Barrack Square but men were mustering at the far end, and faces pressed to the tall fence bars tried to make out what was happening. The children were tired and the crowd pushed them against the roughcast wall, and what had begun as an exciting outing was now boring. 'Look, Mother!' Sidney's clear voice made many heads turn to the main driveway, where men with musical instruments formed into ranks.

'It's a band! They'll play the men out to the barges,' someone shouted. Behind the band came men sitting high in the saddle, leading strings of horses and baggage mules with grooms. The row of poplars, dark behind the men, was aflame at the edge of the setting sun as the theatrical scene consolidated, the horses pulling on the bits, the men curbing them until the drum major raised a hand and the band struck up. Sentries flung back the gates, scattering the crowds to line the route. A woman sobbed and Jane stood pale and silent, holding Emily's hand, her other hand resting on Sidney's shoulder. They stood back on the raised bank behind the crowds and could see over the heads of everyone.

It was there that Walter spotted them, making a picture for him to treasure on the way to Africa. Emily waved, and for a moment Walter raised his riding whip in salute and smiled, then obeyed a sharp command for 'Eyes front!' The swaying backs of the mules moved along the lane, followed by a rag-tag of children and dogs, but Jane hurried back to Newport, passing latecomers who had heard the band. The family returned through the town, avoiding the dark quay. It was enough that he had seen them.

Now I can plan, Jane thought with a new serenity. God willing, I can manage. As they reached the High Street, she gave a deep sigh. 'Run home and get a big basin,' she told her children. 'Here's the money. Go up the road and buy faggots and peas for supper.' She went over to the *County Press* window. Already, Newport was a town without men and the crowd mostly consisted of women. She called in to see Maudie and praised the clean curtains at the windows.

'It's all your doing, Mrs Darwen. I went to the hospital and Lucy's been baptised. She's so much better now. The tube isn't out yet but she smiled at me, and Ben is coming home before he goes overseas, to see her.' She was radiant and Jane felt suddenly lonely. Lucky Maudie. In spite of poverty and a sick child, she would have two precious days and nights when she could give herself in simple love and possibly conceive another child. Was it envy? Jane shook herself. She didn't want to change places with Maudie Dove. She had her own seven children to look after.

Chapter 6

Jack blew on his fingers. It was warm with Bess in the stall after feeding the ducks. She pulled at the hay overhead and the smell and the lantern's glow worked a soothing magic on the boy. Edward was filling the trough with fresh water and the other chores were finished. Jack showed Edward the basket of ducks' eggs. 'They don't wander away this weather,' he said. They locked the stable and pulled their caps over their ears. The river was a stream of black lead overhung with mist that swirled in the rising wind. The boys came out on to the bridge as Aaron threw fish-guts into the river.

'Any news?' he called. 'It's getting on for six weeks now and you should hear something soon.'

'Even from the first landing the mail takes three weeks – and it took Father's regiment three weeks to get there,' replied Edward.

'You'd best take the rest of the fish.' Aaron lugged a huge basket over the stones. 'Garn, you can manage that, but get on home now. You both look shrammed.'

Jane was in the boiler-room. 'You aren't doing laundry tonight, Mother?' Edward asked anxiously.

She looked up from the bundle of twigs she was pushing under the boiler and smiled. 'Not tonight, but I thought I would do the crabs for the officers' mess, ready for the morning.' The water was now steaming, but Jane put back the wooden lid impatiently. 'Boil, can't you!' The crabs lay as if dead but bubbles rose in their bin and they were very fresh.

'I'm hungry,' Jack complained. 'Can't the crabs wait until after tea?'

'You know the water has to seethe. I must wait until it's really boiling.' She looked worried. It was too bad that the boys came in cold after working so hard, and she wasn't ready with hot food for them.

'I'll do them if you want to get on,' suggested Jack. Jane looked uncertain. Her son was a scatterbrain but Walter had stressed that he must be made to take responsibility; meanwhile, there was mackerel to fry and the water under the pudding might have evaporated.

'Be sure it's really boiling fast,' she cautioned him, and hurried back to the house. 'Bring in some good coal,' she told Edward.

He filled two hods from the pile of best coal in the coalstore between the shop and the living room, and brought Ikey the cat to show to his mother. 'She's near her time,' he said. 'She was looking for her spot in the coal.'

'Holy Mary, not another litter? It was only the other day I took two kittens to the piggeries to keep down the mice!' She went on adding water to the steamer. 'Fill all the old buckets you can and put them in the yard. It's no use trying to make her have kittens anywhere but in the coal, so I'll spread a clean sack in there and leave the door open a thread.' She put a huge tureen of floury potatoes on the table. 'What's keeping that boy? Call Jack and the girls.'

The back door opened and Jack sidled in. Jane wiped her hands on the oven cloth. 'What happened?' she asked accusingly.

'It wasn't my fault! I thought it was boiling but I couldn't see for steam. I put more wood on the fire and tipped the crabs in and there *were* bubbles.'

'You know you don't add more wood then,' Edward said in a shocked voice. 'It takes it off the boil. Did they throw their claws?' Jack nodded.

'So they're spoiled. We can't send them to the Mess like that. I'll have to dress them for table and you know how long that takes,' said Jane with annoyed resignation.

'I don't want to spend all evening dressing crabs,' whined Lizzie. 'If it's Jack's fault he should do the work *and* take them up to the Barracks in case he gets told off.'

'Nobody asked you,' Jane said caustically. 'Now eat up, the lot of you.'

Ikey licked the last piece of fishskin from her saucer and Sidney put down a dish of milky tea for Nero. It was Walter's firm belief that strong tea was a preventative of distemper in dogs and Jane was touched to see how Sidney now made a point of doing the same every night: he had not forgotten once since Walter left for Africa. The children worked hard and they were very young. She piled more food on Jack's plate and he knew that the crisis was over.

He gave a sidelong grin. 'Can't we do as Father did once?' he suggested, and Jane smiled. The memory of Walter's face, a study in shame and anger when he discovered two dozen crabs with not a leg or claw between them was very funny.

'No, we're not as clever as your father,' she said.

Jack bolted his pudding and ran out to the yard. 'We can try!' The girls cleared the table and spread clean hessian on the deal top. The crabs had cooled slightly and they graded the claws while Janey made splinters of wood from a piece of orange box. Jane inserted a splinter in each claw and Jack assembled the crabs as if they had all their claws intact. Arranged in the clean basket on a linen cloth, they looked perfect but Jane picked one up doubtfully. 'They never really look at them,' Jack said reassuringly. 'The officer takes one sniff and waves them off to the cookhouse and they don't mind. I know one of the men and he'll only laugh.'

Jane looked at the wooden cuckoo clock on the wall. 'You'd better go up now,' she said. 'There's a lot to do tomorrow.' She sighed. At first after Walter left, the children had worked hard before going to school at the hour Miss Martin had decreed, but although they still did the work they loitered on the way to school, finding the bare withy beds full of fascinating small creatures. They began arriving later than their allotted time and then one day, were just in time for the playtime break when Miss Martin saw them coming up the drive with peeled withy swords.

Jane still smarted at the memory of the sharp note she had received, accusing the children of ingratitude and informing her that they must forthwith attend school at the normal time. Jane could understand her point of view and made them apologise to Miss Martin, but she gave them no other punishment. They were so young and did their work with little grumbling.

The next morning, Jane woke early and shuddered as she washed in cold water. Her breath hung in the unheated bedroom and a film of frost covered the window. She pinned up her bun quickly and put on a warm camisole under her dress and thick handknitted stockings. The living room was cosy and it took courage to leave it to scrub the marble slab in the shop after riddling the fire and putting the flatirons to heat. The gophering iron was hot when she came back and she tried it on a piece of paper. The paper charred and Jane blew on the iron to cool it, then crimped the frills of the stiffly-starched pinafores and hung them over the back of a chair to harden.

'Come down and fetch some warm water and use the washstand in my room,' she called upstairs, knowing how cold it would be for the children in the scullery where they usually washed. When the boys went to fetch the cart, she gave them thick mufflers to wrap round their heads to cover their ears, and brought the thick serge cloaks for the girls into the living room to warm up the red flannel linings. Perhaps today there would be a letter. Walter had scribbled a note and passed it to a bargee who knew Aaron Sheath, when the boats paused at Cowes, but she had received nothing since. To be at sea for three weeks without touching land was a nightmare. She remembered her one journey from Ireland when she was so sick she wanted to die.

Africa was another world . . . She wiped soapy water from the counter and dried her hands, then nibbled a date from the block. When the postman came, she took the mail with trembling hands. The one from Ireland she put aside, then tore open the other, hardly seeing the words for tears. He was safe and well, thank God, after a bad journey, with the horses suffering through the Bay of Biscay and in the wet heat south of the Equator with the ship like a foul-smelling Turkish bath. Some of the men had been off-colour, too.

Jane smiled. Walter was never seasick and thought it a weakness, but horses were different and had all his sympathy.

He described their first camp and Jane looked out at the bleak sky, then remembered that down south it was summer. *'By the time you get this, we shall be mustering and training and even relieving some of the Regulars. Now that General Buller has arrived in Cape Town the men are in good heart and eager to engage the enemy. They call him "Buller the Deliverer". Don't fret if you hear nothing for a while. Our post goes by land and sea but war news goes by telegraph to the press.'* He went on to tell her of skirmishes at the Kimberley mines where the Boers were driven back, with only a few British killed.

Jane ran her fingers over the marble slab and felt as if she was as cold. 'Only a few killed'? But if he had been of that few, what then? She heard the cart and pushed the letter into her pocket. 'I've heard from your father and he's well,' she informed the children. She told them of the camp and the horses but not of the fighting. 'Now that we have a field address, you must all write to him. Even if he moves on, the letters will catch up.'

They loaded the cart. 'We'll go by the town,' said Edward. 'There might be ice on the quay.'

'Put on the drag when you come down Hunney Hill, then,' warned Jane, 'and ask Mr Wray if the shoes are right for this weather.' She went back to the house and saw that Emily was crying. 'Aren't you glad we've heard from Father?' she asked.

'I'm frightened. Soldiers get killed.' Jane hugged her close. If only you knew how terrified I am too, Emmy, she thought, and wanted to weep with her daughter.

As it was Saturday, the children could take longer over the chores, but Jane made sure that they had time to play too. She sent Sidney and Emily out with iron hoops to make them warm, racing by the withy beds, as the only warm place in the house was the living room with the blazing range and the pot of beef bones and vegetables and savoury dumplings simmering on the hob. Sam Walmsley put his head round the door and sniffed. 'If you let that smell out, you'll have the whole of Newport in here for a bite,' he joked.

'Come in the warm, Mr Walmsley,' Jane invited. He sat in Walter's high-backed leather chair and stretched his feet towards the fire. Jane gave him a mug of tea and he tipped spirits in from his flask, then drank the hot sweet brew with satisfaction, reminding Jane of Walter and his enjoyment of simple pleasures.

'You're pale, gal. Doing too much?'

'No, it's the cold gets into me, but the boys have lit the fire in the outhouse and it won't be so bad when I start the washing out there.'

Sam looked at the well-polished brasses, the room swept and clean and he'd already looked in at the stables and knew that the horses were in good condition. 'I promised Walter I'd keep an eye on you, but as yet you haven't asked for help.' He pretended to be hurt. 'If you don't ask a favour soon, I'll think there are others you'd rather have helping.'

'Now who'd be asking for compliments?' she demanded, laughing. 'I heard how you rescued Jack the other day when the wheel locked – and I haven't yet thanked you.'

'Oh, that was nothing. I've brought along a load to save the lads one journey, and I'll take some fish off you while I'm here. The oranges have come and you'll need plenty for Christmas trade and the first batch of apples are out of the Wootton store. They look good.' He took one from his pocket and cut it with his pocket-knife. It was crisp and sweet and had the waxy skin of apples stored in a cool loft.

'I heard from Walter.' She gave him the letter and watched him read it. Sam carefully kept all expression from his face but he thought it was a pity Walter had mentioned the fighting. He should have known Jane would be scared half to death. 'He seems well and hearty,' he commented cheerfully. 'But now to really important matters: have you ordered your Christmas dinner yet?'

'The goose is coming from Folley as usual, there will be carols and the Church social and I expect one or two will drop in.' Her voice faded as she imagined Christmas without Walter singing at the harmonium.

Sam pursed his lips. 'I know it's hard, Jane, but I'll drop by and there'll be plenty of mouths to feed. You'll have no time to fret.' He put on his hat and buttoned his coat high before unloading the cart, and the air cold-fingered its way into the shop. Jane closed the door to the living room to keep in the heat and put on woollen mittens to handle the cold boxes of fruit and to cover the bananas with straw to keep out the frost. Her fingers ached and it would be so easy to let everything go in a tide of misery, but she gritted her teeth and prised frozen fish from the slab for Sam to take home.

Edward and Jack came back bringing the east wind with them, their faces blue and their lips chapped. They shrugged out of their coats and huddled close to the range before going out again. Jack rubbed his chilblains although he knew that sitting by the fire made them worse. Jane went to serve customers and looked up when Edward came into the shop when she was alone. 'I want a word with you, Mother,' he said awkwardly.

'Well, hurry up before we get frozen,' she said.

'I've been talking to Fred Cantor.'

Jane already had her hand on the door, wanting to get back to the warm again. 'I don't like that family, Edward. I thought you had enough of them with Percy picking fights and with Fred getting drunk.'

'He said that I will be fourteen soon.' Edward shifted uneasily.

'How clever of him to know that! Get on with it, I'm freezing.' Edward looked like Walter when he was about to say something he knew that Jane would hate. 'Well?'

'He wants me to work on the railway with him.' The words spilled out incoherently and he had to repeat them.

'The railway! The cheek of it! You still have schooling to finish, my lad, and you'll not leave a minute early. And what would you be doing on the railway, may I ask?'

'They want a boy on the station at Cowes to help with luggage.' He looked at her beseechingly. 'It wouldn't be just yet,' he added.

'And what would your father have to say? You know he

wants you in the shop when you leave, and I don't know how I'll manage when you go back to school after Christmas if the weather gets worse.'

Edward smiled. 'The war will be over by then, Mother, and Father will be home. Fred says . . .'

'Fred Cantor? I might have known he'd fill you with rubbish!' Her eyes flashed and her misery surfaced. She thrust the letter into his hands. 'Read that and tell me if the war is nearly over!' Tears, normally held back until the children were in bed, stung her lids and her shoulders heaved. 'Tell me if your father will be home after Christmas or ever!'

Edward put an awkward red hand on her shoulder. 'I'm sorry, Mother. I thought it was all right – you never let on. I promise we'll all help and he will come back safely. I know he will.'

Everyone had a red nose in the cold and none of the others noticed that Jane had been crying. Edward kept an eye on her and a new note of authority in his voice made Jack jump to fetch more coal and the girls lay up for dinner and look sharp about it. As the hot soup warmed them all, Jane knew that Christmas and Jane Darwen must go on as usual.

Sunday dawned with a red edge to the sky. The wind had dropped and lowering clouds raised the temperature. Jane met the children from Sunday School and they picked their way through the icy mud to Fairlee Cemetery, with Jane holding firmly to the wreath of holly for Caroline's grave. The Websters and the Fosters joined her at the gate, each carrying a similar wreath. There were few families with no tiny grave to tend, with headstones telling of infants dead from diphtheria or infantile paralysis. Jane wiped the simple headstone free of mud and placed the wreath securely.

Caroline Darwen, died in infancy, 1895.

The Websters had lost their only son when he was nine and they'd recently bought a splendid angel of Italian marble to watch over him. Jane imagined it at night, cold with folded menacing wings and she ignored all hints that she should raise a similar monument to Caroline, preferring the simple stone on the grass mound that was nearer to God. Walter never visited the place, and Jane suspected he shared her horror of the memories it evoked, as well as the gossip round the tip where dead flowers were dumped.

Mr Foster was in good form. He'd put on a smart tailcoat and new galoshes and was bursting with news, but most of the mourners had already read the latest bulletin. Now he caught up with Jane. 'Did you know that relief forces have reached Kimberley?' he asked eagerly as she threw away some faded chrysanthemums. 'Lord Methuen has reached the relief column and attacked at the Modder River.' The little grocer was so delighted to be the fount of wisdom that he had learned his piece by heart and sounded like a gramophone record. Jane said she had heard, but still he followed her.

'Have you seen the casualty list?' he asked hopefully, and then stopped as he saw the agony in her eyes. 'I'm sorry, ma'am, I didn't think. There are none from Newport, thank goodness, although twenty British soldiers were killed in the last sortie from Kimberley. That included some Irish, who fought bravely and were a credit to Her Majesty,' he added with condescension. 'Major Scot Turner was amongst them.'

'Major Scot Turner? God rest his soul! He was a good brave man and must surely be missed.' Jane let herself be pulled away by Emily to see the white wax flowers under a glass dome that the Fosters had brought, while the angel from the Webster grave looked down with ice on his wings. There is too much cold and white in death, thought Jane and gathered the children for the walk home by way of the towpath where it was less muddy than the road.

The younger children played leapfrog over the capstans that moored the grey barges and Jack climbed up the sides of stacked planks waiting to be stored. The protruding planks made good swings and Jane tried to ignore the danger. A little innocent exercise was good and she had learned to accept the scrapes and bruises. Sidney ran ahead to open the stable door so that his mother could inspect the horses. They were safe and warm, the hay was lasting well and the oats were dry and fragrant, free from mildew.

'Your father will be so pleased when I write and tell him how well you care for the animals,' she said approvingly. Blackie snorted and Jane ran a hand over his muzzle. He was healthy but lacked exercise. She'd have to ask Sam what to do. The family at Wootton would be glad to have him – Archie could use him on the farm and it would be good for the horse. 'I might send Blackie to Uncle Archie,' she mused.

'Bess would miss him,' Sidney objected. 'She pined when he went to Wootton in the summer, and she even whinnies when he comes back from a ride.'

'Yes, I'd not want her upset. In Ireland we had stable companions for our horses.' She smiled. 'Not another horse, but a donkey or a nanny goat.' She was touched by the sudden radiance in their faces. 'That's not a promise,' she said hastily, 'it's only an idea and it would mean another mouth to feed.'

'With Blackie gone we wouldn't have to feed him,' Jack pointed out logically, and on the way home Jane wondered what she had started as they all argued. The girls wanted a nanny goat and the boys a donkey.

'We could milk a nanny goat and make better cheese than Mr Foster has on the slab,' said Clare.

'And who would end up milking her?' asked Jane dryly as she put out bread and pickles, jam and cheese, but nevertheless she thought back to the little white goats on the Irish hills and wondered.

Sidney brought out paper and pencils for the Sunday letters to Walter. The children finished quickly and turned to games and knitting. Jane wondered what would interest Walter. The shop was doing well, the boys were managing the deliveries and Dan, Bert Cooper's younger brother by fifteen years who lived with him and Annie, helped them with the heavy boxes. Jane was sorry for Dan as he had been an 'afterthought' that had killed his mother; he was helpful, and had a dry wit that delighted Jane and infuriated

Annie. He escaped as often as possible from his sister-in-law's acid tongue and frugal table.

Jane inspected the short notes written by the children. Edward had stated the number of times he had been to the Barracks, and what he'd delivered, while Jack merely added a *'Come back soon'* to that letter. The girls had written about Ikey and Nero, the shop gossip and the fact that they wanted new dresses for Christmas. Sidney managed in a few words to convey all that would make Walter laugh and feel that all was well at home, and had included some drawings. Jane addressed the envelope then banked up the fire, remembering to leave the coalhouse door open for Ikey and her kittens before going up to bed.

Chapter 7

'The Queen's coming!' Sidney rushed in. 'Mother, I saw the outriders but they came down Snooks Hill and went back.' It was Christmas Eve and bitterly cold. 'They must have found ice on the Hill. Emily will be mad to have missed her again. She's up at Mr Foster's with Janey and Lizzie.'

'Well, you know what to do. The rest of you wrap up warm and fetch some buckets, quickly,' said Jane. The children ran to the far end of the bridge and down by the water, filling buckets and an orange box with grit until they were almost too heavy to drag to the top of the Hill. There they shovelled grit over the patches of ice until one of the outriders came back and saw them. He dismounted and took Clare's spade, making light work of the gritting and ignoring his smart livery. When he heard a distant horn, he remounted and rode down the Hill and up the High Street. His companion meanwhile returned to Osborne, to report that the road was passable. The children stood and waited, Clare posing with her spade and hoping she looked pretty.

A light carriage drawn by four black horses slowed as it reached the top of the Hill. The coachman saw the gritted surface and the children waving and threw down a handful of coins. The carriage went safely down the hill and they had a glimpse of a black, crêpe-trimmed bonnet and an old pale face sunk on bowed shoulders. Two tired eyes lit up with pleasure and the Queen kissed her hand to them.

Edward counted the money. 'What shall we do with it?'

'Some is mine,' said Clare jealously.

'*Parson's* sell crystallised fruit and we have enough for a very big box,' suggested Jack greedily.

'No,' said Sidney, looking cross. 'We ought to buy something nice for Mother for tomorrow. We can choose it on the way back from the Barracks.'

Back at the shop, Clare went to the door as soon as she heard her sisters returning. 'We saw the Queen and you didn't! I had to help so I couldn't come and tell you,' she added smugly. Emily looked downcast but then Sidney whispered that they were going to spend the money they had been given on a present for Jane, and if Emily met them at *Tiler's* after the deliveries she could help choose it.

'Wash your hands before the company come,' Jane ordered. She straightened the damask tablecloth and arranged fancy cakes on a glass stand. The brasses and fire-irons reflected the glow of the clean coal fire and she fidgeted until she heard carriage wheels, conscious of her best dark green velvet dress and the neatly coiled coronet of dark hair done as Walter liked it. She made a fuss of Blackie and gave him sugar as he nuzzled her hand, his breath sweet and warm on the frosty air. 'He looks well,' she said. He was leaner and well-groomed and she was now more confident that Walter would approve of the horse being lent to Archie.

Archie unhitched the two horses and took them down to the stables out of the cold while Amy, his wife, hurried thankfully into the warm room, shedding her cloak and gloves. She sat on a straight-backed chair, arranging her new brown serge skirt with care. 'Rose couldn't come out in the cold,' she said. 'Her chest is bad again and she never thrives in this weather.' Jane thought sadly of the lovely little face with its pink and white skin and huge blue eyes. Rose was as light as a feather and had cold after cold throughout each winter. 'I must take back some lemons,' Amy said. 'The doctor says that all I can do is to keep her warm and give her honey and lemon for her cough.' She sniffed. 'He's got a fad that she ought to have goat's milk. Silly man, he knows we have gallons of new creamy milk straight from the cow.'

'If that's what you need, I can give you a pail to take back. Since Blackie went to you, we bought a nanny goat as a stable mate for Bess and now have more milk than we can use.'

Amy smiled politely. Her eyes missed nothing and she

was disappointed: a woman without a man didn't need to be as houseproud and shouldn't look as handsome as Jane did now. She wished she had thought of dark green velvet for her new dress. 'I didn't think Walter likes goats,' she said.

'As Walter isn't here, I have to make decisions on my own.' A dangerous sparkle in Jane's eye warned Amy not to probe. 'I tell him what I think fit, including *not* telling him that you have Blackie on the farm. If you think Walter should know, then I'll write and you may have to bring Blackie back again if he disapproves.' Jane moved the plate of bread and butter half an inch and went to fill the kettle.

'I don't know how you manage,' Amy said in a placating voice. 'If Archie went away I couldn't possibly run the farm all alone.' She twisted the rings on her fingers and looked sly. 'I expect the neighbours help out,' she went on. 'Does Sam Walmsley come in often?'

Jane gave her an old-fashioned look. So that's what they thought! Walter away and all the men visiting her? The men were no problem, but there had been a subtle change in the manner of the wives since Walter's departure. At first they were sympathetic and gave many offers of help, but when Jane remained cheerful and refused their aid, they drifted away, visiting the shop for only as long as it took to buy fish and making sure that their husbands no longer offered to help. Jane had no idea how jealous some women had become when their men spoke of Mrs Darwen with respect and admiration for the way she managed. They liked her cheerfulness and humour and oddly enough, applauded the way she looked after Maudie Dove and women like her.

'Mr Walmsley? Yes, he comes into the shop to take the order and save me a journey. He says that the quay and warehouses are no place for women. Aaron brings the fish and the boys collect the fruit.'

Outside, Archie was laughing with the boys and Jane sighed with relief. She put the kettle on the hottest hob and took a steaming apple and ginger cake from the oven, filling the air with spicy scent. Archie was red with the cold. He hugged her and kissed her heartily on the cheek. Jane caught sight of Amy's face and chuckled inwardly. You needn't think I want your husband, Amy Cheverton, she thought, but it was good to smell the woollen cloth with its faint whiff of tobacco and have strong arms round her again.

Edward couldn't hide his disappointment that Rose hadn't come. It was strange how much he cared for the delicate child, so different from his sturdy and often unemotional nature. Rose was all mercurial high spirits or deep depression. Amy laughed at him and unlike Jane, couldn't leave well alone. 'Do you miss your little sweetheart, Edward?' He turned crimson and stuffed his mouth so full of ginger cake that he almost choked and Jane hastily talked of the little goat and how much the children had taken to her, and took it in turns to milk her.

They spoke of the war and the casualty lists, and Archie watched Jane, admiring her courage and self-control when Amy talked of the wounded with complete disregard for Jane's feelings. 'They say that Lord Methuen doesn't mind how many are killed so long as he has victories,' she sniffed.

Archie frowned. 'Everyone was for him when he didn't risk too many men, but Buller should never have given him command. Buller should lead the attacks himself as he knows Zulu country and their ways.'

'But Lord Methuen is a good soldier, isn't he?' asked Edward.

'Yes, but not to fight these rascals. He's an old army man, used to fighting in line, which is no good against these artful beggars of farmers who come out of the rocks and are gone before they can be caught.'

'We must all pray for peace,' said Amy piously.

'That won't win the war,' objected Jane. 'They've started collecting comforts for the troops and if we give as freely to that as we can afford, it will do more than prayers can.'

'Look, Aunty Amy, I've bought a favour,' said Jack. He showed the button on his lapel: *Buller the Deliverer.*

'I bought a favour for Lord Methuen but lost it,' said Edward. 'I'm glad I lost it now. As the Royal Horse Artillery are fighting close to Kimberley, there's bound to be a victory soon.'

Jane cleared away the tea things and they all dressed warmly and walked up to St Thomas' Church. A huge brazier burned in the middle of the square between the Church and the Wheatsheaf, and patrons from both places stayed to hear the carols and to give to the comforts fund. The faces in the flickering light were of women and children, old men and boys and the few men who had avoided service, like Archie who worked on a farm and Bert Cooper who seemed able to malinger his way out of anything. Jane saw the prosperous manager of the arms factory there and wondered if Walter wouldn't have done better making bombs.

There was little Peace on Earth to sing about and Jane was glad to get back to the warm house, mulled ale and potato pie before Archie brought the horses round for Amy, who had played on the harmonium and seemed more contented now. Jane was sad to see the visitors go and when Archie kissed her, perhaps more lingeringly than was necessary while Amy struggled into her six-button gloves, she had an absurd desire to pretend that he was Walter. Now, she had to face Christmas Day without him.

The morning dawned bright and clear and the family hurried through their work and settled down to porridge and fresh bread and jam. Emily nudged Sidney and they giggled. The others caught their mood and had an irritating air of 'I know something you don't know.'

Jane brought in a basket of presents for everyone – hair ribbons and knitted ties, handkerchiefs and sweets, gloves and figs. The children rummaged in the cupboard and produced presents for her and Jane had to look pleased and surprised at the bead purses, sewn by the girls but often with her assistance. Edward had carved a pair of wooden spoons, Sidney had painted a nativity scene and Jack gave her a bookmark of leather.

She propped the picture against the blue vase on the mantelpiece and picked up the last package. Her heart lurched with surprised emotion as she had no idea what it could be. A wad of cottonwool came from the small box and she picked up a brooch. It was cheap and gaudy, a thin layer of mother-of-pearl on white metal with a red rose painted on it. Across the base was written MOTHER. It was vulgar and yet at that moment was the most beautiful jewel she possessed. She pinned it on her blouse and the children beamed with pride. 'We all chose it,' said Emily.

'Your father left presents, too,' Jane said. From a wicker hamper they pulled wooden hoops, skipping ropes and a set of nine-pins. There was a big coloured ball and a chequer board and dice. Sam had sent over a pretty jar of Chinese ginger and a bottle of sherry wine, and while Jack stoked the fire under the puddings and Janey made brandy butter, Jane opened a package that Archie had given her as he left. Amy's gift lay on the harmonium, a pack of cottons and needles as befitted a woman alone, but Jane felt an almost forgotten thrill as she saw the extravagant wrapping and the colourful box. The girl on the lid had a sixteen-inch waist and was dark-haired and laughing as Jane had been when she came to England. She bit into a Turkish Delight as she read the tiny note. *'Sweets to the sweet'*, it said. She tossed the note into the fire. 'Edward, you can all have one before dinner but no more.'

'Who gave us those?' asked Clare.

'Your Uncle Archie spoils you,' she replied.

'You can have another piece if you like, Mother,' Lizzie said. 'I'm sure he wouldn't mind.'

'No, he wouldn't mind. He's a dear man, a dear man,' she said softly.

'Will he ride Blackie tomorrow?' asked Jack. Jane looked puzzled. 'He said he wanted to ride to hounds,' her son explained patiently. Jane went pink. She had forgotten that she'd invited Archie in before the Meet up at the Square and now she wished she hadn't. The look he had given her as he pressed the parcel into her hands had been expressive. Sure there was no harm in the man, she told herself uneasily, but when Archie came she kept Emily and Lizzie by her side while he drank one mug of ale and ate a hot chestnut. He was well-groomed and as good-looking as

Walter and it was a pleasure to watch him ride up the road on Blackie. Jane pretended that Walter was already there at the Wheatsheaf and would be home soon.

Rivulets of melting ice formed in the gutters and a hunting horn sounded. The Meet of Foxhounds was by the Wheatsheaf this year and Jane buttoned up Emily's coat and gave her the new gloves to wear. It was traditional to watch the hounds move off from the Meet even if they started as they did every other year from Gypsy Hollow in Carisbrooke. The shops in the High Street had a shuttered, Sunday look. Jane spoke to neighbours and customers, but few mentioned war.

Dr Barnes sat a rangy hunter and drank spiced wine. The local gentry in hunting pink, with their ladies in black habits and riding side-saddle, gathered round the landlord of the Wheatsheaf to take a stirrup cup from the silver salver that Mrs Grace held high. Local businessmen on their own horses reined in slightly away from the richer full members of the Hunt, from habit, but today anyone who could sit a horse was welcome for the Boxing Day Meet, if he contributed to the Hunt Purse.

A bow-legged man sitting a saddle-backed mare tried to look as if he didn't drive the coalcart in the working week, and Bert Cooper was on his own highly unpredictable stallion, looking very uncomfortable. Satan was a good name for the beast, but to Bert the animal was more of a white elephant as he was half-scared of him. Jane smiled to herself maliciously. Bert had demanded Blackie for the hunt and was very put out when he learned that Archie had him on the farm. With Walter away, Bert tried to take far too much for granted and refusing him also made up to Jane for Annie's sarcasm.

'Bert Cooper can hardly handle him, Mother,' said Jack. 'Satan was playing up when he brought him down from the brickyard. He's over-fed and under-worked – Bert will be off at the first fence.'

Jane recalled other hunts, with Walter immaculate in a well-cut jacket and top hat, boots that gleamed and his silver spurs earning the respect due to him. He had once brought her the fox's brush, reeking of blood and excreta but his pride had evaporated when he saw the revulsion in her eyes. He never brought trophies home again, and confined his talk to who had fallen and where, and who had made a fool of himself.

The Master whipped in his hounds and cracked a long leather thong over their heads. They moved off, each rider putting a contribution in the Purse. The rich threw in a sovereign and others gave what they could afford. Jane stood tall, remembering that Walter would have given a sovereign, too. The Master of Foxhounds saw her. 'I hope he's with us next year,' he called and saluted. Sidney absorbed the colour and atmosphere, the bright red coats against the grey church and the innkeeper with the silver trays, the horses with coats like polished silk, the immediacy of the horn and the flow of hounds just clear of the hooves. They passed, leaving the smell of hounds and fresh dung on the frost.

Some backed out at Coppins Bridge, saying that the ground was too frosted. Bert paused and Jane called, 'Satan looks in fine fettle. Are you following?' Bert saw her smile and Archie grinning from the back of the horse he had wanted to ride, so he tugged at the reins and followed hounds, to show her that he was as good as Walter.

Jane took Clare and Janey up to Staplers, where they sat on a gate and watched the hounds weave across a meadow in full cry. Horses jumped the five-bar gate, bunching in the gully before gaining ground in Arreton, making a picture that Walter loved, but Jane soon took the girls back to the *County Press* window to see what quarry Walter was hunting this Boxing Day. The news was evasive: mention of fighting on the Modder River and praise for the heroism and sacrifice of the Highland Regiment and the Gordons. *'In spite of heavy losses, the Artillery kept up a fierce barrage,'* she read. What Artillery? Which regiment? The list of casualties was dated 20 December and contained no familiar names.

The news was wrapped up in cautious stirring phrases but indicated that all was not well. Jane's faith in the newspapers had died weeks ago and she longed for the truth from Walter. Some papers condemned Methuen and some praised him, while others pointed out that this was a war he could not comprehend, having an alien code that the British must copy if they were to flush out the skirmishing Boers, who had small sturdy horses used to rough terrain, accurate Mauser rifles and no cumbersome bayonets. They fought and retreated to deep trenches where their big guns were hidden and made sorties like will-o'-the-wisps, mowing down hundreds of men at the Modder.

Clare was cold so they went home to fetch her hoop. Jane carved the rest of the goose and made more apple sauce, reheated the Christmas pudding and cooked potatoes. Suddenly there was nothing to do, and she sat fingering her new brooch.

'Dreaming, gal?'

'Mr Walmsley!' she exclaimed.

Sam looked at the scattered newspapers and the neatly laid table. She can't be on her feet all the time, he thought. 'I hoped that you'd offer me some of that sherry wine, unless you drank it all last night.' She filled two glasses. 'To Walter and a speedy return,' he said. He regarded her solemnly. 'One day he'll walk in that door and expect things to be as he left them.' His voice, though light, held a plea.

'I know it, Mr Walmsley.'

'Why not call me Sam? Everyone does and I've always called you Jane.'

'I don't know. People are strange. They don't believe in friendship between men and women. They might think I was too familiar.'

Sam gave a short laugh. 'So they've dropped hints to you, too?' Jane raised startled brown eyes. 'Oh yes, there have been a few nods and winks and speculation and it's best you know. The fact that I'm almost old enough to be your father doesn't count. They'll make it hard for you if you give them half a chance. Call me Sam and take it for granted that you and Walter are equally my friends and business associates, but take care. Not with me – I wouldn't hurt a hair of your pretty head but there are vinegar faces who think a woman alone is fair game.' He sighed. 'The trouble is, that pretty face and kind heart of yours might lead some to take liberties. Understand me, Jane, you are a lovely woman.'

'What can I do, Sam? I can't go through life with my face buttoned up like Annie. It's not my nature. I can't see where gossip could start as I have the children here most of the time. People like Annie don't worry me.'

'When they go back to school you'll be alone, and the barges will be upriver with the coal; the men can be a rough bunch.'

Jane laughed. 'You've no need to worry about the men from the river. They would never harm me. Walter has been good to them and the Dutch families come in here for vegetables. I save goosegrease for one family who have a child with a weak chest and I often bind up cuts for them.' Her eyes sparkled. 'If I get into trouble, I'll hang a red flag out of the top window and you'll see it from the warehouse.'

'That would really set the tongues wagging.' Sam relaxed. 'They'd swear it was a code of messages.'

'Stay and have dinner,' Jane begged. 'The children are coming down the road. Here, take this jug and get some cider.'

'Mother, you should have stayed!' said Sidney.

'Whisht! I've never heard such noise. You know I could never see the fox torn.'

'The Hunt doubled back to Cross Lanes and Bert Cooper came a cropper by the copse. It was so funny! We all saw it. The horse bolted and he had to walk home.'

'What of the horse?' asked Jane anxiously.

'He ran off after jumping a thorn hedge and stood there, grazing. Mr Cooper could have found him easily but he was too cross and muddy.'

Sam put the cider jug down. 'Where's the horse now?'

Jack smiled. 'When Mr Cooper had gone, we took some carrots from the barn there and called Satan. He came like a lamb and ate the carrots. Edward took the reins and led him to the brickyard, but the gates were barred and we couldn't make anyone hear, so we took him down to our stable in Blackie's old box. He was hot so Edward said he'll be late for dinner as he ought to rub him down and put a blanket on him.'

'You did just as I'd have done,' approved Sam, 'but Bert's an awkward cuss and if you saw him ditched he'll be mad. Might even think you played a trick on him, hiding the horse. I think it best if I tell him.'

'What about your dinner, Sam!'

'I'll be back directly. I'll catch Bert at home if not in the brickyard. Keep my bit of dinner as the wife is in bed again and I doubt if Annie would give me any!' Sam passed by the Shoulder of Mutton and along to Pan Mill, and as he rounded the bend, Bert came out of the saloon bar, glassy-eyed and full of comfort.

Back at the shop, Jane served the family and put vegetables aside to keep hot for Sam and Edward. It was a relief to have Sam take over, as she hated meeting any of the Coopers except Dan, who was a useful go-between. A banging on the door made Jane hurry to open it, thinking it was Sam again, but as she closed the living room door behind her, the outer door burst open in spite of the Closed sign and Bert Cooper lurched into the shop and leaned on the counter. His eyes were as red as a ferret's and he took up one of the heavy weights from the pile by the scales and punctuated his words with blows to the counter. 'SHOP! SHOP! SHOP!'

Jane walked behind the counter and fixed him with an icy stare.

Holy Mother he's as drunk as a Lord, she thought. 'And what might you be wanting? Can you not read the sign? Do I never have a meal in peace with my children?'

He clung to the counter. 'I've lorst me horse,' he said with pathos.

'And do you think I have him under the counter? He's quite safe and you can collect him when you're sober. He was found and put in the stable to cool off.'

'I knew it!' He glared and banged the counter again, leaving deep dents in the wood. 'Those children of yourn stole him. They laughed at me when I took a tumble, too. Sly as foxes, they are.' He leaned across the counter.

'There's a law in the land that says Thou Shalt Not Steal – and I'm going up to Fairlee to the constable to tell him your family are thieves. Those boys need a strong hand but they've no father to give them the strap, that's the trouble.' He was full of maudlin zeal.

'Now listen to me, Bert Cooper,' Jane said, partly frightened and partly furious. He was a heavily built man and to Jane very unattractive, but never more so than now. He reeked of beer and reminded her of the one time when Walter had been really drunk and forced her into bed without care or tenderness. In spite of her revulsion, she looked into his face and tried to reason with him. Holy Mary let someone come in, she silently prayed. 'The boys helped you,' she said, and tried to smile. 'You know how Walter taught them to care for animals. Go home and rest and come back later to fetch him.'

'He's not my horse any more, that's the trouble,' he muttered. 'I want to know what harm they've done to him.'

Jane's eyes glowed pink with anger and loose hair escaped on to her cheek as she made to answer with a vehement retort, but then his words sank in. 'You *have* sold him, Bert? And I suppose you've already taken the money!'

Bert nodded. He forgot his sense of outrage. Now he knew that Satan was safe, his attention was fixed on Jane. Normally he was half-afraid of her but tonight his inhibitions were dulled. 'You're a pretty woman, Jane,' he said. 'Too pretty to be left behind. What's a woman like you doing without a man to cuddle up to? Walter must be mad.' She tried to pull away as he suddenly caught at her dress, his hand hot and hard against her breast. She felt the fabric split and indignation at the ruin of her second-best dress made her think quickly. Her free hand found a wooden skewer, split at one end to hold the price card and pointed at the other and she brought it down on his hand as her Irish temper flared and his drunken breath fanned her cheek.

Bert howled with pain. He released her and she shrank back behind the counter, aware of his fury and realising she was trapped in the small space. She took an orange in each hand as Bert came slowly towards her, his eyes hard and his mouth loose. He picked up the heaviest of the weights and smiled, as if enjoying revenge for the injury and for all the snubs he had endured in the past from the wife of a man he envied for his easy manner, his looks and the making of eight children from this lovely body.

He threw the weight just as a shaft of light came through the opening door. Jane ducked and the weight missed her by a fraction, chipping the marble slab and losing itself among the mackerel and ice. Then she opened her eyes to see Bert flat on his back with Sam Walmsley standing over him, his boot raised and a look of such fury that Jane thought murder would be done. 'No, Sam,' she said with icy calm. 'He isn't worth it.' She caught his arm and forced him to look at her. 'No more,' she said firmly. 'But thank God you came – he would have killed me.'

Sam jerked the man to his feet. Bert put a hand to his jaw and seemed considerably more sober. Sam pulled him up against the wall and shook him, then took a deep breath and Jane relaxed. The worst was over. 'You have an apology to make to the lady,' Sam said softly. He banged Bert's head against the wall.

'Sam!' warned Jane. 'No trouble!'

'Apologise, or I frog march you up to the police station and have you charged with assault and battery.' He slapped the man's cheek, casually but hard. 'Well?'

Genuine regret surfaced as Bert apologized. 'It was the drink,' he explained. Tears of self-pity and a runny nose made him look revolting. 'And it was the worry of the horse. I had sold him to Webster, you see, and thought I might have to give back the money.' He began to beg Jane's pardon over and over again.

'Please get him out of here,' Jane said, faint with disgust.

'We'll take the horse home,' Sam said, and grinned. 'It's a fair old walk to the Websters and Bert needs the exercise.' He pushed him out into the road and towards the stable. Jane cleared away the dinner things and missed the sight of Bert Cooper walking at the tail of the horse that Sam rode. His feet shuffled and his eye showed promise of all the colours of the rainbow tomorrow. Net curtains twitched up Church Litten and by Oystershell Cottages and the next day, everyone in Newport heard that Bert Cooper had been dead drunk after the Hunt and that Sam Walmsley had blackened his eye.

There was much speculation but both men kept silent, Bert from shame and Sam from his care for Jane. 'All right, gal?' he called from the shop door the next day.

'Yes, thank you Sam. I wrote to Walter and told him about the Meet and that the Master asked after him. There was nothing more of interest.'

'No good writing for the sake of it,' he agreed. 'We can sort out anything this end.'

'By the way, you never got your dinner, Sam. I bought some nice boiling bacon today. Come in tomorrow when the children are home, and take a bit back for Elsie if she's able to eat it.'

Chapter 8

Jane Darwen flaked off a thin layer of green paint and wondered whether to ask Mr Damer what he'd charge to paint the shop front; it hadn't been touched for years. There was no end in sight to the war, and Walter was too far away to make decisions – what he wrote these days had nothing to do with home. His letters told of the suffering of the horses but as usual made little mention of the men and their conditions. After the disaster at Magersfontein, however, when he'd seen the Highland regiment and the Gordons mowed down after the British had been made to try a frontal attack on Boer defences, he had written to her about it.

He wrote also of treachery: the Boers had hoisted a white flag over a house when the Seaforth Highlanders went through their lines, but once the Scots had passed through, respecting the flag of truce and submission, the Boers had opened fire from the house, thinking that all Scots were through the gap and could be picked off from the rear. '*They made a mistake there*,' wrote Walter. '*The Highlanders went mad and bayonetted every living thing in that house.*' But mostly he told her of the heat and flies in the African summer, and Jane learned more from the *County Press* than from his latest front-line messages.

Edward had a large map on which Jane tried to plot the events of the war, noting the capture of Spion Kop and the fighting at Venter's Spruit, rejoicing at victory and mourning the dead and wounded. Mr Foster had all the bulletins copied on to the backs of envelopes and old invoices, stored on a spike in the shop. To look up the retreat from Tugela for a customer he had to riffle through dozens of sheets of paper and began to wish he'd never started this service. Far from being good for trade, he now had to waste valuable serving time, and when a customer came in and said: 'Have you a minute to find the date when the Boers wrecked the bridges over the Modder, Mr Foster?' he groaned, as he was already trying desperately to recall where the account of the skirmish at Rhodes Drift could be for someone else.

'You offer a wonderful service, Foster,' said Dr Barnes as he went straight to the counter to be served in front of everyone else. 'I'll have some of my special tobacco, please.'

'I'll be with you as soon as I've served the doctor,' Mr Foster said to the waiting group, but hoped they'd go away.

Dr Barnes drew him to one side. 'Certain civic figures had a meeting last night, and in view of your activities there is every likelihood of you being put up for the Town Council. You are performing a unique and humane task.'

Mr Foster handed him the tobacco in a daze. It was the fulfilment of all his dreams – to be a councillor, to walk with the gentry and be at the Town Hall when Royalty came. He might even be recognized by the Seelys at Mottistone Manor and the titled vicar at Osborne! Caught in the trap of his business acumen, he was doomed to repeat again and again how two hundred and fifty of the best British troops had been killed as they followed Methuen at Magorsfontein – but now it was different. He bought exercise books and copied in the bulletins, even warming to his own rhetoric.

'The enemy have better rifles, ma'am, called Mausers, and the blackguards fire and run away without giving our chaps time to retaliate. Now if I was in command, I'd make sure our boys had the same guns instead of those heavy ones they have to use.'

'Would you give one to my Ben?' asked Maudie Dove shyly. She thought he was wonderful.

'If only I could,' he said modestly. 'That'll be tuppence and the borax will be in tomorrow.'

Maudie haunted the shop. Ben's name was not on the casualty lists after the relief of Kimberley and she took pride in the fact that he had fought at the defeat of Cronje, the famous Boer leader. Pictures in the *Daily Mail* of the defeated man, before he embarked for St Helena and exile, showed British soldiers among the Boer prisoners, and she was convinced that one of the faces was Ben's. More women now spoke to her and she took trouble over Lucy and her own appearance, keeping the rooms in which they lived clean and pleasant. Her daughter grew plump with the fresh fruit and fish that Jane gave them and the little scar on her throat was hardly visible now.

'Cronje is not how I thought he would be,' Maudie said to anyone who would listen. 'He's middle-aged with a beard, and not at all good-looking – *and* his wife is a mess. My Ben was standing right by him, you know.'

Jane felt a mixture of pride and guilt when she saw her own well-nourished children and heard the news of typhoid and scurvy among the troops. The shop was doing well and she made a fair amount of pin money from pickles, jams and potato pies. When the sun shone with more conviction, she went ahead with the order for the painter and knew it was spring-cleaning time.

A reluctant participant in the annual ritual, Clare shook the carpet on the clothes-line with more resentment than enthusiasm. 'Why do we have to work so hard? Dan does all the heavy work for Mrs Cooper, so why can't he do ours?'

'Dan already helps with the animals and the brickyard and I can't expect any more. Annie puts on him, but you live here and your father expects you to help, so I'm not turning this house into a pigsty just because I have a lazy daughter.' She smiled. 'Now tie your head up in this duster, Clare, and put on a sack apron. That carpet is full of dust.'

Janey attacked the bedroom rugs with a wicker carpet-beater, sending clouds of dust billowing up to hang on the sunbeams, while Jack reached up into the corners of the outhouse with a long-handled brush, bringing down the winter harvest of cobwebs. Lizzie wiped a strand of hair from her eyes with a soapy hand. 'I hate spring-cleaning,' she grumbled. Rainbow lights danced in the water as she washed all the china and put the clean pieces to drain on the slate shelf out of doors. Some was never used and other pieces only once at Christmas and they would all go back for another year, but Jane loved her china cabinet and regretted that it had to stay in a dark corner by the pantry door. 'You'll be glad of a few pieces when you get married,' she said, but Lizzie wished every piece would break.

The warm spell showed up every dingy crack. The pampas grass was taken out of its vase and burned, and the limp leaves of the castor oil plant were wiped free of the grime from winter fires. Buckets of strong soda water, fierce enough to remove the skin, waited for the boys to use on the ceiling and walls of the outhouse. The boiler had a good scrub and the bars under it were black-leaded. For once, the smell of fish was banished as doors and windows were flung open. Jane believed that if a place smelled fresh it was healthy, and even on cold days she aired the rooms well.

Now she plunged her arms into the hot soapy water to wash the linen valances from the beds. Briskly, she pounded them with the dolly and rubbed them vigorously over the washboard. When she was satisfied, she eased them out into a two-handled tub and the boys carried them to the outhouse to boil in the copper. 'Will you add the blue?' she asked Sidney, who swished the blue bag in the clear cold water while his mother rinsed the now snowy linen in the big sink. The swirls of dark blue made pictures like waves on the shore until he stirred it and the blue was like the sky at Cowes on a clear day.

He stood by the huge mangle in the yard, watching the water flow down the grimy wooden shute into the bucket. He only touched the wrought-iron pattern and avoided the rollers, as Clare had once crushed a finger-end in it when Lizzie started the mangle too soon. Her finger would never grow a perfect nail again, and afterwards the mangle was chained up when Jane was not there to see what was happening. The first valance was folded and lowered into the blue water, the yellow from the soap counteracted, and Jane sighed with satisfaction. The starch was ready, made from knobbly pieces of starch and borax mixed smooth with cold water and then stirred with boiling water until it turned blue-grey and thick. Jane diluted the mixture until it 'looked just right' and soaked the valances thoroughly to make them stiff when ironed.

Emily took her turn to serve in the shop and knitted if there were no customers. When her friends came in, she surreptitiously prised dates from the block and gave them each a handful which they wrapped in handkerchiefs and stuffed inside the elastic of their bloomers. Smells of washing and dust, of suet pudding boiling and beef broth simmering came from the back room, and customers recognized it as the spring-clean smell that issued from every well-ordered house each year. Janey swept the bedrooms and the beds looked vulgarly denuded without their valances and the boxes usually concealed now in full view.

'You've all done well,' Jane said at last. 'We'll shut up shop and have our dinner now.' She laughed, well pleased, knowing that they had finished quicker without Walter interfering and grumbling about the draughts and wet floors. Even the dinner was better today, as Walter would have come in demanding attention while the children were famished and tired. She felt a pang of guilt: it was wicked to be relieved he was away, and she was glad of his picture on the wall to remind her of him.

'May we do the boxes?' asked Clare, after the last dish was put away and the valances were out hanging in the dust-free air of the yard.

'You don't want to look at old clothes,' Jane teased, knowing full well that they had been looking forward to this all the morning. 'Oh, I suppose we'd better take a peep in case the moths have got in.' One by one, the boxes were brought down and examined by the fire. Long-lost treasures and fine clothes kept for special occasions came to light and Jane put a thick towel on the end of the table and heated the flat irons.

They sorted out what could be worn, what could be altered to fit and what could be discarded. Clare draped herself in Jane's silk shawl, admiring the heavy fringe and the embroidered birds and roses. Jane examined it – there was no mildew and no fading. 'Why don't you ever wear it, Mother?'

'I'll wear it when your father comes home,' Jane said, and carefully put tissue paper between the folds again. She had worn it once when Walter gave it to her and again when they had gone to Cowes Week to watch the foreign yachts. Emily found a tiny chest of drawers filled with coarse sawdust to absorb damp. The papier mâché front was decorated with writhing dragons and it contained rings which Emily put on fingers reddened from serving fish. There were strings of amber beads. Clare put a butterfly brooch in her hair but avoided the rings as she was self-conscious about the maimed finger.

Jane was busy doing a dozen different jobs, serving in the shop and ironing the first of the damp-dry valances, but she was persuaded to put on jet earrings, a choker of paste diamonds and the *Mother* brooch. It was easy to be lighthearted on a sunny day and now she could think of Walter without the usual dull ache; she no longer wished to go to him, together with the ladies who flocked out, intent on giving the soldiers nursing care. At first she'd been envious of the titled women who left full of adventure, their children safe with nannies and servants. As for the other women who went, Jane knew that they were 'no better than they ought to be'! She was familiar with camp-followers from living in a garrison town, and when pay parades took place they haunted the Barracks gates. She fingered the cameo brooch that had belonged to her mother. It was odd to feel closer to her than to Walter. She shook out the wedding dress from the box which was always left until last, and as always the girls were delighted, fingering the tiny tucks and the high collar covered with handmade lace.

'What a tiny waist you had, Mother,' exclaimed Lizzie. She held in her stomach. 'Do you think I'll be like that?'

'You'll all be beautiful ladies,' Jane said. She held the dress in front of her and marvelled at the slender hourglass figure she had once had before eight pregnancies had made her curvaceous but no longer slim. She would never wear it again. Did Walter know that she kept it? And she would never part with it. Perhaps one day, one of the girls might want it, but that was ages away she thought as she looked at the too large and heavy rings on Emily's small hands. They needed more dresses now, but not wedding dresses.

'You're still as pretty as the day you wore it.'

'Archie! You made me jump,' said Jane, and Janey caught the dress as it slipped from her fingers.

'I saw the Closed sign but the door wasn't bolted,' he excused himself.

'This is for ladies only,' Clare reproached. The boys had followed tradition and gone out when the boxes emerged.

'I know, I saw the boys,' he grinned. 'They told me you were slaving all the morning but I don't believe it. You are too dolled up for that.'

Clare picked up a black shawl and draped it round her shoulders while the others showed him rings and necklaces and beads, but Jane felt shy with the man she had known ever since she came to the Island. His eyes showed admiration and something else she sorely missed. She quickly removed the jet earrings and sparkling collar, the cameo brooch and the bracelet of elephant hair, but kept the *Mother* brooch as a label making her status clear. 'Ladies offer tea to gentlemen who call,' she said lightly.

Archie shook his head. 'Shouldn't be here by rights. Had to go to Shide and thought I'd see if you had some more goat's milk.'

'How is little Rose?'

'Tired as usual. How did we make a weakly child like her when you have seven who never have much wrong?'

'I lost one,' Jane said quietly.

That's not the same.' He watched Jane's flushed face as she lifted the heavy kettle. 'Rose isn't even as bright as yours. They work hard and are so grown up that they are a credit to you.'

'Rose is sick and hasn't had a chance,' Jane said gently. 'Mine have had to grow up as there is so much to do. They do more than is fair to them.'

He stood by the shop door with the lidded can of milk in his hand. 'You look better than when you wore that dress, Jane. Better and prettier and more of a woman for a man to love.'

'Sure, I've had enough loving to last a lifetime,' she said, wrapping up the fish for Amy. 'Seven mouths to feed are enough.'

'Not for me, Jane. If I had you, I'd have sons and warmth.'

'Dear man, neither you nor Walter nor any man can have that from me since Caroline,' she said softly. 'And now be gone. Sure we talk a lot of nonsense at times and I have work to do even if my favourite cousin has time to spare.'

'I don't talk nonsense and never discuss you with Amy,' he said. He kissed her cheek, outwardly again a cousin by marriage with no hint of wanting. Poor Archie, she thought as the boxes disappeared under the beds for another year. He has no son to take over the farm.

'I know – we'll walk over to Carisbrooke tomorrow,' she told the children suddenly. 'You deserve a treat.' The look in Archie's eyes was a tonic she wouldn't admit to. 'Archie said that the Queen is at Osborne and her flag is flying, so she may go up to the Castle tomorrow.'

'Can we pick primroses?' asked Lizzie eagerly.

'We'll go to chapel and pick primroses after, and have a late dinner,' promised Jane. She wanted to climb a hill and look into the distance, and in the morning she dressed in her best dark violet coat trimmed with fur. She buttoned on boots and pinned a bunch of artificial violets to her dark green hat. The walk to the Castle passed quickly. Through the town, they went up to the raised Mall with its handsome new houses behind tall iron railings. Some had infant rambler roses and privet hedges and the Mall was level for walking and free from mud and horse manure. Sidney took a stick and ran it along the railings, making a staccato noise that wasn't really fitting for Sunday, but Jane said nothing. They walked by the Shrubbery and up to the moat where sheep grazed and birds shrilled a welcome. Jane was young again. This time next year I shall come here with Walter, she thought.

The huge oaken gates were open and the sweep of cobbles to the Castle chapel was clean and dry. 'Straighten your tie, Sidney,' she said and tweaked Jack's sailor hat to a more reverent angle. Jane blinked in the gloom of the porch and felt confused by her boldness as she had never been there without Walter. Two men stood by the entrance. Were they visitors or the Queen's equerries? 'Please go in, madam,' said one of the men, smiling, and Jane relaxed. He looked like Sam. 'Her Majesty likes to have a congregation,' he added. They were shown to seats behind the Royal pews. Jane frowned at the boys, willing them to behave and nodded curtly when Sidney whispered, 'Is she coming?'

Local residents filled more pews and the choir from Carisbrooke Church rustled anthem sheets while the organist played softly. The simple solemnity of the chapel was enhanced by flags and pennants, and by the coats of arms of long dead dignitaries. Sidney slewed round to read the gothic writing at the back of his seat, tracing one illuminated letter with a finger, trying to remember it to copy later, before Jane nudged him with a sharp elbow.

The gilded side door opened and two ladies-in-waiting hurried in with cushions. The equerries stood to attention, the organist played more briskly and a stout short figure was helped from a carrying chair in the porch. Lizzie coughed and went red and Janey tried to appear unconcerned as she made an effort to keep still so that the Queen wouldn't hear her squeaky shoe. Clare hid her broken nail under her hymnbook as the Queen passed, leaning on a black stick with an ornate silver head. Her Imperial Majesty, Queen of England, Scotland, Ireland and Wales, Empress of India and Sovereign of All Her Dominions Overseas, sank thankfully into the well-worn cushions in her chair.

Queen Victoria had passed the shop many times in her carriage, but she had never been as close as this: the children stared. She was dressed from head to foot in black, with a touch of white at her throat. Her cap was of fine soft lace and the black crêpe made the whiteness stark. Jet beads hung about her like black hail and her eyes wore the expression of one who sees badly. Her face was pale and her mouth turned down at the corners.

She's old . . . old and tired, thought Jane. It was sad to think that with all she had, she was just a tired old lady, weary of the world. She's lost a husband and two children, so no wonder she's sad. The congregation stood for the National Anthem and the fat little woman sat impassively as if she had no part in it.

The children mouthed the hymns, afraid that the Queen would hear if they missed a note and Janey blushed when her shoe squeaked on the sticky polish of the pew. The vicar began his sermon from the pulpit and Clare watched the birds on the hat of a lady-in-waiting, half expecting them to fly away. Jane looked up at the dusty flags, thinking it was just as well the Queen couldn't see them. If she's like me she can't abide dirt, she thought, but the Queen stared at the pulpit and her daughter, Princess Beatrice, smiled helpfully at the vicar who tried to preach a sermon of hope to someone who had already heard the latest casualty figures and news of heavy losses, and was still in mourning for her own beloved family.

The Queen had lost one child with the blood disease, Jane remembered. And she had lost Caroline. She prayed for Walter, addressing her prayers to God, the Trinity and for good measure to the Holy Mother although she was a lapsed Catholic. Her Majesty remained in the chapel until it was empty and when she reappeared in the carrying chair, her mantle was folded neatly and she had more expression as her pale eyes flickered over the waiting women and children who curtsied awkwardly. One child was pushed by her mother to hold out a bunch of primroses. The tired face brightened as the Queen accepted the flowers and pressed them to one parchment cheek. She patted the girl's head and spoke to her.

'I wish I'd done that,' said Clare jealously. 'That girl wasn't in chapel and she didn't sit with the Queen as we did!'

'Is it to be primroses or back home for dinner?' asked Jane.

'Have you brought any biscuits to tide us over?' Jane nodded, and they walked along the steep rough path to the Priory. The grey building looked gaunt against the greens and yellows of spring but through the side window, blurred by frosted glass, figures passed up a stairway, shadows with faceless hoods which sang as the Darwens picked damp primroses by the walls.

'I'm thirsty,' complained Emily.

'You've eaten too many biscuits. You'll have to wait for a drink until you get home.' Jane drew back from the gate feeling guilty as she always did when she saw a priest or a nun. 'Can't you all wait?' she asked uneasily. Emily's lips quivered, Jack looked defiant and Lizzie sniffed. 'It seems wrong to bother the Sisters on a Holy Day,' their mother said.

'That's why they are there,' Edward objected. 'They never refuse a drink to travellers and we are thirsty.' Jane bit her lip and tapped nervously on the postern gate. A grille over a wooden shutter moved and a voice asked if she could help.

'I have thirsty children here, Sister. Could they have a drink of water? We've walked from the far side of Newport.' Sidney stared at the door that talked. The shutter slid back to show a recess in which was a jug of milk and two mugs.

Emily whispered, 'Where is she?' and wiped the ring of milk from her mouth. Jane shook her head warningly and took the mug to fill for the others, and when the jug was empty, the shutter closed again.

'Thank you, Sister,' Jane said shyly, and gave Edward a push so that all the children echoed her.

'God go with you,' the voice said and the small sounds faded.

'Why didn't we see her? Was she a ghost? Does she live alone in that tiny room?'

'There are a lot of them but they never come out as it's a closed order of Nuns, but they help people and pray for the world and bad children.'

'They *must* come out for Christmas,' said Lizzie. Her face was solemn and half-afraid.

'They promise God to stay there for ever and never have children. They have a nice Christmas singing hymns, and I expect they enjoy it,' Jane said without conviction. 'I wish sometimes I was a nun and needn't answer all your questions!'

Gypsies were gathering watercress by the mill at Shide and Jack wanted to stay to see the water-wheel turning, but Jane was hungrier than she'd been for weeks, the children had on their best clothes and her boots had begun to hurt her feet.

'I'm glad I'm not a nun,' announced Sidney when they finally sat down to dinner.

'Boys don't go to convents,' said Clare. 'Emily and Janey and Lizzie and me could go but you wouldn't be allowed inside, so there!'

'Men do!' said Jack. 'I read about it, Miss Knowall.' Jane explained the difference between monasteries and convents and talked a little about the Catholic faith, Confession and Absolution but knew that Walter wouldn't be pleased if she confused them by saying too much. He attended the Wesleyan Chapel twice a year and the parish church for weddings and funerals.

'I like to know,' said Jack, when his mother stopped and refused to answer more questions. 'I'd like to have my sins forgiven.'

'That's because you have so many,' said Janey and he punched her.

'I'll not be forgiving you if you don't eat up your dinner,' said Jane sternly. 'Your father wouldn't like it.' But neither she nor the children felt any impact of that threat. 'Take some primroses to Granny Cheverton. She can hardly walk up her path now and won't see them this year. You can tell her about the Queen,' she added, to make them want to visit the crotchety old lady.

'I'll see to the animals,' said Edward as Walter did when he wished to be let off an unwelcome chore. 'And I'll get the latest news.'

Jane closed the door behind them and put on old slippers. She began to read a romance and lost herself in castles and wicked men and a handsome lover until the children burst in after what seemed like only five minutes. 'What's wrong, Edward? Are you ill?'

'I was up at the *Press* window – there's been another battle with heavy losses! They've rushed up volunteers.'

Jane forced a smile. 'Your father is good at looking after himself. It's bad luck to think of him wounded.' Edward looked as if he believed her and helped her to cut bread and butter and the plum cake for tea, but under Jane's forced cheerfulness, the gold and green of spring had died. After tea, she went up to the *Press* herself and read the casualty lists. One name was familiar, a man from Yarmouth who did business with Walter. The account of how the British forces were trying to clear a corner of the Orange Free State to get to the Transvaal sounded like a game, but a bloody game with forty-one dead in one skirmish and many wounded as they cut off the Boer retreat. She read on: *30th April 1900. Mounted infantry and Smith Dorien's Brigade of the 7th Division reached Houtney, 45 miles from Thaba N'chu and fought Botha who occupied the hills with 7 guns. General French was on his way to meet him. Known casualties 45 dead. Three kopjes taken by the Gordon Highlanders and the Shropshire Light Infantry with bitter fighting continuing.'*

The war was worse than ever. Some politicians said it was nearly over but Lord Asquith had condemned the inefficiency of the Generals: White was in disgrace and Methuen had lost more men with his tragically wasteful frontal attacks using fixed bayonets. How the Boers must laugh at them, Jane thought. The men were heroic but who wanted to die or come back wounded. At that moment, a man limped out of the shelter of the archway and tried to sell her a copy of the poem *The Absent-Minded Beggar*, donated by Rudyard Kipling for the relief of war widows and orphans. 'I have a copy and my husband is at the war,' she told him. She knew the words by heart and had sent a copy to Walter, knowing he liked Mr Kipling's poetry. The children were learning the verses parrot-fashion for school, but they still brought tears to her eyes.

He's an absent minded beggar, and his weaknesses are great,
But we and Paul must take him as we find him
He's out on active service, wiping something off a slate . . .
And he's left a lot of little things behind him!

Chapter 9

Archie Cheverton reached down for the silvery cream churn that he had brought for the goat's milk and Jane handed up the parcel of fruit and fish. The goat's milk had been a great success, although Rose remained frail.

'I'll bring her over now that the days are lengthening,' Archie promised as Jane waved him off.

Maudie Dove would soon be in for her jugful for Lucy, and Mr Foster now took it for his daughter too, as the doctor said it was good for Nellie's consumption. It gave Jane pleasure to give away the milk, which came in far greater quantities than her family could use. She wondered whether Amy knew that Rose had consumption. Amy smothered the girl, keeping her shut in a stuffy room to avoid chills, but Jane longed to get Rose out into the fresh air. Her own family came home from walks with sparkling eyes and pink cheeks and it was difficult to breathe in the room where Rose lay listless, day after fine spring day.

The doorbell jangled and Maudie entered. 'Oh, I forgot to bring the jug for our milk! It's all the excitement over this letter, Mrs Darwen.'

'From Ben?' Jane looked apprehensive.

'No, from the army. Ben is wounded and is coming home. Isn't that good?' Her eyes sparkled.

'How bad is it, Maudie?'

The young woman waved aside all questions. 'I can look after any old wound,' she said. 'I'll have to bring the jug in later. Have you heard from Mr Darwen?'

'Not since last week. He's at the front again and he was at the Modder.' Long practice had trained Jane to keep her voice steady when asked about Walter. 'He's well, thank God.' She hoped that Maudie wouldn't see the trains of wounded before Ben arrived, as she had heard that minor casualties were patched up in the field hospitals – and only the very badly wounded were sent home to the Garrison infirmaries. If Walter was wounded like that, she prayed that he would die rather than be a cripple for life.

However Walter, it appeared, was fine and enjoying himself. The freedom and excitement suited him, he said in his letters, but the horses were a constant concern. Solid in his praise for Lord Roberts and Ian Hamilton the General who fought so bravely at Sanna's Post, he was still outspoken about the leadership. He wrote bluntly that the Generals should be made to unlimber the Artillery themselves, to set up the guns and see firsthand how, as soon as the guns were free, the Boers would swoop down and isolate the men from them. '*If you deal with poachers, you set traps, not stand on the sky-line and hope they come your way,*' wrote Walter, and Jane pictured him fighting with cunning like the enemy, and relishing laying trip-wires and other traps.

These days, Jane was becoming nervy. She feared that conditions for the men were bad. Comforts did arrive at the Cape and base camps but nevertheless, letters home told of dysentery, scurvy, typhoid and the terrible suffering of the wounded before they could get to hospital. There must be some truth in these stories and she didn't know what troubled her most: the suffering and privations, or the other 'compensations' that were hinted at so strongly! Jane tried to stifle her fears. Men away from home lived by a different set of rules and family ties were weakened under the constant threat of death. The urgency of life would colour the desires of the moment, and influence the men to indulge in all bodily needs and lusts. All but Walter, she hoped. He hated dirty women.

Maudie soon returned with the jug and Jane gave her the milk, as well as some shrivelled fruit and fish pieces for Lucy, but she couldn't bear to hear more about the war. When the shop was empty, she locked the door and sat in the back room, drained of all energy, sobbing more bitterly than at any time since Walter had left. The spring flowers set in vases about her were fading and smelled of death: she threw them on the fire. A kind of peace came after the crying, and when she heard a tapping at the shop door, Jane quickly splashed her face with cold water and dabbed her nose with Fuller's Earth to take away the shine and the redness round her eyes. She pinned her hair securely and went to the door.

'Violets? Lovely violets? And watercress fresh from the stream this morning, lady.' Old Mother Lee, the Queen of the gypsies living down by the river, looked into Jane's face, her sharp dark eyes shining with a curious mixture of Romany understanding and cunning. It needed only half a glance to see that Mrs Darwen had been weeping, but Mrs Lee sensed no tragedy in the house. 'You're as pretty as ever, my dear.'

Jane forced a smile. 'You say that every year, Mrs Lee.' In spite of the crying she felt better, as if the tears had washed away bitterness and misgiving and perhaps because the old woman was a sign of spring, like the first homecoming of the birds. 'I've made tea,' she said impulsively. The woman followed her into the back room and put her basket on the floor. She pulled out a red ribbon. 'I want no ribbons but I do need pegs,' Jane said. 'There may be a few pieces to mend, too, if a boy can come for them.' She busied herself at the range and Mrs Lee saw the clean windows and white-stoned hearth. No neglect here even with the man away. Courage was something she respected and she absorbed the atmosphere, part clairvoyant, part psychologist and felt a bond with the Irishwoman.

'Take your tea in a white cup,' she instructed. Jane hesitated, mistrusting her own reactions to fortune-telling, but Mrs Lee would tell her no lies, she knew. Hadn't she said when the twins were on the way, before even Jane knew she was pregnant, 'You've taken, my dear, and there's more than one, both girls.' Walter had scoffed but didn't like to be reminded of that when the twins were born.

Mrs Lee took a large slice of cake with her tea but Jane only crumbled her piece and ate nothing. When she had finished her tea, she swirled the dregs to leave a pattern on the sides of the cup. The gypsy gazed into it, turning the cup slowly, her eyes sinking under half-closed lids.

'There's someone over water, further than the mainland and with death all round him,' she said. Jane nodded. That was to be expected – Mrs Lee must have heard that Walter was in Africa. 'He's in good health but may be hurt in the leg.' Jane drew in her breath sharply. 'It's not much more than a bad bruise. Not enough to bring him home but bad enough to take him out of danger for a while.' She paused, her face expressionless. 'He lacks nothing and will have everything he needs where he is going.' She smiled suddenly. 'I see you surrounded by good friends. There is love everywhere of all kinds, and love will protect you from a man who wants to harm you. He has tried to hurt you and he envies you. Another can be trusted and you may go to him safely for help. You have the sense to say no to the one who wants you as you have nothing to give him.' Jane blushed.

'Give the eldest boy his head. He will ask soon. Let him be occupied in another place before the master returns. This one will deserve it and needs to make his way before he marries trouble. It's a long way off but as plain as day.'

'And the others?'

'You are blessed with good children, my dear. One girl will marry and lose her husband young. It will be hard but she is brave like you. One will make a bad marriage out of vanity and another will marry for a lifetime. The youngest girl will never marry but be with you in your old age.'

'What of the other boys?'

Mrs Lee frowned. 'The wild one will travel far and the other will never marry but you will lose him. Leave him to be happy in his own way. You work hard – it is in your hands and face. You work for others but it brings you joy. You will never want.'

Jane re-filled Mrs Lee's cup. It was only a game! A bit of harmless nonsense, but she'd better not tell Emily she would never marry a prince!

'You forgot to put the green thread in his hussif,' the old gypsy said slowly, 'and he had to borrow . . . He keeps your likeness in his pocket and you will always be the most important woman in his life.' Jane instinctively glanced at the cupboard where, sure enough, she had found the hank of green thread after Walter's departure. Mrs Lee listened to make sure they were not overheard, then came closer. 'Have you thought what to do when your man comes back? He will be as all men are after a long separation, more eager for you.' Jane's cheeks burned. 'Don't be upset, my dear, it's the way of life, but you know you must not bear another child and you must protect yourself.'

'But we don't . . . we haven't since Caroline,' Jane said and it seemed natural to confide in this woman. 'I could sleep with the girls but Walter's a proud man and would be angry.' She sighed. 'He's a passionate man, too, and if he expects his rights, I can do nothing. So far he has been very good.'

Mrs Lee searched the depths of her basket and held up a package wrapped in dark linen. Inside were crude pessaries of yellow fat with specks of colour showing through them. 'These are safe and don't make a man sore like the ones you can buy. They are gentle and are made of herbs. He need never know you use them.'

'I don't know if I could,' Jane began.

'Take them. They will help you through a hard time. Each time you use one you will be protected, but if you miss one and get caught, then you must take this pill at the first sign of sickness.' She took a large grey pill from inside her shawl. Jane started back, revolted. 'It tastes of nothing,' Mrs Lee crooned.

'But that is a mortal sin. The Church says so and it's against the law. Walter begged the doctor to do something when I was so ill with Caroline but he refused.'

The sharp eyes looked angry. 'And if a woman obeys the law and dies, who looks after her family? Who would feed your children and bring them up as good people? You know I never give you bad advice. Trust me. You are a good woman and have done many kind things for me and my family and we never forget.'

Jane put the package deep inside her workbox and replaced it in the cupboard. 'I must pay you for your trouble,' she said.

Mrs Lee put the pegs on the table. 'Pay me for those. The other is a gift, my sister.' She picked up the money and the bundle of old clothes that Jane had ready for her and when the children came home, Jane was absentmindedly winding and re-winding the forgotten green thread on a spool.

'Who came in?' asked Emily.

'Maudie with news that Ben will be home, wounded, and old Mrs Lee who talked a lot of nonsense.'

'Percy Cantor says that a big ambulance train is coming tonight from the boats. They're using the chapel at the Barracks to take some of them.'

'Those Cantors think they know everything!' scoffed Jack.

'I'd know too if I worked at Cowes,' said Edward. 'The train from Cowes will be in Newport by four and they want as many traps and carts and carriages as they can muster to take the men to the Barracks and the hospital. They say there's been another bulletin and Mr Foster is taking it down in his book.'

'War! When will it end?' Jane whispered. The newspapers these days contained leader columns hinting at more bungling, and were critical of what had once been a popular and righteous conflict. The wounded brought back their own version of events, and cartoons were boldly mooting reform. The *Morning Post* was so savage in its condemnation that the Queen apparently refused to have the paper in her presence; even advertisements, like the one for Monkey Brand Soap, carried the caption '*Clean up the War Office, Lord Kitchener!*' *Punch* carried scathing references to the National Debt of fifty-five million pounds. '*What? Run the war on business principles? Good Gad, sir. Hope it doesn't come to that*! declared *Punch*'s General Muddle.

Newport had its share of wounded, some too maimed to earn a living. The workhouse was full and the charity homes for paupers had harsh conditions and still carried the stigma of poverty – that Victorian sin. An army pension was pitiful and if the wounded had to go on the Parish, it meant the workhouse for any who had no able-bodied member of the family to help them.

Jane hated to see the men in corduroy and the women in coarse print dresses working in the workhouse laundry and hospital gardens. How could any hard-working honest person suddenly become a pauper, with no respect, freedom or rights? She shuddered. Pray God none of hers ever came to that.

'Fetch Bess and the cart,' she said to Jack. 'I shall take a few things up to the station later for the men.'

Janey helped her mother to load the cart with fresh bread and shrimps, apples and potato pies. It was a way of expressing Jane's thanks and guilty relief that her own husband was not among the wounded. Emily wound strips of old sheet into neat bandages and the metal jar that Walter used when fishing with Aaron was filled with tea and another bottle with cider. The men might not want it or be able to take it, but Jane needed to give.

The first of the carriages were filled with walking cases. Any man who could hobble – even with a heavy crutch – fitted into this official category. A man with no hands was taken behind the coal heaps by a helper to urinate. Another for the workhouse, thought Jane sadly. She tried to find out if any were from Ben's unit but heard no news. The carriages contained officers and men from many different regiments: they had only their wounds in common, along with the dirt and bloodstained clothing and the smell of stale sweat and blood. Jane longed to clean the men up, to change their soiled dressings and to comfort them, as she hoped that Walter would be if he was wounded.

The stretcher cases were transferred to ambulance carts and delivery vehicles, while local people lent their gigs and traps for the walking cases. Jane walked along the line of men awaiting transport handing out drinks and pies. A pair of eyes, dark with pain like the eyes of dying animals and old men losing their minds, looked up at her. She smoothed the damp hair from the young man's brow and gave him a drink. One of his sleeves was pinned across his chest and the tunic was stiff with dried blood. He gasped between sips and Jane stayed until two orderlies came to put him in a cart. He groaned and she wiped the cold sweat from his face with her handkerchief, and pulled the thin blanket higher over his chest. A sickly offensive smell came from his stump. 'Bad case of gangrene, ma'am,' one orderly commented.

'He looks rough but how do you know?' she whispered.

'That smell. Once you catch a whiff of it, you never forget it.' The orderly spat to rid his mouth of the smell. 'Should never have been brought here. He's beyond help and took a place on the boat that another could have had. Whether you're in foreign lands or British, it makes no difference where you die.'

Jane could bear no more suffering. She took Bess back to the stable, needing to be alone and quiet. The warm stall dispelled the aura of death with its familiar sounds of Bess and the nanny goat, and the house was still when Jane went home. She raked the range vigorously and dropped her handkerchief into the reddest part of the fire. The poor young man had been too young to enlist, she suspected, and death was a poor reward for youth and patriotism.

'Was it very bad, Mother?' asked Sidney, who had been forbidden to go near the station.

'It tears me to pieces, son,' she said but no tears came, only anger. Was it wrong to hope that the dying boy's mother never saw him indecently dirty and in pain? She hated the army and the cynical men who turned a blind eye to age when they wanted more men to enlist. She hated the Generals, too, and the journalists who warped the news – and she wished that women had the care of the money, the better to do the housekeeping. There was so little she could contribute personally but there was something . . . She took notepaper and an envelope, and copied the address on to it from the piece of paper the orderly had given her. The boy's parents lived on a farm near Blackwater, and soon they would receive the dreaded buff envelope bearing news of his death.

She made no mention of their son's real condition but said that she had seen him and talked to him and he was comfortable although very ill. By now, the railmen would have spread the news along the line to Shide and Blackwater that the train was in. 'Edward,' she called, 'take this along to the station and ask the guard to put it on the next train to Blackwater. The porter there can deliver it as the farm is close to the station and I've put something inside for his trouble.'

'If that soldier dies in the night, at least his mother will know someone cared,' Edward said. He looked uncomfortable: 'I had to help, Mother. They let me shift the baggage and I saw him. You see, I knew him before he enlisted.'

Maudie came into the shop, cheerful now that she had learned Ben wasn't on the train. She was still convinced that his absence meant he was not badly wounded but had been treated at a field hospital. Jack meanwhile sprinkled water from an old watering can to lay the dust in the shop and Jane watched, as absorbed as a child as he made patterns.

The evening was warm and the sky tinged with pink clouds and Jane shook off her depression. She put a jar of wildflowers and mint on the counter to keep the flies away but they hung in spiralling circles, either immune to mint or having never heard that it kept flies away. They settled on the dates until Jane covered the sticky slab with butter muslin, then clustered on the fish and walked on the windows until the glue-papers hanging from the ceilings were covered with blue-black bodies.

Bad news and others' misfortunes brought trade to *Darwen's* but Jane avoided being dragged into any discussion about the wounded. At last the shop was empty and she sat in the dusk listening to the pull of the train going up the rise while the bats flitted low from their hiding places in the broken brickwork of the railway bridge. Edward let himself in. 'I took the letter there myself, Mother. The guard let me go free and told the crew to stop on the way back from Sandown to pick me up, so at least you know they got your message.'

Jane put bread and cheese and milk on the table for the family supper. 'It's Saturday tomorrow,' she said. 'You've all been very good and can do as you please once the morning work is over. Edward and Sidney can do the deliveries and there'll be no rush. I shall write to your father and tell him how helpful you are.' She left them to eat and went upstairs, knowing that the mention of Walter had made no impact. He had become almost a name and no more to the children. There were no clean pinafores to iron and tomorrow, Aaron would go to Hamble for the strawberries. I wonder if I ordered enough for the officers' mess, she wondered as she dropped off to sleep, luxuriously alone in the wide and soft featherbed.

Chapter 10

'Hurry up or he'll be gone,' hissed Jack as he held back the bolt and pushed the girls out into the street. 'We've the goat to milk and the hay to pull down and we mustn't be seen.'

Lizzie complained that it was too early and she was tired, but didn't make a real fuss in case Jack left her behind. Bess looked as if she thought the children were mad to be up this early. 'Do you think we should have asked Mother?' said Clare anxiously.

'I left a note and wrote down all the jobs we've done, and after all, she said we could do as we liked today,' answered Jack. They hurried past the warehouses and Sea Street, then along by the iron cranes where Ethel Sheath waited for them, her red hair a second sunrise and her freckled face glowing with excitement. The tide was full and it was too early for Joe Matthews to operate the swing bridge, so his hut was empty and the children had the quay to themselves.

Aaron's barge was tied up below the path to the stables, high on the tide and as silent as the chimneys of the timber-yard. Jack glanced back to the hut and climbed down on to the barge. It was an open boat with a cubby-hole and cupboards, coils of rope in the stern, a few tarpaulins and the buckets and lines needed for fishing. Water seeped in by the keel and a patched sail lay in it, absorbing the water. Jack pulled at a salt-hard tarpaulin but his feet slipped on the deck. 'Give it here,' commanded Ethel. 'I know about boats. Fold it back, not pull it.' Jack grunted but did as she suggested and held the tarpaulin up so that the others could slide under it and hide. It was hot and dark in there and smelled of stale fish. Clare kicked a bucket of rotten bait over by accident and the smell was terrible, making them push even further back under the canvas.

'They're coming,' whispered Jack. 'Don't make a sound!'

Aaron rested his barrow by a bollard and George Crouch put a stone under the wheel before handing down the strawberry baskets to be stacked against the sides of the boat. The men added a couple of jars of cider and one of water, a covered basket of food and a fresh bucket of bait. 'That nipper of yourn wanted to come,' George remarked.

'Young Ethel? Oh yes, she was on to me all day – and she wanted them Darwen children to come too, but I couldn't have that. What would Walt's missus say? She'd have been in a rare old pickle if I'd as much as asked.' Aaron untied the mooring lines and pushed off into mid-stream, taking the barge between the mudbanks. He raised the sail and it flapped lazily against the mast as they drifted into deep water until the offshore wind freshened. Lizzie wished she had brought a bottle of cold tea with her, but dared not make a sound as the barge slapped its way out into open water.

Gypsies by the bend were too busy lighting their fires to notice a barge, while the houseboats on Little London still had their curtains closed. Aaron lit his pipe, tamping down the oily shag with a calloused finger. The smoke drifted back to Lizzie, penetrating even the smell of canvas and fish and as they hit the cross currents of the Solent, she felt sick. She stuffed her mouth with her handkerchief but that only made it worse. She dared not make Jack cross by crying out, since Aaron might take them back before the tide took over and it was too late. She raised one edge of the canvas and gasped a breath of sweet air.

'What was that?' asked George.

'Nothing. Might be a rat – I'll ask Bert to bring down his Jack Russell. It's time he took a sniff round again. Best ratter in Newport, that dog.' Aaron picked up a boat-hook but Lizzie was quiet again. He fixed bait to lines and trailed them clear of the wake. The sail filled and the boat made good time and Jack sensed that they were clear of the Island and Aaron might even be amused by his stowaways.

He clawed a way out of the canvas and blinked in the sunlight, grinning nervously and keeping out of Aaron's range. At the sight of him, Aaron sat down heavily on a locker, his dismay growing as Clare crawled out, then Ethel and finally Lizzie, who stumbled and clung to Ethel. 'How many more on you for the Lord's sake?' he growled. Lizzie sat on the tarpaulin, her face pale and her forehead covered with sweat. She was frightened and queasy although the swell was slight and the weather fine, and Aaron looked stern, like a pirate with heavy brows now close together in a veil over his hooked nose.

The girl's fear and pallor stemmed the tide of his wrath and his eyes twinkled. 'You don't look much of a sailor, my gal,' he said. He picked her up and sat her down on a coil of rope in the bow. 'You stay there. Look ahead and you'll not smell my old pipe.' Lizzie lay back in the fresh air and felt better, enjoying the water for the first time in her life. 'I don't know what your mother will say,' Aaron fretted.

'I left a note and she has Edward and Janey and Sidney to help her. We did our work before we left,' Jack added hastily.

'Well, I can't abide stowaways, so you'll have to work your passage,' Aaron stated firmly. He winked at George. 'And you'll have to work hard as we don't feed tramps. Hope you brought plenty of grub with you?' Jack shook his head and George laughed. 'Too bad then, eh, George? We only brought a bite for us two, so you'm going to be hungry.'

'You've plenty in the basket,' Ethel said, her face going red. 'I saw Mother pack it last night.'

'That's for after the picking – and we might see a few friends.'

'Did you have a good breakfast?' asked George. 'Nothing like a good filling breakfast to stand by you for the day. We had a good feed, didn't we, Aaron?'

The men joked in a heavy-handed way as the children felt emptier and emptier but Aaron eyed them with tolerance. Little blighters, they needed a lesson but he'd go easy. Clare was almost in tears. 'We might give you a bite of ours after the picking and you can eat all the strawberries you want while you pick,' he consoled them. 'You don't think you aren't going to help? You'll fill a good few baskets in three hours.' He made Jack bait the hooks and the girls pull in the catch while he and George sat in the stern, taking turns with the flagon of cider. Lizzie eyed the jar with longing. 'Want some?' asked Aaron. The cider was cool and potent and made Lizzie catch her breath. The sun came up hot and bright in a cloudless sky and she felt sleepy, so she snuggled down on the ropes and dozed off while the boat followed the coast to the Hamble River, past the lobster pots and the men on the beach mending nets. Several of them called out a greeting as the boat drifted by the leafy river bank to the Inn where Aaron tied up under dense shade.

Women in print aprons and sunbonnets were already picking strawberries, filling flat boxes and loading them on farm waggons under layers of straw. The farmer weighed all the boxes and told them where to pick. Trees at the edge of the field gave shade and it was pleasant to work between the cool rows of green plants loaded with ripe fruit. Jack and the girls worked quickly and filled a lot of baskets ready for George to stack once he had swilled the boat clean and cleared it of the stale remnants of fish and bait. He rigged a shelter of tarpaulin sprinkled with water to keep the fruit cool and kept a tally of the weight picked.

The next batch took longer and the sun shifted from behind the trees. Clare's back ached and her mouth felt rough and acid. She stopped eating strawberries. Jack wiped sweat from his eyes and rolled up his shirtsleeves. Lizzie was hot and sorry for herself and Ethel's face turned red and sunburned under the carrotty hair, while the pile of empty baskets didn't seem to diminish. 'Can we have a rest?' whispered Clare.

'No!' Ethel sounded frightened. 'I know he wasn't angry on the boat but just you stop working and he'll be wild with you.'

'Come on, you lot, I didn't ask you to come!' Aaron shouted at that very moment. 'If you don't like it you can lump it. Should've stayed at home.' So they picked until they hated the sight of strawberries and were covered in midge bites. Aaron goaded them until Clare faltered, Jack looked defiant and Lizzie and Ethel began to cry. Lizzie had endured all she could. At best she had less fortitude than her twin, and at worst gave in easily to tantrums but today she had filled almost as many baskets as Clare. She staggered to the hedgerow and was quietly sick. All her tiredness, her vague sea-sickness and a vast number of pulped strawberries spewed out on the grass. She wiped her mouth and felt much better.

Aaron saw her out of the corner of his eye and relented. He'd been really hard on the children, to teach them a lesson, but they had shown real pluck and even that one hadn't whined. He left George to fill the last of the baskets and called, 'Enough! You can have a rest and we'll catch the tide.'

The last few baskets were stacked with spaces between the layers to give them air and George came out of the Inn carrying a large fresh loaf and a flagon of beer. Aaron put thick layers of apple chutney and cold salt pork on to hunks of bread and George unearthed tin mugs from the wheel-house. The children ate and drank in stunned silence and Aaron found it hard to look stern. They were tired and itched all over, the skin on their hands was sore from the sun but somehow the children were happy, and the food was the most delicious they had ever tasted, eaten on the grass with dragonflies skimming the water.

Aaron saw the tops of the trees swaying. 'We'd best be off,' he announced and the children took the rest of the food with them on to the barge. They slipped from the river and the sail filled; a deep serenity came from the gentle tide and they saw the distant Island. Seabirds paused to swoop for crusts and George pulled in line after line of mackerel. Aaron gazed across the Solent. 'She's a lovely old gal today,' he said. Gypsy fires lit the bend of the river after the dusk at Cowes and Folley, and Newport Quay was deserted except for a woman resting on the stone wall by the barrows. She had a lantern against which moths dashed themselves to death.

'Look out! There's your Ma,' said Aaron. George jumped out and made fast but the children hung back. Jack braced himself for trouble, jumping ashore and kicking a stone as if he had no care in the world, but waiting for the explosion.

'I brought them back safe and sound,' Aaron said heavily.

'I don't doubt it, Aaron, and I don't blame you for taking them, but they should have asked me first.'

'We thought you'd say no if we asked,' said Clare.

'And how did you know that if you didn't ask?' replied Jane dryly. Jack kicked another stone.

'Jack left a note and said it would be all right,' pleaded Lizzie.

'Any coward can leave a note,' she said and looked at Jack for the first time, then turned her back on him. 'While you are here, you can load our cart.' Jack looked angry but kept silent. 'You did remember I wanted extra, Aaron?'

'Yes, gal, I remembered. Fine berries this year.' He winked. 'They were cheaper, too, as I didn't pay for labour,' but Jane didn't laugh.

'I'm tired,' said Lizzie, in a voice that usually brought sympathy.

'So am I!' snapped Jane and Lizzie helped the others to load the handcart for the shop and to carry the order for the Barracks to the stable ready for the morning. Aaron carried two of the baskets and walked back to *Darwen's* with Jane. He put one basket on the counter, and Jane looked at it doubtfully. 'That's above the order,' she said.

'It's an extra few,' he said awkwardly. 'Don't be too hard on them, gal. They worked like navvies and I saw to it that they did! They ain't bad and you have to let them run with the tide occasionally. I'll take the lot of them some time if you'll let me.'

Jane's face softened. 'You're sure they weren't in the way?'

'No! It would give you time to yourself and a break for them, too,' he said sensibly. 'They're great pickers and kept at it to the bitter end, all on 'em.'

Jane looked at the dirty faces of the three truants. Lizzie tried to scratch a bite on her bottom without anyone seeing and Clare looked pale and hollow-eyed. Jane washed scratched hands and arms with vinegar and water and dabbed sore places with elderflower ointment, and they went off to bed too tired to eat. 'You'll have some broth?' Jane asked and Aaron sat down in Walter's chair. He ate one bowl of thick mutton broth then filled his pipe, sensing that Jane needed him there just to fill the space, however inadequately. He watched her over the smoke and saw a lonely woman.

'Best go,' he said at last. 'Ethel will have told them we're back and they'll want their berries. It's been a good day. Pity you couldn't come, but the children were really good company. You're lucky Jane, there's not a dud 'un among them.' He hoisted his basket on one hip and walked across to his own cottage. Jane lit a candle from the guttering stub of the last and the acrid smell of the extinguished wick hung in the tobacco smoke. She took a ripe berry and bit into it. The juice trickled down her chin and when she put her handkerchief to her face, the juice was diluted with tears. One day I'll have to let them all go, she thought.

That night she dreamed of Walter. He was back home again – but she couldn't find him. He was laughing but his laughter was cynical and taunting. She couldn't touch him and behind his laughter was a woman in shadow. She threw off the bedclothes and tried to find a cool spot in the bed but slept lightly and woke again. She wanted Walter, needed his body close to hers, his hands caressing her, his swift compulsive love.

Amy had Archie and even the Coopers had each other, although both wives made no secret of the fact that they disliked the physical side of marriage. Jane wept tears of loneliness and frustration and dozed off again only after she had explored her own body and given herself guilty comfort of a kind. As the orgasm faded she prayed, 'Forgive me for I sin,' and fell asleep.

Long before the children were awake, she had a hand wrapped in a towel as she stirred the spitting jam. Dawn was cool and dew hung on the grass and the strawberries smelled heavenly. Nero went back to sleep on the bench in the yard and Jane filled the row of seven-pound stone jam jars and washed the huge preserving pan.

Over the way, Aaron sniffed the strawberry-laden air and grinned. 'Good, gal. That's the best medicine – work and more work. I'll bring you the best of the oysters when they'm ready.'

Chapter 11

Heat shimmered over the bridge and tar bubbled in the gutters. Jane wore her thinnest blouse and skirt and was glad that she needed no corsets in this weather. The heat seemed set to last for days and the children were home for the weekend.

Jack came back from the stables and Jane knew that he had been swimming in the river again, as his socks were inside out and his hair was wet. However, she ignored it, just remarking dryly that he had more energy on Saturdays than when he was in school.

'You work too hard, Mother. Miss Martin should let us off to help you more.'

'And where would you get to? Up in the withy beds no doubt.' She called him back. 'And where are you going now? Not with that Percy Cantor? You stay here, my lad. Your Uncle Archie will be arriving soon and he'll want some help. Did you bring the milk?'

'It's in water in the outhouse,' he said. 'Can I go haymaking with Uncle Archie?'

'I don't know. Amy doesn't like extra visitors.'

'You manage and we have lots of people here.'

'She hasn't my crowd to feed all the time, so it's easier for me to fit in a few extra. Run out now – that's Blackie, for sure.' She followed him. 'Rose! Ah, it's good to see you, dear! But what have you done to poor Blackie?' Sidney gazed in wonder at the straw hat with holes cut for the horse's ears and the spray of mint to keep away the flies tucked into a bunch of poppies and cornflowers.

'May Rose come down to the stables with us? I'll take care of her,' Edward offered immediately.

'Jack must stay and mind the shop,' said Jane quickly, 'and Janey hasn't finished sweeping.' She relaxed. Archie was easy to talk to but she felt safer with others about. She ignored the fact that Sam came alone into the back room, so did Aaron and that some of Walter's business friends occasionally shared a pot of tea with her in there.

'That's a fine lot of plums you've brought,' she told him. 'I've already had a few asking for these as they make such good jam. I'll do mine tonight when it's cool, as I can always sell some to the Mess.' She turned away from the admiration in his eyes. 'You'll be wanting a cool drink. Cold tea or lemonade?'

'Cold tea, please. We've had a glut of fruit this year. Can't get it all picked as so many of the men are away. The hay is good too if we can just stook it dry.' He drank his tea. 'Unfortunately I can't stop for long now – I have to collect maize for the fowls and get back to the fields. We can work late with the light evenings but labour is still a problem.' He sat in Walter's chair unwilling to move, then sighed.

'What about hay?' asked Jane crisply. 'How much of your crop can be put aside for Blackie and Bess? If Walter comes home, we'll need double as he'll want Blackie again.'

'I wish he'd sell. The horse is a good worker and a nice ride.'

'I've never seen him look better, Archie, but you know Walter. Horses are his affair and I can't sell Blackie however long he's away.' She glanced out into the yard where Janey was washing the broom and Archie broke the sudden silence.

'Any news?' he said, and the tension eased.

'Only about the bad food, bad tents and the state of the horses. Walter doesn't write about himself, but he did describe the sieges. People had to eat mules and horses and even rats. They made puddings from laundry starch to help fill up and when the troops went into Ladysmith in March, when it was finally released, the people had been existing on a bowl of something like porridge, called mealies and one biscuit a day.' Jane leaned forward, her face tense with anguish. 'There is fever, too, Archie – it's everywhere. They buried five hundred alone at Ladysmith. I hear the news twice but it's never the same. The newspapers say one thing and then Walter tells me different. Some of the parcels never arrive, and the men are under canvas.'

'I forget that it's winter out there while we simmer in this heat. Cheer up! General Buller saved them and the army is making gains all over the place now. Walter will be home in no time! He doesn't say he's short of food, does he? He must be fine if his only grumble is shortage of baccy.'

'I do miss him, Archie.' Jane gave him a level glance. 'He is my husband and I miss him.'

Archie looked down. 'You worry too much. Why don't you take a day off and come down to the farm? You know you enjoy it there.' Jane looked sad. 'Come on, say you'll come down tomorrow with the family. Bring a bite to eat and you can give the children their grub in the field. There's hay to be tossed and plums to pick and you can eat with us.'

Jane smiled at Archie's tactful suggestion. The picnic for the children would overcome any objection that Amy might have. 'Tell Amy I'll bring all our food and we can all eat in the fields if it's fine, and we can all help.' Jane looked eager and pretty and Archie saw a dimension of femininity that Amy had never possessed. 'Stay and eat with us now,' she suggested, her face alight with warmth and affection.

'Not now, for I haven't time but I'll expect you tomorrow. Rose will be delighted and it will do her good to run wild with her cousins. She is very well just now.' He asked Jack to fetch back the horse and to find Rose for him. It would be so easy to make a fool of himself over Jane Darwen, he thought, but she was married with seven children and must have no more, he reminded himself severely. He saw the lively faces of her children as they settled Rose under a parasol in the trap and wished for a son and healthy daughters and not a lovely hot-house flower. Gently, he put Blackie to Snooks Hill.

On Sunday, the Darwens wore cotton clothes and straw hats for the picnic. Heat made the streets lifeless and the dry gutters were acrid with manure. Edward took the big basket and Jack the churn of goat's milk for Rose, while the others carried the rest of the bundles. The path crunched with coaldust from the sidings as they walked up to the station and Jane tapped on the window of the ticket office. 'One and seven halves to Wootton please, Mr Rich.' He handed over the stiff green tickets, having counted the scrubbed faces, then closed the window and when they reached the iron gate leading to the platform he was waiting to examine the tickets, counting the children again as if he suspected that an extra one or two had crept in. He gave Jane the return halves and compared the time on the station clock with his half-hunter watch.

'The train to Wootton and Ryde will be here in seven and a half minutes,' he announced. 'Please cross the line, using the gates.'

Jane pushed the white wicket gate at the side of the line and held it open while the baskets went through. It was designed to keep children and animals off the line and there was a similar gate at the other side of the track. Although it was possible to cross the line five yards away without using a gate, Mr Rich still thought they were his contribution to safety. The station-master now became porter as he pulled a trolley bearing two red mailbags along to the spot where the guard's van would stop. Edward watched him, his face alight with envy. How important Mr Rich was! He had to do so many duties and did them all with such dignity. Some day *he'd* do that and watch the huge monsters steam into the station. He might even punch tickets if he had some experience. There was baggage to shift, the station garden to tend and the lamps to fill with oil. He dreamed of sternly telling people without tickets to go back to the booking office, but would pause with the green flag and whistle until they boarded the train.

A plume of smoke and steam rose from the bend by the river and hung in a white cloud, dissolving slowly into tiny wisps long after the train had passed by. The whistle blew as the gradient was reached and the brakes squealed in the dry atmosphere as the train found the old bridge, the music of the wheels changing over the metal lattice. Horses and ducks under the arches ignored it and it slid to a gusty halt with the guard's van exactly at the right spot. How did they know, Edward wondered. A crate of young fowls was lifted out and oats for the local chandler. Two long-handled scythes, their blades wrapped in sacking, followed, with a mass of harness. A few passengers alighted and walked to the exit where Mr Rich examined their tickets with deep suspicion.

Carrying less than twenty passengers, the train breathed asthmatically out into the open and Edward saw the privileged station-master cross the line without using the gates.

Jane sat in the centre seat, enjoying the short journey. She read all the advertisements framed in heavy mahogany and looked at the gaudy views of the Island that were in every compartment. She could just see the reflection of the pink flowers on her hat in the flyblown mirror. Edward secured the window on the middle notch of the leather strap but smuts came in through the opening and Jane moved slightly to avoid soiling her dress, 'Don't lean out of the window,' she told the children. 'You'll get your heads knocked off when you come to the bridge. A man did once because he wasn't looking the right way. Or you'll get smuts in your eyes,' she added. She said this each time they went on a train and the children loved it, venturing just so far and falling back long before they came to the bridge.

Jane watched them indulgently. Hedges along the river fields were covered with dog roses. Clumps of cow parsley dotted the sides of the track and patches of burned gorse showed where sparks from the engine had fallen. Cows brushed flies away with long tails and a gypsy girl stared at the train as it passed the encampment; in no time at all they were at Wootton.

Wootton Creek was still and cool against the soft rise of the green hill on the way to the farm. Lizzie picked flowers that wilted as she bunched them and Jack threw stones into the Creek, but Clare and Janey kept their dresses clean so that Rose would see how smart they looked. Sidney lagged behind, pulling a leaf to bits without tearing the veins.

Amy was at the gate. 'Thought you'd be on that one,' she said. 'Rose is in the lower field with your Uncle Archie and he wants you to help him there.' She smiled at Jane.

'It's such a nice day we'll all eat in the field. Run off,' she told the children. 'We'll bring the food down later.'

Jane loosened the ribbon tying her hat and watched a dragonfly flash blue fire back to the Creek. 'I love this place,' she enthused.

Amy, who had been up since first light making butter, was hot. 'It's all right in summer,' she admitted, 'but it's cruel in winter, with the damp rising from the Creek.' They went into the low-ceilinged, flagstoned kitchen where the copper pans gleamed in the sunlight and the deep bowl of wild flowers looked attractive, but Jane could imagine it in winter with draughts coming in under the doors and through the ill-fitting window frames.

Beyond the kitchen was the room with a high, tightly-shut window above the couch by the fireplace, where Rose spent most of her life. Brown marks left by condensation streaked the walls and to Jane it was no better than a dungeon. 'How is Rose?' she asked.

'I can't understand why she is so well,' said Amy. 'She's been out in the open more than I think is good for her, but she has more appetite and energy.'

'She may be over the worst,' Jane suggested. 'She's growing fast and it takes all her strength.'

'Sometimes I think she won't make old bones,' said Amy. She finished her cup of tea quickly.

'I don't want to hold you up,' said Jane. 'Just tell me what to do to help.'

'Have you ever skimmed?' Jane shook her head. 'All you need is a steady hand.' The stillroom-cum-dairy was lined with slate shelves and contained stone kegs and ewers, and silvery cream buckets with heavy lids and brass hinges. Milk, ready for skimming, had a thick layer of cream on it: Amy pulled a skimming spoon across the surface, puckering the cream as it was gathered and put it into the cream jar. Jane washed her hands and put on a print apron. She took the skimmer but made it bite too deeply at first, then caught the knack and separated cream from blue-white milk evenly. She remembered her aunt in Ireland doing this and enjoyed the smooth rhythm as ladle after ladle flowed into the jugs and the skim-milk that nobody but the very poor would drink went in a bucket for the pigs.

The goat's milk for Rose was kept in an earthenware jug covered with wet butter muslin. 'It looks the same as our cow's milk,' said Amy, 'but Rose does seem so much better for it. We'd better scald the churns now.' She poured boiling water and soda into each one, scrubbing away any smell of milk as she knew that new milk in unwashed vessels went sour quickly. Nobody knew why – it was a fact of life.

Then Amy took a pair of butterpats and dipped them in cold water, cut butter from the churn and tossed it from one pat to the other, beating out surplus water and shaping it into a neat, criss-crossed square. Jane stacked the squares neatly, covering them with wet muslin and taking them in batches to the cool dark pantry where the walls were too thick to know winter or summer. Now, Amy filled wooden butter moulds and forced out all the bubbles to make the pattern clear, before tapping it out on to a wet plate. There was a rose design on one, a thistle on another and a cow with mournful eyes on the third. 'The big house have three every week,' Amy said, and left the washed churn upside down to air. They stacked bottles of cold tea and cider and one of goat's milk in a basket with the food that Jane had brought and packed another with more food and water. She put the baskets on a yoke and Jane was amazed to find how easy it was to carry a heavy weight in this way, as they walked through the fields and saw the butterflies on the nettles by the cesspit. With perfect weather and no bad news, her fears receded.

Emily ran to them with a bunch of scabious and clover and Clare took the cloth from the first basket and spread it under a tree. The others came running, the boys with sleeves rolled as high as possible and the girls bare-legged in the dry grass. Janey picked hay from Jack's hair. 'I was only doing what Uncle Archie said, to throw it as high as possible,' he grinned.

'We can stook it after dinner,' Archie said. 'Do you want to be rid of them, Jane? I could do with them full-time, and every handful of hay will be used if the war goes on.' Archie flung himself on the grass, his working shirt open at the neck and his dusty corduroys tied with string at the knees. He wiped his face with a red handkerchief and his strong teeth were creamy against the brown skin. He was much better-looking in these clothes than when he was tightly suited with a necktie and Jane smiled, thinking herself lucky to have such nice connections by marriage.

Amy clicked her tongue. 'Archie, you look like one of your own labourers. Those corduroys are as bad as those they wear in the workhouse!'

But Archie only smiled and accepted the cockles that Jane had brought specially for him as Amy never bothered to pickle them in vinegar. He laid back, enjoying being spoiled by the girls who brought him what he wanted and tickled his neck with long grasses. He watched the two women with lazy eyes. Amy was a good wife, always willing to help with sick animals, but his eyes turned again and again to Jane, whose face was flushed and whose hair hung down in curling tendrils from her usually severe bun.

An instinctive alarm made Jane get up and brush her skirt. 'This won't do! We are here to help. Put on your shoes, girls, and come into the orchard. If you want jam this year, you'd better pick a lot of plums. I've made some for the Barracks but we need quite a bit too.'

'The lower branches have already been picked. I'll bring a ladder and the boys can go up,' said Archie.

'You've the hay to finish,' Amy put in sharply. 'Jane and I can carry a light ladder. We're not made of putty!' She smiled maliciously when he was gone. 'Take no notice of him, Jane. I'm afraid my husband is fond of the ladies and has to be kept in his place.'

Jane raised her eyebrows. 'You *do* surprise me, Amy. I would never have thought so. Archie's a good husband, isn't he?' She looked directly at Amy. 'Has he ever given you cause to doubt him?'

Amy looked down. 'No, he's a good husband,' she admitted.

'Then you've no cause for worry.'

Amy called to Rose, 'How many more times have I to

tell you to put on your hat? You'll be burned and have a bad night again.'

'Don't be cross, Amy,' Jane smiled. 'It's a lovely day and you've been so kind, teaching me to skim. You know, you ought to be proud of such a handsome husband. Everyone speaks well of him and he's faithful to you. There's never been a word of gossip, and I don't think there ever will be. I'm very fond of Archie but I have a husband of my own, a good man, and I need never look at another man however long it takes Walter to come home.'

Amy changed the subject quickly but insisted on making a special pat of butter with the cow's head on it, for Jane to take home.

Emily slipped a hand into Jane's on the way back to the station. Midges hung in clouds and a woodpecker tapped a hollow tree. 'I do love Uncle Archie, don't you, Mother?'

'Sure he's a good dear man with a big heart,' Jane said. On a day like this, she was more at home with Archie than with Walter, who would never lie about in the hay and fool with the boys, but she wished that Amy hadn't hinted at something that she tried to ignore.

'Uncle Archie thinks you're pretty, Mother.'

'And so I am!' said Jane firmly. 'So is Aunt Amy and Janey and Lizzie and Clare and Rose and you.'

In the train the wheels said, '*Walter has gone, Walter has gone, Walter has gone*,' and her sadness flooded back, but it was more of an objective sadness for a set of circumstances than for herself.

Everyone was grubby and when they reached home, had to wash all over to get rid of the harvest mites. 'That'll teach you not to run barefoot in the grass,' Jane admonished as one by one they cleaned themselves up, had salve dabbed on sore places and sat down in their nightclothes to eat supper. Edward washed in the tin bath in the outhouse to show he was a man and didn't share with the children. Jane sorted plums while the wasps were away and filled a jam jar with sugar water to trap them on the outhouse roof, away from the shop. The dusk was warm and the smell of jam everywhere when she went to bed. She stripped and washed all over, patting her skin dry and scenting her underarms with Attar of Roses as she had done when Walter was there to notice and caress her, his face at her breast, but tonight no tears came, no sadness. He was a long way away and she had learned to skim milk and make cream.

'Plum jam? I smelled it from home and knew you were up early.' Maudie Dove brushed aside a wasp and looked hopeful as she closed the shop door behind her the next morning.

'I've kept a pot aside for you and Lucy,' Jane answered brightly.

'Have you heard anything lately, Mrs Darwen?'

'Not for weeks now, Maudie. After Ladysmith, the troops moved so fast that they can't have had time to put pencil to paper.' Maudie looked tired and drawn. The men coming home had no news of her Ben or if they had, they refused to comment. Rumours were being spread of troopships lost and convoys of wounded drowned. 'No news is good news, they say, so make sure you have everything clean in case Ben should turn up suddenly. Make Lucy a dress from this one that Emily has outgrown.'

'If the Queen is at Osborne, we'll have the news quickly,' said Maudie, brightening as she fingered the good Madras cotton. 'She's ever so good as she knows that we all have someone in the war. Poor lady, they say her sight's going.'

'That's why she stays here, where she feels at home and people don't bother her,' said Jane. 'And it's not far to see her daughter at Carisbrooke. I think of her sometimes, all lonely in that big house at Osborne. It's stuffed with paintings and tapestries and ornaments from every outlandish place on earth and she's left it all just as Prince Albert had it.' She wondered if men dominated everything, even after death.

'Have you ever been inside?' asked Maudie. 'It must be nice to have all those rooms.'

'Once,' Jane said shortly. She remembered with horror the collection of marble hands and feet that were on view, all replicas of the hands and feet of the Royal infants, and the cold marble reminded her of the cemetery. The bronze statue of the Duke of Wellington wasn't as bad but she never wanted to go inside the place again.

Edward called out that the carriage was coming from the Castle. Maudie smiled. Any news, if it wasn't her own bad news, made life exciting. 'The Queen must be ill again,' she said, and in next to no time the town buzzed with rumours. The *County Press* issued a guarded bulletin that the Queen was very grieved at the death of the Duke of Coburg and that the Princess Beatrice was in attendance at Osborne.

'Holy Mary keep her safe,' prayed Jane. 'It's her fourth bereavement.' She told Jack to put the black shutter in the middle of the shop window and a picture of the Royal Family on the counter, but apart from the conventional mourning in churches, the local people were unconcerned about the fate of remote members of the Family; children told not to make a noise wanted to know who this Duke was, who upset their play.

To make matters worse, the next Sunday was very hot. Tight collars and button boots were intolerable and Jack sat at the end of the pew in church and slipped out during the singing of the last hymn. With any luck he could swim in the river before he was noticed. He went to fetch a towel, but Aaron was waiting by the shop door. 'Thought you'd taken root in there,' he said, and waved a stiff mackerel in Jack's face.

'Is it a glut?'

'Certainly is. Sandown Bay's black with 'em. I've brought up one load and I'm going back for more but your Ma ought to know. I need some help, and wish your father was here as he'd be off like a shot.'

Jack gave a war whoop and rushed inside to change into thin old cotton trousers and faded shirt. He put on rope-soled shoes and grabbed a straw hat.

'A glut is it?' Jane smiled when she got back to *Darwen's*. 'Edward, put Bess in the shafts and load up from the barge using plenty of ice, then take it all up to the Barracks. Jack, tell the foreman at the ice factory we'll need more ice and bring some back for the slab. Janey! Clare! Take Sidney and the push-cart up to the Town Hall arches and sell this lot cheap. Keep the fish in the shade, mind. We'll have to open the shop, even though it is the Sabbath. Jack, tell Aaron to put the next lot on the train and Edward can collect it when he comes back.' She speedily cleared the window of fruit and vegetables and washed down the marble slab, putting zinc trays of ice under the cascade of stiff blue-silver fish. She changed her Sunday dress and put on a sacking apron; the air smelled of the sea.

Already, local women converged on the shop at the prospect of cheap fish. They brought Delft dishes or buckets as they knew they would have better measure if the fish was roughly weighed and tipped into a container. The innkeeper's wife and Mrs Grace came, still in church finery but wearing pinafores and took two dozen fish for sousing and serving in the taproom. They ordered more smoked, and as they left, the women from the Bugle came with the same idea. Maudie turned up with her bucket and offered to serve, while Lucy sat and nursed Ikey the cat.

Jane was up to her elbows in fishguts as some people were too squeamish to clean their own, and Emily heaved buckets of the refuse down to the river. Maudie weighed and took money, tossing it into a bucket of water so that it wouldn't stink when taken to the bank, and all thoughts of Sunday dinner faded. Jane swiftly put a dish of mackerel in cider and bay leaves into the oven with scrubbed potatoes on the top shelf and by two o'clock, there were few fish left. They washed their reeking hands and Emily sprayed water over the shop floor before sweeping it out with a yard broom. Maudie put her own fish in a tray of ice and laid the table. They sat down and ate soused mackerel and stewed plums, while Lucy had a banana from the shop.

Jane gutted and put the remaining fish to souse, the only way of preserving them for a day or so in hot weather. Then she found the long bamboo rods on which to impale the next batch for smoking. 'Maudie, will you go up to the brickyard for me and ask the men to make up a smoking shed? Tell them I want it ready for smoking by early tomorrow morning. It takes all that time for the oak chips to settle and heat the house.' Walter would enjoy these when he came home, she thought. 'On the way, leave this dish of soused fish in at the surgery. Dr Barnes likes them and it's a way of saying thank you.' She wished that Maudie had had the idea as she had so much to thank him for.

As it was Sunday, this was an extra day of trading and allowed only because mackerel was traditionally a twenty-four hour fish and no one would eat it unless smoked or soused after that time. Bert Cooper came in, and for once Jane was glad to see him as he offered to make another smoke-house quickly, using old iron sheets to back the bricks. 'You've a good eye for business,' she conceded.

'We could make a good partnership,' he said, more boldly than at any time since the Hunt.

'We're already business partners, Bert,' Jane said. 'That works very well.'

'I hope you tell Walter that.'

'I'd never tell anything I couldn't say to your face,' she said. 'The good and the bad.'

He seemed relieved. 'I'll take some smoked over to the mainland – get a good price there. How are you off for sticks?'

'With two smokers we'll need more. Can I leave that to you? Green willow sticks would do.'

He sniffed. 'Annie never cooks soused fish as she can't bear the smell,' he said.

'Not much smell to that,' said Jane with a malicious smile, knowing it was Bert's favourite dish, and one he enjoyed with Walter when they sat over their business accounts. She saw too that he was tired. He'd helped Edward load the cart from the train and chivvied the men at the yard to get the smoke going before she even asked for it. 'You can take this lot up to the yard and have some yourself,' she relented. 'And if you break that dish, I'll murder you!'

'I wouldn't dare!' he said, but went red with surprised pleasure.

Maudie washed the marble slab and swilled out the hand-cart ready for more fish and Lizzie told people in the town that more was on the way. Jane scalded some pieces for the cats and dog and sat down to drink tea. Maudie drank her fourth cup and reluctantly took Lucy home. It was peaceful at last. Jack had gone with Aaron and she was glad to know his energies were harnessed usefully on the boat. There would be fish to gut and string up when the barge came in and everyone was hot and tired, but unable to settle. 'Is the tide in?' she asked Ethel who sat on the counter, drumming her heels.

'It's on the turn. Mother says the barge will be up about nine.'

'Come on,' said Jane. 'Let's walk down the river fields to meet them. We'll find a breath of air and see the gypsies opposite. You can bring something for supper and Nero can come.' Janey packed jam sandwiches and cake and fruit and the boys filled haversacks with bottles of cold tea and lemonade. Birds drifted low after gnats and the fields were empty and not a leaf moved, but the tide pushed its way over the mudbanks to hiss on the warm gravel of the shore. Dry rushes quivered as the water eddied round the roots and a family of moorhens swam for an islet of reeds as the children waded in the shallows.

Jane tucked the girls' dresses into their knickers and quietly removed her own stockings and shoes, wondering if Annie Cooper had ever paddled in the river. Nero hunted every sound and splashed wet fur over Sidney. A water rat disappeared and owls started hunting, and Ethel shouted that she could see the boat. Aaron's sail flapped limply but the tide was strong. They went out to a finger of gravel and waved like flowers in the dusk and he pulled over so that they clambered on board. The boat was full of fish and Jack had salt caked in his eyebrows. He grinned happily and helped himself to a hunk of bread and jam.

Aaron took a swig of tea. 'Parched I was.' He jerked his head towards Jack. 'Young 'un did well. Worked like a man. We sold all but this load but knew you'd want a few to smoke.'

'We'll have a grand settling tomorrow, we will,' said Jane. It would be more funds for her own store of pin money, her perquisite over and above her shop duties and one that

Walter looked on with amused approval, never dreaming that she made as much as she did, imagining that it was on a level with Amy and her pin money from raising sickly piglets. Aaron saw the peace in Jane's face and knew that she'd manage even if Walter never came back.

A distant rumble of thunder over Pan Down came with flickers of lightning. 'Someone's having it tonight,' said Aaron. 'Might clear the air a bit but I don't think we'll get it now. Best get these in smoke though or we might catch it tomorrow.'

Chapter 12

Bad news came with the thunder. Jane looked out at the streaming gutters and turned back to the misery inside the shop. Ben Dove was dead. The fine weather and the sense of holiday had broken, and the reckoning had to come. Maudie Dove sat in the back room, sobbing. His last letter lay on the table beside the official buff envelope and, after convincing Maudie for so long that Ben was being cared for in Africa, Jane was lost for words.

Ben had written to his wife while recovering from a slight wound after Bloemfontein. He told her that the local medical services were bad, and that more and more wounded were left in poor shelter while waiting for doctors and orderlies to come from the Cape. '*I'm feeling weak*,' he wrote. *'My leg aches all the time and I can't stomach the native food. The fever has come to the camp and never an hour goes by but someone dies of it.'* Typhoid was already affecting him, poor man, and he died a few days later.

This news brought the war closer again, but somehow Jane knew that Walter would return safely. She believed Mrs Lee's prophecy and in her own Irish feyness – and anyway, there was too much to do running the shop and making sure that Bert Cooper didn't cheat her over the brickyard to have time to worry.

Maudie looked up out of swollen eyelids. Her face was blotchy with tears and in spite of her youth, suddenly ugly. Jane saw with distaste that the girl's blouse was grubby; not with the grubbiness of new dirt on a hot day but with the greyness of bad washing. She's a dabber, Jane thought. She handed her the panacea for every crisis, a cup of hot, strong and syrup-sweet tea which Maudie sipped between shuddering sobs and gradually took comfort from Jane's strength.

Jane read the typed information in the official letter with

indignation. It painted a very different picture from the one described by Ben. It sounded as if he had died with a smile and a 'God Save the Queen' on his lips! *He will be remembered as one of our country's heroes,'* the letter stated. Maudie was very impressed and Jane said nothing of her own feelings. Already, the girl was brighter and returning to normal as Jane filled the cups again. She's an easygoing girl, and when she's clean and not crying, she's pretty enough, thought Jane. She could marry again.

'I shall have a pension,' Maudie said with relief.

'It won't be enough to keep you and Lucy and buy clothes. You'll have to get work. What can you do?'

'I can scrub,' said Maudie without enthusiasm. 'I'm not a very good cook, and when I tried a job on the Mall, the missus was very unkind and said I didn't clean in the corners.'

'I believe that Mrs Anderson at the laundry needs more hands,' said Jane. 'Mind you, it's very hard work,' she warned her.

'I'd like that. I know some of the girls there and I want to keep Lucy nice. When she goes to school in September, I could work half-time.'

'Remember that Lucy is still small and needs you at home in the evenings. If the School Board Inspector caught you leaving her alone after dark, he'd be after you.' Maudie bit her lip. In the summer she had spent a lot of time on the quay, laughing with the men. It was harmless but tongues wagged and everyone knew what went on after dark down there.

'I do try, Mrs Darwen, but people think I'm no better than I ought to be and it hurts.'

'You'll be judged by the company you keep, Maudie. I know all about that. A woman on her own is a target for gossip and you have to be careful. You've left Lucy alone now. Bring her over here for a bite to eat while I go up and see Mrs Anderson, and come to me whenever you need advice or to leave Lucy for an hour if you want to go out.'

The laundry was in a back street between the bonemeal factory and the bakery. In hot weather the smell was bad, for the smoke and the steam mixed with the stench of stale soda, bleach and soap, but today the breeze took away the worst. The office was above the cat-walk by the workroom and the huge zinc baths of linen tended by girls in drab dresses covered with rubber and sacking aprons. Mrs Anderson shut out the noise and steam. 'It gets everywhere,' she said and showed Jane mildew on the leather bindings of the account books. 'What can I do for you, Jane? Is it the big damask tablecloth?'

'I haven't used that since Walter left. Do you need extra hands? Maudie Dove has just been widowed and needs work.'

'A slip of a thing, isn't she? Would she be strong enough?' Down in a bay where hot sheets were dragged from boilers into sinks using wooden tongs, the girls looked hot and some had arms bandaged from wrists to elbow where the scalding water had run off the sheets. 'She'd have to have her wits about her and not gossip. They have only themselves to blame if they get scalded.' Others folded half-dry sheets to put into the huge mangles and Jane thought of Clare's crushed fingertip. What a terrible place, she thought. Please God none of mine come here. 'I'll give her a week's trial,' decided the manageress. 'Tell her to come on Monday and do mornings, as school-term starts then.'

That Monday, the children went back to school reluctantly after the freedom of the summer. Sidney rubbed soap round his stiff collar to prevent it from chafing and the girls looked prim in their starched pinafores.

Edward was fourteen and ready to leave school. He was good with his hands but hated learning from books and Jane had to decide what he must do. When he came home for dinner, she sent Jack to do the deliveries and asked Edward to stay behind. 'You'll be leaving school soon,' she began. Edward looked sullen. 'I thought you hated school!'

'I do, but I don't want to work in a shop for ever,' he said.

'Anyone can see that,' she replied dryly. 'Now, I've been thinking: with the others coming on and your father back soon, God willing, it might be best to get you settled.

However, if he does come back and decides that he needs you here, you'll do as he says or it rebounds on me.'

'You mean I can really, really work on the railway?' He hugged her ecstatically. 'I'll help all I can when I come home, and see to the others. Tomorrow I'll get them up early to pick mushrooms.'

'Good boy. I can sell all you can pick.' It was sad to think of autumn and bramble jelly and chestnuts, and to know that a very happy summer was over.

When the shop-bell rang, Jane held out a hand in warm greeting. 'It's so good to see you again,' she exclaimed.

André Duval grinned, Jane's smile dispelling his fear that she might have forgotten him. 'I bring the first onions from Brittany for you as usual, madame. It has been six years now, and you have a better bargain each time!'

Jane laughed. The onions were hard and fleshy with purple between the layers and crisp brown skins. Walter loved to talk with André and bargain, both knowing that they would strike a good deal and enjoy the meeting. André was a farmer in France but lived on his barge while selling his crop in England. Now he produced a bottle of wine and put it on the counter. Jane hesitated: this was a part of the ritual, to share the fine wine and nibble a biscuit like taking wine with the gentry but this year, Walter was away. Oh, where was the harm? She picked up the bottle and led her visitor to the back room, and while she polished two thin glasses, he talked of the war and how sad he was that Walter was away. 'We were sure it would be over after they took Pretoria,' he lamented.

'They said the last of the Boers captured would take a vow of allegiance to the Queen,' said Jane, 'but there has been more fighting since then.' She sipped the wine and closed her eyes.

'It is good, yes?' André chuckled. He helped himself to the cold rabbit pie that Jane set before him and told news of his family in Roscoff, of his daughter's marriage and his uncle dying, as if she knew them all. He saw Jane's sadness. 'Walter will be here before the barge is empty and I have to leave,' he reassured her. 'We shall drink together again.'

He produced another bottle. 'For you when I am not here. If Walter is not back when I leave, I will bring you more wine for his return and you must both drink to me and my family, n'est-ce pas?'

Jane put a hand over her glass as he tried to fill it again. 'I would be light-headed this afternoon,' she demurred. 'Come back to supper when the children are here.'

He rose to leave. 'I shall bring the onions then. You are très gentille. I like very much to come back again.'

From the acid triumph in Annie Cooper's eyes, she had been in the shop for a long time. 'Why, Annie!' Jane exclaimed. 'Why didn't you knock on the counter as you always do to bring me running?'

'I was up at the butcher and saw you had a visitor so I didn't like to interrupt your entertaining.' She smirked. 'Good at feeding the men, aren't you? Even my Bert gets fed on soused mackerel up at the brickyard when my back's turned.'

André saw the sour looks and Jane's discomfort. 'Les femmes!' he muttered and left the shop.

'Now you are here, what can I do for you, Annie?'

'He's foreign, isn't he? Sounded *very* foreign to me.' Jane smiled grimly. The old cat – she'd make a meal out of this. Jane wondered who had told Annie of the mackerel in the brickyard.

'Mr Duval is an old friend of Walter's and they do business.'

'A friend of Walter's – or yours? I didn't think he liked foreigners off the barges.'

Jane clenched her hands under the counter. 'Walter's, of course, Annie. When my husband is away I must do business on his account. I have to deal with old customers, new ones, old friends and even with people I heartily dislike and would never have over my doorstep except in the line of business!'

Annie sniffed. 'Well I suppose you think you know best, but I'd be very careful Jane. Some might think the worst if they knew you had men in the back room, *drinking*.

Foreigners, too.' She opened her purse. 'I'll have a pen-n'orth of potherbs.'

Jane found a carrot, an onion, a piece of turnip and some herbs. She thrust them across the counter and Annie gathered them up hastily, her eyes malevolent coals of excitement. 'Any order I can leave with Mr Foster?' she asked, to make sure that Jane knew where she was going. The grocer's shop would be crowded with housewives ready to hear any juicy piece of gossip.

Jane washed the glasses and corked the bottle firmly. I might need a drop more tonight, she thought grimly, and scrubbed the marble slab with such vigour that streams of water flew out through the drainage hole on to the pavement.

Aaron came in, heaved a basket on to the counter and tipped the fish on the marble, topping them with a huge skate. Jane put the cockles on the counter with lemons and parsley. 'Will you be taking tea?' she asked, and Aaron looked at her more closely. Whenever she sounded so Irish, she had something on her mind. 'I could do with a cup myself,' she continued wanly. Two men in the back room in one day! Annie should have waited. Aaron sat carefully on a whitewood chair, conscious of the trail of fish smells. He helped himself to sugar and stirred the cup until Jane wanted to scream.

'You don't look yourself, gal,' he began. 'Missing Walt bad?'

'No.' She gave a guilty start.

'Saw Annie Cooper go up to the grocer's,' he said. He sucked his tea noisily. 'Don't lose much time spreading gossip, does she? Oh, she loves a bit of mischief,' and he laughed maliciously.

'It's no laughing matter, Aaron. Tell me what she said.'

'That Annie's a tartar and no mistake.' He seemed to have a private joke.

'What have you done, Aaron?' Jane put down her cup. 'You have a look about you that I know means trouble!' She was very pale.

He laughed until the tears ran down his face and the

smell of fish came in waves. His red hair bristled on his head, his eyebrows and in his ears. The reddened face and bulbous nose made him ugly but now the fierce expression that frightened babies gave way to a sparkle of mischief. 'I settled she!'

'Aaron, what have you done?'

'Never could abide her, hikey old faggot! Can't never forget that her father made a bit of money – that's why Bert married her. She gives herself too many airs.'

'*What happened?*'

'I saw the Johnny Onion man come out o' here and she come after, so I went up the shop to get some flour. She'd just opened her mouth to tell them a tale about you, Jane, but you know Annie – can't tell it until she's spun a fine old yarn, so they didn't hear anything but the warming up, so to speak, about how you had to meet all sorts now that Walter was away.'

'She isn't the only one to spin things out!' Jane said meaningfully.

'Women like her make me puke, and there were plenty to listen.' He slapped his knees at the memory. 'I gave a sort of cough like, to make sure everyone saw it was me, and then I went and kissed her. I said as Bert was away I'd be up to see her as usual. "Let me know," I said, "and when he goes to Portsmouth again I'll be up there with a nice bit o' jellied eel".' He roared with laughter as he recalled Annie, stricken in his rough and odoriferous embrace. 'She was all of a heap, my gal.' He gave Jane a penetrating look as she protested. 'She took it hard and she knew what I wanted, so she won't be spreading lies about you for a while.' He guffawed again. 'Frightened to death she'll be every time she sees me now.'

Jane cut him another piece of cake. 'Aaron, you are an old devil!' She shook her head. 'You're a dear man, so you are, but be careful. Annie's petty and backbiting and I wouldn't have you harmed by her for the world.'

Aaron heaved himself to his feet. 'Don't you fret – her can't hurt me or mine. I owe nothing to nobody and I give their Dan work sometimes. He's the best out of that stable and I like him. He said once he'd move away if he got a good job, but she's got him under her thumb.'

The shop-bell rang and Jane laughed. 'You'd best be going or they'll think the worst as you have such an eye for the ladies!' All morning, women came in and hinted at what had happened in Mr Foster's shop, but Jane served and smiled and refused to be drawn. She was warmed and comforted by the real friendship she had experienced and almost felt sorry for Annie.

The back door had been left open but Clare still sniffed. 'Mr Sheath has been in.'

Jane laughed. 'Can't I do anything without you knowing the minute you come in that door? Mr Duval is back and coming to supper, so you'd better be able to say good evening in French.'

That evening, André wanted to hear about the Queen so that he could tell his family, who had never seen a Royal person. Sidney described her carriage and the times they went to church at the Castle.

'Carisbrooke will never be the same once she goes,' Jane said regretfully. 'She may have riches but she's a sad old lady and has to rule her country alone.'

'She has a parliament,' said André firmly, 'while you, Jane, rule your little kingdom without Walter and do well.'

When Walter came home, he would take control again. The unwelcome thought took Jane unawares, as she seldom considered it now. Everyone worked hard and was healthy, and sexual security gave her contentment. No longer did loneliness nag at her at night. It was like being a widow, but without the grief. Even the idea of women in Pretoria giving men comfort no longer appalled her. It could be a solution of sorts, she decided – but surely, Walter would never go with another woman . . .

Chapter 13

Christmas came and went, clouded with mournful expectancy as the Queen was in poor health; as her concentration failed, audiences were cancelled and few people saw her. Lord Roberts, the hero of the war, was given an audience on 14 January. The country assumed by this that the Queen was better, but by 19 January, rumours came from the staff at Osborne that she was ill again. Two days later, many members of the Royal family gathered, including some from Europe who had travelled in luxurious ships anchored off Cowes, and an amused ripple of disbelief greeted the news that Kaiser Wilhelm had insisted on seeing her.

'I didn't believe it,' said Aaron, 'but he's here all right! Never seen moustaches like it, and he looks as if he's got a rod up his backside. Poor old lady. Him coming will do her a power of good, I don't think! She never could abide him near her.'

But Her Majesty was beyond caring who fought over protocol, and a whole Empire mourned when she died peacefully on 22 January. It was the passing of a century – and the end of a great era.

Jane dusted off the black mourning shutters and Edward gave them a fresh coat of paint. *Puller's*, the draper shop by the Mall, ran out of black crêpe and black-edged handkerchiefs when the gentry hastened to show respect by selecting the expensive ones with the wider black border. The printing works in Chapel Street churned out black-edged visiting cards and memorial cards with angels and marble urns and lilies in abundance, and pictures of the Royal Family appeared in every window, draped in black, with vases of Christmas roses and evergreen. There was no call for waste, however patriotic they were, so Jane searched the boxes for clothes that could be adapted for mourning. She hung out a dress of black velvet to air and looked out black ribbons and gloves for the girls, armbands and ties for the boys. She trimmed a hat with black tulle and purple flowers and wore a miniature of the Queen on a black velvet band at her throat. Only the rich went into full mourning and Clare sulked, lost in envy of the girls who dressed in hideous crêpe, but she managed to unearth a huge black shawl in which she enveloped herself. A rash of embroidered Union Jacks appeared on muffs, coats and dresses, and jewellers did a roaring trade in cameo brooches and charm bracelets hung with sovereigns. Jane was tempted to buy a cameo of the Queen from her pickle money, and then wore it every day.

Flags at half-mast and guards in ceremonial dress marked the funeral. Jet beads and earrings jingled and black velvet chokers with yet more jet adorned the matrons of the nation. It may have been a sop to convention, but there was satisfaction in making a show during the horrors of war, and those on the Island revealed a genuine sorrow and affection for the Queen. Black horses, some dyed for the occasion and decked with black ostrich feathers, paraded with muffled hooves at the Barracks.

Sam Walmsley twisted his hat in his hands and looked at the picture of the Queen Jane had placed on the counter. 'I'm glad she came home to die even if they took her to the mainland to bury her,' he said, echoing the thoughts of all on the Island.

With the coming of spring, the country became tired of mourning. The bright sun showed up uneven black dyes and the efforts of home-cleaning on patches of underarm sweat which weakened the fabrics and left stains. Jane took out a white blouse and grey skirt then removed the black tulle and tired flowers from her best hat, replacing them with white flowers. But dare she wear it to chapel? Dr Barnes' wife had emerged in pale mauve with a purple hat, and the gentry were already in half-mourning. Jane pinned the hat to her bun and smiled. Local shops tempted with light fabrics in mauve and grey and hats trimmed with pale ostrich feathers from the farms in South Africa. Granny Cheverton splashed out on a black satin apron – exactly like her old one – and even sour Annie Cooper put fresh curtains at her windows.

Jane had a lump in her throat when Edward started work at Cowes. It was only five miles away and he'd be home for supper, but he was the first of her brood to fly the nest, and she let him go with love and understanding. She turned back to read the news but found little to cheer her. Although the Boers were officially beaten they still gave trouble, and more horses and men were shipped out even when the Generals came home with the wounded. Walter's last letter was scanty and a tear made a blister that dulled the ink as Jane read it again.

'Bad news?' Sam Walmsley popped his head round the shop door.

'Oh, Sam, I didn't see you there. No, Walter is fine, but I just feel low somehow. Edward went off today and I wish I had some idea when his father would be back.'

'Tears – with Walter coming back soon?' He regarded her steadily. 'Perhaps it's been *too* long, Jane.' She had blossomed into a fine businesswoman capable of handling farmers and customers, and even Bert Cooper admitted that she had a full say in matters concerning the brickyard, never giving an inch where money was concerned. 'Bert may find Walter easier to handle than you,' he went on with a grin. 'He's a slippery one but you've been his match, my dear. You get more with a quiet word than Walt used to get in half an hour's fight. Aye, it'll be strange and none too easy for you when your man comes home.'

'It's not that I don't want Walter home, but Sam – I just don't know how I feel,' she admitted, touched by his sensitivity. 'I'll pay you now,' she added, and entered their transaction in the ledger with speed and efficiency. He gave her a good hand of Canary bananas, saying it might be the last for a while if the convoys didn't bring fruit. 'Then it's certainly time the war was over,' she joked, peeling one and offering it to him. Sam went home wishing that Walter could stay away for even longer, but a few days later when Jane was washing a blouse in mild soap, Sidney came in with an envelope with a field postmark on it. She dried her hands and her heart beat painfully. Nero thumped his hind leg on the floor and the children gathered round the table.

'Your father is coming home in five weeks' time,' she said in a low voice. Janey and Clare went on eating and Jack frowned, but Emily ran to her and hugged her. 'That's wonderful,' she said and the tension broke.

'Does it mean that Blackie will come back? Did he say anything about me?' asked Edward anxiously.

'I told him how well you had settled and I think he'll let you stay,' Jane said.

'That's a relief!' Edward caught up his satchel and ran to catch the Cowes train. He had just three minutes from the time the whistle blew at Shide to get to Newport station.

The letter was warmer than the last one, and contained more news. Walter was excited and his humour came through the words. Unconsciously, Jane began to tidy the room as if he might walk in there and then. She folded linen and took out her mending and looked for a shirt button. Under the cottons, she found a package. Slowly she unwrapped the herbal preparations that Mrs Lee had given her. She made a movement as if to throw them on the fire but something seemed to stop her. She wrapped them up again and put the package in her bedroom drawer under the handkerchiefs, a few trinkets, a lock of Caroline's hair and a rosary.

Over the next weeks, Jane was quiet and busy; she bore an air of gentle resignation that Sam admired, loving her for her courage. Troops came home but some stayed behind to hunt for pockets of resistance in the isolated Lagers and homesteads. In April, the war was still costing one and a half million pounds a week.

Over a thousand leading soldiers were gazetted for meritorious service, and Alfred Milner in his *Blue Book* gained fame and spread the belief that the Boers would eventually accept the loss of their independence. Mrs Botha, the wife of General Botha, resumed peace negotiations with the British, and now only scattered groups of Boer commandos wandered starving and ragged from ruined farm to empty compound in a land laid to waste. With the winter rains, the Peace Party begged the dissidents to work for a representational government that might be superior to a Republic in a Transvaal dominated by the Hollanders, while in England, the returning wounded could expect only a welcome with bands at Portsmouth, the shadow of the workhouse and disillusion.

'Did you see how firms have been hammered on the Stock Exchange?' Bert asked while Jane scrubbed the counter. 'I got my money out early.'

'Check the book,' she said, still scrubbing to let him know that he must do business in the shop and not in the living room. 'I'm sorry for those who were caught with their life's savings,' she said. 'I'll stick to the shop and not dabble in things I don't trust.'

'It's about time Walter got back, and then I might be asked in for a mug of beer or a cup of tea,' he said bitterly.

'Annie wouldn't like it if I entertained her husband,' Jane replied smartly.

'Nothing is going right these days,' grumbled Bert. 'Some of my men wanted to form a Trade Union! I told them that they were lucky to have work and not to work under the Contract system like the Americans. They are treated like slaves over there.'

'Men coming back have a right to better times,' said Jane, wringing out the wet cloth. 'Many are making mischief, though, and I hope it never comes to real trouble. Someone in Germany even threw an iron bar at the Kaiser!'

Every feeling but excited expectation faded as the day came when the troops returned to the Island. Flags flew on public buildings and Newport High Street was a mass of bunting. The town band was lined up under an awning on the newly-swept station approach, and the coal-dust was hidden behind a large placard bearing an out-of-date and tactless advertisement calling the men to arms. The wooden partition in the booking office stuck as the fresh paint hadn't dried, and the green seats were still tacky. Mr George Foster, resplendant in a magnificent silk hat, stood proudly with the Mayor under the arches of the Town Hall where it was cool and away from the bubbling tar of the station approach. Emily bent to pop tar blisters until Janey stopped her and wiped her fingers on a handkerchief. Jane noticed nothing and nobody could read her thoughts, standing in her Sunday best with her handsome family around her.

The Mayor, chosen for his business ability and not for looks or eloquence, had begged the schoolmaster to write his welcoming speech and was terrified that he would lose his place, stumble over the long words and be robbed of his moment of glory. The same busy schoolmaster had composed a song set to music just two notes uncomfortably high and the children had shown little aptitude for learning it. The head boy of Barton School rubbed the dusty toecaps of his shoes on his socks and tried to remember the words of *The Absent-Minded Beggar.*

The new barmaid at the Bugle wore a red hat, white blouse and blue skirt. 'Know what they say,' said Aaron, 'red hat and no drawers!' All the local girls were out to catch the eye of any unattached soldier and Maudie stood giggling with the girls from the laundry, wearing too much rouge, a low-necked blouse and her hair fluffed out like a doll. And Ben not dead a year, thought Jane, and Lucy not with her.

White smoke was glimpsed and the crowd cheered. Jane clutched her bag so tightly that the clasp snapped. The children were pale in the heat and a pulse beat deeply in her head, until she thought she might faint. The men formed to march up to the Town Hall. Their uniforms were spruce and two officers from manor houses in the West Wight led them. 'No horses!' said Sidney. 'Where is Father?'

'They can't bring horses on the train,' Jane explained. Some men were foot soldiers and some from mounted regiments but all had come home to the Island. 'Wait, there's a lot more on the train,' she said, and it was with a sense of anti-climax that at last she saw him, his hat at a rakish angle, lean and tanned with his spurs shining in the sunlight as he marched with disciplined ease, while the men kept eyes front as the crowd followed them to the Square, in spite of women calling some by name.

The schoolmaster relaxed as the Mayor remembered

most of his speech and the vicar droned a long sermon about self-sacrifice then rest after labour, which made the girls from the laundry giggle. A bugle blew, the officer in charge barked a command – and the men were finally free. Emily rushed forward and tugged at Walter's tunic. He swept her shoulder-high and kissed her. The other girls pulled at his hands and the boys stood grinning a welcome. Jane met his gaze over their heads and smiled. He had the same bold look about him that was there in the days before their marriage, as if he saw her for the first time – a good-looking woman among a crowd. His eyes took in every detail of her dress, her face, her shining hair and with growing satisfaction, her figure. He pushed the children aside and embraced her. 'How's it been, gal?'

'We managed,' she said. As they walked home, stopped many times by people wanting to shake his hand, she watched Walter's face, looking for something she badly needed to see but couldn't find. What she didn't care to see was there, however. His mouth was harder, his eyes smiled less than his lips and even his handshake had a new controlled ruthlessness. At last he dragged himself away from the well-wishers and took his wife by the arm. 'What's for tea?' he asked, and was now warm and like the man who went away.

The afternoon was a confusion of eating, drinking and visitors. Boiled ham and potatoes and fresh apple pies disappeared with endless pots of tea and ale, and Walter was in his element. He said little about the campaigns but spoke of the men, the Boer prisoners, the native Africans and the horses. 'We found a broken-winded nag left by the Boers to die when we over-ran a Lager. We kept him for a lark and let him run with the mules and when anyone came scrounging a horse, we offered him as our only spare. We called him Jeddah after the Derby winner.'

The children hung on his words. 'Is it true that the black children wear no clothes?' whispered Emily.

Walter laughed. 'Some go without, but they're glad of a few rags to keep them warm and dry when it pours out there. The natives are a poor cop but they found us mealies and buried our dead.' Jane gave him a warning look as Lizzie looked sad. 'We had one nice fat little black boy who I nearly brought home to serve in the shop!'

'And what would I be doing with another mouth to feed of any colour?' commented Jane dryly. She stacked dishes while the boys slipped away to work in the stables. Janey went to milk the goat and Clare tidied the shop. Emily helped with the dishes and Walter smoked and talked until the air was blue, unconcerned with the time. The boys returned and put the shutters over the shop windows. Jane brewed fresh tea and Bert Cooper arrived with George Foster and Sam to talk even more.

'So you are a free man again,' Bert began.

'Not quite. I've to report to Albany every day until I collect my campaign medals, tie up loose ends and be demobilized.' He looked apologetic. 'Give me a week or so and I'll be ready to take over.' He saw Jack sitting at ease and frowned. 'What about the stable, my lad? It's late.'

Jack stayed where he was. 'It's all done, Father,' he said. 'They're bedded down for the night.'

Sam was about to fill his pipe but suddenly put it away. 'Tomorrow will do to catch up on the news,' he announced. 'You'll be up early, no doubt.' When Jane followed him to unbolt the door, he pressed her hand. 'Don't let him see how well you've done – not yet, Jane. Don't be too efficient in the shop.' She nodded, having seen the fleeting look of annoyance when Walter realized that everything had gone on well without him.

The smoke haze thinned as Jane opened the back door while she filled the kettles and the tank by the range. She took her time, hoping that Walter would go to sleep in the chair, leaving her free to get to bed first and pretend to be asleep, but he poured more ale into his own tankard and leaned back, dreamily. He was becoming maudlin although she had pressed tea on him so that he drank less ale. Nero lay with his head on his master's slippered feet. 'Good old dog. You remember me, don't you. It's as if I never went away.'

'What will I do? Holy Mother, what now?' Jane whispered

in the dark scullery. He had watched every move she made in the night routine and now called her into the room.

'How have you been? In yourself, I mean.'

'Well enough. Tired at times but you know how much there is to do here.'

He took her hand. 'You're prettier than ever. Do you think, as I do, that Dr Barnes is a silly old fool?'

Jane turned to stone. He had come out with it soon enough! 'I don't know, Walter. You heard what he said and I've been in good health without that worry.'

'That was long ago. After all this time you'll be barren. Women find they don't have children after such a gap without a man.'

'That's a wicked old wives' tale,' gasped Jane. She saw his cold eyes. 'I'm still seeing. I'm still normal in that way.'

'Are you today?' She shook her head, dumb with misery. 'There must be ways other than those things I brought from Portsmouth that made me sore enough to think I had the clap.'

'The doctor can't give us anything. It's against the law and against God's law.'

'What do you know about God's law? You aren't a papist any longer and where was God when we were on the Modder and Bloemfontein? Where was He in the hunger and death of Ladysmith and Mafeking? Where was God when they raped and humiliated women?' He paced the room and ignored her. 'I'll tell you where He was! He was with the women who followed us from camp to camp, looking after their dirty tails. They never got caught! Never with child, even if they did have plenty of disease. Was disease their punishment or didn't He care about that, either?'

Everything about him said 'It isn't fair!' He was like a spoiled child used to having his way, and Jane tried to block out the bitter blasphemous voice and the echo of violence between them. He was a man with a sense of injury and a new selfishness built from deprivation – a man without faith. Jane prayed, and at the moment when she needed to ignore her old faith, she called on the Virgin Mary. Dimly-recalled dogma and her own commonsense fought and gave her no salvation. The peace and security of the future depended on her, and she braced herself to trace the hard lines of his mouth with a gentle finger. 'Perhaps the doctor *is* just an old fool,' she said.

Walter filled the coal buckets and Jane went to the bedroom. She took out one of the herbal pessaries and inserted it, tense with an agony of fear. It felt cold and unfamiliar and she could not relax, so when Walter was in the backyard she poured out a full tumbler of the wine that André had left and drank it down, almost choking. Then she drank another, so that when Walter came to her, she was all soft arms and whispered comfort and wifely love.

At four o'clock, she woke on a tear-soaked pillow. Her head ached and her thighs were sticky with cocoa butter and semen and she felt dirty and lonely, deep in an abyss of sorrow.

Chapter 14

'I can milk her all on my own,' said Janey, wishing that her father wouldn't sit on the straw and watch her, but Walter just smiled, content to close his mind to matters that troubled him. Jane had come to him in bed and so he had no need to look elsewhere for sexual relations. I'm clean, he told himself. I had a clean bill of health and the women I went with were the superior kind, not the sluts by the camps. The woman in Pretoria had stayed with him all the time he was on leave after his accident.

He bent a straw. She would have found someone to fill his place by now, but she'd been good and taught him a thing or two. Why did those women never get caught? Or if they did, they knew what to do about it. He followed Janey and took the full bucket from her. There were things he'd miss about South Africa but he could never force whore's tricks on Jane. He glanced uneasily up at the windows in Sea Street. They said that a dose of clap or the pox made a woman barren, but surely the clean ones couldn't have had it. He walked on. He was fine. There had been only that one bit of soreness ages ago and nothing since, and Bert Cooper had never got anything from his fancy piece in Portsmouth.

Janey hurried back to the shop. It was good to have Father home but he did get in the way and Mother didn't seem happy, unless tears in the scullery were a sign of joy.

Gradually, Walter did more to help but Jack still delivered many of the orders and Sidney went with him, but Aaron took them fishing and they had more time to play. 'That one needs a long rope, a bit like you do,' Aaron said when Walter frowned over Jack. 'Let him wear himself out. It'll do him good and do you good, too, to come back into things slowly.' No mention was made of the troubles with Bert and Annie, and they both tried hard to be pleasant to Jane in case she decided to tell Walter. Eventually Bert relaxed and soon the two men were back playing cards in the brickyard while they were supposed to be going over the books, and Jane wondered what Bert was up to now that she no longer kept an eye on the accounts. Still, it was a relief not to have to deal with Bert on her own, and to have more time to herself when Walter would be finally free from military service in two weeks' time.

The depression that had built up in her over the past two days made her bend over the dolly tub and work furiously to dispel her heaviness. I might even have time to go down to see Amy, she told herself in an effort to feel better, but the blinding headache and tense pelvis made her dry her hands and go to her bedroom, leaving the ironing until later, if ever. She knew that she must be pregnant. The heat of the boiler had made her perspire and her linen drawers stuck to her. Hating to smell of sweat, Jane took them off and found them quite wet. She turned the garment over and saw the beginning of a period. With rising joy, she changed and put on a cotton diaper.

'I'm not pregnant,' she told Ikey when she put the soiled drawers into a bucket to soak in the outhouse. 'Glory be, I'm not caught!' She laughed hysterically. They had made love four times and she had used one of the pessaries each time. Dear wise old Mrs Lee! Dear witch or saint or whatever she was, she'd saved Jane's life. There were more pessaries in the package and a week's grace while she lost blood, but she must get extra ones to be safe.

On Saturday, it was a lovely day and she suggested that as the children had been so good while Walter was away, she would take them down to the river fields for a picnic while he sat with Bert over the books in the living room. Walter was pleased. It was good to be alone with Bert and tell him tales that could never be mentioned before Jane or any respectable woman.

Jane walked through the fragrant fields, the trees heavy with late summer. She had seen the gypsy men with their bright neckerchiefs in the town so she knew they were back from the summer fairs and would be making more pegs and baskets, or trading in horses and donkeys at the Agricultural Show in Nine Acres field.

She spread the food on a cloth under a tree by the ruined tower at the bend in the river, and when they finished eating Jack brought out rags soaked in paraffin to burn at the foot of the tower and watch the bats fly out. 'I think you're cruel,' said Sidney. 'I'm not staying to watch.' He followed Jane along the towpath and she was secretly glad of his company, suddenly shy of meeting Mrs Lee again on her own. Rough piebald ponies were in the stockade, bred for hard work and good health and Sidney climbed the fence, calling them with words he had learned from the gypsy boys at horse fairs, and the ponies came to him and ate the apple pieces he held on a flat hand.

Jane braced herself to walk to the main waggons where dogs cringed under the tailboard and children stared with dark eyes in expressionless faces. The open door of the painted waggon reflected sunlight in its highly polished brass and the coloured glass windows. Mrs Lee sat on the bed at the back and smiled a welcome. 'I expected you. I saw it this morning,' she said. 'Don't be afraid. There's nothing *here* to harm you.' Her eyes were as dark as sloes and she opened a wooden box. 'You came for these.'

'Mrs Lee . . . you . . . I can't tell you what it means.'

'I help when I can, but soon I can help no more. The young ones know little and there isn't time to teach them everything I know. I can't live for ever.'

'How can I thank you?' Jane asked.

'I know how it is, none better. Men are the same the world over. Take care.' Her fingers dug urgently into Jane's wrist. 'You have the other pill? Keep it safe for if I can't help you there may come a time when you'll need it.'

'But you will be here all winter?'

'The waggons will be here.'

Jane pushed the large package into her reticule, and Mrs Lee looked at the money she offered. She hesitated then waved it aside, and Jane was astonished. What gypsy ever refused money? But she knew she must not offend by pressing it on her. Impulsively, she took the cameo brooch with the Queen's head in relief from her neckband and pinned it to the other woman's shawl. Mrs Lee smiled sweetly. She touched the brooch gently. 'May Sweet Sara and Mary go with you,' she said.

Sidney was sketching the gypsy boys with a stub of pencil and a piece of paper. He had given them apples and dates and had learned new words and was completely at ease with the wild-looking dark-skinned boys. Now he jumped off the gate and gave the sketch to the smallest boy. 'I like them, don't you, Mother? I like the colours they wear and their waggons. Your hair is dark like theirs. Are we like them?'

'They are good people,' Jane said. You don't know how kind, she thought. Mrs Lee saved my life.

'Bert Cooper says they are bad, but they care for their horses and he doesn't. May I wear an earring like they do?'

'Indeed you can't!' retorted Jane, laughing. 'What would your father say? I wonder if Jack has burned down the whole tower by now.' Jack was covered in smuts and had seen only one bat, but the children were happy and sang all the way home.

When they got back, Walter winked and nodded over towards Annie who sat straight and annoyed in a hard-backed chair. Bert, too, looked cross. 'Did you want me for anything, Annie?' Jane asked, surprised.

'I thought you'd be here,' Annie said sulkily.

'Now that Walter is back there's no need for me to entertain on business and I have more time for my children.'

Annie blushed and seemed about to make a retort but Bert broke in, 'Come on, Annie, we can't expect Jane to make tea for both of us after being out.'

'Please stay,' Jane said, beaming at them. 'Now that Walter is back it makes it easier to have people in for a chat.' Walter looked pleased and Jane poured hot water into the big brown teapot from the singing kettle. She brought out a fresh lardy cake, safe in the knowledge that Annie could never make one as light and was stingy with the fruit and the sugar crusting.

'I can see you got on well while I was away,' said Walter.

'We had our ups and downs but I had a lot of help from

friends,' Jane said. Annie took another piece of cake and pushed the plate over to Bert. Jane smiled. That would make sure she didn't have to give him supper. Silly woman, she drove him to the Wheatsheaf and Mrs Grace's smiles and the good potato pies they served there. In her new euphoria, Jane regarded the pair with pity. She had her husband home and was able to be a wife to him, and there was a certain pride in knowing that she had managed the business so well.

Walter began one of his interminable African stories while Jane cleared the dishes. The Coopers looked bored and Jane smiled, knowing that if they knew nothing about the country the stories meant little. In the Wheatsheaf, these days, many sighed with relief if Walter retired to a corner with Mr Foster to talk over the campaigns. Everything will simmer down as it was, she told herself, but looked thoughtfully across at Walter. He was harder, and when he made love to her, it was with new haste, almost a fury; he had hinted at new methods of intercourse. So far she had only a dim idea of what he wanted but her mind and body were revolted. Where had he learned such things? Who had taken her place and shown him?

'Blackie will be back tomorrow,' said Walter. 'He'll come in double harness and bring the feed. Archie will need a bite to eat.'

'I know it,' said Jane shortly. 'I'll leave you plenty but I have to see Miss Prentice about the girls' winter coats.' She dreaded being with Archie when Walter was there.

'You seem glad to be rid of all Walter's friends,' said Annie spitefully.

'I'm glad to see anyone but I need more time for the girls. They grow so fast and like new clothes.'

Annie sniffed. 'Miss Prentice is good at making over old clothes,' she said.

'Yes, you know all about that, Annie. I remember that coat the doctor's wife gave you for charity. That came up well with a bit of fur at the neck – I hardly recognised it!'

'Yes, now I'm here you must take time for yourself, Jane,'

said Walter expansively. 'You used to go blackberrying about this time.'

The autumn days were dry and fine, summer lingered and life was less demanding. They picked berries and crab apples, the girls draped themselves in old man's beard and Walter said it looked like the ostrich feathers from Africa.

When Jane went to the cemetery each Sunday, she gazed across at the plumes of smoke from the gypsy fires and made sure that Sidney took fruit for the children and as many clothes as she could spare, and when the boys came with pegs and baskets, she gave them stale buns and more fruit and often a lardy cake for Mrs Lee.

The last of the sweet chestnuts were gathered from Parkhurst Forest and a mushroom smell in the woods told Jane that time was passing swiftly and she must go down to see Mrs Lee. Walter would be at Wootton that Sunday and the children in chapel, so she put on a warm serge skirt and jacket and packed a basket of fruit and cakes. Sidney caught her up on the quay. 'Why aren't you in chapel?' she asked.

'I said I'd meet someone in the river fields,' he admitted shamefacedly.

'You know you should be in chapel,' she said severely. 'How can I bring you up well if you don't go to church?'

He grinned. 'Father never goes and you don't really like it,' he said.

'That's neither here nor there, but I suppose it's too late now.'

He caught her hand to make her hurry. 'I want to show you something,' he said. 'Come on, we'll get a good view from the next bend.'

'I don't want to see the bats,' she told him.

'Not the bats, it's the camp. Be careful not to be seen, as we aren't Romany and they don't let Gorgios watch. Haven't you heard?' She shook her head. 'Old Mrs Lee died in her waggon, so they have to burn it. It's their law,' he added.

Jane put out a hand to steady herself. His voice came through a mist of pain and fear. Pain? Stupidly, she looked at her hand where it had clutched at a branch of thick bramble thorns. Drops of blood welled from the bluish wounds and she had a vision of the crude pictures of the Sacred Heart and the flames and thorns on her mother's bought indulgences. She shuddered. 'Holy Mary, Mother of God, be merciful,' she whispered.

'Are gypsies Catholic?' Sidney asked. He dabbed the blood away with his handkerchief. 'Only, you did pray for the old lady in the way you told us went with the Rosary.'

'She said, "Sweet Sara and Mary go with you," when I went there.'

Jane sat on the bank, unable to walk, and they watched the distant flames. The shell of the waggon stood empty. The glass splintered, the colours erupted, the painted wood curled and the oil-lamp exploded. The roof fell in a shower of gold sparks and the flames died. Summer died too, and with it, all Jane's peace of mind, her hopes and happiness.

She couldn't recall walking home but somehow, she was there with her apron on, ready for Walter to bring the roast from the bakery. He had worked up a good appetite and the glossy beef was succulent, surrounded by baked vegetables. Jane stirred gravy and ladled out potatoes and nobody noticed her silence. How soon would it be before she had to leave them all? Or could she make Walter understand?

Walter's face was flushed. Since his return, his appetites were grosser as if to make up for deprivation. The family grew tired of him saying at every meal, 'Better than mule's liver. Better than mealies and flour with weevils in it.' He talked of little else at meals and drank far more than before he went away. He's changed, she thought. He wasn't the man who had been tender that first night back, and Jane hated the coarse laughter she interrupted when he was with his friends. Sam and Aaron came less frequently now and his new friends had fought in the same campaigns. Some were interesting and told her of the birds and beasts of the Veldt and the houses there were in Pretoria, and she listened fascinated to tales of the Boer women who fought as men did, wiry and tough and determined to protect their way of life. However, when the others came, eyeing her as just another woman and speaking roughly, she went off to see Granny Cheverton or took the children to chapel concerts.

From snippets she overheard, Jane was now convinced that Walter had been with loose women.

Jane spooned custard over stewed apples and cleared away the meat. Tonight he would want her, ending a day of self-indulgence with a love that was no longer tender, and the added 'refinements' that he demanded filled her with revulsion.

The rain came in cold glassy sheets and Walter said it was too wet to go to the Bugle, so he sat at the harmonium all the evening, drinking and becoming sentimental. Five more, thought Jane, watching the thickened neck as he played. Five times to be safe and then what? Long after he was asleep she lay awake, stiff with misery and frustration as he had taken her with rough urgency, leaving her bruised and her breasts sore.

The last leaf fell and the river lapped the parapet of the bridge in the autumn storms. Jane searched her workbox for the third time but found only the grey pill. She had kept Walter away for two weeks, pretending to be asleep or making the excuse that she didn't want to give him a cold. If I can keep him away until my period I have another week, she thought, as he never touched her during that time.

That night, Walter wound the clock and put Ikey in the outhouse. At the stair door, he took Jane's hand and squeezed it. His eyes were bloodshot. 'Not tonight,' Jane pleaded. 'I've had a heavy wash and my back aches.' His grip tightened and he half-dragged her to the bedroom, put a candle on the chest and looked at her closely. 'I'm too tired,' she repeated.

'Are you sick?'

'No, I'm frightened.'

He laughed. 'After all these years? You enjoy it. What's to frighten you? We've proved that I was right and the doctor is an old fool. You're barren! The last lot left you barren and I can have you whenever I want you. You are my wife and my property before the law and I'll do what I damn well like with you, in spite of your lady-like objections!'

'Listen, Walter. Since you came home I've used some herbs that Mrs Lee gave me. I was afraid you'd be cross so I never told you. I thought I could always get more but now she's dead. Dr Barnes could be right. I've used the last and I don't know what to do.' She sobbed and sank on to the side of the bed.

'You've been with me regular for months!'

'I was using the herbs.'

He laughed. 'Are you telling me that a few herbs stopped it? It's the same as I said, you can't get caught now. Your body won't grow any more babies.' He shrugged. 'What's a man to do? Get into bed and you'll see. You can't take now.' He slipped out of his clothes and unbuttoned Jane's dress, pulling it roughly from her shoulders and covering her breasts with moist kisses. He pulled down her skirt and drawers, leaving her naked.

'No, Walter! Do you want to kill me?'

'Be still. Can't you see that I must have you?' She tried to cover her body with the ripped skirt and Walter grabbed her arms from behind and came up close. 'No! Not that,' she begged.

'It's one way or the other,' he gasped. 'Some of the men took mules but I drew the line there. It's front or back, gal, and I don't care a damn which!'

Jane collapsed on the bed. 'That's a mortal sin and I couldn't.' She shivered with revulsion and cold as he rolled on top of her. It's a judgement on me, she thought. I've sinned against nature. She lay like a log until he had used her, then groped for her shift and turned away to the well of darkness.

A combination of drink and Jane's passive resistance had thwarted Walter's climax. His head had cleared but he dared not touch her to say he was sorry. If this was Pretoria, at least she would have helped me now, he thought.

Chapter 15

Christmas came and went in a foggy drizzle. Boots were muddy and the dog had distemper and dragged its weak haunches to the backyard in the damp air. Sidney dosed Nero with the mixture that Sam had given him and the dog was recovering now, but the boy couldn't forgive his father for having neglected him. Since his return, Walter had said that Nero was *his* dog and he was the one to look after him, but he forgot to give him the strong tea each day and Sidney was convinced that this had caused the distemper.

Walter wondered uneasily if there was truth in the old wives' tale and if so, was there truth in others? Jane had changed. She hadn't been the same since the night he had raped her. Now she came to him quietly, with never a show of affection or encouragement and it was like sleeping with a tailor's dummy. He was torn between anger and shame. He caught her once with the old Rosary in her fingers and he tried to forget how tired and drawn she had looked. It was the weather getting them all down – see the sun and they'd all be smiling again. An evening in the Wheatsheaf would do him good, he decided, and he'd get away from Sidney's accusing eyes.

When she heard the door slam behind Walter, Jane took out the gophering iron. Lizzie watched her and wanted to try it, so Jane gave her a piece of paper to crimp. 'You and Emily are quite little housekeepers,' she said. Clare and Janey washed their hair and Emily braided it in coloured ribbons. They giggled and pretended to be music hall artistes while the boys were putting wood ready for the boiler in the outhouse after the stable work and milking was finished.

If I should die, they could manage well without me, Jane thought. Would they miss her, and if so, for how long? All the hard work they had had to do, at a tender age, might have been fate, so that they could carry on without her. Then Lizzie gave a cry of pain, tears pouring down her face as she held out a burned finger to her mother. Jane crooned over her as if she was a baby and put butter and rag over the burn so that Lizzie felt important. Perhaps they do need me, Jane decided, but it only added to her despair.

Walter rose early the next morning to take the cart to the Barracks. Before leaving, he sluiced his ale-thick head under the tap and heard a noise in the privy as if someone was being sick. A child must have stepped on Ikey, he thought and then forgot all about it. Jane was pouring tea when she heard him return. 'Just what I need and so does Nero,' he said with the false heartiness he now assumed. Nero managed to wag his tail but Jane remained silent. At least the dog still likes me, Walter thought resentfully. Anyone would think I'd half-murdered her the way she sits like a plaster saint. He ate breakfast and left hurriedly and Jane swept the shop, sending dirt from the potato sacks into the gutter where it sat like a sandcastle slowly washed down by the rain.

Annie stepped over the mud and walked into the shop, shaking her cloak. Jane beat down the nausea that lasted longer each morning. 'You look seedy, Jane,' she said in a prying manner.

'The cold gets into me, that's all,' Jane shrugged.

'Cold? I thought how muggy it was. I'm far too warm in this cloak but it's hard to know what to wear.'

'What can I get you, Annie?' If only she would go! The woman's eyes were everywhere and missed nothing.

'You do look peaky.' Annie noticed the pinched look about Jane's nose, her pallor, and suddenly she knew. 'I'll take a cabbage and some herbs and come back for the fish. I must get up to Mr Foster's.' She grabbed the cabbage and hurried out, her bottom waggling with importance. Jane looked in the mirror. It was there for all to see. None of the married women in the town needed a doctor to diagnose pregnancy. She pushed aside the memory of Caroline's small dead face. 'I'll feel better after the sickness goes,' she told Nero. By dinner-time, her colour was good and she was hungry. She craved something really sharp and the children found her sucking a lemon.

Walter called in at the brickyard on the way home, and Bert grinned maliciously. 'Annie said that Jane looked really rough this morning.'

'She was fine when she gave me my breakfast,' Walter said.

'She never makes a fuss. Was she all right early on?'

Walter recalled the sound from the privy and forced a smile. 'You know women, down one minute and up the next.' He hurried home.

Jane sat with a half-lemon on a saucer on the table and Walter buried his head in his hands. Whenever she'd been pregnant, he had made sure she had the finest lemons that money could buy. 'Oh, God! What have I done?' he whispered. Jane didn't seem to hear but went on preparing food for tea, cutting bread and butter and arranging cold meat in a neat pattern on a dish, and arranging knives and forks carefully, then she sat with her hands folded on her lap.

This meek acceptance, so foreign to her personality, was too much. He put his arms round her, his tears running into her hair. 'We'll go to Dr Barnes! That's it. He'll have to help us.'

Jane smoothed his head as if he was a child. 'No, he can do nothing. He says it's against the law. I have already asked him.'

Walter shook her gently. 'There must be a way. Aren't there certain women who could take care of this?'

A flicker of Jane's former spirit surfaced. 'And would you have me messed about by some dirty backstreet abortionist?'

'Some women manage alone. *Gin* – that's it!' He ran to the Jug and Bottle and returned with the biggest bottle they had. Feverishly he poured some into a cup, spilling it on the clean cloth, but Jane moved away.

'I've the children coming in for their tea. Do they have to see their mother swilling gin out of a cup during the day?'

'You must, Jane. Oh God, you must drink it,' he begged.

She was surprised how much he cared, so after the family had finished tea Jane climbed upstairs with the bottle and a jug of lemon juice and drank herself into a stupor; Walter prayed as he listened to her drunken snores.

In the morning, her tongue was furred and she felt like death. After being sick she felt better than she had for weeks but she remained pregnant, performing her duties as if in a vacuum. Walter took over all the heavy work and tried clumsily to show how much he cared, but the barrier was still there between them. And then Jane began to feel less well. Slowly her brittle defence cracked when Dr Barnes examined the old varicose ulcer scars and shook his head. Jane bound up her legs to stop them swelling but the thumping in her head told her everything. If I could fade away with dignity it wouldn't be so bad, she thought, and her natural resilience now made her feel anger and hate.

She hated Walter for forcing this pregnancy on her, and she was angry that women must put up with this because a law, made by men who knew nothing of the suffering and humiliation involved, offered no way out. Walter was right: where was God? Where was justice? She had managed better than most men while he was away and yet she was still a chattel to be used worse than the animals. Walter talked to Dr Barnes himself and then seemed resigned to doing nothing: society and respectability must be observed.

Jane removed the wedding ring that was fast becoming too tight. Walter was in the outhouse, the children at school and Edward wasn't due home for hours. If she had to die let it be before she was too gross and ugly and the baby wasn't like a human being. She dragged herself upstairs, dabbed her aching temples with eau de cologne and took out the grey pill. Her throat constricted. It was enormous. She sipped some tea and the pill was cold and heavy in her mouth as she tried to swallow it. She gagged and swallowed again until it slid painfully down her gullet.

Walter opened the door. He saw the cup. 'Why bring tea up here? I've made fresh and it's warmer downstairs.' Jane drank cup after cup of tea and hoped the pill had gone right down. She had no idea what would happen now and wondered if it was a drastic aperient that might make her have the runs but leave the baby. Women did take castor oil, she knew, and it sometimes worked, so that night she put a chamberpot handy in case she couldn't reach the privy in time.

At three in the morning, Walter heard Jane call out in her sleep. He lit a candle and saw her grey face covered with sweat. She shivered and he patted her hand. 'Wake up, gal, you're having bad dreams.'

She moaned and turned away, tossing her head to shake off the pain and when he turned her face towards him, she looked through him without recognition, her eyes dull like the eyes of dying men and horses on the Veldt. He was terrified, and put a hand under her to draw her to his warmth and the hand met a patch of oozing sticky blood.

Walter ran to the boys' room and pulled the bedclothes off the nearest bed. 'Wake up! Run for Dr Barnes! It's your mother, Edward. Jack, get more candles and Sidney, light the lamp in the shop and bring it up here.' He pulled back the curtains in the bedroom but the night was too dark to give any light, so he lit candles and put them in every holder in the house and brought wood to light a fire in the grate. He glanced at the still face on the pillow and wanted to weep but there wasn't time.

Dr Barnes came running in his nightshirt under a long overcoat. 'Put bricks in the oven. She must be warmed,' he ordered. He put down his bag and drew back the bedclothes. Jane clenched her teeth as talons of pain clawed through her subconscious mind. She was floating above her body looking down at the pale woman in such pain that she screamed. She sank down through the bed in a whirlpool of darkness that throbbed like a heartbeat. Her head was lighter than it had been for days but she knew only this other pain.

Hands were pulling, pushing, pressing her distended abdomen. The stickiness had gone and she recognized the face of a woman she knew. Mrs . . . Mrs . . . she had something to do with Dr Barnes. Caroline was there with other babies, all waxen-faced, and she held out her arms to them but other arms thrust her down to become one with the woman on the bed and she gave up fighting. A cup was put to her mouth, and Jane struggled against it as she thought it contained more grey pills.

'That's better.' Dr Barnes tucked back the cuff that Jane had ripped from his nightshirt. 'The bleeding has stopped and she'll sleep now.' He felt in the basin of blood and took out a small bag of transparent membrane. He slit it with a scalpel and held it for Walter to see. 'Yes, you must look,' he said sternly as Walter turned away.

Walter saw with horror the little human being that might have been his son. It had tiny perfect fingernails, but the skin looked as if it had a rash.

'What did she do?' The doctor's voice broke through the horror.

'Do?' Walter said stupidly.

'Yes,' the doctor repeated. '*Do*, man! She obviously used no instrument or a knitting needle but she must have done something.'

Walter stared without comprehending. 'You said she could do nothing and you couldn't help her.'

'That's right. The law and the Church would be down on me like a ton of bricks if I did anything.'

'She drank a bottle of gin but that didn't seem to help,' Walter said.

Dr Barnes grunted. There was no instrument used and he wanted no fuss, so he wrote '*spontaneous abortion aggravated by alcohol in excess*'. 'No puncture exists so there's less likelihood of infection. It now depends on you, Mr Darwen, Mrs Gregory who will stay with her, and your wife's hold on life. Give her more laudanum when she wakes, Mrs Gregory. Stop her threshing about and starve her. If she asks for food give her thin gruel. The blood loss may have done good and her mind may have escaped undamaged as she had only the one fit. If she has another, make sure she bites on a towel. She has a sore mouth from the other one.'

Walter watched as Mrs Gregory washed the pale face and tidied the room. The heavy dose of drugs had calmed his wife and she looked as she had done when Caroline was born. Walter wished that he was dead. Clare made him up a bed in the boys' room while Janey took him firmly downstairs and made him drink hot tea, looking so like Jane that he could hardly bear to glance at her. He wakened Nero, who thought he was mad, and tramped the river fields until daybreak, wishing he had stayed in South Africa and saved his family this pain, but he couldn't walk for ever and went home to light the boiler and make up the orders that had to be delivered even if the sky fell.

Chapter 16

Emily put the first primroses in a china bowl and carried it carefully to the chest of drawers in her mother's room. She took a deep breath once she saw that no water spilled on to the polished surface and noticed that her mother was still propped up in bed, staring into space.

Jane was aware that the sun shone and it seemed like spring, but what had happened to her? Kind hands and voices, and terrible dreams of pain were fading and she ate and drank and slept and was content.

Sidney saw that she glanced at the primroses although she had taken no notice of the pictures he had drawn for her. 'Primroses, Mother,' he urged gently.

'The Queen loves primroses,' Jane smiled. 'Did you know that she picks them every year at Osborne? I heard that she died but I don't know if that's true.' Emily looked blank but Sidney sat on the bed and took her hand, and told her that the Queen had died last year before her illness.

Jane wrinkled her forehead. She recalled Walter coming home and Emily popping tar bubbles. She thought of Maudie with all that paint on her face and wondered if Clare had remembered to milk the nanny goat. 'How is Rose?' she asked. 'She should be out of that steamy little room.'

'Rose is well, Mother.'

'Let me smell the flowers,' Jane said and Emily made a small bunch to pin on her bedjacket. 'I need my cameo brooch to pin them on.' She put a hand to her throat. 'Have you seen it anywhere?'

'Don't you remember? You gave it to old Mrs Lee at the camp. You said that she admired it and you gave it as a keepsake,' Sidney tried to remind her. 'We went there one day and I sat on the fence with the gypsy boys and learned more Romany words, but you wouldn't let me wear an earring like them.'

'I should think not!'

'Jack tried to smoke out the bats,' Emily said eagerly, and Jane tore at the webs clouding her memory, until Emily slipped away to tell Walter that Mother was restless again. Sidney went on talking about the gypsies, the piebald horses, the picnic and the blackberry hedges. His hands were comforting and Jane clung to them. There was something about Mrs Lee and Walter that had to do with her illness.

Mrs Lee died and they had to burn her waggon, Sidney told her. 'We saw it and you were upset and said a nice prayer.'

As Walter appeared in the doorway with the draught to make her calm, the last shreds of the veil lifted and Jane wept for her lost babies, her sins, her illness and for Mrs Lee. She cried as if the flood would never stop, and it washed away her guilt and desolation until she was exhausted, then she slept restfully for several hours.

From the darkening room she knew that it was evening and she smelled fish frying. 'I'm hungry,' she told Janey. 'It's time I got my strength back. I've been lazy long enough.'

All her old friends wanted to see her as soon as Jane was well enough to be downstairs, but they were welcome for only short visits as Jane found lots to do. She reclined on the couch organizing the family again, and sewed new shifts for the girls. Annie came and was surprised at the serenity in the living room and the way that Walter worked hard and brought in a girl from the Barton to clean the house. The shop had new cabinets for herbs and dried peas, and Walter replaced the flyblown mirror for a new one, adorned with a painted scene of Table Mountain and a voluptuous girl with oranges – which Jane suspected was a sop to his nostalgia for South Africa.

There must be changes, Jane decided. Walter must never again be tempted to take her in bed. Edward was settled at work, and Jack was still happy to help his father but Sidney needed a place of his own where he could paint and read and keep out of his father's way. Jane climbed painfully to the attic, a room used only for storage. It had a window and a skylight and a good big cupboard. She pulled rubbish from the room and called the girl to take it all downstairs and then to sweep the floor and wash the furniture. Without the clutter it seemed quite big. 'Sidney,' she called. 'Would you like this room all to yourself and have somewhere to put your paints and things?' He hugged her, his surprised joy too deep for words. 'You'd have to distemper it yourself and keep it tidy,' she went on. 'You can choose the colour and go and get the distemper now.'

He came back with a large pot of mauve distemper. 'Well, it's a bit bright but you'll have to live with it,' said Jane and wondered what curtains would tone down the colour, but when the warm hook rug was on the floor and the table put under the window, even Jack was envious. She wanted to make all the changes while Walter was at Ashey Races for several days with Bert, leaving early and coming back late, no longer anxious about her. She tried to think he had changed and he was certainly more considerate, but as he had swung into the seat of the smart trap, with his hat at an angle and a bright buttonhole in his good suit, he had the same swagger of old, looked just as virile and just as selfish. The boxroom was also turned out and its contents stored in the new shed in the yard. Lizzie was entranced by the pink roses on the new curtains of the tiny room where she would now sleep. Finally, Jane took all her clothes to the big cupboard in the room she would share with Janey.

'There's no need to talk about it,' she warned the children. 'You needn't spread it all over Newport that I sleep badly and don't want to disturb your father.'

'Uncle Archie was up by the Town Hall,' Sidney said. 'He asked after you and said he'd come and take you up to the Castle in the trap one day.'

'Your father will do that soon,' she replied. Dear Archie, to whom she could always go if there was any need, but whose love she could never return.

Annie tried hard to see some hint of conflict in the house, but gave up, baffled. She had worries of her own as Bert went more often over to Portsmouth now, coming back with a self-satisfied look on his face.

When Walter came home from the Races, he smelled lavender polish and Sunlight soap, and hoped the house was back to normal. 'Humbuggen nonsense,' he muttered as he went upstairs, but he sensed a difference. The valances were crisp in their bedroom and the clean curtains moved gently in the breeze, but there was a bare patch where Jane's hairbrushes should have been on the chest. He opened the top drawer. The ribbon box and gloves were gone. The other drawers were empty, too, and they were lined with fresh paper as if awaiting another tenant. Jane's wrapper no longer hung behind the door.

In the big room he saw Jane's thick gown where Lizzie usually hung her own and Jane's brushes on the washstand. He touched the gown, remembering the nights when Jane had worn it during teething troubles, chicken pox and measles, and he wept. She no longer trusted him. His emotion was worse than sorrow. She was casting him out for ever.

At tea-time, she gave him an apprehensive glance but hummed as she cut the bread and butter. It was done now and she felt released. I'm free of all that, she thought, but found a warm maternal feeling developing in its place for Walter. He was a good man and a good provider, and he did care about her and the family. Holy Mary, she prayed, thank You for Your intercession and God rest the soul of Mrs Lee who didn't sin but helped me according to her lights. Jane thought of all the pin money she had put away with Sam's help – it gave her some independence. The girls would need extra things, she thought. She could buy them without asking for every penny, and when she was stronger, she'd walk up to Carisbrooke again.

PART TWO

The Family

Chapter 1

The ragged line of young men marched up to the Barracks square. Walter Darwen pulled the reins tighter. It was a pleasure and a pain to watch and he turned the cart to follow them to the quarters. 'Pick 'em up,' he muttered. Who was responsible for this shambles?

'Lost sixpence and found a ha'penny, Mr Darwen?' asked the sergeant from the cookhouse. He pulled aside the linen cover to the basket. 'You've got some nice crabs there.'

Walter winced at the civilian address. He still resented being a plain 'Mr', even ten years after the old Queen had died and the war in South Africa was over. Memories were short and ex-soldiers were worth nothing, even after their years of sacrifice. 'You'd better get the mackerel cooked soon,' he said gruffly. 'They were fresh this morning and stiff as a board but it's a warm day and they don't keep.'

'I'll get the men to souse them,' the soldier said, and Walter looked at him sharply. Was that false humility, as if humouring an old fogey? 'Where's that lad of yourn?' he went on as they unloaded the cart. 'They grow up, I suppose, and should leave you time to spare.'

'I'm not one to keep idle,' Walter said sharply. I could teach this young whippersnapper a thing or two, he thought. If I was still in uniform he wouldn't dare have that top button undone. 'You've got a lot of rookies over there,' he observed in a superior tone. 'They wouldn't have lasted a week out there on the Veldt.'

'Territorials, they are. Nice lads off for a week in camp to get the stuffing knocked out of them.' He eyed Walter with new interest, seeing the firm set of his shoulders. 'The officers were talking about you, Mr Darwen. They need men like yourselves to go and train these lads in camp. You had a good rank and a very impressive record, so one said, and he'd jump at the chance of using you.'

'I was mentioned?' Walter flushed when he heard the officer's name. 'I was in his battalion in the Royal Horse Artillery. Now *he's* what I call a professional soldier.'

'Nearly due for retirement but never misses a thing,' the sergeant admitted. He shrugged. 'I'm not in the fighting line myself if it comes to war, but I see what's what. That lot need sharpening up by men who have had experience in the field. They say that the next war will be different but the men will still need to know all the old tricks.' He put the empty fish-baskets back on the cart and hauled down a box of apples. 'Why don't you leave the cart in the shade and go and look in at the guardhouse. At worst you may only chat, but I think they might mention the camps.'

Walter instinctively drew in his waist before he tapped on the door of the guardhouse. A single bugle note and the roar of a drill sergeant sent him into a dream, and as he glanced up at the light blue sky, he saw a heavier blue one over burned grass and sniffed again the smell of Africa. There, a man could be different, free of stifling Victorian morals. He suddenly longed for friendships with women that lasted a day, a week or a month or even just a night, with no one to condemn him. An hour later, he walked back to the cart in a bemused state, and let Blackie have his head. Back at the shop, he replaced the boxes and baskets in the store and then took the horse and cart to the stables under the railway arches beyond Coppins Bridge.

The smell of hay and the sweet breath of Marigold, Blackie's new mate, made Walter want to sit and think but he knew he must meet Bert Cooper at the brickyard, as the smoke-houses for the mackerel had to be checked or the fish might be ruined. He hung up the tack and slapped Blackie on the rump. 'I'll show 'em,' he said aloud. Reluctantly, he thought of the accounts. Jane had done them when he was away in Africa but since her illness she had been the perfect housewife and nothing more. He dared not suggest that she should take over the books again as she still seemed to dislike Bert and wouldn't go near the brickyard, but Bert did get the accounts in a sorry tangle – mostly to his own benefit.

The morning's events had made other matters come to the surface in Walter's mind; the years that Jane had spent sleeping in Janey's room and the nights when he had burned alone. He walked round by the warehouses in Sea Street to see Sam Walmsley, and glanced up at the windows there. A woman shook a duster out of an upper floor and he touched his hat to her when she smiled. Maudie Dove had filled out and her fair hair was thick and shining. He was shocked to feel a tightening in his loins. She was a dirty little strumpet and he could never become involved with the likes of her, at least not in Newport where he was so well-known and respected.

He grinned ruefully. Even if he went to the other side of the Island there was bound to be someone who would recognize him. Already he was jibbing at the bit, thinking as the soldier he had once been. What would be the harm in having a woman in Portsmouth like Bert did? Bert managed to keep his own doorstep clean, and even if people talked they could prove nothing. Walter finished the business of the morning thoughtfully and went home, where the smell of mutton stew and dumplings made his mouth water. Jane might not fill his bed but she couldn't be failed on other skills. 'Grub up?' he asked.

Jane smiled. 'You look pleased with yourself, Walter.' She brought out the huge bowl of mutton chops, the carrots, swede and potatoes and the fluffy dumplings. 'Did they take all the fish?'

'I could have sold another cart-load, and nothing to throw away now the weather is so hot.' He poured ale and broke off a piece of fresh bread. 'Where's that lazy rascal?' he asked.

'Jack's not lazy! He hobbled up to the brickyard and took bread and cheese with him. He said his foot would be better tomorrow but I don't want him doing the deliveries just yet.'

'I could have done with him today. You know I have to spend a lot of time with Bert. He gets the accounts wrong every time.'

'I *do* know,' Jane said with spirit. 'I did them all the time you were away!'

'And you might have to again. With Edward married and the others grown, you have the time,' he said, his voice taking an edge that meant growing bad temper. 'And you might see less of me in future. I've been asked to see to the young Terriers in camp. They need men who have fought in the field and have experience. You can't get that from books!'

'That's wonderful, my dear!' Jane said, then seeing his expression stopped smiling and hastily added, 'if you can spare the time. It means a lot of hard work for you but I'm sure we can manage something. Do they supply uniform?'

'I said I'd wear my own,' he told her with a grand gesture. 'You haven't let the moths get at it, have you?'

'I'll air it in the yard to get rid of the mothballs,' she promised. 'When do you want it?'

'Not yet. I have to talk to them first in the Drill Hall. That might be every week and then there are three big camps in the summer.'

'So often? There isn't going to be another war, I hope. We have treaties with South Africa now and no other fighting.'

'There'll be a war all right, but not in Africa: Germany is no friend of ours.'

'But the German Royal Family are related to our King!' She relaxed. If grown men wanted to play at soldiers it kept them out of mischief.

'We are building heavier ships and many men are on the reserve now. They even talk of fighting in the air.'

'That's impossible!' Jane laughed. 'Do you mean in aeroplanes like the one that Dr Barnes flies? The Flying Corps could toss rotten apples at the Germans but not much more. Just because that mad Frenchman flew the Channel in a contraption of wood and string doesn't mean they can fight like that.'

'You know nothing about such matters,' Walter said sternly. 'They've even tried a submarine out on a boat moored in harbour and they'll use such vessels in the next war. They could destroy a whole fleet.' He tapped the side of his nose as if he was in the know. 'Lord Fisher says they'll be very useful and deadly and we must have them ready in case the Germans have them too, but we won't use them any more than we'd use poison gas.'

'They've filled you up with a lot of rubbish, Walter Darwen,' Jane said, laughing. 'If you've finished eating, I'll put this back to warm in case the others come in, then I'll give your uniform a shake.' The lift to his chin showed that he imagined himself to be as he'd been years ago, and she smiled sadly. So much had happened that could never be the same, but pride played a great part in a man's life and this would help. It was a relief to hear Bert in the shop and the girls back from shopping. Jane served food and listened to the chatter.

Lizzie giggled. 'I saw two of the Attril boys marching with the Territorials. Harold has pigeon toes and can't keep in step.'

'He's not old enough,' Jane began, but they were all growing up. Edward had married young and although she thought of him as a man the others were still children. Jack might never grow up to be a responsible adult, as he was still harum-scarum.

'It's not fair,' said Clare. 'They are going to sleep in tents out at Ventnor and have a good time. Why can't girls go, too?'

'Because men like playing at soldiers,' said Jane. 'Your father is going to help drill them, so never laugh at the Terriers in his hearing or you'll be in trouble.' Janey nodded, soberly. Walter had violent fits of rage these days, short-lived but frightening.

'Mr Foster was talking about war,' Emily confided. 'Not the Boer War but the next one. He said he'd keep diaries like before and maybe this time they'll make him Mayor! They say he's made so much money that he could buy a Lord of the Manor!'

They talk as if war is just round the corner, Jane thought with dread. Not again, please God. 'Do you like these?' asked Clare, poring over a magazine.

Jane glimpsed shorter skirts that showed off ankles, and wide hats with veils. 'I like the hats,' she said, 'but the skirts are disgusting! A veil is flattering to the skin but any woman who wears a skirt like that away from the golf course is asking for insults.'

'I'm saving for a bicycle,' Clare said with an air of defiance. 'I have the money from Granny Chevvy and my Christmas money and I can look after Mrs Minn's children a few times and soon have enough for a secondhand one.'

'Just don't let me see you on it with one of those skirts,' Jane stated firmly. 'You can hitch up the side as you do for evenings in the wet.'

'Mrs Barnes wears one,' objected Clare.

'She's older and she plays golf!' But Jane was shaken – Mrs Barnes had been one of the first to come out of mourning for Queen Victoria after only four months and heads had turned in church when she went in wearing a pretty mauve feathered hat and lilac dress, and many had followed her soon after. If Mrs Barnes wears the new styles, they can't be so bad, thought Jane and looked at the pictures more carefully.

Walter came in for a cup of tea. 'The smoke-house is lit and I'll want everyone gutting mackerel,' he announced. Jane busied herself at the range and when she turned he was still there.

'I'll do the uniform as soon as they start on the fish,' she said. 'Sidney can bring it in a wheelbarrow but until the oak chips have died down they are better kept on ice.' But Walter lingered, looking uneasy.

'Bert is going to Portsmouth tomorrow,' he said.

'And surely the whole town knows it, and I'll have to put up with Annie's grumbles,' said Jane briskly, anxious to get on.

'I might cross over with him. There's a bit of property I want to see – it could bring in a sovereign or two,' Walter said. 'Can you manage?'

'When have I not?' He looked uncertain, as if he wished he wasn't going. 'You work hard, Walter. You need a change if you are to drill those lads. You go and I'll see that you are really smart for parade.'

He turned away and took an apple from the shop. 'Better check my hussif,' he said. 'I haven't used belt Blanco for years.'

The house and shop became quiet. The girls gutted fish in the outhouse and the Jack Russell that had taken Nero's place sniffed at the drain. Mick, one of Ikey's descendants but twice as fierce, licked a saucer of scalded fish and Jane turned out her old sewing-box to find Walter's hussif. The needles could do with passing through an emery pad to remove the rust, Jane thought, and then she came across the hank of green yarn that Walter had forgotten to pack for the Boer War. Memories of old Mrs Lee flooded back. Somewhere, Jane had her forecasts written down but she had mislaid the piece of paper. At the time, the gypsy's words hadn't seemed important, but now Jane recalled some of them. Edward was doing well on the railways but had indeed married trouble – if that meant a fragile girl unfit to bear a baby and of little use in the home.

The rest can take care of itself, she thought firmly, and brightened the needles. The uniform had been close-fitting even when Walter was slimmer. She brushed it and put it on his bed. Let him find out how tight it was – that would make him really mad.

Chapter 2

The whistle from Shide station sounded clear, so Jane knew that the wind had changed and the rain had stopped. 'Edward will be over in the dry,' she said, and glanced at her daughter-in-law. In this heat, Alice looked as if a breath would blow her to eternity, she thought. 'Will you have some broth now or wait for the others?' she asked.

'I'll wait.' Alice half-reclined on the horse-hair couch, her purse and shopping bag beside her. 'Emily could slip up and get my order,' she suggested.

'Emily has to mind the shop while I make pancakes,' said Jane rather firmly. 'Go up to Mr Foster now before dinner and get it over. Walter wants to be away early so I must be ready.'

'Where's Father going?'

'Where do you think?' Jane shook the frying pan vigorously over the hole in the top of the range. 'He's over to Ventnor again teaching them how to fight!' A dribble of hot fat made the fire flare and she slapped the pan over the hole and pushed the damper back with the ease of long practice. 'You can bring me some saltpetre and brown sugar while you are at Mr Foster's,' she said in a tone that stood no nonsense. It was difficult to know when Alice was ill and when she was just bone lazy. Alice sighed and left, and Jane poured batter into a cup then swirled it into the pan, watching it coat the surface and bubble. She turned the pancake when it was just golden underneath and squeezed lemon juice over the brown sugar and butter before sliding it on to the pile already made. 'If I had a penny for every pancake I've made, I'd be rich,' she said aloud.

'And better every time.' Jack crept up behind her and hugged her. 'What's for dinner?'

'Cold meat and potatoes and pickles. If your father is back go to the Jug and Bottle.'

'He had enough on the way,' Jack said, 'so I'll get cider.' He grinned, knowing that Walter never mixed ale with cider and would have to drink water with his dinner. Jane exchanged a long understanding look with her son. 'It's all right,' he said. 'We've had a good enough morning. I went to the Barracks with the fish and Ethel had the crabs ready cooked. I took some smoked before I left so I didn't have to come back here and Sam Walmsley helped me load the fruit. Aaron may be stuck in a chair these days unable to walk but his tongue works well enough.' Jack grinned. 'He's on to Ethel, wanting this that and the other all day long.'

'Don't laugh at him,' Jane begged. 'He's been a grand man in his time, a grand man, and a good friend to me all the while your father was away. I never forget a friend or a good deed to me and mine.'

'Nor a bad one, Mother,' he said softly. 'I'm the same. It's the Irish in me. We love and hate, don't we, Ma?'

'Get away with you! I hate nobody. You can put a masher to the potatoes and stop making me burn the pancakes.'

'You never forgave Bert,' he ventured.

'Bert? He's no more than a bag of wind with no real evil in him, even if he does make my son drink too much and make eyes at the new barmaid at the Bugle!'

Jack beat the potatoes but wouldn't meet her eyes. 'I suppose Father told you about that. Is this enough? I'll go and get the cider.' There was a dangerous tension as he left the shop and Jane wondered just how long it would be before Jack and his father had a real battle. Hastily she put the last pancake on the pile and left them in the warming drawer of the range. Voices from the shop told her that Walter was back.

'I found young Lucy up by the Square,' Walter said, pushing the girl into the room. 'Her Ma is over at the laundry so I said she could eat with us.' He glanced at his wife and she did up the three top buttons of her dress that she had undone in the heat, and pushed the tendrils of hair away from her pink cheeks. He shouldered past her roughly, to get to the backyard and wash away the smell of the piggery from his hands. 'Get it on the table,' he commanded. 'I haven't got all day.'

'Is Maudie working today? I thought this was her cleaning day at home.'

'She wasn't there when I came back from helping the little ones at school,' Lucy said, 'so I thought she'd gone to work.'

'You leave school soon, don't you Lucy?' Jane asked. The girls were chattering over a picture of a woman dressed in what looked like a waterfall of diamonds and a feather headdress. Jane couldn't believe it was real, but some women did wear the most outrageous clothes now. 'Don't let your father ever see you wearing anything like that,' she warned.

Clare tossed her head. 'Unless we marry rich men we'll never wear nice clothes like the gentry.'

'That's not gentry! They have a bit more pride than to go out in public showing off their ankles and worse!' She wished she had cooked more vegetables. Lucy ate ravenously as if starved and Alice took a lot of meat and carrots but refused potatoes, saying they made her feel heavy. Lazy she might be with those slightly sunken blue eyes but there was nothing wrong with her appetite, Jane noticed. She took some of the rich broth she had made for Edward and cut thick hunks of bread and cheese.

Walter was in fine form and Jane suspected that his 'little drop' had been more than enough but he looked at the cider and took only water. Lucy sighed with repletion and had time to gaze at Sidney with loving eyes. Walter laughed coarsely. 'You look just like your mother, Lucy. She's got an eye for the boys, too.' Lucy blushed and Sidney looked embarrassed. Jane gave a warning cough but Walter was feeling relaxed and looking forward to the camp. 'He's a pretty lad, isn't he, Lucy? Nice wavy hair just like one of them actors on the moving pictures.' He smiled without warmth. 'Too pretty by half.' If his youngest son had been in South Africa he wouldn't have lasted five minutes unmolested with the rednecks there, he thought.

'Leave them alone,' Jane said in a low voice, and handed

the oven cloths to Clare while she and Janey cleared the dishes.

'I wish he wouldn't,' Janey said. Clare put warm plates on the table and Janey took the carving knife to slice down through the pancakes, after counting how many she had to serve. The lemony butter oozed from the slices and she handed the portions out carefully.

'You'll make a grand wife for someone, my gal,' said Walter, eyeing the serious sweet face and budding figure of his eldest daughter.

'Time enough for that,' said Jane sharply. Walter tried to swallow quickly to answer her but she went on, 'The train goes in fifteen minutes, Walter. Are you changing into uniform?'

'Not this time.' He pulled out his half-hunter watch, then stuffed his pockets full of his Boer War souvenirs to show the lads what he had brought back from a real war, and left the room without a backward glance.

'Aren't you going to eat your pancakes, Alice?' Jack asked.

'I don't think they agree with me,' she said, 'and I'm full.'

'Give it here. You know what they say if you get faddy about food,' he added, grinning suggestively. Jane had wondered often enough about Edward and Alice, married for a year and no sign of a baby. Even now, she had no instinctive feeling that the girl was carrying and shook her head at Jack. Alice certainly had likes and dislikes with regard to food, and there were times when she sat about all day half-asleep, but her figure remained the same.

'Clare, you can help Alice home with her groceries and then come back and take the mending up to Miss Joyner.' Jane plucked at her sleeve and whispered, 'Make sure the house is tidy for Edward. He doesn't want to come home to a pigsty.'

Clare looked annoyed. It was bad enough having to serve in the shop and help about the house, but the thought of cleaning the two-up and two-down cottage where Edward lived by the withy beds with Alice was more than she could bear. 'And take the broth with you,' Jane added. 'If I know her, she's in one of her moods and will have nothing ready for him when he comes off the boat.'

'Yes, Mother.' Clare cheered up. At least she could escape the washing-up and the afternoon chores. If Aaron was asleep, Ethel might even be free to go with her to the woman who did the mending and made simple dresses and blouses for the girls.

'Have you time for a cup of tea?' asked Alice, when they reached the cottage. Clare noticed that the kitchen was nearly tidy but the fire had gone out. She smoothed down her clean print dress and made her escape before Alice saw that more coal must be brought in and fresh sticks laid.

Ethel Sheath almost pushed Clare from the house when she called there, and hurried after her. She looked back as if afraid that her father would call her. 'He gets worse every day,' she confided. 'Nothing is right for him and he's that heavy it takes me and Mother and the lad to lift him into his chair. Sometimes he can manage a bit on the level, but he can't climb the stairs alone. The doctor says he's on the mend but then other people say that one stroke follows another, and Mother is frightened.'

'When he's better we can take him out in the trap,' Clare promised. 'He must miss his trips over the water.' She looked at Ethel's long straggly carrotty hair. 'Will they let you put it up soon?' she asked.

Ethel's pale face reddened. 'I don't want to. When you do, the boys get after you. I don't want that!'

'You do! In that picture we saw, the girl was younger than us and she had that handsome man after her.'

'That's pictures,' said Ethel glumly. 'It doesn't happen in real life.' She stuck out her lower lip and looked very unlovable.

'When it's our turn we'll have lots of choice, not like in the war when most of the men were killed.'

'Soldiers from the Barracks?' Ethel made a face. 'It'll be farmers or fishermen more like, unless you can get one of the gentry to take a fancy to you.'

'There are others,' Clare said. She undid the button on her glove and tossed back the thick dark plait of hair over her shoulder. 'I went to the bank with Father and there's a new clerk there from the mainland. Further than Portsmouth,' she added to impress Ethel. 'He's got fair hair like that hero who rescued the girl in the castle he gave me A Look!'

'Oo-er! Is he there now? Can we have a peep inside the door?'

'On the way back,' Clare said. She hadn't really been impressed by the man and hoped that Ethel would have forgotten by the time they had taken the mending. 'I want to go to *Tyler's* to buy ribbons,' she added, knowing that Ethel would enjoy this.

'You trim lovely hats,' Ethel sighed, 'and you look so nice in them. My mother says you think you're a lady because you wear gloves all the time.' Clare did up the glove button. She hated to show the split nail and hated her sister Lizzie even more for crushing it in the mangle when they were small; even now when the weather was hot she wore gloves.

Miss Joyner's house was covered in roses and Ethel wanted to pick one but the door was opened quickly and they went inside the untidy parlour where piles of cloth and samples filled two tables. 'It's Clare, isn't it?' Miss Joyner said. 'But I don't know you.'

'This is Ethel. I've brought the socks to darn and two shirts that need collars made from the tails. Have you finished my petticoat?' asked Clare impatiently.

'First things first! I haven't had time to do yours yet. My Ivy is off sick and she does the mending, so I'm all behind. When your Pa came in, I dropped everything as he was in such a state, but I had to tell him his uniform wouldn't be ready by yesterday. I've finished now so you can take it back with you. Proper put out he was when I said he'd gained three inches round the waist, but I had a bit of khaki by me so we made do.' She held up a pair of army trousers and Clare giggled, knowing Walter would be angry if he knew she'd seen them. 'The tunic wasn't so bad as I could alter the buttons and let out the side seams.' She draped the tunic on a dummy and brushed the frogging on the front. 'Fine figure he cuts in it still. Can't think why they want to be reminded of war, though,' she said, with the lack of illusions that a life of spinsterhood had given her after her fiancé had been killed at Spion Kop.

'If he said he'd collect them, maybe I'll leave them,' said Clare doubtfully.

'Take the blouses for your mother, then, and I'll not breathe a word that you saw these,' Miss Joyner said conspiratorially. 'Men are a vain lot.'

'Come on, I want to see your film star now,' said Ethel afterwards.

'He isn't really that wonderful,' said Clare. 'I only saw him over the partition.'

'He's a new face and I want to see him before our Amy does,' insisted Ethel. The bank door was half-open and Ethel stepped on the mat to look inside, trying to seem poised but inwardly in awe of the place.

'Can I help you?' A man holding envelopes as if on his way to the Post Office came out, smiling.

'Oo-er!' stammered Ethel. 'I was looking for someone but she isn't here.'

He looked beyond her to Clare, who blushed and fiddled with her gloves. 'Miss Darwen, isn't it?' he asked. She looked almost scared. 'I'm Joseph Manning. If you could wait for a moment, I have some papers for your father.'

'He called you Miss Darwen – and he knew you,' said Ethel, deeply impressed. 'And he wears a nice suit to work.'

Jane Darwen walked over to the Sheaths' house and glanced across at the tiny house by the withy beds. Edward hadn't called in on his way from the station, which showed that he was worried about Alice. 'I wish I knew if she was ill or just putting it on to gain sympathy,' she said.

'What's that? Talking to yourself?' His voice was only slightly slurred.

'Aaron! You're sitting out!' Jane said with real pleasure.

'Can't stay in there for ever,' he said gruffly, but he smiled. 'What's the matter, gal?' She shook her head. 'Nothing, eh? Never was, was there? That'll be the day, when you start wingeing about life.' He nodded towards the withy beds. 'You never were a curtain-twitcher but he's safe home, Ethel saw him. *She* looked half-baked, but you know that as well as I do. What makes a big strong lad like Edward marry so young – and to a weakly milksop like that? Never learns, does he? She's the image of that poor little dead Rose he liked when they were children. This one won't make old bones, either.'

'Aaron,' said Jane in dismay, 'I never thought that she had taken Rose's place.'

'Some women marry brutes and when they die they marry another. Some men like their women frail.' He shrugged. 'You and Walter got it just right, or nearly. Seven live and two dead ain't bad.' He chuckled. 'Now the real strife begins.'

'What do you mean? The children have left school and soon I might be on my own.'

'Push me along a bit. I asked Ethel to but she went off with that Clare of yourn. She won't be back until she thinks I'm in bed.'

'If the wheels have been oiled, I can take you down to the quay.'

'Dan did them. Runs a treat now; hardly a squeak.' Jane wheeled her old friend along Sea Street by the warehouses and the shuttered houses and past Maudie Dove's rooms. Lucy was left alone so often that everyone assumed that she could manage, but she was only a bit younger than Emily, just fourteen. Emily had seen her first monthlies recently and Lucy must be due soon. Jane bit her lip. With a mother like Maudie, how could a girl learn right from wrong? 'Proper little trollop,' said Aaron, as if reading her thoughts.

'Aaron, you must be careful what you say about people!'

'You know I mean Maudie Dove. When George goes down on the tide if it's a late one, he sees her laughing with the bargemen. It don't stop there, neither! He's seen her coming off the boats.' He sniffed. 'Give her her due, she never fouls her own nest. That little nipper of hers needs better than that, though. She's a nice little thing and needs someone like you to look to her.'

'I'm not her mother! I've girls enough of my own,'

objected Jane. She laughed. 'You say I'm in for a rough time with my own so why should I take on another?'

'Because you have a heart as big as two.' He grinned. 'So has Maudie, but she gives a leaf to everyone.'

'You are a wicked old man, Aaron! It shows you are better, praise be,' she added happily. 'With Janey cooking up at Staplers now, Lizzie and Clare have to do more at home. I could take Lucy in the shop one day a week or when the girls want to go out.'

'Does Walter like his brood about him?' Aaron's shaggy brows came together, now iron grey instead of red. 'You've got a powder keg there, gal. Too many men in a house is as bad as two women in a kitchen. He was very tetchy the last time I saw him. Is he all right?'

'He's always been healthy,' said Jane. 'The boys rub him up the wrong way at times but he's never had a day's illness unless it was an accident like the time in Pretoria.'

'Still got the scar?'

'I . . . I don't know.' Jane put off the brake and clung to the handles of the chair. 'When a thing like that is there you don't notice it after a while.' Artful old devil, she thought. He knew that they hadn't shared a bed for years. 'It's getting cool. I'll take you back.' She felt her skin grow hot and was glad to be in the open air. The flush died down and she hoped that the change of life would be over soon. Please make me barren, dear Mary, and take away this fear, she prayed silently.

Maudie went with men and didn't get caught. Some men refused to wear the sheath, though, so how did their women manage without something like the pessaries that Mrs Lee had made?

'Look! In broad daylight, too,' said Aaron. A man was helping a woman to alight from a boat and she turned to wave to him. 'He goes over to Hamble,' said Aaron. 'Makes a good day out for her, if she ain't fussy.'

'I'll take on Lucy,' said Jane softly. 'Poor little soul.' She called in at the shop to fetch some small cakes that Aaron liked and then pushed him back home and helped his wife Ruby to put him to bed. 'Ethel not back yet?' she asked.

'She's with your Clare.' Ruby Sheath poured tea and Jane sat back listening to George's thin whistling as he piled boxes on the cart to take to the Quay. 'Growing up they are, those two, and your Lizzie isn't far behind.'

'Lizzie's still a baby, even though she is Clare's twin. She still cries if I expect too much of her and hates weighing potatoes, but she has to do her share.' Jane sighed. 'I'd hoped to finish with the copper for this week, but Alice brought Edward's thick shirts for me to do and he needs some by tomorrow. He managed when he worked at Cowes but now he's on the mainland, he has to take plenty with him to last the week.'

'She's had all week to do them,' Ruby said. 'Lazy little baggage.'

'She's not well,' said Jane, instantly defensive of anyone connected with her family. 'I might ask Dr Barnes what he thinks when I go up for Walter's medicine.'

'Is Walter ill?'

'He keeps a bottle of that white medicine handy in case he has a stomach upset. He won't go himself and tried to make me say it was for me!' Jane pinned her hat on firmly, said her goodbyes, and walked through the dusk past the ice factory where two figures pressed back into the shadow. She was curious to know who was at this end of the town so late but it wasn't nice to stare at courting couples. A high-pitched giggle made her pause, then she walked slowly on back to the shop.

Clare and Ethel were talking as if they hadn't seen each other for weeks. 'Is everyone in?' Jane asked.

'No, but we know where Lizzie is,' said Ethel, then blushed crimson as Clare gave her an angry look.

'And where might that be, that's so interesting?' Jane said dryly. 'It's time you all had your cocoa and went up and Ethel, your mother was asking for you.'

'Father will be out,' announced Clare. 'Bert Cooper told Jack up at the Bugle that he is staying at the camp tonight.' Just then, Lizzie rushed into the shop and through to the back room. 'I'll make the cocoa,' Clare offered hastily, and Jane went upstairs to put the mending away. She fingered the two new blouses that Miss Joyner had made for her, wondering if the red one was too showy. It was brighter than it had seemed from the tiny swatch she had chosen, and had very modern puffed sleeves. She hung it in the cupboard then put the plain poplin one with a summer dress. It was highnecked, and of a soft mauve that would match the ribbons on the hat that Clare had trimmed for her.

Back downstairs, she noticed that Lizzie sat well away from the table in an attempt to look invisible, her nose in her mug of cocoa. 'Can I go to Cowes with Ethel on Sunday?' Clare asked. 'I've money enough for the train, and there's a big ship anchored in the Roads.'

'You're too young to be looking at sailors,' Jane said.

'We hate sailors,' Clare said self-righteously. 'We just want to see the ship.'

'They aren't all bad,' Janey said, smiling. She handed Jane a biscuit. 'Taste that, Mother. Mrs Neville shows me how to make these and they just melt in the mouth.'

'That's three days you've worked there this week,' Jane observed.

'I like it and they pay me well,' Janey told her. 'It isn't like being in service. I have a girl to clear away and do the washing up, and so far I have learned a lot. I cook for dinner parties twice – once for the family and, if it's all right, I do the same for the guests the next day using more fancy trimmings. Mrs Neville said she wished I was there all the time.'

'Now isn't that grand?' said Jane with pride, then sat straight in her chair. 'They must think a lot of you, and why not? Any of my girls are good enough for the greatest family in the country!'

'I suppose Father is still in the Bugle, telling them how he won the Boer War,' said Clare, yawning.

'He was a brave soldier,' Emily said defensively. 'He has silver spurs and medals.'

'That was a long time ago and please God we'll have no more fighting,' Jane put in.

'I'd never fight,' Sidney assured them all, on his way to

wash the paint from his hands. 'War is wicked.' He came back for his cocoa. 'I've nearly finished the stage,' he said.

'And the puppets?' Emily asked eagerly. 'Will you give us a show when it's finished? Is Herbie going to help? He's so clever with the voices and the way he makes the puppets move.' Her eyes shone with admiration.

Jane watched the family talking, completely at ease now that Walter was away. They sat up late, and Jack teased his sisters about the boys they knew. He took three of the new biscuits and stuffed his mouth full when Clare made a remark about girls in the Bugle. 'You can talk,' he said. 'Lizzie's courting. He wants to come to tea and get his feet under the table!'

Lizzie's face was bright red. 'It's none of your business, Jack Darwen!'

'It's Harry French and he works down at Folley in the boatyard,' said Clare, unwilling to be left out.

'Then he's got a long walk back tonight,' retorted Jane. 'It was you by the ice factory tonight, wasn't it? No mistaking that giggle of yours, Lizzie.' She sighed. 'You're too young to be walking out, my girl. And far too young to think of him seriously.'

'I'm sixteen! Alice was married at sixteen to our Edward,' Lizzie said.

'Who's talking about marriage? Edward had a good job and prospects and can support a wife, but I've seen the boatyard and it can't give that lad enough to feed himself let alone a wife!'

'I didn't say I wanted to marry him,' Lizzie said in her hard-done-by voice.

'Marry or not, you'd better bring him to tea on Sunday so that your father can take a look at him.' Jane sensed that Clare was about to protest. 'You will *all* be here!'

'I'll make a nice tea, and Mother can rest after dinner,' said Janey.

'Will Father be away?' queried Lizzie hopefully.

Jane smiled. 'I doubt it. I hear thunder and bell tents aren't that comfortable in the wet. They'll all scuttle home if it's bad. Now Jack, bolt the door and the rest of you go up.'

She washed the mugs and saw the candle still alight in the shop. 'Did Bert sell the piglets?' she asked Jack. 'I hope he saved mine for me, as I've the crock ready for it and the saltpetre and sugar. There'll be brawn and haslet to make and pies from the trimmings. Mrs Caws at the Bugle sold all that I could let her have the last time and she asked for more, so you can tell her there'll be some next week.'

'I'll tell her,' he said, and blushed.

'What's Nellie Stone singing this week – *The Merry Widow*? She sings just like a music hall artiste and trails around in the hats to match it!' She watched his face and knew that something she had dreaded was happening. 'What is it, son? Your father's out and we have time to talk in peace.'

'How much do you know?' he muttered. 'Everything, I suspect. Newport doesn't miss a thing. Have the others been talking about me?'

'No, they haven't breathed a word.'

'You know already, Mother. You mention her often enough and Father hints.'

'Nellie Stone.' Jane sat with her face clouded with a sorrow just beginning.

'She's all right, Mother. She's just so beautiful that all the lads fall for her. She can't help it! But it's me she wants, she said so.'

'She's older than you.'

'I'm a man! I'm twenty. If Lizzie can go courting at sixteen and Edward married young, why not me? I slave away in the brickyard and the stables and earn my keep and more, and I want to get married.'

Jack's dark eyes were tragic and he laid a hand over hers in the loving gesture she remembered from the time she was so ill and nearly died. Jane tried not to cry. Edward was different. He had been serious and a man before he was out of sailor suits, and was rapidly making a place for himself in the smoke-filled railways that he loved. 'What will your father say? It's one thing to laugh with the rest of you and join in the singing, but when it comes to the altar he might sing a different tune.'

'I can marry – Nellie said I can marry as soon as I'm twenty-one.'

'And where would you live?'

'We'd be together,' he replied, as if that said it all.

'But *where*? You do earn a wage here but you could earn twice as much if you worked for Uncle Archie as he suggested last year. You need more money if you're to feed two and have a roof over your head.' He couldn't bring her here, she thought with revulsion. It would be as if Maudie Dove came to stay the night under her roof, although Nellie wasn't like that, as yet.

'Nellie would like to stay on at the Bugle, playing the piano and singing, but when we're married I shall make her give it up and keep house,' he said with pride.

'Go and see Archie. He hasn't been well and needs some help. There's a cottage on the farm, and that might do,' she added.

'I knew you'd be on my side,' he exclaimed, hugging her. His smile was wicked and very young, like the boy she had loved through all his tantrums as a child.

'I'll have to know a lot more about that lady before I'm on any side,' she warned him.

'Wootton would be a good idea,' Jack said, his smile now tender and sweet. 'I can just see Nellie in a print sunbonnet with a pail of milk on her arm. Good night, Mother. Shall I put out the gas?'

'No, I shan't sleep. I'll make tea and sit here for a while. You've given me nightmares, Jack.' Nellie Stone, she thought. Older than Jack by three years, flaunting her low necklines for all to see who wanted to look. There might be no harm in her – but a barmaid for one of Walter's sons?

Chapter 3

'Foot regiments!' Walter loosened the starched linen of his collar and wondered why it had shrunk.

'But the Wessex Howitzer Brigade was there and some horses,' Emily ventured timidly.

Walter grunted. 'None of my lot. The uniforms were sloppy and I know a few sergeant majors who would soon lick them into shape. Wouldn't have happened in the old days.'

Jane sighed. At any moment he would start on about the Boer War, and talk of the Queen as if she were still alive, refusing to accept that anyone had taken her place. King Edward he ignored completely – unless it was to laugh at his exploits before he married and came to the throne.

'When do I get my tea?' Walter was hot and the smart collar rubbed and he missed his long afternoon nap. 'Who is this friend of Lizzie's?' he asked for the third time. 'Harry French? That sounds foreign. Do we speak his lingo?' He laughed and Jane hoped he wouldn't repeat it when Lizzie came in with Harry to tea.

The thunder had done nothing to cool the air and Jane propped open the back door, letting in flies that tried to get to the cakes under the butter muslin. Janey peeped at the soda bread to see that it didn't scorch and Sidney sat reading. Jane put herself between him and his father as Walter had fixed views about clothes and disapproved of the soft floppy tie that looked smooth and romantic under the starched collar. At only seventeen, Sidney was handsome and many girls sighed for him. Lucy Dove openly adored him.

Edward was married, Lizzie was on the way there and Jack was waiting to leave. I'm getting old, Jane thought, but her reflection showed no change even with the hot flush that now made her want to undo her neckband. She was as she had been yesterday, only more dressed up.

The shop-bell rang and Jack went to bring in Lizzie and her guest. Harry walked straight over to Walter, hand outstretched, and Walter stared. This wasn't a callow boy who could easily be brushed aside as unsuitable for his Lizzie. Harry looked completely at home and gazed fondly at Lizzie, who smirked triumphantly at Clare.

'Well, sit down,' Walter said, and Lizzie pointed to the chair next to hers. 'Janey, the lad wants his tea and so do I.'

Harry sat with head slightly bent then looked up. 'Will you be saying Grace, sir?'

'Humbuggen nonsense!' Walter grunted and reached for a slice of soda bread and jam. His face reddened, the collar grew tighter and a pulse beat fast in his neck. He was putting on weight again, Jane thought. She looked at Harry. He had good eyes but was a lot older than Lizzie. Obviously he thought her the most beautiful creature on earth, but his mouth was firm. He might even manage her in a tantrum, Jane thought, and relaxed.

When the chenille cover and the vase of summer flowers had been replaced on the table and small-talk had dwindled, Walter sighed, knowing that there were still hours to get through. 'Let's have a bit of music,' he said jovially.

Jane took the family pictures from the harmonium and Jack looked through the music in the stool seat. 'Isn't there anything new?' he asked impatiently, and shoved it all back untidily.

'Those are fine songs,' said Walter. He looked at Harry. 'Don't you agree?' He looked more closely. 'Didn't you sing at the concert last year?' The young man nodded and Walter selected *The Lost Chord*. Harry stood with one hand on Lizzie's shoulder, the other in his jacket – like Napoleon, thought Sidney – and sang in a reedy tenor, song after song. Jack squirmed in his seat. How could Lizzie look so adoring when he sang *Home Sweet Home* like that, as though he meant every word and wasn't making fun of it? He dreamed of Nellie and her white throat as she sang the latest songs and looked beautiful, and wished he hadn't promised his mother not to say anything until he was fixed at Wootton.

Jane slipped out to the scullery and Janey followed to do the washing up. They closed the door and giggled and Jack sidled in to join them. 'Go back and talk about the war,' Janey suggested. 'Father is getting sentimental about the songs they sang out there.'

'My duty is with the washing up,' Jack said firmly. 'And I have something to tell you.' Janey poured away the soda water, scouring the sink as it went down the drain and Jane dried her hands.

'Have you been to Wootton?'

'Yes. Archie is better but now Aunt Amy is sick. She wants to know if Clare can help over the jam season.'

'Clare? I suppose she could. She ought to do something and refuses to go to Annie Cooper. What did you say to Archie?'

'I start there next week,' said Jack with a tremor in his voice.

'So soon? Have you asked your father?'

'It might not be a question of asking. Bert Cooper was up at the Bugle last night and he knows. Come tomorrow, he'll tell Father.'

'Then you must tell Walter yourself tonight or there'll be murder done!' She found that her fears were not for the boy leaving home but for those left to face Walter's moods.

'What about Nellie?' Janey whispered.

'You knew?' Janey nodded. Everyone but Jack knew that Nellie Stone boasted of his devotion to her and bets were laid as to when they would marry or get together and another book was on how fast Nellie would be caught.

'Archie says I can have the cottage if I do it up myself,' Jack informed them. 'Sidney can help me as I don't know one colour from another and he knows what pleases a woman's taste.'

'He'll have to do it on the quiet,' Janey said wisely. 'Father would be mad if he knew you had it so easy. I can help with curtains when Mrs Neville is in Scotland, and when Father is away at camp we can all go over to the farm.'

'Wootton is a long way from the Bugle. I can't see Nellie in the country,' Jane said doubtfully.

'She'll love it,' Jack assured her, with the same disregard of fact that Walter showed when he wanted to believe something.

'Take these sweets in to them. It might stop them talking about the war,' said Jane. In the living room the air was thick with smoke but the men seemed to be enjoying themselves as Harry listened and nodded at all the old stories and Lizzie giggled if they made a joke.

'So you want my little Lizzie,' Walter said at last. 'Bit of a cradle-snatcher, aren't you?'

'I know I'm older than Lizzie, Mr Darwen, but I can give her a nice home and I'd be good to her.' Harry looked down at Lizzie cautiously as he hadn't meant to say that yet. 'Of course,' he added hastily, 'I don't expect to get married yet as Lizzie will need to make her bottom drawer, and I have a lot of work on hand at present.'

Lizzie looked less than pleased. It would have been exciting if Harry had said he couldn't wait and wanted to sweep her off to church now. She had embroidered four pillowcases with flowers but had never taken it seriously, for who wanted to turn in bed and have raised French knots digging into their cheeks? Then she brightened: if she had to sit with an embroidery frame, she couldn't serve in the shop. 'I'll do some of it next week,' she promised, and Harry smiled as if a kitten was learning a new trick.

He looked at a huge silver watch. 'I ought to get my train, Mrs Darwen,' he said.

'Where do you live?' she asked. They knew nothing about him.

'East Cowes but I help at Folley sometimes. Now though, I've started at White's and shall work there fulltime. They pay well and I can save. I work on engines – the internal combustion engine is the horse of the future, Mr Darwen,' he said, his fingers in the armholes of his waistcoat as if about to deliver a lecture.

'Nine days' wonder,' Walter said, getting annoyed. 'Never replace the horse.'

'You'd better walk with Harry to the station, Lizzie,' Jane suggested hastily, 'or he'll miss his train.' It would be a pity if the first good impression was ruined!

'Engines,' muttered Walter as Jane made fresh tea and set it before him. 'Out at the camp they had two lorries with canvas sides as ambulances.' He laughed. 'One got bogged down in the mud and it took four horses to pull it clear. We used the laundry cart after that. They'll never last in battle, and take an army of their own to service them. That lad has a lot to learn and he'll be back in the woodyard before the next war starts.'

'There are plenty of yachts with engines off Cowes, and even old Aaron has one to beat the tide,' said Jack.

'That's different.' Walter tore off the tight collar and flung it on the floor. 'Do you want to throttle me, woman?' he muttered. Inwardly, Jane flinched but showed no emotion. He had a strange look about him again.

Emily looked frightened. 'You won't go away to war again, will you, Father? Whatever would we do?'

'It won't be in Africa this time but in Europe,' he replied grimly. 'You'd just have to manage the shop and look after your mother like you did last time.'

Emily hugged him, which put him in a good mood again. 'I never want to leave home,' she said fervently.

'Do you want help with the animals, Father?' Jack asked, looking down at the man who now sprawled in the big chair.

'No, I want to see Bert about payment for the pigs and about going over to Portsmouth on business. I must get out of these clothes first into something lighter,' and Jane knew that 'something lighter' meant a pale grey, slightly raffish suit that he wore these days when going out with Bert Cooper.

'Will you be looking in at the Bugle?' Jack asked hastily.

'What if I am?'

Jack bit his lip. 'I'm taking a job on the farm,' he blurted out. 'Archie wanted me some time ago and now I've said yes. Sidney can do the deliveries here and Clare doesn't mind helping with the horses. He will pay me well.'

'So it's more money you're after, eh?' Walter smiled, a sneer lurking in his eyes. 'To buy pretty things for that gal who is setting her cap at you? Don't think I haven't seen her getting round you and you making sheep's eyes at her while she plays the piano, showing all she's got! Can't have the father so tries it on the young 'un.'

Jack clenched his fists to stop himself hitting the mocking face, and Jane ached for his self-control. 'She isn't like that. I want my own place and my own life,' he said quietly.

'You see, Walter, Archie hasn't got over his back injury yet,' Jane ventured in conciliatory tones. 'And Amy was bad the last time I went down. There's all that hay to toss and fruit to pick, and Clare is needed to help out with the pickles and jam-making.'

Walter ignored her. 'If you go, you go for good,' he said to his son. 'Think about that. You stay here or go to hell in your own way.'

Jack sat with his face in his hands after Walter had disappeared upstairs. 'Take no heed,' Jane whispered. 'He means only the half of what he says and he knows he'd miss you, so that puts him in a bad mood.'

'When is he in a good one?' Jane saw that Jack was deeply upset. 'What's to become of you when I go, Mother? He's changed. He isn't my father any more and I hate him.'

Jane put a soothing hand on the dark head of her beloved and wilful son. 'I'll be fine, just fine,' she said. 'I understand his funny ways, and you'll only be down the line at Wootton.'

Jack smiled up at her, reassured. 'Just think of it, Mother. Me on the farm in my own cottage with a lovely wife. You can take the train on Sundays and after you've seen Aunt Amy, you can come over to our place for tea. We'll have a real sing-song and not that old-fashioned stuff you have here.'

'Can Nellie cook?' Jane asked cautiously.

Jack dismissed this. 'All women can cook. Janey does and Lizzie can – and even Clare does when she has to.'

'But not all girls learn from their mothers, and you like

your good hot dinners,' she said, but he had already gone off to find Sidney.

Clare was annoyed. The Sunday ironing included the thick working shirts that Edward wore on the railway. 'I don't see why I should do them while Lizzie swans off and does nothing but walk to the station with Harry, and Edward has a wife to do them now.'

'You didn't touch the washing up,' Jane reminded her, 'and poor Alice is bad again. When you have a young man you can walk to the station with him.' She sighed. 'I thought you would be the first as Lizzie is still such a baby at times, and you look so grown up.'

Clare thawed. 'I was called Miss Darwen the other day,' she admitted. 'The new clerk in the bank gave me papers to bring home to Father and he knew my name after seeing me only once.'

'Now that's what I call a proper job of work. It's good and safe and a lot of people from banks go on the Council.' Jane was impressed.

'When it comes to my turn, I want someone better than Harry French,' Clare sniffed. 'Some girls take the first offer and I don't want a factory worker like Harry, or a farmer.'

'The first might be the best,' Jane said sharply. 'Some girls fall between two stools and end up with a sore backside! You know what Pride did!'

Clare tossed her head defiantly. 'You married a soldier and had to work hard all your life.'

'And we've given you a good home with plenty of everything! Don't let your father ever hear you talk like that.' Jane had a lump in her throat. Yes, life had been hard but there had been the good years when she was a true wife and the children were small. Perhaps when she passed through the change of life she could go back to bed with Walter and he'd be better-tempered, but for her, all desire had fled when she recalled the night he had raped her. She folded a shirt and smiled. 'Maybe you are right. Wait for the right man, Clare. You'll be able to pick and choose.' They put the clean shirts into a hessian bag and the front door opened.

Edward looked relaxed, which meant that Alice was feeling better. He was dressed in his Sunday suit although nearly due to catch the boat back to Portsmouth for the coming week's work. 'I have to see someone tomorrow and must look smart,' he explained. 'They want me back at Cowes for Cowes Week while the Royal Family are here. I shall be assistant stationmaster.'

'But Cowes is smaller than Portsmouth,' protested Clare.

'After that I might be given the same job on the mainland.' He blushed. 'I shall have to wear a silk hat and lay down the red carpet when important people use the train, and arrange transport for guests at the Castle.'

'You'll see the Queen, and the whole Family will be there for Cowes Week with the German cousins, and they'll visit Princess Beatrice at Carisbrooke,' Janey said, and blushed when Clare looked cross and said she hadn't seen the notice in the *County Press*. 'I'll know more later, about whether they will come by train to Newport or by carriage from Osborne,' Janey continued. 'One of Mrs Neville's sons is a cadet at Osborne and will be on duty for the Week. He tells his mother anything of interest.'

'They have a son at Dartmouth, too, haven't they?' Clare asked.

'That's the older one,' Janey said, her eyes downcast and her hands busy riddling the fire. She seemed to have difficulty in speaking clearly. 'Mrs Neville will be back from Scotland for the Week and wants me to get the place ready for them all. There will be someone there to let me in the day before they arrive, apparently, and I shall cook food for them and their house party.'

'They are such nice people,' Jane said. 'I'd be really proud if one of my daughters married a naval officer.'

'Would you? Would you really, Mother?' Janey smiled softly. 'It's a pity that Clare doesn't like sailors.'

'An officer would be different. I'd like a husband who was away a lot and didn't get under my feet all day.'

'Bank clerks get sent away,' said Jane meaningfully.

'I wouldn't marry a clerk,' Clare replied derisively.

'Nobody has asked you,' said Emily in surprise, 'so how

do you know? *I* want to stay at home for ever.' She listened and went through to the shop. 'What's wrong?' she asked Lizzie, who was leaning on the counter drying her eyes.

'Nothing,' said Lizzie, as if a great catastrophe had occurred.

'Did you slip on the coaldust?' Emily led her into the living room.

'No, it's just that . . .' Her mouth took on the square shape Jane remembered from when Lizzie was a child and a cry that was more a moaning bellow came out. 'It was Harry!'

Anxiety made Jane rough. She shook Lizzie into silence. 'What happened?' They had walked in daylight to the station, she knew, and couldn't have been there long as the train whistle had blown a few minutes after they left the shop. Jane jerked her head towards the scullery and the others filed out obediently, leaving the door open a crack to hear what was said. 'Now, my pet, tell Mother,' Jane said gently, smoothing back the damp hair from Lizzie's brow.

'He put his hand . . . here,' said Lizzie in a loud whisper, placing a hand over her left breast.

Jane waited for more revelations but there hadn't been time for more, surely? She looked away to hide a smile and saw Walter lounging in the doorway in the light grey suit, and for a second they shared the rapport of earlier years. He stepped forward. 'Just that?' he asked, and Lizzie blushed scarlet. 'Well, at least he's more of a man than I gave him credit for, or a bit of a one, anyway! You'd best get him to the altar my lass before he loses control completely.' He laughed coarsely. 'Why don't you teach your girls something, Jane? She'll have more than that to put up with before she's through. What is she? Sweet sixteen and never been kissed? Never been touched – never been . . .'

'That'll be enough, Walter! She told me and that was the right thing to do. There's no call for you making it worse and there's no harm in the lad, that's for sure.'

Walter looked at the colour in his wife's cheeks and the glittering dark eyes and his mouth softened. She was still the handsomest woman he'd met – and the cleanest. The woman he'd made love to in Portsmouth made him shut his eyes while his body found release. 'I'm off,' he said. 'Don't lock up, I'll be late.'

Lizzie was annoyed at the lack of impact her news had caused. Harry had often kissed her, but this time his hand had wandered further and more masterfully, but it had been nice. 'I forgave him,' she said piously.

Clare giggled as the others came back into the room. 'You'll have to wear two pairs of drawers and a bust bodice,' she suggested, but made up for it by lending Lizzie her copy of *Weldon's Magazine* and they dreamed of the time when they would be rich.

Chapter 4

Annie Cooper hammered on the shop door until Jane came to open it, ignoring the Closed sign. 'It's only me,' she announced, as if that gave her a right to intrude. 'That Mr Foster told me it was dinner-time and he was shutting, and he almost pushed me out of the shop.'

'Well, some of us do like to eat,' said Jane sharply. 'What can I do for you, Annie? If it takes long I'll have to put our dinner back to keep warm.'

Annie ignored the sarcasm. 'I hear that your Lizzie is looking at patterns for wedding dresses.'

'Lizzie? They all look at patterns. What do you want – a few specky oranges and a penn'orth of potherbs?'

'No, I want a cabbage and some carrots.' She put her sacking bag on the counter and rubbed the worn surface where a series of dents showed in the polished wood. Jane smiled. Annie would look less superior if she knew that Bert had made them with the weights from the scales when he had attacked her while Walter was in Africa.

'Is that all? It is the biggest,' Jane said, seeing Annie eye the pile of cabbages. 'That'll be threepence.'

Reluctantly, Annie gathered her bag and purse. 'Is Walter home?'

'He's out the back,' lied Jane, knowing that Annie wouldn't try to beg a cup of tea and a bite if he was there, and she hoped that he wouldn't suddenly appear from the road. The rest of the family were out and complete solitude was precious, but still Annie lingered, rubbing her hands together and complaining of the cold at night. 'I hadn't noticed it,' Jane began, but then saw how swollen Annie's hands were with rheumatism. They looked painful.

Jane sighed. Why didn't Annie go to Dr Barnes, instead of expecting her to make homely remedies? 'I can't stop now,' she said, 'but come tomorrow and I'll give you some of that cream for your hands.' She bolted the door after Annie left, knowing that as usual, Bert's wife had got nearly everything she'd come for. She filled a bowl with good thick beef broth and cut a hunk of bread, savouring the time alone but starting up in a small panic when she realised she was late opening the shop again. Walter had forgotten to wind the cuckoo clock and so she had not heard one o'clock strike.

'I'm sorry, Mrs Barnes. I didn't know you were waiting,' she said hurriedly. 'You should have knocked.' The doctor's wife had been waiting on the pavement.

Mrs Barnes smiled warmly. 'I would never do that. I know how busy you are, and how much we resent having our meal-times interrupted by people who call at the surgery on some trivial errand out of hours. Ah, I see you have grapes.'

Jane picked a blue-black berry and handed it to her to taste. 'They're from the hothouse at Carisbrooke. We have some peaches coming at the weekend, too.'

'Good. I have guests and a nice basket of fruit dresses the table well. Can you send them over on Saturday?'

Jane hesitated. 'I might bring them myself at surgery time,' she said.

'Is something wrong, my dear?' Mrs Barnes looked anxious. Had Walter Darwen been up to his tricks again and made his wife pregnant?

'I'm fine,' Jane said quietly, sensing what was in her mind. 'I just wanted a word about my daughter-in-law.' She saw the raised eyebrows. 'No, she isn't expecting, although half the town have totted up dates since they married, but Alice isn't strong and sometimes I think she may have something seriously wrong with her.'

'I'll tell my husband that you will come to the surgery at six on Friday. Do you want to bring her, too?'

'No, I had a word with Edward and said I'd see the doctor first without telling Alice. Edward has to be away a lot and has been made assistant stationmaster at Southampton, so it looks as if they'll have to live there. I just don't know how Alice will manage alone. We do all her laundry and bake her a cake now and then.'

'Which means you do all her cooking and make sure your lad gets fed when he comes home!' Mrs Barnes laughed. 'Mothers are silly. I do the same when Alex comes home, as if he has had nothing to eat for weeks. He'll be with us this weekend and hopes to bring his friend with him.'

'Would that be young Clive Neville? They grow up so fast. Who would have thought they'd be old enough to be in the navy?' Jane looked thoughtful as she tidied the shop and pulled the blind down halfway to shield the fish from the still-warm September sun. Walter spent a lot of time at the Barracks and up at the Drill Hall these days, and grumbled when asked to do anything. He said that if they wanted a roof over their heads, the family could earn it and work harder.

With Jack gone, life had lost both a barb and a joy for Jane but increasingly, Walter eyed his youngest son with animosity. Sidney made puppets and helped the local drama society when he wasn't working hard with the animals and delivering supplies to Albany Barracks, and Walter thought him a fool. Harry French arrived for tea every Sunday and took Lizzie for walks but there was no talk of marriage, to Jane's relief. Walter liked the young man as he was willing to listen to the war stories and Lucy listened too, hungry for any news of the war that had killed her father, so Walter tolerated her presence when she worked in the shop.

'The evenings are drawing in, Mrs Darwen.' Mrs Foster stood at the counter, puffed up with pride. 'When my husband had to meet the train to take the Royals to the Castle it was nearly dark.' Jane wondered secretly how it would be when Walter had more time to stay in at night unless he went to the Wheatsheaf or the Bugle, and Sidney's room grew too cold for her son to work in. With Jack gone, Sidney had become her husband's target for spite and taunting. Walter was easily crossed and only the trips to Portsmouth with Bert made him better-tempered. Jane closed her mind to those visits. Bert shared business and friendship with Walter, so why not women? Annie knew full well that Bert had a woman over the water but seemed relieved that he now left her alone completely, and Jane knew that she must learn to feel the same. At least Walter kept it away from the Island and the gossip-mongers.

Emily ran into the shop, looking very self-important. 'I saw Clare talking to that man in the bank,' she told her mother.

'Very likely. Your father asked her to leave some papers with the manager.'

'They weren't *in* the bank, they were in the side alley and he was asking her to go to the chapel social with him.'

'So, Miss, you were eavesdropping on them, were you? You talk to Arnold sometimes, but the others don't rush home to tell me. What's more, you are going to the social and so are Janey and Sidney and Jack – it would be strange if the young man hadn't asked Clare if she is going as I expect to see the whole of Newport there.' Jane buttered bread and thought quickly. The social was on Saturday and she must make two huge apple pies to grace the tables. Jack would be there so that meant Nellie, too, making their friendship public. Janey would go with Clare and Lizzie and Harry would escort them, repeating again and again that he was a rose among thorns, and making Lizzie giggle at his wonderful turn of phrase.

Sidney emerged from the scullery smelling of carbolic soap. 'I've finally finished the new Punch and Judy,' he beamed. 'They want Herbie and me to give a show at the social.'

'Then it's as well that I've made the clothes, then,' said Jane. 'The ruffs were not as hard as I expected and they do add the finishing touch.' She watched the sensitive fingers picking at his cake and wondered again where Sidney's artistic talent sprang from. I'm like him in many ways, she thought, and I have a special love for him, but I feel that he is fast outstripping me.

'Someone who saw the show we gave a few weeks ago is coming to see us again this time. He wants Herbie and me to join his troupe.'

Jane stared. 'You're much too young to traipse about the

country with travelling artistes. Your father wouldn't like it.'

'He'd be glad,' Sidney said calmly. 'If this comes to nothing then I'll have to think of something else as I can't stay here much longer. Jack has gone, Lizzie is walking out and the others will do what they want, so I must go before he gets really mad.'

'Not yet,' she whispered. 'There's plenty of time and you do like the animals.' Not you too, my dearest boy, she wanted to say. Not you, who brought me primroses and coaxed my mind back from near madness . . . as gentle and tender as a woman. 'Where would you go?'

'There's a cheap passage being offered to America. Herbie wants to go and I want to go with him.' Sidney took her hand, his eyes shining. 'America is the land of opportunity, Mother – they all say so. I might even get into moving pictures.'

'You aren't an actor,' Jane objected.

'I know a lot about stagework, enough to get started – and I can dance.'

'When I wanted to go to dancing lessons, you wouldn't take me,' Emily interrupted resentfully.

Sidney blushed. 'I didn't go to ballroom dancing classes,' he said. 'This is different. They said I was very good.'

And with your handsome face, you could end up in moving pictures, Jane thought. 'Keep quiet about it until you find out more,' she said firmly. 'That means you too, Emily. Your father mustn't hear a whisper until it's all settled. If it fell through, then Sidney would have to bear the brunt of his sarcasm. He hates failures.' She shuddered to imagine Walter's face when he heard that his son wanted to make a career of dancing and puppet-making. 'I can see that you must do what you wish, but promise you'll be here for Christmas,' she begged, when Emily went to fill the kettle in the scullery and they were alone.

'I promise. By the way, Jack is coming to the social. We have finished two rooms in the cottage and he talks of getting married soon. He doesn't want to stay under this roof overnight so Archie will bring him in the trap and take him back again to Wootton. I thought I'd better warn you!'

'Thank you. Archie might like to stay for the social. He enjoys dancing and a bit of music, and at Harvest Festival there is always food to spare for extra guests.' It would be like old times. Walter would be in the Wheatsheaf at a reunion of army men and she could relax and talk to old friends. It was a tonic to look forward to the social, and Jane felt lighthearted as she took the carefully arranged shallow gilt basket of fruit over to the doctor's house and went on to the surgery.

'I haven't seen you for a very long time,' Dr Barnes said. He was as brusquely kind as ever but greyer, Jane thought.

'I'm fine, just fine,' she assured him, 'but it's Alice, my daughter-in-law I've come about, as she refuses to see a doctor.'

'Off her food? Being sick?'

'She's not carrying, Doctor. This stems from the time just after they married when she got wet and cold at Sandown. She had a fever for two weeks and you said she had a chill on her liver.'

'I do recall that.' He leaned back and regarded Jane with warm interest. 'I respect your judgement, Mrs Darwen. Since then? Any trouble with her waterworks?'

'She goes down the yard more often than we do to pass water but she's not off her food, or not all of it. Sometimes I think she has worms!'

He asked more questions. 'Tell me, have you smelled her breath lately?'

'Sometimes, in one of her sleepy fits.' Jane laughed. 'It sounds silly but it reminds me of a field of new-mown hay.'

'How very observant; that's what the textbooks say. You *are* the last patient, I think?' She nodded. 'I must look at this paper and this book. No, don't go away. I told you a long time ago that I would have liked you as my assistant: you show such intelligent interest that it is a pleasure to hear what you have to say. Alice has a disorder of a gland called the pancreas. Only a few years ago a man called Sharpey-Schafer discovered that the sugar disease is caused by a lack of something given out from that gland. Animals deprived of the pancreas cannot digest sugar as it runs through them and leaves them tired and eventually very sleepy as if they'll never wake up, and they die.'

Jane was pale. 'Alice sleeps a lot and drinks a lot of water and tea. If she eats sweets and puddings, she feels ill and sleepy and often refuses sweets even though she likes them, as she knows they disagree with her. Can you give her some medicine?'

'It isn't as easy as that. We know about this hormone they call insulin, but the people doing research haven't yet found a way of giving it to patients. They've tried to extract it from dead glands, but when scientists fed patients with raw pancreas as we do liver to people with anaemia, it just got digested as a food and was not effective as a medicine. The only way of treating these patients is to stop them eating sugar.'

'No sugar in her tea?' Jane smiled. 'Alice likes sweet tea but she'll have to see sense.'

'There must be no sugar in anything – and that includes all you bake containing sugar and honey,' he reminded her. 'And remember, Mrs Darwen, this is the time when you must think of yourself after all you have suffered. Alice has a husband now. Tell Edward what I have said and leave them to manage it for themselves.'

'Thank you, Doctor. I'm well in myself and so is Walter even if he gets bad-tempered at times when he can't do as much as he did at twenty.'

'If that's your only worry you are blessed! I saw your good-looking girls in the High Street and they are a credit to you. We never had a daughter and my wife is hoping that Alex will bring back a wife soon. If he finds one as well-brought up as yours, I would indeed be happy.'

Jane blushed, her eyes bright with pride. To think that Dr Barnes, from an important county family, wouldn't object to one of her daughters for his son was praise indeed.

'What's so amusing?' Walter said mildly when she went home.

'Just something Dr Barnes said.'

'You aren't sick?' He started from his chair then sank back. It was ridiculous: Jane had slept alone and there would never be another baby to cause this tremulous joy she now showed.

'I'm not sick.' She was glad to see he retained some care for her. 'You would have been proud too, Walter.' She repeated the conversation and although he tried not to look pleased he was more like the man she remembered.

'Well, he can't have Lizzie as she's taken, and Emily will stay here with us as she's the youngest. Do you think Janey would fancy Alex? Old Barnes' boy would be lucky to get one of mine,' he added complacently, and Jane hoped he wouldn't boast in the Wheatsheaf.

'There was some bad news, though,' she said, to take his mind off the subject. She tried to recall everything the doctor had told her.

'Bad blood!' Walter said at last. 'Can't think why Edward ever married her.'

'She was fine when they wed but the chill got into her liver,' Jane explained. 'Poor Alice, I've been too sharp with her, thinking she's lazy.'

'And so she is.' But Walter wasn't cross. The drills had gone well and his uniform now fitted, as he walked more and ate slightly less. He would wear his silver spurs to the reunion. Now he had a meeting on at the Drill Hall. Jane picked a few grapes from the box and sat down alone to read the paper. Life did have certain compensations, and when Walter appeared on the night of the social, smart and in a good humour, she was proud of him.

'I've been asked to say a few words,' he said. Jane pulled a loose thread from his tunic. Miss Joyner wasn't good at finishing seams, but it was firmly stitched and nobody had let on that they knew he'd had to have the uniform altered. 'I wish you could be there to hear me,' he said. 'You're still the best-looking woman in Newport!'

'It's a man's night and it wouldn't be fitting,' Jane said primly. 'You go and enjoy yourself and I shall hear all about it in the shop. Will you look in at the social on the way home? I could ask them to put something nice aside for you.'

'No, I'll get something there,' he replied hastily. 'I might be late, so go out and enjoy yourself, gal.'

Jane washed in warm water, carefully patting her breasts dry and dabbing them with Attar of Roses as she had done years ago. Her hair was as dark as the day she was married and she remembered that apart from the redheads, all her Irish relatives retained dark hair into old age. Annie Cooper, by contrast, was quite grey by now and hinted that Jane had hers touched up. Would Sidney meet any kinsmen in America, she wondered? Many young Irish had left to find fate or fortune there but Jane had never returned to Ireland since her wedding and so had lost touch with all her relatives. She looked out her new red blouse and knew that it would be warm enough in the crowded hall even though it felt chilly in the small of her back. She smiled to herself. What was the mother of seven children doing, dressed up in a red silky blouse, with scent on her skin? She pulled on a huge woollen jumper over the blouse to wear until she was ready to leave for the evening.

Walter was at the bottom of the stairs. 'I'm off,' he said and looked with approval at the shapeless dowdy garment, then sniffed and frowned. 'I thought you'd finished with that rubbish years ago,' he muttered.

'I found some and wondered if it had gone off.' She wished she had left it in her top drawer.

'It smells the same,' he said shortly, and left without another word. The door slammed and half an hour later, Archie arrived with Jack, who called for Sidney to help take the horses down to the stables.

'So you managed to come,' Jane said. 'Is Amy fit to be left?' She talked quickly, hardly waiting for his replies, suddenly aware that she was unused to being alone with a man even if he was Archie, her dear friend. She pulled her cloak about her over the thin blouse and turned away, feeling that he was about to kiss her. He had loved her once, in words but not in touching and she was afraid. 'I hear the boys coming back,' she said with relief. 'I hope they wash the stable smells from them before they go to the hall.'

'You should give them some of your scent,' Archie said softly.

'Carbolic is more manly,' she replied and followed Jack into the scullery. 'Is it too strong?' she asked him swiftly. 'Both your father and Archie noticed that I'm wearing scent.'

He leaned towards her. 'Wearing that blouse and smelling like a red rose, you'll have all the men after you,' he said and laughed. 'I'm fetching Nellie now. We want to be married soon, Mother. Tonight, you'll see how right I am about her and you'll love her. She wants to meet you as she has no family of her own.'

'I'll make her welcome Jack, but you'll have to get round your father. How can a body survive without kith and kin?'

'Thanks, Mother, but you'd better get used to the idea that Nellie and me are to marry on the mainland. I hate to see you torn but I don't want him there.'

'You'll marry in a church, though?' Jane felt sad although she had little time for organised religion. However, people married, were christened and buried with the blessing of the church and Jack should not go against the grain. He merely smiled and ran up the road towards the Bugle, leaving Archie to take her arm and Sidney to carry a box of equipment. Jane shivered. Holy Mary, save us from destruction and Jack from folly, she silently prayed.

'You're cold,' Archie said, and made her walk faster.

'It will be warm in the Hall and I'll be better,' she said.

A rich smell of baked bread and fruit came on a wave of sound as the door opened for them. The tables were covered with food and Mr Foster was carving a boar's head with great expertise. Jane went to the kitchen to make sure her pies would be hot enough and came back to Archie who was talking to the horse doctor, which gave her time to nod to old friends. Lizzie and Harry held hands by the bandstand and Janey and Clare and Emily talked to Ethel and another friend so there was no need to keep a place for any of them. Archie plied her with sweet cider, said to be free of alcohol and so acceptable on church premises, but Jane suspected it wasn't as innocent as all that and sipped it with caution.

'It's only crushed fruit,' Archie said, and thought how Jane looked just as she had done one day on the farm long ago, with bright cheeks and sparkling eyes. Jane avoided looking at him directly and tried to believe that it was Walter by her side waiting on her and enjoying her company. Many people came over to talk and some complained that the tea was tainted by the metal urn. One left over from the war, no doubt, Archie suggested.

'Walter would know about that,' a man said.

'He's probably telling them all about it in the Wheatsheaf,' she replied dryly. Brown china teapots replaced the rejected urn but the man called out not to throw it away as it might be needed again soon. 'Why does everyone talk of war?' Jane despaired. 'We have treaties with South Africa and are respected all over the world. You don't believe this nonsense, do you, Archie?'

He shrugged. 'I couldn't go last time as I had to grow food and I'd be too old for the next even if they'd let me leave the farm.' He helped clear the trestle tables and make a space for entertainment and dancing, then came back and touched her arm. 'Don't worry, Jane. Walter wouldn't have to go this time and although there are rumblings, it may come to nothing, even if they are training more men and building bigger motor vehicles for the army.'

'That won't please Walter. He hates motor vehicles.' She watched two girls dancing with ribbons and dressed as Japanese while their dancing teacher nodded in time to the music. 'The Royal Family wouldn't let there be war. Many of their foreign relatives come over here in great ships quite frequently for pleasure, and the Kaiser is often at Cowes.'

'Those ships could be turned into warships,' Archie commented. 'Have you seen our latest – the *Dreadnought?*'

'It looks big enough to mow down anything, like that barge did to poor Fred Cantor.' She recalled the awful day when Fred had been nearly crushed to death between a barge and the sea wall. By a lucky chance, Jane had been on the spot, and had reached down and held on to Fred's hand until help arrived, then she had staunched the blood from an artery in his thigh while Dr Barnes applied a rough tourniquet. The incident had occurred before Aaron had his stroke but it still made her shudder, and wonder why so many men had just stared until she gave them orders to fetch the doctor, and why it was her who ended up covered in Fred's blood! He still walked with crutches and she liked him no better then she had ever done, but resolved to ask after his health if Percy was as the social.

Across the room, Nellie was singing songs from *The Merry Widow* and Jane hardly recognised the girl in the neat dress with the modest neckline, her hair piled high and gleaming in a simple chignon. Her face was devoid of make-up and when her songs were done Jack brought her over to his mother. A juggling act took the attention of most people and only Mrs Barnes and Annie Cooper saw that Jane was talking to Nellie Stone.

'You have a lovely voice,' Jane said sincerely. She was pleasantly surprised. Nellie was certainly older than Jack but had the same easy manner and charm and a boldness that was oddly attractive. Two strong wills could get on, but it could go badly wrong. Sadly she realised that if she invited Nellie into the house, Walter would be furious, but Jack almost devoured her with his eyes. If they didn't marry soon, who knew what might happen? 'Have you made any arrangements, Jack?' she asked.

Nellie smiled. 'I'm going over to Portsmouth to friends for three weeks while the banns are called. Jack doesn't want to wait and we can be married a month from now, Mrs Darwen.'

'Jack has worked really hard on the cottage,' Archie said. 'When are you coming down to see it, Jane?'

'I'll come next week to visit Amy and I'll see it then,' Jane promised.

'I hope you come to the wedding,' Nellie said, and Jane sensed that it was important to her.

'I'll bring her if it's possible,' Archie assured her, 'but

you understand how it is?' Nellie nodded, having no illusions about Walter Darwen.

The Punch and Judy show was greeted with enthusiasm and Sidney seemed transformed as he concentrated on his art. He came to her breathless after the show, with eyes shining and Jane wanted to hug him close and keep him from leaving across that great ocean. Lucy Dove followed him shyly and put a hand on his arm. 'You were wonderful,' she said. Sidney smiled, gave her shoulder a friendly squeeze and turned to Percy Cantor, who asked him if he'd do the same show for the school treat. Jane blinked. She hadn't seen Percy for a long time, not since he and Jack fought over school, the Boer War or anything else that called for a bloody nose.

'Is Fred better?' she asked.

Percy shrugged. 'Drinks all night and grumbles all day and says he wishes you hadn't pulled him out of the river.' He eyed the red blouse. 'You ruined your clothes that day, Mrs Darwen. How did it feel to be covered with Cantor blood?'

'It washed out, like any other blood,' she replied evenly, but knew why he rubbed people up the wrong way and realised why Jack had fought him.

Jack smiled, seeing his own glint in her eyes. 'Are you coming to my wedding?' he asked. Percy nodded and Jane decided that she couldn't go against Walter's wishes. If the riff-raff from the Bugle were there, she would stay at home and hear about the wedding from Archie. Everywhere she looked, she saw her family. Lizzie was laughing with Harry, Sidney was packing up his equipment with Herbie and three pretty girls whom he ignored unless he wanted their help, and Janey was watching two young men in the white duck breeches and dark blue reefer jackets of Royal Navy midshipmen.

Clive Neville was laughing, his face creased with infectious humour. It was a good face, Jane decided, and saw that although they were far apart in the room, an invisible thread linked him with Janey – but of course, they met often when Janey was at Staplers with his family. I'm being fanciful, Jane thought. I shall believe that Clare is smitten by someone soon! She smiled, seeing Clare toss her head when the bank clerk offered her a cigarette. He was no knight on a white horse whom Clare would think worthy of her attention.

'I'll take Nell back as Archie will want to leave soon,' Jack said.

'I wish he would stay on at the farm,' Archie confided to Jane on the way back to the shop. 'Jack and I get on fine and I always wanted a son.'

'But he will stay! He's being married and has done up the cottage. Surely that's enough for a start!'

'He'll get restless and want to spread his wings further.'

'It's Nellie who might want more excitement. Singing is her lifeblood just as the stage is Sidney's. I like her but I can see that they might have their ups and downs,' said Jane. 'Fetch the mare, Archie, and I'll make tea. Walter isn't back yet.'

When Archie returned, she was wearing the old jumper over her blouse and pouring tea. I can't even offer my own son a cup of tea tonight, she thought sadly. Once he had left, Jack dared not set foot in the shop again while his father was there.

'Come down soon,' Archie said. 'Amy likes to talk to you and it does me good just to see you. Walter doesn't know how lucky he is.'

'Not as lucky as all that, my dear. If you asked him, he would say he wasn't lucky at all.'

'It would be enough just to hear your voice and smell that scent of roses.'

'That I can give,' said Jane, 'as well as loving friendship and help for Amy when she needs it. I shall come then, Archie.'

'If *you* need help, promise me that you will look no further than Wootton?' he asked tenderly.

'I promise, but when have you heard me asking for help, Archie?' She laughed. 'If I come running to you it will be about the horses or Walter or the business, but thank you all the same. It's good to know that you care. Ah, there's

Jack with the other horse and the trap. You'd best get the mare into the shafts before Walter sees Jack.'

Chapter 5

The motion of the ferry from Southampton to Cowes was sluggish and Jane Darwen felt queasy. The girls sat still and silent and Jack had gone to watch the vanishing shoreline fading into the mist.

'It's like the day when we went strawberry-picking with Aaron to Hamble,' Lizzie remembered. 'I felt sick until we reached open water, but I'm all right today.'

Jane said little except to tell them to button up their coats. This trip was as sad as the first time she had crossed the sea from Ireland as Walter's bride. The cedar-lined army chests on the troopship had been stacked neatly on deck, almost hidden by the more disorderly collection of belongings of the wives and families, and Jane had felt sick enough to die, but it was nothing to the agony she suffered now. The mournful note of the bell-buoy came clear through the mist and the lights along Southampton Water flickered as night fell.

'Do you think he really wanted to go?' asked Emily, snuggling up close for comfort.

'He knows it is right,' answered Jane, but the memory of her youngest son would be with her until the day she died, with his huge dark eyes dull with misery and his fine-drawn face pale and tight-lipped.

'It will be dark on the boat,' said Lizzie. 'Why did he have to go so late?'

'The ship sails on the morning tide,' Jane told her. It was impossible to imagine just how far he had to go, in good and bad weather, by day and night, until he reached America. 'Did you give him your biscuits, Janey?'

'I put them in a tin in case the boat was damp.'

'I gave him a new tie,' said Clare.

'I gave him pencils and paper,' Lizzie added. Jane smiled. In the days to come, she hoped he would be pleased by the small gifts she had hidden among his clothes, just as she had done for Walter when he left for the Boer War.

'I thought that Herbie would jump off the boat,' Clare remarked. 'He looked so frightened. Do you think Sidney is frightened?'

'Yes, a little but when he reaches New York he will be interested and busy and the feeling will pass.' Jane tried to sound cheerful. 'Everyone says America is the land of opportunity for young men of talent.' Tears could come later when she was alone, but now she was the centre of the family and the faces turned to her were the faces of children again, needing reassurance. Thank God they still needed her.

Sidney had looked smart and more like travelling gentry than a young man out to seek his fortune. By now he might have opened the letter she had told him to keep until they had said goodbye and he was alone. It might comfort him even if he had the companionship of Herbie and several others going from the town. In it she told him that she had hidden, sewn inside his waistcoat, twenty golden sovereigns that he must keep for when he was in need. She blessed all the years of jam-making and pickle-bottling that had earned her good pin money, kept carefully without Walter knowing how much she had. When Walter had turned on the boy at last, calling him a bloody pansy, she had started to sew, one at a time, the money that could buy her son freedom.

Soon after that, Sidney had come home with papers and told her that he had a passage booked. Walter then admitted that the lad had more spunk than he gave him credit for, and in a mood softened by beer and before he once again lost his temper, had handed Sidney far more money than Jane had dared hope for. Now she knew her son could exist for a long time, even if he found no work.

'We can write to him and he'll send us letters with funny stamps,' Lizzie said, more cheerful now that the ferry was docking.

Walter had refused to come to Southampton, saying that someone must see to the shop and he had a man to meet about a contract of bricks. He hinted that there were enough of them to say goodbye to a lad who was leaving his country just when there might be another war.

In the winter of 1913, the politicians of Germany and Great Britain exchanged verbal threats like neighbours disagreeing over a garden wall. The Kaiser was lampooned and dubious tales spread about him. His arm, withered at birth, gave him a sense of inferiority, and now that King George was the monarch of England, with none of Queen Victoria's awe-inspiring majesty, he could make mischief. Shipyards rang with the sound of heavy saws and hammers, the docks showed signs of increased activity and pleasure boats gave way to more sinister grey outlines in the harbours.

Jack came back to the others. 'It's too dark to see now and we're nearly home,' he said. 'What a life, eh? Lucky old Sidney.'

'Married men like you can't do that,' said Lizzie, shocked to think he envied his brother. 'You've a wife and the farm to look after!'

'I know.' He moved restlessly. 'All the same, it's a great adventure.' He teased them. 'Why don't we all go? Get on the next boat and surprise him. Imagine his face if he saw us just when he'd thought to see the last of us!'

'We couldn't go, not without Father and he'd never leave home,' said Emily stoutly.

'No, just me and Nellie and the baby when it comes,' Jack said. 'Nellie wanted to come today but I didn't want her stomach upset, and I didn't want my son to be born in Southampton even if I had to get married there.' Jane relaxed. Marriage might be the making of him. He was devoted to Nellie and worked hard on the farm, anxious about the baby and more settled than he'd ever been before. A first grandchild! It was life starting all over again, and Nellie had no family of her own to care for her and the baby.

'Have you named the day yet?' Jack asked Lizzie, knowing that Harry was content as things were. 'Let me know and I'll hang up a white flag of truce if Father will let me come to the wedding.' Jane saw that he was half-serious. 'If we do turn up, do you think he'll speak to us, Mother? If he doesn't, he'll never see a hair of my son.'

'It's time you made it up,' she replied. 'I'll do what I can but I'll have to choose my time as he's very touchy.'

Jack shrugged. 'If it wasn't for Nellie and the baby, I'd be on that boat.' He laughed. 'No, perhaps not that one; it's going the wrong way. When I go it will be to Australia. There are lots of sheep there and I get on with animals.'

While they were walking to the station after alighting from the ferry, Jane caught up with a woman in a dark coat whose eyes were red with weeping. 'It's Mrs Peachey, isn't it? You went to see off your sons, didn't you?'

'Yes. Now it's just me and the girl left – all the rest are gone.'

'Mabel stayed with you?'

'She has a sweetheart here but on the ship she wanted to change her mind and go with the others. She clung to the rail and cried but she had no papers and no passage booked and had to be sent off.'

'She can go later after they marry, and take you too,' Jane said gently.

'I could never go that far. Who would look after the graves down at Sea Close? I was born here and I'll stay here and die soon, please God.'

'That's wicked talk. Mabel will need you when the babies come.'

'They'll all be gone, all the young 'uns when the war comes. Your Sidney may be the lucky one, to get out now. Didn't Walter come with you today?' Mrs Peachey straightened her shoulders and put away the black-edged handkerchief reserved for mourning.

'He had to stay at the shop. The talk of war and his work with the recruits keep him happy enough, but now that so many are leaving, I think he remembers South Africa and is a bit envious of them all. Anyway, he hates goodbyes,' Jane explained.

'Sometimes I wonder just what did go on out there in the war when the old lady was alive. It wasn't *all* fighting and sickness.' The woman chuckled. 'Some brought back a few things they'd rather not have, and I don't doubt that some women over there landed up with little packages.' She eyed Jane with respect. 'Your Walter came back whole, of course, and there's never been a breath of scandal against him.'

'I'm lucky,' Jane agreed, but wondered why she too felt the impulse to follow Sidney into a new world. She could do without adventure, but everything was dwindling away and soon her family would be split for ever.

'You'll soon have enough on your plate with Nellie's baby and your own family. How is Alice now?'

'Better. She nearly died last year after eating a bag of sweets given her by the Dutch family on the barges, but now she knows that sweets are poison to her she's been very good.' Jane tried to forget Walter urging Alice to eat 'just one more' and then another as if he wanted her to suffer, and his derision when Jane asked furiously if he wanted to kill her.

'She'll go soon,' he'd bawled, 'so why make her linger? Edward could marry again and have a bit of comfort. I suppose you'll go running to Barnes now and tell him it's all my fault she's ill! Can't you keep away from him? I like my family to be private!' Walter had slammed out of the shop then to join his army friends who were common and lewd, leaving Jane shivering with misery in the back room.

'I want to go with them,' wailed Mabel as they reached the train to Newport.

'Should have thought of that afore,' Mrs Peachey said with an air of finality. 'Come on, gal, we'll have a cup of tea when we get home.'

The crowded train was quiet, and many women were still weeping as they knew they might never see their children again.

Jack stayed on the train that went on to Wootton from Newport station. 'We are a house of women now,' said Jane, 'but maybe Nellie will have a boy.' It might make all the difference to Walter: he had been good when the babies were small.

'He's gone, then?' Walter said when they opened the door. He looked at Jane's stern face, dry-eyed and proud. 'You'll say I drove him away, I suppose.'

Jane peeled off her gloves. 'Not entirely. All men need to leave home. It's only natural.'

'That's all that's natural about that one,' Walter muttered.

'I don't know what you mean and he's gone now,' Jane said flatly. 'The girls are hungry. Have you had your supper, Walter?'

'I made do. You didn't worry about me so long as you could see your dear little boy on the boat.'

Jane answered gravely, 'You enjoyed your pie at the Wheatsheaf, I hope? I went in and told Mrs Grace to save one of Mrs Bell's pies and I know they are good.' She hid a smile and he stumped off to let Alice into the shop.

'I heard the train,' Alice said. 'Edward told me you'd have no time to cook today so I brought you some savoury ducks when I fetched mine. The peas are underneath.' She held out a basin of the firmly packed pig's fry, cooked in balls wrapped in pig caul and covered in thick gravy, bought from the pie ship in Pyle Street.

'That was really kind.' Jane blushed with pleasure.

'Do you think they'll give Sidney any supper tonight?' asked Emily, nearly in tears.

'Hard tack!' said Walter firmly. 'Hard tack and water and a bit of salt beef.'

'What nonsense! The food is better now and tonight he won't starve. I packed up fresh bread and cheese and smoked mackerel. Would you begrudge your own son a bit of food on a long voyage because you had bad food when you were in the army?' Jane asked, her glinting eyes forbidding his usual tale about weevils in the biscuits as if it had been her fault. 'You're rid of him now, Walter. None of us may see him again.' A drip of gravy flowed down on to the clean cloth. If I weep now, the whole family will suffer and make this a house of mourning, she decided, and kept the tears away until she could escape to the privy and give vent to her sorrow. 'Edward came in his uniform as it was only a step from the station,' she added cheerfully. 'He's easier in his mind now you are better, Alice.'

Walter knocked the spent tobacco from his pipe and put it on the mantelpiece, muttering a 'Goodnight' and left them to finish supper. The pipe was warm and Jane ached with fresh grief. Walter smoked a pipe only at times of great stress and sorrow, like when baby Caroline died, when he had to go to the war and when Jane nearly died. On her way to bed, she paused by the door of his room then went on. It wouldn't do to comfort him now, even if he would ever admit that he still loved his son.

She heard the wind rise. 'Holy Mary have mercy. Dear God look after Sidney and keep him safe.' She tried to forget what old Mrs Lee had prophesied: she had been right about Edward, and her voice came from the grave now. '*One will go across the sea and you will lose him.*' Jane turned in bed restlessly. What of my wild boy, Jack? A baby in a week or so might tame him. She closed her eyes. A baby was a wonderful tie and a blessing, but Nellie might be lonely now that the doctor forbade her to sit and chat to Amy, for fear of contagion. Only another week or so, and the baby would be born.

'Mother has been gone a long time,' Lizzie said. 'Shall we start tea? I wonder if they've called the doctor.'

'Yes, get the tea, gal. I can do with a cup and so can Harry after all that talk,' Walter added resentfully, beginning to think he could have too much of Harry's company on a Sunday.

'As I was saying,' Harry went on relentlessly, 'they've fitted the very latest wireless telegraphy to the new boat launched from White's.'

'What's the use of that if the batteries run out? You'll be glad of the old morse code and heliograph.'

'Morse and flags can't be seen in fog and the enemy can read morse just as we can so it isn't safe,' Harry retorted smugly.

'We've enough of those contraptions up at the Barracks,' Walter replied – thinks he knows everything, does he? 'They rigged up motor vans full of the stuff with enough wire to scare the birds even if the enemy aren't. One mortar bomb and you'd be back to flags and mirrors!'

'Harry went all over the ship. Tell Father about it,' said Lizzie, with pride.

'It's all iron-clad with revolving turrets and oil-burning engines capable of twenty-five knots.'

'What guns do they carry?' Walter asked, interested in spite of his disparaging remarks.

'Eight fifteen-inch guns made of lighter but stronger metal that the scientists have discovered, so that the ship can carry more men and supplies. The oil is easier and cleaner to store than coal.'

'Oil? That can go up in smoke if the ship's attacked. What's wrong with coal? They'd never use submarines with those torpedoes the Germans boast about.' Walter got up to put more coke on the fire.

'Do you think they've sent for the doctor?' fretted Lizzie, ignoring their talk.

'Doctor Barnes said the baby wasn't due for another week, but he wrote to the doctor at Wootton to take over, just in case,' Janey said. The train whistled over the iron bridge but ten minutes later there was no familiar footstep so they knew that Jane was still at Wootton. 'If there is news, the doctor there will telephone Doctor Barnes, and they promised to bring us a message.'

'Him or young Mr Barnes?' Walter asked with a grin.

'Alex is back in Dartmouth,' Janey said shortly, and wished her father would stop making heavy remarks about Alex Barnes when she had no feelings for him apart from friendship.

Lizzie poured tea and made the most of the tiny diamond in the broad gold band that was her engagement ring. She was disappointed that the others paid no attention to it. It might be nice to be married and use the pretty tea service that Jane had bought for her birthday. The pile of linen in her bottom drawer was becoming impressive but Harry seemed in no haste to take her away from her family. He came each week and talked of his work and the coming war and lately he had said he didn't want children yet and couldn't they wait a little longer before they married? It was all Nellie's fault, Lizzie decided spitefully. If she hadn't been caught so soon after marriage Harry wouldn't have thought about babies and drawn back.

'Where is she?' Walter poked the fire yet again and looked distracted. 'Your mother's place is here with her family, not gallivanting off on her own to Wootton!' He watched Janey clear away but leave a plate of soda bread and cakes for Jane if she came in hungry.

'She's needed there,' Janey said quietly. 'Nellie has no mother of her own and Jack was very worried. It's only natural that Mother should want to see her first grandchild.'

'Her first *what*?' Walter stared as if the relationship was impossible.

'*Your* first grandchild, too, Father.' Had he grown so completely self-centred and resentful over Jack's marriage that it meant nothing?

'I think I'll go now,' Harry said, suspecting that storm clouds were gathering in the warm living room.

'I'll walk you to the station,' Lizzie said. 'We might meet the next train and I shall be the first to hear the news!' She glanced triumphantly at Clare, who never walked with them as she made fun of Harry behind his back and said he was boring.

'I can wait,' said Clare. 'It's either a girl or a boy and makes no difference to me.' She moved her head to make the side curls spring and smoothed the sleek dark bun in the nape of her neck. 'I'm going for a walk too. I said I'd call in to see a friend.'

Emily took out her crochet and the pattern, trying to follow the instructions for turning a corner, and asked Janey to help her. 'I can cook, but all that is foreign to me,' Janey admitted. 'You seem to have the knack, though.' She watched Clare come downstairs wearing her best coat with the fur collar and the hat newly-trimmed with poppies. 'Isn't it a bit late in the year for flowers?' she observed, and Clare looked annoyed. 'I suppose Joseph Manning said he likes flowers,' she added wickedly.

'Other people have admired them,' Clare said. 'You don't suppose I care what he thinks, do you?'

'I think he's very nice,' Janey said. She giggled. 'Hurry up or you'll be late meeting him!'

Clare walked through the shop past the boxes of Christmas fruit and the tangerines covered with silver paper. A fresh block of pressed dates gleamed in the background and the shop smelled clean and inviting. She went out into the darkening evening with no fear of the empty streets, and walked quickly to the Town Hall and past the Victoria Memorial where the marketplace met the High Street. A man slipped off one of the horizontal bars that flanked the market and came towards her. 'You managed to get away then,' said Joseph Manning.

Clare walked with Joseph along by the Drill Hall and on to the path by Priory Fields. 'They were far too busy worrying about Nellie and the baby to wonder about me,' Clare said, laughing.

'Has the baby come?' Clare saw the gleam of white teeth and thought that although there would be better fish in the sea, Joseph was quite good-looking. He sounded almost as concerned as the family. 'Perhaps something is wrong as your mother is still there.'

'Nellie is strong,' Clare said carelessly. 'She'll breed like a rabbit.' She sensed a moving away, physically and mentally, so added hastily, 'Or that's what I try to think now we're worried.'

They walked and ate the grapes she had brought, spitting the pips into the blank hedgerows, then Clare threw the empty paper bag into the ditch. Joseph dusted a seat with his glove. 'Let's sit here,' he said. 'It's not very cold and I'll keep you warm.' His arm slid across her shoulders and held her in a firm and very masculine way, and when he turned her face to his and kissed her, Clare was more responsive than she thought possible. Her eyes closed under the spell of his warm but disciplined passion and he held her tightly in a close embrace.

'We shouldn't,' she whispered.

'Why not? You know how I feel about you. Lizzie is

getting married so why not you? You are twins so a double wedding would be wonderful.'

Clare gasped. It was like this on the films, but in more glamorous settings than on a hard wooden seat at the back of the bonemeal factory on a cold night! She felt cheated. Joseph ought to tell her first that she was beautiful and he couldn't live without her, instead of hugging her with the comfortable familiarity of an old friend and nibbling the lobe of her ear as if she were a grape.

'I do love you, Clare, and I can provide everything you want. I don't want to rush you, though. We don't have to be married before Christmas – what about Easter?'

That was better but not good enough. I need time to meet more exciting men, she thought and recoiled from the trap she saw opening before her. 'Give me time,' she said melodramatically. 'I must think it over.'

'We might go to war. I want to marry you before I get called to the flag.'

'You aren't a soldier! You aren't even a Terrier and we are safe from war; a lot of people say so. The papers just print things to frighten us.'

'They are building ships as fast as they can in Cowes and new factories have been made to be switched to munitions when war breaks out. And why are people like your father still training recruits at this time of the year, in camp?' Clare was alarmed at the firmness of his voice. 'I'm in the bank and know which firms have borrowed money to expand and to which firms the government has given orders. A lot of people will make a great deal of money if war comes. Your father will do very well if he leaves his shares where they are, but I mustn't tell you details as the work is confidential.'

'Bert Cooper will make money,' she said.

'Who wants to talk of Bert Cooper?' he said, kissing her again.

It would be nice to be a child bride as the magazines described, Clare dreamed as she rested in the warm embrace . . . marriage in the spring wearing a wreath of flowers and her hair down on her shoulders and a pretty sprigged muslin dress instead of more formal clothes. On the other hand, she had seen a wedding at the parish church when the bride had a huge hat with sweeping plumes and softly draped tulle with a flattering veil over her face. The dress was a two-tiered tunic edged with fringing and the gloves were dove-grey calf.

'We'd better go back – it's getting colder,' said Joseph, his words breaking into her thoughts. 'I expect you are eager to know if you are an aunt.'

'An aunt?' The vision of a child bride stepping out on to a carpet of rose petals faded. 'Yes, it's cold,' she snapped and avoided his goodnight kiss, and when he hinted that she might ask him to tea one day, pretended not to understand. It was too bad of Jack to make her an aunt!

'You'll pop into the bank tomorrow and tell me if the baby came?' he asked when she insisted on being left by the corner of Sea Street and no nearer to the shop.

'I'll tell you,' she promised, and slipped away. The back room was brightly lit and Clare knew that her father had settled in there for the evening. She passed through and up to her room, taking off her hat as she went. She glanced in the mirror: some said that once a girl had been kissed in a certain way it showed in her face. When she came downstairs, Emily was in the scullery and Walter fast asleep in the chair. Clare picked up a book as if she had been there for ages and heard the train slowing at the station, but thought little of it until the door opened and to her horror, she saw Joseph with her mother.

'Joseph was very kind,' Jane said. 'I hate Sea Street after dark but it does save time, and he insisted on walking home with me.' She took the pin from her hat and smiled. 'He heard the train after he left you and wondered if I'd be on it and waited.' Clare bit her lip. Now they all knew that she was walking out with Joseph Manning.

'Nellie had a girl,' Jane went on. 'A lovely little girl, praise God. It was difficult but they are both fine, just fine.' She beamed and looked young and excited. Walter yawned and opened his eyes. 'Nellie has a baby girl,' Jane repeated. 'It's difficult to say who she's like as babies all have blue eyes and her hair is still wet, the dear little thing.'

Walter gathered his wits. 'Well, let's hope she takes after neither of them,' he said heavily, and went off to bed.

'You'll have a cup of tea, Joseph?' asked Janey, already pouring it from a fresh pot.

'I'd like that very much,' he replied firmly. Emily brought out bread and cheese and soda bread and jam, and Jane said she was starving.

'There was no time for food,' she explained happily, 'and I wanted to catch the last train. Help yourself, Joseph. It's very nice to have you at our table at last.' Clare busied herself cutting bread, avoiding his reproachful gaze. Now he knew that she had lied when she said that her family didn't approve of the girls taking friends home with them.

'Did you give her the binders?' Janey asked.

'Wasn't it lucky I had them with me! She's very slack and needed a tight one and the dear little flannel belly binders for the baby came in just right. I sewed her into one and they can leave it until the midwife wants to see the cord stump.' Jane's eyes sparkled. 'I'm sorry to make you hear such details, Joseph. I know that men aren't usually interested in such matters,' she added as an apology for Walter's indifference.

'I'm fascinated, Mrs Darwen. I'm an only child and always wanted to be in a big family. I would like several children,' he said, looking at Clare, who reddened and went to the scullery for more plates. He stayed for half an hour and Jane thanked him again warmly and told him that he was welcome at any time.

'Why haven't you brought him home before, Clare?'

'He's only a friend and if I brought him here everyone would think we were really walking out and about to be married.' She wiped a plate and wrung the dishcloth with venom. 'I don't want to marry anyone yet.'

'Girls do marry young, and if war comes, you might be glad to be married. It's a comfort to be loved and to have a man about the house and a family growing,' Jane said seriously.

'I don't really like babies. When I look after Mrs Minn's

family they are noisy and smelly and dribble all over my bodice.'

Jane dried her hands. 'Never bring a child into the world that you can't love, Clare. If that's the case, you'd better wait until you are sure, but don't be a tease and lead that poor young man on.'

Chapter 6

George Foster was puffed up with pride. 'I volunteered when they asked for a representative from the Council and it's my duty to go.' Walter Darwen looked annoyed. Trust George to be first with the bit of news about the drumming-out ceremony at Albany Barracks. George would stand on the dais, wearing white gloves, while Walter shepherded his men on the outer fringe; they were raw recruits best kept away from the attention of the inspecting officers and gentry. 'There's going to be war, you know,' George fussed, as if that was real news.

'Well, you needn't get your notebooks out yet,' Walter replied acidly. 'I know the rumours and my son-in-law who has a very important job at Cowes told me about the work they're hurrying up there.' He edged closer as if sharing a confidence. 'They've built seventy-four submarines in various shipyards and thirty more are on the stocks. Admiral Percy Scott says that Germany will use submarines to torpedo our shipping and we must be prepared. Now, that's a *fact*!' he said when George looked impressed. 'When it comes to facts, you ask Walt Darwen. I've the right contacts and could tell you a thing or two not generally known.' He tapped the side of his nose and looked solemn. It was easy to forget that he was never really pleased when Harry came with such snippets of news, and he saw no reason to thank him for the information.

'Doctor Barnes told me about the aeroplanes,' George said, to even matters up. 'He's a full member of the Royal Flying Corps now and has a licence to fly. Do you know they have parachutes, things like huge umbrellas they strap on men's backs when in those observation balloons in case the things catch fire and the men have to jump for it? Doctor Barnes said that they will use them in aircraft as well, when they fight in the air. The balloons are made in a place called the Royal Aircraft Factory.'

Walter grunted. Perhaps he'd better collect his own indigestion mixture in future and hear the news at the surgery. 'Are you sure you are up to the ceremony?' he asked maliciously. 'Some men faint or are as sick as dogs.'

'They don't hurt him, do they?' George paled.

'Depends what you mean by hurt,' and Walter refused to say more. He had seen similar ceremonies in South Africa when soldiers were dismissed from the service, cashiered for dereliction of duty, a criminal offence or immorality, stripped of all rank and drummed out of the Barracks during a service in full view of the public and various dignitaries.

'Must you go?' Jane asked anxiously when he went back for dinner and to change into uniform. 'It's a terrible thing to do to any man and I never want to see it again, although I caught only a glimpse before.' It was no day for standing in a cold Barrack square, let alone seeing that terrible happening. 'Put on the thick vest I left on your bed,' she urged.

'Expecting company?' he asked as he saw Jane clear the table and lay fresh plates and cups.

'Nellie is bringing the baby. They'll be gone before you come back,' she added tartly, but her face softened. 'Walter, she's such a dear little thing and I think I see a bit of you in her. You were always fond of the little ones and you'd soon grow to love her.'

'I'll see her when I'm good and ready,' he said and went to fetch Blackie who was still a smart horse and sat him well. In February 1914, the signs of war were there and only wanted a match to the paper to send the whole affair sky high. I could go again, he thought with satisfaction. Not to Pretoria, but out to the other British dominions in Africa: they'd need men like me with my record.

A keen wind scoured the Barrack square and bent the bare skeletons of the poplars against the cold sky. The uncompromising starkness of the buildings showed no pity, as if there was no heart, no hope there for the man about to be drummed out. The band struck up a march and the first of the units of infantry came across to their places. Horsemen followed with officers on well-polished mounts to make up the full complements. The civic group turned up, out of step and conscious of their unmilitary bearing. Walter grinned. They had been like that the day he returned from the Boer War and had to listen to the rubbish they said before he could even kiss his wife.

But why think of her as she was that day, when now he was here to witness the disgrace of a non-commissioned officer in the Regulars? He flexed his right hand in the gauntlet glove and found it stiff. He flexed and unflexed it a few times and although he could still grip the reins his hand had suddenly lost all sensation. He exercised it again. The day was cold and he had obviously held the leather too tightly. Gradually the feeling returned and Walter breathed freely. It wouldn't do to collapse with cold on parade!

The band stopped playing and then began a slow march. From the Barracks came a small procession consisting of the prisoner, his escort and an officer preceding them. A sword flashed in salute to the dais and a much-decorated senior officer descended as the drum began a relentless slow roll.

An NCO saluted and the indictment and judgement was read in a hoarse and unintelligible voice. The prisoner stepped forward. His cap with the badge of his regiment was removed, the flashes on the shoulders of his uniform were ripped away and every button in turn slashed until all sign of rank disappeared. The drum began again, slowly with the sinister regularity and precision of a metronome. The escort of four each seized a limb and held the prisoner face down. As slow as fate, the drum beat a way to the Barrack gates where a crowd waited to watch the man frog-marched out of the army, drummed out of his regiment with ignominy. There was only the beat of the drum, no music, and only the tread of the escort in time and step and the grunt of the man who tried to keep from crying out and to maintain a shred of dignity in an effort not to soil his trousers. Walter shut his eyes. In time of war the man would have been shot for that indictment.

The crowd melted away, ashamed of being a part in these proceedings, and Walter dismissed his men and set Blackie for home, over the frosty hill down to the town, aloof and seeing nobody even when people greeted him by name. He was cold and needed comfort: he needed Jane's warm arms and tender words as if he had suffered that gross humiliation himself. He swore softly. The woman in Portsmouth gave physical release but nothing more. It was early and he needed to think. He took Blackie back to the stable and thawed out in the animal warmth. He loosened his tunic and pulled hay down into the rack while Marigold snickered softly to greet Blackie. A load of hay had been delivered in a mess and he stacked it, glad of the exercise. The smell was a breath of summer in the cold grey day.

Halfway through his task, he sat on a bale of hay to get his breath then looked over the half-door. The river was in full flood but on the ebb, and a solitary figure sat on a capstan as if waiting for a barge. He saw Maudie Dove stand up and shiver, stamping her feet to keep warm. There were two boats tied up, a Norwegian timber boat now awaiting ballast of gravel and cement and chalk while the crew slept away for a break, and a French boat just leaving. Whoever was late coming into harbour had lost the flood and could be caught on a sandbank if they tried to leave the estuary now. It must be the Dutch boat with a father and two sons on board who came to Newport regularly. He grinned. Maudie wasn't there in the cold to buy a Dutch cheese!

She looked down the river for the last time and her shoulders drooped. She saw Walter watching her and raised a timid hand. If he was in one of his moods he would refuse to recognise her, even if she went into the shop.

Poor little trollop, he thought and impulsively called to her, 'Want a few duck eggs for Lucy?' She wouldn't get anything from the boats now and her widow's pension and the bit she earned at the laundry didn't go far.

'Thank you, Mr Darwen. I was wondering what to have for tea. Mrs Darwen gave me a nice bit of skate yesterday but I'm a bit short until my pension comes.'

'Take this basket and you can have any they've laid outside the run. I'll have to fix it as the fox got in one night and they lay away.' He almost regretted his gesture but thought of Lucy, only a little younger than Emily, his favourite child. What chance had she of a good life with such a mother? He couldn't bolt the stable until she had gone so he began to clean the tack. The lamp gave out heat and he hissed through his teeth as ostlers do and found the same satisfaction in the rhythm of cleaning as a child does when running a cane along railings, or humming to match the rumble of wheels.

Maudie pushed open the half-door. 'I found eight,' she said. 'Can I take four?'

'Take the lot. The ducks are laying well and we've far too many. I'll kill off some of the old ones and my wife can make potted meat. It keeps well under a layer of duck fat.'

'I know, Mr Darwen, I've tasted it. I think she's ever so clever.' She came further into the stable. 'It's nice and warm here.' She held her hands out over the lamp and Walter went on polishing the harness. The light shone upwards in a circle of rose and gold making the young woman's pale cheeks soft and translucent. Her hands were slender and her fingernails trimmed and she enjoyed the warmth with a child's sensual delight, relishing the moment and giving no thought to the bitter wind outside, and the fact that she would be cold again in five minutes.

'How are you off for coke?' Walter asked abruptly.

'We'll be down to driftwood if the weather stays cold,' she answered.

'And Lucy? Is she over that chill?' He recalled that Jane had sent soup and fish along for the girl when she hadn't turned up to serve in the shop.

'I make her stay in bed until the fire is lit,' Maudie said, with no hint of whining or begging, partly because she knew this man thought she was dirt and partly because she resented having to accept so many favours from his family. However, she eyed the fine eggs with anticipation and saw no reason for refusing anything offered. 'I can earn my keep and enough for Lucy,' she added. She sat on a bale of hay and watched the silver emerge from the chamois leather as Walter held up a bridle to inspect it. He gave a short laugh of satisfaction. 'It all looks so bright and clean,' Maudie said, and smiled more naturally. 'But soldiers are like that. You must have seen many sights in South Africa where my poor Ben died.'

'He died for his country, Maudie,' Walter said, but wondered what Jane would have done if he had died, too. She could have managed quite well without him, he decided bitterly, but this poor little slut hadn't the spunk or knowledge to do more than survive. She looked at him as if expecting an oracle to speak and although she was common, she was pretty and cleaner than most. She looked like the kind of woman who respected a man and knew her place. 'Some die fighting like your Ben, some live to tell the tale if anyone will listen, like me, and some go bad as that poor devil today.'

'I wondered why you were in uniform. You look very smart.' She opened her purse to take out a handkerchief as the warmth made the tip of her nose moist and Walter thought that she was moved by what he said. He leaned closer. She was quite a tasty bit in the dim light.

'If war comes, they'll need me again,' he said. 'Do you think I'm past it, Maudie?'

'You're the smartest man in Newport,' she told him without the respect she usually showed. She opened her purse again to discard the handkerchief and Walter clumsily took it, to drop a half-sovereign inside.

'Take it for coke,' he said. 'Lucy needs warmth, and we've got plenty.' Maudie made a feeble attempt to pull the purse away and refuse, and the contents spilled on to the hay. She blushed crimson as Walter picked up a small package and grinned.

'I carry it in case,' she said defiantly. 'My friend is on the boats and we may get married one day.'

'But he likes a slice or two to be going on with?' Walter felt his loins tightening. Maudie, looking confused and strangely innocent, was not like the whores he had known, nor like the woman in Pretoria. He read aloud the printed words. '*Mother's Help and Friend.* Very fitting. Do they make a man sore?' She shook her head. 'So that's why you don't take!' He tossed the package over to her, envying the man for whom she had waited in the cold.

'I'm putting away the harness and filling the trough. I've to lock up the ducks and fowls and have a look at Marigold as she's likely to foal soon.' Maudie looked at him in silence. 'I have to go home and have my tea late as my son thinks he can dump his wife and infant on us whenever he likes, and then I may go to the Bugle. Tonight I shall go to bed alone as usual.' He hung up the harness. 'If you aren't out of here before I finish, I might forget what I am in this town, Maudie.' He smiled grimly. 'I can't afford a breath of scandal, so get out of here and back to that gal of yourn, and take the eggs.'

When she'd gone, Walter filled the troughs and looked up at the bleak sky. That man today had suffered, slung inches above the cold mud as they carried him and now, what comfort was there for Walter Darwen? Jane would never come back to him after the way he had treated her, even if she used pessaries like Maudie's, and he couldn't go with her after taking whores. Bert had been scared last month and the doctor had cleared up whatever it was, but the danger was still there. He put his head against the flank of the mare and felt the tense life within. Was every living thing able to enjoy life but him? Even Lizzie might enjoy the marriage bed once she was over the shock! He hung the bucket on a nail and had almost forgotten Maudie. He couldn't go home yet, though. Nellie might still be there and he would have to wait for a while.

In the stable, he saw a movement and peered into the hay. Last week there'd been a rat there and Bert's terrier had caught it, but there might be more. Transfixed, he saw Maudie, half-reclining on the hay, her bodice undone. She smiled and put up her arms. Walter sank down beside her. Her skirt was almost up to her thighs and her hips curved on the soft couch that smelled of summer. 'You unwrapped it and they only go soft,' she whispered. 'A pity to waste it,

I thought.' She pushed him away. 'First bolt the door and put out the lamp.'

Chapter 7

'It must be the spring!' Jane didn't know whether to laugh or cry. 'You said only last week that you wanted to wait.'

'There's no point in waiting now,' Harry said firmly. 'Lizzie is ready and so am I. You won't be losing a daughter, you'll gain a son.' Jane smiled weakly. Harry French might be a good engineer but he had not a single original thought in his head and it was as well that Lizzie admired his platitudes. 'We thought Whitsun would be nice,' he went on, and Jane wondered what Walter would say when he came back from the stables. He spent a lot of time there these days, taking over Jack's work and seeming content to see to all the animals.

'Father spoke quite nicely to Jack at the market, so he will be able to come, but Sidney won't be here,' Emily said sadly. 'He's been gone such a long time and still we haven't heard, but Mabel Peachey has had a letter from her brothers. They had to move away from New York as there was no work there.'

'Young men alone travel fast,' Jane said. 'We'll hear once he's settled down.' She closed her mind to all the disasters awaiting immigrants in a new country and hoped Sidney was strong enough to resist the pressures.

'No news is good news,' Harry contributed, and Lizzie beamed.

'I shall be married in a hobble skirt.' Lizzie glanced at her mother to see her reaction. 'They make them shorter now to show off soft button boots and spat tops.'

'You'll trip,' warned Clare. 'It takes practice to wear one of those. I saw Mrs Barnes in one and she had to walk very slowly even with a split in the back of the skirt.' Jane closed her mouth and the girls smiled, wickedly. If the doctor's wife wore anything, it must be respectable! 'I shall have a hat with crossed birds' wings on the front,' Clare announced. 'What will you wear, Mother?'

'Mrs Darwen looks smart at all times. She is an example to you all,' Harry pontificated and Jane wished she felt more flattered. If the weather was fine at the end of May, Miss Joyner could run up something in the lighter fabrics on sale for summer.

'You'd look well in a tunic dress, Mother. Mrs Neville wore one of pink and mauve to the Passing Out Parade and looked very smart,' Janey said.

'So young Clive Neville will be on his first real ship of the line,' Harry said, as if he had been at the parade and knew it all.

'When they got home in all their finery, he nearly tripped over his sword,' Janey said, giggling.

'Too busy looking at you,' Harry said with heavy humour. Janey blushed and went into the shop as if she heard a customer, then slipped back to prepare tea and cut bread.

'Where's all the money coming from if you want so much?' Jane asked with growing irritation. Walter might be fond of his daughter but he wouldn't waste money on fripperies. She had noticed how Harry eyed the silver tea service and good china that came out at Christmas and special occasions and wondered if he thought he was marrying into a well-to-do-family!

'We could take the chapel hall, and *Baine's* cake shop do a lovely spread,' Harry said. 'You'd want the best for Lizzie.'

'And who do you think would fill that hall? I'm not asking the whole of Newport to see Lizzie wed!' Jane wondered why they were in such a hurry so suddenly, and gasped as she thought why haste might be needed. Janey shook her head, and as so often happened, an unspoken message flowed between them.

'Come into the shop, Mother,' Janey whispered, and laughed when they were alone. 'It's simpler than that. Harry wants to be married before war breaks out. He heard at White's that all the unmarried men will be conscripted first. He has nothing to worry about, though, as Clive said that all aircraft workers and shipyard engineers will not be *allowed* to enlist. Those are reserved occupations and Harry is a good engineer.'

'Poor Harry. Lizzie thinks he just can't wait for her any longer.' Jane giggled. 'I hope she gets that ring on her finger before he finds out. Edward might be safe too, as he says the sidings are full of rolling stock in readiness for a sudden need and his work is important. It may not come, but I'm glad that Sidney is safe and Jack is tied to the farm.'

'So long as he remembers that he has a wife and baby and keeps away from the enlistment booths,' Janey said quietly. 'He's like Father and will do what he wants to do.'

'I feel sorry for the mothers of young Regulars,' Jane stated.

'I wish I was a nurse,' Janey said wistfully.

'I often envied the women who went out to the last war, but there was too much to do here. They had servants to look after their families.'

'The lucky ones had a mother at home to cope as you did,' Janey said warmly. 'I've met some people who have never had family love. We managed when Father was away and could do even better now that Emily and I are older.'

Jane smiled. 'It couldn't happen again, love. Your father would want horses and mules, and the cavalry is not used as much now they have motors. They'd say he was too old.'

'I think Jack might go,' Janey said slowly. 'Nellie was in Newport the other day at the Bugle, showing off the baby to the customers. She stayed until after opening time and even played a few songs. Then Victoria began to cry and Mr Morris drove them to the station in that big car to catch the train.'

'Holy Mary! And where was Jack?'

'Out the back of Wight buying sheep,' Janey said.

'There'll be murder done if he finds out,' Jane predicted. 'He forbade Nellie to go back to the Bugle and said the mother of his child would never sing for common tipplers again.' She composed her face. 'Sure it was just a mother's pride that made her want to show the baby. Haven't we all done that?'

'You didn't play for men in a public bar, Mother. She

bought one of those Tango dresses with the low neck and a slip of a skirt, and she taught Mr Morris to do the dance.'

'Is she mad?' Jane heard movements beyond the door to the living room. 'They're coming out. Now don't tell another soul – and please God make Jack deaf and blind.'

The front door opened to let Harry and the glowing bride-elect out. Harry came more and more frequently and ate enough for four, making Jane wonder if he ate anything between visits. The small house they would rent was cosy and convenient and although Lizzie could cook plain fare and make bread, he would miss the lavish table at the shop on Coppins Bridge.

Walter came into the shop, frowning. He slammed the door and glared. 'What's happening all of a sudden? Church Hall indeed! Busy spending my money as soon as my back's turned?'

'You met them? Harry didn't waste much time, did he. He told me what he wanted and I said they'd have a few friends back here after the church and no church hall or a caterer!'

'So he went above your head? That one has a mean streak,' Walter said more calmly. 'Lizzie is like him, selfish to the core, so they might deserve each other!' He put the eggs basket on the table. 'Not many today but they laid away again. That foal will have to go to Wootton. I can't swing a cat in the stable.'

'You have brought half the hay with you,' said Jane, picking bits from his coat.

He moved away. 'I saw Maudie and Lucy and told her she could take any eggs that were outside the runs as there's no time to hunt for them.'

'That was kind,' Jane said. 'Come through, I saved some nice lamb stew for you. Harry sniffed and said it smelled good but I told him it was only scraps for the dog!'

'So our Lizzie has made him come up to scratch at last!' Walter laughed when Janey told him that Harry wanted to escape the army and they all talked companionably now that he was not resentful and had no frustrated desire in his eyes. He's more contented these days and no longer goes to Portsmouth with Bert, Jane thought with relief. He's finally found out that life has more to offer than bed and beer.

'Harry should be proud to go in the army,' Walter said. He held out the big moustache cup for more tea, but his hand was stiff again and the cup fell off the edge of the table and smashed to the floor.

'Sweet Mary! You had that cup on our wedding day.' Jane gathered the pieces in newspaper and put them on the white hearth ready for the ashcan. It was only an old cup, she thought sadly, but it was part of their marriage and part of Walter. He was flexing his fingers again and again. 'Did you catch your hand on it?' she asked, taking the hand and smoothing it.

'It slipped.' He held the fresh cup in both hands and sipped carefully, then put it down and wiped away the dampness from his moustache.

'I'll buy another,' Jane offered. 'You don't want your moustache turning ginger from the tea, like Bert. He never uses a moustache cup. That's unless you shave it off,' she teased him, knowing how unlikely that would be.

'I might get rid of it,' he said casually. 'Only old men have full moustaches now, or hadn't you noticed what goes on around you?' He made it sound as if she was old-fashioned.

'I notice,' she replied dryly. 'Isn't your own son a real masher now with his hair slicked down and parted in the middle and something like a thin worm asleep on his upper lip?'

'Jack? That woman and he make a good pair together,' growled Walter. 'Didn't take long to get a name for herself again, did it.' Jane regarded him with apprehension. 'Up at the Bugle, she was, and then singing and dancing in the Castle Inn, doing the latest dance there. She thought she was safe from Jack, knowing that neither he nor I go to the Castle Inn.'

'Walter! This is serious. I heard a whisper but I didn't know it was as bad. There must be something we can do. They were married in church and marriage is a communion before God.' Jane twisted her own wedding ring, too tight now to slide over the slightly thickened knuckle. It had been cut off twice in the past when her fingers swelled but had been repaired each time she was better. Walter watched, seeing the small marks that showed recovery from near death each time. 'I'll have to see Nellie before it gets worse and Jack finds out. Everyone has ups and downs in marriage but the good times should outweigh the bad,' she added softly. 'Now they have a duty to the baby.'

Walter walked about the room, more moved than he liked to admit. Jane was still the best-looking woman he'd met and she never nagged as other men's wives did. Even now, she was his best and most loyal friend. 'You've been a good wife,' he said abruptly. 'None better – but if you'd done that, I'd have thrown you out!'

'If I had to do that to fill my heart you would never have kept me,' she said slowly. 'Until . . . that last time, we were real partners, Walter. Don't ever forget that.' She looked at him with candour. 'Whatever you do now can never take away what we had, and thank God we still have more than most.'

He looked away. How much did she know? Maudie was too scared to breathe a word and they met only in the stables for a tumble in the hay; he hadn't even told Bert. 'I can't take on their troubles,' he said quickly. 'If Jack goes away it will sort itself out and mark my words, if he wants to go nothing will stop him, not me nor you nor Nellie nor the farmwork.'

'And you know why? He's your son, Walter!'

'Are my army shirts ready? They need me in Ventnor next week for a drive to enlist men in the Territorials.' He saw her shoulders sag. 'It's no use looking like that, gal. War is on the way and we must be ready. We can't avoid it with honour.'

'Honour? Where's the honour in fighting so far away and dying or coming back maimed? Have you seen the man with no legs and only one arm, sitting on that sled, selling papers all weathers? It's wicked.'

Walter sneered. 'Women! We've a camp at Easter and

one at Whitsun and they've put anti-submarine nets out from the forts at Puckpool and Spit Fort and the same on the other side of the Solent. They've built a huge turning circle for big guns at Puckpool Battery to cover the whole reach of the sea. It's in a sandpit and the big gun can be moved by one man at a finger's touch. That looks like business to me, and I hear they have more victuals stored than we used all the time in South Africa.' He laughed at his wife's stricken face. 'We'll all be out there again,' he boasted. 'The quarter-master at Albany took in pith helmets and white ducks – which means Egypt or British East Africa or I'm a Dutchman.'

'They've said they'll take only the young unmarried men, Walter. You couldn't go again.'

'I can if my country needs me! They still need horses and I'm fit and vigorous and can show them a thing or two.'

'It's easy to crow from your own dung-hill,' Jane said quietly and picked up the bundle of smashed crockery.

'We're going to walk to Carisbrooke,' Emily said when the girls came down ready to go out. 'Why don't you come, Mother?'

'That walk gets longer each time and I have work to do. I said I'd go to Wootton tomorrow to see Amy as I have some things for her. You'll be in the shop then and I can take my time.'

'You should let Archie take you out in the trap,' Clare said. 'You know you enjoy it and he offers enough times, but you never go now that Aunt Amy can't go with you.'

Jane looked thoughtful. Amy had caught tuberculosis some years ago from her little daughter Rose and was now very ill; Archie showed only too plainly his delight when Jane could go out with him. 'You go and enjoy yourselves. Emily should get out more, but I'd never keep up with you even in those tight skirts! You look very nice,' she added with pride. 'I have pretty daughters.' Clare pulled on her gloves and turned in a circle to show the looped skirt that was almost a hobble but cunningly gave room for walking by having slits at both sides. Janey looked more demure with a filled-in neckline under the deep V neck and a longer skirt, but her eyes were bright and full of warmth like her mother's, and Emily looked sweet-faced in a delicate way that often made people overlook her prettiness.

Janey laughed, 'All dressed up and nowhere to go! We shall walk on the Mall and show off in front of the boys to let them see what they are missing! By the way, Lucy said thank you for the fish.'

'Fish?' said Jane to the empty room. Maudie hadn't been to the shop for two or three weeks and Lucy wasn't due to serve until the next day. She shrugged – Maudie must have come while she was out.

Jane packed the basket ready for Wootton and put in some cakes for Nellie, too, and all the time she was on the train she wondered about her children. Everything in the railway carriage was as it had been when the children were small; the pictures of Alum Bay picked out in coloured sands and the views of Freshwater Bay in the thick mahogany frames, but today she felt lonely. She looked out at the gypsy caravans but there were fewer now, huddled behind the cow parsley and stunted bushes, as many Romanies now worked in factories and had gone into the bricks and mortar trade.

Mrs Lee was dead and Sidney was in America. She touched the letter in her pocket, but hearing from him had made him no closer. Vaudeville was the same as Music Hall but Sidney seemed to think it the way to fame and fortune. His descriptions were graphic and excited, giving her a picture of all he met and worked with, and the fast-moving and sophisticated way of life he saw there. It showed more happiness than he had ever managed to find close to home, and this saddened her.

She stepped from the train at the halt and braced herself to meet Amy as she walked along the lane sheltered by dog-roses and unkempt brambles. A woman greeted her at the door. 'I heard the train,' she said. 'Mrs Cheverton has looked forward to seeing you. The others are working over in the lower field but they'll be back for dinner.'

'How is she?' Amy's housekeeper looked tired. She was

a poor relation, glad of a home and work and had been good to Amy. 'Any worse?'

'Not worse, but she eats nothing and is so thin a breath would blow her away. Still, you can't make a body take what it doesn't want.'

'I have brought some jelly I made from good beef and calves' feet and some dainties that Janey does so well. Where is she?'

Ivy sniffed. 'That young doctor said she must sleep out in the open unless it rains, but not in the full sun. He's got some funny idea that this is the new treatment for consumption. He also wants her to drink goat's milk – and I am the one who has to milk the creature!'

'I'll milk her today,' Jane said. After half an hour sitting with Amy it would be a good excuse to have a change, she thought guiltily. Amy lay on a day bed in the doorway of the parlour. The thin muslin curtains moved in the warm breeze and Amy held up a thin and painfully weak hand in greeting. The hair that had been so thick and dark and abundant was now wispy and grey and she looked twenty years older than her age. Jane refrained from kissing her as the doctor had warned that once Amy spat blood she was infectious.

'You look better,' said Jane, seeing no sense in making matters worse. She recalled with revulsion the small foetid room where Rose had spent her days and nights and blessed the new doctor for bringing air and light and, please God, better health from natural things, but Amy had left it all too late.

'Tell me about the family,' Amy said, and seemed to enjoy hearing about Edward and the house rented above the railway station close to his work in Southampton, the way that Harry changed his tune when the coming war threatened his liberty and small snippets of gossip about people she knew. Then her eyelids drooped and Jane slipped away to milk the nanny goat. It was like old times, with the warm flank by her cheek and the milk flowing into the bucket. Life on a farm was hard but she envied Nellie in the pretty cottage with a new baby, and made up her mind to go down to see them later, after dinner.

A hand on her shoulder made her nearly spill the milk. 'It's good of you to come,' Archie said, and she wanted to hug away the tiredness and dejection from his face, but she only picked up the bucket and slapped the goat on the rump to send her back to the yard. Archie took the bucket from her and held her close. 'She's dying, Jane,' he said and kissed her cheek. Dear God, his arms were warm and loving but he let her go as if even that contact and touch of life was denied him.

'She seems pleased to see me and took quite an interest.'

'She likes you, Jane.' He smiled wryly. 'She trusts you more than she's ever trusted another woman. Do you know, she thinks that Ivy wants to take her place – Ivy! who is as fetching as a cow and whom I've known for years. If it was you she hated, I could believe it, as you know how I feel about you.'

'Long ago I told her that I had a man of my own and didn't need hers,' Jane said steadily. 'You know I can never give myself to any man, not even my husband after the last baby.'

'But you do have some feeling for me, Jane?' he asked humbly and with pain.

'If things had been different,' she admitted, 'we could have found something, but now there is someone in there who needs us both.'

Archie looked at her silently, then, 'Jack's here,' he said. 'I came to save you the walk down to the cottage.' And then he strode away to stop Ivy from beating the dinner gong to death as everyone had heard it.

Jane set the milk in a silvery churn covered with damp butter muslin to keep it cool and washed her hands before taking in the tray of jelly and thin bread and butter to Amy. She waited until Amy tried a little and began to eat with more interest then went back to the table. Jack stared. 'What on earth are you doing here, Mother? You must have missed Nellie. She went up this morning to Newport.'

'Which train did she catch?' Jane asked with instinctive caution.

'The one that gets in at ten. Don't you remember, you promised to look after Victoria today while Nellie visited a friend and did some shopping?'

'If she took that train then I'd have missed her,' Jane lied. 'Oh dear, I must have got the day wrong. I am sorry.' If Nellie had caught that one, they would have met on the station, Jane thought – and when would she ever forget to see her own grandchild? She helped Ivy clear away and asked if Nellie came up to the house often.

'She doesn't bring the baby close to Amy and so we don't see much of her, but the baby is bonny and Nellie seems like a very good mother.'

Jack came back. 'I can't do more to the barn until the timber comes, Archie. I could go back with Mother, call at the chandlers and leave the broken harness in for repair before collecting Nellie.'

'It will give you time to talk,' Archie agreed. 'Don't go yet, though. Amy wants to see Jane again and I have some nuts to send back for the girls before they dry out.' He made to follow Jack but Jane caught his sleeve.

'I may be wrong and please God I am, but Nellie said nothing about coming to me today.' Archie looked shocked when she outlined what she had heard of Nellie, but she made no mention of her dancing in the revealing dress.

'I'll make some excuse for him to stay,' Archie said, frowning. 'Silly girl, she doesn't know when she's well off. Ivy keeps grumbling that she would like the cottage and expected to have it for looking after Amy so well and to tell the truth it is rightly hers, but Sidney and Jack did a lot to it and now he can have it rent-free for as long as he likes.'

Back in Amy's downstairs bedroom, the invalid nibbled a thin biscuit and sipped her tea. 'I'd soon get better if you lived nearer and brought me food like today Jane,' she said. 'Ivy is a very plain cook but you give me some of your strength.'

Jane felt anything but strong. Archie did his best to persuade Jack to leave the trip to Newport for a day or so until they had a full list of things to get there and raised his shoulders with an air of 'I did what I could' when Jack refused to budge and began to look annoyed.

'We might as well catch the next train,' Jane said, resigned to what might happen if Jack found that Nellie had not left Victoria at the shop. His face was so like Walter's and his temper short at times but she knew that he must find out one day. In the train she showed him Sidney's letter and he read it avidly.

'Lucky, lucky boy. How wonderful to be free.' Dear God, she wanted to say – if you feel like that now how will it be when you know about your wife?

'He's far from home and may one day need love and caring,' she reminded him. 'You have so much more than most men of your age.'

'You mustn't worry about Sidney, Mother. He will be fine – and never worry about me, either. I'm the cat that always falls on its feet even if dropped from a great height. You're the one I worry about. With Edward gone and Lizzie soon, and me down here away from you, and Sidney not coming back in a hurry, you need care and to have a decent man around. I wonder sometimes about Father . . . He's getting worse, you know. I have a temper like yours, soon over, but he seems to smoulder inside like a fire in a haystack that only needs a wind to fan it into an inferno.'

'I know him well,' Jane said, 'and I'm just fine, but you and he are best kept apart.' She smiled at her son reassuringly. 'If I need you, I'll come running.'

'Not to me, Mother. If he did anything to you, I'd get into a rage and kill him. If you need help, go to Archie – he's the one to look after you.'

She gave a slight shudder. 'And what would I be doing, running to Archie with my troubles?' But she saw how serious Jack had become and had a premonition of evil. Archie had said almost the same. What did they see in Walter that she missed, seeing him daily?

Jack grinned. 'Father may go away again. He boasted in the Bugle that he would be one of the first to go as they couldn't run a war without him! He taunted Bert with being a coward in the last war and too old for this one.' Jane stared out of the carriage window and felt no sense of shock or dread at the thought of Walter leaving her again.

The gritty station yard crunched under foot and smelled of coaldust and spent ashes. New shops had opened by the end of Quay Street and Jack stood for a minute before a shop selling paintings of ships. He stared at the billowing sails over a rough sea in the Solent and sighed for the freedom and vision of speed it conjured, then followed Jane back to *Darwen's*.

Emily was half-asleep in the golden sunshine streaming through the window. 'There haven't been many customers and I did quite a lot of crochet,' she said.

'Where's Nellie and the baby?' Jack demanded. He stood over Emily as if sensing that Jane might influence her to tell him less than the truth.

'She hasn't been here,' Emily replied, puzzled. 'She might be on her way now, I suppose, after seeing her friend up by the Priory, or she may be on her way home and you missed her.' She smiled. 'If she comes in for tea I must put the kettle on, as I'm sure we could all do with a cup.'

'*Where is she?*' Jack asked in a voice that sent a chill down Jane's spine.

'Sit down and cool off, Jack. You'll do no good getting into a state.' Emily fussed over him as he sat ready poised for flight and offered him his favourite seedy cake and bread with thick butter and jam. Jane tried to soothe him as she had done a hundred times before, but this wasn't the child who fought Percy Cantor, this was a jealous husband whose pride of possession had been threatened. At five o'clock there was still no sign of Nellie and the uneasy silence became oppressive.

The shop-bell clanged wildly as Clare burst in, but she bit back her words when she saw Jack. He leaped up. 'You've seen Nellie. Where is she?'

'In the High Street,' stammered Clare. 'She's on her way home.'

'Right,' he said grimly, and made for the street. 'I'll meet her on the platform and we can talk in the train.'

'Nellie needs to see her friends sometimes,' Jane pleaded.

'It depends which friends she sees,' Jack called back as he almost ran.

'I hope the train has left before he gets there,' Clare said, and they heard the whistle blow.

'It may give him time to calm down,' Emily said.

'That's not it.' Clare looked frightened. 'Nellie isn't going by train. I met her and Mr Morris on the Mall and they were just leaving in Mr Morris' car to get back to Wootton before Jack finished work. If she thinks Jack won't find out she must be mad, for at least five people we know saw her get into that big car.'

'There's no harm in accepting a lift, especially with a baby to carry,' Jane said hopefully. 'I was once driven into Ryde by Dr Barnes who heard I was taking some papers to the bank there and he was going to the Infirmary. Very comfortable it was. I didn't have to walk to the station and get my feet wet, although it was raining hard.'

'That's different,' Clare said and shrugged as if she had no further interest in the matter. 'By the way, I chose the patterns for my dress and Miss Joyner says she can make it up with fringing on the layers to look like the latest lampshade dresses. I chose deep pink and I know it will suit me.'

'I wonder if Jack caught that train,' Jane mused.

'Who?' Clare said. 'Oh, them! They make me angry. All they think about is going to bed, and when they aren't making love, they are quarrelling. When I get married I don't want all of that, or not so much of the time.'

'Then you are best unwed,' Jane said shortly. She made a list of guests for Lizzie's wedding and decided on twenty to come back after the ceremony. Lizzie confided that she was going to Bournemouth to an aunt of Harry's for two nights' honeymoon before returning to their tiny house in East Cowes.

'He's getting you cheap,' Clare said acidly.

Chapter 8

'Let them all come.' Walter was in an expansive mood. 'Let Jack and his woman see what a real wedding is like and not some hole-in-a-corner affair like theirs.' He'd made sure that Bert and Annie were on the list, along with two army friends and now had no further interest in the arrangements. It would be a day of stiff collars and a stuffy suit and people he neither cared for nor wanted to see.

'You'll have a new suit?' Jane asked tentatively. 'One of the new cut would suit you so well, Walter. They make a man look slim and tall.'

'I might think about it,' he replied, pulling at the end of his moustache. Maudie had hinted that he would look younger without it, and it had become a nuisance since he broke the special cup. She had also said she would like to see him in one of the new suits, so he had a good excuse to splash out for the wedding. Lizzie blushed with pleasure and insisted that he also bought pale grey gloves. He smiled indulgently. Let little Liz think it was all for her benefit. Poor child, she'd not have much excitement married to Harry, and Jane's firm management had saved him a packet over this wedding. 'Buy yourself something nice, lass . . . within reason,' he added hastily.

'Get the extras now while he's in the mood,' Jane whispered, then aloud, 'Give them the money now, Walter, and the girls might leave us in peace. It will be done then and they can't ask again! I think you are very generous.' The eager faces gave him an unaccustomed twinge of paternal pride, and he handed over more than they expected. 'Get a smock for Victoria and something pretty for Nellie,' Jane hissed to Janey. 'And go now, before he regrets it!' She smiled. If he was as generous as this, she could keep her own store of pickle money. Giving Sidney his share had made her realize how important it was to have something in reserve about which Walter knew nothing.

'I'll stay in tonight,' he said. 'They'll want to show us what they bought.' Jane raised her eyebrows. 'Janey can look in at the stables on her way up to Staplers and I did all that was necessary this morning.'

Jane picked up the mending. 'Lucy said that she can't help tomorrow. She's going with Maudie to visit a friend at Shanklin for two days. It will be a nice change for them.'

'Hope it keeps fine for them,' Walter said. 'I might look in at the Wheatsheaf later but that can wait.' He walked out to the yard, moving stiffly. Jane smiled indulgently. He'd hate it if she suggested he had a touch of rheumatism. He did work hard and nowadays seldom grumbled. In fact, he seemed unwilling to let the girls do anything in the stables. 'Will you be bringing Marigold and the foal back soon?' Jane asked when he returned.

'Archie can use her with the hay and the foal is better left with her mother,' he replied. 'I might bring Marigold back for the wedding but the foal will be old enough to stay on the farm.' Even now, he felt embarrassed to have a horse looking down on him and Maudie when they were in the hay.

'Call and see Nellie when you go down, Walter. She's such a good mother and I don't think it's all honey between her and Jack.'

He touched her hand. 'All right, gal, if it will please you. Has she said much to you?' he asked.

'She was very pale the last time she came in and told Janey there had been a terrible row over her visits to the Castle Inn, but at least Jack didn't know that Mr Morris had brought her home the day he missed her.'

'She's a fine-looking girl, but the wrong one for him,' Walter grunted. 'They're too much alike and it will go from bad to worse. See them if you must and have them to Lizzie's wedding but don't meddle. They must sort out their own lives.'

'You have a camp at Whitsun,' she reminded him, in case

he suddenly remembered on the day of the wedding and made a scene.

'I know,' he said testily. 'I shall see our Lizzie wed and then go down for a day or so. They don't need me for the first two days as they are drilling with grenades and the new mortars, using motor transport. Humbuggen nonsense! Get a wet period and they'll soon need horses. They think if they lay down bits of wood nailed together, they can get the wheels moving over the mud.' He chuckled. 'The tide caught one and it took two lorries and four horses to pull it out!'

'I'll order a nice few flowers for the shop next week,' Jane said. 'It brightens the place up and there'll be many coming to hear about the wedding.' The sale of flowers was her idea and Walter had told her to do what she wanted. He would be surprised at the profit I make, she thought and was amazed how many people bought flowers at weekends and for the cemetery.

'Just keep the floor clear of leaves. They get slippery,' Walter said. She glanced at him sharply. Something about him disturbed her, like the transient loss of power in his hand and the way his eyes were angry and suspicious when he couldn't hear what people were saying but thought they were talking about him. He had slipped twice on patches of wet but also when the road was dry. 'You'll be making wreaths next,' he said.

'Not wreaths. I don't mind making bunches of flowers for weddings and special displays for Mrs Neville, but never a wreath. I've seen enough of death and if I'm not mistaken there's more in the offing with Amy so bad.'

'Then Archie will be a man alone,' he said, as if he disliked the thought. 'In need of a kindly woman and her interest.'

'He'll get that from his many friends,' Jane said quietly. 'They'll flock to help him.'

'And will you join the other sheep?' he sneered.

Jane raised her chin defiantly. 'I shall be the first to offer help. I've told him that if Amy is taken really bad I'll go there for a day or so. I know you'd want to help your cousin as he's been a man to trust and he helped us a lot when you were absent.' She set her mouth firmly and Walter looked away. Jane had never deceived him and yet he wanted to put her in the wrong for once, to assuage his own guilt.

Lizzie almost danced into the room and Walter enjoyed an hour of giggles and flattering attention as he inspected the purchases. Jane sighed with relief as he approved of everything they'd bought and even suggested items for the wedding breakfast. 'You make the best drop scones I've tasted, so don't let all the strawberry jam go to the Barracks and I'll bring cream from the farm,' he offered.

Later, he changed into his smart suit and walked to meet Bert before going to the Wheatsheaf. It was Bert's day for Portsmouth and Walter had no desire to visit Annie and wait for him, so he strolled through the town looking up at the pink and blue flecked cloud above the Town Hall and along the narrow road by the old burial ground of Church Litten before turning towards Shide.

The white scar of the pit on Pan Down where chalk had been quarried for centuries showed starkly against the green and yellow gorse and Walter sat on a wall watching the birds fly low. Bert's house was visible up the side road and looked very handsome. Walter grinned wryly. If I'd been as astute and as sharp as Bert we could have had a house as big, he thought, but it didn't destroy his good mood.

Bert might have a knack with money but not with women. Annie grew more shrill and suspicious each day and had never been a cosy armful, and the paid women who warmed Bert's bed were rubbish. Walter felt complacent. He'd fathered a big family with a lovely wife, and now had Maudie with whom to pass the time of day in the surprisingly erotic setting of the stables. He wiped the grin from his face when Bert came hurrying down the hill. It wouldn't do for him to find out about Maudie as Annie would worm it out of him in no time and then the fat would be in the fire.

'Well, Bert, how was it on the mainland?' he asked. They walked towards the town.

'She was away.' Bert grunted with disgust. 'The old

woman gave me a name and address on a bit of paper but when I got there, I couldn't stomach it. It smelled worse than a goat in rut in that room and she was filthy.' He quickened his steps and glanced with apprehension at Walter. 'I called on your friend and spent some time with her.'

To Bert's surprise, Walter only laughed. 'You could do worse,' he said mildly. 'I've decided I'm not in the mood these days for such amusements, so give her my best and enjoy yourself.' He tipped his hat to an angle and drew in his stomach. 'She'll teach you a trick or two you didn't know, Bert, and she's clean.' He saw Bert's puzzled expression. 'In any case, I have to give up my visits over there as we are so busy in the camps. If I have time and want her again, I'll fight you for her,' he added, roaring with laughter. 'So don't wear her out!'

Bert was relieved as just lately he never knew which way Walter's temper would go, but Walter had already forgotten the woman and thought only of Maudie's white skin. They talked business in the snug of the Wheatsheaf and Bert explained about some government stock he was buying. 'It's time you invested in arms, Walt. The ones who get in early will make a pile.' Walter pulled at his moustache. 'Come on, Walt. You can afford it. You don't pay wages any more to Jack or Sidney or Edward, and Lizzie will be off your hands soon. I don't know how you manage with so little help. Shall I ask Dan to give you a couple more days to do the stables?'

'No! I like to see my beasts get the best.' He gulped his beer. 'Now don't mistake me, Dan's a good man and one I trust, but the girls do their share and we have Lucy to serve in the shop for a bit each week now. To tell the truth I like to get away from a houseful of women at times. Dan can do an extra delivery to the Barracks instead. That would be a real help, and I'll look into those stocks if you'll give me the details. It's time I put something aside for Jane, in case I get sent away again and never come back.' He grinned as if that was impossible and Bert eyed him curiously, wondering why he was in such high spirits.

'Annie said that Amy is bad again,' Bert remarked.

'Yes, Jane might have to go down for a day or so if she's really ill,' said Walter as if it was his idea. 'Clare helped out with the jam and pickles last autumn until Amy began to spit blood and the doctor sent Clare home, saying it was infectious.'

'And what of Jane? She could catch it.' Bert sounded really concerned.

'No, there are some women who can walk into any house and not catch a thing. They are like doctors. Jane is very clean and believes it helps and I've always said she has a kind of healing gift and a protection from somewhere.'

'Jane is a good woman,' Bert said. 'Annie says she prays.' Walter lifted an eyebrow. 'I mean she cares about people and calls on the name of the Lord.'

'All that Holy Mary talk is an echo of her life before we met and I have none of that nonsense in my house.' He sat in silence. If Jane wasn't so good, it would be easier to deceive her.

'Look who's here! Were you expecting Jack?' asked Bert.

Walter bent over his tankard in case Jack wanted to avoid him but his son came over, smiling, and Bert motioned him towards a chair. 'Mother told me you'd invited us to the wedding,' Jack said.

'That deserves a drink,' Bert said and went to order them. Peter Fry spoke to him and Bert paid for his drink, too, so relieved that Walter wasn't mad because of the woman in Portsmouth that he felt generous. Peter, now almost crippled with rheumatism, took this as an invitation to join them. Jack made more room and realized that he was glad to see his father. I've missed the old devil, he decided.

Peter Fry was in his element. It wasn't every night that Bert bought him a drink or tolerated his company and he responded by being over-anxious to entertain with news. 'How's the baby?' he asked at last and Jack started up on seeing the time.

'I'll have to go or I'll miss my train,' he said. 'Nellie will expect me soon and I don't fancy walking all that way to Wootton at night.'

'Why don't you ask for a lift in a motor car?' Peter's nose was red and his eyes held a cold pleasure.

'Because I haven't a motor and I don't know anyone here with one,' Jack replied sarcastically, and turned to ask when Jane might be visiting the farm again.

Peter saw that Jack had taken no heed of what he said and went on, 'Why not ask Monty Morris, then?' Jack stared, bleakly. 'He's the one with the big car and he is free with his lifts, isn't he? He knows the way to Wootton.'

'What do you mean?' Jack was white-faced and he clenched his fists.

'Come on, we've ten minutes to catch that train.' Walter tried to push Jack towards the door, but was shrugged away.

'What do you mean?' Jack repeated quietly.

Peter saw that he had gone too far and began to whine, 'Nothing. He knows Archie and Amy, that's all. Everyone knows them. He gets fruit from the farm, you see,' he lied. 'Give them my regards and say I hope Mrs Cheverton mends soon,' he added, backing away.

'I'll run down alone,' Jack said. 'I have to catch that train.'

'Leave him, Walt!' Bert caught the other man's arm. 'You'll do more harm than good if you interfere. It has to come out soon and he's the last to hear. Annie saw Monty taking Nellie and the baby back to the farm the other day – and you know what she is! I saw no harm in it. I'd be the first to offer if I had a motor car.'

'So would most, Bert, but Monty is a different kind of fish.' He saw Peter gulping the last of his beer. 'Yes, drink up, Pete. Get back beneath the stone you were under before you crawled out tonight!'

'Men like that should be locked up,' Bert said self-righteously. Walter grinned. With Annie the troublemaker as a wife how could he say that? 'I thought of asking Jack to Ashey Races,' Bert went on, 'but Monty has his bookmaker's stand there and I hate the sight of blood! Let's hope it blows over. It means nothing, Walt. Dr Barnes gives Jane lifts, after all, and Monty does for many who need one

– says it's good for trade. Stands to reason that if he gave a person a lift, they'd have to place a bet with him out of gratitude.' Bert laughed. 'I might buy a motor myself if my dividends come out well. I may want to drive over to the West Wight more as I'm buying property there.' He laughed again. 'And they say the back seats of a motor are good for a cuddle.'

'Yes, so they say.' Walter recalled that Maudie had recently had a small win on a horse and wondered if she used the street-corner runner or had gone to Monty Morris.

'Well, I'm for home,' decided Bert. 'It's been a long day. When this scare is over, you ought to come with me again, or they'll think you're past it.'

'They can think what they like and so can you. Make the best of it, Bert, while you can.'

'I've years yet,' Bert said with a superior smile. If Walter was impotent, then at last that was something he had over him.

'I don't mean that, Bert. Think! If war comes you'll be cut off from the mainland, and you'll need that motor!' Walter laughed. 'See you at the wedding.'

Chapter 9

Emily Darwen brushed the damask cloth with the brush and crumb set and Annie Cooper sniffed, but decided that she would buy one too, like the ebony and mother-of-pearl set that lay among Lizzie's presents in the upper room of the house. 'You'll stay for another cup, Annie?' Jane asked. 'Most have gone now and I'm parched as I haven't drunk a full cup all day.' She sighed and folded the cloth carefully and put the sprigs of roses and myrtle on the harmonium top. 'It was a pretty wedding, wasn't it, and Lizzie's friend as bridesmaid looked very nice.'

Annie settled back. Bert obviously agreed as he was laughing with that chit of a girl half his age now in the shop, and Annie wasn't leaving without him.

Lizzie had looked so happy, and even Harry had said his vows in such a loud voice that Walter whispered it was too late to back out as the whole of Newport must have heard him promise. Jane had glanced at Walter several times in chapel, wondering how the loss of his moustache could alter him so much. That and the new suit with peg-top trousers and well-fitting jacket made him look slim and taller, but his mouth and chin, now exposed from the shelter of the heavily drooping moustache, looked almost brutal. He was still good-looking and knew it.

Some of the furniture had been manhandled out into the shed to make room for more guests and now that Lizzie and Harry had gone with Jack in the newly-painted trap drawn by Marigold and Blackie to the ferry, the house seemed bare. The twenty guests had become thirty, with many more uninvited dropping in after the ceremony to wish the couple joy, and who Jane felt had to be offered refreshments as most of them brought small gifts.

Lucy Dove had come to the wedding but Maudie had kept away, pleading a bad attack of hay fever. Walter laughed to himself. If she wasn't used to hay by now, she never would be, but he was glad she saw sense and stayed away. Jane put a fresh cotton tablecloth on the end of the table and filled the biscuit and cake plates again as she suspected the day wasn't yet over and more friends might call to admire the bouquet that she had made of roses, love-in-a-mist and maidenhair fern that everyone said was better than the ones they'd seen over in Portsmouth. Clare still wore her dress and could hardly walk in it but seemed to be enjoying Joseph's attentions after Jane insisted on inviting him, and Janey seemed quiet, glancing towards the shop door and starting when new faces appeared.

Now Janey blushed and Jane looked up curiously. Two men in naval uniforms stood in the doorway. They came in, caps across their chests to greet Walter with courtesy and then Jane, solemnly but with a wicked twinkle that gave the lie to their ceremonious entrance. Walter smiled with pleasure and Annie Cooper gaped as she took in every detail of the smart reefer jackets with brass buttons, the close-fitting white trousers, the proud bearing and the deep blue eyes of Clive Neville. 'Mother asked me to bring this for Lizzie,' he said, and Dr Barnes' son also handed over a package.

Janey poured tea and handed a cup to Clive with a gentle smile on her lips. He took it without speaking but his eyes gleamed as he saw the girl in the yellow dress who looked so like her mother, then he turned away abruptly to speak to Clare, teasing her about her skirt and challenging her to race him up the Mall and back. Clare saw that Joseph wasn't pleased and it made her happy. She had the attention of two naval officers who seemed to prefer her to any of the girls present.

Janey gave out tea and biscuits to everyone and made her mother sit down again but Jane sensed the bond building between her daughter and Clive even while he teased Clare, and didn't know if she wanted to laugh with joy or cry. If Janey fell in love with him, would the Nevilles approve? Rumour had it that Clive had been encouraged to court the daughter at one of the Manors near Atherfield, and the girl had been seen at Staplers many times when he was on leave.

'I thought Nellie looked pale – is she expecting again?' Annie asked Jane in an aside. 'And Jack seemed more interested in looking at his wife than at the bride in chapel.' Annie had found the one sore spot that had marred the day, and she went on to rub sand into the raw patch. 'I asked him if he was cross about something but he was quite rude to me.'

'Little Vikki is a handful now and wears them out, that's all,' Jane said. 'A sister or brother might make her less demanding but that's their affair.'

'He seemed very put out,' Annie persisted.

'He's got a lot on his plate,' pointed out Jane. 'Amy is very ill again and he had to help Archie from early this morning so that he could get away to the wedding. He wanted to drive Lizzie and Harry to the boat, bless him. Archie couldn't spare the time to come as they are short of labour again up there. We'll see Jack again later after he's stabled the horses to save Walter changing his clothes and getting dirty.' She spoke calmly but was secretly filled with dread.

'It would be a pity to spoil that suit,' Annie said maliciously. 'Quite the masher, isn't he? You'd think it was him getting married.' She recognized the same lift to Walter's step that Bert had each time he came back from Portsmouth; she wondered who the woman could be that made Walter Darwen walk with such a swagger.

'Walter is like a warhorse smelling gunpowder,' Jane said and laughed. 'All this talk of fighting is a tonic to him, but if there is war, Annie, it will play havoc with money. I doubt if there'll be any market for luxuries and I may have to stop selling flowers.'

Annie looked sour. Bert had just invested in the fur trade which wasn't doing well as people now drew back from such extravagance. 'What goes on over there can't affect us,' she said.

'That's what I thought the last time,' Jane said, 'but the young ones take no notice of the bad side of war and want to fight, and that affects everyone with a son or brother in the services.'

Mr Foster joined Walter in a corner to talk of strategy and more people drifted in for lemonade or tea. When Sam Walmsley left, Jane hugged him, remembering all his kindness over the years. She was shocked to feel how thin he was and how much he had neglected himself since his wife Elsie had died. He's old, she thought with a sense of loss. I must go and see him tomorrow and make sure his housekeeper is feeding him properly. It depressed her even when seeing her daughters all bright and pretty. What did the future hold for them? Clive was laughing, eating a drop scone and glancing at Janey but teasing Clare. He would go to war with high hopes of victory and honours but the navy was vulnerable to the new torpedoes and deadly howitzers.

Nellie was upstairs feeding the baby and Jane saw Jack in the shadow of the scullery door. She left Annie and drew him from view and closed the door. 'What's wrong?' she asked.

Jack paced the floor, tried to speak then shook his head as if angry at his own weakness. He tried again in a broken voice. 'I can't go on. I've had enough, Mother. I know I'm impatient, but I've run out of all I had and I can't stay here another night. I never want to see her again!'

'Jack – you can't mean that!' She looked at her son closely but saw he was cold sober. 'Tell me what people have been saying to you and I'll let you know if there's an inch of truth in it.'

'She danced with that rotter Monty Morris, wearing the dress I told her to burn as it isn't decent, but she kept it and danced at the Castle Inn. When we married, she promised to give all that up and I can't have men like Morris making free with my wife!'

'Nellie loves to sing and dance,' Jane said, her smile threatening to crack her face with effort. 'Give her time, Jack. She's a good mother and she loves you dearly.'

'Do you love Vikki enough to care for her as your own for my sake?'

'What do you mean? Stop this! You frighten me.'

'I frighten myself if the truth be known,' he said, more calmly. He plunged his hands into his pockets and looked even more pale and grim. 'What happens when something comes to an end, Mother?'

'You make do,' said Jane firmly. 'You pick up the pieces and make something that still holds water even if the cracks are there. You have a wife who loves you, a healthy baby who looks to you for her future, and Archie says he wants to leave the farm to you when he dies.' She gulped back her emotion. 'You have me and the girls and you are friends with your father again. Let Nellie see how much you care about her and then she might never be tempted.'

'Tempted?' he said softly. 'Before we were married, Nellie smiled at other men to make me jealous and how do I know if it stopped there? She's my wife now and a mother but it didn't take long for her to go back to them, did it? My Nellie will always be an entertainer at heart and no rules will tie her down.'

'But you *do* love her, Jack?'

'I love her so much that I can't wait here and see it happen, or one day, when she smiles up into the face of another man I shall go mad and kill her.'

'Holy Mary, Mother of God help us,' whispered Jane.

'You said that when Father came back from the war and he made you suffer. I couldn't have the strength that you had. It would end in mayhem and both of us know it. We've talked until we are exhausted, so don't tell me we haven't tried enough. I'm leaving, Mother.'

Jane recalled how envious he'd been of Sidney and she put a hand to her throat to stop herself from crying. 'You wouldn't leave the country?'

'I went to the office in Cowes where they give out cheap passages to Australia. I asked Nellie to come with me and make a fresh start but she refused to leave England. I booked a passage for one but I haven't told her yet as I wanted to spare you all before Lizzie's wedding.' He hugged her tight. 'I'm glad I stayed for this. I shall remember this day for ever.' He was weeping.

'How will she manage?'

'She can go back to what she did before or stay on the farm, but she hates the quiet and the novelty has worn off now. She'll be fine.'

'And you?' Sidney had planned and saved for his adventure and had her gift of money to help him but Jack was as harum-scarum as usual over practical matters.

'I want you to have this,' he said and handed her an envelope. Jane turned pale. So he *had* planned. 'It's a paper giving you the care of Victoria if the need arises. I'm her father and this is a legal document. I wanted it cut and dried so that if Nellie has no time for her, you will take Vikki.'

She saw that no words could affect him now. 'Wait!' she ordered, and hurried up to her room and back again. She couldn't cast off her wild son as if he no longer mattered. She thrust the small package into his hand and blessed the fact that she kept some of her pickle money in the house. 'Take it and no questions or thanks. You are my son and I gave the same to Sidney. It's mine to do as I please with. I can't bless you for this, but you have my love, Jack, and I hope you write when you are settled and this has lost some of its bitterness.' She controlled her sobs. 'When do you go?'

'Tomorrow. The ship sails the day after that.' He kissed her cheek. 'I can't say goodbye as there will always be something of me with you if you have Vikki. Tell the others after I'm gone,' he added, and walked calmly out through the front doorway.

Jane sat in the dark scullery for five minutes to gather her wits. It was typical of Jack to walk out and leave her to tell the others and her eyes were hot with unshed angry tears as they had been long ago when he had left a note rather than face her wrath. This time, he had told her – and it took real courage, she conceded, but she wondered if Nellie really believed he would leave her. She'd better sleep in Lizzie's room tonight.

Nellie was sitting on the bed buttoning up her bodice. Victoria bubbled back some milk and smiled up at her grandmother. 'Jack's gone,' Jane said softly. It could mean that he had gone home to the farm or something far more.

She saw Nellie's mouth tighten. 'So he told you?' Nellie put Vikki to her shoulder to bring up the wind. 'Don't look so tragic, Mother. It couldn't last and it's good to have it over.'

'Don't you care for him at all?'

'I care, but he's jealous and destructive. He's accused me of everything possible and wouldn't believe me.' Nellie looked up with wide and lovely eyes and Jane saw her pain. 'None of it mattered. If he had left me free to see my friends, this might not have happened but he couldn't bear me to even look at another man. I shall love him in some ways for ever, but we tear each other to pieces and in time we would come to hate each other. I like to sing and dance and see people enjoy themselves – is that a sin?'

'You'll stay tonight in Lizzie's room?'

'For tonight,' Nellie replied.

'For as long as you like,' Jane said firmly. She took the baby to change the diaper. 'I have an old crib in Sidney's room. You can sort out what you need tomorrow.'

'Thank you. I'd like to stay for a few days until I know that Jack has definitely left, then I'll get someone to take me back to the farm to sort out my things and make up my mind what to do.'

'Tell me if you need anything,' Jane said. She hugged the baby. My son has done this, she thought. My wild and beautiful son for whom I have this special love has left his wife and baby and I shall live with the shame of it for the rest of my life. 'Walter is a hard man but he'd never see you want for anything,' she added.

Nellie took the baby and cradled her in her arms. 'I don't want charity,' she said. 'You are different and I don't know what I'd do without you, but I'll make my own way after I've settled down.' She wrapped the baby and put her in the big open drawer in the bottom of the chest until the crib was ready, and tears began to fall for the first time.

'I stayed through the bad and good times and we made

a good life,' Jane said. 'Love and pain go together. It isn't too late, Nellie.'

'For us it is. I'd go mad staying on the farm picking daisies! Victoria would grow up in a bad atmosphere like the one I suffered as a child in a house with fights and no real feeling. I was greedy enough to want Jack and take him, but in my heart I knew I was a fool.' Nellie sighed. 'Give me the sheets and I'll make up the bed. I'm exhausted.' Jane put her arms round her daughter-in-law and kissed her, trying to give her strength and love, then fetched the clean sheets.

Annie was seething with curiosity. 'You were a long time,' she said. 'I nearly came up but I can't manage your stairs any more.'

'I wanted to see Vikki before she went to bed. It's late so I suggested that Nellie stayed with her overnight.'

'You see enough of her, and will see more I've no doubt, the way some people put on you.' Annie sniffed. 'Nellie spends time in Newport that ought to be spent cooking her husband's dinner, but if she's lucky enough to have a nice big car to take her back, it does save time . . .'

'I know what you are getting at, Annie, and I won't have such hints made under my roof. If you can't speak well of Nellie, it's time you went! Bert is kicking his heels in the shop and wants to get away from George Foster. It was nice of you to come and wish my Lizzie joy. We do appreciate that, but I will not have my daughter-in-law insulted.' Annie picked up her bag and called angrily to Bert to take her home. They would all know soon enough, Jane thought, but tonight they could all go away with a picture of the Darwens that would remain untarnished.

Some of the pleasure of the day returned. She was proud of her family and glanced up at the big photograph that Clare had insisted on propping up on the mantelpiece; it was of Sidney, dressed in a soft white shirt open at the neck, his fine features in profile and looking like a moving picture star. All the evening, people had admired it and Lucy Dove had stood entranced before it, but Walter had glowered and wanted it put away, muttering to Lucy, 'Forget him, gal. He'll be no use to any woman.'

Chapter 10

'Mark my words,' said Councillor Foster with a gleam of excitement. 'There'll be fighting before the year is out. I've seen it coming and so have people in the reserve like Walter Darwen.'

'They know less than we do!' retorted Bert Cooper. 'You had no idea that this Archduke what's-his-name would be assassinated, did you? Who thought that the Austro-Hungarian Empire would declare war on Serbia, of all places. It would have been a storm in a tea cup but for the Ruskies spoiling for a fight for years, just like the Germans. It's the excuse they've waited for and it won't be long before we are in it, too, unless we have enough sense to stop them dragging us in.'

'You'll be all right,' said George. 'I put something by on your advice but not enough to make me as rich as you.'

'Yes, I'm not so bad,' Bert agreed complacently. 'Not that I want war,' he added hastily. 'Men like Walter are the fire-eaters; I'm a man of peace.'

'Peace and profit.' Walter Darwen came up behind him in the grocer's shop and grinned. 'What happens if they can't do without you and you have to come with us?' Bert made a derisive gesture. 'I was in the last lot and I train the lads. They think a lot of me up at Albany. I'm fit and not too old.'

'We've trouble enough in Ireland without going overseas to fight strangers,' Bert said. 'Some say the Irish are close to civil war but they could have chosen a better time if we have to send troops elsewhere.'

Walter sat on the edge of the counter and picked at the cheese on the tasting board. 'Nice and close,' he said. 'Did Jane take one?'

'Took one and ordered another for next week. If war comes I must get more local supplies like that, as we might not be able to obtain Dutch cheeses if they fight in Holland. This time, the fighting might be a bit warm and too close to home.'

'If the Russians keep them occupied on the Eastern border we have nothing to worry about,' Walter said, 'but France is getting edgy and has built forts along her boundaries in case the Germans invade the land.'

'With Belgium as a buffer and her being neutral, the Germans can't ever cross to France,' Bert surmised. 'Belgium makes a good shield.'

'Look, Jane is busy and Emily up to her elbows in flour so I said I'd fetch the dried fruit.' But Walter munched raisins from the thick blue-paper poke that George filled and stayed on to talk of the war. 'What's new up at the *Press* window, George?'

'Just the reaction to the assassination on June the twenty-eighth, 1914 and the Declaration of War on Russia on the first of this month,' George announced as if reading a bulletin. 'It isn't the same as when the old Queen was here and let us have the news firsthand from Osborne.'

'We'll get it soon enough,' Walter said. 'The bases at Ventnor and the Needles have enough equipment to electrocute the whole island.'

'And to think that only a month ago your Lizzie was wed and Jack went off. One thing is certain, there'll be no time for gossip about them if war comes.' Bert smiled maliciously. 'Where is she now, Walter? Back with her own kind?'

'Nellie is on the farm where she belongs, with the baby.' Walter put up a hand to tug at his moustache but found it gone. He missed it more than he had thought possible but Maudie liked him without it and Jane had said only that now she had no need to buy another moustache cup.

'You kept that quiet,' Bert said with grudging admiration. 'It was nearly a month before we knew Jack had gone as we thought he was on the farm, then someone said he'd been seen getting on the liner at Southampton with his luggage the day after the wedding. Even my Annie didn't ferret that one out! I suppose it was best for him to go out first and see if it was fit for a wife and baby.'

'Yes, it makes sense,' Walter said shortly. If people took it for granted that Jack had gone ahead to Australia to find a place for his family, it was better so. 'Is Dan at home? If I go away I might need him full-time, tell him. We can afford help now and Jane is managing well,' he added carelessly.

'She had plenty to protect her the last time, Walt. She had Sam Walmsley to fight for her.' Bert sounded savage for a moment, then added, 'And she had your three boys and Archie too, of course.'

'Well, if she gets to rock bottom, she can always ask you for advice,' Walter said, laughing. He knew that at some time when he was away Bert had suffered the sharp edge of Jane's tongue – and maybe there was more that he hadn't heard about – and it amused him. 'I'll go over the books with her and make sure she knows about the investments,' Walter went on.

'Maybe that isn't necessary. We may not go to war,' Bert said nervously. Jane could run a finger down a ledger and spot the errors that Bert had made to his own advantage whereas Walter let things slide.

'Any more news?' Jane asked when Walter went back to the shop. 'As usual, the papers don't say much but are full of pieces written by men who know nothing about war. It's August the second and we're still in the dark about what's happening in Europe.' She was pale but as always in a crisis kept busy. The ironing was done and the banked-up fire made a homely nucleus to the room even on an August day, with Emily ready to put the fruit cakes in the oven. The back door was propped open to let out the heat. 'You'll be off to camp?' she asked.

'I'll go up to the *Press* first and leave tomorrow.' Walter tried to smooth his moustache again and Jane knew that he was uneasy. It was a recurring nightmare. Was it so long ago that he had sat like that, before going to the Boer War? Surely they wouldn't take Walter a second time? None of the boys would be involved, she thought with guilty thankfulness. Even Edward was safe unless he volunteered. As for the girls, Janey had said she wanted to be a nurse and Clare refused to believe that anything as unpleasant as war could interfere with her life. Lizzie was cosy and squirrel-like in her tiny house and seemed happy enough, with Harry secure in a job of national importance. Walter had laughed when he heard that Harry had been informed that he must not volunteer as he was not eligible for service. 'Our Lizzie caught him just in time,' he said.

'I'll go up to the *County Press* again now, I think,' Walter decided when they were eating the evening meal. By the Town Hall he bought a paper. GERMANY DEMANDS THE RIGHT TO CROSS BELGIAN SOIL, he read.

'It's a bluff,' someone by him said. 'They can't violate neutrality.'

'If the Kaiser does that, then it's war,' Walter said and the waiting crowd stopped to listen to the man who knew about the Boer War, and the training for another. He raised a fist. 'We can't let them violate little Belgium.'

'Little Belgium!' the crowd repeated, and this took the public imagination, not just on the Island but wherever the words were spoken across the country; the idea of a small neutral country being overrun was received as if they heard that a child had been raped. Walter rushed home and caught the night mail-train to the camp, taking the latest newspapers with him

Clare and Joseph paused on their way home and listened to the murmuring crowd. Clare turned up her nose. 'That means more troops on the Island. I hate rough soldiers.'

'Does that mean you'd hate me if I volunteered?' Joseph asked, trying to smile. Clare was such an enigma. When she allowed a kiss or two he imagined her with a home and family, but at times she seemed so distant that he despaired of ever possessing her.

'It depends on the service,' she said. 'The navy has the smartest uniforms.'

'I get seasick,' he replied shortly. 'Anyway, I might not have to go at all as they want me to study foreign exchange and the investment market.'

'Only fools volunteer.' Clare was oddly relieved that Joseph might not have to go. He was good company and, apart from the barriers she imposed against any real emotional contact, they were walking out. 'Father will be in his element,' she said. 'He'll come back with even more boring tales to exchange with Mr Foster.'

'Aren't you afraid for him?'

'No. We had a lot more freedom when Mother was in charge and although she'd never admit it, Mother was happy then.' Clare believed that this had something to do with sex: she dreaded any man touching her in certain ways. Lizzie had told her about marriage, the shock of the first night and the growing liking for love-making, with the sensation that she had power over a man's feelings and actions, but to Clare it was as repulsive as the copulation of beasts in a barn.

'Even the King and Queen do it so it must be all right,' Lizzie had said defensively. 'I like it.'

Joseph put an arm round Clare when she wasn't thinking and she snuggled closer. If this was marriage, the hugging and kissing and nothing more, she could enjoy it. 'I couldn't bear to go away and leave you, Clare,' he said in the dark doorway when he kissed her before they went into the shop.

'Then don't volunteer,' she said and let him kiss her twice more before pushing him away and straightening her hat.

Jane pulled on her coat and her hat looked as if it was taking a flying lesson. 'Clare, make the cocoa. I'm off to the *Press* window but I'll be back as soon as there is any fresh news.'

George Foster had reappeared, and was bobbing about on the fringes of the crowd near the Town Hall, secretly deploring the advance of technology and communication and the fact that most of the people could read and had no need of him. The Board Schools had a lot to answer for, he thought.

Tired and dispirited, Jane returned home. Janey sat sipping her cocoa as though lost in a dream, but sadly the dream was incomplete or threatening. 'Has Clive gone back?' asked Emily.

'Yes, with Alex,' replied Janey. 'They reported to Portsmouth.'

'They didn't say goodbye.' Clare was annoyed as she was certain that at Lizzie's wedding both of the smart naval officers had been attracted to her. It wasn't fair that Janey went to Staplers and heard all the news about them.

'Clive sent his regards to everyone,' Janey said. 'Any news, Mother?'

'No, it may yet all blow over.' But everyone knew matters had gone too far for peace. 'Try to convince your father that he must not volunteer,' she begged them. 'He thinks he can do what he did years ago and I know it would be too much for him.' I have to say the words, she thought, but would it be so bad if he did go? The girls listened politely as if talking about a stranger but they made no promises to speak to him, except for Emily who was nearly in tears. Joseph left and Jane asked Clare if he would volunteer.

'What if he does? We are only friends; we aren't courting,' Clare said.

'You'd miss him, Clare. He's one of the nicest men I know and you're very lucky.'

'You're welcome to him. I shall wait for someone better than Joseph Manning.'

Jane saw that Emily sat looking into space. All girls dreamed, she thought, but Emily was a homebird who wanted nothing better than to stay as she was, and was sad because she loved her father. As the youngest female child it was recognized that she must stay with her parents to help them in old age. 'Get some rest,' Jane ordered. 'Dan will be here early in the morning for the deliveries and we must make up the orders.' She felt as if Walter had gone away. This is how it will be again, she thought. If he went, Nellie might come to live above the shop and bring Victoria with her. They would all get on well together, and Vikki would say her first words in her grandmother's house.

Dan arrived at dawn to swill down the front of the shop

and pavement and the bucket stopped clanking when he left for the stables. Jane dressed quickly and went up the road to buy the first newspaper of the day. She read GERMANY DECLARES WAR ON FRANCE and felt suffocated. War was now inevitable.

The next day, Germany invaded Belgium and on 4 August 1914, history recorded that GREAT BRITAIN DECLARED WAR ON GERMANY. Newport seethed with troops and the man from the ferry told of hundreds of trains converging on Southampton overnight, set in action as if a giant switch had been pulled, bringing supplies and men with a terrible efficiency as if they were mere packages to be moved along a line.

Lorries rumbled on to transport vessels and men bedded down on decks as the flotilla of the British Expeditionary Force got under way. The sea off Cowes and Ryde was dark with ships and the smoke from countless chimney-stacks, and sails billowed in any wind that helped them. Barges, as yet empty, waited for horses to be loaded from the horse slip at Ryde. Nobody knew what would be needed. Warfare might need cavalry or a more mechanized approach. On the broad Veldt of Africa the British had learned from the Boers, wearing khaki to blend with the earth, making sorties and withdrawing instead of launching costly and laborious attacks from a massed front. Was the terrain of France suitable for either type of attack?

Aaron's righthand man came up on the tide, grumbling that the fish had been disturbed by all the activity, so Jane didn't complain that the shrimps were late, but took what he had and thanked him. 'That great hulk, the Dreadnought *George V* was out there,' he said.

'Ready to sail?'

'Too high on the water-line for that. She isn't loaded. All leave has been cancelled except for some who can go home from Portsmouth by launch for a few hours. I met a man in Cowes who told me they have to register to an agent every day but it looks as if they've come to say goodbye.'

'I'll take some shrimps up to Staplers,' Janey decided. 'Mrs Neville wanted some and these are nice and fat.'

'You go,' said Jane. 'I can manage.' She sensed that this was important and knew that Janey never shirked her work in the shop. She thought of the man with the devil-may-care eyes who wanted Janey and prayed that all would be well.

Janey walked up the hill with the rush basket covered with butter muslin. It was hot and sultry and the woods were heavy with dark green in the depths where she picked Spanish chestnuts in autumn and bluebells in spring. The house she now knew so well was set back behind laurel hedges and the drooping fronds of weeping willow, and gravel crunched under her feet as she approached the front door.

Violet the maid opened the door and stepped aside. Miss Darwen came in by the front door even if she was carrying fish. 'Mrs Neville isn't at home, Miss,' she said.

Janey saw a movement on the stairs and looked up. She held the basket on one hip like a peasant girl in a picture and her smile was radiant. She didn't know that she spoke but she used the words her mother used when in trouble or great emotion. 'Holy Mary,' she said.

Clive Neville came downstairs, two at a time. He took the basket and thrust it into Violet's arms. 'Take these and prepare them for table,' he said. 'I hate to find shell in mine.' Violet went away with obvious reluctance to do the fiddly job that would take a long time, and Janey shook her head at Clive, laughing, knowing he wanted the girl out of the way.

The kitchen door closed and he came to her and took her in his arms. Janey seemed to melt and cleave to him and they kissed, a deep slow kiss of commitment. 'Well, when's it to be?'

'I can't tell when you'll be called away,' she said, puzzled.

'I know that.' He traced the edges of her mouth with a finger and kissed her lightly. 'When do we get married, Janey?'

'We can't! You have to go away and there isn't time. Your mother and father wouldn't approve and I can't leave my mother to look after the shop while Father is away.'

'I have thought of all that.' She had never noticed how firm his mouth could be and how steadfast his eyes. Usually he was laughing and charming everyone he met, rather like her brother Jack, but Clive's face was stronger and she knew that if he asked her, she would go anywhere with him, ignoring friends and family and local gossip, just as her mother had done when she left Ireland to marry an English soldier.

'You can't work miracles,' she said.

'Tomorrow, you wear the yellow dress you wore to Lizzie's wedding and meet me at the top of Snook's Hill early before the rest are about. I shall have the car waiting and we can get married.' She gasped. 'You remember meeting my cousin? He's the vicar of Calborne and I have made all the arrangements.'

'I shall have to tell Mother and you must say something,' she said slowly, looking troubled.

'If we do, we shall never get away. Trust me,' he said. 'I must make you my wife before I leave. I love you, Janey, and we may have no time beyond tomorrow.'

'What shall I say at home?'

'That there's a crisis in the Neville household that requires you there all day!'

The front doorbell rang and Violet came from the kitchen, drying her hands. 'I can't!' Janey said in an agonized whisper.

'You must,' he said and left her to see herself out.

Jane looked up as Janey came back into the shop. 'Is Clive going away?'

'Yes, Mother.' Janey leaned on the counter and watched the golden oranges drop one by one as Jane sorted them. She picked up a large one and peeled it carefully, leaving the peel in one continuous curve as she had done so often as a child, throwing the peel over one shoulder to see what initial of a lover's name it made as it fell to the floor; this time, however, she didn't drop it on the floor but placed it on the counter.

'You already know his name,' Jane said. 'Don't look surprised. I've known for a long time and I think his mother has too. She doesn't object and nor do I. Why should we? The men may have other ideas but men often do for reasons of their own. If Clive married into the Manor, the Nevilles would move up in society but Mrs Neville sees a woman who will always love her son.'

'Mother . . . oh, Mother!' Janey burst into floods of tears.

Jane led her into the back room and smoothed the damp hair from her face. 'I ran away with the man I loved and never regretted it in spite of all the suffering and the rest. At the time, he was what I wanted and that was all that mattered.' She took a deep breath. 'Wanting brings a kind of madness like between Jack and Nellie but if you love equally with no cause for jealousy, it is good and nothing can take its place.' She laughed softly. 'You of all my children are the most like me. Edward is a throwback to old Parson Bright with not a bit of Irish in him, Lizzie will never feel passion and Clare loves Clare. Do you have any time?' she asked.

'No. He wants me to marry him tomorrow.'

'Then you have no time at all,' said Jane briskly. 'You'll need to iron your yellow dress and thread ribbons through your new petticoat. I'll wash your hair and you must go to bed early.' She gave Janey a sharp tap on the shoulder. 'It's to be in church?'

'Yes. His cousin will marry us.'

'Thank the Lord! It's a good thing your father is away and I'll say nothing until you tell me to do so. You will come back here to wait for him?'

Janey nodded dumbly and they clung together for a minute. 'I do love him so much, Mother,' Janey whispered.

'I surely hope you do, or it's a day wasted,' said Jane dryly.

Chapter 11

'It isn't fair! I could have worn my pink dress.' Clare was sulking.

'There wasn't time,' Janey explained. 'We had only a day and a night together before Clive went back to Portsmouth. He may sail on the *George V* but he doesn't know. As he said, he might spend the war ferrying troops over to France on a paddle-steamer for all they tell him now!'

'You did the right thing,' Jane said firmly. 'I approve and although his mother was hurt that she wasn't told she gave them her blessing.'

'What about Father?' asked Emily. 'He should have been told.'

'There wasn't time.' How often would that phrase be used in the future, Jane wondered. There never was time to live or catch breath and show their real feelings when the men had to leave their loved ones. Janey had changed from a girl into a woman in a day. Sweet Mary may it last for ever, with good health and joy.

'Nothing here has changed,' Janey said. 'I shall live at home until Clive comes back, and if Father has to go I shall stay to help until the war is over. I shall still go up to Staplers to cook for Mrs Neville, though.' She picked up a pile of clean linen. 'I'll put this away and start on the pickle jars, Mother.'

Pickles and jam, Janey thought with a sense of unreality. Did Clive think of her every minute of the day? She had said that nothing had changed, but how could the clock be put back after having lost her virginity with such shattering intensity? She touched her sore breasts through the thin blouse, remembering the flood of passion that had committed her to Clive for ever. Her body glowed with a sultry fire that needed only his touch to burst into flame. She folded the linen carefully. Had this ever happened to any other girl? Lizzie was married but surely she and Harry had never felt such passion after courting for such a long time. They had been in no hurry to marry, either. She laughed softly. That wasn't fair. How could Harry ever make a girl cry out with love? What other man could match the hard but gentle desire mingled with boyish uncertainty? She might have no bottom drawer saved up, but oh – what jewels to recall!

'Keep all the money you earn,' Jane insisted once they were alone packing sliced apples into the big metal jam boiler. 'Put it safely where you can get at it in a hurry. If Clive sent word to follow him you'd need money to buy clothes and to travel, and we don't want to have to ask your father!'

'No, he was furious when I told him today. I didn't think he'd be like that – half the time he resents us being here, but when we go our own ways he behaves as if we are insulting him personally.' Jane pushed a handful of cloves under the apples and added enough water to prevent them from sticking. Together they lifted the heavy pan over the fire and Jane wrapped her right warm in a thick towel as the jam came to the boil and spat over the wooden spoon.

'Clare was upset, too,' Jane reminded her. 'It wasn't that she wanted Clive, but her pride was hurt. That one likes attention from the men but isn't ready for marriage by a long chalk. Poor Joseph doesn't know if he's coming or going! One minute she's all honey and the next she can hardly bring herself to speak to him. If he says he will volunteer she says he's a fool and if he doesn't she hints that men who hang back are cowards.'

'She'll lose him,' warned Janey.

'She may stay with us like Emily,' said Jane.

'Or instead of Emily? Why do we take it for granted that Emily will be here for ever, unmarried.'

Jane moved smartly to avoid a spat of jam and slid the pot away from the direct heat. 'Don't say such things when I'm stirring jam,' she joked. 'Emily will stay at home as she likes it too much to leave, and she is the youngest.'

'If I'd been the youngest, would you have expected me to stay?'

Jane unwrapped the sticky towel from her arm. 'Emily isn't as pretty as the rest of you,' she said, but sounded uncertain. 'We always thought she'd stay and I haven't seen many boys after her!'

'Arnold Churcher is fond of her.'

'Arnold?' Jane laughed. 'He may dance with her at socials and they are in the same group of friends at chapel but he isn't her beau. Can you imagine your father if a man wanted to take his Emily away?'

'I can, Mother – that's the trouble. I doubt if Emily would be strong enough to go off as I did. Please remember what I say. Clare would be better fitted to stay as I can't imagine her in a man's arms!' They smiled, two women who had experienced passion as tempestuous as a spring storm.

'She'll never marry,' Jane said with sudden conviction. The recollection of Mrs Lee comforted her. 'Years ago, old Mrs Lee told me that one would stay with me into my old age. She read my tea cup and a lot of it has already come true.'

'Did she say anything about me?' Janey asked eagerly.

'And what would you be wanting to know now that you have the handsome prince she saw that day and you'll live happily ever after?'

Janey blushed. 'I'm glad,' she whispered, and put thick layers of newspaper on the table under the heavy earthenware jars hot from the oven ready to receive the jam, and dipped the circles of greaseproof paper in cheap brandy to keep the surface of the jars from mould.

Jane nodded and smiled as Janey told her about the wedding service and the two witnesses brought in from the village, quite bemused by it all, but she wasn't really listening. Over the years she had made a barrier between her mind and what Mrs Lee had told her but glimpses came through. It wasn't good to dwell on what happened to the children but most of what the gypsy had foretold had come true already. It wasn't clear exactly which of her girls would make a bad marriage – and she prayed that it wasn't Janey.

One look at Janey's face reassured her. Clive was gentle and loved her and had none of the coarse elements that Walter showed. She no longer cared that Walter had raped her but prayed that Janey would never suffer as she had done.

'Father is thinking of joining the Expeditionary Force,' Janey informed her. 'He's gone off to see Dr Barnes to get a clean bill of health to make his claim certain. Apparently, they are accepting men five years younger than him and each day the age seems to go up, so he could still go.'

'He'll do as he pleases as usual, but I shouldn't think they are that hard up yet,' Jane said and washed her hands before looking at the magazine with the latest recruitment poster in it. 'Lord Kitchener has sent out thousands of these to attract young men, and a special letter to men of the Island.' She was impressed that a man as famous as Kitchener should bother to single out the Island.

'Clive says they send one like that to each county to make them feel important,' Janey said. The headline was flanked by fingers pointing to the sharp capitals. MEN OF WIGHT, YOUR KING AND COUNTRY NEED YOU!!! ANOTHER 100,000 MEN WANTED!

'They are taking them young,' Jane said sadly, reading an article on the next page. The age for enrolment was nineteen to thirty-five years, with ex-soldiers up to forty-five. Then her heart nearly stopped: ex-non-commissioned officers up to fifty could join up, but must be physically fit and over five feet three inches in height. Now she understood why Walter had braved the idea of an interview with the doctor . . . Apart from the motives for his check-up, Jane was secretly relieved that he was to see the doctor. One evening recently he had sat and stared at her with hot eyes and then accused her of talking about him behind his back; she often saw him standing behind the bead curtain these days listening to conversations as if waiting for his name to be mentioned. If worry about the war was making him like that, Dr Barnes might give him a tonic.

'Father went up the road in his new suit a long time ago,'

Janey said. 'He must have gone on somewhere from the surgery and not come back to tell us the result.'

The shop-bell clanged and Emily burst into the back room. 'It's the maid from Doctor Barnes,' she said in a hoarse whisper. 'He wants to see you straight away, Mother.'

Jane snatched up her knitted coat and pulled her close-fitting hat nearly down to her eyes. 'Holy Mary, what now?' she murmured and rushed out of the house and up to the neat house behind the laurel bushes. The maid panted behind her but managed to say that there had been no accident or anything dramatic so Jane arrived breathless but calm.

In the waiting room, she took a deep breath. She knew the room so well . . . She had come here heavy with her first child with joy in her heart, and later with the others, each time with less enthusiasm when her health suffered. When the children were young she had sat on the faded red velour chair in the corner to wait for news about Emily when scarlet fever made them take her away to the Isolation Hospital at Fairlee, when Jack had run a nail into his foot, and now she had no idea what lay beyond that door.

She waited until she was called and meanwhile absent-mindedly tidied the tablecloth to make it hang straight, and looked at the pictures on the ochre walls. At least we finished the jam, she thought, and Janey could organize Emily in the shop before going off to Staplers. Then the door opened and Dr Barnes smiled and asked her to come in.

Walter sat in his shirtsleeves and the look of horror on his face could not be hidden now that he was cleanshaven. 'What is it, Doctor?' she asked, as if politely enquiring about a sick neighbour.

'Your husband is ill, Mrs Darwen,' he said. He put up a hand as if to stop her speaking. 'I never like to beat about the bush as you know. This condition has been coming on for years and is nothing new. With treatment, he will be able to overcome a great many of the symptoms.'

Jane tried to think clearly. Walter had none of the symptoms of tuberculosis or the wasting disease like the man on the Mall who jerked and fell and had to be put in a chair when he was very bad, and Walter had only the occasional twinge of rheumatism.

Dr Barnes looked less confident under her calm scrutiny. Why did this have to happen to the best woman in the entire neighbourhood, who had already taken more from her husband than most women could endure? Perhaps he need not tell her the exact nature of the disease. He moved some papers on the desk and looked at her again. Her eyes missed nothing and he had to tell the truth. 'It started a long time ago when your husband was in Africa,' he said. 'It happened to many men out there fighting and away from their loved ones.'

Jane felt frozen. He's making excuses for Walter, she thought, and regarded her husband coldly. If it's what I suspect, I don't want to know, she decided and her flesh began to creep with fastidious revulsion. He had been with her since then, slept in her bed and made disgusting love to her, making her pregnant and nearly killing her. The hostility that had lain dormant for years showed in her eyes and Dr Barnes thought it was aimed at him.

'I can tell you the facts, Mrs Darwen, but I am not a man of the cloth to make moral judgements, and men were exposed to many temptations away from home.'

'I understand, Doctor, but you haven't told me the name of the disease.' If he doesn't say the words I know that Walter will try to deny it when we get home, she thought. 'I must know,' she added firmly. Both men looked away, Walter silent and ashamed and the doctor red-faced. 'Are you trying to tell me that my husband caught syphilis when he went with women in Pretoria?' Dr Barnes nodded. Jane took a step towards Walter and her fingers pulled at the knitted coat. Her eyes blazed with a fire as dark as hate but her voice was clear and steady. 'Are you also going to tell me you wanted me here to say he most likely gave it to me, too? That he brought this . . . corruption into our home among our children? That the baby I lost would have been tainted? That the whole house is defiled?' She felt the knitting give and knew that two wide ladders had run in the garment that Emily had taken two months to knit.

'Happily you aren't infected. From what your husband says, all the first and infectious symptoms appeared when he was away and the second stage occurred when he was sent from Pretoria on active service, and was no longer in contact with . . . well, he wasn't re-infected. The third or tertiary stage is not contagious unless he has some form of ulceration on the surface of his body.'

'Happily?' Jane gave a short bitter laugh. 'And *unhappily*, he still has it in him. What does that mean?'

'I found some knots of fibrous tissue in certain muscles which led me to investigate further. The later symptoms may already have occurred. Have you noticed any changes in your husband?'

'He dropped his moustache cup because his hand was numb,' she said. 'He's bad-tempered more than I'd think likely even with middle age and he thinks that people talk about him and distrusts even his friends at times. Has that anything to do with this?'

'You always were observant, my dear.' It was as if Walter was a tailor's dummy with no voice or mind. 'There may be other changes.' The doctor moved away and Jane followed him. 'Bursts of irrational bad temper and even violence, or apathy, or loss of muscle power, depending which part of the spinal cord is affected. Try not to cross him, and with treatment he may get no worse unless his blood vessels are affected. Mr Darwen may improve, but some men have trouble suddenly.'

'Could Walter have a seizure like Aaron?'

'Not quite,' was all he would say. 'It wouldn't lay him up for long.'

Walter regarded them both with open hostility. 'So you refuse to sign my paper, is that it, Doctor? Just because of something that happened years ago and was no one's fault, you take away my chance to serve King and Country!'

Trust Walter to put the blame on the doctor, Jane thought. 'What do we do, Doctor?' she asked and Dr Barnes smiled.

'I can ask the district nurse to give what is called mercurial inunctions; this means she has to rub ointment into the skin each day for half an hour to make sure the mercury compound is absorbed. I can also make up preparations of arsenic and iodide of potassium that will act more quickly and which he can take by mouth.' He smiled warmly. 'I asked you here, Mrs Darwen, in case you would rather do the treatment yourself. It's monotonous, though, and whoever does it must wear a glove to prevent the mercury from being absorbed into their own hands.'

'Thank you, Doctor. I can collect the medicine from you and it will not be the talk of Newport,' she said bluntly. 'When do I start and what do I do?'

'Apply it to a buttock or thigh, changing the site each day to avoid soreness. Any glove with no holes like a chamois leather or a calf glove will do and I'll check your husband once a week to see that he is not getting too much. If he complains of a metallic taste in his mouth or has bad headaches, tell me. You must clean your teeth well, Mr Darwen,' he said to Walter.

'How long does it take to kill me?' asked Walter.

'The disease will be arrested and you can live a normal life knowing that unless you develop a gummatous ulcer you cannot infect another person.'

'Not the disease, Doctor, the treatment.' Walter pulled on his jacket and fixed his tie. 'I'm not afraid of the disease – I've had it long enough to know it isn't a killer. How long before *she* poisons me with arsenic?'

'There'll be no talk like that, man! If I hear another word, I'll send you to the infirmary where the nurses will have less patience than your wife, and everyone will know what you have!'

'I was joking,' Walter said, but Jane knew he had meant every word. She waited for the white-wrapped bottles and ointment boxes sealed with red sealing wax while Walter went back to the shop alone.

'I think we have caught it in time,' the doctor said. 'Another stern test for you, I'm afraid, but you have courage.' Jane smiled. What was so wonderful about putting on ointment? 'If at any time, he . . . changes for the worse, promise me you'll leave the house at once and come to see me or go to a relative or close friend.'

'I know his funny ways, Doctor, but thank you for being so kind.' She walked home slowly. He was the third person to hint that she might need help in the future, but why? There was nothing on earth that could make her want to leave her home, and no danger there.

Chapter 12

The paddles of the ferry dripped its last load of water in Southampton Docks and Jane Darwen stared at the change in the port. The warehouses were busy even on a Saturday and on each slipway grey shapes with shrouded gunturrets and lifeboats lay waiting, making the one liner look vulgarly bright against the grey. The trip on the omnibus to take her to Edward's home was a novelty but she turned up her nose at the dust and grime everywhere, as each passing train covered the buildings with smoke and grit. She ran a gloved finger along the sooty ridge of Edward's door and wondered how anyone kept clean.

Alice seemed pleased to see her and helped her unpack the fish and fruit from her basket. They sipped tea and spoke of everything but the two things on Jane's mind: Walter and the health of this girl who looked too bright-eyed and hollow-cheeked and today had the new-mown-hay smell about her. Yet Jane was enjoying the visit and felt free away from the shop and the need to justify Walter's ill-humour to everyone by saying he was disappointed that his bad back kept him from the army. 'I'll cook fish for dinner and make a pie,' she offered, and Alice smiled gratefully. She made no effort to help but seemed eager for all the family news.

'It's very dull here,' she confided in her mother-in-law. 'I don't go out much as I feel tired and everywhere is dirty. I wish I was back in our little house by the withy beds. I miss you all and have only Edward to help me do the washing. He's up half the night with it sometimes,' she added, as if it was something to boast about and Jane set her lips, not knowing how much was illness and how much pure laziness.

'I hope you don't leave everything to him – a bit of hard work can bring colour to your cheeks.'

'I'm just too tired to work,' Alice repeated resentfully. 'Have you brought any journals today?'

Jane handed her *Weldon's Journal*, wondering if the girl sat with her feet up all day reading, then busied herself in the kitchen making apple pies. At least Edward would have one good feed this week, she thought grimly, and the other pies would keep well in a cold larder. She heard her son's familiar whistle and smiled. He sounded cheerful enough but when he came in he looked thinner and his eyes showed signs of strain until he saw his mother. He hugged her and grinned. 'I might have known that the smell of cooking along the road was from here,' he said. He kissed Alice tenderly and said she looked better for a bit of company.

'That's not as important as keeping away from sweets,' Jane said. 'Remember what Dr Barnes said?'

'I can't help it and I'm going to have some pie,' Alice said sulkily.

'I've made you stewed apple on its own without sugar. You like sharp things and that will be better for you,' Jane asserted. It did her heart good to see Edward enjoy his food and Jane pressed him to more. At last he stretched and yawned. 'I could go to sleep now, but I have to clear away and get back.'

'I'll make tea now and wash the plates after you've gone back. Help me bring in the tray and then sit down for five minutes.' She closed the kitchen door so that Alice couldn't hear and told him about Walter. 'You've troubles enough of your own but you are the eldest and I had to tell someone or burst,' she said anxiously. 'I don't need help, Edward, but I wanted you to know, and I don't ever want to tell the girls. I can do the treatment myself and Doctor Barnes has promised your father will not get worse.' She went on to ask him about his work which made him animated, so that Alice couldn't guess at their conversation or become suspicious by his long face.

'We saw all this coming,' Edward told her. 'The day before war was declared, they moved thousands of Territorials and Reservists from camps to their bases. The whole of the Ist Gordon Highlanders, stationed at Plymouth, and four hundred units from other depots were mobilized on orders received at five-twenty pm on August the fourth, two hundred and thirty-five Reservists from Aberdeen on August the sixth, and two hundred and ninety-six Reservists from there too were brought by rail and reached Boulogne by the fourteenth. In five days, eighteen hundred special trains were run in Great Britain and Ireland. On the busiest day, the equivalent of a whole division was moved in eighty trains to Southampton Docks! Ships are sailing all the time and one day there were thirteen full of troops.'

'Good heavens! You sound as you did when you wrote to your father in Africa. You told him then to the nearest pound what you had delivered to Albany and kept him up to date with the figures.'

Edward smiled proudly. 'I'll come over to see you as soon as I can, so try not to worry,' he promised, 'but I work every day of the week now and we'll have to wait until things calm down. Alice enjoys your visits and it's a breath of fresh air for me, too,' he added rather wistfully.

On the way home, Jane wondered if Alice could go on living as she did. The rooms above the shop were emptier now, and perhaps she would be better off under her mother-in-law's roof. Jane could not admit to herself that her own fear of being alone with Walter was growing. A cargo ship steamed up the Channel flanked by smaller naval vessels bristling with guns. The convoy made the war more real, more threatening and infinitely sad. Men in khaki stood about the deck of a ship ready to sail and Jane could see their white faces and the smoke from their cigarettes under the drab caps. She wondered if their mothers and sweethearts knew they'd be in France by the next morning. It was as sad as when she saw Sidney leave and sadder to know that she didn't see Jack sail. It would be so easy to let go and weep now, but she took hold of herself and by the time she reached home, had mentally made arrangements to be ready for Nellie and the baby and Alice to live above the shop if the need arose.

'Did you see the docks?' asked Janey eagerly, as soon as

Jane took off her hat. She poured out the strong tea that was brewing ready for her return.

'There were two of the new cruisers that Clive told us about and one of the fearful Dreadnoughts looking like someone's worst nightmare and lots of smaller boats with men in them.' She shook her head. 'Edward told me so much that most of it has gone. I don't know how he remembers all those figures, but he seems very happy at work. I remember that he said the railways were now under national control and Admiral John Jellicoe has become Admiral of the Fleet.'

'I should hear from Clive soon. In his last note he said he could have stayed here for another day or so as they are still in port but unable to visit anyone.'

'Jellicoe?' said Walter, who had come in silently. 'He's fifty-five if he's a day! How does a man of that age take command when they refuse men who have already served their country well?' He seemed to have forgotten the reason for his being denied a place among the volunteers, although he still remained an instructor. He had taken to wearing his Boer War medals again whenever he drank in the Wheatsheaf and spent more and more time with George Foster poring over the news. Janey handed him a cup of tea and sat back silently.

'Alice and Edward sent their love,' Jane said brightly. 'He's very busy, just as you are, Walter. They can't spare men like you to go away from training the recruits, and Edward can't go and leave his work, either.'

'Humph! They refuse men like me, born and bred an Englishman and yet they bring over thousands of Canadians and Indians to fight in places they haven't even seen on a map!' He slurped his tea noisily and took a piece of currant cake from the plate. 'They're mad,' he said through a mouthful of crumbs. 'Those poor devils of Indians will freeze in this climate with winter not far off and some of our boys will swelter under the suns of Africa, trying to get cool in tropical kit. Let the Canadians go back home and warm their backsides by their own fires and bring back all the men who escaped the war by emigrating, then we could fight our own battles!'

Janey smiled. It was common knowledge that the local girls had been put in a flutter when the husky and virile Canadians arrived. The newcomers had put a lot of local noses out of joint among the men of Newport and Cowes. The Canadians didn't even have difficulty in communication like the French or Spanish.

'The first wounded have come back,' Walter announced. 'Not here, but on the mainland.'

'I wanted to be a nurse but if Clive comes back I must be here,' Janey said.

'We shall have plenty to do at the chapel,' Jane told her. 'Mrs Barnes is arranging entertainments for the troops in the Hall and I said I'd help with refreshments and assist some of the men who can't write letters to their families. If you can cook some of your cakes and biscuits, Janey, that will be grand, just grand.'

'Remember you are a married woman now,' warned Walter.

'I'm not likely to forget that,' Janey replied with spirit. 'Clive would want me to do all I can to help. I know if *he* needed help I'd be grateful for people like Mother and Mrs Barnes to give him entertainment.'

'Some forget they have husbands. One who slept under my roof, for instance,' he added sullenly. He had resented Nellie staying with them for a while and when she left, he resented that, too.

'Nellie will do what she does best, singing and dancing for the men. There's no harm in making people happy,' Jane said.

'She does that, all right! Throwing her legs about for all to see and leaving her child in an inn kitchen while she goes whoring.'

'Sing she may, dance she does but a whore she is not!' said Jane with such fury that Walter knew he had gone too far and was silent. He found few ways to rile her these days even when she did his treatment and she had to touch him.

'It's high time you did the ointment,' he reminded her

spitefully, as if she had kept him waiting all day. He knew how much she dreaded the contact.

'Is your back getting any better, Father?' asked Janey. He glanced at her sharply but saw only concern. Jane had obviously kept her word that none of the girls would know why he had been refused his clean bill of health, and a bad back, massaged with cream each day and examined by the doctor at intervals, was a good excuse.

'I'll be up in a minute,' Jane said. 'I have a fresh pot of the cream.' Cream sounded better than unguent or unction, she thought. It was like the precious substance poured over Our Lord's head by the Magdalene but this ointment, though precious in its own way, was unholy – poisonous to all but those it treated for something even more unholy. She took the pot and a towel with a rag to wipe her glove clean after the treatment and went upstairs. Walter lay on the bed with his shirt covering his thighs. He usually kept on his underpants but today he had taken them off to embarrass her with his nakedness. He half-smiled but her fear made her seem aloof and very controlled.

'Turn over,' she said briskly. 'I'm doing the right buttock today.' She made no attempt to touch him until he had assumed the position she required and he didn't see her relief. She massaged the cream, adding more when it was absorbed until she had used the amount prescribed. She turned away at last, wiped the glove clean and screwed up the soiled rag ready to burn. It would be easier if she had access to the rubber gloves now used in hospitals as she could wash them, but she had to make do with old calf leather gloves. Quickly, she left him to dress and escaped the underlying menace of being alone with him, and when Walter came down ready for supper, she had washed her hands and was dishing up the food. As usual she asked, 'Have you any funny taste, Walter? You'll say if you don't feel right, won't you?'

'It takes longer than this to kill a man with arsenic,' he said, and Emily chuckled thinking he was joking. 'I've enough mercury in my blood to fill a barometer and get the latest weather.'

'Oh, Father, you do make me laugh,' Emily said.

Walter, who was usually very fond of Emily, now frowned. 'Make you laugh, do I? I know someone who will laugh on the other side of her face if I catch her with that Arnold Churcher again.'

Emily blushed scarlet. 'We're only friends, Father. We both belong to the chapel and go about with lots of other people.'

'Keep it like that and don't let him get any ideas. You stay at home, my girl. I'm having none of that sniffing round my Emily. At the rate we're going we'll have nobody left in this family. Why don't you teach your children where their duty lies instead of letting them run off to marry the first Tom, Dick or Harry they meet?' Jane clenched her hands and walked into the scullery in case she said something she might regret and Emily burst into tears. Only Clare sat calmly, looking superior. She fetched more plates for the pudding and seemed in a hurry to get the meal over, then dressed carefully in a long loose coat over a tight skirt and white blouse and put a deep clinging toque hat on her head.

'Where are you going?' Emily asked miserably.

'Up to the Drill Hall with Ethel Sheath. They have whist and games and someone is coming to talk about Carisbrooke Castle.'

'You never play whist and you hate history,' Janey said, laughing.

Walter belched and stood up. The mixture he had to take under Jane's stern gaze made him full of wind and he was due at the Wheatsheaf so he didn't stay to hear the rest. 'Can I come, too?' Emily asked when he had gone.

'If you like,' Clare said carelessly. It suited her to have a paler sister who was a foil to her own luxuriant hair and bright colour, and as for Ethel with her mop of red hair, she was no rival. Emily ran up to change into something more suitable for a social evening but Janey said she'd stay in as it was no fun without Clive.

The Drill Hall was brightly lit and over three dozen people stood about, chatting. Clare saw Joseph but pretended not to and made for a boy she had known at school and never really liked. Ethel joined three girls who by their expressions of doom knew they'd be eternal wallflowers while Emily slipped away to meet Arnold Churcher by the first whist-table. They smiled, and Emily blushed. At first glance, Arnold was plain and unimpressive, but he had a kind mouth and eyes, and made anyone talking to him think he cared about them to the exclusion of others. They refused all offers of whist and sat by the stage talking, and Joseph claimed Clare and took her off for refreshments.

'I might volunteer,' Arnold confided to Emily. 'My father doesn't need me now in the business as my two brothers have come in and they are too young for the army.'

'I hope you don't,' said Emily.

'Would you miss me?'

'Yes,' she whispered as if Walter might hear. 'I'd miss any friend who went away.'

'I know you are too young yet,' Arnold said, 'but if I went, would you write to me and be my special friend?' She nodded. Surely there was no harm in that? 'I want to think of you Emily and to know that when I come back you'll be waiting for me.' He brought out a box containing a ring made of plaited hair, lacquered to stiffness. 'I had this made for you. It doesn't tie you to anything but when I come back I want to ask your father for something special and very precious. Keep it until I come back.'

'Oh, Arnold, you are going away!'

'Yes, I go next week. I had to enlist. I can't stay here and watch the Germans tramp all over Europe and let the Kaiser beat us just because men wouldn't volunteer.'

'My father wanted to go but he has a bad back and they wouldn't take him,' Emily said.

'I could never look men like your father in the eye if I shirked this. Brave men like him fought and won the last lot, and so must we. I have to come back with my pride intact before I meet him.'

'I'll write,' Emily said. She was confused and numb inside. 'I have to look after Mother and Father, Arnold, but I'll keep your lovely ring for ever.'

They walked back from the Drill Hall in a group, with

Clare and Joseph in front, laughing. Ethel and the other girls ran on when it started raining and Arnold drew Emily into a shop doorway and kissed her. 'Remember this evening,' he begged. 'Please, Emily, and when I come back I want to marry you.' He kissed her again and wondered why she had tears on her cheeks. Clare called impatiently as she didn't want to be alone with Joseph in the dark and knew that he couldn't kiss her in the doorway of *Darwen's* if Emily and Arnold were there. She pushed Emily into the shop and waved a casual goodbye, leaving the two men frustrated and lost.

Emily crept up to bed and put the ring in a box that had once held chocolates. The girl on the lid had a sweet smile of utter happiness and Emily ran a sharp fingernail over the face, ruining the smile. I can't marry him, she thought sadly. I can never marry but tonight I know how Janey feels. It isn't fair, but how could I anger Father who has always been so kind to me?

Clare loosened her hair after its confinement in the tight hat and felt free. Joseph was becoming persistent and now kissed her in a different way that made her gasp. His hands wandered deliciously over her body and she mistrusted her own growing response. Half her mind told her that he was a good catch and that she was fond of him but the other half pined for excitement and a far more handsome and rich husband. If he went away to the war, she could meet other men and decide what she wanted from Joseph when he came back.

Ethel had told her about girls who played a game, handing white feathers to men out of uniform, thinking it a great joke. It was the mark of a coward to be given one and many innocent soldiers on leave had been embarrassed by being insulted in this way, but the custom was growing to near hysterical heights and Ethel wanted to give some to men she knew had avoided enlistment. Everyone was so serious these days. Lizzie was no fun and seldom came to the shop unless she was after free fish and Emily did little socializing. Janey dreamed of Clive and her mother hardly heard her say good night, but sat with the last two letters from Sidney open on the table; Clare knew that Jack hadn't even sent a forwarding address.

Gulls' feathers were white enough, Clare thought gleefully. That might be quite exciting.

Chapter 13

George Foster tried not to panic. It was all very well for the Council to take it for granted he could write a book about the Boer War, but what did they know about his difficulties through lack of education, leaving school at fourteen and having no literary background? The vicar blandly said, 'You have all your valuable notes, more than any man I know, George, and it will be a forerunner to the one you must write about this war – a slimmer volume this time, as the war will be over soon.'

In February 1915, however, most knew that this was a pious hope as war was not only a reality that showed no sign of abating but crept closer with each day, the news bringing fresh losses and terrible happenings that had no place in civilized warfare. The Indian Corps had gone to France in November after war was declared, heroically defending the still-undamaged town of Wytschaete, in the first battle of Yprès. Walter respected men like that who came from foreign countries but were fiercely loyal to the Crown and fought under the banner of Colonialism. He still read the poems of Rudyard Kipling and knew that the Indian troops . . . Baluchis . . . were like the regimental *Bhisti* or water-carriers in the poem *Gunga Din*. This poem could still make Walter's eyes wet when it was declaimed at chapel concerts.

'A quarter of a million Indians came to fight for our Crown,' he mused, sitting over a pint with George and Bert in the Jug and Bottle one day.

'Savages,' snorted Bert. 'They may send numbers but can they fight?'

'You know nothing about war, so why don't you shut up,' Walter shouted in one of his now frequent bursts of temper. 'We thought the Boers were a bunch of gypsies but we had to learn from them and we train our lads in a lot of their ways now.' He drank his second tankard of ale and lit a Red Hussar cigarette, not because he liked them but because they were the issue to the troops, even more than Wild Woodbines.

Bert lit a Passing Cloud and puffed at the more fragrant and sophisticated elliptical weed. He grinned and touched the black armband on Walter's jacket. 'Still in mourning for Lord Roberts, eh? Will you leave that off before the end of the war? He's been dead for months now.'

Walter became maudlin. 'He was a good man. They called him Bobs and Bobs he was to all the men. He didn't want war but he was like me, ready if called. He fought with us, did Lord Roberts, and didn't sit on his backside and give orders from the Veldt, not like the generals we have today. He fought again this time and was killed before he could look round.'

'Someone has to stay behind the lines to keep the wheels turning,' Bert said mildly.

'And make a pile out of death!' Walter sneered. 'Have you shares in mustard gas yet?'

'The German gas attack was on the eastern front,' Bert said uneasily. 'It wouldn't be allowed in France, and we've dug in well with mortars and heavy guns so they'll have a job to come any closer.'

'Oh yes? And who thought they'd drop bombs from a Zeppelin? They even raided England and killed a few people on the mainland. My son-in-law was in the Gallipoli raid, you know,' Walter said with a pride he never showed to Janey. 'He was home on leave for a week afterwards and is now in a cruiser carrying torpedoes and hunting German U-boats. If one of them gets caught in the nets we have round here, I wouldn't say much for their chances if our people find them. They do the work of the devil. They are like conger eels, the carrion of the sea.'

'We bomb from aeroplanes, too,' George put in, 'but at least the enemy can see us coming and run for it. The Aircraft Factory turns out some wonderful machines now and a lot of local lads are learning to fly. I think they are the heroes – they can't get them to France fast enough.

And we have balloons to keep the German airships high. Sir James Grierson was saying in the paper that if we don't achieve mastery in the air, then present-day warfare will be impossible.'

Walter grunted. 'In all that mud in Flanders, they still need horses.' He smoothed the thin line of his newly-growing moustache. Maudie admired the narrow line of hair adopted by many of the officers and Walter had to keep up with the young men who had the pick of the women. Maudie had not come to the stables on several occasions recently, her excuse being that Lucy was at home and she couldn't get away, but he thought she was lying.

'It's getting difficult to go to Portsmouth now,' Bert said, as if echoing his thoughts. 'That silly bugger taking the tickets for the ferry, who has known me man and boy for years, asked what I was doing there and if I was going on business.' He gave a short laugh. 'I soon put him in his place! I said I'd mind my business if he minded his, and if he thought I was a German spy he needed his eyes tested!' They laughed but it brought the war too close for comfort. Everything German was hated and local people, formerly well-respected but with foreign names, now faced outright suspicion and ridicule, and the wife of one of the publicans was in tears when her dachshund dog was poisoned. 'He was so brave and acted like an English gentleman,' she sobbed. 'Everyone loved my little Fritzy and he would never hurt a fly.'

Foreign workers and waiters who had been on the Island for years were rounded up and interned, bemused by their treatment after so much loyal and honest service. A woman carrying field-glasses while walking on the cliffs was harassed until it was proved she was the wife of a serving officer. Spy mania was rife, with men like Peter Fry on the look-out for scandal. 'Flappers' in London sold war bonds and, Jane suspected, also sold their bodies – but this was dismissed as being all in a good cause.

To be a civilian was a crime if a man had two arms and legs and fairly good eyesight, and many enlisted because they feared the acid tongues of neighbours more than they feared the Bosch. If they came home after missing being blown up, with a battle-stained uniform and the elementary gas mask slung over one arm, they were heroes, even if they had done no more than tend the baggage mules.

The first of the concerts for the troops had gone down well, with Nellie singing in a throaty whisper, 'We don't want to lose you but we think you ought to go, for your king and country need you . . .' and other fervent songs destined to send hundreds of young naive men to death on a wave of patriotism and the proud glow of the girls clinging to their arms.

Duty to one's country was preached from pulpits and platforms, and the public bars and music halls rang with patriotic songs, but by closing time, fights broke out between men from the Barracks and sailors, boasting of the respective merits of their services. Although he didn't use his fists, Walter strongly defended the old ways and said that if the Royal Horse Artillery was good enough for Lord Roberts, it was still good enough for him.

'Wipers we call it,' said a man from the Western Front. He removed the froth from his mouth and enjoyed the free beer offered in each bar he visited. 'Wipers is hell on earth. Thank you, I don't mind if I do have another. Your health, sir. You'd never believe the half of it.' He told them of the stench of decaying corpses on the barbed wire where the soldiers couldn't retrieve them without being strafed by the Germans. Nobody believed him, however, when he told of the Christmas Day truce between Germans and English, and he got more free drinks by dwelling on the dirty tricks of snipers and machine-gun teams.

With a great show of drama, the man struck a match to light his cigarette, but first lit the one that Walter held. He lit Bert's from the same flame then blew it out, leaving his own unlit. 'Bad luck to light three from one Lucifer,' he said.

'Garn! Old wives' tale,' said Bert.

'Not if you've been where I've been,' the man said. He lit his own Woodbine with a fresh match and inhaled deeply. 'You light a match and the Bosch sees the glow. You light the fag of the next man in the trench with his head near the top of the wall and the Bosch takes aim. You light the third fag and he fires and your brains are spilled over the duck-boards for some poor bugger to slip on and break his neck!'

Walter sobered, realizing that this war of attrition was not his kind of war. He couldn't think of staying in a slit trench for days on end, making no progress but banging away at an invisible enemy and scarring the landscape with craters soon filled with stagnant water and dead bodies as sorties were made into no-man's-land. Even he had to admit that horses would be useless in that scenario and at risk except when transporting supplies; the Artillery would be unlimbered more quickly using vehicles that couldn't be killed by machine-gun fire.

'Another five minutes and you'd have been locked out,' Walter said that night as Jane and Janey returned from a chapel concert. They ignored his surly tone and talked about the evening. 'Lucy was there with Maudie and she has a really nice voice,' Jane told him. 'She didn't go on the stage but she joined in the community singing.' Walter stared. Maudie had told him she was going to Sandown for a few days. 'And Lucy is growing up well,' Jane went on. 'Maudie makes her money go a long way and puts a lot on that girl's back. Lucy said you give them fish quite often. I think that's really kind, Walter. She's filling out a treat and Maudie looks better these days.'

'I might go to Portsmouth with Bert again some time,' Walter said. It was obvious that Jane had no idea about Maudie and if the little slut didn't fancy him now, he could find someone who would. Perhaps he had been too free with his money and might do well to keep her short for a while until she came to heel.

'It's getting difficult to go over to the mainland,' Jane reminded him. 'I had to show my ticket twice the last time I went to see Edward. I suppose as it's impossible to hide big ships like the *Invincible*: they have to be careful. I have a note now to say I am visiting my son.' She hesitated. Alice was ill again and needed a strong person to make her stick to her diet: Edward couldn't resist her when she pleaded for 'something nice in my mouth to take away the nasty taste'. She told Walter that Alice was ill and that Edward had to leave her for two nights to go to Waterloo.

'I said she was bad stock,' Walter replied. 'We don't want none of that here. You've done your share for them all, gal, and so have I – and as far as I'm concerned they can stew in their own juice.'

'What can I do?' Jane asked as Janey helped her with the dishes. 'He was bad enough over Nellie and Vikki.'

'Vikki is so sweet and I could love her as my own,' Janey said. 'I hope I have pretty babies.'

'With Clive and you as parents, you will,' Jane reassured her. 'Still, I'm not sorry you didn't get caught before Clive went away. Being the wife of a serving officer is bad enough without having a baby to consider.'

'You worry in case I am widowed,' Janey said bluntly. 'We have talked about that and when Clive comes home again, I hope to become pregnant as I want to have something of his to keep forever if the worst happened.'

'Don't! Jack said that I would have something of him for ever in Vikki if she had to come to me and it's true she has a lot of Jack in her eyes and hair.'

'That's all he left her,' Janey said dryly. 'He got away scot-free and didn't look back. We may never discover if he lives or dies out in Australia. Anything special you need me to do, Mother? I haven't to go to Staplers tomorrow. I keep an eye on the place while they are in America visiting Clive's sister who is having her first baby, but I have no cooking to do until May when they come back.'

'Where will you go when Clive has leave? There's room here for as long as you want it but if Clive has other ideas, I shan't be hurt. I have my daughter all the time he is away and he needs to see his own parents. You must follow where he leads.'

'As you did, Mother.'

'As I did, and the good years were worth it even when I lost my roots. I could never go back as my family hated

Walter for being English and a soldier. Stick to your man and never look back.' She poked the fire viciously and filled the kettle to put by the hob ready for the morning.

'So I may have Irish cousins I have never met?'

'Oh yes – Sidney found one in New York. He'd get on well with them as we are all gypsies at heart. Jack has their restlessness and so has Clare, but in a different way and I ache for her at times.'

'Clare will do as she pleases! She makes me really cross the way she treats Joseph, Mother. She's incapable of really loving anyone, just like Sidney, but he is at least kind.'

'Sidney? You are wrong, Janey. Sidney just hasn't found the right girl to love yet and although Clare is a cool one, she'll fall on her feet like Jack.' Jane looked up at the photograph of Sidney that Walter dared not remove. 'I must have that framed,' she said.

Janey tidied the room and picked up a bag, thinking it was hers. She opened it and stared. 'Oh, no!' Jane looked into the open bag as Janey took out a handful of white feathers. 'It's Clare's, and I wish I'd never touched it,' Janey said, with agony in her voice. 'Did you hear about Herbert Grace? He received one through the post and then killed himself!'

'Holy Mary, what wickedness! That poor dear soul had a weak leg from a riding accident as a child and the army turned him down. To think that anyone could do that to him.' She smoothed the stiff quill and soft feather. 'You don't think that Clare would do something like that, do you? I suppose Ethel Sheath is in on this somewhere, and it amounts to nothing worse than giggles and talk.'

There was such a lot of suspicion and hate about, Jane thought as she went to bed that night. Annie Cooper seemed almost human beside some of the present scandal-mongers and jingoists. For the first time in years, she took out the rosary and prayed in the old way as she had done as a child in Ireland. She prayed for Walter's mind and health, the well-being of her children, the end of the war and the baby that Jack had left, until she fell asleep with the beads in her hand, having prayed for everyone but Jane Darwen.

Chapter 14

'There are no oranges and the banana boats can't get through.' Jane was serving in the shop and chatting to her latest customer, Mrs Barnes. *Darwen's* was one of many shops experiencing shortages of their normal lines.

The other woman pursed her lips. 'I suppose we are better off without luxuries if it means risking innocent lives, but each week we seem to be short of something. If only we could send good things to the boys out there it would be different, but they have other worries on their minds. One lad when asked what he needed said a hundred spades! They are needed to dig the many trenches, some of which are only decoys to attract German fire.'

'Is Doctor Barnes still flying?'

'He's at the airport three days a week, teaching young men to fly the new Avro aircraft, which is one of the best yet. The designers have invented a way of using a machine-gun, firing it between the revolving blades of the propeller without damaging them, but my husband thinks the Germans brought down one plane fitted with this device and are now copying it to use in their Fokker planes. The flying men would rather fight one to one as a point of honour but now they are being taught to fly in groups in certain patterns to protect each other.'

Jane picked off a leaf of yellowing cabbage and sighed. 'This last year has been sent to try us for sure. Joseph went off to enlist and came back last month in a terrible state. He wasn't badly wounded but you can imagine what effect all that dirt and noise and killing has on a sensitive man. It made me weep to see him and I can't help feeling that men like that show more courage than the "heroes" who secretly enjoy the violence.'

'I really came in to hear your news,' said Mrs Barnes. 'Janey looks cheerful now she knows that Clive is due home.' She took the cabbages and inspected the fish. 'It must be terribly sad for him to come back to that house now and know he'll never see his parents again.'

Jane shuddered. 'I wonder my hair wasn't white in a night. Those wicked, wicked people, to torpedo a liner!'

'Alex said that the Germans had warned us they might attack any ship sailing between England and America if they thought she carried arms.'

'How could they think that? The *Lusitania* had a very distinctive long prow and four smoke-stacks and no guns! All I know is that Clive has no parents and only his brother left. At least he doesn't have to return to that huge empty house, though. As his brother Andrew will inherit Staplers, Clive is to have the Lodge and Janey is making it comfortable for them to stay there during his next leave. Emily has given her a hand and even our Clare was impressed by the oak panelling in the hall. Joseph worked there like a navvy to wear himself out so that he could sleep at night, and Arnold Churcher has been a godsend.'

'Is he walking out with Emily?'

'Emily says not and we daren't mention his name to Walter as he insists that she will be the one to stay home and never marry.'

'You should have had plainer children,' the doctor's wife replied. 'You are lucky to have so many, all healthy and safe.'

'I am very lucky, but handsome is as handsome does and I can't exactly praise Jack. We've still had no word and he's been gone for two years. Nellie isn't happy and Vikki grows so fast. She's a lovely child to be sure, but a millstone when it comes to her mother's future. Nellie can't marry for seven years unless Jack is traced or is found dead, which heaven forbid, and I can't see her waiting all that time.'

When Clare came in with Joseph at midday, Jane was in the back room and had put knives and forks on the table ready for dinner. 'Here I am again, like a bad penny,' Joseph joked.

'Rubbish! Clare – bring a cushion for his poor back and fetch in some cider.'

'I thought they'd send me back today,' Joseph went on, 'but the medics say not. I'm to stay on until next week.'

'So long as there is nothing really wrong,' Jane said. 'You just need more rest.'

'Nothing wrong?' His voice was bitter. 'I have nothing here for me and out there is a mortar with my name on it.' Jane helped him to fried fish and vegetables and saw how his hands shook. 'If you saw it, you'd know what I mean, Mrs Darwen. Endless mud and misery with the men dispirited and rotten with gas and trenchfoot. The Germans send the gas over in green and yellow clouds and when the wind is right, the gas settles on our trenches and makes them foul for days. It burns any skin it touches.' He tried to smile, but his mouth quivered.

Jane gave a warning look to the others and they went quietly into the scullery, each carrying her plate of food. 'Tell me,' she said softly.

He began to shake violently and she cradled him in her arms. 'It's hell,' he whispered. 'I hate going back but I hate it even more here as nobody seems to know what is happening. We thought last year that Asquith would make a compromise to stop this insanity but Churchill and Lloyd George had their way and with Kitchener dead now, and some say good riddance to him, and half a million dead or wounded it all still drags on. Politicians won't have a coalition and the munition barons don't want peace.'

He shuddered. 'Out there on a dark night with rain dripping into your boots it's as cold as the grave, even wearing a thick greatcoat. One night I went into no-man's-land and stripped three German corpses of their coats to cover some of our wounded but we can't do that often, for fear of snipers. We had no communication with the medics as that trench had been bombed, together with the First Aid Post.'

'No rest, no comfort,' murmured Jane, as he clung to her, forgetting that she was the mother of the girl he loved and who should herself have given him this help; he needed warmer arms and a kinder heart now.

He went on as if in a dream. 'Verdun was important or

so they said. It's a big fort along the Western Front with the Germans firmly entrenched there. The French pound away at them and they return the fire, with guns every few yards going off from dawn to dusk and sometimes at night, giving neither side time to bury their dead. Have you ever seen a corpse fully dressed but swollen to twice its size and stinking?'

'My poor, poor boy,' she crooned.

'Not just one but everywhere,' he muttered feverishly, 'even being used as sandbags to fill the gaps in the line. Sandbags! The Western Front is seven miles long with every mile the same, and the Generals sit in the safety of the dugouts, court-martialling men for not being smart enough or for disobeying their stupid orders.'

'You are an officer so surely it isn't as bad for you?'

'I wish I *was* a sapper and could just drop into a kind of coma and do as I'm told and die without feeling any responsibility.' His face convulsed. 'I was ordered to hold the trench at all costs and when I was wounded, I praised God for that bit of shrapnel that put me beyond such decisions. I'd had orders to shoot any man who ran away and if I didn't obey, then I knew I'd be shot for disobedience.'

'The blessed angels preserve you,' she said.

'Angels?' He drew back, suddenly ashamed of revealing his weakness. 'Some say they saw angels at Mons, flying in a cloud and frightening the enemy but I saw no angels there or anywhere else in Flanders, nor at Verdun. If there's a God He's forsaken the whole of Europe!'

'Now then, Joseph. Eat up your dinner before it gets cold,' Jane ordered him gently. 'We'll have no more talk of the war today, and after dinner you can rest for an hour or so in Lizzie's old room.'

'Clare wanted to go to Ventnor on the train,' he said.

'Then Clare can think again! You must be worn out walking back from the social late last night and you need rest.' She knew that Joseph had been at Clare's beck and call ever since he came home from hospital and Annie Cooper, who slept badly, had seen him one morning at dawn pacing the path up to Pan Down and staring at the red sky over the chalkpit as if he was in torment. The girls came back for pancakes and plum jam and Joseph was tucked up in bed, although Clare complained that fresh air would do him more good.

'He's ill,' Jane explained patiently. 'He's badly shocked by all he's seen and suffered out there.'

'He didn't say a word to me,' Clare said resentfully.

'I don't suppose he could. I can't think why he ever volunteered – the bank wanted to keep him and he was due to be made cashier soon.'

Janey nibbled an apple and Clare reached out for one, a fruit she seldom ate as she had a tender tooth. 'He was sent a white feather,' said Janey, her eyes hard.

'Who would do such a wicked thing? A man killed himself after receiving one.'

'I wonder who did?' Janey said and made the tea.

'Well, my lady?' Jane asked in a voice she had used when the children were young and very naughty. 'Who sent it?'

'Not me, Mother.' Clare went beetroot red and twisted her hands in her jacket pockets. 'I swear it wasn't me.'

'But you knew who did, and let it be.'

'It was Ethel,' Clare whispered and when she looked up, she was crying. 'I would never do that to Joseph. I know you all think I lead him up the garden path but I do . . . I am fond of him.'

'Did you send any?' Clare hung her head. 'Did you, Clare?'

'I put three through letterboxes but they weren't wrapped up and they could think it was just a feather blown in,' she mumbled. 'I don't think there were any young men in those houses and we did it for fun.'

'But Ethel saw that Joseph's was delivered?'

'I swear I didn't know until afterwards. She said she wanted to walk by the bank and slipped in to give an envelope with Joseph's name on it to one of the clerks. When I saw him he was as white as a sheet and I couldn't say anything in case he thought it was me. He enlisted the very next day before I could pluck up courage to tell him it was Ethel, and by then it was too late.'

Jane stood tall and elegant in her righteous indignation. 'This is partly your fault and yet you offer him no comfort.'

'What could I have done? Rush off and get married?' Clare replied defensively.

'Oh no, not you, Clare. Not you, my beauty! You could never cuddle a toy doll and mean it!' Emily came in and stared and listened, aghast at her mother's fury. 'Don't you *know* when a man needs human warmth, Clare? There's more healing in a woman's touch than in all the bottles of medicine a doctor can give him, but Joseph will go away cold and beaten before he even sees the German front again.' Jane tugged at the tablecloth to remove it and forgot two saucers still on the table. They crashed to the hearth and she found the breakage satisfying. Clare silently picked up the broken pieces and took them out to the yard.

'She'll never pick up the other pieces if she lives to be a hundred,' Jane said bitterly. 'How did I ever come to make a cold child?'

'Is Joseph really ill, Mother?' asked Emily.

Jane folded the tablecloth with care. 'They've healed his body but who knows what is left in his mind?'

'If Clare had let him . . . kiss her, would it have helped? Even if she didn't think she would ever marry him?'

'Emily dear, you are still very young and can't know about men, but women have always sacrificed a lot for the one they love.' She added cold water to the hot soda water in the sink and thought of her own sacrifices, of how she had risked her life for Walter's love. 'I'm not saying we are always right to do so, but it's difficult to know which path to take at times.' She dipped a tufted cotton mop in the water and swirled it about. 'In the last war, many women went out to South Africa to be with their men, but those without wives had to take comfort from women who were often dirty and bad. Sometimes I wonder if it isn't better to follow your man and leave everything behind, to prevent that from happening.'

'You couldn't have gone, Mother. We needed you too much and Father hates dirty women so he was all right.' Emily smiled. 'I think it helps men if they come to our social evenings and talk to the girls there. Then they can go back knowing that someone is thinking of them. I gave Arnold a penknife with his name on it,' she added, her cheeks pink. 'You won't tell Father, will you? I do like Arnold but we are only friends.'

'Send him away happy,' Jane said, smiling. 'You are more like Janey and me than Clare is. I can't think where she found her funny ideas.'

'I said I'd go up to the Lodge today with the curtains,' Emily said, changing the subject.

'Can you manage? They're very heavy, but they'll keep the draughts out a treat.'

'Arnold offered to take them in the wheelbarrow as Father is using the trap and won't be back.'

She carried the curtains into the shop and waited for Arnold to bring the barrow. Jane watched them push the heavy load up the hill and wished she had stopped Arnold to say goodbye as he was due to go to Aldershot the next day and then on to France.

'Keep going or we'll never get started again,' Arnold panted and they laughed, but by the time they reached the house and had unpacked the barrow they were breathless. 'Do we have to put them all up?' he asked in dismay, looking at the tall windows.

'Only in here as there aren't enough curtain rings in the other room.'

'Good! I want to talk to you Emmy, as I haven't much time left.'

'The steps are over there,' Emily said hastily. 'If you take the weight of the curtains, I'll go up and fix them.' He did as he was told and then Emily made tea in the pretty kitchen and they sat on the one comfortable piece of furniture – a large settee covered with green velour with ochre cushions. Emily felt strangely nervous. Arnold seemed different today although when he helped her from the steps, she had enjoyed the feeling of strong arms round her.

'I've finished my training,' Arnold began, 'and after two weeks at Aldershot I shall be just another ant, digging my way through all the mud we hear about out there. I might get lost.' His mouth laughed but his eyes were blank as if he actually saw what he had heard about the Western Front.

'You'll come back a hero,' Emily told him. 'We shall all miss you very much.'

'Because I help with the curtains?'

'Of course not.' She blushed. 'I think a lot about you, Arnold.'

'You'll keep my ring until I can change it for another and put it on a different finger?'

'I like this one,' she said softly. He looked so sad, she thought, and couldn't imagine him in the uniform of a corporal in the sappers. Those clumsy boots would be so heavy and could he put on puttees the right way? 'As you aren't commissioned, at least you can't do the terrible things an officer like Joseph is told to do,' she said.

'Does it matter that I'm not an officer? Clare puts great store by that.' He took her hand. 'A soldier can love as faithfully as any officer and I do love you, Emily.'

A wave of tenderness made her eyes damp and she drifted towards him until he was holding her close and kissing her with a desperation that both excited and filled her with a dread that was not fear but the instinctive caution of a vulnerable woman. His hands touched her breasts and a shiver of wonder flowed over her. She loved him and her Arnold was leaving for some terrible battlefield. Mother said I must send him away happy, she thought, and we are happy like this in each other's arms as if nothing can ever part us.

Everything dissolved into warmth and wanting and the need to be closer, ever closer as she felt his body harden in a strange way. Arnold groaned and tried to turn away but she clung to him. Waves of a delicious tingling joy after the first sharp and glorious pain made her want to cry out, and then it was over as he made the crucial decision to withdraw before ejaculation.

'Oh, what did we do?' Emily moaned, frightened not of what they had done but of the future.

'Emmy?' He held her close and kissed her tenderly. 'That was a part of it, and when we are married it will be even better, but I made sure that you will not be left with a baby. Make no mistake, I love you too much to leave you in that state but each time I close my eyes I shall think of us together and die happy, if that's my fate.'

'Don't die, Arnold. I love you,' she said shyly. She rearranged her clothes and combed her hair and saw him looking disconsolately at the stained ochre cushion.

'What can we do about that?' he asked.

Emily smiled and picked up the cold teapot and poured strong tea all over the cushion. 'You are clumsy, spilling the tea, Arnold,' she admonished him. 'Now I'll have to leave it to soak in cold water until I come back again.' And she knew that she had grown up.

Chapter 15

The snug in the Wheatsheaf was full of soldiers who listened but laughed when Walter Darwen began yet again about the Boer War and the use of horses. 'Even the German Generals at the start of the war said they should use our "open spaces" attack with skirmishes in unexpected places.'

'What open spaces?' jeered one laconic sergeant. 'There ain't none, just two lines of trenches with no-man's-land in between. We take a trench, they take a trench, we take prisoners and interrogate them if it's a good night with no rain or we shoot them if we need our rum ration and can't feed them.'

'That's murder!' Walter was horrified. 'We didn't stoop to that in Africa.'

'They do the same to ours and by the time you've been there for a few months with your feet rotting and your lungs bubbling with gas, you'd do the same, or do yourself an injury to get a blighty one.' He gave a coarse laugh. 'They say there are more dead through dysentery, the French Pox and shell-shock suicides than ever die in clean fighting. The French have a brothel in Béthune and others at the back of Wipers that would give you a dose before you crossed the doormat.'

Walter thought the man was staring at him. Did the disease show in his face? He dragged on his overcoat and made for the door, followed by laughter. He ground his teeth in anger but was too restless to go home. He walked down to the stables where he had found happiness and amusement over the past year or so, but the evening was sultry and the manure smelled rank. He lit the lantern and sat on the hay watching the lights of barges. Only local boats came now as one Norwegian barge had been sunk;

the Germans were now eating the ripe Dutch cheeses that had once come across the Channel.

'How's Aaron?' he called to George Crouch.

'On his feet, which is more than I can say for Sam Walmsley. He was taken bad in the ripening shed today and they don't think he'll last.'

Not Sam after all the years they'd known each other! 'I'll go down,' Walter said.

'No use. They've taken him up the hill as he has nobody to look after him except for the woman who does the house.'

'I'll go up on Marigold,' Walter decided.

'Your wife might have news. I went there first to tell you and when I left she was talking to Victoria beside that big car and I think she was taken to see Sam.'

'What's Monty Morris doing outside my house?' Walter shouted, then harnessed Marigold and rode home.

'You're back early, Father,' Emily said. 'I was just coming up to the Wheatsheaf to find you. Mother has gone to the hospital to see Sam.'

Walter cursed aloud and Emily looked shocked. 'I heard she didn't have to walk. She couldn't wait for me, could she, but then I don't have a fancy car! Hasn't that swine done enough?'

He met Jane at the door, and she saw at once that his eyes were red and his whole body tense. 'I was too late,' she said sadly. 'Sam's gone. It's chilly now and Marigold has no rug so take her back and bed her down Walter, and then we can talk. Emily, put the soup to warm.' She unpinned her hat and laid the table.

Walter calmed down as he saw to the horse, and on the way home glanced up at the dark windows of Maudie Dove's rooms. He had never been there as someone might see him, but knew that if she was in as she said she'd be tonight, the light would be on.

'I thought I'd have time to say goodbye,' Jane sobbed when he went home. 'Dear Sam, he was such a good friend.' Emily ladled out thick soup and put bread on the table. Walter grunted and tore his bread into pieces, making a noise when he ate.

' "Dear Sam",' he imitated. 'Yes, he was dear to you, wasn't he, woman? He used to be my friend until I went away and then he changed sides.'

'There were no sides, Walter. You were his best friend and he helped us because of you.'

'But it was you who saw him today! Nobody bothered to tell me he was ill. Nobody came in a fine car to collect me – and no doubt brought you back, too?'

'Holy Mary, there wasn't time and Emily was going to the Wheatsheaf to find you.' She gazed into her untouched soup. In a few days, Sam would join his family under the green turf of Carisbrooke Cemetery. Inwardly she shuddered. The place repelled her with its huge granite tombs and the sea of Celtic crosses stark against the sky where the ground curved to set them high among cypress trees and weeping willows. The rich and famous were buried there in opulent surroundings to match their station in life, while lesser mortals slept down by the river in a smaller field with the salt breezes blowing and the larks singing over simpler plots.

'What did Morris want here?'

'He brought Nellie to see us, but she didn't stay when she heard I had to go to the hospital. She took Vikki back with her to the rooms and said she'd come again another time.'

Emily sensed the growing tension. 'I said I'd borrow a book from Ethel, Mother. Can I go down before it gets too late? Clare is up at the Drill Hall and Janey is with Mrs Barnes teaching her to make brandy snaps.' She sidled away and her parents were alone.

'And the rest of it? Come on, woman, you never could tell a lie properly. What did they want?'

'Nellie is leaving the Island.'

'Good of her to let us know,' said Walter sarcastically. 'What did she expect – a pat on the back?'

'She is going to work in a munitions factory.' There was pleading in Jane's voice as she searched her husband's eyes for some humanity. 'She can make regular money there and be able to bring up Victoria with a good start.'

'What's she going to do with her? Vikki is a bit big to carry on her back while she works like the Zulu women carry their babies. I suppose she'll park her with some drunken old woman who will smother her most like, or give her gin to keep her quiet.'

'She wants us to have her.'

Walter threw down his spoon, leaving a trail of soup over the white cloth. 'That bastard wants *us* to have Nellie's kid?'

'You were fond of the child when they stayed here and she liked you, too. She always smiled when you came into the room.'

'Laughed at me, most like, just like the rest of you.'

'Nobody laughs at you, Walter.' Sweet Jesus, she prayed. The doctor had warned her about brainstorms, when he would think that everyone was against him. She recalled a time before the doctor had said she could stop the treatment, when Walter accused her of poisoning him and made her drink a dose of his medicine before he would touch it, but he had been better over the past few weeks and she knew that something had angered him apart from Monty Morris and Nellie.

She backed away but he followed until the wall was behind her. From the street, she saw the lights of one of the few motor cars in Newport. It must be Dr Barnes returning from the airfield, she thought, just before Walter struck her.

'Get your clothes off. *Now!* You and me are still married and the doctor says I'm clear. I can't get to Portsmouth any more and the woman I have here has run off with some other fool.'

'Stop it!' She wrenched away and ran to the stairs but he was after her.

His laughter was worse than the blows he had given her. 'Good, gal – can't get to the stairs quick enough, eh? Did you think I'd finished with you, my dear wife? Missed me all this time, did you?' He grabbed the front of her dress. 'Come here.' She smelled his beery breath and began to retch but she had eaten nothing and her throat closed painfully on air. He relaxed his hold for a second to open the door to the stairs and she ducked beneath his arm and ran for the front door, snatching up her purse and hat as she went.

Jane had no clear idea of what to do but she ran down the dark short cut to the station, a lane she never used at night when soldiers had their girls in the shadows or laughed and jingled money at any woman passing by. A train whistle blew and she ran as fast as she could up the station approach. She waved to the guard, who stopped with his whistle to his lips, and collapsed into the nearest carriage as the whistle blew and the train wheels began to turn. She gasped until her breath came more calmly. The trees and hedges could have been beside any track and she couldn't recall if she had crossed the line to the train or not. She closed her eyes for a second: what did it matter? She might have to sit on a bench all night but it would give her time to think. The kettle was nearly empty, she suddenly remembered. Would Emily and the others return before it boiled dry?

'Wootton,' called the guard. 'Wootton Halt.'

Jane stepped off the train with her veil pulled over her face and her hat tilted forward. She apologized for not paying her fare and gave the man the money. 'That's all right, Mrs Darwen. I heard your cousin was worse. She's lucky to have you come here at all hours.' He smiled kindly. 'Now don't rush so, but if you had missed this train you would have been stuck as they cancelled the later one.'

'Yes, I have to get to the farm,' she agreed, and walked along the muddy lane. A small light glowed in the kitchen and another in the room where Amy now lived. Jane's eye watered where Walter's gold ring had caught it and she kept the veil low as the door opened.

Yellow lamplight flickered and the one gas-mantle flared as the draught followed her inside. Archie stared, then seized both her hands and covered them with kisses, as tears flowed down his face. 'How did you know? I was going to send you a message tomorrow. She's so much worse Jane, and I'm at my wit's end.'

Jane forgot her battered appearance and unpinned her

hat. 'What does the doctor say, Archie?' She heard him gasp and he turned her face to the light. 'It's nothing. Worse things happen at sea,' she said crisply. 'If you've some flour, I'll powder it a little and then see Amy.'

He made her sit down and brought arnica and soft soothing balm and tended her gently. She felt tired but under it was a kind of happiness as the tension flowed away. 'Tell me about it later,' he said grimly. 'Now, Amy needs us.'

The window was wide open but still Amy gasped for breath, looking bloodless. Jane glanced round and saw what was needed. 'I'll wash her face and hands and we can turn her to rub her back as the doctor instructed,' she said softly. 'That will soothe her.'

Archie brought in a bowl of warm water and the spirit and powder for her back and Jane washed the thin face and shrunken arms. Amy showed no surprise. 'I knew you'd come,' she said. 'Don't let that one in again,' she added. 'She's after my Archie.'

Archie smiled for the first time, the lines in his tired face softening. 'Poor Amy made me promise not to marry Ivy,' he said while Jane emptied the basin and wiped it dry with the cloth. 'I promised! She still thinks I can be fooled by any woman who looks at me, except you.' He emptied the spittoon into the cesspit and put fresh Jeyes' Fluid in the bottom. The clean hard smell of the disinfectant was as healthy as fresh air or water bubbling over pebbles.

'We all cling to something when we are at a loss,' Jane said. Her mouth trembled and the delayed shock made her shake as she recalled every moment of her conflict with Walter.

'You need to eat,' Archie said firmly. 'She'll sleep now. It's only bread and cheese but it's our own cheese and Ivy makes good bread.' He regarded her with concern. 'And you will drink stout. You look as if a lamb could knock you over.' He looked more closely as the bruises began to show. 'And a bull did knock you down.'

She sank into a chair with a sigh. 'It's nothing, but I can't go back tonight. There are no more trains.'

'You'll stay until I know a lot more about this,' Archie

said. 'It was Walter, I suppose?' He set his jaw and looked more furious than Jane had ever seen him.

'He's ill,' she said weakly.

'He'll be worse before I've finished with him,' Archie vowed, and Jane was comforted. As she drank the dark stout and ate bread and cheese, she felt strengthened and cherished.

'Where's Ivy?'

'In the cottage. I sent her off to rest as she's had no proper sleep lately. I said I'd sit up tonight. She'll be here for breakfast.'

'We'll take it in turns,' said Jane. 'You get some sleep now. I couldn't – I have too much to think about. I'll wake you in a few hours.' She patted his sleeve. 'I'm grateful to have this place to come to, so do as I say and don't thank me.' She went into the sleeping woman, whose chest rose and fell lightly with too little air to rinse away the disease. Her hand lay white with blue veins dark on the back and Jane smelled death in the aura round the bed. It would come slowly unless there was another gush of blood, she thought, and cut small squares of old linen to wipe Amy's mouth, and put more disinfectant in the chamberpot where the soiled linen could be discarded.

Amy would never look across the fields again, she thought. There was a last time for everything. She rocked in the bentwood chair. *A last time.* So many of them, with Jack gone and Sidney seen for perhaps the last time, and Janey would one day sleep a last night in the house above the shop before leaving to live in the Lodge. Nellie wanted to make a life with Monty and leave her child behind: if that happened, there must be the agreement Jack wanted, for Nellie must give up all claim to the child. It was easy to think dispassionately here and Jack had shown unexpected wisdom. Jane set her lips. If Walter wanted her back as his housekeeper he must bow to her wishes in this.

From the window, she saw trails of travellers' joy hanging in ghostly shapes from the eaves of the barn. The air was fresh and the horses were cropping grass. It's good here, she decided. If Walter doesn't want me back, I might stay.

Amy called and she went to give her a drink. 'Where's Walter?' Amy fretted.

'Someone had to stay in the shop. I couldn't bring any lemons for you as we haven't had any for a long time,' Jane apologized, and smiled grimly to herself. There hadn't been time to snatch even an apple in her rush to get away! It was as if an abscess had burst and she was free. There was a last time for everything after being at the crossroads so often, doing what others wanted. I shall go back on my own terms for Emily's sake, she vowed.

The birds woke Amy at six and Jane made her more clean and comfortable than she had been for days under Ivy's strong but vigorous hands. She took Archie tea in bed and stood for a full minute before waking him, watching him tenderly. He had never cheated on his wife. Jane wondered if Maudie had angered Walter. I'm not that much of a fool that I don't know what's happening, she thought. What was unsaid could be left that way but if Walter thought she didn't know about Maudie then he was really mad!

Jane washed all over in the privacy of a small room but had to put on the clothes she had worn when she arrived. To ask Ivy was impossible and to wear the clothes of a dying woman was equally repugnant. Ivy came over, sleepy but refreshed and Archie sat down to bacon and eggs and fried bread with a good appetite and said he felt fine again. Jane avoided Ivy as her face was still bruised even after dabbing it with cold water and powdering it with Fuller's Earth, but she called out that Amy was comfortable and needed nothing for a while and she herself was going to bed for an hour or so.

Later, she woke and found the swelling less, and when Archie saw her he said, 'I'm going to see the local doctor. He has a telephone and will ring Dr Barnes.'

'I don't want a fuss,' Jane said. 'I'd be glad if Janey can be told where I am, but don't let Walter know unless he asks. I was ready to come here if Amy was taken bad as everyone knew, so you can just say I shall be too busy to go home for a while as you need me. I have no fears for the girls but I think that Walter isn't right in the head any more, so I'd like to know if Dr Barnes thinks he is safe to be about. It's a terrible thing for a wife to ask to be sure, but it's come to that.'

'I'll tell him what happened, but there's more to it than a man hitting his wife when he's in drink.'

'Only Dr Barnes knows,' Jane said. 'And Edward as the eldest, but now, you should know, too. It takes them in different ways,' she added when she'd told him and saw his agonized horror. 'It isn't so bad,' she said. 'The doctor said they've killed the disease and it can't get worse, but certain changes can't be put back and mended. He hopes that Walter will never have to be . . . restrained.'

Archie's voice was broken. 'Does he force you to share his bed?'

'Not for years now, as it wasn't safe for me to have more babies. If only I could have been a true wife, I think that none of this would have happened.'

Archie looked as if he might explode. 'You not a true wife? Jane, you are everything a man could wish for – and more. You have given him what I never had, a happy, healthy family and he should have been glad to sit and watch you for the rest of his days without so much as molesting you with one little finger!'

She touched his arm. 'Tell the doctor the truth but don't let anyone make a meal of it,' she requested.

Ivy came in and stared. The bruises were fading, the eye less bloodshot and Jane looked better but still battered. 'When did that happen? Archie really must chop off some of those branches in the lane. It's a death-trap in the dark.' Ivy fussed over her but when Archie left the farm to see the doctor, Jane missed him. Together she and Ivy turned Amy again, and she said she had no pain at last after days of agony that the drugs seemed to dull but not control.

'She's on the mend!' Ivy said and went about her work singing, 'Keep the home fires burning!' Jane's eyes filled with tears: Noël Coward could twist a woman's heart. She wanted to go home, not be here in safety. She must be back at Coppins Bridge to pick up the pieces in case any of the family ever needed to return. Even Sidney might come back one day. He hadn't forgotten them and at Christmas had sent jewellery for everyone – a gold-plated necklace for Emily, a bracelet for Clare, brooches for Lizzie and Janey and a wide amber and bronze bracelet for his mother, which Annie had sniffed over and said it was the kind of thing a man gave his fancy woman.

Jack was a ghost who never wrote and might be dead, yet at times he felt close. He was her wild boy who loved life but not responsibility. Who did need her now? Only Emily, the favourite child whom Walter would never hurt. She could stay away forever and they'd manage, she thought and wept, but was dry-eyed when Archie returned and took her into the small office where Ivy was not allowed to go.

'You were right to come here,' he said. Jane put a hand to her throat as if to feel the cameo brooch she had given long ago to Mrs Lee. The old woman seemed to be with her now, giving her courage. 'Dr Barnes has given Walter a sedative, but he is in such depths of self-accusation and depression that it wasn't really necessary. The doctor knows how to treat him and is very glad you came here. He will keep an eye on him. Janey is there to help out in the shop and Emily will manage well. You have a girl who helps too, I believe?'

'Lucy Dove? Yes, she's a great help.' Jane looked at him stonily. 'I could disappear and they'd still manage.'

He gave her a quick hug. 'Never! You have a lot to do, Jane, and if Vikki comes to live with you permanently, it will be a busy time again.'

Indignant hens scattered before the car belonging to the Chevertons' doctor and he entered, removing his driving gauntlets. 'I've brought something for Mrs Cheverton's pain but use it sparingly as it depresses the breathing,' he said. 'How is she?'

'The pain's gone,' Jane said, thinking it was better news.

'Gone?' he said sharply. 'Bring hot water and towels immediately, and boil up these instruments, please. When she was in pain we knew that the lung surfaces were rubbing together but now she must have fluid between the layers and probably a collapsed lung. I must drain it.'

Jane rushed to do as he said and later, was too engrossed to notice Walter in the doorway of Amy's bedroom. He was horrified. He had seen men die of wounds and some with maggots crawling in dead tissue, but this was different. Jane was dressed in a huge white overall such as the men used when milking the cows, and she held a rubber tube mounted on a wooden box with a U-tube of glass perched on the lid as it stood like a book open on its ends. A sweet smell of purulent discharge filled the room as the greenish fluid flowed sluggishly down into the bottle from Amy's lung. The doctor carefully pumped a measured amount of air back to replace the fluid and noted the pressure during the paracentesis. He turned the tiny tap leading to the bottle and withdrew the wide-bored canula.

'This should have been done in hospital,' he said in a low voice as Jane dabbed the tiny hole with collodion to seal the skin, 'but she was too weak to move and we can't risk ether or chloroform.' Amy seemed apathetic and allowed them to do as they wished and Jane settled her in a warm clean nightdress and soft pillows.

'Will it do any good?' she asked. 'What do you want me to do when you aren't here?'

'You will stay?' He smiled. 'I could ask for no better nurse. First of all, you must dispose of this with all care as it is very infectious.' She picked up the bottle and turned to go to the cesspit with it and saw Walter. She stiffened and the doctor saw her distress. 'Who are you?' he asked, annoyed. 'This is a sickroom and I don't recall giving permission for people to come and gawp at my patient!'

'He's my husband, anxious about Amy but he isn't stopping,' Jane said clearly, and swept past Walter with the tray of infected dressings for burning, leaving him with the irate doctor.

'I didn't know she was so bad,' Walter mumbled.

'Your wife did.' The doctor collected his apparatus and clean syringes, went to the wash basin and scrubbed his hands, picking up the spotless huckaback towel ready to use. 'Your good lady is an excellent nurse and I am very relieved that she is staying as I shall have to repeat this treatment several times and must have everything clean.'

'How long will it be for?' Walter asked, convinced now that Jane was really needed and was not just trying to rile him.

'You don't wish it to be soon, I hope?' the man said piously. 'Life is precious even at the end and with pain. Your wife will be needed here until I say she can come home,' he added sternly. 'She is willing to stay and is a tower of strength.'

Walter shifted uneasily as the doctor packed his bag, and he watched Jane clean the apparatus under the yard tap before filling it with disinfectant until it was used again. The smell of carbolic acid sweetened the sickroom and she hung the white smock on a hook and scrubbed her hands as the doctor had done. 'I'll be back,' she said, and followed the doctor to the car. 'Did Dr Barnes send any message?' she asked.

'He gave your husband a piece of his mind. That episode was not entirely due to the disease but in his opinion was mostly spiteful temper after drinking. The Bible tells us that such outbursts are wicked and he would do well to read the Good Book and repent.' Jane smiled, knowing that Dr Barnes would never say such a thing. 'Give Mrs Cheverton fluids only and I will come again tomorrow. The air we introduced will act as a splint to the lung for the meantime, although I may have to introduce more and drain away anything left. She is very weak, however, and may leave us at any time. We must pray for her.'

Jane smiled enigmatically, wishing she had Dr Barnes to deal with and not this stiff-shirt. Walter was watching Ivy skim milk in the dairy: she still used the old way as she distrusted the new separating machine and she ignored Walter's hints to leave them. Jane sat on a stool as if she had no intention of being alone with her husband and asked if everything was running smoothly at home. She noticed that he had shaved carefully and trimmed the new moustache to a thin line. He wore the new suit and looked very smart.

'We need you back,' he said curtly.

'That depends on Amy mostly, as poor Ivy can't do all this work *and* nurse her. It depends on a lot of other things, too,' she added softly when Ivy left the room to fetch another cream bowl. 'Some things must change, Walter. I can stand by and know that you and Maudie Dove are enjoying yourselves in the stable, and I can forgive what you did to me, but *if* I come home, and at present that is a big if, then Victoria will come to me and no questions asked! I can run the house and help you with the business once more but if ever you lay one finger on me again, I shall leave you.'

'You can't do that!'

'I could and I shall do so, if necessary. I've had time to think: Emily is capable and neither she nor Clare look as if they'll marry yet and Janey will be living just up the road. You can afford someone in to help and I could share the cottage here with Ivy.'

'You'd go to *him*?'

'I'd go to no man as well you know, Walter Darwen! Don't you ever forget that! I leave that sort of dirt to you. Why not ask Maudie to help? It would save me having to clean hay and worse from your shirts.' The anger of years began to bubble to the point of erupting, but Ivy came back, singing *Tipperary* to please Walter and settled down to skim again.

'I'm off,' he said in a strangled voice.

'Walter!' He spun round at the peremptory tone of her voice. 'Take this note to Janey or Clare to bring these things for me by train. If they are busy, they can put them on the afternoon train and I'll collect them from Wootton. I need a change of clothes.' He said nothing and his anger was because he knew that the house was empty without her.

'Walter looked a bit pale,' Ivy said.

'Men hate sickness and I doubt if he'll come again while Amy is so ill.' Jane hardened her heart. He had come all dressed up, taking it for granted that she would return as soon as he beckoned. The last time for that was long overdue and it would never happen again. She was glad that Archie was down in the lower field and hadn't seen him.

The days passed quickly as Amy took more and more nursing care. Twice a day she had to be blanket-bathed as she sweated badly and grew cold if left damp, and a woman from the village was brought in just to wash the pile of soiled linen sheets and towels. Heavy sheets hung over the range to dry as rain now added to the gloom and the smell of carbolic from the drying linen and the floors was everywhere, an amulet against infection. The sickroom was dry and bright with a good fire burning and fresh candles after dark, but the yard was muddy and the cattle pens awash and Jane thought of the men living in such conditions in France under the constant barrage of howitzers and the huge gun they called Big Bertha.

In the shop she had been able to hear the news and had no time to dwell on her own thoughts, but here, rocking by Amy's bedside or trying to knit, her head buzzed with unwelcome memories and a dread of the future. Jack seemed close, as if he had never left the country, and she read of Australian and New Zealand troops on the tragic beaches of Gallipoli, on land that would be for ever Anzac Beach, and of Australians coming to England wounded or on leave. He couldn't come over, she decided, and it was wicked to wish him involved in the war, but if Nellie didn't hear from him, Victoria would grow up like Lucy, with a mother but no father and few to care if the Darwens didn't take her in. Lucy was another niggling worry. She must know soon what kind of a mother she had, and would be better off away from her influence.

Janey had come out for half a day, telling Jane the news and helping with quiet competence. She even made Jane laugh: 'Lizzie came for Sam's funeral and stayed to tea,' she said.

'But of course she didn't have time to stay and do the washing up!'

'How did you guess? She had to get back to cook Harry's supper and as she had wasted so much time being noble, she took back enough free fish to last a week.'

'And Clare – is she doing her share?'

'I am quite surprised. She delivers orders in the basket

of her bicycle and is very quiet since Joseph went back to France. I think she realizes how ill he is as they went out one day and a motor back-fired and he went to pieces, but even then she refused to marry him. I'm so glad that I married Clive. There's all the difference in being committed to someone for life and just being a girl in love.'

'Is it true that meat is now rationed? At least we don't have that worry on the farm and you must take some pork back with you.'

'As the Germans ignored their own pact to stop torpedoing merchant ships, the navy have regular convoy duties, but meat from abroad is a heavy cargo and one we must do without.' Janey laughed. 'Annie says she doesn't know what all the fuss is about. The meat ration is more than she uses normally! Poor Bert will be hit by the ban on big hotel meals. Who would have thought the war would go into its third year? In spite of a change in government with Lloyd George as Prime Minister and Jellicoe and Beatty in charge of the fleet, all we hear is unrest in industry, and now the Russians have started fighting among themselves and we have fewer for the war. Clive said that when they murdered Rasputin, the mad monk, it took ten men to kill him and many Russians think he was a wizard who caused all their troubles.'

'Did you see Clive?'

'Only for two hours, Mother. I met him off a naval launch at Cowes when he was on official business and we sat in a shelter for an hour. It was freezing but at least there was no one as crazy as us and we had Cowes front to ourselves. He can't wait to see the Lodge and I long to cook for him, care for him and bear his children.'

'The war can't go on for ever,' Jane said soothingly. 'Even the stupid and wicked politicians have to run out of time and money and men. Has Emily heard anything from Arnold? I've been thinking over what you said Janey, and I know that if Emily wants to marry she must be allowed to do so. I shall make sure of that when I come home as I shall have more say in what happens from now on.'

'Father is very sorry,' Janey said cautiously.

'And hasn't your father always been sorry when he can't have his own way and has to back down?'

'He asked me to say you can come back at any time with no hard feelings.'

Jane's laugh was frightening in its bitterness. 'I can come back, can I, and with no hard feelings? Now isn't that grand, just grand? Isn't that kind! Tell him that I'll come back when I feel like it and not before – and *if* I do come back there will be many changes. He knows what they are and he knows I mean it. There are some things a woman can't forgive and should not forgive, in case matters get worse. He hasn't taken it out on any of you, has he?'

'No, he's been very quiet and when he gets angry it's against the government or the shortages but never against us. Dr Barnes said he's improved a lot so his back must be better.'

'His back? Oh, yes.' The facile lie was still important.

'Lucy comes in but says she wants a regular job, living in if possible, to be independent of Maudie.'

'Why not have her at the Lodge? You can afford to pay her board wages until you live there and then pay her in full. She can work in the shop until Clive comes back but live at the Lodge. Wait until she comes to the shop again before you tell her, though. Don't go near that house! It's a dirty district,' Jane added and Janey looked surprised at her vehemence.

'I hoped you'd say that. I like Lucy and we get on well. She's a good worker once she's been shown anything.'

It might solve many problems, Jane thought. She would have no need to see Maudie, and yet she felt a kind of gratitude to the woman who had for so long taken away Walter's lusts and left her with peace of mind.

Janey departed with a big joint from the newly-killed pig, some butter and cheese. 'Give Aaron a slice or two,' Jane called as the train left. She walked back through the muddy lane. Spring has deserted us all, she thought. April and no good weather and the crops late. 'I'm thinking like a country woman,' she said aloud, and went back to the spotless sickroom. Amy coughed and Jane tapped her chest to bring up the phlegm. She gave her oil and rhubarb to cut the mucus and was glad that there was no blood in the sputum for the third day. 'I'll read to you,' she offered and Amy smiled and nodded, too weak to talk but content to lie back in comfort.

I'm all she has, Jane thought. Daughters were good to have and she knew she would never be left alone if she needed one of them, unless Emily married Arnold. She contrasted the cleanliness and order of this room with the scene she had found on that first night, with a soiled counterpane and bloodstained nightdress. It must be terrible to die alone. She looked up from the book. Amy was asleep, and she was free to wander about and do other tasks of her own choosing, but Archie insisted that she didn't do any more than she wanted to do, and he showed his devotion in many ways.

Now that the load was shared, he was relaxed and fatalistic about his wife but saw that she had everything she needed. He indulged her whims for sweet-smelling scents and delicacies to tempt her appetite, and for Jane this new way of life had great attractions. It was good to see a man come into the room and know how his face would look, and in spite of the hard work, she enjoyed a deep tranquillity that showed her just how far she had travelled along a road of fear with her own man.

The next day, Amy moaned and complained of fever. She was bathed in perspiration and her chest hurt again. The doctor came, as solemn as a priest and shook his head as she was too weak to take more treatment; the sick woman's lungs gradually filled with fluid. Jane had no sleep for twenty-four hours but Amy smiled, her chest cushioned by the fluid, giving no pain now.

A bird sang with the special clarity that comes after rain and Jane stretched and yawned. It had been a quiet night and she had dozed in the chair and didn't feel as tired as she expected. Ivy insisted that they had breakfast before washing Amy again and reached up to the flitch of bacon to cut thick slices for frying. Jane regarded the other two with wonder. We all want Amy to live for as long as possible, she realized. They like me here and I like to be here, but when she dies, all this will end.

'I'd better go in and see Amy before I go to work,' Archie said reluctantly.

'I'll be bringing fresh sheets and Ivy and I can settle her for the day,' Jane said. She pulled down the sweet-smelling sheets from the airing rack and followed him. Amy opened her eyes and tried to sit up. She coughed and tried to swallow. She reached for a handkerchief as the paroxysm came and blood poured from her mouth. It was all over quickly. Archie held the hand that was covered with her own blood long after every pulse had died and Amy was past caring for him or for whom he married, even if it was Ivy.

The doctor suggested a woman from the village to lay her out but Jane shook her head. 'Archie wouldn't want strangers pulling her about,' she said and rolled up her sleeves to do this one last duty of love.

'This is a very Christian act, Mrs Darwen,' the doctor pontificated. 'One that will be rewarded in heaven.'

'No,' she said, 'I'm doing this for Archie and for me. It's neighbourly and that's all that matters. I never was one for heavy crowns.' But when she had composed the pale limbs after washing them with care, using sweet-smelling soap, she did kneel to pray before pushing every stitch in that room that could be burned into a huge linen bag, and she pulled down the curtains and put them on the mattress ready for the fire.

Then Jane bathed her body in the long zinc bath in the scullery and dressed in fresh clothes. She put the ones that smelled to her of death by the pile ready for burning and walked back into the kitchen.

Archie was ready with a cup of tea laced with something strong and Jane sat down and looked about her. This was another last time. 'I'll be getting along,' she said.

'I'll take you,' Archie said, and made no attempt to stop her.

'No, there are things for you to do here and papers to see to. I've done my bit. One of the farmhands can help me to the station with my bags and we'll be down for the funeral. Ivy can see to the food and I'll bring something, too.'

He didn't touch her. 'You know where I am if you need me,' he said.

'I know that,' she said and smiled, and walked straight-backed to the station.

Chapter 16

Clare changed into her new dress and wondered if the hemline was too short. She needed to go out and be with other people as the letter from Joseph had upset her. Many place names had been crossed out by the censor and she resented having another person read the tender words that he wrote but most of all, she knew that he should never have gone back.

The newspapers told of the seven months of barrage and misery culminating in the terrible massacres at Verdun and Passcendale and the Battle of the Somme, when the proud boast of the Generals came true, that if the Bosch carved a way through the French and British lines it would be over a pile of bodies. There were 57,470 casualties in one day during that summer and unrest reached a climax when the French, who had taken a severe blow, threatened to mutiny.

Too much time had been taken the previous winter for rebuilding trenches and dug-outs and the Germans made the most of the delay. They launched a great effort as soon as the thaw came, attacking a fifty-mile front from the Oise to the Sensée Rivers in the second Battle of the Somme. There were 200,000 British casualties and somewhere out there, Joseph and Arnold were fighting.

Returning troops brought no news of local men except of casualties, and families continued to receive the buff envelopes that told them their son or father had died a hero's death, regardless of whether death had resulted from wounds, venereal disease, dysentery or from the influenza that now swept Europe, taking servicemen and civilians alike without prejudice.

Joseph was there, Clare knew. He had left soon after they quarrelled and now she almost wished she had promised to marry him. Perhaps when he came home he would be suitable, with a good job in the bank and the status of an ex-army officer. We could have a maid and a girl to do the rough work, Clare thought as she matched gloves with the scarf tied loosely at her throat to make her dress more modest. 'Going up to the Drill Hall?' Emily asked.

'Mrs Barnes said a new batch of men has returned and she wants help with the refreshments.' Clare removed the scarf, suddenly thinking it made her look matronly.

'I've seen some of them and they all look so young,' Emily said. 'I know I'm not old, but some look young enough to be still in school!' Her hair was tied up with a ribbon that made her look like a child, too. 'I'll come with you. Mother says we must look after them in the same way we want our boys to be treated, wherever they are.' She sat on the bed. 'Janey and me made a lot of potato pies and took them out to Shide yesterday for the soldiers coming back from that awful route march they do from Albany to Arreton Down and back. They are allowed half an hour to rest before marching through Newport and back up to the Barracks. Arnold says that they wait for a band to play them in and smarten up their steps. They even make them sing but some of the words they use are very rude!' She sighed. 'I wish they allowed other ranks to wear good boots. Arnold has trouble with his feet and his boots are so heavy.' Emily mentioned him often to convince herself that he existed and that the wonderful, frightening and completely shattering experience they'd shared was no dream.

Emily looked at her sister and wondered if Clare had let any man do that to her. 'Well, get ready if you're coming,' Clare said.

'I'm ready. I'm not out to catch anyone and I'll be behind the tea urn, I expect.'

'Is Mother going up?' Since her return, Jane had sensed a protective urge to include her in their plans whenever the girls thought she might be left alone with Walter. She went out more to visit friends, did her housewifely duties, seldom sat down if Walter was in the room but read or knitted by her bedroom window, and Emily continued to serve meals as she had done when Jane was away.

'Nellie came in today,' Emily said. 'Vikki is beautiful. Do you want many children when you get married, Clare?'

'I never think of it. How do you know if you want them until they arrive?' She picked up her long knitted coat and Emily straightened the lace on the dress under it. 'You make lovely lace,' Clare said casually, ignoring all the hours that Emily spent in making it for her. 'If I ever marry, I'd like a bedspread with some of your bolder designs all round the edge for at least five inches deep!'

Emily looked surprised. 'Would you really like that? I can do it but it would take a long time.' She laughed. 'You'd better stay single for years if you want it as a wedding present, but I'd rather you married Joseph now. He's very nice.'

'There are as good fish in the sea,' Clare said but tried to forget the look in his eyes when he told her he wanted her so much and she realized he wanted to make love to her before he went back to the war.

'Are you asking me to do something immoral?' she had asked.

'All those lucky devils who got married, like Clive, have memories to take back with them and hope for the future but I have nothing. I love you, Clare, and you needn't feel tied until after the war if that's how you want it. You've no idea what I have to face out there.' He shuddered and hid his face in his hands while they sat on a damp seat by Carisbrooke Castle. Clare reached out to touch his hair but drew back, partly in fear and partly because she had no real idea of his urgent need. If I give in now he'll expect more, she decided and although she let him kiss her with passion enough to illuminate the world, she merely smiled and gave him the impression that she was being kind to allow it at all. He had buried his face in her bosom and held her close. 'Say you'll marry me on my next leave and I'll make you love me as much as I love you.'

The letter had echoes of his words and Clare felt guilty. Life in the battlefields was full of noise and fear and dreadful sights and Joseph was completely demoralized, depressed and hopeless.

Jane hurried to catch them up when they reached the door of the Drill Hall. 'Clare,' she said urgently, 'come out here for a minute. I must speak to you.' Emily shrugged and went into the Hall to find Mrs Barnes, who was giving out orders like a company commander.

'What's wrong, Mother?' Clare felt suddenly apprehensive.

Jane clasped her daughter's hand. 'I met Joseph's mother on my way here.' Clare leaned against the hard stone wall and found it cold. 'Joseph is missing, believed killed.' There was no gentle way to tell her and Jane knew that of all her children, Clare was the most self-controlled in times of drama or sadness. Her own eyes were filled with tears and she was torn by the expression of despair she had seen in his mother's eyes. Even if Jack is dead, she thought thankfully, I haven't been told and until that happens I can believe I have a living son.

'That's impossible,' Clare said. 'I had a letter today.'

'I saw the postmark. It was posted the day before he disappeared. They don't tell us many details yet but he went over the top and his whole platoon was captured or killed.' Jane gave a tired smile. 'They said he died a hero, but they say that about everyone.'

'I don't believe it! He can't be dead, Mother! They took him prisoner. He didn't die out there! Joseph couldn't die there! He just couldn't!' A sudden panic seized Clare: what would she do if he was dead? A deep and painful grief shook her and she wished that she could cry but no tears came, only a burning in the throat and at the back of her eyes. 'He's a prisoner. That's it, Mother. He'll be back after the war pestering me again to marry him.' She gave a shrill laugh. 'I have his letter. He said nothing about going on a dangerous trip and he tells me everything.'

'I know.' Jane spoke softly. 'That's what happened for sure. He will be back again some day. Now come in out of the cold and have some strong tea. We've all had a shock.' She decided that it was better for Clare to be with other people than to send her home to brood, but it was almost a relief to see that Clare did have some feeling for the poor young man. She signalled to Emily and whispered the news to her. Emily burst into tears and ran to the cloakroom and Mrs Barnes raised her eyebrows as her best helper deserted the tea urn, but when Jane told her, she took charge of the situation.

'Clare,' she said firmly. 'There are dozens of poor hungry men wanting tea, so will you see to the urn while I fetch the sandwiches?' She slapped the kettle-holder into Clare's hand. 'The tap gets hot so take this.'

Clare poured tea with the regularity of an automaton, handing the cups to brown hands, white hands and hands with dirty nails, but seeing no faces but Joseph's, which she might never see again and now decided she loved.

There was barely room for all the men to sit down. Many uniforms were stained but brushed and pressed, and the boots shone with mirror brightness. Emily stayed in the background, pale and silent, busy making bully beef and ham sandwiches. She was deeply distressed both by the news and her own guilty inner voice that said that Clare might now be the one to stay at home and when Arnold came back they could be married.

Many of the men found Clare's aloofness intriguing but she ignored them all. How could he be captured? How could Joseph be a prisoner when he knew she needed him at home? How could she face life without the devotion that made her feel wanted and important?

She handed a plate of sandwiches to a man who continued to wait and she looked up. 'They want more over there, miss. If you have a tray I'll take them, and four more cups. Some of them can't stand about so I'll take theirs.'

Clare smiled briefly. She recalled seeing the man several times that evening, handing out plates and cups and bringing back dirty ones to the kitchen. She saw that he walked with a limp and one arm was stiff as he held the tray. Walking wounded . . . one of the lucky ones, she thought, but he might be suffering as much as the men on whom he waited.

The entertainment started with the vicar praying and announcing a hymn which most of the soldiers ignored, then Mr Foster told a funny monologue and the men relaxed. Nellie came next, dressed in a long gown that would have graced a West End party, cut to leave her shoulders bare and shapely. The fishtail of the deep blue skirt swung after her, revealing the front of her legs to the knees and the stiff bows on the patent leather shoes. She carried a long cigarette holder and tossed her short crop of curls in a way that made the men stare and stop eating and the women murmur 'Huzzy,' but even Clare admitted she had style.

'And who paid for that lot?' asked Annie Cooper, who as usual came to watch but never to help. There was complete silence when Nellie sang the much-loved songs from the latest Noël Coward revue and as the applause came, Nellie went to Jane and sat down.

'That was beautiful,' Jane said. 'I hope that Vikki has your voice.' She saw the torment in the other woman's eyes. 'It's all right, Nellie,' she said softly. 'I know how it is. You've put it off as long as you could but Monty still refuses to take Vikki too?'

Nellie inclined her head as if it was suddenly heavy. 'Monty has arranged for me to sing in a big club at Ascot near his business, and I think I must go or lose him.'

'If you can accept the terms that Jack wanted, then you can bring Vikki to me tomorrow. She's my own flesh and blood and we all love her.'

'If I go, I go for good,' Nellie agreed. 'When she is older you can tell her I died of the Spanish 'flu or whatever you think best.' She blinked to stop the tears running down her powdered cheeks. 'I shall love her for ever just as I still love Jack in many ways.'

'Jack was wrong and impetuous but he is my son and will be until I die and Victoria is part of him, but mostly I do this for you. You have been a good mother and I swear that Vikki shall hear nothing from my lips about you that is bad. Bring her early tomorrow,' she whispered as Clare came over, followed by a soldier.

'I think your dress is lovely,' Clare said and seemed less

tense. 'I wish I had the courage to have my hair cut really short and waved like that.'

'Don't do that!' Jane and Nellie stared at the staff sergeant who stood by Clare's side. 'You have beautiful hair, Miss Darwen,' he said. He nodded to the other women and began to clear away the cups. 'They want these in the kitchen,' he said.

Nellie laughed. 'Who is he? I saw him following you around. He's quite good-looking but I assume he's married.'

'He didn't say he is,' Clare said quickly.

'So he told you his life story?'

'Of course not.' Clare sniffed. 'He helped a lot with the men who have crutches and we chatted while the water boiled for more tea. He comes out of the army next week for good as he has a piece of shrapnel in him that they can't reach yet and he asked for his discharge.'

'I like that kind of quiet voice in a man,' said Nellie. 'Nice hair and eyes, too,' she added with the air of an expert.

'He's a deep one,' Jane said, but didn't know why she thought that. He was sturdy and well set-up with a smile that reached his eyes and he found Clare attractive, but she was reminded of a bull in a field, as quiet as you like for a very long time, but watching and making straight for what he wanted over any obstacle when the time was right. She smiled, sadly. A bit like Walter when they first met: 'Well, are you coming to England with me or not? I have no time to waste and I have a shop and a business that needs a mistress.' This man had Walter's determination but she sensed that he lacked something of Walter's early appeal and she felt suddenly uneasy.

'His name is Alan Dewar and he thinks he saw Jack at Gallipoli,' said Clare. 'I said it was impossible but as soon as he heard my name he mentioned that he'd met a man called Jack Darwen in the Australian contingent who was wounded and taken to the same hospital.'

'Holy Mary, I must talk to him,' Jane said, forgetting her first impression.

'He asked if he could visit my family,' Clare said, looking faintly puzzled. 'He seemed to take it for granted that he'd be welcome.'

'I must ask him to tea on Sunday when Lizzie and Harry are there,' Jane said and hurried after him.

'Be careful,' said Nellie. 'It's the quiet ones who get their feet under the table and stick.'

Clare looked horrified for a moment. 'I had forgotten about you and Jack, Nellie. What if he comes here?'

'What if he does?' Nellie said, taking a Balkan Sobranie cigarette from the silver case in her purse. She put it in the long holder, lit the gold paper and drew in the smoke. 'As far as I'm concerned, Jack died when he left me. I wept all my tears long ago and I'm going away to a new life where he can never find me. Only one person whom I trust above all others will know where I am and Victoria is coming to live with you for always, Clare. If I needed anything to make up my mind this news does it. I have no place in my life for Jack now.'

Monty waved from the door and she picked up her silky shawl. 'Tell your mother I'll be down early – and be careful, Clare. Joseph will let you have your own way but that one is different.'

It was only when the whiff of Phul Nana scent was all that Nellie left behind, that Clare remembered that Nellie knew nothing of Joseph's disappearance. Clare followed her mother, the first shock over and now convinced that Joseph was a prisoner and would come back to her. The helpers cleared the Hall as men drifted away to find ale before the pubs shut, and outside the fog gathered and drivers of army transport called for everyone due back at Albany to get in the lorries before the fog closed in completely. Clare saw Alan Dewar look in as if searching for someone but she turned away and pretended not to see him. The last lorry left with him in the back.

'It must be Jack,' Jane said emotionally. 'Dear God and Sweet Mary be praised. Alan talked to him, he told me, and saw all our pictures. I know that Jack took them with him. He had one of me and your father taken at Wootton and one of you girls sitting on a log with Sidney pulling a face.' She glanced at Clare. 'He said he recognized you from the picture and that must have been taken at least three years ago.'

Clare shrugged. There was something about Alan Dewar that crowded her. Joseph wasn't like that; not exactly pushy but tenacious. So the man wanted a free tea and a bit of home comfort? The whole family would be there and Walter would be in his element with a man from the Western Front. With any luck Harry wouldn't have time to sing and the women could go and chat in Clare's room.

'You'll go and see Joseph's mother, Clare?'

'I see no reason for that.'

'They looked upon you as their future daughter-in-law, and it would mean a lot to know how sad you are about their son.'

'I'll go,' said Clare resentfully. What could she say to the Mannings? She'd never said she'd marry Joseph so why should she weep with them? It was bad enough to have her own private grief and he might still be alive. She bit her lip, confused by her emotions, and somewhere among them was a sensation that Alan Dewar knew far more about her than she liked.

'He didn't walk you home, then?' asked Ethel Sheath.

'Who?'

'The man who followed you round all the evening and couldn't take his eyes off you, and is going to tea with you on Sunday!'

'My mother asked him, not me! He thinks he may have met Jack, that's all. I have other things to think of.' She told Ethel about Joseph and Ethel began to cry. He is my friend and yet other women weep for him, Clare thought, but before they reached the shop on Coppins Bridge, she was weeping too, and hating the void he would leave in her life.

'You should have married him,' Ethel said more cheerfully as she recovered over a cup of cocoa in Clare's room. 'You would have had a nice pension. If Fred Cantor asks me, I'll marry him and if he doesn't come back, I'll still be all right. Any man is better than none and they'll be in short supply after the war. He's not bad and he's the only man Pa lets near his boats.'

'I don't want just any man,' Clare objected. She imagined herself at some future date, consenting to marry a man as yet hazy in her mind if Joseph didn't return. It could be rather beautiful and sad if her one and only true love was dead. She smiled in a rather wry way to practise.

'We can't afford to leave it too long,' Ethel went on. 'Neither of us is getting any younger. I don't want to be left on the shelf like old Miss Scovell!'

'That's silly,' Clare said. 'We're young enough to pick and choose.'

'You might not have a chance like Joseph again,' Ethel said. 'I'd better go. Ma wants help to get Pa to bed these nights even if he is walking. Let me know what happens.'

'They may not have any more news for ages,' Clare said. 'You know what the army is like.'

'Not about Joseph, I mean the other one. I'd snap him up. He told one of the girls that he had property up north and a good job to go to when he leaves the army.'

'I don't even know him!' said Clare.

Chapter 17

'So you saw our Jack!' Walter was more moved than he let on. 'How was he?'

Alan Dewar shrugged. 'He had a few bits to be taken out before I left for Blighty. I can give you the address of the hospital.'

'Clare, get a piece of paper,' Jane said. 'I must write tomorrow. Jack has enough love left for his old country to fight for it,' she said, with a sharp look at Walter.

Harry sulked. Nobody asked him to sing, the girls spent the time in Clare's bedroom gossiping and Walter and the new man talked over his head about the war.

'Who would have thought that it's nearly a year since General Plummer captured Vimy Ridge,' said Walter, beginning to warm to Dewar.

'A lot has happened since then,' said Dewar. 'Remember the RAF were given some fine planes and this year we shot down the German ace pilot Richthofen who was a kind of idol to them.' He then paused to let Walter have his say which pleased him, as these days he was increasingly ignored in the Wheatsheaf.

'The Americans have done us proud,' Walter said. 'Just think, for them it is like me going all that way to South Africa, leaving everything they love behind to fight for what is right! They are battling hard at St Mihiel and Chambrai alongside our own lads.' He sipped his tea. 'Janey, this is cold!' But Janey wasn't there. 'We need something stronger than this,' he said disgustedly.

'Later,' said Alan Dewar. 'You can show me where you drink.'

'Right, we can wait.' Walter smiled, and pontificated about the war, painting a highly-coloured and exaggerated picture of the Russian uprising, the birth of the Royal Air Force after years of the almost amateur Flying Corps and the fact that he had it on good authority that Lloyd George would end the war in a matter of weeks.

Dewar eyed Clare as the girls returned to the room. 'And all the prisoners of war will be repatriated,' he said thoughtfully.

'Thank God,' Jane rejoined. 'What will you do when you are discharged, Mr Dewar?'

'I have a house further north and am an engineer by trade.'

'How far north?' asked Clare.

'Not so far that friends couldn't visit me,' he said boldly.

'Not by a river and the sea like here,' Clare said.

'It's by water and near the most beautiful of the grouse moors where Royalty shoot,' he replied.

'We see plenty of Royalty,' said Jane. 'They are a nice family,' she continued, as if the Queen bought fish regularly at the shop. 'We take them as they come.' She'd noticed that Alan Dewar boasted about things he enjoyed and about people he had met. He told them he had met the poet Robert Graves when he was with the Welsh Regiment, and bragged about rescuing a man from the barbed wire under fire. He seemed to have been in several theatres of war which were very far apart and had little communication with each other apart from telegraphy.

Jane caught her breath. What if he was a real liar and his story about Jack was untrue? No, that could not be, as he had described the family photographs accurately. 'I'll fetch Victoria,' she said. 'She must have woken by now after her nap.'

'I'll go, Mother.' Clare escaped. This man frightened her as he seemed to think there was a tie between them. Victoria was playing with a rag doll and smiled. Since Nellie left she had settled well, having had so many people look after her in the past and she had been fond of Jane since birth. Clare stayed to play with her for a while and the men continued to talk, until Lizzie came to complain that Harry wanted to go home.

'You said you were an engineer,' Harry remarked, when he could get a word in. 'I'm a marine engineer with White's.'

He puffed at his pipe and looked important. 'We've enough orders to last for at least ten years. They wouldn't let me go to fight even when I wanted to volunteer,' he lied. 'They can't get enough skilled men.'

'I have a good job to go back to,' Dewar said quickly. 'We build aircraft and that's the thing of the future, not ships.'

'We build flying boats too, so we have the best of both worlds if you ask me.'

'Limited but useful,' admitted Dewar, 'but you should see our factory in the Midlands.'

'We turn out good stuff,' said Harry complacently. He could afford to make allowances for a man who would have a lot to catch up on when he came out of the army. It was the men who had stayed behind who had been promoted. 'When do you go home?' he asked.

'I get my discharge papers after one more medical and then I shall take a holiday before I go back up north.' He looked at Lizzie as she came into the room. 'Quite the family man, aren't you, Harry?' he commented. 'Is the little one yours?'

'No,' said Lizzie hastily. 'She's my brother's. We are going to wait until after the war.'

He looked at Clare who held Vikki by the hand. 'What a waste,' he said. 'You twins are born mothers.'

Clare flushed. 'I have better things to do than provide cannon fodder, and I may have to wait a long time before my fiancé is free again from a prison camp.'

'Oh, I didn't know you'd heard he was safe,' Lizzie began, but stopped as Clare gave her such a withering look that she went to fetch her coat and purse. She didn't dare say now that she had no idea that Clare was actually engaged to Joseph.

'I believe he is safe,' Clare said.

'What if he doesn't come back?'

Clare regarded Dewar with disbelief. He was talking about Joseph as if he was a parcel lost in the post, inconvenient to lose but not irreplaceable. 'I haven't even considered that,' she said with dignity.

'Well, you'd better think about it,' said Alan Dewar. 'I have to leave now, Mrs Darwen. Thank you for asking me to tea. I hope you have news of Jack soon but I stress it was some time ago and he may have moved on. In fact, he could be back in the fighting again, wounded again as some are – or anything.'

Jane smiled coldly. He was hardly the soul of tact and she suspected the man had little warmth. He had wormed his way into her house with promises of news of Jack, but had given her no more details than he had volunteered at the Drill Hall except for the address of the hospital.

Walter was more cordial. 'Come again,' he said. 'You know where you are welcome, isn't that so, Clare? We must make your leave a well-earned rest. What will you do? Do you like boats or fishing? I can take you to Ashey Races for a day or some shooting over the Downs.'

'My leg might not hold out for that,' he said cautiously. Clare smiled. So there were things he couldn't do!

'Come and see what a well-run yard turns out,' Harry invited, not wanting to be ignored. He lingered in the doorway on the point of leaving. 'As you are a serving soldier they would let me take you round,' he said with condescension.

'When can I come?' Dewar asked quickly. 'Shall we say Wednesday next, if that's convenient?'

'Well, yes, I suppose that would be all right,' Harry said as if the wind had been taken from his sails. 'Make it after dinner about two and ask for me at the gate. Better bring your identity papers or they might not let you past the door.'

'With your influence they will let me in,' Dewar said, smiling as if well-pleased with himself. 'I've enjoyed meeting you, Lizzie.' She simpered and found herself inviting him for a cup of tea after he had been to the yard with Harry. 'I will if Clare will show me the way to the yard. I don't know East Cowes and might get lost.'

Walter went with him through the shop to the door. 'Make a nice day of it. Clare can meet you at the station, take the train to Cowes and go over on the chain ferry to East Cowes, and the yard's quite near.'

Clare bit her lip. It would be rude to refuse but she felt

that Alan Dewar wanted more than a day out inspecting oily engines.

'We can go shopping, Clare, and have tea ready when the men come back,' Lizzie said eagerly, as she hated entertaining and thought that Clare could bring some cakes.

'Are you sure you can spare the time?' Harry asked in a last effort to get out of the arrangement.

'I have plenty of time. I have only one more important piece of business to see to.' Dewar set his uniform cap firmly in place.

'What's that?' asked Lizzie.

'I shall look for a wife.'

Walter laughed. 'There are plenty of women about without men,' he said. 'You'll find them five to one after the war.'

'Just any woman won't do,' Dewar said quietly. 'I know what I want.'

'He thinks he can pick a wife at Newport market,' Jane said furiously as she slammed plates into the sink, then shrugged. 'He did bring news of Jack so we must make allowances,' she added.

She took the blue and white plates to return them to the dresser and found Walter looking annoyed. 'He said he'd come with me to the Wheatsheaf tonight and he didn't make an arrangement for Ashey Races, but I suppose he has a lot on his mind with leaving the army. Take him some baccy when you go to Cowes, Clare.'

'I'm going to see Lizzie and I'm not his nursemaid! He could easily have found his way there. He's far too pushy for me.'

'If you don't push, you don't get,' Walter said. 'He's a fine figure of a man and the type to get on – better than some namby pamby who never soils his hands and is frightened of the dark. You could do a lot worse, my gal. There's no comparison between him and the other one.'

Clare pulled on her gloves. 'You're right, Father. There *is* no comparison. I shall wait for Joseph. Now I'm going to chapel with Ethel.'

'Well, don't say one for me. I can do without that whey-faced crowd. Give me a real man to talk to!'

Clare flounced away but when she saw Ethel she took a deep breath and wondered how she could get so upset over one man.

'I know I look like a dog's dinner,' said Ethel cheerfully, 'but a bit of colour might make Fred look at me as he's in the choir tonight.'

'You look very nice,' Clare said with some truth. The pale green ribbons on the leghorn hat toned down Ethel's florid complexion when she blushed and jollied up her pallor when she wasn't blushing. Her soft cotton dress showed a plump creamy neck and curves that Fred couldn't ignore. 'I thought you said that only loose women wore powder and scent,' Clare added with amusement.

'I meant rouge and lipstick,' Ethel said. 'We go to the minister's house after the service and I said I'd help Fred carry the hymnbooks for a prayer meeting tomorrow.'

'I promise to find a stone in my shoe and have to come on more slowly so you can be alone with him,' Clare said.

'I saw Lizzie with Harry,' Ethel giggled. 'They looked like an old married couple. If I don't get Fred soon, he will find someone younger. It's all very well for you, Clare. You are much prettier than me and could wear a chamberpot on your head and still look nice.'

'You have a few years to go yet,' laughed Clare, but she felt uneasy. Most of her schoolfriends were married or engaged, and some had children. 'I do miss Joseph,' she confessed, 'but I know he'll come home.'

'I saw that soldier who went to tea with you walking with Harry and Lizzie to the station. He didn't see me so I had a good look at him. He's quite handsome and apart from a limp holds himself well. Is he trying to court you, Clare?'

'He'd better not try! He said he was with Jack after Gallipoli in hospital and so Mother asked him to tea and Father was all over him,' she said with disgust and Ethel looked amused. 'It isn't that I dislike him,' Clare said, slowly. It was difficult to know how she felt. 'He talks well and tells funny stories that make Father laugh, and he seems to come from a good background, but somehow he makes me want to back away.'

'That means you are attracted to him, as they are in the films,' Ethel said solemnly. 'You'll fall in love with him next.'

'Don't be silly,' said Clare and joined in the Sankey and Moody hymns as if to free her mind of all thought. Lucy joined Clare to walk to the manse and Ethel and Fred strolled there together. Lucy told her how much she enjoyed working at the Lodge with Janey, and Clare let the words flow over her without really listening. She thought of Alan Dewar again and how he had looked when he said he wanted a wife. She had seen that look pass between Nellie and Jack before they were married and recognised it as a deep earthy desire which she had always dismissed as slightly disgusting, as if two animals circled before copulation. It could never happen to me, she thought defensively. Clare Darwen was in full control of her emotions and would carve a future for herself with a man of her choice who demanded nothing but what she was prepared to give. Sex wasn't important. She knew that her parents had slept apart for years and Lizzie only used it for her own purposes. Janey was different, while Emily never spoke of such things.

'I must never allow him to touch me,' she said aloud.

'What did you say?' asked Lucy, startled.

'I said it was time I had new gloves,' Clare said, showing her the hole that had appeared as she twisted the soft calf leather.

Rooks made a background chorus to the manse lawn where a trestle table was covered with food and lemonade. Clare sat with Lucy on a rustic seat and war seemed a distant nightmare as everyone laughed and talked and acted as if the world was young and pure again and the late July evening would last for ever. Janey arrived, looking bright-eyed and pretty. 'Clive is coming to Osborne for a week or so. He didn't tell me he had been slightly wounded and the first I heard was that he was going there to convalesce. Wouldn't it be wonderful if the war ended and he didn't have to go back?'

'Do you think they'll let him come over to the Lodge?'

'They must! He had a leg wound, apparently, which has healed well and so he can drive the car in two weeks' time.' Janey tried to damp down her delight. 'Have you any more news of Joseph, Clare? I hope you pray hard for him tonight in chapel. If you have faith he'll come back.'

'I hope so.' I need him to protect me from the magnetism of a man I dislike, Clare thought.

Dusk brought midges and the sly silence of bats and Lucy put a scarf over her head in case they got in her hair. Ethel came to speak to Clare briefly, squeaking with excitement. 'Fred asked me! I said yes and I'm taking him home now to tell Pa and Ma before he can back out!' She led Fred away in triumph.

Clare experienced an unpleasant shock. If any girl was a typical old maid it was Ethel. I'm the last in my school class, she thought with sudden fear. As if to make it worse, Lucy talked of a girl marrying at sixteen and being widowed at eighteen and now marrying again. 'I can't think why my mother doesn't marry again,' Lucy said. 'I know that men admire her. I hope she has friends to the house now that I'm not there as she must be lonely. She did talk of going to the mainland to work in munitions and said I could go too, but I'd hate the noise of the factories and the rough people you meet there.' She smiled. 'I like working for Janey and she's teaching me to cook all sorts of nice dishes. One day I may be able to cook in a big hotel if I learn enough now.'

Lucy and Janey branched off down the hill and Clare walked home alone. The full force of her future struck her as she pictured no Joseph to tease and order about. The prospect of staying to look after Walter now that he grew more and more garrulous and bad-tempered appalled her. She was weeping softly as she reached the shop and saw the light in the back room. She dried her eyes and went in.

'Did you go to see Joseph's mother today, Clare?' Jane sounded reproachful. 'I know she is suffering and you are a link with him just as Nellie is a link with Jack.' She saw the dried tears and smoothed Clare's arm. 'I know it's a strain but you should go. Come in now and we'll have some cocoa.' Clare let the fragrant fumes tickle her nose as she held the hot mug between her hands. For years she had imagined leaving home to seek adventure but now, the cocoa and the warm room and the familiar homeliness made a rock to which she clung.

'Does Nellie know about Jack?' Clare asked.

'No. I promised only to write in an emergency and Nellie has finished with Jack for good. He is still my son but they are better off apart. They tear each other to pieces and Monty will make her a better husband.'

'But they aren't married! How can you talk like that? You are the most moral person I know and have always spoken out against infidelity.'

'As I grow older, I see a lot of unhappiness that is swept under the mat because of what people will say. I would never leave your father or deceive him, but for some it could be right and only God can be their judge. Be very careful whom you marry if Joseph doesn't come back.'

'He *will* come back!' Clare's hands were tense and her desperate wish deceived neither of them.

Chapter 18

'The tide is turning,' George Foster said as he weighed out sugar carefully so that he couldn't be accused of favouritism. 'With the Royal Air Force we are pushing the Germans back where they belong. Look at Amiens on August the eighth and the crossing of the Ancre a few days later. They're on the run but it takes time.'

'It sounds as if it's better out there than here,' Annie said acidly. 'First the munitions strikes and then the police agitating. We've more enemies on this side of the Channel.'

'The long and short of it is that we are tired of being told what to do. I don't like telling you ladies that I haven't any currants and good flour and other things we took for granted. I hope we don't have another winter like the last and as for the men, I doubt if they could bear it; we'd just have more mutiny.'

'The Russians are savages,' Annie rapped out. 'They were on our side, then signed a treaty with our enemies, turned on their own people and killed their Royal Family.'

'We don't know what they had to put up with,' George said defensively, as he had preached about the valour of the Russians for years.

Jane put her basket on the counter as two women moved away. Annie was following but stayed to see what Jane bought. 'I'll have what I'm due, George,' Jane said and tasted a sliver of cheese. 'At least we have plenty of local cheese. I'll take some of that.'

'Don't you get enough from Archie?' Annie asked slyly. 'I hear they make it there now.'

'I prefer Folley cheese,' Jane answered equably. She blessed Archie for staying away since Amy's death, knowing that Annie was avid for news of his plans.

'Have you heard from any of your family, Jane? There

can't be many places on earth where you won't find one of them now.'

'Jack is closer to home,' Jane replied. 'The Salvation Army is trying to find him as they have posts all over the Western Front and we do know for sure now that he came over with the Australian forces.'

'And what about Janey and that smart young officer of hers?' asked Annie as if Clive was something from under a stone.

'Janey's husband is back on convoy duty but he is well again,' Jane said politely, but she raised her eyebrows as if awaiting the next personal question in a way that suggested she'd had enough.

'I'll be off,' Annie said but paused at the door to make one last sarcastic remark. 'It's no use asking him for extra jam when the shop's empty!'

'I still have plenty of home-made,' Jane rejoined sweetly. 'If you get really short, Annie, you can have my share of shop-bought jam.' She turned back to George. 'Do you think we are nearly at the end of all this?' she asked. He might be an old windbag but he did know a lot about events.

'Don't rightly know, me dear. We are winning on most fronts, but there's the Far East and Mesopotamia to be taken into consideration and we lack supplies after all those ships went down. Even if peace came tomorrow it takes time to pick up the pieces. There are a lot of local names again on the latest Casualty List.'

'Holy Mary, with so many we know there can't be a family left without a black armband.' Jane went home, troubled despite the American help which was having a sweeping effect on the war. The personal traumas were still bad: efforts to trace Jack had so far failed and Clive was doing dangerous work. Emily heard from Arnold at intervals but had seen nothing of him since he left England as he neither got wounded nor sick and was posted too far away for home leave.

Even Alan Dewar had gone back after being refused his discharge, and now wrote to Clare as if he owned her. Jane tried to be fair, knowing that he had no close family but she couldn't like him.

She saw the list of wounded and dead and when Clare came home and saw her mother's white face, she finally knew that Joseph was dead. Emily came in, dragging her feet as if she had no energy left. She was tense and almost in a trance. Jane put an arm round her, touched by her concern. 'We all grieve for Joseph, Emmy, but we half-expected it. Put the kettle over and make some tea.'

'It isn't Joseph,' said Emily. 'Arnold died of Spanish 'flu last month out in Egypt.' She brushed past Clare and shut herself in her room.

Her grief was too deep to share and she wanted to die. Dear Arnold, who had to wear thick army boots that made his feet sore and who never wanted to hurt anyone. Dear Arnold, who had shown her a glimpse of paradise that made her feel as if all the angels in heaven were pouring warm treacle down her back when he loved her. Dear Arnold, who hadn't even died a hero's death but had succumbed to the killer that struck old and young, soldier and civilian. Dear Arnold, dear Arnold, dear Arnold, she murmured as she cried herself to sleep.

'Did you really love him?' Janey asked later. Her own eyes filled with tears when Emily nodded and she hugged her sister. 'I never knew.'

'It's all right, Janey,' Emily said in a calm voice. 'I did love him and I know that I shall never love another man as long as I live but don't worry about me.' She gave a sweet smile. 'Nothing has changed, as I always knew it would be me who stayed home to look after Father and Mother. Victoria will help and I shall care for her as if she was mine.' She shrugged away as if avoiding all physical contact. 'Go to Clare; she is really upset.' And in the weeks that followed, it was Emily who had dignity beyond her years. She was the youngest of the Darwen children and almost a generation away from Edward but she didn't weep again and went about her duties with her feelings hidden.

Clare was distraught as she saw that she was the only one of her contemporaries left without a husband or sweetheart. She didn't count Emily who sat each evening with a crochet hook and mercerised cotton, making the crochet edging she had promised to Clare for a bedspread.

Even Ethel was no comfort as she spent every spare minute with Fred and was planning her wedding for two weeks' time, determined that neither 'flu nor calamity should rob her of the title of Married Lady. As a consequence, when a letter came from Alan Dewar saying that a fever had put him back in hospital and he would definitely have his discharge soon, Clare was glad to hear from him. Lizzie reminded her that when he had gone to Cowes to see Harry, the two sisters had spent a pleasant afternoon together, and after the first half hour the men had found a lot in common. Clare had enjoyed Dewar's company as he talked quite well and made no attempt to touch her.

'When he comes to the Barracks here he can grub with us as often as he likes,' Walter said, taking it for granted that Jane liked him as much as he did and ignoring her pursed lips.

'That one won't wait to be asked,' she said. 'He'll come as Harry did when he courted Lizzie, eating me out of house and home until I wondered if he loved Lizzie or my soused herrings best.'

'I don't want to hear a word against him,' Walter said, but without heat as he was half-scared that Jane might go away again.

'He'll be here next week in time for Ethel's wedding,' Clare said, relieved to know she would have a male escort, and she wondered what to wear. No one would be able to pity the girl left behind by Joseph Manning now.

'Clive can't get back yet,' Janey said sadly. The two short days they had spent at the Lodge alone had been bliss tinged with agony and the accounts she heard from Alex who was on leave, when he told her of the convoys and bad weather and the work of mine-sweepers that cleared the way for merchant vessels, did nothing to make her less anxious. Lucy now lived with Janey at the Lodge and Emily went there often to take refuge when she wanted to be quiet; she knew that Janey understood.

The family watched Alan Dewar when he looked at Clare and Jane was afraid that Clare might be caught on the rebound from Joseph.

Walter spent less time in the stables and Maudie Dove was often seen leaving the laundry late where she was now a supervisor and more independent. She dared not refuse Walter too often as he had influence in the town and could make life hard for her and for Lucy, so on the evening before Ethel's wedding Walter walked home by way of the town, well-satisfied and in a good mood. He brushed dust from his jacket and fell into step with Bert by the memorial.

'It's a nice evening and Annie's in one of her moods so I thought I'd take a stroll,' Bert said.

Walter grinned, seeing the well-cut suit and rakish bowler. 'Out to get a flapper?'

'Not much chance of that. There are eyes everywhere and I heard that Matthew Beard has been tossed out of his club for having a bit on the side. I can't afford scandal if I'm to stay on the Council and in the Masons, but I do miss my trips to Portsmouth.'

'You could go to the other side of the Island.'

'If a local tart was seen there on the same day, the tongues would clack. I want this war to be over soon!'

'That's a change. Does it mean you are pulling out of munitions?'

'I've done that for the most part. Bricks and mortar are the thing now, Walt. The men coming home will need houses and we must expand the brickyard. I've bought up some nice cottages out at Totland and some at Bembridge and I advise you to do the same.'

'There's enough empty houses. Fill them first. Why Bembridge, anyhow?'

'Before the war many of the gentry came for holidays here and they like to sail in boats and stay by the sea. I could make enough from holiday rental in three summer months to let me shut them for the rest of the year.'

'I might buy up that row behind Staplers,' Walter said slowly. 'I'd rather have full-time tenants but what you say makes sense, Bert,' he conceded.

Bert eyed him quizzically. Walter made fewer decisions these days and twice, Jane had persuaded him to follow Bert's advice. The animosity of years had mellowed into a cautious mutual respect as far as business was concerned and Bert resolved to mention the cottages to Jane. Walter had definitely changed. Just look at him now, Bert thought. 'Been rolling in the hay?' he said, and picked some bits of straw from his sleeve.

'What do you mean?' Walter's eyes were hard.

'Nothing. You look a bit dusty, that's all.'

'I slipped on some muck and landed in the bales. If you've nothing to do with your time, I have! I'll be getting home.'

Bert watched him go rather unsteadily down the road. It was too early to be the worse for drink and he wondered if Walter didn't have a nice little bint somewhere as he seemed to have no interest in Portsmouth or in finding a girl nearer home. Who was there to fill the bill who could keep her mouth shut about a conquest as important as Walter Darwen?

At Ethel's wedding there was no hint of anyone to interest Walter and Bert thought he must be mistaken. Ethel looked surprisingly pretty in a white dress and veiled hat and Fred was in a blissful stupor, after being congratulated so often that he began to believe he was a lucky man. Clare had refused to be a maid of honour in case people sang 'Always a bridesmaid and never a blushing bride,' as they did on the music halls, but was elegant in a daring dress of lilac with handkerchief points on the skirt that drifted as she walked. Her bodice was filled in with a diaphanous scarf to make it modest and Alan Dewar never left her side.

He wore a civilian suit and together they made a good-looking pair. People whispered to Clare, 'You'll be next,' and she didn't contradict them. Alan was polite and she felt would never make demands on her that she was unwilling to meet. It was strange. When they had first met she had felt threatened but now when he continued to hold back, she wished he would make love to her, and she didn't flirt with the other men at the wedding as she might have done when Joseph was there.

Ethel waved goodbye and Fred went red in the face as he crashed the gears of the tiny car he had borrowed to take them to Gurnard, six miles away, for their three-day honeymoon.

Alan took Clare by the arm. 'Would three weeks be too soon?'

'For what?'

'Our wedding. We just have time to put up the banns and get away that weekend.'

'Where would we go?' She sounded breathless.

'To my home, of course.' He looked pained. 'You did know, Clare. I wanted you as soon as Jack showed me your picture and I came looking for you. I held back before you knew that Joseph was dead but now that is all over and your family will expect us to get married.'

'I haven't said I will,' Clare replied weakly.

'No, that's what you say at the wedding,' he joked, and pulled her back into the Sheaths' house and called for silence. 'We didn't think it right to tell you before Ethel's marriage but Clare and I are to follow their example three weeks from today.'

'Took the wind right out of her sails by the look of her,' said Aaron. 'Don't think he bothered to tell her first.'

Emily rushed forward, crying, 'I'm so glad for you, Clare.' It could never happen to her now but she wished her sister joy.

Jane listened to the buzz of comment and well-wishing and knew it was wrong but then wondered if that was true. Lizzie and Clare were alike in many ways and might both want settled, unpassionate marriages. They had even chosen men in the same trade, engineering.

Clare blushed and became quite excited as more and more people asked about Alan's home and prospects. 'What an adventure,' Lucy said enviously. 'I've never been further than Portsmouth.'

Walter was delighted and sent for sherry wine; by nightfall, Clare wore the engagement ring that Alan had brought with every confidence that it would be worn, and his kisses were warm on her lips as she went into the shop. Dewar was a nice name and the ring was a good one, Clare decided. She closed her mind to what came after the ceremony when she wore a gold ring and vowed 'Till death do us part'.

'The journey to Nutbourne takes a long time,' Alan warned her, 'so we'll be married early in the morning and catch the train north. We have to cross London to another station but we can nap in the carriage if the train isn't crowded.'

Where was Nutbourne? Where was London? One thing became clear: this was not a holiday from home but a final severance from all she knew. If she wanted to come back the journey would be very long and she might not manage to leave him. For as long as she could foresee, Clare would be tied to this man wherever he wanted to make his home.

On their wedding day, the chapel organ played and the slanting September sun was as warm as a blessing. Clare held her husband's arm as they stepped out into the fresh air. 'Hello, Mrs Dewar,' he said.

The family went to Portsmouth to see them on the train and Edward managed to be there to help them into a reserved compartment, apologising for Alice as she was too ill to attend the wedding but was well looked after by a reliable woman. Jane felt as sad as when Sidney had left but tried to think of Clare's happiness. She wondered if she had been silly to sew twenty golden sovereigns into the lining of the trinket box that held Clare's bits of jewellery. I did it for the boys, she thought, but why not for Edward or Janey or Lizzie? Was it because they had no need to escape?

A mist settled over the Solent hinting at autumn and Janey peered into it to make out the silhouettes of naval vessels. She shivered. Since 1 January that year, the Germans had sunk 530 British merchant ships and protecting convoys. She saw Jane's anxiety for Clare. 'Try not to worry,' she said gently. 'Clare isn't like you and me – she's like Lizzie. She's forgotten that Joseph ever existed and if her marriage isn't what she wants she'll find something to fill her life to her own satisfaction.' She laughed, softly. 'I wasn't at your wedding, Mother, but I think it was like mine. Clive and I could hardly keep our hands off each other and must have looked ecstatic, beaming from ear to ear and making the poor vicar stammer.'

'Yes, that's what they lack,' Jane agreed slowly. 'They stood like ramrods and hardly touched. Alan Dewar wouldn't have suited me or you – but he might be just right for Clare.'

Chapter 19

'I shall put it away for Victoria,' Jane said.

Janey picked up the cap badge, the stained leather belt and the wallet of papers. 'It should go to Nellie. She's his wife.' Her shoulders shook with weeping.

'Nellie *was* his wife,' Jane replied slowly, 'but Victoria is his flesh and blood and he told them I was his next of kin.' The knowledge warmed her now that the first bitter blow was over. 'I shall send Nellie the proof that she is a widow and can marry Monty. It's her due and I like to have things tidied up.'

Jack's last letter was as if he was there talking to her in the same room. He made jokes even when he knew he was dying, and his handwriting wandered all over the page. My wild boy is finally at rest after heeding nobody, but loving life and people to the full, Jane thought. She put the letter away to read again later. To think of him lying in pain was intolerable. Birds and creatures of the open should be free and he must have hated being restricted. Victoria had no father now, but could be proud of the man he had become.

'This will give me an excuse to write to Clare, and then perhaps this time she'll answer it,' Janey said, then put a hand to her throat and turned pale. 'I feel sick again,' she said and rushed out to the back yard lavatory. She returned looking normal again.

'Have you seen Dr Barnes?' Jane asked.

'I can't be sure yet.'

'I can. I've seen that look too many times not to know. Have you told Clive?'

'Not yet. He wrote from Dover and may be home a few weeks from now, once the Armistice has been signed. The German delegation left Berlin on November the sixth and Field Marshal Foch met them two days later, so it can be only a matter of days now before the war is over.'

'Sweet Mary, let no more lives be lost,' breathed Jane.

Crowds gathered each day by the *Press* windows, restless and uneasy. 'Hang the Kaiser,' one man shouted.

'He's skulking in Holland,' said another, 'but we'll soon have him out of there.' Rumours spread that Lloyd George had gone to the meeting and the King was ready to receive the Generals soon. Soon! It was said everywhere as if that made peace come quickly but as politicians talked, men still died and guns fired across the deadly fields of blood-red poppies in Flanders and France.

Shopkeepers brought out old stocks of bright bunting and ribbons of red, white and blue. Royal Family pictures were dusted off and the frames re-gilded. Even potato and turnip soup no longer seemed so unappetizing and Jane imagined Nellie bringing tears to every eye when she now sang of hope and pathos in the music hall and clubs.

Emily sat and crocheted and the lace for Clare grew slowly. It gave her something to do and she looked after Victoria, imagining that she was the child that Arnold could never give her. Clare wrote seldom, and when she did she never described the grey stone cottage on the edge of the canal in a small mill-town. It was comfortable and clean and as Alan had said, was by water and close to the moors, but the sea was not there and the air was full of factory smoke that smelled worse than the smoke from steam engines. Nor did she say that Alan went away often to work on engines in other towns and she was very lonely, but she tried to give a good impression to make Ethel envious.

Jane woke with a start and heard drunken voices. It was like the days when the troops stationed at Albany still had the energy and spirit to carouse but she assumed it was from the crew of the first foreign barge she'd seen on the quay for ages.

It certainly wasn't Walter. She could hear his stertorous breathing through the wall and lately she had noticed that he walked heavily and his face grew mottled after exertion. She slept again and woke to a foggy morning that needed thick stockings and woollen gloves. The calendar, given by the traveller in dried peas and brown sauce, was hanging in the shop, its picture of a smiling woman serving a huge bowl of incredibly big and bright peas which had never seen a packet dominated the wall. She tore off the date and saw that this was 11 November 1918. Today, Peace would be official and the drunks had celebrated early.

In spite of her sadness over Jack, Jane felt a surge of life and hope. Janey was expecting and Victoria was bright and healthy. There was a future, after all. The counter was dressed in red, white and blue to greet the early customers who Jane knew would gather to await the Maroon and the bugles from the Barracks giving the signal that war was over at eleven o'clock.

Janey came down early after she had been sick and Emily made her weak tea and toast. George Foster, resplendent in top hat and tails, was ready to join the Mayor on the steps of the Town Hall, and the girls from the laundry were allowed out for an hour to join the singing crowds who ignored the fog and the drips from balconies, and men from the farms who had come in with produce stayed to drink a toast as Mrs Grace, albeit frail now, insisted on serving them in St Thomas' Square as she did for the Hunt, from a silver tray.

Walter and Bert joined the official party on the stand and Jane felt cold even with the extra clothes. A wave of emotion swept through the garrison town of Newport as the Maroon went off and the bugles played, clear as silver. Women cried and the church clock struck the hour. Guns from the forts in the Solent boomed out and were answered by others in Portsmouth and the small racing cannons outside the Royal Yacht Squadron at Cowes.

The guns faded but the bugles still stabbed the air with Reveille over the now silent town. Suddenly it was over and they didn't know what to do next, then someone began to sing *Tipperary* and the whole town went mad. Jane hurried home and raked the fire. There were potato scones to make and enough smoked mackerel to feed an army as she knew that people would drop in all day. A row of blackberry and apple tarts lined the dresser and shelves and Jane thought how Clare would have enjoyed it all. Emily made tea, dressed in a spotted muslin apron, and Mr Foster sent down a whole tin of biscuits he had saved for this day; Annie Cooper eyed them with suspicion as he had told her last week that he had none left.

Jane was happy and Janey, now the sickness was over for the day, ate well and looked blooming, eating enough for two to obey the old wives' tale. The doctor's motor horn shattered the air every time he passed the shop, and Alex came from the surgery to help just as Clive would have done. Janey treated him as a brother now that his fiancée had died of 'flu while nursing in France and it was good to see him smile again.

'The whole town is in my back room,' Jane laughed. 'Annie, if you could move a little you can make room for one more on that seat.' Annie moved a couple of inches and sat as if she intended staying all day but doing nothing to help.

'The men will be up to their little tricks again as soon as the Solent is clear of mines and the ferries are in service again,' Annie said sourly. 'It will be easy for Bert to go over on urgent business again and I expect your Walter will go with him.'

'There is a lot of business to be done,' Jane answered, ignoring the innuendo. 'Bert has bought property over there I believe, and holiday cottages over in West Wight. Walter has bought some too and they'll take a bit of organizing.'

'I never go on holiday.' Annie sniffed.

'You could go to Totland,' Jane reminded her. 'They make a good investment.' Jane had been surprised how easy it was now to convince Walter to invest in anything she or Bert suggested and decided that it was not weakness but the dread of her leaving him again that made him amenable. Jack's death had made a great impression on him, reminding him of his own mortality. He made a will, lodged with the lawyer in the stately house by the Priory, and at the same time made over a row of cottages to Jane, to use as she saw fit. Bribery, she had thought at the time but had kept quiet, saying only, 'Thank you, Walter. If we ever have to leave the shop they will come in handy to sell.'

By six that evening, there were just two potato cakes left and the tins were empty of cakes and biscuits. Jane scraped the last of the fish into the cat's bowl and made more tea as she had been too busy to think of her own needs. Even Annie Cooper had gone home and Janey nibbled at the last of the tarts as Walter came back from the Barracks. He was in high spirits at the thought of yet more celebration in the Wheatsheaf. 'Bert said he'd meet you later,' Jane told him. 'He had to take Annie home as she isn't safe on her legs now.'

'It's all that sitting about all day doing nothing,' Walter said. 'There's nothing wrong with her eyes or her tongue.' He took the cake that Jane had saved for him. 'Pity that Alan and Clare aren't here: Alan would have liked to come up to the Wheatsheaf tonight.'

Jane handed him another cake kept hidden for him. Walter never did see that all Alan Dewar wanted was to be fed and to stay at home every evening! Clare had made her bed and must lie on it, she supposed, but hoped that if her daughter ever had a family she could return to the people who loved her, at least for a while.

The fog lifted to show windows lit by gas or oil-lamps and some by electricity, with flags and paper streamers in red, white and blue everywhere. Soldiers crammed the Drill Hall where Mrs Barnes worked late to supply them with food and tea, but Jane said she was too tired to go there. Janey insisted that she wrap up warmly and go as far as Mount Joy just to see the fireworks. 'Alex has a car and has offered to take us,' she said, 'and this might never happen again. We can see the ones at Cowes and those at Clatterford from there. Come on, Mother, I want to see them and an old married lady expecting a baby can't go off into the night alone with a handsome young sailor.'

'It's only Alex,' Jane began. Sweet Jesus, she thought. With his fiancée dead this could be Archie and me all over again! Alex might well fall in love with Janey and have his heart broken. 'I'll fetch my hat,' she said quickly. Emily went with chapel friends to Arreton, while Lizzie and Harry, who came late and found all the food gone, went home at once to see the fireworks from there.

Walter waited by the church for Bert and listened to the music. Never one for religion, tonight the music seemed good to him and familiar, and he was almost sorry when Bert appeared. He saw couples kissing in public and soldiers from Albany whistling after girls and he felt old. The overflow from the taprooms spilled out on to the square and kept the barmaids busy, and even Walter Darwen and Bert Cooper couldn't find a seat inside but had to sit on a wall. Walter was pleased he had worn his medals. Others wore theirs, too, and it was one in the eye for Bert who had never won anything in his life, not even for fishing.

They toasted the King and Queen and all the members of the Royal Family and the Members of Parliament that they could remember, and included the Archbishop of Canterbury for good measure. Nobody felt cold and by the church buttress, Walter saw Maudie Dove, dolled up and laughing. He left Bert suddenly and followed her into the gloom. Bert thought he had nipped out to bedew the old burial-ground, but when Walter didn't return, he was annoyed at being abandoned among strangers. He recalled his friend muttering something about seeing to the horses, so decided to take a bit of a walk to get over the ale fumes before facing Annie. He strolled through the town to the stables talking to friends and hearing their news about returning relatives, and taking his time.

Walter had followed the pale flash of Maudie's coat as she hurried down Quay Street. He quickened his steps, knowing that there was at least one Dutch boat at the quay and maybe others, and Maudie had once had a Dutch lover. She stopped by the dark boat and saw that the crew had left for town but as she turned, Walter gripped her arm. She gave a low cry and pulled away. 'It's only me,' Walter said.

'You frightened me,' she said crossly, but her heart beat fast with apprehension. 'I wanted to get away from the noise,' she said, hoping that he wouldn't remember that she had once been with Hans, and fly into one of his rages.

'Looking for me in the stables?' he asked.

'Yes, I thought we could have a walk down the fields.' He reeked of beer and his voice was slurred.

'I've a better idea.'

'I've got my best coat on and I haven't come prepared,' she objected.

'But you don't mind not being prepared with him, eh?' Walter jerked a hand angrily towards the boat.

'I don't know what you mean,' she whispered. 'I'll look in my bag and see if I have something.' New coat or not, she must placate him and she tucked her hand in his arm and smiled. 'Warm me up, Walter.'

He unlocked the stable and lit the lantern and swore at a mouse that scuttled across the floor, knowing that Maudie hated them, but this time she seemed not to notice.

'Put out the lantern,' she begged.

'Not tonight. You look too pretty and there's not a soul to see us.' He gave a short laugh. 'If they see a light in here from the barge, what of it? You belong to me, Maudie, and don't you ever forget it!' He took off his coat and let his braces hang down round his ankles. Maudie lay back on the hay and he unfastened her blouse, grunting as his desire grew and the buttons seemed stiff in his numbed fingers. Her flesh was as soft as he remembered and tonight was fragrant with a scent that made him groan.

'Jane,' he murmured into her breasts. How dared this trollop wear the scent that Jane had worn when they were happy and in love? 'Where did you get that scent?' he asked harshly.

'Nice, isn't it? It's some your wife threw out. She said it had gone off but Lucy brought it home and I think it smells nice. Attar of Roses, it is, and too expensive for me to buy.'

Walter shut his eyes and tried to think of other nights in a warm and clean bed with his wife smelling like a flower. He lunged into the woman on the hay and she submitted to his violence, waiting for it to be over. She felt the weight of his body on hers, heavy and spent with effort. She tried to move but still he lay over her, crushing her deeper and deeper into the soft hay. 'Walter, get up, you're suffocating me,' she pleaded. 'You are too heavy! I can't move.' The mouse ran across the floor again but the horses were silent. 'Walter!' She pushed against him in panic and horror. 'Walter, get up!' She sank back and listened for his breathing and the silence of death made the horses snicker with unease.

From the quay, Bert Cooper heard a woman scream and saw the flickering light. He ran down, furious that someone should have more courage than he to use Walter's stable to rape a woman of the town, and thrust open the door. He took hold of the man's shoulders and heaved him away from the screaming woman.

Maudie sat up and gazed at the tall, smartly-dressed pillar of the community. 'He's dead, isn't he?' she asked. Bert turned the body over and stared at Walter's agonized blue face. 'Oh, Mr Cooper, what shall I do?' cried Maudie.

Bert saw the dishevelled body and agitated exposed breasts. 'Get dressed,' he said tersely. Maudie buttoned her clothes and dragged a comb through her hair as he felt for a pulse but found none, and when he looked up, she appeared almost normal. 'How long has this been going on?' he asked.

'A long time.'

'The old devil. No wonder he didn't want to come over to Portsmouth with me!' He closed the staring eyes, then eyed Maudie with cool speculation. 'Walter and me shared a lot but he never said anything about you.'

'He was very good to me,' Maudie said, her lip quivering with real feeling. 'I don't know what I'll do now.'

'So would any man be good to you. You're a nice-looking woman and I'm sure you have a generous and grateful nature.' It was almost a question and Maudie looked at him wide-eyed. Walter was not yet cold and here was Bert Cooper already asking to take his place. 'I suppose I should go away now and leave you here until the doctor comes,' he said.

Maudie put her hands to her mouth. 'I can't stay here! What would people say? If they find out, I shall have to leave the town.'

'You're quick – I'll say that much for you,' he said, and

she saw his relentless eyes that would show no mercy if she refused him. 'You go home quickly while I fetch the doctor and tell him I found Walter here dead of a heart attack.'

'Would you do that for me?'

'I might, but we'd have to come to an arrangement. If I never say anything about how he died, you must do me some favours from time to time or the whole town will know and you'll be driven off the Island.' He looked round the stable. 'I couldn't use this place but supposing you take the train to Ventnor sometimes and I pick you up to help me hang curtains in my cottages, would that do?'

She nodded, and her glance was filled with hatred and submission. 'We'd better get him dressed,' Bert said, 'then you slip away and I'll fetch the doctor.'

He left Walter as if he had collapsed over a heavy bucket of water and closed the stable door. An inquest might be tricky and apart from Maudie, Bert wanted no other person to know. We've been friends for years, he thought as he walked along the road. We've had good times and bad and I wouldn't want Jane to know about this. She's a good woman and I'll see she has no idea. It was probably the most generous thought he'd ever had and he was truly upset when he hurried back with the doctor.

'He'd been drinking hard and I thought he looked ill so I followed him when he left to water the horses, but I was too late.'

'You've known him for years, you say. Did you have any inkling of what might happen at any time?' Bert stared. Did the doctor know about Walter and Maudie? 'I see that you have no idea,' Dr Barnes continued, 'and I want this to go no further. I want your word of honour on that, man! I refuse to have his wife embarrassed,' he snapped.

'Anything you say will remain with me, Doctor. I promise not to tell a soul, not even my wife.'

'Least of all your wife! Walter Darwen had a disease he contracted during the Boer War that affected his blood vessels. Tonight a big blood vessel called the aorta swelled up and burst. It could have happened any time he exerted himself, and lifting a heavy bucket is typical of what can cause it.'

Bert was flabbergasted to think that Walter had had syphilis all these years. He wondered if going with Maudie might be a bad idea after all. 'Was it infectious?' he asked.

'Not since he left South Africa, so his wife had no marital relations with him at the critical stage.' Dr Barnes smiled. 'It's good to know you are so concerned for her.'

'Yes, it was Jane I was thinking about,' Bert said hastily. Maudie was clean and he could look forward to many years of pleasure with her. 'Shall I go to the shop?' he suggested.

'They are all out at the fireworks,' Dr Barnes said. 'My son Alex took Mrs Darwen and Janey there. We'll get them back as soon as we can save her this sight,' and by the time that Jane came home, Walter was lying in his bedroom and the ambulance had departed. Janey and Lucy had decided to stay the night as the Lodge would be cold. As they entered the shop, Jane smelled something intangible that made her catch her breath and her hand sought the security of the old cameo brooch that she no longer possessed. Dr Barnes was sitting in Walter's leather chair.

'Walter?' she whispered.

'A heart attack. He was caring for his beasts and collapsed. He didn't suffer and we've brought him home. Mr Cooper found him.' Janey and Lucy put their arms round each other and sobbed. 'It was as I said it might happen,' the doctor said quietly to Jane and she nodded.

Jane went to look at Walter's face but left him to the women who came to lay him out and didn't touch him. She'd done that act of love for Amy but she couldn't touch the flesh up there. Calmly she wrote to Clare and Lizzie and a note to Nellie and put them ready for the post in the morning. Dr Barnes drank cocoa with her and marvelled at her calm and dignity and wished she would weep.

He left after half an hour and a car stopped outside soon afterwards. She hoped it wasn't another late visitor on their way home. The car door slammed and she stepped back into the shadow among the smell of chrysanthemums in the shop. Sweet Mary leave us in peace for this is a house with death in it, she prayed.

'Jane?' The door opened and Archie came in. 'I took Ivy to the fireworks and met Dr Barnes on the way back.'

The first sob came hard and unpractised. 'Archie,' she wept as he held her close.

'Leave everything to me, Jane,' he said. 'It's my turn to look after you now.'

PART THREE

Ebbtide

Chapter 1

Jane Darwen pushed back the black veil and took the pins from the tight-fitting black cloche hat, wishing that she had time to brush her hair and remake the knot in the nape of her neck but Janey looked frozen and needed a hot drink.

'There's hot potato pies and cake enough to sink a battleship,' she said. 'And plenty of ale for the men.'

'And ham and tongue, Mother,' Lizzie noted with satisfaction. 'Now just you sit down and let Harry and me cut up the ham in the scullery.'

Jane smiled weakly. Lizzie never changed. Her father was just in his grave and she still thought of number one first. She would see that she took the best of the ham back to Cowes when she and Harry left.

'I'm chilled to the bone.' Annie Cooper pushed past Bert and held her rheumaticky hands out to the fire, firmly taking the best chair.

Bert grinned. 'I told you not to come but you can't bear to miss anything.'

'I went to pay my respects,' Annie said with real emotion. 'We've been friends for years and even if I never say much, I'm fond of you Jane, and always respected Walter.'

Jane reached inside the cupboard for the pot of cream she had prepared from pounded herbs on Armistice Day, the day that Walter had collapsed in the stable and died, and Annie took it quickly, muttering her thanks.

'Are you all right?' Bert asked awkwardly.

'Fine, just fine,' Jane said softly. 'It's as if Walter was away at the war and will come in that door with his hat on one side demanding attention.'

'But this time he'll never come back and you'll have to face that, Jane.' Annie reverted to her usual acid tone, and Bert's indulgent smile faded. He moved away to get some ale and Annie pulled on Jane's sleeve. 'I wondered what you'll do with his clothes,' she whispered. 'Dan could do with first pick if they're going begging.'

Bile rose in Jane's throat. 'Let it be, Annie. I've not had time to draw breath.' She felt Janey's hand on her shoulder and relaxed. 'I'll see. Just give me time.'

'You look more like your mother every day, Janey,' Annie said. 'Oh, you do look poorly.'

Jane gave an exasperated laugh. 'I'm not poorly and I'm not carrying!'

'She has that same look,' Annie recalled complacently. 'I knew before you did more often than not, and after seven I should know how you were.'

'Nine,' Jane said so that only Janey heard. 'Aren't you having a cup?' she asked, as Janey handed her fresh tea. She smiled at her daughter. 'Tastes funny, doesn't it? I couldn't drink tea for months but your father brought me fresh lemons and I loved the sharpness.' She stared into the fire. That had been another man, surely: the good husband and father of her children who cared for her, not the heavy-handed brute Walter had become. 'Perhaps now that the war is over we'll have some lemons again. I've a bottle of Camp Coffee that takes away the blandness of plain milk – do you think it would help?'

Annie put down her cup as if Janey had intruded. 'I'll be down tomorrow for cabbage, Jane,' she said importantly. 'Bert is out at the West Wight and it isn't worth lighting a fire for one.'

'I should stoke up at home,' Janey said gently. 'It's a long walk down here and Vikki is having some little friends in to play with her. The noise would only get on your nerves, Aunt Annie.' Annie opened her mouth but Janey went on, smiling, 'I know we are in mourning but as you say, life goes on and we must make the best of it. I'll pick you out the biggest cabbage now.'

Bert wiped his moustache with a silk handkerchief. 'Annie, get your coat and basket and wait for me in the shop or in the motor,' he ordered, and Janey gently but firmly propelled her through the doorway. 'I'm sorry, Jane,' he said, at a loss.

'No need for that, Bert, after all you've done over the past few days. I'm glad it was you who found him.' She pressed his hand between both of hers. 'We Irish never forget a good deed or a bad, but as I get older it's the good I remember and there's plenty of that in folk.'

It was a truce and a forgiving and Bert went bright red, stammering, 'I only wanted to say the books are in order and there's plenty there for you and the girls. Walter signed a paper a few days before he died making over more cottages to you as well as a big house he bought on the Mall. I'll talk about the shares later when you have a minute. I could come down here to save you going up to the brickyard office.'

'You made him put a lot in my name, Bert. Don't think I never knew. It was kind when he began to lose his grip on things; you made sure I was secure. I know we shall be fine, just fine.'

Bert blew his nose hard. 'At least you have them off your hands except for Emily, but I never had those blessings. Sometimes a man has to take warmth where he can find it. Walter . . . going, made me think that I must make what I can of my time left.'

'But Walter was ill! You are in your prime, Bert, and healthy too.' She gave him a smile that had a touch of mischief in it, as she wondered if he was about to go back to his visits to Portsmouth. 'Don't try to confess to me, Bert. I know all about men.'

He relaxed and winked. 'I promise not to burden you with my sins but if you hear bad about me, promise to take it with a grain of salt and I hope we can be real friends.'

'We can be that,' she agreed. 'Good friends and business partners. Business always did interest me and we had to be partners once with Walter away, so why not now we are older, wiser and more tolerant?' She regarded him with something akin to affection. Yes, I can do business with you now Bert Cooper, she thought. I'm not the girl you fancied years ago and I know now that you'll never cheat me. 'Bring Annie next Wednesday for a bite to eat and we'll discuss things then,' she said with a twinkle in her eyes. 'We can't have you losing your reputation with a widow, Bert!'

He went an even deeper red and turned away. Now what's making him so uncomfortable, she wondered?

'I'll be off,' he said. 'Annie will be cold waiting in the motor.'

'A long ride would do her good,' Jane said kindly. 'Brook Bay is pretty but I suppose it's too cold for that until the spring.'

'Don't suggest it!' he said with unnecessary urgency. 'She might want to go now and then grumble if she took a chill.'

Many of the others had left, just waving goodbye as they went, seeing that Bert was in such close conversation with her and Jane saw Lizzie sidle out to the door with Harry. Janey laughed and looked pointedly at the heavy shopping bag loaded with food that the pair had taken. 'I'll just take a cabbage as I leave, Mother. Harry has to get up early for work so we'll go now. We've done all we can for you,' Lizzie added kindly. 'You had a nice rest.' They left before anyone could suggest more washing up.

'Lucy is here to help, Mother,' Janey said. 'She can come down when Vikki has her friends here as I think they are too much for you this week. I have two girls in from the workhouse to do the rough work up at the Lodge and Lucy hasn't a lot to do when Clive is away. I do most of our cooking and I have a lot of energy now.'

'Janey tells me how well you look after them at the Lodge,' Jane said as Lucy came in with Emily.

Lucy looked very pretty as she smiled at Janey with affection. 'I love working there, Mrs Darwen. Janey has taught me such a lot.'

'Vikki is in bed and there's nothing for you to do now, Mother.' Janey held up a hand to stop any disagreement. 'Why not walk up to the *Press* and see if there's anything fresh? It's too dark for anyone to see you even if it is the day of the funeral,' she added. 'And you might have a chance to talk to Clare as she is getting ready to go up there now.'

'Why don't you go with them?' asked Jane.

'I shall have a good walk when I go home,' Janey said. 'Lucy and me can go together after we've cleared away here, and it's too chilly up by the Town Hall. I get so cold across my chest. Were you like that?' She bit into a pasty as if she had eaten nothing all day, and Jane warmed to the daughter who was so like she had been and now talked to her as an equal. 'You go and get some air,' Janey added.

'There's no need to coddle me.' Jane touched Janey gently on the cheek. 'You are a real blessing but I feel fine, and so I should for I've been waited on hand, foot and finger all day. Even the cemetery didn't make me as tired as I thought it might. It just didn't seem to have anything to do with me . . . or your father. You and Emily prepared the food and I noticed that our Lizzie didn't leave anything to go bad!' It's true, she thought guiltily. I do feel fine but all that may come later.

Clare came downstairs wearing her hat and coat. 'Hurry up, Emily. I heard shouting up towards the *Press*. There might be news about the election.'

'Wait for Mother. Take care of her and see she doesn't get cold and I'll have cocoa ready when you come back,' Janey said.

Jane was glad that her hat hid her face and she slipped into an old warm velvet coat that had nothing to do with mourning. She breathed deeply in the mild evening air and Clare put a friendly hand under her elbow as they walked up the road. As in all times of change or crisis a small crowd stood by the *County Press* windows and now the buzz was about the coming election.

'Alan said they'd have an election as soon as peace was declared and he was right,' Clare said. 'But he didn't think it would start this soon, even though they had to have one before we found out what a fraud old Lloyd George is. The papers say it will be finished before Christmas, only a month away, and the posters are out everywhere for the candidates.'

'You mustn't talk about the Prime Minister like that.' Jane drew away and pointed to a mud-splashed placard. THE MAN WHO ENDED THE WAR, they read. 'At least he brought our boys home again. It may have been a coalition government but he led them. Walter says . . . well everyone knows he's a fine man.'

Emily bought a paper and her eyes were misty. VOTE FOR ME AND HAVE A COUNTRY FIT FOR HEROES TO LIVE IN. Heroes like Arnold who never fired a shot in anger. She gave a shuddering sigh. 'Some heroes never came back,' she said.

'What do you know about it, Em?' Clare's voice was harsh. 'You were never in love as I was, but you are right, some never came back.'

'We must all look to the future,' Jane said firmly. Her head was clear and the air was good, but she felt strangely irritated by her daughters. Surely hers had been the greatest loss and the most recent – and she felt nothing but optimism. The war was over, Janey was expecting and she was once again her own mistress as it had been when Walter was in Africa. I can have help in the house and choose who comes to see me, she decided with a kind of awe. 'What about the horses?' she asked them. There were matters that couldn't wait for the future. 'Has anyone given them a thought?' They walked down Quay Street and over the quay. The high arches of the railway loomed above them in the dark and a soft murmur came from the duck-pens. The door set in the next arch swung open as they drew the bolt and they went into the warm stable. Emily lit the lantern and set it high and Jane saw that the trough was full of fresh water. There was plenty of hay in the racks and even the manure had been swept away.

'Bert Cooper said he'd look in,' said Emily, 'but he seems to have done it all already. Dan will be here tomorrow and until you find someone permanently.' She hesitated. 'Bert told me to keep you away from here but I knew you'd want to see that everything was being done,' she said almost apologetically.

'Quite right, Emmy, but I'm glad you are with me for the first time.' This is where it happened, she thought in horror. This is where my husband died after drinking heavily and lifting a bucket of water. Dr Barnes said it might happen at any time and it had. So be it. Goodbye Walter, I shall never know the half of what really went on in here. She saw the horses bending to the specky fruit that Emily found in the basket. 'You saw more than I'll ever know,' she murmured.

They hurried back across the bridge to the shop and to the warm living room. 'Vikki is sound asleep and Lucy and I will be off now. There's cocoa made and if you've finished with the paper I'll take it to see what ships are in the offing. Clive could get home at any time now for leave.' Janey yawned. 'I'll sleep tonight, Mother. I did enjoy the Camp Coffee.'

'Take the bottle with you and make sure you pick up some fish. It's good for you and easy to digest.'

'If Lizzie has left me any.' Janey laughed. 'Did you ever see such scroungers? Harry and she make a good pair. I hope she has a baby and can't eat for weeks – it would kill Lizzie if she lost her appetite.'

'I'll bank up the fire so that we needn't be up so early tomorrow,' Emily said cosily, and emptied the tea leaves to hiss on the hot coals.

Jane looked in the scullery and then back in the living room. It was neat and tidy with everything put away and even the dishcloths rinsed out and hung to dry on the airer. Hot cocoa in a big jug sat on the hob and cups were ready on the table. For the first time since the funeral, Jane wanted to weep. Not for Walter or her own loss, but in gratitude for her daughters.

Emily poured cocoa and hummed softly, and even Clare looked less sharp-faced and more as she had done before she married Alan Dewar and went to live in the cottage by the canal in Nutbourne. The tall case clock that had replaced the cuckoo clock when he finally choked on the passing of time, gave a mellow reminder that it was late and Clare switched on the light above the stairs, knowing that Jane often forgot that they had electric light. Jane undressed and lay awake, luxuriating in the soft feather mattress in a room that was entirely female, with scented soap, fresh floral curtains and clean clothes. Would Sidney from his busy and sophisticated world grieve when he heard the news? Walter had never been fair to him. Tomorrow she would turn out Walter's room, she decided, but tonight she'd dream a little and cast her mind back to the good times.

She tossed and turned, recalling everything said to her over the past few days. 'I'm being pulled too many ways,' she said to herself. Annie Cooper told her to sell the shop and move into one of the cottages, Archie wanted her to marry him and live on the farm and Clare nagged about everything. At six o'clock, she dressed and stirred the fire into life. 'I'll please myself,' she told the ghosts of the past as she pulled out the damper. 'I know what I shall do and nobody shall stop me, but I'll bide my time.'

Chapter 2

'Take down that black shutter, Jane. It's bad for trade and nobody wants to see mourning signs after the war,' Bert advised. 'It's a month now since Walter went.'

'Do you think I could? I feel that people hesitate before coming into the shop and it depresses me. They aren't as easy with me as they were and I miss the gossip.' Jane looked relieved.

'Get me a chair and a screwdriver and I'll take it down now,' Bert offered.

'Take off that smart jacket first. You look all dressed up and nowhere to go,' she teased.

'I've business out in West Wight and I wanted you to have these deeds before I left.' He avoided looking at her directly.

'Perhaps I should come too and see the properties that Walter left me,' she said, turning away to fetch the tools and smiling wickedly.

'No call for that,' he replied hastily. 'You want to leave that until you feel better.'

'I'm not going into a decline, Bert,' she said dryly. 'I've had too many shocks in my life for that and I like something to fill my mind apart from Vikki.'

'You make yourself sound too old, Jane.' He regarded her seriously. 'You've kept your looks and wear widow's weeds like other women wear fashion. Any man would be proud to have you as a wife.'

'Thank you, Bert.' She smiled. He sounded like a brother these days and she wondered how he had discovered this new protective attitude. 'How's Annie?' she asked.

'Middling. Grumbling as usual and carping about expense and shortages but she knows she has no need to stint herself or me for that matter. I'll be glad of a few hot dinners at the Bugle once they start up again.' Jane held the chair steady while Bert unscrewed the board, and caught it as he passed it down to her.

'That's your good deed for the day. Now you can go off and enjoy yourself,' she said.

He looked at her sharply. 'What do you mean?'

'Well, you do enjoy driving that great car of yours, don't you? It must be a wonderful feeling going along the Military Road. What does Annie think of it?'

'I never take her,' he replied shortly. 'There's a lot to do out there and I've had to hire a woman to make up the curtains and a couple of lads to see to repairs.' If Maudie Dove was seen so far from home he now had this excuse.

'How sensible,' Jane said. 'Annie was never a good seamstress and you need a woman on the spot to measure up, as the curtains never hang right unless you do.'

'Is Clare staying for Christmas?' he asked, to change the dangerous subject.

'Yes. Alan sent a wire to tell her he was home again from his work but she sent one back saying I needed her here.' Jane shrugged. 'I think she just wants a change. It's even foggier up there than it is in Hampshire just now and Clare never did like winter.'

'Foggy across the water but clear on the Island so I have to make the most of it as the weather might close in,' Bert said. 'Here are the addresses and deeds of your cottages.'

'Are they close to yours?'

'No, mine are on the other side,' he said vaguely. 'Yours are nearer Colwell.'

After he'd gone, Jane swept the pavement at the front of the shop and saw Janey approaching. 'I didn't see you walk up,' she said.

'I didn't. I took the motor and it's over there. I'm getting quite expert but I need a longer run for practice. Good, you've taken the shutter down and now we can be back to normal by Christmas. Is Clare about?'

'She's ironing her blouses and Emily is making puddings.'

'Then you and I have nothing to do. Can I come for dinner and take you out in the motor car?'

'I don't know. Is it safe? What would Clive say?'

'Clive is away, Mother, and I have to make my own decisions just as you did when we were little. Anyway, he's anxious that I shall be able to drive well once the baby is born. I'll just motor up to the Lodge and tell them where I am and be back to collect you in half an hour.'

Jane walked up to the shop that sold newspapers and magazines and bought *Jungle Jinks* and *Tiger Tim* comics for Vikki and a gaudy journal about American film stars for Clare. Emily had her *Weldon's Journal* and when Jane added a half a pound of Sharp's Creamy Toffees to her order, she knew that the girls would be content to stay at home and serve the customers.

They dressed warmly although the new Singer motor car was covered and draught-free, and Jane put a basket of cakes and lemonade and a flask of cold tea in the small luggage compartment before Janey started the engine. 'We aren't going for a week!' Janey said.

'You never know,' Jane replied darkly. 'If this contraption breaks down I'm coming home by train!'

'Where on earth do you think we're going? I thought a trip to Carisbrooke was all we could manage this time!'

'I've been to Wootton with Dr Barnes and to Cowes with Monty Morris so Carisbrooke would be nice.' Jane was pink-faced with pleasure.

'We'll be fine,' Janey said. 'This car has a handle as well as the self-starter and we can use it if we have to.'

'You mustn't wrench yourself with that!'

'Don't worry. There's always a man somewhere dying to get his hands on one of these cars, even if only to crank up the engine,' Janey said cheerfully, then saw her mother's shocked face. 'I'd only ask a very respectable gentleman,' she teased.

'Don't go too fast.' Jane settled down with a delighted smile on her face and they didn't stop to buy a newspaper although the placards screamed of election news. 'They can't have any results yet as the polling booths are still open, but Bert says that Lloyd George will have it all his own way with no coalition this time.'

Janey pressed the hooter to scare a dog in the middle of

the road and several people looked at the couple in the car. 'Quick! Think of something sad, Mother. We look far too carefree for women bereaved.'

'Holy Mary! I'm a wicked creature to be sure, coming out with you for pleasure so soon but I can't pretend, Janey. I have my bad moments alone when I dwell on the past, but I can't help but smile when Vikki says something clever and you so blooming with the baby coming,' but Jane assumed a solemn expression and when they passed the car driven by Dr Barnes they were able to incline their heads with unsmiling dignity.

'Shall we go on, Mother? We're past Carisbrooke and on the Clatterford Road and I still feel fine. I drove with Clive as far as Freshwater once and that was when I was sicky!'

Jane watched the hedges slip by and the bare branches of winter give way to scrubland and patches of faded gorse and she thought of the farm. 'Do you still crave turnips?' she asked. 'They will be getting potatoes and turnips from the clamps now and Archie promised to come in with the swedes and carrots soon. I'll save you a really nice turnip. Clive must be glad that you don't crave strawberries or something else out of season!'

Janey glanced at her and saw the sweet smile. 'Archie's a good man, Mother.'

'And don't I know it? He's a good friend but don't try to marry me off yet. Half of Newport is wondering which way the wind blows, and I shall say nothing until after Christmas but I do have an idea or two.'

'I'm glad you don't want to change anything.'

'I didn't say that. There will be changes and a few shocks for some.'

Janey chuckled. 'You have the same look you had when Father went to South Africa.'

'Keep your eyes on the road and you'll see nothing to make you think!' Jane replied cryptically.

'We're nearly in Freshwater. Where shall we go now?'

'Could we see my cottages? I have the addresses in my purse and I think I have a measure with me. If I am to let them this summer I shall have to see inside and make a few notes of what is needed. Bert has a woman to do all his sewing but even if I did the same, I'd still want to see what Walter bought. If Bert purchased them all, he might well have sold Walter the worst!'

A train whistle blew and Jane looked at the addresses. 'I've only been as far as this on the train,' she said. 'Do you think you can find the way to Colwell?'

After losing the way twice, Janey drove slowly by the village green and the row of empty cottages. Jane checked the numbers and produced the first key, feeling as if she was trespassing. 'Did you see those curtains twitch?' asked Janey, with a stifled laugh. 'Do we look like burglars?'

They were impressed by the size and quality of the dwellings although they were chilly without furniture or fires; Jane realized that she had a bargain. They measured windows and walls and noted what would be needed and sat in the car to drink lemonade as if they were on a picnic. 'Bert said that his were on the other side, which means nearer Yarmouth, I think,' Jane commented.

'We'll drive back that way, but if you don't know the addresses, you can't expect to see them,' Janey replied. 'Still, it will be a change to go back another way.'

'He has property in Totland and Ventnor and now here. Soon he'll own half the Island,' Jane said.

Janey slowed down by the railway station to avoid a car blocking the main entrance. She frowned. 'That's Bert's car! If he drove here, why is he at the station?'

'Drive on and don't look back,' Jane urged. 'I saw who he's meeting off the train. Now I know who is doing his curtains and probably a lot more! Not a word to anyone, Janey. Certainly not to Lucy.' They were quiet on the way back. Walter had shared many things with Bert but Jane couldn't take in the fact that Maudie Dove had been left as a kind of legacy to his friend. No wonder he was upset at the thought of her coming out here today.

'Where have you been?' Clare sounded cross. The magazine wasn't as interesting as she'd first thought, a lot of customers had come into the shop all wanting potatoes which Clare hated weighing out, and Vikki had cried over a broken toy.

'Just for a drive,' said Jane. 'We saw our cottages and took measurements and Janey made a sketch of the rooms. You can choose the material for the curtains if you like, Clare,' she added to placate her.

'They are quite big, aren't they! I wish I had one – I like the West Wight.'

'You have a nice home of your own and a husband,' Emily said quietly and bent over the lace edging again.

'I know that,' Clare snapped, and flounced out of the room.

'What's wrong with madam?' asked Janey.

'A wire came after you left from Alan. If Clare can't get home for Christmas he's coming here.'

Jane raised her eyebrows. It had been in her mind to invite him but Alan Dewar never seemed to need an invitation. 'He has a right to be with Clare,' she said mildly. 'We must get the big room ready.' She sighed and spooned tea into the pot. There was no excuse left now for putting off turning out Walter's room. 'When you go, ask Dan to come here tomorrow. I may have some clothes for him.' She thought with guilt of the many maimed and destitute men she saw daily and knew that she must not keep a stitch of Walter's clothes that could help someone else. Vikki came in pink-faced from her wash and Jane hugged her, thinking of the pale faces of the children in the workhouse. 'And tell Dan I want him to take some fruit up the hill when he goes to Albany, as they never see so much as an apple,' she added. 'I think I'll start on that room now. Janey, put your feet up for an hour before you go home, and Emily see to the shop. If it's Clare's man who's coming, she can help me.'

The room was cold and well-aired; when Clare complained she told her to put a match to the fire and be quiet. Together they stripped the clothes from the big wardrobe and laid them on the bare mattress. Jane selected three suits and some warm shirts for Dan with ties and socks enough to satisfy even Annie Cooper, then put sets of trousers, shirts and jackets or warm woollen cardigans in bundles. Shoes she put in a laundry bag as she couldn't bear to see them. They more than anything bore the imprint of the man who had worn them.

Clare helped in silence. 'It will be done soon and then be over,' Jane said kindly. 'Your father didn't die here so there'll be nothing to remind you when you sleep here with Alan.'

'Can't I have Sidney's old room?'

'Vikki is in there and you can't sleep alone. You haven't been married five minutes!'

'I know.' Clare turned away. 'I wish that Joseph hadn't been killed.'

'Wishing won't take the lumps out of your bed. You have to accept what is of your own making, Clare. Alan wanted you and you married him – now you have to make the best of it.'

Clare's eyes were bright with tears. 'We aren't right for each other. Not everyone is like you and Janey, wanting to fill the house with babies!'

'I loved every one of you,' Jane said. 'And Janey and Clive have made a happy marriage. Your marriage hasn't even begun.'

'I wish I'd gone with Sidney and made something of my life,' Clare said defiantly.

'Alan will be here tomorrow and while you are under my roof there'll be no quarrelling or you can pack your bags!'

'It might be better if we did fight,' Clare said in a tired voice. Angrily she put the bundles out on the landing and helped to make the bed. Even she became more cheerful as the room grew warm and the bright patchwork bedspread lay neat over the blankets.

'You take that bundle to the man under the Town Hall selling papers,' Jane said, 'while I turn out the drawers in the bureau.' Clare looked as if she wanted to refuse but saw the glint in Jane's eyes and went meekly. Inside the desk were papers that the solicitor hadn't needed and old letters over which Jane wept. Walter had kept all that she had written to him in Africa and she found a lock of her hair that she had cut off one summer's day on impulse and sent him. It lay raven black on her palm like a living thing and for the first time she cried bitterly and her heavy loss melted with the tears.

She burned the letters and watched the hair curl in the heat of the fire as if in agony then lined the drawers with fresh newspaper and put writing paper ready for use by whoever used the room in future. With a sigh of relief she surveyed the warm and comfortable room where she had conceived so many babies, some in joy and some with dread and one in hate. Walter was gone. It was done and the tide could not be held back.

'I bought two papers,' Clare said on her return. 'They are full of the latest fashions and all about films.' She seemed to have forgotten that she was angry and hurt.

'Did you give that man the clothes?'

'Oh, yes. He was very pleased,' Clare replied carelessly. 'Did you know there's to be a pantomime up at the Drill Hall given by the travelling company that used to put on plays like *Murder in the Red Barn*?'

'That sort of thing might cheer people up but it does nothing to help those in real need,' Jane said.

'The war is over and we need a bit of fun,' Clare said sulkily. 'If I can stay on here, I could have some new clothes made up from some of that material you collected before things got so difficult to buy.'

'I thought you lived next door to a mill! In any case, that is Emily's share. You had yours the last time you were here.'

'Emily never goes anywhere and the mill makes stuff that doesn't hang well.'

'Well, we haven't time for that now before Christmas if we are to make it happy for Vikki,' said Jane but made a silent vow to take the material to Miss Joyner to make up for Emily. 'I want to decorate a tiny tree for her and surprise her on the day.'

'We never had a tree when we were little,' Clare complained.

'It was the old Queen who made them popular,' Jane said, 'and you had brothers and sisters to amuse you, unlike

Vikki.' Jane took a fresh towel from the landing to put ready on the wash-stand for Alan, and Clare followed her back into the room and decided to move in straight away as it was so warm.

'Have you seen Ethel yet?' asked Jane. 'As Fred is still with the occupying forces she might like to come over at some time.'

'Yes, and she said that the soldiers are having a lovely time now. They travel free on all the trams and have nice food, even though there is nothing to buy in the shops and food queues are worse in Germany than at any time here during the war.'

'Poor creatures. It's winter and the little ones must be hungry.'

'The Germans? Serves them right. We won the war and they should pay! You are always on about the wounded who came back and the people sent to the workhouse – so why should we worry about the Germans as they caused it all?' Clare put on the expression that Jane had come to dread. 'They killed my Joseph, didn't they? They killed many of our friends and now expect our pity.'

'Don't ever say that in my presence again, Clare! When Joseph was alive you hadn't a good word to say for him. It was you who sent him off to the war. It was you and Ethel who sent him a white feather and nearly drove him mad with shame, and so if anyone is to blame for his death, look a little closer to home! You could have stopped him enlisting.'

Jane went downstairs. The old healed ulcer on her leg dragged, and her head ached after weeping. Vikki came and snuggled up on her lap and she didn't send her to bed but held her close, more for her own comfort than for the child's.

Chapter 3

'If you're going down to the bridge, you can take this for Jane Darwen.' George Foster took a packet from under the counter and Bert eyed it curiously. 'It's the first batch of dried fruit I've had for years and I'm saving it for regular customers.'

'I'll take Annie's share too,' Bert said and George bent reluctantly to find another. It was one thing to be polite to Bert as he was a fellow Council member, but Annie was a different cup of tea. 'I shall give it to Jane and say nothing to Annie,' Bert said calmly. 'I like my cake second-hand and Jane gives away most of what she cooks.'

Bert sat on the edge of the counter picking idly at the cheese until George asked him how much he wanted to buy, and passed over the newspaper to keep him occupied. 'We've got the Peace Treaty ready for signing,' George told him. 'Lloyd George says we are in for a boom now they've removed the blockade from Germany and trade will freshen up.'

'Don't be so sure. With peace they need fewer armaments and rolling stock. Who wants guns and tanks now except to keep the peace? Ireland takes some and other pockets of rebellion across the globe but there's no trench warfare, no Verdun, no Somme, so no guns!' He saw the Councillor's fraught expression. 'Don't tell me you hung on to your shares in munitions? Walt and me got out months before it all ended and made a packet.'

'I sold most of it but now I have the money lying idle and don't know what to do with it.' George looked hopefully at Bert.

'Bricks and mortar!' Bert exclaimed. 'Or, if you are feeling brave, then one of the new fashion houses.' He popped a sugared almond in his mouth.

'Do you know a yard of ribbon from a string of liquorice?'

George asked with a superior air. 'Did Annie try to make you buy into fashion? She's hardly a fashion-plate herself!'

'She wears the fox fur I bought her for Armistice and fur can make any woman look pretty.' Bert thought of the simply coney tippet he had bought at the same time to give to Maudie the first time they met at the cottage and of the sight of it against her fair skin. How would she look in full-length chinchilla?

'The Americans talk and talk but they take their time and Woodrow Wilson's "Fourteen Points" hold everything up. We all want disarmament and peace but there are ways of doing it. Freedom between trading nations would be good – if we can be sure that some won't just dump their goods on our shores and refuse to take ours. I'm all for the League of Nations, too, but we should keep our hold on the seas.'

Bert loosened his collar slightly. 'Well, they are signing it now and I hope it isn't as hot there as it is here.' The June sunshine made the jars of rice and lentils shine on the high shelves and dust hung on the sunbeams as the shop door opened and shut.

'If you aren't busy, I'll give you my order,' Jane said. She smiled at Bert. 'Shopping for Annie or putting the world to rights?' George put out a chair for her; he thought she looked thinner than she had before Walter died, but knew that she was a busy woman as she still cooked for Janey and Emily and ran the business and took dishes over to Edward's wife, and now had Vikki to look after.

'How's Janey?' Bert asked.

'Fine, just fine – the baby is the image of Clive. The monthly nurse leaves on Tuesday, with Janey sitting up and feeding the baby well.'

'Don't wear yourself out,' Bert admonished.

'Babies are no trouble until they are walking,' she replied. 'I love the smell and feel of a clean baby bubbling with milk and Janey has Lucy there full-time and a girl in to do the rough. Even Vikki tries to help and calls in on her way home from school to see the baby.'

'Has Clive seen his son yet?' A twinge of envy made Bert

feel miserable. Janey would be just like her mother, fruitful and loving and everything he had never enjoyed.

'He came home two days after the birth. He was at Scapa Flow when those wicked men sank the German fleet, and his ship was one that escorted the Generals and Members of Parliament to France before the signing. It's lovely to see them together, but Clive goes back tomorrow.'

'You should have a picture of them, Jane. I haven't given them anything for the baby yet so I'll go up the High Street and organize the photographer to go to the Lodge before Clive goes away.' He saw her hesitation. 'He can make several prints and you can send one to Sidney and one to Clare.'

'It would have to be today, Bert. I'll hurry back and up to tell them, to give Janey time to brush her hair and change.' It was a kind thought: Sidney would be pleased and it might make Clare feel more maternal.

At Christmas, the atmosphere between Alan and Clare had been strained. His eyes had seemed to follow Clare everywhere with an expression of disappointment, although he was polite and attentive. Clare had tried to send him home alone but he had insisted on her returning with him. Twice Jane heard raised voices in the bedroom and often Clare pretended to work in the scullery rather than be with him. She had left behind her a bundle of movie magazines about stars like Clara Bow and Rudolph Valentino and the new jazz musicians, and Lucy read them avidly, hoping to see a reference to Sidney.

Alan had bought gifts for all the family, including fine woollen dress material for Emily and a length of best quality worsted for Jane that Miss Joyner had exclaimed over and transformed into a smart two-piece suit with a long jacket. However, he had taken back with him a wife who still tried to live in a dream world that had failed her.

Up at the Lodge, the sound of a baby crying made Jane hurry into the nursery. Clive sat on the floor with the baby on his knees and Janey was buttoning up her blouse after feeding him. 'You'll make him sick if you jog him about like that,' Jane said, laughing.

'If he's to be a sailor he must get used to it,' Clive said.

Jane picked up the baby. 'He's full of wind, the dear,' she said. 'Look at the blue round his little mouth!' She put the baby to her shoulder, loving the softness and small movements and the satisfying belch that followed her gentle tapping. 'There, you can have him back now.'

Clive looked amused. 'Do you always close your eyes when you de-wind a baby? That's what Janey does when I kiss her.'

Jane saw the tenderness between them and wanted to cry. 'It's all a part of the same thing,' she said. 'Women are all like that.'

'Only the best ones.' He held the baby away from him. 'But the best ones never leave a smelly bundle like this with a helpless man.'

When Jane told him about the photograph, he was delighted. 'Can I take a picture back with me?' he asked.

'If Bert can't make him do it in time, then nobody can,' Jane asserted. She had changed the baby, dressing him in fresh crisp frills and a tiny bonnet while the others got ready.

'Clive wants me to wear my yellow wedding dress but I can't get it to meet at the back now,' Janey protested.

'The back won't show – I can pin it,' Jane promised her, and when the photographer arrived with his tripod and the dark curtain under which he disappeared before squeezing the bulb to take the pictures, Janey looked as she had done on her wedding day, with Clive now resplendent in the full dress uniform of a sub-lieutenant in the Royal Navy. The man rushed off to get the first prints ready, spurred by the incentive of the promised bonus that Bert had offered, and Jane resisted the temptation to stay to dinner when Clive suggested it.

'I'll come again when you have your long leave,' she promised.

'Look after them for me whatever happens, Mother,' he whispered as he kissed her cheek, and Jane wondered why she felt suddenly cold.

'Clive will be busy on the Day of Jubilation,' Janey

grumbled. 'He has to be on board, among the ships dressed over all in the Solent. I wish I could go to London to see the march. They say that Marshal Foch will take the salute and the Royal Family will all be there.'

'There'll be plenty to see here,' said Jane. 'After the last war beacons were lit on all the hills and they have planned fireworks and games for the children just as they did then. Vikki was told at school to bring a Union Jack and she wants to wear red, white and blue ribbons in her hair, and so she shall, the love.'

'I heard from Sidney at last, Mother. Our letters must have had to follow him for miles. He was with a travelling circus and went to a place called Hollywood to see some people working in the movies.'

'Why go there? Sidney isn't a movie actor like Valentino.'

'At first he is to dance and act small parts but he says he may get bigger roles if the public like his face.' Janey looked impressed. 'He could be a movie star one day, Mother, and we can all go across the Atlantic to visit him!'

'No wife of mine goes there,' said Clive firmly. 'You are twice as pretty as Mary Pickford and much more intelligent! I'd lose you in five minutes.'

Jane slipped away, their love and spontaneity catching at her throat. She sighed. Clare could never look like that for any man. And then she blinked in the strong light. 'Alex! I haven't seen you for a long time. How are you?' she asked gently as he shook her hand.

'Better, Mrs Darwen, but I'll be glad to be back at sea.' He nodded towards the Lodge. 'Anyone at home?'

'Don't be alarmed! Clive is in uniform but he hasn't to go back until tomorrow. They've just had their photographs taken.'

'I wouldn't want to go back if I was in his shoes,' Alex said, sadly. 'Look in on Mother sometimes, Mrs Darwen. She enjoys your company.'

One day he'll find another girl, Jane decided as she walked home, but it must be agonizing to see how happy Clive and Janey are. Life without love wasn't right for any healthy young man. She closed her mind to Archie. It was about eight months since Walter's death and soon she must make the effort to arrange her own future. Archie would be coming to Sunday dinner with an eager question in his eyes. He would hand her ripe cheeses from the farm and choice fruit from his own greenhouse and say nothing of the love he felt for her, but soon she knew he would ask her again. She didn't know how to tell him that she could never live on the farm where Rose and Amy had died.

The notice that Edward had made for the window stood out well: FISH SOLD ONLY ON FRIDAYS. With Aaron dead and his family giving up fishing except for George who supplied one shop in Cowes and her once a week, it was a good excuse to shut up one side of the business that had become a burden. Jane sighed with relief at the thought of never having to supply the Barracks again and never again to lay out fish on a freezing slab in winter. Tomorrow, she would put up the final notice that only fruit, vegetables and flowers would be obtainable in future at the shop on Coppins Bridge.

Lizzie had been appalled at the news. 'Surely you'll keep some for special customers and the family?'

'You'll have to buy your own fish now,' Emily told her. 'It will be nearer for you to buy from Fred at Cowes and he'll give you good measure as he knows us all.'

Lizzie smiled hopefully. 'You'll still have to buy yours, Mother. You could buy mine at the same time.'

'No, Lizzie. I shall buy what I want when I want it and not on a regular basis. I like a bit of rabbit for a change and a good round of beef and Emily is partial to lamb chops if they are young and sweet and some mutton and capers if we have visitors for Sunday. We never had chops when your father was alive as he grumbled that they had no meat on them.'

With Archie at the farm, the family never suffered from shortage of meat. Jane had asked him to bring marrow-bones and off-cuts of meat to make into soup for the people at the chapel soup kitchen, where a hymn had to be sung before the hungry mouths were given food. Each Monday, the huge copper that once had seethed with crabs boiling, now made gallons of thick nourishing broth containing meat, turnips, onions, pearl barley, potatoes and carrots.

'Bert Cooper called in with some more papers for you to sign, Mother. He gave me two tickets for the cinema and said he thought you'd enjoy it,' Emily told her.

'If it's one of those Lon Chaney frighteners, you can find someone else,' Jane said.

'This is a new Mary Pickford movie called *Daddy Long Legs*, and they say it is ever so sad.'

'Then we'll get there early and take those sweets that Mr Foster gave me and have a lovely cry,' Jane said, and felt more cheerful. The High Street was busy, with men in new suits bought from gratuities, sure of better times when full employment came again, and the shops held stocks that had been unobtainable for years. However, Jane knew of the real poverty beneath this surface elation, among the maimed and sick and those without pensions, while men like Harry prospered in the engine division at Saunders Roe and looked down on those who had given everything for their country.

'Thank heaven that Lizzie has a good provider,' Jane said when she saw respectable women in shabby clothes. 'Clare is lucky, too,' she added.

'I don't agree,' Emily replied slowly. 'I'd hate to be married to Alan. She must have wanted him at the time but now I think she regrets it bitterly and she hates the house where they live.'

Jane shook away her doubts and fears and the story on the screen took over and after the last poignant scene, the audience shuffled out, wiping away tears and smiling. 'Lovely, wasn't it?' said a woman whom Jane knew. She fell into step beside them. 'If you are going home now, I'd like some fish, Mrs Darwen,' she said.

'Haven't you heard?' asked Emily. 'We aren't selling fish any more.'

'But you must! What can I do if there is no shop open when I want it? It's so handy to be able to knock on your door after the cinema and take fish home for the family's supper.'

'We did put up a notice to give people plenty of time to get used to it,' Jane said. 'I have some bloaters and smoked fish left but no fresh and no more at all after tomorrow.'

'You aren't closing down altogether?' The woman looked annoyed. 'I like your shop.'

'We have enough to do with the fruit and vegetables and now the men are coming home, I am busy making posies and bouquets for weddings,' Emily said. Later, Jane served the last customer and locked the door. No more late-night sales, she resolved. Should they close down altogether? It was a thought that had teased her for months and now someone had come right out with it. She tasted the soup keeping hot on the range. Ethel had offered to look after Vikki and might like some before she went home even on a warm night, but tonight, the girl turned away and shivered.

'What's the matter?' Ethel was never pretty but tonight her skin was mottled and her eyes rimmed with red.

'Is it cold out?' she asked, and held her hands close to the hot stove. 'I'll get home and go to bed,' she said in a weak voice.

'Now where did you catch cold this fine weather?' Jane wanted to know and her apprehension grew. Ethel had hot dry skin and a fast pulse. She was obviously very unwell.

Ethel was almost a dead weight as Jane and Emily half-carried her through the shop. It seemed terrible to let a sick and very pregnant woman sit on the doorstep but she was too heavy for them to carry further. 'Ethel, wake up!' Emily urged her half-conscious friend. 'We have to get you home! Oh, dear, we need two men and a trestle.'

'Get the wheelbarrow,' Jane suggested. 'At any other time there would be curtains twitching but now there's nobody about.'

'What if they see us?' giggled Emily nervously.

'If they see, they can help,' Jane retorted as they bundled Ethel into the wide-based barrow. The wheels needed oiling and the rise of the bridge made them breathless as they pushed the inert form home, and struggled until Ethel was lying on the sofa inside her front door. 'She'll have to stay there until George gets back,' Jane said breathlessly. Emily held water to the parched lips and Ethel drank greedily. Upstairs, her sister Ruby was snoring and her face was covered with sweat. She obviously had the infection, too. 'We can't do more now,' Jane decided. 'I'll leave a note for the doctor on our way back and ask if he will send a woman to nurse them tomorrow.' The evening air smelled clean and fresh outside after the stuffy room and Jane breathed deeply. 'We must wash well and change all our clothes and hang them out to air, and have something to eat,' she said, and long after Emily was in bed, she hovered near Vikki and wondered if Ethel, who was very fond of the child, had kissed her and hugged her that evening.

Dear Mary preserve us, she prayed. So many people like Arnold had died from this terrible 'flu and now it was close to home. Ethel was not in the best of health with her first pregnancy, so what was in store for her and Ruby?

The early train rattled over the bridge and Jane packed a basket with clean towels, soap, disinfectant and cool lemonade and walked over the bridge to see what was happening.

Chapter 4

The door between the living room and the shop was firmly shut in spite of the heat, and Emily stopped Archie from entering. 'If I ring this bell, Mother will come out to you,' she said, 'but she doesn't want to spread the infection. No, not even you may go in, Uncle Archie,' she added firmly as he stepped forward.

'I'm here.' Jane closed the door behind her and Archie took her hand, seeing how pale she looked and how drawn her face.

'You aren't ill, too?' he asked anxiously. 'You must take care, Jane.'

His hand was comforting and Jane clung to it. 'Vikki is my own flesh and blood, Archie, and I'll take nothing bad from her any more than I did from your Amy.'

'Are you eating enough and sleeping?'

'I eat well,' she said but her mouth trembled. 'The poor mite is so thin now. Dr Barnes says she is over the crisis but it's a terrible scourge that's sweeping the country and even now we can't be sure of her.' Her eyes filled with tears. 'When does suffering end? I sometimes wish I could run away to the farm again and shut myself in the cottage where Jack and Nellie lived and not come out until the world is well again.'

'Why spend your life here? You know the farm is ready for you at any time and I've made a lot of improvements that Amy wouldn't have at any price.'

'No.' Jane smiled weakly. 'I say these things but my place is here. I have Emily and Vikki, and Janey and little George just up the hill.' She caught her breath to hide a sob. 'Archie, I wonder if the doctor is telling me the truth. Vikki is so weak and thin and eats nothing but slops and she could slip through my fingers at any time.'

'Does Nellie know?'

'Nellie?' Jane looked uncomprehending.

'She is her mother and should be informed.'

'Nellie swore that she would never come here to upset Vikki and Jack made her my sacred trust.'

'What if she came too late?' Archie asked quietly. 'You know you would never forgive yourself, Jane.'

Jane sat down heavily on the wooden stool where customers rested their baskets. 'I don't know her address now. I did ask Edward to find out if she was still living in Southampton when Vikki was first taken ill but he found no trace of her.'

Archie showed her a cutting from a newspaper. 'I had no idea that Vikki was ill but I brought this to interest the girls.' He showed the advertisement for a music hall, with Nellie dressed in furs over a silk dress with a wavy hemline just above her knees. Her hair was expertly waved and hugged her well-shaped head in a way that added to the elegance of the picture. 'She's been further north but is now starting in Southampton again. I could write to the theatre.'

'So long as Nellie keeps her promise not to unsettle her, she could come once and stay at the Bugle,' Jane conceded.

'Emily can help me unpack the lettuce and flowers and then I'm going to the Jug and Bottle to get some stout for you. I shall come back and have dinner with you so it's no good saying I can't come in!'

'You'll see that we do eat well, Uncle Archie,' Emily said. 'That's one thing Mother makes sure of and there's enough Irish stew today to feed ten. We've far less to do now that the fish has gone and the whole place smells sweet with the flowers.' Archie ran up to the Post Office and sent a telegram to the theatre before returning to the shop with the stout and sat down to dinner.

'I'll write today,' Jane said.

'It's done – I sent a wire,' Archie replied. 'You'll be glad to see her, Jane.'

'I shall hate every minute! If Vikki knows who she is we'll have no peace. Look at that picture! Could any child resist that face bending over her sickbed? Vikki has something of Jack in her and would see only the romantic side of Nellie.'

'I said I'd meet her boat and I'll make sure she understands how you feel, Jane.'

'Mother, Lucy came over to enquire when Janey and the baby can come here again,' Emily said. 'I told her to stay away until we tell her but she's in the shop in case you have any special message for Janey. She also said that the doctor went into the Sheaths' house again.'

'Make up a big dish of stew and ask Lucy to hand it in from the door, but not to go inside the house. Ruby is on the mend and needs nourishment but the nurse is no hand in the kitchen. They can't live on savoury ducks from the shop up the road and porridge.'

'Don't you give away enough at the soup kitchen?' Archie asked.

'And would you have me see my old friends starve?' she answered with a burst of temper. She wouldn't admit it even to herself but Archie had put her in the wrong by taking over a duty she should have done.

She went off into the shop herself with the basket of food and came back smiling. 'Lucy always asks if we've heard from Sidney,' she said. 'She was always sweet on him and blushed every time we mention his name. I do wish they could meet again. He could do worse. Lucy is pretty like her mother but has more refined features, from her father, I suppose. Nobody believes that Ben Dove was her father and she looks more and more like the blonde Scandinavians who owns the barges. Janey has taught her a lot and she can play simple tunes on the piano and cook really well. She loves any talk of films because of Sidney and never looks at other boys.'

It was a dream, Jane decided. Mrs Lee had told her that one of her sons would never marry and Sidney was the only one left. She watched Archie sit in Walter's chair and fill his pipe. The rest of the prophecies she shut away and hoped she could forget but today, she thought of the old lady as if she was still alive. I could do with you now to tell me about *me*, she thought.

Emily called down to say that Vikki fancied a fried egg. 'That's the first time she's asked for food,' Jane said, her face aglow. She reached for the frying pan. 'I'll put in some snippets of bacon and some tiny pieces of fried bread.' Archie sensed he was in the way and got up to leave. 'It's a pity you didn't wait,' Jane told him curtly. 'There was no need to send that wire and now I'll have all that trouble again.'

Vikki dipped the fried bread triangles in the yolk and ate most of the bacon while Jane watched every mouthful and sent up a prayer of thanks. She took away the tray and washed the child all over, changed the bed-linen and night-dress and when the room smelled of lavender and cleanliness knew that the infection had gone and she could open the door to the shop again.

The man who collected her rents came into the shop, smelling strongly of eucalyptus and Jane backed away. 'It's not me,' he explained. 'I was told to use it to keep away the germs when I have to go into people's houses. I saw the doctor in with Ethel Sheath again. The baby came early and is poorly and they've put straw down outside on the road to deaden the noise, so Ethel must be very ill, poor lass. They have a nurse day and night now.'

Jane and Emily stood on the bridge and watched the house where they had been so often. A scream came from the upper rooms and Jane turned pale. 'Is it the 'flu again?' Emily asked.

'That may have started it but this is different, although I hope I'm wrong! There's a kind of madness that comes after a difficult birth and high fever.'

Emily seized her arm and stopped her from rushing across to the house. 'We can't help her now, Mother. Look!' They watched the ambulance arrive and saw Ethel taken to the hospital where mental illness was contained if not cured. The baby lay in a wicker basket with the mother and Ruby looked down helplessly from her bedroom window.

Back home, Jane and Emily worked quickly and silently, as if cleaning the house and turning out dead flowers and bad fruit were the most important things on earth. They were determined to show a tidy house, free from infection, when Nellie arrived the next day. The last post of the day brought a package from America and Jane sank into a chair thankfully to read the letter in it.

'*I travel a lot but now I am in a show in New York and may stay for three or four months*,' Sidney wrote. There were references to famous stars he had seen or met and the fact that the ban on alcohol was total. '*Sales of liquor are prohibited, with heavy penalties for breaking the law but already clubs are being set up for private parties where people drink behind locked doors*.' Jane frowned – Sidney had never liked drink and she hoped that his new life hadn't changed him – but she smiled when he mentioned the things he knew would interest her; the flowers, the places he had visited and the magnificence of the vast countryside.

'It sounds grand, just grand,' she sighed. 'Now, what has that rapscallion sent us this time?' It was a relief to turn to the small packages within the big parcel and forget for a while that Ethel might have puerperal insanity. Emily went to put the Closed sign over the door and Jane heard voices and laughter.

'Mother?' Clare sounded unsure of her welcome.

'Clare? What has happened? Why are you here?'

'I haven't come all that far,' Clare complained. 'Alan said that if I went with him to Winchester on business, I could come over here for a few days. I have to meet him in Portsmouth for the Victoria train the day after tomorrow.' She smiled and her face relaxed. 'It was worth it.' She regarded the gleaming brass and shining china and the air of comfort with affection. 'Have I missed a birthday?' She picked up one of the small packets.

'That came just now from Sidney,' Emily explained.

Clare sniffed. 'Do I sleep in the room we had at Christmas?' She picked up her small case and made for the stairs without a glance at the package with her name on it.

'Clare is jealous of Sidney,' Emily said softly. 'She says she wishes that she was there in America with him, but she can't sing or dance and knows nothing about the theatre. It's as if she bargains with Alan for a bit of freedom: a few days and nights where he wants her and in return she has a short time away from him.'

'How can you bargain with love and marriage?' Jane asked sadly.

Clare came down again and sat by the window. 'It's good to be back,' she said.

'Why doesn't Alan come down too and stay for a while if his work allows it?' asked Jane.

'I said I'd meet him at Portsmouth station and I'll keep my word,' Clare said icily. 'Now what rubbish has my brother sent us?' She ripped open her present and laughed, bitterly. 'This is for someone he loves, not for a sister.' She threw down the dainty chain with a cluster of marcasites in the shape of a heart on a wide bow of small pearls.

'It's very pretty.' Emily was reproachful. 'I had the sweetest pearl brooch and I can wear it on the side of my cardigan as they do in fashion magazines. He loves us all, Clare.'

'It is very pretty,' agreed Jane. 'You must send him a nice little note of thanks.' She gathered up the torn paper and left Clare's necklace where it was, then pinned the filigree brooch that was her gift to her blouse. 'Make the tea, Clare,' she said coldly, and turned back to the letter. Sidney referred to the old days as if homesick; things he remembered like the smell of Christmas puddings and the scent of primroses. He mentioned many of his old friends and asked after Aaron, the Coopers and Mr Foster, the girl on the Mall who helped him with the puppets, and Lucy Dove.

The shop-bell rang and Lucy came in with an empty basket. 'Ethel didn't know anyone when she left,' she said with tears in her eyes. 'Some say if you go into that place you never come out alive.' Lucy shuddered and Jane held her close and Clare looked wide-eyed.

'It's the infection and the baby,' Jane said. 'Don't take on so, Lucy. She may be better soon but if she's violent now she could hurt the baby.' She told Clare what had happened over the past few weeks and Clare seemed genuinely upset and wondered if she could see her friend. 'I'll ask the doctor,' Jane promised. 'Wait while I get some flowers for Janey,' she added to Lucy. 'Clare has made tea so stay and have a cup.'

She gathered flowers and fern and wrapped them in tissue paper but before she could return to the back room, several customers came in to be served and Lucy had to fetch the flowers. The girl was bubbling with a kind of joy and her smile erupted into delighted laughter that had nothing to do with the beauty and scent of flowers.

'Lucy looked pleased with herself,' Jane said later.

Clare poured her mother a cup of tea and went to sit by the window again without speaking. Her face was pink and her eyes over-bright and Emily jabbed at her crochet as if to kill it. 'What's the matter?' Jane saw that the necklace had gone from the table.

Clare twisted her cuff down to hide the split nail she detested. 'Nothing. I think I'll go to the surgery and ask when I can see Ethel.'

The shop doorbell pinged behind her and Emily looked up. 'Sometimes I think that Clare loves to hurt other people,' she said in a low savage voice.

'She's upset about Ethel,' Jane ventured. 'Has she been rude to you?'

'That doesn't matter, but I can never forgive her for what she's done to Lucy.'

Jane laughed. 'Lucy looked as if she had a handsome husband and a thousand pounds a year!'

'I wish she had, but she has nothing but a dream based on a lie!' Emily was pale. 'At first I thought Clare was joking and it happened so quickly that I couldn't make it right. Now it's too late and would make matters worse. She said that Sidney had written and sent Lucy his love. We all know how fond of him she is. She blushed, which made Clare go on about it.'

'He is fond of her and he did send his love to all his friends,' Jane said quietly, but she felt the muscles in her face tighten.

'Clare picked up the necklace he sent her and gave it to Lucy, saying she had opened it in error and it was for her. She pointed out that it had a heart on it, and Lucy took it and kissed it and rushed from the room. She really believes that Sidney sent her a token of love.'

'Sweet Mary, what devil is in Clare that she is so unhappy she must hurt others? She's no right to fill the girl's head with such ideas. Janey needs her and if she's swayed by romantic nonsense she'll be no good to anyone.'

'Leave well alone, Mother. She loves Janey and little George and we all have our dreams.' She bent over the crochet again, her face shadowed by the smooth but unfashionable knotted plait of hair. Emily took a deep breath. 'Lucy needn't know the necklace was for Clare. It's time she had something to call her own that we haven't given her and it might do some good to have a keepsake from someone she loves.' She was aware of the finger-ring of hair that Arnold had given her, now hidden in the locket round her neck.

'I'll look out a good dress for tomorrow. We can't have Nellie thinking we are poor relations!' Jane said, changing the subject, and Emily put up the new light shutters over the shop windows and banked up the fire.

The scent of roses in the closed shop met Clare as she returned, reminding her of the scent her mother had used when they were children, and she went reluctantly into the living room. Emily looked up from her book but said nothing and Jane put the kettle over the fire. Clare relaxed – perhaps Emily had kept quiet and of course Lucy would forget about the gift in time. 'Dr Barnes said I can go to the hospital tomorrow and look at Ethel through the window to see if she recognizes me,' Clare announced, 'but apparently she's asleep under a heavy dose of something now.'

'Go later on,' Jane said. 'I want you around when Nellie comes so that I can forget the shop while she's here. Now you've invited yourself, you can make yourself useful,' she added dryly when Clare looked annoyed. 'You will say nothing to Vikki, remember, and that must be a promise. No hinting! Do you understand, Clare? I won't have half-truths spread about in my house.' Clare looked away and mumbled a promise, knowing now that her mother was very angry with her.

'I wonder what Nellie will wear?' Clare asked, in an attempt to sound normal. 'I hear that she is quite well-known now. Monty gave up his business to arrange those photographs in the magazines and see to her bookings.'

At midnight, Jane made arrowroot and lemon for Vikki and watched her eat it. It was late but what did it matter? If she had asked for roast lamb Jane would have stoked up the fire and cooked it. She settled the child under a light covering and dimmed the light, dreading the disruption that Nellie could bring.

My children are close tonight, Jane thought as she unpinned the brooch from Sidney. Jack seemed to be with her in spirit and she was aware of the trust he had given her, but there was only Emily and Vikki left at home now and the future was cloudy with far too much work for two women alone to do in the shop.

In the morning she dressed with care in clean underclothes as if going to see the doctor, but her fresh blouse and skirt could wait until later in case she spilled something. She touched her hairbrush with jasmine oil and put peach powder on her nose.

Jane unlocked the old bureau in the living room and took out the papers referring to her considerable properties. She had no need to be beholden to a living soul and if Nellie had any ideas about paying towards Vikki's future, she could refuse with dignity. The deeds of the big house on the Mall lay open and she studied them, dreaming of sitting on a real lawn in the summer or standing by the wide French windows. There was a small front garden, she recalled, and a larger one at the back with flowerbeds and fruit trees. Bert said that it was wasteful to keep the house empty, and he wanted to sell it for her. She knew she must decide soon.

Jane locked the desk and made porridge before calling the girls as she had done when they were late for school.

Chapter 5

'She's sound asleep,' Jane said with relief, and smiled. 'You look as if you need a cup of tea, Nellie.' She warmed to the lovely woman who had come soberly dressed in a neat grey costume and white blouse and a hat that hid most of her face under a wide brim.

'You are so kind, Mother,' Nellie said, making no attempt to hide her tears and holding her cup in both hands as if to warm them.

'We all love her,' Jane said. 'She has your looks and Jack's humour.'

'Not too much of our temper, I hope. Seeing her asleep, I can't believe she is my child. I haven't seen her for so long that this is unreal.' She glanced up, pleadingly. 'Am I wicked, Mother? It's far too much to expect you to look after her for ever, after raising your own large family and if you find it too much you must let me know. Even if Monty raises the roof I'll take her back.'

'If she can't have a loving father, she's better off with us,' Jane asserted with a feeling of elation. Nellie was on her very best behaviour but definitely didn't want Vikki. There must have been quite a tug when the wire came and a panic in case she was expected to nurse her own daughter! 'If it's what you want, I'll never send for you again, Nellie, whatever happens, and you can get on with your life with Monty.'

'He hates me to mention Jack but he often speaks of you with affection and sends his best regards.' Nellie fiddled with the clasp of the huge crocodile handbag on her knee. 'In a way, I'm glad you sent for me. Monty wants us to go away for good to America.' Emily took the empty cup and saw the rush of colour to Nellie's face.

'You must go where your husband leads you,' Jane said quietly. 'He's a better husband than my son was to you.'

Nellie flung herself into Jane's arms and sobbed. 'If only

you were my real mother. If only you could come with me. If only we could start again!'

'If only never got you anywhere,' Jane said as if to Vikki when she was naughty. 'You must look to the future. What are your plans?'

Clare listened with a half-smile and was cross when the shop-bell rang and she had to go and miss the conversation, but she came back with Lucy Dove who stared at Nellie and smiled. 'I have all your pictures from magazines and I remember you singing when you lived here! You look wonderful, Mrs Morris.'

'I'm here for only a few hours and came to say goodbye.' Nellie looked at Jane for approval and she nodded. 'Monty has arranged work for me in several American nightclubs and we leave soon.'

'Will you see Al Capone or any of the gangsters?' Lucy was wide-eyed.

'That's Chicago. We are going to New York. Monty would never book me into any of the speak-easies that have trouble with the law about Prohibition and the illegal sale of liquor.' Nellie gained confidence. 'It's a different world – and I can't wait to be a part of it. They really want me and have even booked a suite on the *Mauretania* for us. I shall do cabaret work on board and get known by a lot of rich Americans who may have influence in the theatre.'

'It sounds wonderful.' Lucy was wistful. 'I wish I could come, too.' She touched the thin chain at her neck that held the hidden heart and bow.

'Can you find a place for me too, Nellie? I could do with a change,' Clare announced.

'That's impossible,' Emily said sternly. 'You have a husband and a home here.'

'As it happens, I *do* need someone but you wouldn't do, Clare. It's not all bright lights and excitement, you know. I need someone for the boring jobs like ironing my dresses and mending the costumes I wear for dances like the Tango and the Black Bottom, since they are made from delicate materials and get torn easily.'

'You don't dance the Black Bottom? One of the bishops

denounced it from the pulpit as immoral,' Emily said with awe.

'It's only a dance,' laughed Nellie, 'but when I ask the men for a volunteer to dance with me I get more offers than I need!'

'What else would this girl have to do?' Lucy edged closer.

'Check luggage and see it all arrives at the hotels safely and dress my hair before performances if there isn't a good hairdresser there.'

'Would she have to cook?'

Nellie laughed. 'That would be heavenly! Late at night, that really would be wonderful. Monty often feels hungry then and I am too tired to cook at the best of times. It's not so bad when we take an apartment and I have scope to prepare meals earlier, but where could I find such an angel to do all this?'

'I can cook – ask Janey.' Lucy was pale with excitement. 'I can sew and make things and often do Janey's hair, and once or twice I've done it for Mrs Barnes before a dinner party.'

Nellie leaned back. 'You are Maudie Dove's girl!' She took in the slim dress and shining hair and the air of gentility that Maudie lacked. The finely-chiselled features were Nordic and the innocent mouth showed the influence of Janey and the Darwens and not the house in Sea Street. 'Are you serious, Lucy?'

'If only you'd take me, I'd work and work and you'd never regret it.' She spoke with passion and Jane sought comfort from the long-vanished cameo that she had once worn. Clare looked at her hands and Emily hid her face over the crochet. 'Sidney is in New York,' Lucy said clearly. 'If possible . . . that is . . . I'd like to see him again.'

'A ready-made friend would make a difference, as when I am working you might feel lonely at times. With someone you can trust, New York is a wonderful city to explore.'

'New York is a very big city,' warned Jane. 'You might never find him.'

'What does he do?' Nellie caught sight of the picture on the mantelpiece and laughed. 'Of course! Why didn't I think? He's at the Broadway Theatre. I saw the programme and Monty says he's an up and coming star, but I never thought it was your Sidney. He's only a few blocks from where I shall be working.'

'You seem to have it all planned and settled,' Jane said dryly. 'Arrangements like that usually take more than five minutes.'

'Monty went over last month and brought back all the programmes.' Nellie blushed. 'We decided to go some time back, but it wasn't settled until now. I wouldn't have gone without saying goodbye, or I'd have written to you. I can write and tell you about Sidney now,' she offered, to hide her embarrassment.

How alike they were, Jane thought. Jack and Nellie, two of a kind, who left notes rather than face the music. 'Leave things as they have been and just let me know where to find you from time to time,' she said. 'Sidney writes his own news.'

Nellie turned to Lucy. 'Do you really want to come with me? If so, write to this address by next week and be ready to leave England for at least a year the week after that. You must promise to stay for a year or it isn't worth the expense of taking you.'

'So soon?' Emily was shocked. 'What is Janey to do without you, Lucy?'

'It's more a case of what can Janey find for me to do now she is well after the baby. The girl who comes in is good with George, and she does the housework. I know that her sister wants to come as nanny and wishes I wasn't there!' Lucy hung her head. 'I shall miss you all but I must go. It's . . . it's fate,' she whispered.

'Monty can't wait to get there,' Nellie went on. 'He says he would like to manage movie stars once we have made an impact and he really longs to see the Dempsey-Carpentier fight. He could even end up as a boxing promoter.'

Archie popped his head round the door and looked at the clock. 'We'd better go now, Nellie, or you'll miss the ferry. I'm later than I promised but I had to show a sample of oats that had mildew in it to the chandler, and so I was delayed.'

Nellie drew on her gloves hastily then listened to Vikki calling from upstairs for her Gran. Jane said, 'Do you want to go up?'

Tears fell on the powdered cheeks and Nellie shook her head. 'No, Mother, she's not mine now and if I touched her, I'd regret leaving her for the rest of my life.' Quickly and fiercely, she hugged Jane then ran out of the shop. Archie held the car door open and she didn't look back.

Jane climbed the stairs slowly. 'Vikki, what are you doing out of bed?'

'I was watching the lady get in the motor car. I couldn't see her face but I think she was pretty. Who was it, Gran?'

Jane tucked her up warmly again and sat on the chair. 'Just a lady who came to say goodbye,' she said. She wanted to hug the child and shout that she was hers alone now, but she only smoothed the light hair and told her to stay in bed or she'd be poorly again.

'Clare went up to the hospital,' Emily said when Jane came down again. 'Dr Barnes sent Alex to take her in the car and he'll bring her back later.'

'I thought he had to join his ship.'

'He has extra leave as he must go to the Mediterranean Fleet and be away for at least six months.'

'That means he and Clive will be parted. They've been together for such a long time and are so alike that it seems sad. Alex needs someone to remind him of home until he finds another girl to love.'

'Instead of Janey?' Emily bit off a cotton thread.

'Rubbish!' Jane objected. 'Janey is happily married – he can't fall in love with her.'

'Men do,' Emily said and laughed. 'I hear Archie's motor horn, Mother.'

'You had no need to come back, Archie, but I'm glad you did,' Jane said.

'I saw Nellie on to the ferry but at the last moment I think she regretted leaving and made them wait to take the gangway down for a minute.' He took Jane's hand. 'She's gone and she'll never come back.'

'I'm glad you sent for her. You were right, as until now I never really believed that she would keep her promise not to interfere. The Atlantic Ocean is very wide and America will offer her much more than she could have here. Now, Archie, I've made drop scones for Vikki, so do stay if you have the time. We won't wait for Clare as she is visiting Ethel.'

'I could have taken her there. Surely she didn't walk all the way?'

'Dr Barnes asked Alex to take her.'

Archie raised his eyebrows. 'Alex driving alone with a married woman? That's more than I dare suggest! No, leave the scones and come and sit down while Emily is up with Vikki. You know how I feel, Jane, and isn't it time you married me and came to live on the farm? Warm my heart and warm my home, Jane, for both are very empty.'

'My dear,' she began. 'I shall love you until the day I die.' She checked his effort to kiss her. 'It's a special love, a dear and deep love that I don't deserve to feel for any man after all this time, but it isn't married love. I could come to you and give you less than you deserve and make your years of wanting turn bitter. I have borne seven live children and two dead. I have been a faithful wife to Walter, and although the Good Book says "Till death do us part," I shall never be free. I married one man and he is here now, watching me.'

Archie made an impatient gesture. 'Walter is dead and gone, and for years never deserved you.'

'As long as I am in this house, he is with me.'

'Then sell the shop and come to me, Jane!'

'What about Emily and Vikki, and Janey so near?' She laughed. 'Don't suggest again that I learn to drive one of those terrifying monsters, and I never did find a pony and trap comfortable in bad weather! No, Archie. Everyone has tried to say what I should do. You take it for granted that one day I'll live on the farm. Annie wants me to live in the wilds to get me out of the way as she never could see an inch further than her nose and suspects that I might set my cap at Bert! She ought to know by now that apart from business we have nothing in common and he has other fish to fry. Clare suggested I live with her and Alan for three months to see if I like it there, and most people who come here think that Emily will marry some nice man and take over the shop.' She smiled. 'Even Sidney asked me to visit him but I'm sure it would be a shock if I did!'

'So what have you decided?'

'On none of these things. I shall sell the shop and move up on to the Mall. Emily can still make bouquets and when Janey has to join Clive at any time, there will be room enough for George and his nanny if necessary. I shall never work as hard again and I'll enjoy making a garden with your help, Archie.'

'So I may come to see you?' he asked wryly.

'As often as you wish, my dear. We've shared far too much to lose each other now.' She stood close and reached up to kiss him on the lips. 'You're a dear man so you are. Now hand me that basin of batter and I'll make some more scones.'

Clare brought Alex back with her and Jane fussed over him. 'How is Ethel?' Archie asked.

'Very bad,' Clare replied. 'The nurse said she ripped the uniform from an orderly and they had to take the baby into another ward as she was so violent.'

'Holy saints,' breathed Jane. 'It isn't her fault.' She dimly recalled the time when she was deep in a trough of incomprehension and pain with her heart beating sluggishly but hard enough to stifle her, and her subsequent fight back to reality. Please God I was never violent to my own, she prayed. Surely I never raised a finger against any of them? But she had never found out as nobody would talk about that time.

'They'll know more in a day or so,' Alex said. 'The afterbirth didn't come away whole and that caused the fever.' Clare looked away. How could a man as good-looking and unmarried as Alex talk about such matters, even though he was a doctor's son?

Jane felt the painful past close to her in Ethel's pain and saw Archie tense with memories of sickrooms and death. Suddenly she wanted to take him upstairs and comfort him as she knew she could but not, she thought, not in Walter's house among their children.

'Dr Barnes has written to Fred's Commanding Officer to get him compassionate leave,' said Clare. 'There's less to do in Germany now the blockade is lifted and more for the people to eat, not that I have any sympathy with them. They'd have done far worse to us if they'd won.'

'They certainly murdered a lot of people in every country they overran,' Archie agreed. 'Even now, there is the terrible news of that mass murderer.'

'You mean George Grossman – "The Butcher"? Oh, he is mad and will be executed,' said Alex.

'What did he do?' asked Emily.

Alex gave a ghoulish laugh. 'Better not walk alone in Berlin or the Butcher will get you and cut you up for meat,' he said.

Emily gave a small scream and covered her face, then asked, 'Did he really do that?'

'Yes, to dozens of females, and there's another who killed men by biting through their windpipes. They haven't caught him yet, but they know who the Butcher is. If you go there, it's better to be a vegetarian until he's behind bars!' Alex tried to make Emily scream again and looked more boyish and relaxed as he teased her.

'Europe is a very sad place compared with America,' Archie said. 'Nellie will do well there but I hope that Lucy has made the right decision. It's taking a chance to leave everything you love just to try to meet an old friend so far away.'

'Yes. Sidney was fond of Lucy, but only to give her a hug at Christmas and smile at her when she did something for his costumes.' Jane didn't look at Clare as she spoke but noticed that her daughter slipped away to the scullery.

Archie got up to go. 'Nellie left something for you in the car,' he said. 'I was to keep it until she left on the ferry.' He fetched a large black box and lifted the lid.

'It's one of the latest gramophones,' Alex said with growing excitement. 'Father wants one but he can't get an American one like this. Monty must have bought it over there. Look, the handle goes in here and the horn on this bit. You wind it up, take the record from this compartment and hey presto – music!' He swivelled the head of the arm on to the record and grinned. 'These are Nellie's songs that she must have used for practice, but there are some more under the lid.'

Clare came out of the scullery. 'That's one of the tunes they play at the Kit Kat Club where the Prince of Wales goes dancing. I read about it in a magazine and they gave away the sheet music for it. It's called the *Shimmy*.'

'I wonder our Prince lowers himself to go to such places,' Jane said disapprovingly. 'It sounds indecent! The women who dance there are all legs and no bust and I can't stand skinny women.' Clare turned away to hide the tight binding that made her breasts conform to fashion. 'Does Alan like you looking like a stick of rhubarb?' Jane asked. She'll never feed a baby wearing that thing, she thought.

'I think this one is for you,' Alex said, and Emily giggled as the sober strains of *In a Monastery Garden* filled the room. Jane tried to smile, remembering that Walter used to sing it while playing the harmonium, but she knew that when alone she could never play that record again.

They found excerpts from *The Merry Widow* and Jane hummed with the rest. 'Now that *is* lovely, and I'll play it over and over again if you'll show me how it all works, Alex.'

'Have you an old sock that you can put in here if the music is too loud?' he asked.

'What will they think of next?' Jane said, as if this was the height of scientific discovery. He showed her how to change the needle after about twenty records had been played and then laughed, starting the record without winding it enough. The music played fast and then began to slur and slow down, grinding to a halt and making weird noises.

'It's better like that!' Emily said. 'Let's try the others.'

Jane went up to dress Vikki and bring her down for half

an hour and found her dancing to the music. 'It's too slow now, Gran. I like it fast. One day, I'll dance and dance.'

Jane thrust the small arms into the sleeves of the dressing-gown. 'Put on your slippers and come down to see Uncle Archie,' she said. Vikki ran down showing none of her former weakness, and Jane watched with growing apprehension as the small energetic figure danced more and more like Nellie Morris.

Chapter 6

'I've tried to stop her,' said Jane. 'And Archie has told her just how far away America is.'

'Clare has a lot to answer for,' Janey said crossly as she watched her mother fold baby clothes. 'I really think that Clare has convinced herself now that the necklace really was for Lucy! She can't bear to be in the wrong and is prepared to swear black is white if it suits her. Lucy has been upset, as Maudie who never usually cares what happens to her, has suddenly turned nasty. She's always been jealous of Nellie and the way she has with men. Anyway, it didn't work – it only made Lucy even more stubborn.' Janey picked up a tiny sock and put her finger through the hole in the toe. 'Still, Mother, I'm no one to talk. I'd go to the end of the world for Clive, and if Lucy loves Sidney she must find out for herself if he can love her back.'

'What worries me is that Lucy is starved of love. If Sidney doesn't take her on she might turn to someone bad in desperation. She's pretty enough to attract men and it's a strange world she's entering.'

'Nellie will look after her,' Janey said firmly. 'I shouldn't worry about that. She's a woman of the world and can smell danger before it happens. After all, she's had plenty of practice in getting rid of men who follow her after her performances. Will Monty Morris be good to Lucy?' she asked bluntly.

'Yes, he's a good man at heart and might even like the idea of having a grown-up daughter who has nothing to do with Nellie's husband, and he adores Nellie.'

'Will you see them off?' Janey asked.

'No, Nellie left the day she went from here, but if you want to see Lucy safe on board I'll look after George and you can take Emily for a treat. You are allowed on board to look round until the bell tells all who aren't travelling to leave the ship. Take care of Lucy, as she will be frightened when it comes to the pinch, but I just can't bear to see another ship leave with anyone on board that I care for.' Her eyes had a faraway look as she remembered another ship, a troopship in the rain with rows of white faces over the khaki uniforms lining the decks and the band playing stoically with rain dripping off the nose of the band-master. Fear had seeped out of the grey iron decks and she had felt sick.

'The ship will look beautiful,' she mused. 'All bright paint and flowers everywhere and streamers to send them off, but you'll need a warm coat. Look out anything you think that might be useful to Lucy and buy a few extras. I'll do the same, and the saddler is making a good cabin trunk that will do as a parting present. I'll write to Sidney to warn him they are coming.'

'Letters go on the same ship, Mother. Lucy could post it when she gets there.'

'No, I'll send it.' Jane didn't say that she had sent a telegram to the theatre where Sidney was acting. 'I want to be sure he'll get it. Think what a shock he'd have if people from the Island turned up out of the blue with no warning!'

'Warning? You make it sound as if he must brace himself for an invasion,' Emily said as she came into the room.

'He should be warned,' Jane said quietly. 'Lucy is going there with stars in her eyes and I can't see any future for her with Sidney, although he was fond of her and has never said he has a sweetheart.'

The next day, Jane picked up a newspaper and read of the opening of the Cenotaph in Whitehall, London. There were pictures of the King and the Prince of Wales following the coffin of the Unknown Warrior on its way to Westminster Abbey. It was meant as a gesture to all who were buried in a foreign unmarked grave in the stench and ordure of the Somme and Verdun and Ypres, and the other senseless battles that had laid a generation of young men to waste among the bright poppies. A hundred men, all with ribbons and medals of the Victoria Cross, formed the guard of honour and the King himself sprinkled earth on to the lowered coffin. And then she read of the Assembly of the League of Nations in Geneva, from which America and Germany and Russia were absent.

'What's the use if they don't all join?' she asked Bert Cooper when he came into the shop.

'It's a start, and while the politicians are wrangling, it's the businessmen who will set the pace.'

Jane watched him take a polished apple from the display and bite into it. 'How many shall I weigh?' she asked sweetly. 'Less the one you've had, or a few specks if you are short of a copper.' She eyed his smart suit with interest and wondered where he was going today.

'I want some flowers for Annie,' he said. 'Her rheumatics are bad today and she can't get out.'

Jane weighed the apples and made up a bunch of flowers. 'Give her these from me,' she said. 'How is the new maid getting on?'

'You know Annie! Hates to pay out anything but she can't do it herself now. I pay the girl over the odds and don't let on to Annie as I think she'd leave as soon as wink the way Annie goes on to her.'

'What is it, Bert? You've a bunch of flowers and the best grapes and you still stand there shifting from one foot to the other.'

'I've seen Dr Barnes,' he said throatily. 'He says it's more than rheumatism: Annie will get steadily worse.'

'Dear God!' Tears sprang to Jane's eyes. 'It's a shock but I think I've known for some time that she was really ill.'

'If you could pop in sometimes? She thinks a lot of you, Jane.' He picked a grape from the bunch. 'You do her good.'

'You surprise me. She's been the first to gossip and I've felt the edge of her tongue often enough.'

'It's her life's blood,' he admitted. 'Both of us might have been better people if we'd had a family. As it is, she vents all her bitterness on me, you and poor Dan – who bears the brunt of it now that you have sent the horses to Wootton and he can't escape to the stables. What shall I do about the animals, Jane?'

'Get rid of everything. I don't want a pony and trap and I never want to go to the stables again.'

'I'll see to it. You are a lady of property now but you must make sure of your profits. What about that house lying idle on the Mall?'

'I'm going to live there,' Jane replied breathlessly. 'I have told Archie but even the girls don't know yet, so you are honoured! Don't tell Annie before the girls know, or it will be all round Newport.'

'After two wars and a lot of unhappiness you must be glad to leave, even if it is a wrench,' he said wisely.

'A lot of happiness too, Bert.'

'Walter was a lucky man. You trail warmth wherever you go.'

Jane looked pleased. 'I want your help, Bert.' She saw him redden. 'I know I don't ask for it often but now I want you to draw up papers so that some of the cottages are made over to Emily while I'm still alive. She'll never marry and I want her to have something of her own so that she need never have to ask for every reel of cotton. The rents bring in quite a nice bit.' She lifted her chin defiantly.

'She can be like you were with the pickle money,' he said and grinned.

'Emily makes something from the bouquets and can go on doing that in the big greenhouse at the back of our new house. By the way, we went out to the West Wight ages ago and measured up for curtains.' Bert nearly swallowed a grape pip and coughed. 'We shall go there most Fridays until the cottages are finished,' she added with a slight smile. He had been so kind of late that she thought he'd feel safer if he knew which days she might be there, to avoid meeting him and Maudie.

I'll have to tell everyone now, Jane thought as the family returned from seeing Lucy and Nellie on board ship. Next year, she dreamed, I'll have an asparagus fern by that path in the new garden and try to grow a peach tree.

'Why can't I go on a big ship?' Vikki asked, coming into the scullery.

'Away from me and Aunt Emily?'

'You'd have to come, and Aunt Janey and George and Uncle Archie and my friends.'

'That would fill a ship! But we *are* going away – to a nice house with a garden where you can have your little friends in to tea.'

'Can I have a *rocking horse*?' Vikki asked in a sibilant whisper. 'A real rocking horse?'

'A wooden horse, is it?' But Jane agreed that they didn't bite and they stood still when not needed, unlike the pony that Archie had suggested. She made tea and put fancy cakes on the stand. 'Now tell me about Lucy,' she invited her daughters.

'Everything was fine,' Janey said. 'Lucy was overwhelmed by the splendour of everything and even I was surprised at the wooden panelling and the palm trees in the lounges. It was like being in a luxury hotel.'

'We saw the cabins and the restaurant and where they play the band for . . . the people who work in the cabaret.' Emily bit her lip in time. 'We met some nice people who will look after Lucy,' she added, and Vikki had no idea that they were her mother and step-father. Emily began to cry. 'It was beautiful but so sad, Mother. We were with Lucy and the others when the ship's hooters went and a voice called, "All ashore who goes ashore," and we had to leave. Lucy didn't want to stay on the boat but the lady with her held her hand tight and said nice things to her, so I think she'll be all right.'

'A member of the Royal Family was travelling and so the band was a very smart one from the Guards. They played *Auld Lang Syne* and streamers were thrown from the deck but as the ship drew away, they broke and fell into the water.' Janey shrugged. 'It was sad but I brought a piece back for you.' She produced a length of bright pink paper but Jane made no attempt to touch it.

'I want it.' Vikki snatched it and rolled it into a ball, then tried to straighten it but it was damp. She screwed it up again and threw it into the fire and nobody tried to stop her.

'So that's that,' said Jane.

'I'm going to have a rocking horse,' Vikki announced. 'I shall play with it in the garden.'

'You'll get it muddy in the backyard,' said Emily indulgently.

'There will be a garden,' Jane told her quietly. 'I want to move into the house on the Mall. The shop is too much for you and me and we don't need it now.'

'I wish it was this side of town but I'm glad,' Janey announced.

'I'm glad, too. I secretly hoped you'd decide to go there,' Emily agreed. She grew quite excited as the possibilities opened out. 'It means we are free to have trips to Portsmouth, see our friends and never have to stay in to mind the shop, although I can still do the flowers.'

'I hope you'll stay with me unless you marry and have a place of your own, Emily, but until then I want you to feel independent. I've made over some cottages to you and that, with your flower money, will make life comfortable even if you leave home. There are three cottages up at Cross Lanes which bring in good rents from clean reliable people and Bert's agent will collect for you.'

Janey nodded her approval and Emily was pink with pleasure. 'I can buy nice presents for people now,' she said. 'Oh, Alex called in to say goodbye,' she added, more seriously.

'When was this?' Janey asked sharply.

'Yesterday. He called at the Lodge but you weren't there.' Emily regarded her sister solemnly. 'We shan't see him for six months, but Clive will be here soon and you'll have eyes only for him.'

'He'll miss us,' Janey said almost defensively. 'Now that his fiancée is dead, I think we help him.'

'Did you mind me giving the cottages to Emily?' asked Jane. 'You are secure and so are the others and Emmy will never marry.'

'I think it's grand, just grand,' Janey said, cheekily imitating her mother when excited. 'Don't ever tell Lizzie or Clare, though, and I'll see that Emily doesn't either.' Janey prepared a feed for George and Vikki held the bottle carefully so that he didn't take in air as he sucked and George was content.

'They were talking on the ship about work here,' Emily said. 'A lot of people are leaving for America as engineers are losing jobs in the midlands and at a place called Jarrow men are starving. So many ex-servicemen are out of work.'

'Alan and Harry will be safe,' Jane said stoutly but looked anxious.

'Harry boasts about the orders they have for the next ten years,' Janey remarked. 'He was impressing Alan the last time he was here, and it made Alan quiet, I thought.' A motor cycle raced up the road, making George start and cry. 'There are a lot of them for sale secondhand,' Janey said. 'Silly things! The men bought them with their army money and now have to sell them to make ends meet.'

Jane felt restless. She hated to think of any of her family losing their pride. 'How did Nellie look?' she asked.

'Very pretty, all in pale blue. Even her fur was dyed blue and she wore very thin silk stockings. Her scent was very heady as if she had all the flowers in the world in a bottle.'

'I hope that Lucy is safe. We don't know if she has much of Maudie in her yet.'

'She's different,' Janey affirmed. 'She hated the house in Sea Street and her mother's friends.'

'Blood tells,' Jane said cryptically. 'I just hope she hasn't too high hopes of New York and Sidney.'

Chapter 7

The throbbing grew louder and Lucy felt the surge as the *Mauretania* turned by the Needles. The porthole framed the lighthouse for a moment and then green sea and clouds, and she knew that she had seen the last of England.

The scent of Californian Poppy made her turn. Nellie stood by the cabin trunks, her hair flattened by the discarded cloche hat and her make-up ruined by tears. Wordlessly the two held each other close and shuddered with emotion. Monty Morris coughed. 'I'll just see the purser and arrange about supper,' he said, and escaped.

'I was fine until the streamers broke,' Nellie sobbed. 'I never want to hear *Auld Lang Syne* again, or I know I'll cry.'

Lucy began to recover. 'You'll feel better soon, Mrs Morris,' she said and patted her back. 'I'd better do your hair as I heard your husband say he wanted you to meet some people in the lounge in an hour.'

'You sound just like Jane Darwen,' Nellie said and gave a watery smile. 'You're quite right, though, I do look a mess.' She washed her face in the small basin they found under a mahogany lid and put on fresh cream and powder from her beauty case. 'I'm glad you came, Lucy. It's wonderful to have another woman with me. Monty gets fed up if I cry and we can talk about things that don't interest him. You must call me Nellie. Come next door to our cabin while you do my hair as there's more space. You will be cramped here as we have so much luggage but I think it's quite comfortable for sleeping. Considering that this is a ship and not a hotel, we have a very big suite.'

Lucy brushed the lustre back into the copper hair and stuck two kiss curls to Nellie's cheeks. 'You look lovely. What shall I unpack for you to wear?'

'I shall wear this as it's just a business meeting and I have to change for the cabaret tonight. Here is a map of the ship. Wander about and if you want tea or coffee or a drink, just sign the chit with this suite number. It's all included in the agreement and we have only to buy our own souvenirs or personal shopping. There are shops here so take this and buy me some more Larola Rose Bloom and a jar of Larola cream.' She gave Lucy five shillings. 'The rouge is a shilling but I'm not sure about the cream. Buy the largest pot they have.' She laughed at Lucy's surprise. 'In a day or so, you'll forget you are at sea. They have everything on board, including beauty parlours, clothes shops and a doctor.'

'But when do I make myself useful?' Lucy asked.

'Don't worry, I shall work you to death! Meet us in the Veranda Café at half-past six and we can have coffee there.'

Lucy checked where to find the Veranda Café and the shops before clutching her bag nervously and leaving the suite. She wandered through luxurious flower-filled lounges and up wide stairways and stopped by the barrier separating First Class passengers from the rest of the ship, realizing for the first time in her life what it was like to have the respect that money could buy when a steward asked if she needed a lounge chair and rugs, and would she like any refreshment on deck?

With new-found dignity, Lucy smiled and asked him to show her where she could find the Veranda Café. 'My friends will expect me,' she said, and he led the way down flights of stairs and through corridors until he could point out the wide entrance through which she saw cane chairs and soft drapes. Being alone was odd when all around were families and couples but she sat straight and arranged the marcasite heart on the front of the pale beige dress and tried to feel secure.

'You found it!' Monty sounded pleased. The girl had class and it had added to Nellie's status to speak casually of 'my dresser' when they talked business. He rubbed his hands together. 'Now for a drink. What will you have?'

'I'd like some tea,' Lucy replied. Monty made a face but snapped his fingers for a steward and gave the order.

'I'll have whisky. What about you, Nellie?'

'I'll have tea, too.' She laughed. 'Lucy will be a good example, I can see. I shall drink wine tonight but gin during the day depresses me, and it's one way to keep my schoolgirl complexion.'

'Don't forget there's Prohibition in New York,' Monty warned her. 'I intend making the most of this voyage.'

'Do you good to go dry,' Nellie teased.

'Sufficient to the day!' He winked at Lucy. 'They sell a good line in the shops here – two, in fact. It's a good thing that walking sticks are fashionable again. I'll have to pretend to have a limp.' He picked up the stout cane by his chair and unscrewed the knob to show them. 'It's hollow and holds more than you'd think. I'll fill this flask, too. See, it fits snugly under one arm.'

Lucy giggled. 'You'll be like a gangster with a holster under his coat.'

'Be careful, Monty. If you get frisked, they'll find it and you'll be in trouble.'

'Frisked? I didn't know my wife knew such unlady-like American sayings. Have a cake or something, Lucy. Dinner for us will be very late as Nellie has to do her show and then repeat it for the other diners in Second Class. We might as well get used to eating late as they do in America.' Nellie watched as Lucy ate two cream cakes with all the pleasure and hunger of a slim child, and Monty smiled indulgently.

Nellie lit a Sobranie and Lucy said shyly, 'You are both being very nice to me.'

'You don't know me,' said Monty with a grin. 'I can be terrible! But if you have any problem, come and tell me or Nellie and we'll sort it out for you.'

'I can't think of anything likely to happen to me,' Lucy said innocently.

Monty looked at the slim, almost boyish figure and translucent skin, and picked up his glass. 'Just remember all the same, and you'd better call me Uncle Monty.' Nellie nodded agreement. 'We never meet trouble halfway but be careful. Drink up that tea or it will be cold.'

Lucy sighed with contentment. It was like having a proper

family who cared for her and she didn't see the looks that some men gave her as they drank more and lost their inhibitions. Monty treated them to a basilisk stare and they turned away.

When they went to change Nellie asked, 'Did you leave a special friend behind?'

Lucy put Nellie's dress on the bed. 'I'll press it before I hang it up,' she said. 'I shall miss the Darwens and one or two old schoolfriends who gave me nice gifts before I came away.'

'I mean men friends. Lucy, you're a big girl now!'

'Of course not.' Lucy fingered her necklace. 'I dance with boys and we have picnics with Clive and some of his friends but I'm going out to find Sidney. He sent me this, with his love.'

Nellie filled the bowl with warm water and began to wash her breasts and underarms, completely unselfconsciously. 'Has he said he wants you?' she asked abruptly.

'He sent me this heart and his love and anyhow, I wanted to come and work for you, Nellie.' Lucy seemed less confident.

'Hold back a little, Lucy. Men hate women who run after them. It pays to let them make the running.' Lucy brushed Nellie's hair with vigour. 'He may have changed and then you'll be hurt,' she went on cautiously. 'You've known him all your life and he is fond of you, but what if he doesn't love you in a special way when you meet?'

'I know he hasn't a sweetheart and I think I'm quite pretty,' Lucy said. 'If he doesn't love me now, I'll make him learn to do so. He sees a lot of beautiful women, I know, but I have to see him. I have to have a chance to make him love me – don't you understand?'

'Yes, I do,' Nellie said. 'Now hand me that slip or I'll be arrested if I wear nothing under this dress.' She powdered her body with scented talcum powder and handed the long-handled swan's-down puff to Lucy to finish her back before sliding into the close-fitting dress.

Monty sat Lucy in a dimly-lit corner at the back of the dining room. All the women were smartly dressed and she felt like a schoolgirl in her plain frock, but when she remarked on the dresses, he laughed. 'Tonight they aren't really trying. First night out is a casual affair but tomorrow they try to outdo each other like peacocks.' He regarded her with amusement. 'You needn't worry. Most of the old bags need two layers of paint to fill in the cracks and they'd give their eye teeth to have your complexion.' They watched Nellie warming her audience, singing and dancing but never making her manner vulgar or too much directed at the men, and always performing with humour and style. 'She's got them in the palm of her hand,' he said, and chuckled. 'America, you'll love her. Here we come!'

Nellie walked between the tables to the shadows at the back and sat down to have her own dinner while the applause died and conversation resumed. Lucy was tired and hungry and the room was stuffy with the smoke from a hundred cigarettes. She looked at the menu in disbelief. 'Do they serve all of this?' she asked.

'Not all at once,' Monty said. 'Choose what you like. It's fish at the beginning and meat after that. They write it in French to confuse us and it's just a bit of snobbery, but get Nellie to lend you a phrasebook so you can read a menu.'

'What are you having, Nellie,' Lucy asked.

'Melon and grilled salmon and salad. No potatoes.'

'But you didn't look at the menu!'

'There's always salmon and salad and if there isn't, there should be! It takes snotty waiters down a peg if I demand it,' Nellie confided.

'That sounds lovely but could I have some potatoes? I'm so hungry,' Lucy said.

'I suppose you'll eat more than both of us and not put on an ounce.' Monty looked at Nellie and smiled.

White wine appeared in a silver bucket and Lucy ate until she could eat no more and was in a dream, accepting half a glass of wine and some fresh orange juice.

'I'm exhausted,' Nellie said at last. 'If I'm to be up early I must sleep. Come on Lucy, you look tired too.' As soon as Lucy sank into her narrow berth she fell asleep, lulled by the gentle movement of the ship but at dawn the ship rolled and from the next cabin, she heard Monty swearing and moaning. Lucy washed and dressed and timidly knocked on the other door. Nellie was bending over her husband at the basin. 'What can I do to help?' asked Lucy.

'He's better now he's been sick but stay with him and mop his face until I get dressed. I have sent for the stewardess and she'll take over.' Nellie put on a smart blouse and long woollen cardigan over a pleated skirt and when the dumpy little stewardess arrived with fresh towels and a tray of remedies she smiled at her ravishingly. 'I'm so glad to see you. Do you mind if I leave you to see to everything? I have to go down to breakfast with my dresser and then see some people.' She pressed a coin into the woman's hand.

'Shouldn't we stay?' asked Lucy.

'They prefer not to have me breathing down their necks,' Nellie said lightly. 'I hate sickrooms and Monty loves a bit of fuss. I may be queasy later but I doubt it. I have never been seasick, have you?' She noted with satisfaction that the bloom had not left Lucy's cheeks. 'It sometimes runs in families.'

'My mother is never sick but I didn't know my father as he was killed in the Boer War,' Lucy said.

Nellie smiled. It didn't matter if Ben Dove had been prone to seasickness; Vikings were good sailors. 'Wrap up warm,' she told Lucy after breakfast. 'We'll find a couple of chaises longues and rugs in a sheltered spot and have some beef bouillon later. I might even snooze as I was up half the night with Monty groaning.'

The four large funnels seemed even larger now she was on deck and Lucy felt pampered and happy under the warm rugs with a cup of hot broth beside her, but soon felt stifled.

'Go where you like but meet me for lunch at one,' Nellie said sleepily.

The deck took on all kinds of odd angles and Lucy buttoned up her thick blue melton coat against the wind. Two children ran about, sliding as the deck tipped and laughing at their nanny who ran after them looking slightly green. Lucy noticed a man watching, smiling at her own amusement. She went below to the shops and marvelled at the pretty but very expensive garments there, longing to buy but having enough sense to keep the ten pounds that Jane had given her safe until she could buy real bargains in New York. Janey and Emily could look at a dress and copy it in cheaper material that looked as good, or if it was complicated Miss Joyner was clever at tucks and pleats. Suddenly she was homesick and dabbed her eyes with a handkerchief.

She made for the Veranda Café as the most familiar place on board and sat by a trough of flowers. 'Coffee, miss?' She looked up, startled, and nodded. Nellie had said, half-joking, that she must get used to drinking coffee as they did in America. It arrived in a silver pot with a small jug of cream and a dish of brown sugar crystals and the cup was of thin china embossed with the motif of the Cunard Line.

She sipped the coffee, more to savour a new experience than because she was thirsty and saw a man at the next table who seemed familiar. Yes, she recognized his shoes. She smiled faintly. Who could forget them? She had seen similar ones in magazines and knew that they were called Correspondent's shoes. They were white and black in shiny leather and laced with wide silk bows. The man wore a well-cut suit and his tie was brighter than any she'd seen worn even by Monty, who favoured colour. When he sensed that Lucy had noticed him, the man smoothed back his brilliantined hair and smiled, showing very white teeth under a neat moustache.

Lucy looked away and shifted her chair slightly so that she could no longer see him. He had been on deck previously, strolling past Nellie and her and then again by the shops. Several men had tried to get into conversation with her but her aloof manner discouraged them and Lucy had no time for lounge lizards, as Clare called men who dressed in that way. She glanced at the clock on the wall. Nellie would be ready for lunch in a quarter of an hour. She walked past the man with her eyes downcast and found Nellie, rested after a good sleep.

'I feel wonderful,' she said. 'Let's go down and see that Monty is all right and then have lunch. I'm starving.' Nellie noticed the man now leaning on the rail. 'Monty hates those shoes,' she whispered. 'Americans wear them a lot but they are too flashy for his taste. That man probably owns a speakeasy or a gambling casino or poolroom.' She swept past him with Lucy in her wake and he threw his cigarette stub in the sea and followed them.

Monty was feeling better but still groaning. The portholes were open and the linen fresh but the idea of eating made him feel queasy again so Nellie hastily left him to sleep. The dining room was half-empty and they lingered over the meal, with Nellie telling Lucy about people she'd met on her tours. When Lucy said she'd be afraid to speak to a movie star, Nellie laughed.

'All you need there is a pretty face and lots of nerve. Those people are human like the rest of us and who knows, I may become a star one day! Sidney Darwen will be a star if this revue is successful, so you'd better get him before the Broadway vultures dig in their claws.'

'Now I'm here, I do get nervous at the thought of meeting him again. I shall come over all shy, I know.'

'Well, that's a novelty in this profession! Stay as you are and you'll have half the stage-door Johnies drooling after you.'

'I'm not in the theatre,' protested Lucy.

'Oh, yes you are. As my dresser, you will be there for several hours a day and be seen with me wherever I go without Monty. You may laugh but I am really quite shy unless I am performing and I need you with me.'

'I promised to stay with you for a year,' Lucy said.

'I may have to remind you of that,' Nellie said. She saw the man with the too-smooth hair watching them. 'Be very careful, Lucy. Men like that one can be beasts. Have fun and dance with them if you must, talk to them but never be alone with one like that who looks as if he wants to eat you for dessert.'

'You are funny!'

Lucy's light innocent laughter made Nellie feel very experienced and world-weary. 'Go and do what all horribly young and healthy creatures do on board. Play shuffle-board or something and look even more fresh and make me feel tired! Be ready for cocktails with the doctor and First Officer at six, as Monty might not be fit and I'll need you there. Don't be scared, but you'll need something smart to wear. I'll lend you something. Clothes do make a difference but look beyond them at all times Lucy, to see the real person there. Look at eyes first and the mouth gives away a lot.'

'I shall try to act a part,' Lucy said. 'If I wear borrowed clothes it might be easier and I feel a different girl to the one who looked after little George.'

'You still have to wash and iron and mend.'

'It's different,' Lucy insisted. 'Crêpe de chine is more difficult to press than cotton but much more exciting. Have I time to go to the library and get a book to read and a French phrasebook?'

'Yes. Find me a nice light novel,' Nellie requested. 'They have the latest books there, quite as good as any subscription library ashore.'

Lucy found a Nick Carter novel and sat down in the library to read it. Sidney is like Nick Carter, she decided. Nick never swears or smokes, drinks or tells lies and he respects all women. The book was full of drama and suspense. Sidney never ran after girls but like Nick Carter would one day find the right girl. She flipped over the pages to the end, but no, Nick Carter was still pure and unattached, unsullied and suddenly boring.

She had every intention of studying French but the array of magazines on the glass-topped table was inviting; she saw *True Romance, Love Story Magazine* and others with a similar theme where the heroine found romance with a fine incorruptible man. The stories were beautiful and as she imagined real love to be. Another stack contained American periodicals like *Ladies' Home Journal*, sold for ten cents a copy. How much was that in English money? There were so many new things to learn and so much that was confusing.

On deck, the wind had died and more people walked cautiously in the fresh air. A girl of her own age came up to Lucy. 'I'm Dulcie Weinburg,' she said with a pronounced American accent. 'My parents are sick and I'm bored. Come and play shuffle-board.' They joined four other young men and women and when Lucy won, they teased her and insisted on taking her to the bar to buy her drinks.

'Only lemonade, please,' she said and looked at the clock.

'You have a date?'

'No, but I have to go at five to get ready for the cocktail party. I'm with Nellie Morris.'

One of the boys gave a long low sigh. 'She's gorgeous. Do you sing, too?'

'No, they've . . . brought me along to visit a friend in New York and Uncle Monty said I could help Nellie and be company for her.' Somehow with these rich people she couldn't bring herself to say she was Nellie's dresser.

'See you at the party, then! I bet you'll wear something really dramatic to the fancy dress?'

'I haven't decided yet.' She envied their easy manners and laughter, but was annoyed to see on her way back to Nellie that the man was there again as he had been while she played shuffle-board, leaning on the rail as if waiting.

'Monty isn't up yet so you'll have to come, Lucy. Don't look so frightened. Just let the men talk about themselves and nod sometimes and they'll find you very intelligent and attractive!' She threw a gown on the bed in Lucy's cabin. 'Wear this. It's tight on me and I was going to get rid of it so you can keep it.'

The pale green silk flowed into a series of soft points over a satin underslip, the low waist was trimmed with rosebuds and the modest neckline gave a hint of far more that was unrevealed. 'It's lovely and I'll take great care of it,' Lucy breathed.

'It's yours now and you mustn't worry if someone spills wine on it. I have lots more that you can have, but it's refreshing to find someone who hasn't seen or done everything yet.' Vikki would grow up with the same care that Jane Darwen had given Lucy, and Nellie felt a trace of maternal feeling as she brushed back a tendril of hair from the girl's face.

A burst of music from the salon greeted them as Nellie stood by the door waiting for someone to introduce her, and she was ushered in with respect as everyone had heard that she was no ordinary cabaret artiste but had a contract with some very smart venues in New York. Her perfect make-up and pale lavender dress made heads turn and she was quickly swept into a group of admirers. Lucy watched the faces of women who had heavy make-up and sparkling jewels, and men who had hard and expensive expressions as if money ruled out any sign of human kindness. Dulcie and two of the men from the morning came to ask her to join them, but Lucy explained that Uncle Monty was sick and she had to stay with Nellie.

'You sure look pretty, Lucy,' said Dulcie. 'Where did you get that lovely dress?'

'I have to look smart if I travel with Nellie,' Lucy said and turned away reluctantly. 'I'll try to see you later.'

A man with a silk handkerchief and an elegant matching cravat took her hand and squeezed it. 'What a pretty little thing you are,' he said. 'With the cabaret?'

'I am not on the stage,' she said, 'I am travelling in the care of my Uncle Monty.' She dragged her hand away and turned to find herself staring into the face of the man she wanted to avoid. He made no attempt to touch her but asked politely, 'May I fetch you a cocktail?'

Lucy glanced with agony at Nellie who was lost in a group of men. She was laughing and talking in a throaty voice that was very attractive and not looking at Lucy. 'I don't know what to drink. Something lemony would be nice. Lemonade?' she asked without much hope as a waiter passed them with a tray of tiny funnel-shaped glasses, each filled with a different coloured liquid with olives or other strange things floating in it.

'I'll do my best.' His accent was American but had an added sibilant softness, and she felt reassured. His hair might be over-polished and his eyes hooded with heavy lids, but she felt safer with him than with the man who tried to hold her hand and breathe all over her. 'Try this.'

She held up the pale yellow glass with the sugared rim and the twist of lemon. 'It's pretty,' she said and sipped.

He smiled and watched her drain the glass. 'More?' She

nodded and he took the glass. She was aware of a growing warmth and a sense of well-being and much more confidence. Even the hard faces lost their edges and Lucy smiled.

Nellie saw her and came over quickly as the man brought the second drink. She took it from him and sniffed. 'You worm,' she said quietly. 'If you as much as look at this girl again, my husband will throw you to the fishes!'

'It's delicious,' protested Lucy.

'So it is.' Nellie poured the contents of the glass into a potted plant. 'I've asked the steward to prepare fresh orange juice for us and he's bringing it now.' Lucy looked back at the man who was now tapping a cigarette on a gold cigarette case and his face was like a mask.

'I can see that you need me,' Nellie said. 'Cocktails are poison. They make you drunk quickly and ruin your looks. You can never be sure what they put in them and with men like that they make sure it's strong to make you an easy prey. Who is he? Did you make any arrangements to meet him?' Nellie sounded shrill.

'He asked me to look him up in New York and his name is Frank Garsey,' Lucy said sulkily. The aftertaste wasn't so nice now and she wanted to belch but it wouldn't be polite.

'More like Franco Garcia with a complexion like that,' Nellie said scathingly. She looked at Lucy's eyes. 'There was more in that drink than even I thought. You are going to bed, young lady.' She called for a stewardess and gave her a big tip to make sure that Lucy locked her cabin door and stayed there alone, under the care of the woman who had seen it all and showed no surprise.

Nellie smiled again and dismissed Lucy from her mind, once more the beautiful woman who charmed and entertained and was rapidly becoming very popular.

Chapter 8

'I met Janey and she says that Clive is coming home,' Emily said as she burst into the shop. 'She's on her way here with the perambulator and she's very excited.'

'It's ages since he had a good leave,' Jane said, pleased. 'George is a very good baby and they could leave him with us for a few days.'

'Three whole weeks, Mother,' Janey said later as she fed George and ate a piece of fruit cake. 'It's the most we've ever had together and he wants to get to know his son properly.'

Jane said nothing about taking George off their hands but wondered if after a few days Clive might want his wife alone and would be glad to leave George with her. 'Has he heard from Alex?' she asked.

'Poor Alex is very unhappy; he can't get home leave and he misses his friends.'

'He'll find himself,' said Jane. 'Men do.' She saw Janey take out her shopping list. 'Now help yourself to anything you want in the shop,' she said. 'Lizzie and Clare make free with everything when they are here so why not you? You are still my daughter!'

'I like to keep things straight,' Janey said and weighed out apples and ticked the amount on her list. She laughed. 'It won't be as much of a shock to me then when you give up everything. Lizzie will be furious to lose her free food. By the way, Clive will be home in time to help you move.'

'No! You are not to suggest it. When I need strong arms I shall hire them. It isn't fair to do it ourselves when there are so many men who need to earn a few days' work, and Dan will see that it runs smoothly.' She thought of the bitterness in the eyes of the men on the dole and the thin children who lined up for soup each day. More and more she added nourishing ingredients to the soup she made for the chapel and wished she could feed them all.

'It's not as bad here as it is up north,' Janey said. 'Another engineering firm is laying off men in Wales and the miners are thinking of going on strike.'

'More trouble, just when we thought that peace would bring plenty for all.' Jane looked sad. 'Ireland is in the news again as well. There'll be trouble there for ever. The Irish have memories that are far too long; I know and I've suffered from it. They never forgave me for marrying an English soldier and they never forget that the British brought the Black and Tans over.' She sighed. 'There's blame on both sides in a country where they should be working together, not fighting the past.'

'Right – I have everything I need,' Janey announced. 'I'll get back as I want to have a good baking session today and tomorrow morning so that I am not in the kitchen for too long when Clive comes. I sent Maisie away to her mother who is ill and to tell the truth I don't need a nanny. We shall be much more private without her and she isn't like Lucy. I can't wait to hold him close,' she whispered as she hugged her mother goodbye.

'I shall keep away until you want me,' Jane said firmly. 'Give Clive our love and enjoy his leave.'

Janey pushed the heavy pram home and put George upstairs for a nap. Clive wasn't due yet but she had no idea at what time he would arrive the next day. She made pastry and a cake and got up early to make bread and to chop vegetables for soup which she put to simmer. A bird flew across the window making an alarm cry and she brushed the floury hair from her eyes but no familiar step came along the drive.

The lamb chops were ready, sprinkled with rosemary and pepper. The cut glass bowl held an enticing array of fruit and on the sideboard a bottle of French wine was ready with glasses. Janey tidied the kitchen. The navy might keep him until tomorrow, but she must be ready and the food would keep well. George was asleep and she left the front door unlocked in case Clive came while she was upstairs.

She ran warm water in the bath that to her was still a real luxury and she hoped that Jane would have a bathroom installed in the new house. Her hair was damp so she lay down and washed it while she was in the water to get rid of the kitchen odours. George cried and she wrapped her head in a small towel and pulled on her dressing gown over her lavender-scented skin. It was early for his feed but he grew hungrier each day and nothing would stop his cries but food from a spoon or from his bottle.

George smelled her warm flesh and tried to reach her breasts but she held him away and fed him by spoon although she ached to feed him even now her milk had gone. I want another baby, she thought. I'm like Mother. I love to have a baby to feed. She rocked the child and made him bring up wind then held him close to make him sleepy. A sound at the doorway made her start and she saw Clive leaning against the lintel. She caught her breath. In the smart uniform, he was more handsome than she recalled. She blushed deeply. 'How long have you been there? I thought I'd be ready for you. Please don't look at me now! My hair is all wet.'

He took his son in his arms and laughed. 'You deceived me, woman! This monster isn't the baby I left.' George burped a thin trail of milk over the smart uniform but Clive didn't notice. He tucked the baby into his cot and turned to Janey. 'You really have deceived me,' he added. 'You are far more beautiful than I remember.'

Janey hung her head, the exquisite dread of her nakedness making her shy and she gasped when he took away the towel and ran his hands through her damp hair. He kissed her as if he had needed her for a very long time. His hands were gentle but irresistible and he carried her to their bed and undressed, shedding his rank and uniform, becoming husband and lover with a passion and reverence that made them complete.

'Soup!' Janey said as they lay relaxed and spent.

'I heard you talking to your lover so I turned it off and came to see what was happening.' He kissed the lobe of her ear. 'What did I find? My rival locked in your arms.'

Janey stopped as she began to put on her gown. He was half-serious. George was asleep and didn't need her and she remembered her own father being jealous of each new baby that took Jane's attention away from him, so she kissed her husband on the lips and whispered, 'It's been so long. You go and see that your son is still breathing while I prepare food for my real lover.' She dressed and when Clive came downstairs in old comfortable clothes, he was singing softly and came behind her, cupping her breasts in his hands.

'Open the wine,' she said and giggled. 'Not that we need any, but it will keep you occupied while I stir the soup.'

'It smells wonderful and so do you. We have three weeks together and I want you all to myself.' The cork came out with a plop. 'The baby too, of course,' he added.

'There's a lot to be done here,' Janey said. 'I need your advice badly.' Clive looked pleased and she knew that she must make him feel important in his own home. She glanced at him from under her unruly, newly-dried hair. 'Is it very wicked of me to want my husband all to myself for a few days? Say if you want him here all the time but I'd like to leave George with Mother for a while. Emily would help with him and they'd have him if I asked them.'

'Not yet,' Clive protested. 'I want to get to know him first and then you shall leave him and we'll walk across Tennyson Down and Afton and along the beaches and make love.' But she noticed that the strain was fading from his eyes.

'All at the same time?' she teased him. 'Anyway, just let me know when you've had enough of one squawling boy.'

'He's crying now. I'll fetch him.'

'You'll spoil him if you pick him up each time he murmurs,' Janey said, when Clive reappeared holding George.

'At least he stopped and I think he likes me.'

'Of course he does! I show him your picture every day and say that it is Daddy. You brought him down so you look after him while I serve the food.'

Later, Janey stacked the plates in the sink ready for the girl who came each day to clean the kitchen and nursery. 'We'll take him for a walk,' Clive said. 'We can go up to the Mall and see the house where your mother is going to live and call in at the shop for a cup of tea on the way home.'

Janey smiled to herself. Clive was doing everything she wanted but thought the ideas were his own. I'm learning fast, she decided and asked him about his ship when they were ready for the walk, with George in a new blue coat and a leather harness to keep him from falling out over the high-sided perambulator.

'There are hundreds of mines in the Channel and the Atlantic that get brought to the surface after storms,' Clive said. 'A fishing boat caught one in the nets last week and it exploded, killing all hands. Our minesweepers are busier than ever although the war has been over for nearly three years.'

'We're thankful that Lucy got to America safely,' Janey said. 'We had one letter but nothing since then and I hope she isn't too homesick or too disappointed in what she finds out there.'

'In what way?' Clive inclined his head to acknowledge a neighbour who smiled at the child.

'She was set on meeting Sidney again: she believes that she is really in love with him.'

Clive gave a short laugh. 'Bad luck, little Lucy.'

'What do you mean? You never knew Sidney really well and haven't seen him for a long time. He might be just the man for Lucy and may be glad to see an old friend who is now a very pretty girl.'

'He never had lady friends, did he?'

'Sidney was very popular,' Janey said, slightly annoyed. 'Girls hung on his every word.'

'He'll make a perfect matinée idol,' Clive said and smiled. 'I doubt if he's the marrying kind. Don't worry your pretty head about them. They'll sort out their own lives, and there are some things you don't understand.'

'I know about real love and marriage,' Janey replied.

'Yes, you are the answer to every dream that a real man could have,' Clive agreed.

'You sound as if Sidney isn't a real man! Don't be silly!'

She knew that men often distrusted others who danced too well or were too handsome so she changed the subject and pointed out shops that would be convenient for her mother to use when she moved to the new house. 'I hope that Mr Foster doesn't feel put out if she leaves him, but she can't be expected to walk back with heavy baskets all the way. He might deliver of course as she's a special customer, and now he has a van, distance doesn't matter so much as when the boy had to use the bike with the big basket on the front. I'll have a word with him.' She laughed. 'He refused to deliver to Annie Cooper as her order is so small.'

'Does Bert Cooper deal fairly with your mother's business?' Clive asked.

'I've been very surprised. He seems to feel he has to be protective these days and has suggested many improvements to the shop and taken the burden of much of the paperwork that Mother had to do alone. I don't think he's being kind just because Annie is so ill and Mother helps her.'

Janey produced a key to the house that Jane had given her in case she wanted to go there alone. 'Mother gave each of us one but Lizzie gave hers back as soon as she saw that there was nothing worth having from the garden, and said she didn't like the house.' Janey looked up at her husband. 'I come with George sometimes to make sure the house has something of our happiness,' she said. 'Houses do absorb atmosphere so it's as well Clare and Lizzie don't come here yet.'

'If that's the case you must show me everything here and it can have a little of our love.' Clive put the pram in the hall on the bare boards and closed the front door then kissed Janey tenderly. 'You're right about houses. I knew as soon as I stepped inside the door that you were there in the Lodge – your warmth was everywhere. When I am away, never let my memory grow dim, Janey. I want to dream of you there for always, waiting for me.'

'Some day you'll come ashore and we'll have a big family and live like normal human beings,' she promised.

'I can't see ahead that far,' Clive said softly, 'but this is enough for the present.' He sniffed. 'Linoleum smells for a long time when it's new. What is this room?'

'This is the morning room where Mother will have breakfast and do her sewing and mending. She chose a nice warm turkey red rug for the floor and they've made the wallpaper look nice.' She ran a finger over the crimson velvet flocked wallpaper. 'If I know her, she'll spend all her time here instead of sitting like a lady in the drawing room.'

'Where does my son sleep when I come and take you away?'

'There'll be plenty of room here. If we had six children she'd make room for them all! She loves babies.'

'Just as well. When we go down to see her I shall ask if she will take George for a while. Suddenly, three weeks seems like no time at all and I need you to myself, Janey.' He hugged her almost roughly. 'I want to walk on the Downs and feel the turf under my feet and smell the gorse again. We'll take a picnic even if it's raining.'

'We'd better get on,' Janey said. 'George will want his supper. I brought a bottle and he can have an egg.'

Progress was slow as one person after another stopped the pram to gaze inside. George objected to staring faces thrust in on him and began to cry so Janey took the path down Quay Street and along the lane by the quay. A girl sat on a bollard as once Maudie Dove had done and Janey told Clive that Maudie now put on airs and was hardly ever in the tenement in Sea Street. She also thought she fooled the town about her comings and goings to the West Wight to meet Bert.

At *Darwen's* George was taken upstairs by Vikki and Emily who offered to give him supper after changing his wet nappy, and Jane kissed her son-in-law. 'Let me look at you,' she said and fussed round them with tea, bread and butter and jam. 'This is to fill a gap but you'll need supper later,' she said. Once again, Jane refused all offers of help in the move and repeated that she wanted to give work to the unemployed. 'I have the curtains fitted and the floors covered and I want to take my time over it and have it just right,' she said.

'You'll be very busy,' Clive began.

'Not too busy to take George if you want time to yourselves,' she answered firmly. Her dark brown eyes were tender. 'Take this time away with you and leave Janey happy,' she told him.

'No wonder I love your daughter.' He hugged her and tried to lift her into the air. 'If I'd seen you first she wouldn't have stood a chance!'

'Put me down and stop talking like that! I'll have you know I've refused better-looking men than you.' She blushed and treasured the feeling of the strong young arms and the smell of his skin. 'Go and fetch your son and take him home and Janey can bring him here tomorrow when she returns this dish. It's only a rabbit pie for supper but you don't want to cook tonight, Janey. It's ready to warm up.'

'Am I being selfish, Mother?' Janey whispered.

'That will be the day! No, enjoy him while you have him here. Nobody knows what lies ahead and you may be parted for a long time if he goes to the Mediterranean like Alex.' Jane felt cold and wanted to cross herself in the old way but fiddled with the button on her blouse instead, hating the vision of old Mrs Lee who had died so long ago and should be forgotten.

'I see you have turned out the cupboard by the range,' Janey said.

'Take anything you fancy before Lizzie gets here,' Jane advised. 'There's a cloth or two I never use. Lizzie said that Harry admired my best blue and white dishes but I told them I wasn't dead yet and still needed to eat!'

'I could take those old sheets as dustsheets after you've used them for moving in,' Janey said, and Emily picked up the old army hussif that Walter had used in the Boer War.

'I'll keep this and the box of Father's medals,' she said. 'Look, it still has some webbing Blanco and a hank of green thread for mending. It's strange to think of him mending anything.'

'That's from the Great War. He forgot to take any to Africa,' Jane said. 'He had to borrow.' Her mouth felt dry.

Why couldn't Mrs Lee lie still and not remind her? Clive *must* come home to Janey and stay for ever, making babies and *living*. 'George drank too fast and has the wind,' she said brusquely. 'Get him home and up to bed and bring him nice and early tomorrow.'

'The new furniture comes at the end of the week,' Emily said later. 'The chairs are nice with really soft down cushions and my bed will be very modern.'

'So long as you don't expect me to give up my comforts and lose my featherbed,' Jane warned her. 'I shall put the dresser in the kitchen there and keep this table and a few other things so that I feel I live there and am not on a visit. I'm glad you chose a pretty piano, as the latest ones are so plain. That dark green silk behind the frets and the brass candle-holders would look at home in Queen Victoria's drawing room.'

'I've ordered the last of the flowers to be sent here tomorrow. When we leave, Lizzie and Janey can take what's left, that is if Lizzie comes when there's work to be done, and I can start with a fresh load the week after we move. My piano lessons start next week, too, and I'm getting really excited.' Emily looked happier than she had done since Arnold died and Jane knew that she had made the right decision to leave the shop.

'I never thought I'd leave here until I was in a box,' she said, and sighed. 'There's a time for everything, they say, and this is the time to leave and please ourselves a bit more but I feel sad just now and very tired. I think we'll open a bottle of that sherry wine and ask Ruby to have a glass with us. Poor soul, she hasn't much of a life with Ethel still in that place.'

'Did Ethel know Fred the last time he came?'

'He went in to see her but she attacked him and they had to lock her away again. Now that the baby's dead, it's no wonder he stays away and doesn't even ask after her, apart from when he sends her money.' She stood up, wearily. 'There's a goose walking over my grave, Emily. Go and fetch Ruby for a bite with us. If I'm going to be miserable I might as well share hers as well.'

Ruby slammed her door behind her and hadn't even bothered to comb her hair. 'Sometimes I think I'll go mad too, alone in that house doing nothing,' she complained.

'You know you can come here,' Jane said gently. 'You're always welcome.'

'I know, but we are alike and don't sit in each other's pockets, Jane. I go up to the hospital twice a week but it's quite a long pull walking up from Blackwater and when I get there Ethel doesn't know me, and if she sees poor Fred it's like waving a red rag to a bull! I don't blame him for signing up for the Regulars. It's no life for a man, having that on his mind.'

'It took two to make that baby,' Jane commented dryly. 'Ethel is the one suffering, but he's wise to stay away. Clare was upset because she didn't recognize her either, and she doesn't want to see her like that again.'

Ruby slumped over the table sipping the sweet sherry wine and grew more and more complaining until Jane felt impatient. Emily served the pie and fresh hot vegetables and Ruby ate without showing any pleasure. 'At least you have your health and strength back, Ruby. There's many without proper beds and enough food to fill their stomachs. You've a bit put by from Aaron's fishing and the sale of the boats and you haven't enough to do. If I didn't have Emily and little Vikki to fill my mind, with Janey up the road with George, I'd need something more to do.' She poured more wine, not because she really wanted it but Ruby was getting on her nerves.

Ruby pushed her own glass forward to be filled. 'I'd go to church more but they don't want me there. At one time I know we smelled of fish but even the house and cellars smell sweet now.'

'There's plenty to do at the chapel,' Jane said. 'I'm worried that when I go up on the Mall the soup won't be made properly. It's one thing to fill a belly with bread and something hot but they water the soup down if I don't keep an eye on it. I caught that Maisie Daws last week doing just that.'

'She needs taking down a peg or two. She's another Annie Cooper, as mean as they come.'

'Why not take over from me and see it's done as we'd like it?' asked Jane, knowing that Ruby and Maisie had been sworn enemies for years. 'You don't have to carry heavy jugs as they have a boy with a barrow to collect the churn and he can bring you the vegetables and beefbones instead of bringing them here. If anything, your copper is bigger than mine.' Her expression softened. 'It's good to see the faces when they eat something really good and to know you are doing your best for them. It would be a real weight off my mind, Ruby.'

Ruby sat straighter. 'I hoped things were getting better but they are laying off more workers at Cowes now. Lizzie's Harry will be all right, though, as they repair a lot of boats and make minesweepers for the navy, and they had a lot of orders before this slump happened.' Ruby took another helping of pie as if she had regained her appetite. 'They are building more of those horrible submarines but not at Cowes,' she said. 'I saw one in the Solent on trials and an uglier thing you can't imagine, like a big grey slug in the water. How can men live down there with no fresh air?'

'Clive was talking about mines,' Jane mused. 'Please God he never meets one at sea. Some are ours and some are German but they both kill people and Walter never approved of them,' she added as if that set the seal on public opinion.

'Janey did well for herself,' Ruby said, 'and your Clare never looks as if she wants for anything. Is she coming down again soon?'

'Alan doesn't like her to be away when he's at home,' Jane replied. 'Or that's what she says. I hope it's that she's liking it better there and doesn't want to get away so much.'

'Perhaps he's close with money and refuses to give her the fare.'

'She can get away if she wants to,' Jane said, but saw no reason to tell Ruby about the twenty gold sovereigns that Clare had for emergencies.

Emily listened and said little but finished a corner of the

intricate crochet that was now long enough to cover one side of a double bedspread. It was exciting to find that the rose pattern came in just the right place and she could now continue along the next side. 'That's pretty,' Ruby remarked. 'I know people would pay a lot for such nice work. It's a lovely thing for your bottom drawer.'

'It's for Clare but I don't know when I'll finish it as I do other things in between like lace edging for Mrs Barnes who has it for her maids' starched caps. I've made some pretty doileys for the new house.' She smiled. 'They grow faster and look lovely on pretty plates.'

'The vicar's wife has them but nothing much else on the plates! I'd rather have something to eat,' Ruby joked.

Emily went to peep at Vikki and Jane lowered her voice. 'You know I'm not fond of frills Ruby, but when you come to tea you shall have cake and doileys on the plates and you must put up with it! She's gone to a lot of trouble!' They giggled with the understanding of old friends. 'She's a wonderful comfort to me and I think will never marry. She deserves her piano lessons and nice clothes if she wants them.'

'She's lucky to have you,' Ruby retorted. 'Many unmarried daughters ruin their eyes over typewriters or get varicose veins standing in shops all day and work all hours for next to nothing, but are glad to have something. Mr Foster is right. If the government reduces wages any more and put more and more on the dole there will be trouble. All that money being spent on that big exhibition in London would buy houses and food for thousands! He's been to see it. They've built roads just to lead up to the exhibition at Wembley and invited every colony to take a pavilion to show their own goods. A waste of money, I call it.'

'Bert took a few shares in it, saying it was good for trade but I refused. It's too big to work.'

'I'd like to see it,' Ruby confessed. 'I might take the train there one day if they run excursions.'

Jane laughed. 'If it would get you further than Ryde pier head, I'd come with you! It took all my persuasion to get you to Ryde Pavilion to see Clarkson Rose's show and then you saw *Twinkle* three times.'

'It was lovely,' sighed Ruby.

'They are busy doing the pantomime now at the Drill Hall,' Jane said. 'I'll take Vikki there as it is done by amateurs, with no smutty jokes. Someone said that Sidney should have stayed but he's doing better where he is,' she added with pride. 'He's really acting now and they write about him in the papers, like this.' She showed Ruby a press cutting: CHAUTAUGA WEEK IN MAINE. 'They take a huge tent all over America and act everything from Shakespeare to musical revues and have politicians like Edgar Hoover to speak there. Sidney said they have magic shows and even cookery demonstrations so there's something for everyone. Clive bought me a record of a jazz singer called Ruby Green. She sings in those tents, too.'

'She's a black woman,' Ruby said.

'With a name like yours? And Green, too? I don't believe it, but I like her voice.'

'She is black, Mother. Negroes sing jazz better than anyone and often have lovely voices and a fine sense of rhythm,' Emily said. 'I read a lot about America now that Sidney is there.' Jane looked at her daughter curiously. So much went on in that quiet head that seldom surfaced.

'America is so huge that Lucy and Sidney may not meet for ages. He's been travelling for months,' Jane said.

'I hope it takes a long time so that Lucy is used to America,' Emily replied.

Chapter 9

'March is a treacherous month,' Jane said. 'I hope that Janey wraps up well as the wind has turned cold again after they've had such lovely warm weather. Still, for the last few days of his leave, Clive may be glad to stay in the warm and play with George. Put the basket of his clothes on the table in the shop, Emily, and don't give George anything but milk as Janey will want to give him supper at home.'

'It's time that Clive saw what he can do,' Emily commented. 'George was dragging himself along by the table today and he could walk if he gave his mind to it, but Vikki helps him all the time. I think that Janey is getting restless and wants her boy back again and Clive should see the first real steps.'

'I love having him here but I think he's safer at home now as I have a lot to do at the other house and George is into everything. Dan must clear up the broken glass from the conservatory where the wind took it and I have to be there to say where the rest of the furniture should be.' For the first time, I'm thinking about my own future and putting other people off, Jane thought with wonder. I can't wait to move, as without most of the furniture, this is no longer home. The long dresser had gone and the wallpaper where it had stood was bright and unfaded, as were patches that had been behind pictures. 'George, Mother and Daddy are coming to take you home.' She handed him his favourite toy so that he would laugh when Clive picked him up. We have spoiled him a little, she decided guiltily. We must make sure he wants to go home, and to her relief, George laughed and showed every sign of being pleased to see his father.

'Put him in the baby carriage,' Jane said. 'He can stay there until we've had tea and then you can take him home and put him to bed in his own cot. He looks so beautiful, asleep first thing in the morning, and you have so little time left with him this leave to see all his pretty ways.'

Janey came out into the scullery for plates and said softly, 'Mother, you've no idea what this time has meant to us. It was even better than my dreams and Clive has been completely happy.'

'I know,' Jane whispered. 'I do know.' She thrust the clean plates into Janey's hands. 'We'll start eating now so that you can get home. I've put a bottle of gripe water in the pram as George has a red patch on one cheek that shows he's teething and may get restless.'

Clive teased her about being without house and home and offered a tent in the garden. 'The next time I see you, you'll be a fine lady and I'll have to wipe my feet before coming into your smart hall.'

'You surely will,' Jane said. 'I'm pleased with the runner in the hall and the new carpet-sweeper to keep down the dust.' Everyone was happy and Jane shrugged away any dark thoughts that lurked in her mind, smiling as she waved goodbye from the shop door.

'Did Janey tell you?' Emily began.

'She isn't expecting again so soon?'

'No, it isn't that. Clive has to go north for training.'

'But he's an officer now. Isn't that enough?'

'I thought I'd tell you now so that you don't show your feelings when Janey tells you. He's going into a submarine. It means a big promotion.'

'Dear Mary! Not under the water.' Jane sank into a chair.

'They say they are as safe as any other ship and now that the war is over, they have no fighting to do and have nothing but a kind of playing at war and basic training to do.' Emily sounded more calm than she felt as they sat by the fire in the old range for perhaps the last time. 'Did you open the letter?' she asked. 'George took it and chewed one end so I put it under a weight in the shop. It's from Clare. I wonder what she wants as she doesn't often write.' She saw her mother's growing alarm. 'What's wrong?' she asked.

'I don't know. Read it and tell me what you think.'

'Alan wants to work on the Island? I don't believe it. It's

more likely that Clare wants to come home! You saw the other bit?' Jane nodded. 'I knew that he and Harry were as thick as thieves and they had long talks the last time they were together, but obviously they write to each other and Harry has got a position for Alan in his works. They are sneaky! Not a word to us until it was settled.' Emily was red in the face. 'Where will they live?'

'Not with us!' Emily sighed with relief that the couple wouldn't be allowed to spoil the lovely new home that she and Jane had planned. 'Christmas and Easter and any holidays they are welcome, but not to live with us, Emmy. We deserve a bit of peace.'

Emily still looked apprehensive. 'She does ask if we have any ideas,' she said. 'I know Clare, and she'd be back with us in a wink if we let her as she hates living alone with Alan.'

'She's left it late so that we haven't time to think.' Jane got up and walked across the room but suddenly realised that the bureau was in the new house and all her papers with it. 'If he works at Cowes he needs to live there or here in Newport, I suppose. I must think! Archie is away buying lambs so I can't ask his advice. Tomorrow after the men have moved the furniture, I'll ask Bert. I think he owns a small house near Shide with a few sticks of furniture that he wants to rent out. If Alan Dewar got his feet under this table there's no knowing when we'd ever get rid of him, so he isn't coming here!'

The effort to speak was painful but Emily forced herself to do so. 'They could have one of my cottages. One of the tenants is leaving soon.'

'No, Emily. Don't you dare mention that again! Those are no more than you've earned over the years and are your security. If necessary I can sell one of the West Wight cottages and buy again in Cowes.'

Emily looked pleased. 'Lizzie hinted that you ought to pass on something to all of us girls as you had so much property now, but I said nothing about mine as you made me promise and I'm glad I kept quiet.'

'Oh, she did, did she? Or was Harry putting ideas into

her head? When my time comes you'll all have what I think you deserve. It's all signed and sealed and I'm not going to die yet, and what I do now is my business.'

'Alan starts work in two weeks' time and Clare wants to stay here with Alan at the Bugle, if we haven't room for him with us! They know this is a busy time and they have no right to bother you now.' Emily was more cross than Jane had ever seen her. 'I suppose they could rent the shop as we haven't sold it yet.'

'I couldn't bear to come back again after we leave and I think that Bert has a buyer. He said he'd make sure it didn't go on as we had it, even if we lose the goodwill, but he'd find a draper or an ironmonger or a chandler to take it.'

That night, Jane plumped up the pillows on the bed and smiled. Tomorrow this bed would go to the other house and even if she wanted it, Clare could not return to the shop on Coppins Bridge as it would be completely empty. Even the big double bed where Clare had slept with Alan at Christmas had been dismantled and was waiting to be rebuilt in the new house. Perhaps Emily and I should stay in the Bugle for a week or so to show that *we* aren't settled – that would shock Clare, she thought.

After a hurried early breakfast, Emily pulled on her coat and wheeled out the bicycle. 'I'll go up to see if Bert is there and if not I'll go on to the brickyard, unless he's left for the West Wight this early.' Jane pulled the last of the boxes from under her bed and thought dispassionately of the contents. Emily might like to look through the old dresses and the samplers made by childish hands and the box with Jane's wedding dress and veil, but the smell of mothballs was unpleasant and she shut the lids again and took the boxes down for collecting later.

Bert sat down an hour later to fresh bread and butter and jam. 'I knew you'd have the kettle on,' he said. 'As soon as Emily arrived, I didn't hang around but came as soon as I could.' He grinned. 'Don't look like that. I promise you that Annie doesn't even know I'm here and she won't be told anything you want kept quiet. You've enough on your plate without her gossiping.'

'I never knew how kind you could be, Bert,' she said mistily, and pushed the jampot across to him.

'You're the one who's kind,' he muttered. 'I don't know what Edward and his Alice would do without you and as for Annie, well she'd be dead by now. I hear things that you never let on and I respect you more than any woman I know, Jane Darwen! Now what's young Clare got up to? Gone sour, has it?' He took the letter and began to read. 'Never thought it would work. Can't see her sitting on a canal bank for months on end twiddling her thumbs.'

'She has a nice home. She drove us all mad at first, boasting about it.'

'She'd best have that house of mine. It's got a good enough lot of furniture to make it cosy and it's clean. They can rent it until they see what they want or they can buy it later if it suits. I wouldn't ask over the odds. You don't want to be littered up with them just now, do you?'

'Give me the keys and I'll see it's ready for them,' Jane said. 'You're a good friend so you are, and I can move into the Mall with an easy mind. How's Annie?' she added, and it sounded like an afterthought.

'Middling. She wants me to take her to Ryde in the motor car today. I was going out to the West Wight but she had this bee in her bonnet that she must see a relative she hasn't met for years and cares less about.'

'Family feeling does tell at times,' Jane said soberly, but her eyes twinkled as she wondered how much of Bert's dalliance had reached Annie's ears. 'I'll not have time to go out to my cottages for three weeks, Bert, so if you are out there on the Fridays when I usually go, I'd be grateful if you'd see that they are safe.'

Bert laughed. 'Friday would suit me fine. Annie has the girl washing paintwork on Fridays and likes to be there to see it done.'

It was odd to be helping Bert Cooper to adultery with Maudie Dove but Jane felt no guilt. They discussed business and Bert promised to ask about the engineering trade at Cowes. 'If Alan wants to work here there's more to this than Clare is telling me,' Jane said.

'She needs a baby and so does Lizzie. You brought a couple of cuckoos into your nest when you had the twins, Jane. They should learn to give and not take all the time.'

Jane flushed. 'They aren't as bad as that!'

'Good. I see I can still make you mad! You look really handsome when you're riled.' He smiled. 'If you have to make changes to the house at Shide, tell me and I'll get them done quickly. It will be good for the property when I want to sell and they might as well start off right, with no cause to make them move in with you! You know where it is, close to Shide Mill?'

'I can walk there, given plenty of time,' Jane said.

'But not too close for comfort when you get to the other house,' Bert surmised. 'You should have kept the trap and a pony. It's none of my business but people talk and wonder when you are going to marry Archie Cheverton. Don't you think you need a man about the place? Even Annie has no idea and it's killing her!'

'I managed well enough when Walter was away and it's easier now. I like to go over to help Alice and I like to be independent. There's talk of a cure soon for diabetes but Alice needs it now.'

'Poor old Archie. Men need their comforts, Jane.'

'Comfort should be given with love and enjoyment or there's no virtue in it. I'm glad I'm not young and don't need that. I like it as it is, with my family and friends.'

Bert turned back at the door. Jane stood tall against the light of the window; her hair was still raven black and her figure curved and supple. 'You could make a man very happy, Jane,' he said and left abruptly. Damn, he thought. Half an hour with her and she made Maudie seem like trash, but his step was light as he walked back to the car. Friday would do very well.

Jane opened the door to Dan who had come to get his orders as she hadn't yet gone to the house on the Mall. 'I called at the station to pick up some goods and the station-master gave me this note from Lizzie. He said it was urgent and she had it put on the train to get to you fast.' Jane smiled. Lizzie would put others to endless trouble to save herself the price of a postage stamp.

'She says she's very ill,' Jane said, turning pale.

'Lizzie can't be ill if she walked to the station with that note,' Emily said calmly when she read it. 'She feels left out now that Clare is descending on us.'

'I think I'll have to go down and make sure though,' Jane said, anxiously.

Emily sighed. 'Yes, you go down, Mother. You won't rest until you know and I'll cycle over to the house at Shide and make a few notes about what's wanted there. After the cottages, I shall know at a glance what we need.'

Jane pulled her hat on and stuck a hatpin in so roughly that it caught the skin. The train to Cowes was on time and she sat watching the fields and farm animals and tried to think of Lizzie, but she was eager to be in her own home, attending to her own affairs. The narrow road where Lizzie lived looked even more dismal than usual as Jane knocked on the door. She wondered how anyone could choose a house there with the view of the gas-holder and the back of a building yard. Harry could afford better, she knew. She knocked again and then pushed on the door which opened at her touch. From the back garden she heard laughter and paused to watch Lizzie, giggling with her neighbour as they hung out clothes to dry. Lizzie bent easily to pick up her basket and peg bag as if she hadn't a care in the world and came into the kitchen with the basket on one hip.

She saw Jane and burst into tears. 'What's wrong, Lizzie?' Jane asked briskly. The hatpin *had* gone into her scalp and made it sore. 'What's this rubbish about you being ill? You look well and I heard you laughing out there.'

Lizzie brushed a hand over her eyes dramatically. 'I may look well but I'm not.' Jane recognized the familiar pathetic expression. 'I get terrible stomach upsets and feel as limp as a rag.'

'Well, you aren't limp now, so put the kettle on – I'm parched. I hurried over thinking you were at death's door when I feel worse than you do! Emily has to do all my errands now and we have to get ready for Clare.'

'They aren't coming to live with you, are they, Mother?' Lizzie enquired sharply.

'You know more about her than I do according to the letter,' Jane said sternly and Lizzie turned red and went to put the kettle to boil. 'She will have one of Bert's houses and let me get on with my own move.'

'I can't think why you ever wanted to leave the shop,' Lizzie protested. 'It should have been precious to you and it was so convenient for us all.'

'Convenient for you to take whatever free fish and vegetables you wanted,' Jane retorted, really angry now. She leaned over to put two more spoonsful of tea in the pot that Lizzie always made too weak. Her head ached and she was hot and tired but she eyed her daughter with growing speculation, and laughed.

'It isn't funny,' Lizzie said sulkily. 'I do feel ill and this morning I nearly made Harry send for the doctor.'

'You are expecting, Lizzie.' She laughed again at the horror on Lizzie's face. 'It's what I prayed for and I hope it makes you as happy as Janey is.'

'I can't be!' Lizzie wailed. 'I don't want a baby yet and nor does Harry. He said we wouldn't and he's very careful.'

'Not careful enough.' Jane sipped her strong tea with satisfaction. 'I'm glad I came now. It's put my mind at rest and you must see the doctor soon, but you look blooming. You'll love it when it comes. All babies are sent from heaven and made to be loved.'

'What can I tell Harry? It isn't fair.' Lizzie was in tears again.

'Wash your face before he comes home and comb your hair. Tell him as soon as he sits down. I shall catch the next train back and if I have time I'll come down next week but I don't promise anything.'

'If I'm pregnant I shouldn't do housework,' Lizzie said petulantly.

'Dr Barnes says that housework is the very best exercise,' Jane assured her heartlessly. She hugged Lizzie and picked up her bag. 'Learn to love it even before it is born and you'll be a happy woman, my dear.'

On the train she unpinned her hat. I'll buy Lizzie a nice pram and baby clothes, she decided. The trees seemed greener now and she saw celandines and buttercups in the hedgerows. New life was everywhere and she smiled at mothers pushing their infants in deep baby carriages as she went home from the station. I'll tell Annie first, she thought. It might make her walk a bit more just to spread the news.

Emily took the news seriously. 'She'll put upon you, Mother. She isn't a natural mother and neither is Clare.'

'We aren't short,' said Jane.

'Money is easy I know, but she'll sap anyone who helps her and make them believe she's frail. Lizzie is tough and has more strength than most.'

'Is the house ready for Alan and Clare?' Jane asked.

'The girl scrubbed the floors really well and I ordered groceries from Mr Foster to be delivered there to start them off. I can cook a round of beef to last them a few days cold, and the shop close to the house sells vegetables.'

'You can't cook beef yet until we know when they are arriving.'

'They come tomorrow: another wire came.'

'They'll be so surprised and pleased to have a nice house ready to walk into,' Jane said. Her face glowed. 'Everything is working out fine, just fine. With Lizzie's news what a homecoming it will be.'

'They'll be surprised but not pleased,' Emily said. 'They think they are coming to live with us. You read the wire.'

'I can't read the small writing – tell me what it says.'

'It says that they arrive tomorrow night and that Clare is in an interesting condition.' Emily tossed the telegram on the table. 'Only a man as insensitive as Alan could write that so baldly for everyone to see in the Post Office! I think if they had come here to live I'd have left and gone to one of my cottages.'

'Two babies! A double blessing,' Jane said. 'I shall buy two prams now and they'll be such company for George and Vikki.'

Emily sighed. It was happening again. Just when she thought her mother might take things easy, she would be tugged at from all sides. 'I asked Mr Jenkin to meet the train and take them straight to Shide,' she said.

'Clare might be tired,' Jane ventured.

'Start them off in their own home, Mother. We have enough to do with our own move and if they'd had any sense they'd have made sure it was convenient for us. I'll take them a pie and light a fire to welcome them but we don't want them with us.' She laughed. 'We're talking as if they *could* come here but we have only our beds left and we're off tomorrow. We need to leave the shop,' she said quietly. 'You and I have a lot of things to forget.'

Chapter 10

'Dr Barnes says that Harry needn't be careful now so long as we wait another two weeks,' Lizzie said and giggled.

'I wonder you didn't go to the doctor in Cowes. Dr Barnes doesn't know everything. Mother nearly died when Caroline was born, and again the last time.' Clare shivered and her face was pinched and tense. 'I feel ill not only in the mornings as they say you do, and I hate the thought of having a baby.' The proud lift to her head had gone and she twisted her handkerchief round the split fingernail. 'Alan did it on purpose because I said I wanted to get on a boat to America and leave him.'

'You are always saying that, Clare. You say you want something just because you can't have it and if you couldn't have a baby, then that's what your dearest wish would be. I'm sure you'll want it when it comes. Harry is very pleased now and wants a son.' She looked about the bright room with curiosity. The table was one that Jane had handed on and the new linoleum must have been put down and paid for before Clare and Alan arrived.

'You'll see if I want this baby if I feel any worse soon!' Clare retorted. 'I'd like to get rid of it. Ethel is in a mad-house because she had a baby!'

'That was because she had the 'flu and an infection,' Lizzie said. 'You know you don't mean it.' She added accusingly, 'I wanted that table and I suppose Mother paid for all the things here?'

Clare looked less angry. 'It was the least she could do unless we were to be without a roof over our heads. I hate the house and you are welcome to it if that's any consolation, and in future I shall never let Alan touch me again in that way.'

'That's silly. I like it now and I use it when I want

something or if Harry gets cross if I buy something expensive. It always works!'

Clare smiled and they looked very much like twins with their malicious smiles and speculative eyes. 'That's right. Alan still wants me badly. He takes no for an answer most of the time but is good-tempered for days afterwards if we do.' She handed Lizzie the cake tin that Emily had filled with fruit cake. 'I fancy a bit of cake now with my tea,' Clare said. 'I feel much better.'

'We must eat for two now,' Lizzie said piously, and took two slices. 'Now I know I can get out at Shide station I shall come more often. It's a drag right up to the Mall to see Mother and I'd rather come here. I've never used the train this way very much except for gathering watercress when we were children. The train was crowded with schoolchildren off to their Sunday School treat at Sandown but I managed to get a seat easily.'

'It's nice to see you, Lizzie. I don't go to the Mall often either, as George is always there and he's so spoiled.'

'I'll make my child behave,' Lizzie promised. She looked superior. 'It is a long walk for you and I think that Janey should collect you and take you there. *We* have the motor cycle and sidecar so we can go and see Mother whenever Harry is free, but last week we went there and Emily said she was too busy to sit and talk. She had to keep getting up to see to the cakes she was making after I said we expected to stay to tea. I never make cakes on Sunday and she might have known we would be coming.' She sniffed. 'It isn't as if we can take back a bit of fish for our trouble,' she added. 'We never have the nice teas we had when Father was alive and Harry was courting me. He said how he missed them and Mother wasn't at all pleased.'

Clare glanced behind her as if Jane could hear. 'Nothing is the same,' she said. 'Nothing has been the same for me since the man I really wanted was killed in the war. I think I'd like a nice little shop of my own if I can get Mother to help out. Not fish or anything smelly, but ribbons and artificial flowers and materials for baby clothes.'

'You can't expect Mother to set you up,' Lizzie said,

then wondered if Harry could tell her how much such an enterprise would cost and maybe it would be wise to encourage Clare. If she had something, then Lizzie must too, or it wouldn't be fair. 'I suppose that Mother is quite well off,' she agreed. Even the name of the house, Briony Lodge, was more suitable for someone like Mrs Barnes than her mother. The well-polished dark grain of the front door and the brass knocker in the shape of a dolphin was decidedly classy and Harry had wiped his feet on the new coir mat in the hall so many times that Lizzie had felt like screaming. The sun, shining through the picture of sailing boats on a blue sea in the stained glass windows, rainbowed the hall, showing up one of Emily's best flower arrangements.

Jane had been delighted to show them round. 'They didn't buy this cheap,' Harry whispered as he saw a table he had seen in the window of the best furniture shop on the Island. Most of the old chairs were now replaced by solid ones upholstered in crimson velvet.

'We could have stayed there,' Clare said crossly. 'If I was ill they could have looked after me. All Mother thinks of is Vikki and George and any letters from Sidney.'

'Has Lucy met him yet?'

'No. By the time he was back in New York, Lucy had to go with Nellie Morris to Baltimore where she is singing in a jazz band, like Helen Morgan does – you know, the torch-singer who sings all those sad songs. Perhaps they will never meet. I had no idea how big America is until Alan got out a map and showed me.'

'So you do speak to him sometimes!'

'Yes, it's only the times in bed I hate. At other times he's quite interesting about places and people.'

'Alan didn't have to leave his work, did he?' Lizzie asked.

'No, they wanted him to stay but I said I was coming back here whatever he decided and he had to come too if he wanted to keep me.'

'You couldn't leave him! How could you pay the fare? And if Mother wouldn't help there would be rent to pay!' Lizzie sounded appalled.

'I have some money,' Clare replied. Wouldn't you like to

know, she thought as she saw her sister's curiosity growing. 'You should make pickles and jam like Mother taught us,' she said carelessly, determined to say nothing of the twenty gold sovereigns that she still had safely tucked away.

'I didn't know you did that.' Lizzie looked disappointed. 'I can't start now with the baby coming.'

'I think I'll collect my old bicycle,' Clare said. 'I can get to the Mall quite quickly on that.'

'You aren't allowed to ride now! It's dangerous.'

'All the better if it gets rid of this. Don't look so shocked. I don't want this baby and if it comes I might give it away.'

'I think I'll go now,' Lizzie said. 'I want my baby and that's wicked talk.'

'I'm sorry, Liz. I don't know what I'm saying half the time. Are you going to Mother's on Sunday?'

Lizzie looked sulky. 'No. Janey said that Mother needs a good rest and she's taking her out to see the cottages before the next lot of people move in. Emily is going too and they may go somewhere every Sunday if the weather holds. The girl will look after the two children.' She sighed. 'Harry does like his Sunday high tea but he can't expect me to do it all in my condition.'

'You can come here,' Clare said impulsively. 'It would pass the time for me and I quite like cooking sometimes.'

'We needn't have George crawling over us and Vikki making the floorboards creak with the rocking horse.' Lizzie beamed. 'The men get on well and we can knit baby clothes together. We'll catch the three o'clock train. Just look at the time! I must get the train back to cook Harry's tea. He's working overtime and gets tired.'

Clare heard voices and looked out of the window in time to see Alan helping Lizzie into the seat of a sidecar. Minutes later, when she had cold meat on the plates and boiled potatoes hot in the pan, he arrived home, took off the new goggles and thick jacket and said, 'I took Lizzie to catch her train. Come and see what I've bought!'

'It's second hand,' Clare said dismissively.

'I'm not made of money and I thought you'd be pleased.

We can go into the country or visit your mother on Sundays more easily.'

Clare tossed her head. 'We can't go there this Sunday. Janey has taken it on herself to say that Mother needs a rest and they are going to Colwell.'

'Saturday will do just as well,' he said easily. 'Now they've settled in they'll be glad to go back to those nice teas we had before we were married.'

'They don't want us at any time! They're going to the farm on Saturday. If they'd wanted us they'd have welcomed us to live on the Mall.'

'I like it better here. With the baby coming we must get closer again, Clare. Now let me have my food; I'm starving. We can try out the motor bike afterwards and show your mother. I thought I'd take her a bottle of sherry wine to celebrate the new houses.'

'You seem to have a lot of money all of a sudden,' she said.

'I saw Bert Cooper at dinner-time and he sold me this house dirt cheap. I got a good price for the one up north.'

'You did that without telling me? This is not the kind of place I wanted.'

'You wanted to come back here and I gave up a good job. If you don't like it you can lump it.'

Clare felt limp then realized that she had eaten only a slice of fruit cake all day. She took some meat and a large potato and felt better. The colour came back to her cheeks and she smiled. After all, he had done this for her and she couldn't wait to show the new sidecar combination to her mother and Emily and to be even with Lizzie.

'Aren't you having any?' Alan asked when Clare helped him to apple pie and thick yellow custard.

'I'll just have the custard skin. Pastry gives me heartburn,' she said, anxious to go out. 'I'll get my warm jacket and scarf.'

In the sidecar, she was amazed to find how large it seemed and how free from draughts. Alan sat very straight on the motor cycle and she felt a frisson of the attraction she had felt when she first met him. He looked very masculine and reminded her of her own father. She shivered. Walter Darwen had been a real man who took what he wanted. She put a hand over her as-yet flat stomach. If I give into Alan now when it can't matter, he'll want me when the baby comes, she thought, but at least she'd have the excuse that she was tired out with the infant. She relaxed. The baby wouldn't arrive for months and months and she could enjoy the summer.

Alan helped her from the vehicle and up the steps on to the Mall. 'I came the long way round to let you test it,' he said. 'It's got a very good engine and I bought it cheap as the man was on short time and needed ready money.'

'Are many being laid off?' Clare asked with a twinge of anxiety.

'Not in our factory, but down the road a shed has closed. We should be all right for years but the ones who supply big firms with spares and parts will go to the wall if they can't get fresh orders.' He held her arm as they walked over some rough stones and she welcomed the firm and reassuring touch. Poverty might be far away for them but the threat was everywhere.

Emily opened the door before they had time to raise the dolphin door knocker, and Vikki stared at the motor cycle wide-eyed. 'What a family for contraptions you are,' Jane declared.

'It's the best make of motor cycle combination that there is,' Clare said with a superior air. 'And it's very comfortable and safe.'

'I want a ride in it,' Vikki said and smiled at Alan, who seemed flattered and asked Emily to go with them to make sure that Vikki sat still.

'Safe as houses,' he said, putting the goggles on again and handing Emily into the sidecar.

Clare turned away and followed Jane into the house. 'They'll be fine,' she said. 'Alan wouldn't let me ride in it if it wasn't safe.'

'Yes, he cares about you, Clare,' Jane said quietly. 'He is pleased about the baby and with him you'll never be in need for the essentials of life. Enjoy this time, Clare. It's a blessed thing, a baby. Come and see what we have done. I'm quite good in the garden now, with the boy to cut the grass and Dan coming to fetch and carry the heavy things.'

'The house is far too big for just you and Emily,' Clare said resentfully.

'There's Vikki and when Janey goes to Scotland to see Clive soon we'll have George, too.' Jane brought out a cake tin and suggested that Clare might enjoy milky cocoa instead of tea. 'I went off it when I was carrying,' she said.

'I don't think I'm normal,' Clare said. 'I can't stand the smell of onions cooking, and usually I like them.'

'That sounds very normal to me.' Jane laughed. 'Women have cravings for peculiar things. I wanted sharp lemons and Janey ate loads of turnips. Ethel wanted strawberries when there wasn't one to be had.' She paused, wishing she hadn't mentioned Ethel who had recently tried to kill herself and was very ill.

'I like all fruit but pastry gives me terrible heartburn.' Clare found it enjoyable to talk about her condition and was in a good temper when the others returned, flushed and laughing.

'I want cocoa like Auntie Clare,' Vikki demanded when she was given her nightly glass of cold milk before bed.

'You are too hot and the milk will cool you before you sleep,' Jane replied firmly, knowing that Vikki was self-willed and took advantage if she could.

Vikki pouted but looked sideways at Alan with the charm of Nellie Morris. 'I'll drink it up if Uncle Alan comes to see me on my horse first,' she said. The huge rocking horse stood against the evening light from the window, its mane thick and bright over the dappled neck. Bright blue eyes stared forever from the carved face and the flared nostrils gave an impression of speed and power, even when the horse was still. Alan settled Vikki on the saddle and Clare touched the horsehair tail and gilt trappings.

'It's just like a fairground horse,' she said. The sweep of the rocker was diminished by two big blocks, so that Vikki couldn't make it gather too much momentum.

'Archie got it from the man who makes them for fairs

but we need a more permanent block to stop Vikki. I'm quite afraid of it if I see it in the half-light and we keep the door locked so that she can't come in here alone to ride. Vikki is as stubborn as Jack and Nellie put together when she gets something into her head.' Emily took Vikki off to bed while Alan opened the bottle of wine and told Jane about the house. Jane inwardly blessed Bert, knowing that he had sold it for less than he gave for it and Clare tried to seem pleased.

'It looks as if we are in for a happy time,' she said. 'Two babies on the way, everyone in good health and Emily is great on the piano after only five or six lessons. Now who can that be?'

She went to the front door and Janey handed her sleeping child to Emily while Jane took the basket of clothes into the hall. 'Take George up, Emily. It's already late,' Jane said crisply. 'Now come in and sit down – you look tired.'

'Clive is going into submarines and has a week's leave. I want to go up to Scotland to see him so that he doesn't waste two days travelling. I sent a wire to Edward to book me on to the train and I'll take the first ferry across in the morning,' Janey said. 'Is that all right, Mother?'

'That's fine,' Jane said. Clare put on her gloves. 'Are you going now, Clare?'

'I'm tired too, and Alan has had a busy day.'

'I saw the sidecar,' said Janey. 'It's very nice and you'll have to learn to drive now.'

'I can't do that. It would be bad for my nerves,' Clare said.

'You sound like Lizzie.' Janey laughed. 'I can't wait to see your babies. It's so exciting. I wish I was expecting, too.'

'You don't! I'm sure that one will be quite enough for me. It's time we went, Alan.'

'You'll want more after the first,' Janey said, smiling. 'I want a big family.' She called to Clare. 'Why don't you go to the farm with Mother on Saturday? I can't drive you now but Archie said he'd collect the others so you could come here to be picked up.'

Clare hesitated and Alan spoke quickly to accept. Clare

shrugged. It might be pleasant and it passed the time. 'Give my regards to Clive,' Alan said. 'One day I'd like to see over one of those ships. They say that they have more engines than room for the crew.'

Emily and Janey set the table for supper and Jane listened at the bottom of the stairs but the children slept. I have the two best-loved of my children here tonight and two beautiful children up there, but I feel uneasy, she thought. She closed the door of the morning room where supper was ready and dismissed her miseries. Janey looked happy and there was a letter from America waiting to be read. Surely that was enough?

In the train to Cowes the next day, Janey counted her pieces of luggage and thought back to the warmth and love that had enfolded her the night before she left, when she ate supper and Jane pressed her to drink some of the wine to bring the roses back to her cheeks. At the station, a porter came to take her heavy bag to the ferry and she tipped him, then saw a boy with a thin neck and frayed cuffs waiting hopefully to earn a copper, so she handed him her small bag and the coat that she might need in Scotland and gave him sixpence. He smiled and said nothing and she wondered if he would earn any more that day. If he was my brother or son I'd be heartbroken she thought, and knew that he was only one of many.

On the boat, she bought a roll and butter and a cup of tea as she had been far too excited to eat breakfast, and at the jetty was glad to see Edward's solemn face brighten when he saw her. 'It was good of you to come,' she said. 'Have I a reserved seat?'

He led the way to a clean compartment and the porter, who was impressed that the deputy stationmaster conducted the lady personally to her seat, stacked her luggage safely on the rack. 'Take a taxi in London as you have to cross over to the London Midland and Scottish line.' Edward grinned. 'It's not as good as our Southern Railway but quite efficient. I sent word that you would be arriving and a friend will look out for you and see you installed in a reserved compartment.'

'How is Alice?' she asked as she hung out of the window to say goodbye. 'Mother says she will be over to see her next week.'

'I'm glad. Alice is only middling but she gets better when she sees Mother and even takes her advice for a while.'

The trudge of engines and clouds of steam took over and Janey closed the window against the grime and smuts. She felt different today. Yesterday she had been the mother of an active and demanding little boy, worried over clean linen and fresh milk but now, with every turn of the wheels, she was a woman about to meet her lover. She moistened her lips and the words on the page of her book made no sense.

London came and went and the express train bore her swiftly north. At Birmingham, she looked out and saw grey houses with grimy washing hanging in smoke-laden backyards. Old baths and bits of rope, battered chairs and thrown out fireplaces littered many of the yards but in others an effort had been made to raise flowers against the gloom. Runner beans clung to bamboo poles and roses climbed over one water butt and soon the houses gave way to open fields again. Janey dozed through the midlands and rubbed a patch of window clear when the train reached Manchester where the city lay under a pall of grimy fog as if spring and summer were not allowed to penetrate. She felt more sympathy now with Clare. How could children grow up healthy in such conditions? How could anyone be light-hearted under that fog?

Janey had never believed that people in England could starve but seeing the pale faces waiting for nothing to happen convinced her and she could do nothing, so when she reached Glasgow, she was weary and her earlier elation had dimmed. She held the address of the hotel in her hand and the porter put her bags on a small trolley and went towards the taxi rank. A hand on her arm made her turn and Clive lifted her clear of the ground and kissed her. 'I ran,' he said breathlessly. 'I heard the train from half a mile away, and now I'm here!'

The porter grinned. 'Home on leave, sir?' He found a taxi and Clive took Janey's hand tightly as soon as they sat in it. A spark of intensity smouldered and she glanced at his face. He looked older, with a line between his brows that she had not seen before. He was quieter, like the men who came back from the war or like those who watched the trains.

'I love you so much,' he said as soon as the hotel room door closed behind them.

'I love you too, Lieutenant,' she said. Gently, she pushed him away. 'I need a good wash and I smell of trains,' she said.

He laughed. 'I'll go down and order dinner. We'll be first in and first out.'

Janey blushed. 'They'll think I'm your fancy woman.' He laughed again and left her to change. She stripped and washed all over, and without knowing the past, she did as her mother had done years ago when she was young and in love. She dabbed Attar of Roses over her breasts and in the soft creases of her thighs and felt her body soften ready for love.

Chapter 11

Nellie Morris stepped out of the dress and the bugle beads encrusting the bodice clicked on the floor. 'Thank heavens that's over. Either I'm putting on weight or that dress has shrunk.'

Lucy laughed. 'You are as slim as ever. I knew that the dressmaker made it too tight. She had no idea what it's like to sing in a tight bodice. If you don't need me tomorrow morning I can let it out a little and maybe insert an extra beaded piece.'

'Ready?' Monty put his head round the door. 'C'mon, Nellie, get a move on or we'll be late. What's the point of having good seats if you can't be ready?'

'We have at least an hour. They wanted another encore and I couldn't refuse. I'll get ready faster if you keep away. Fetch us both some fresh orange and soda and I'll be ready as quick as I can.'

'Well, wear something that won't stop this show! You may be the star of *Spangles and Butterflies* but we are going to the big fight.' He couldn't hide his pride in Nellie, and he looked indulgently at Lucy. 'You are good for my Nellie: no alcohol, and you both have the original schoolgirl complexion!'

Nellie showered and Lucy could hear her even from the next room, singing songs from the show. She emerged dressed in a loose-fitting gown with a matching coat of pale beige trimmed with bands of dark fur. 'This will be the fight of a lifetime,' Monty said, rubbing his hands together.

'I hope you haven't bet too much on it,' Nellie remarked without anxiety, knowing how shrewd he was in such matters.

'I hope not, too,' he said and sipped his drink as if he needed it. 'I'm banking on Dempsey of course, but a lot of people are yelling for George Carpentier. I don't think he'll last more than six rounds, though.'

'You know best but Lucy and I might leave if there's much blood.'

'Close your eyes but stay,' he replied firmly. 'We go on to a party after the fight and there will be two English Dukes and some of the best Boston families there. They say that even Randolph Hearst might show up and he's a man I'd really like to see.'

Lucy tried to hide her own excitement. 'Perhaps tonight Sidney might be there.' Nellie eyed her with interest, seeing the pink cheeks and sparkling eyes. She realized just how much Lucy had matured and now dressed well, with taste. Her silk stockings and the crocodile bag, a birthday present from Monty, made the simple dress of deep rose pink look more expensive than it was. How long would it be before Lucy stopped searching for her childhood love and actually saw the men who looked at her?

'Does he like fights?' Nellie asked.

'He said in his last letter that he hoped to be here for the fight and we might meet, but every time we've been almost there, something has prevented our meeting. He's famous now, like you Nellie, and has to be seen in public even if he doesn't like fights,' Lucy went on.

'Coppins Bridge was a long time ago and people change,' Nellie said gently. 'I still remember them with love but you have to see the future now, dear.'

Lucy held up a small mirror. 'You have a trace of powder on your eyebrow but you'd better do it,' she said.

'Come on, you two perfectionists. All the boys will be jealous of me tonight with such beauties, one on each arm!' Monty tipped his silk hat forward and grinned. Lucy followed slowly, aware that she was the perfect foil for the vibrant beauty who had taken America by storm. In the car, Nellie put a Lucky Strike cigarette in the end of an ebony holder studded with paste diamonds, and Monty looked disapproving even though he was smoking a cigar. 'They don't like women smoking outside here. It isn't like New York,' he said.

Nellie waved a spiral of smoke towards a large advertisement hoarding. 'I believe that – and it never affects my voice,' she said.

Lucy read: TO KEEP SLIM, NO ONE CAN DENY, REACH FOR A LUCKY STRIKE INSTEAD OF A SWEET. 'I'll put it out before the public see me,' Nellie promised, and when the car stopped at the stadium, she stepped out in confidence, knowing that her picture was in all the glossy magazines on the East Coast. People murmured when they recognized her and Lucy followed like a lady-in-waiting.

They sat among a glittering company of the rich and famous, honest and criminal brokers, smooth gangsters and social climbers, all in well-cut evening suits, with the women in furs and silks and fine jewellery. At the back, away from the arc lights that stabbed the smoke-filled air and illuminated the square of canvas, hundreds of people sat or stood in the cheaper areas and shouted encouragement to the as-yet unseen contestants, their throats lubricated with illicit liquor and the illegal bookies doing brisk, last-minute trade.

A man climbed between the ropes to check the corners and was met by ribald laughter before he hastily slid back to obscurity. Next, the referee came to talk to one of the promoters sitting by the Dempsey corner. By the other corner sat the trainer and friends of 'Gorgeous George Carpentier', hardly less famous and eager for the World Title. The atmosphere was good-humoured and Lucy wondered how men could stand and fight each other just to entertain. She recognized many famous faces and tried to put a name to others which were familiar but illusive. She puzzled over one face: the smooth hair could belong to any of a thousand men but the dark brown eyes that seemed to burn into her could only belong to the man who had served her the drink that had given her bad dreams and a splitting headache on the *Mauretania*.

She turned away and forgot him as another face rose from the smoke. The longish wavy hair and pale complexion, the deep blue eyes and mobile mouth were as she remembered from the pictures Sidney had sent to his family on the Isle of Wight. Even the carelessly tied cravat seemed familiar, as if it was one she had seen him wear long ago. A faint cry made Nellie look at her sharply. 'Are you feeling too hot, Lucy? Take off your jacket.'

'I'm fine,' Lucy whispered. 'I've seen him! Look, Sidney Darwen is over there.'

'Oh!' Nellie showed none of Lucy's delight. 'I suppose you had to meet some time,' she said and whispered to Monty, then put a restraining hand on Lucy's arm. 'You can't leave your seat now but I promise to let him know we are here. Sit down, the boxers are coming in.'

The first fighter sprang into the ring, his loose robe bright and wide and his hands high in salute to the crowd who went mad until he sat in his corner. The other man came in and repeated the performance but Lucy had no idea which was which. She saw nothing to excite her in the two shining bodies, stripped to the waist and heavily muscled, exuding masculinity. Sidney's face, pale and romantic and slightly effeminate was the only one she wanted to see.

'Wonderful bodies,' Nellie breathed. 'No wonder all the girls go mad for them.'

'I wouldn't,' Lucy said. 'They look like common dockers to me,' but Nellie was shouting with the rest of the fans as the two men slogged at each other, with heavy shuffling and hard breathing until the first bell rang and they returned to their own corners. Lucy smelled the sweat and heard the noise but sat silently. Monty clenched his fist every time a blow fell on the smooth body of Carpentier as if he wanted to add his strength to it, and he chewed desperately on an unlit cigar. He mopped his brow as if he was in the ring too, and as the bell rang for round two he sat forward. Nellie watched him anxiously when it looked as if Carpentier might win and Monty almost stood on his seat as the fight progressed.

'I must have been demented,' he muttered. 'I bet that Dempsey would win before six rounds and they've done three already!' He loosened his dress tie and Nellie tried to fan him with her evening bag. 'Stop that,' he said testily. 'It was that hooch I drank – more like wood alcohol than whiskey.' He sank back as the men appeared again, both tired and Carpentier with blood on his face. Monty wanted to die. He had got tremendous odds when he bet that the fight wouldn't last six rounds and that Dempsey would win. It didn't matter if Dempsey won after the sixth round, the bet would be over and all that money lost.

Monty put a shaking hand over his eyes as the new round commenced, then heard a shout from the crowd – of triumph, disbelief and agony mixed. He looked up in time to see the referee in the middle of the ring holding Dempsey's hand high. Monty badly needed a drink but that could wait and he closed his eyes again to regain his composure. Dollar signs floated behind his closed lids as he calculated the odds he had bet. 'Are you ill?' asked Nellie anxiously, and Lucy forgot her dreams in the tension of the moment.

'Ill?' He laughed hysterically. 'I'm fine, my girl, and so are you. I've just made a hundred thousand dollars.'

A man in a long pale overcoat handed Nellie a note and waited while she read it. 'We have already been invited,' she told him, 'but I shall be happy to meet Mr Hearst at the party.'

'Mr Hearst has sent a car for you, madam,' the man said, and Nellie inclined her head as if this was nothing more than her due. Monty gave his card to one of the attendants, and told him to send their hired car away and he'd be in touch with the firm later. Lucy looked about her but saw only strangers milling around trying to reach the exits. Monty took her firmly by the arm and made her follow Nellie and the man, who seemed to have at least ten huge henchmen creating a path for the Hearst party to reach a side door.

The opulent car awaiting them reduced even Monty to awed silence. Fresh flowers in silver vases hung by the windows and a small table dropped down in front of the seats of padded leopard-skin upholstery. A set of fine crystal decanters nestled in velvet-lined sconces and the guide offered drinks; Monty savoured fine malt that could have come only from Scotland. Lucy stared out of the window after refusing a drink. Everything was happening too fast and Sidney had been swept out of sight and away from her again, perhaps for ever.

'Cheer up,' whispered Nellie. 'He's sure to be at the party. The hotel is big enough to take far more than the eight hundred invited guests. They won't even notice the gate-crashers,' she added dryly.

'Sidney wouldn't do that!'

'I wasn't thinking of him. Just be careful tonight, Lucy. The place will be full of wolves ready to offer a girl the moon.' Lucy relaxed and they chuckled. It was a joke between them. Three men so far had tried to get to know Lucy on the pretext that they were from film studios and could make sure she had a fine career in Hollywood. Lucy had become almost as adept as Nellie in the gentle art of the complete brush-off.

'There will be far too many real stars there to bother with me,' Lucy said, 'except for Sidney. Do you think he'll like my dress?'

'It's time you realized how much people change, Lucy. Look at yourself, for instance. Who would recognize the little mouse we took on the *Mauretania*? You may find you no longer have anything in common.'

The car stopped and Lucy saw men in dark coats with hats pulled well down over their eyes waiting by the entrance. Invitation cards were checked and cold eyes took in every detail of the occupants of the cars before they were allowed further. 'They are Mr Hearst's men,' the guide said.

'But it isn't his party,' Monty said. He stared at the bodyguards who were everywhere.

'Any party Mr Hearst attends is his party,' the man said flatly. He nodded to the doorkeeper and they were ushered through into the foyer.

Monty followed Nellie, filled with pride and jubilation. 'We might even meet the great man himself,' he whispered. 'To be escorted here at his invitation is something special. *Wow*!'

Lucy laughed. Monty tried to adopt Americanisms but

still sounded very British, while Nellie could copy an accent and idiom successfully. Who was Randolph Hearst? And where was Sidney Darwen? Her eager gaze raked the crowds. Skilfully, Nellie was detached from them to meet the Hearst party while Monty and Lucy were introduced to some film producers who were interested in Nellie's singing. From her chair Lucy could see the entrance where the rest of the guests were massing to show their invitations, and Monty drank more fine liquor with no hint of Prohibition in the hotel.

Four men came into the light, dressed in a stylish but casual, almost Bohemian way. One had his arm round the shoulder of the tallest and they were laughing. A waiter offered the tray of drinks but the tall man shook his head and asked for fruit juice, then saw that the pretty girl by the pillar was taking a glass from a tray and stepped forward to help himself.

'Hello, Sidney,' Lucy said.

'I beg your pardon,' he began, thinking that she was another fan who had waited to catch him. He stared, first in disbelief and then smiling broadly with evident pleasure. 'It's Lucy! It's little Lucy Dove all the way from the Island!' Lucy nodded, her eyes bright with unshed tears of joy. 'Lucy, my other dear little sister.' He turned to the men who regarded them with amused curiosity. 'Let me introduce Lucy Dove from my home town who grew up with my family and helped me when I needed her to dress my puppets.' It wasn't the introduction she might have wished for but she was too overjoyed to notice. He bent to hug her and kiss both her cheeks in the manner of stage people and the French, and her heart was ready to burst. The fruit juice spilled over the table as her dress caught the glass when Sidney embraced her and one of the men saved it from falling completely. 'It's so wonderful to see you, Sidney,' she said breathlessly. 'I've looked forward to this from the moment I left England.'

'We've been so unlucky,' he said kindly. 'First they changed my schedule and after that we went round in circles missing each other.' He glanced at his companions who seemed bored. 'I'm here in New Jersey for another week. Can you meet me for lunch tomorrow? I can't wait to hear all about home. Any cab will take you to this hotel.' He scribbled a note and handed it to her.

'Who's the lady, Mr Darwen?' A reporter sidled up and took a picture just as Sidney embraced her again to say goodbye. They saw the flash and turned, their heads close together and their faces showing mutual affection. The man took another shot, swiftly.

'They get everywhere,' Sidney said, no longer smiling, and one of his companions grinned. 'I'll see you tomorrow, Lucy, and we'll talk and talk and talk! If you have any photographs of the family, bring them and think up everything you can recall since my father died. It's so good to find you again.'

The reporter made a great play with adjusting the camera after Sidney had gone. 'I thought I knew most of his friends,' he said. 'You're new round here, miss?'

'I'm with Nellie Morris and my Uncle Monty,' Lucy said as she had done so often to reporters now that Nellie was famous. 'They took a booking in New Jersey as my uncle wanted to see the Dempsey fight.'

'You don't say! And Mr Darwen? You and he seem very . . . friendly?'

'I've known him all my life,' Lucy replied simply.

'Well, who would have thought it?' The man scribbled again. 'I couldn't help overhearing that he said, "It's so good to find you, Lucy." Am I right?'

Lucy blushed. Those words were singing in her heart. 'It's wonderful to meet again after so long and we're having lunch tomorrow.'

'Where would that be?' Lucy paused. Sidney was getting well known and might suffer as Nellie did from persistent reporters so she said that she didn't know but had to get in touch by telephone. She smiled sweetly. 'You'll have to excuse me as Mr Morris is beckoning me.' She hurried away but the reporter took another picture as she joined Nellie and Monty, then he slipped away before two men in dark suits could reach him.

'Isn't it wonderful? Mr Hearst has invited us all to one of the Hearst estates for a whole week!' The party had been going on for several hours and Lucy was desperately tired. She looked at Nellie's jubilant face.

'When do we have to go?' If I can't see Sidney again I'll die, she thought frantically.

'After the final performance here at the weekend. It's come at the right time as I need a break and we are booked for only two guest appearances on the way back to New York later.' Nellie was bubbling over. 'I didn't meet Mr Hearst in person as he didn't appear all evening. He's a bit of an elusive legend, but I talked with Marion Davies and an invitation from her is as good as one from him – better in a way, as she invites only people she thinks have real talent. To let the papers know we're going there will give me a lot of kudos, not only here in the States but all over.' Nellie spoke in a low voice. 'They say she runs everything for him and they've been together for years,' she added, with a meaning glance, 'but nobody dares speak about that as the last time someone called her the Hearst Mistress he had a very nasty accident!'

'I thought Mr Hearst was married,' Lucy yawned.

'He is, but his wife is never mentioned as she's a Catholic and can't divorce him. It will be so nice to live in a house again instead of hotels. I thought when we bought our property in New York that we might actually stay there sometimes – but I've only ever slept there for two weeks. I know you thought it was an investment, Monty, but I do want to live there sometimes.' She tried to look unconcerned. 'Lucy, Monty saw you talking to Sidney Darwen.'

'Yes, isn't that wonderful? He asked me to have lunch with him tomorrow, or today, rather! I can alter the frock first and leave everything as you like it, Nellie.'

'Don't look so worried. I work you into the ground and there's no need to beg for time off.' Nellie was still elated by her success with Marion Davies and Monty's big win. 'You'd better have that new suit I can't wear. In spite of what you say I must have put on a little weight but fortunately in all the right places. Look as nice as you like as I doubt if you'll be in any danger with him.'

'No, Sidney treats women with respect,' Lucy agreed. 'He's so kind but he did kiss me as soon as we met.'

'And when you parted, he kissed you on both cheeks?' Nellie shrugged. 'You'll be quite safe, Lucy, but don't expect heaven. It is often hell upside-down.' She shook away her own sudden depression. Marriage with Jack Darwen had been like that, all passion and joy one minute and jealous recrimination the next. She looked at Monty and her face softened. 'There are men who can make you happy without the anguish that tears a woman in half.'

Lucy gave a deep contented sigh. 'I know. Sidney is the most gentle, nicest, loving person I've ever met.'

Monty took a long drink and exchanged a hopeless glance with Nellie. 'C'mon – it's time we were all in bed. If I stay here I'll drink too much of that fine malt. It's all settled. They gave me details about the time we have to get there and the address, and you still have a show to give tonight, Nellie.'

'Promise me you'll make no snap decisions without telling me,' Nellie said to Lucy. 'I can't look after you for ever, but I do care what happens.' She settled into the car and hoped that the rose-coloured spectacles wouldn't break in too traumatic a fashion. Yellow cabs like the ones in New York were busy taking people home from the party and the first newspapers were already on the stands. Monty insisted on buying every edition available and sank back half-asleep, unable to read them without his glasses. When they were back in the hotel suite, Lucy took the sports pages and put them neatly on the table ready for Monty to see later that morning. She turned to the other pages and saw with astonishment that her photograph with Sidney had already appeared on an inner page of the first edition of a popular daily.

Delighted, she cut it out with nail-scissors and resolved to go down to buy some more copies to send back to England. They'll be so thrilled, she thought. She crept down to the foyer and out into the street where the boy had the papers, bought two copies and hurried back. A man pushed on the other side of the revolving door as if to stop her and she let it go, knowing she could get inside just as fast if it swung the other way. She walked quickly to the elevator and was relieved to see a middle-aged couple join her in the lift. She looked up at the indicator and ignored Frank Garsey, who stood and watched the lift ascend.

Later, Lucy showed Nellie the papers and proudly cut out the extra two pictures. Nellie riffled through the other papers when they were brought up and gave a sigh of relief. Only one reporter had seen Lucy with Sidney Darwen, and so the incident might fade into obscurity without a follow-up. There were several photographs of Nellie with Marion Davies and other famous names and she felt excited, knowing that this was important to her career. Lucy put the cuttings away in her handkerchief sachet while Nellie peeked at the caption that Lucy hadn't bothered to read: *"A GIRLFRIEND? Well, well, what will the faithful Ivor have to say about that? Watch this space and we'll bring you more news about America's newest matinée star."* Swiftly, she crumpled up the scrap of paper to join the others in the waste-basket.

Chapter 12

'Letters from home aren't nearly as good as hearing it all from you, Lucy,' Sidney laughed, as if he was still a boy amused at the antics of his sisters. 'Clare expecting a baby is really funny!'

The first excitement was fading. Sidney had asked eagerly about people and places and even old buildings he remembered, but had said nothing about Lucy and him meeting in this miraculous fashion. 'All women want babies,' Lucy said.

'Do they?' The blue eyes were sad. 'Some don't and that goes for men too.' He looked away. 'Have you found someone to give you all that you want from life, Lucy?'

'I can do all the things a man would want from me and I know I'm attractive,' she replied defiantly. Look at me! she wanted to cry. Look *at* me and not through me at your childhood! I'm a woman and I'm in love with you!

Lunch was over and they sat drinking cream sodas under a tree in the park while the hours flashed by. 'You must think I'm rude,' he said at last. 'I haven't asked after you. How is your mother? Does she still work in the laundry? Mother said she was in charge of some of the girls and did very well for herself.' Lucy bit her lip. Over the last few months on the Island she had realized that someone was keeping her mother as she had given up her job but dressed well and seemed to have money to spend. 'I'm sorry,' Sidney said gently. 'That was foolish of me, but if Maudie is happy who are we to say anything?'

'Don't you think it matters that my mother is no better than she ought to be?'

He smiled at the old-fashioned euphemism. 'Now you sound like *my* mother. Has it made you distrust all men?'

'I could never distrust you, Sidney. I've been longing to meet you again.'

'Well, here we are,' he said lightly.

'Here is the cutting about last night.' She handed him the picture. 'Isn't it good?'

He gave a short laugh. 'Very good. I wish my father was alive to see it.'

'Of course, you couldn't be at the funeral,' Lucy said tenderly. 'It was lovely, with six black horses and ostrich plumes and a really old-fashioned hearse just as he would have wanted. Your mother was very brave and didn't shed a tear but many did. Even my mother cried and there were two of the gypsies from Wootton there, dressed in their best. The whole town respected Walter.'

Sidney's face relaxed. 'That makes sense. Gypsies came to the house often and he went to them when he wanted advice about horses. I used to ride their piebalds and learned some Romany words from the boys. Thank you, Lucy. I had forgotten that I had anything in common with my father and it's good to remember that. It's been wonderful talking about home, but I have to go now and I expect Nellie will need you if she has a show.'

Lucy gasped. 'Yes, look how late it is! When can I see you again, Sidney? We have to go to Florida next week to a place with a very funny name owned by Mr Hearst. Miss Davies invited us all last night.'

'Do you mean *Vizcaya*?' Sidney sat back and stared at her. 'Everyone longs for an invitation there. It means Nellie's really getting recognized and it does wonders for a career in the movies. I'd give a lot to be in your place, Lucy.'

'But you are already well-known. The reporter last night asked questions about us and there are two photographers over there now. One of the men is the same reporter. I told him that I'd known you all my life and he was very interested.'

'I'll bet! They'll make a meal of that but I don't mind if you don't.' He smiled wickedly, and stood up to go. 'I'll telephone the hotel later,' he promised and took her hands to draw her to her feet before kissing her firmly on the lips, just long enough for the cameras to catch it. 'Take a cab from the rank there. I have to run,' he said.

Lucy sat in the cab, trembling with delight. 'He loves me,' she whispered, then forced her mind back to her duties.

Nellie was too preoccupied to ask about the lunch. 'Miss Davies has taken a box for this evening,' she said triumphantly. 'The management has asked her to take champagne with us after the show and to bring her party.'

The performance went well and Nellie sparkled as she greeted the guests afterwards. Lucy sipped a little champagne and a man from the Davies entourage came across to her. 'Haven't I seen you somewhere?' he asked. 'Do you sing?'

'You may have seen my picture in the paper with Sidney Darwen,' she replied. 'I had lunch with him today,' she added shyly.

'Is that so? I thought he didn't go for girls.' The pale blue eyes tried to read her thoughts.

'Sidney is a gentleman!' Lucy declared. 'He doesn't date just anyone but he's the nicest man I know and I've known him for years.' She sensed a certain disbelief. 'He has a lot of women after him but he knew I was coming to America and he prefers my company. He said that it was wonderful to be together again. We just can't stop talking!'

'Is that so? Maybe Miss Davies got the wrong idea.' He went over and whispered something to Miss Davies who looked at Lucy with ill-concealed surprise. They talked for another minute and then she smiled at Lucy and nodded. The man returned. 'Sorry to go off like that,' he said. 'Miss Davies didn't understand that you had a boyfriend here. You can ask Sidney Darwen to join your party if he can make it and stay for the week with the rest of you to give you time together. See you on Sunday in *Vizcaya*.'

'I know he'll be pleased,' Lucy said with engaging candour. 'He said he'd like to be invited there and he's becoming quite well-known as an actor, isn't he?'

'Sure. They invite many of the promising talents if they're

straight. Trouble was that Miss Davies thought he was a pansy.'

Lucy frowned. She'd heard that expression before, but where? She must ask Nellie, she decided, but was too busy to think of it as one of Nellie's costumes had a snag in it that had to be mended before the next performance.

'That was even better than before,' Monty said proudly.

'Thanks to Lucy I could move in that beaded dress. No, don't offer me sweets – I have to trim a little for the swimming pool in Florida. They say it is enormous and we sit in the sun by the side and talk to really famous people! I'm terribly excited.'

'So am I. Miss Davies has invited Sidney too and suggested he travels with us on the train.'

Monty tipped the ash from his cigar into his drink. 'That . . . man?' he said lamely, after a warning glance from Nellie.

'Were you going to say "that pansy"?' asked Lucy. 'What *is* a pansy, apart from being a very lovely flower?'

Nellie gave another warning glance and Monty shut his mouth. 'A pansy is a man who doesn't like women and goes with men instead. If they sleep together it's against the law and against society,' Nellie said bluntly.

Lucy exploded into silvery laughter. 'You *are* funny. What does it matter if they don't like all women? There's always one to fall in love with. Men do sleep in the same room if there aren't enough rooms to go round – so do women. Clare and Lizzie shared a room. Are they pansies?'

Monty coughed and went puce. 'It's a matter of sex,' Nellie went on. 'Men who never have sex with women but have it with men are pansies.'

'I can't see how they can,' Lucy said, still amused. 'I know how babies are made and I've watched animals mate, but how can men do that together?'

'Oh look, forget it. Some day when I am feeling strong and you have a little more imagination I'll tell you. For the present we have his amusing company which I shall enjoy. You will be safe, Lucy, and something has convinced Miss Davies that Sidney is straight. Telephone his hotel as he will have to arrange a substitute for the next week and of course, will need to pack his bag.' Nellie smiled. 'I think it's a good idea, Sidney coming. He's amusing and decorative and with him we can relax and talk over old times and get really nostalgic.'

The girl in reception at Lucy's hotel was very impressed. 'You really know him, honey? I think he's far more handsome than Valentino. I saw his last movie five times and cried every time. Nobody sees him with a girl so maybe he was just waiting for you – isn't that romantic? You are a lucky, lucky girl, Miss Dove.' She called Sidney's hotel and Lucy waited impatiently. 'Call for Mr Darwen from Miss Dove,' she droned. 'Yeah, I'll hold the line.'

Lucy picked up the receiver that the receptionist indicated. 'Who wants Mr Darwen?' a male voice said.

'It's Miss Dove . . . Lucy. He was going to ring me but I have urgent news for him.'

She heard music and another voice in the background, but the man said sulkily, 'He's busy.' The line crackled as someone else took the receiver. 'Sidney Darwen here.'

'Oh, Sidney, I'm glad you are there! Your friend said you were busy.'

'Why didn't you say it was you? Ivor must have misunderstood. Of course I want to speak to you.' She tried to hide her own excitement and sensed that he was almost shocked by her message. 'Are you really serious?' he asked at last. 'You *do* mean it? I've longed for this for ages as most of the movie moguls go there and come from Los Angeles and all over.'

'It was the picture in the paper that did it,' Lucy said. 'One of Miss Davies' party talked to me and then she asked if you'd like to come too as I said we might not be able to meet if I went to *Vizcaya* for a week.'

'Clever little Lucy!' Sidney cleared his throat. 'Do I come alone?'

'No, you travel with us in the special train.' She laughed happily. 'I think they imagined I might be the odd one out with no escort. It happens when Nellie and Monty have to talk business.'

'I see.'

'Sidney? Have we been cut off?'

'I'm here. It's just so sudden and I have to make . . . certain arrangements.'

'That's why I rang. Nellie said you'd have to find a substitute at the theatre.'

'I'll telephone later but whatever happens I'm definitely coming to *Vizcaya*!'

Lucy walked back to the suite slowly. The 'other arrangements' sounded tiresome and she wondered who the sulky man was who had answered the phone. A dresser, late getting away from work? She shrugged off the feeling that Sidney was uneasy. He had said he wanted to be with her, he had kissed her just as he kissed his leading ladies and couldn't be more attentive. The music from the hotel ballroom came faintly. She had heard it when she talked to Sidney on the telephone and she smiled to herself. '*Avalon, Avalon, where you go my heart goes with you.*' It would be wonderful to dance to that tune, held in Sidney's arms.

'Hello!' Monty barked into the telephone. 'Don't you know it's late?' He listened for a moment. 'No, she isn't here – and I'll thank you to leave us alone whoever you are!' He slammed down the receiver and glared at Lucy. 'Oh, there you are! I said you weren't here,' he admitted more calmly. 'This man rang before and I didn't like the sound of him. Go dancing with a stranger at this hour? What does he think you are? He could be one of those white slavers we hear about.'

'More likely one of those boys in the lobby who stared at Lucy,' Nellie said with a yawn. 'Just as well to say no, Lucy. It isn't safe to go dancing alone with a man you don't know even in the same hotel. Did he give a name?'

'Garden . . . Gardel . . . Barcie. That's it. Sounded foreign.'

'Then it's a good thing you answered, Monty. That little rat was on the *Mauretania* and is staying here, and I don't think it's a coincidence. His name is Garsey.'

'Oh, I've seen him and I just ignore him,' Lucy said

airily. 'In any case, he can't follow me to *Vizcaya* and with Sidney around no other man will trouble me.'

The next few days flew by in a flurry of work and packing, with shopping trips to buy smart clothes for the poolside and pretty dresses for Lucy so that Marion Davies wouldn't think that Nellie Morris was cheese-paring when it came to her dresser's clothes. Sidney called twice but seemed preoccupied, but what did it matter after all the years they had been apart? They would have a whole week together, and by nightfall on Sunday, the four were sleeping in comfortable berths as the train rushed through the American countryside to Florida.

Heat struck them as soon as they left the train and it was a relief when the car drew up by the wide gates protecting *Vizcaya*, the home of Jim Deering, a close friend of Randolph Hearst. Even Nellie gasped as she saw the white marble Venetian house set in huge manicured gardens like something from a fairy tale. Servants ran out to take the luggage and to escort the party to their suite. The planning was faultless: Nellie and Monty had a double room with its own bathroom, there was a general sitting room, and two smaller bedrooms with connecting doors and optional bolts. A shower room catered for the two rooms.

Lucy ran to the windows and saw green trees, smooth lawns and the sparkle of fountains. 'It's wonderful,' Sidney said in a broken voice. 'You brought me luck, Lucy. A very important director saw my name on the guest list and rang to say he'll be here and wants to see me about a part in a new movie. It means I'm accepted by the people who matter.' He put an arm round her shoulders and Lucy reached up to kiss his cheek. He held her close and rested his head on hers but didn't kiss her.

'Come on,' urged Nellie. 'There's so much to see and if we want something to eat or drink we may ask for anything we fancy, just anything! Dinner is at nine.' They walked over the black marble floors of the main hall and gazed up at the black pillars. A huge marble ship was set into one side of the house and on the other side was a sandy beach that only needed the sea but made do with a vast swimming pool set half in and half out of the house. Everywhere there were pictures of Marion Davies in her latest movies. 'They say that hundreds of men are in love with her but she remains faithful to Mr Hearst,' Nellie whispered.

Sidney looked about him. 'Is it any wonder? Many men would give their souls for all this, and women would sell their bodies. Not you, Lucy,' he added hastily. 'You aren't like that.'

'I'm a woman,' she said and blushed, but Sidney was absorbed in examining a statue that must have come from Italy and cost a fortune.

'We aren't tourists and they said we must make ourselves at home so order us some muffins and tea, Monty,' Nellie suggested and subsided on to a comfortable sunbed under a huge umbrella. Lucy longed to be in the pool. She watched Sidney bite into a muffin and lick the melted butter from his fingers. It was a new experience being with the man of whom she had dreamed for so long and to know the reality of wanting him so much, aching to be kissed by him with passion, to have his hands explore her body and to go away and make love together.

'I'm going to have a swim,' she said with sudden determination. 'I'll fetch my swimming costume and change over in those cubicles as those people have done.' Nellie went back to talking to the group of actors who had found her, and Monty lay back with his hat over his eyes. Sidney brushed the crumbs from his shirt and said he'd swim, too.

'See you in the water!' he said.

There were a lot of huge rubber animals in the pool, and once in the water Lucy felt really happy. Sidney was like a boy again, splashing anyone who tried to push him off his favourite rubber horse. More people joined them and they played a kind of water polo with no rules and a lot of laughter. Lucy noticed how the women tried to brush against the handsome man and saw that although he was pleasant to everyone he came back to her after each break in the game.

'What a good sport you are, Lucy,' he said as she came up spluttering after a bad dive. He held her close while she regained her breath and kissed the tip of her nose. 'You are the prettiest girl here.'

'Do you like my costume?' she asked.

He eyed it with the same approval he had given the statue. 'The cut is right and the colour suits you and you have a very nice body, Lucy. Better get dressed or we'll be damp at dinner.'

Lucy found soft towels and scented soap and shampoo in the marble changing rooms and took her time over her toilette. Her hair dried quickly into a pale nimbus and her cheeks were pink with effort and excitement when she went back to Nellie to ask what she would like her to put out to wear. 'Sidney says he will meet us at dinner,' Nellie told her. 'I take back all I thought about him. He's fun and even made Monty laugh with a very funny story.' She gathered her belongings together hastily but couldn't avoid what she had dreaded – Lucy's questions.

'You promised to tell me about . . . men,' Lucy said determinedly.

'It doesn't matter now. If men are too good-looking, people say they are too much like women and can love women only as sisters but they fall in love with other men.'

'Sidney isn't a bit like a woman! He has broad shoulders and a fine figure.' She blushed, remembering his maleness through the thin swimming costume.

'Look – forget it! Just have a good time while you can. If I lost my voice or did badly on stage these people wouldn't give us a second glance! Enjoy it all while it lasts but marry a man who can give you love and security, and take luxury for what it is – a toy.' Nellie smoothed down the dress that clung to her figure and had made Monty blench when he'd seen the bill.

At dinner Lucy was seated away from Nellie and Monty but almost opposite Sidney, far enough away to make conversation difficult, so she had to talk to her neighbours. One was a forbidding-looking man, much older than the rest. He ignored her until he saw her refuse wine and ask for fresh orange juice, then turned to look at her. 'Does me good to see a pretty girl refuse alcohol,' he said. He glared at the flushed and laughing faces. 'This house is a sink of iniquity! If Randolph wasn't one of my oldest friends I'd have the FBI down on this place!' Lucy smiled, remembering an evangelist who had visited the Island and had a voice just like him. 'Keep your virtue and your morals, my dear. They are dearer to God than all this.'

Sidney leaned forward and raised his glass. 'The lobster reminds me of home,' he said.

'Do you know that young man?' The narrow lips clamped together.

'We came here together. I've known him since I was a child.'

'Is that so? Sidney Darwen, isn't he? Good-looking and a nice profile. English voices come over well on films,' the man conceded as if inspecting a prize bull.

'Do you think the new talking pictures will take on?'

'I make them.' He watched Sidney help his neighbour to relish. 'Is he married?'

'Not yet.'

'I like my actors to be safely married even if it's only for the publicity, and none of my films corrupt the young.'

'Sidney is a wonderful man. I came all this way from England to be with him and we are getting to know each other again.' Sidney sensed that the powerful man who had very rigid ideas about morality was talking about him.

'Tell him I want to see him in the poolroom at eleven tonight,' the man barked and turned to talk to his other neighbour.

Sidney laughed in disbelief when Lucy passed on the message. 'I don't understand. I went for an audition and he refused to see me. What did you say to him?'

'Only that we grew up together and are really good friends. He was impressed that neither of us drank wine. Is he some kind of Hot Gospeller?'

'Come with me, Lucy. That man scares me,' Sidney said. Lucy slipped her hand in his and they went together to the poolroom.

'Do you want to work for me?' the man said bluntly. 'I can make you very famous, my boy!' Sidney clutched Lucy's hand and nodded, dumbly. 'There is one condition – that you get married!' The black cheroot waved menacingly. 'Can't have a leading man labelled queer. The press would do it, given half a chance.'

'But I'm not even engaged,' Sidney said desperately.

'Ask her! This is as good a place as any and mighty good publicity. She *is* your girl?'

Sidney shut his eyes for a second and saw his future shining bright – or dull with routine and second-rate shows. He looked into Lucy's eager eyes and wondered if it was possible. He *did* love her in many ways and she was the sweetest girl he knew.

'Will you marry me, Lucy?' he asked.

Chapter 13

'Isn't it wonderful?' Jane Darwen spread the cuttings over the embroidered teacloth. 'Our Sidney engaged to Lucy and you expecting again.'

'We've always known how Lucy felt about him and now they'll be as happy as Clive and me.' Janey regarded her mother with curiosity. Her joy held an element of relief and her happiness was greater than at any time in the past when she heard of her children's plans for marriage. Sidney had been special, Janey knew without feeling envious. He was affectionate and caring and now she could tell Clive that he was mistaken in his judgement of her brother. 'I can't see Lucy coming back here again to work at the Lodge!'

'I wonder if Maudie knows?' Jane asked. 'I haven't seen her for ages, so could you leave a note in at Sea Street for me?'

'Haven't you heard? Bert took her to London and they ran into a group from the chapel so it's no use them thinking they are hiding anything now. Bert set her up in one of his houses in West Wight and she doesn't come to Newport much any more.'

'I'll give the news to Bert then to pass on. He wants me to see Annie today and is coming for me in his motor. Annie knows that he goes with other women but she has never said anything about Maudie. She's like Amy at Wootton, who never could see what was under her nose. She'll like to hear about it, nevertheless, and grumble that Lucy Dove never did know her place!' Jane fetched her hat and sighed happily. 'It's a great burden off my mind in more ways than one,' she said enigmatically, and hurried out to the steps leading down to Bert's car.

Sweet Mary, the spell is broken! she told herself. Old Mrs Lee is dead and gone and the other two prophecies can't happen now. Clive will be safe and Sidney will marry and be happy. Perhaps Emily might yet marry!

'Annie's much worse,' Bert said sombrely as soon as the motor started. 'We have a day nurse and a night nurse now.'

'Is she in pain? Does she know how bad it is?'

'The medicine makes her sleep a lot and this nurse has the knack of making her comfortable, not like the last one who lifted her like a bag of potatoes and dumped her on the pillows all anyhow. I got rid of her sharpish. I can't have Annie treated like that.'

It's a bit late for consideration, thought Jane. A bit late for anything – including guilt. 'I can stay for a few hours if you like,' she said aloud. 'Has the doctor said anything new?'

'It could be weeks or it could be hours. The morphia often gives the patients periods of recovery followed by a relapse but some thrive on the big doses for a long time.'

'If it kills the pain it's good,' Jane said firmly. 'The time doesn't matter so long as she dies with an easy mind.' She smiled. 'I know you've done your best lately, Bert. You haven't been out to the cottages for a few weeks and she has everything she can ask for.'

Bert reddened. 'I know I've led her a dance sometimes but she's my wife when all's said and done.'

'I've some news that will make her take a bit of notice if anything will. Our Sidney is engaged to be married!'

'Sidney?' He laughed. 'Wonders never cease!'

'He's marrying Lucy Dove. Can you tell Maudie that for me?' He glanced at her, knowing that it was common knowledge now that he and Maudie were together.

'She never wanted Lucy to go to America, but now she ought to be pleased. They don't usually write to each other, her and Lucy, but I'll suggest she sends a note. How's Janey?'

'Fine, just fine.'

'Do you worry about Clive?'

'No, not any more,' she said quietly. 'He's due home after sea trials next month and I don't think he's in danger in peacetime, even if I do hate the thought of him being in submarines. Alex will be home at the same time so they will have a really good time.'

Bert's house with the view of Pan Down and the white scar of chalk was quiet, with the curtains half-drawn to keep out the sun. Jane wanted to fling them back and let in the light but Annie had lived in shadows all her life and it was too late to change. Jane bent to kiss the tightly stretched skin of the yellow cheek and for a moment, pin-point pupils showed in the drugged eyes. 'She's had her injection and will sleep for a while, then have a lucid period when you can talk to her,' the nurse said. Jane approved of the quiet efficiency and the neatness of the room and sat to sew more tiny garments for Lizzie and Clare, until Annie stirred and opened her eyes.

'How long have you been here?' she asked. Jane held a feeding cup to the dry lips and Annie glared at the retreating form of the nurse who tactfully left them to talk. 'She spies on me,' Annie said. 'She's after my money.'

'She makes you comfortable,' Jane said mildly. 'Bert can't do that.'

'He's been so good. When I'm better we're going to Southampton to see my aunt, and I'll come up to the Mall to see what you've been doing behind my back.'

'We bought new curtains and a lovely chair from *Wadhams* for the drawing room.'

Annie tried to sit up. 'Nothing but the best for the Darwens!' she croaked. 'That must have set you back a few pennies.'

'You will see for yourself, Annie. I have another bit of news, too. Sidney is engaged to be married to Lucy Dove.'

'Lucy Dove?' Annie sank back exhausted. 'Bad blood! Sea Street – remember, Jane? A man there keeps goats in his backyard. Don't let it happen, Jane!'

'They are very happy,' Jane said in a soothing voice. 'Sidney will appear in one of the new talking pictures, and they will work hard for a year until Lucy is free to leave Nellie and get married.'

'That's another one – Nellie Morris! What do they get up to over there, I'd like to know.'

'If they are happy and Janey and Clive are safe, I don't have a care in the world,' Jane said.

'What's wrong with Janey?' Annie picked at the sheets, her hands threaded with corded veins and she became more restless.

'Nothing. They are both fine. Let me get you a piece of thin bread and butter or a little of the jelly I brought.'

'I fancy a boiled potato.'

Jane hurried to the kitchen where Bert stood talking to the nurse. 'Get a pan with water and put in a couple of potatoes, whole. I know they'd boil quicker cut up but Annie likes them whole, split down with butter, making them floury. She's getting restless,' Jane told the nurse who went back to the room. 'Can she manage alone?' she asked Bert.

'She likes to do everything,' he said. 'Annie weighs no more than a breath of air. Stay with me, Jane. I need you at this moment more than she does.'

'The waiting is bad but you look as if there is something more on your mind,' she said gently. 'Is it business worries? Shares?'

'I've got myself in a terrible muddle, Jane.' He put his face in his hands and groaned. 'I've never done better in business and yet I'd give a lot to put back the clock. If Walter was here he'd advise me, but he isn't. I need you to tell me what to do – I need your . . . sanctity, if that's the word.'

'I'm not a saint, Bert, and the good Lord will not hold anything against you if you've done your best now for her.'

'Not Annie! Maudie and me went to London for a few days six weeks ago just before Annie was taken this badly.' He shook his head in disbelief. 'All this time and now Maudie says she's taken.'

'Maudie?' Jane didn't know whether to laugh or cry. 'It's too early to tell, Bert. She might just be late.'

'She's sick.' He gave her a hard look. 'It's happened to me, Jane – but think what it might have been like if it had happened to Walter!'

It was like a slap in the face but true, all the same. 'Why

now, Bert? She could have prevented it as she has done for ages. Did she do it on purpose?'

'Does it matter? It could have been my fault. After all the years with Annie having no babies, I might have thought it wasn't in me.' Suddenly he grinned. 'At least that's one thing off my mind. I *can* father a child!'

'The potatoes!' Jane lifted the lid. They were just beginning to split, showing the creamy floury inside, just as Annie liked them. She lifted one carefully on to a dish, added a generous knob of butter, put a silver spoon on the tray and a dainty napkin and carried it off to the sickroom.

The nurse straightened her back. Annie lay flat with the dull eyes closed and no pulse in the withered throat. Bert stood in the doorway then walked across to kiss the cold cheek, and the nurse took the tray and tipped the potato into the pigbin then brought a glass of whiskey for the bereaved husband. She left the room and heated water for the last washing.

'She's gone.' Bert's voice trembled with almost superstitious fear. 'Poor Annie. What do I do now, Jane?'

'The nurse will see to everything,' Jane said with relief. This time she had no need to touch the still form as she had done for Amy, and there was the living to consider. She packed away her sewing and the photographs from America and went to the larder. 'You'll have formalities to see to later so eat now, Bert.' She found cold meat and pickles and added the boiled potato that was left, just as Annie would have liked it, and he swallowed everything she put before him, without noticing what he ate. Then she slipped away to her own home, where the curtains were drawn back and the light came in, even if it risked fading the wallpaper.

Vikki was on the rocking horse in the playroom and Emily sat close by, doing more to the crochet edging. 'Here is a sweet,' Jane said. 'Your horse is tired and needs to go to sleep, so go into the garden and pick a nice flower for Gran's small vase.' She put the horse away and locked the door firmly, as the new blocks for the rockers had not yet arrived. Then she put the key in a safe place.

'How was it at Bert's?' Emily asked, seeing her mother's tense face.

'Annie died an hour ago and even that didn't make their house more cold. This house is our home, Em, even if we've been here such a short time but that one was never warm and Annie never knew what love could be.'

'I'll cycle over tomorrow to see if Bert needs help with refreshments when the relatives come,' Emily offered.

'There aren't many,' Jane said wearily. 'She talked of an aunt in Southampton who I know died years ago. Bert has cousins and there'll be neighbours and business people but no real grief and Annie would have begrudged every penny spent on food! I feel sad because I knew her so well but all she did was make mischief and find fault yet she said I was her best friend.'

Emily made her mother sit down and handed her a cup of tea. She offered the biscuit tin and stirred her own cup. 'Bert ought to marry again,' she said.

Jane gave an involuntary laugh. 'Maybe he will,' she said. 'Maybe he'll have to marry. No, I'm not matchmaking – he's done that for himself!' She told Emily about Maudie Dove. 'She'll either have to get rid of the baby or brazen it out, but now that Bert is free he ought to make an honest woman of her.'

'They can't marry five minutes after the funeral,' Emily said, 'but they could slip off and marry quietly in a few weeks' time. The baby won't show for months yet. Still, Bert may have his own ideas.'

'That lace is getting heavy, Emily. Why not put it away for a while and do something lighter for yourself?' Jane knew that it was meant for Clare but she wondered if Clare even recalled that she had once said she'd like it. Anything new, however cheap and gaudy suited her and her bedspread now was a cheap Indian one with colours that ran in the wash.

Lizzie and Clare came together the next day when they heard the news and settled in for the day. Lizzie brought out the cake that Emily had baked to have for tea with Mrs Barnes, and cut it into generous slices, filling her own mouth before handing it round. She said self-righteously that Harry insisted she ate little and often to keep away heartburn; at dinner-time, she ate ravenously. Emily sighed as all the food for the next day vanished from the plates of her two uninvited sisters, but Jane gave them cups of tea in the garden after the meal and was glad to have them there both looking so well.

Clare made caustic remarks about Lucy setting her cap at Sidney and scheming to get him, and Emily wondered what she would say when she learned about Maudie but sensibly kept quiet.

Janey arrived later, leaving the car at the bottom of the steps to the Mall. She held George tightly by the hand as he wanted to swing on the rail by the edge of the six-feet drop to the road. Clare pursed her lips as soon as she heard him yell. 'Janey should know better than disturb us all with that spoiled boy,' she said.

'I promised George a ride on the horse, Mother,' Janey said.

'I'll get the key,' Emily offered. 'We keep it locked up until we can have the fixed blocks to prevent Vikki going too high. I usually sit with her while she plays on it but now you are here, you can keep an eye on them, Janey.' She went back to the garden.

George stared at the painted face of the horse and backed away. He buried his face in Janey's skirt and refused to look again even when Vikki went as high as she could to impress him. 'You couldn't wait to get here,' teased Janey. 'It's a nice horse! He's made of wood so he can't hurt you.'

'No, Mummy, he's a bad horse!' George struggled to free himself from her restraining hands and dived for the open door. Janey ran after him, wondering about the front door, then saw that he had reached it. She raced after him, and caught him just as he began to climb the rail. Panting heavily, her heart beating fast, she dragged him screaming back to the house and out into the garden.

'I must have left the front door open, Mother,' she gasped. 'He nearly climbed the rail.'

Emily started to her feet. 'Vikki didn't get out too, did she?'

'You do fuss over that child, Emily,' Lizzie said crossly. 'When I have my child it will never be spoiled like these two.' Emily ignored her and went into the hall and Jane smiled when five minutes later, Emily returned with the little girl. It was good to see how Emily cared for her.

'George is crotchety and needs a rest. May I put him in the cot upstairs?' Janey took him away and Lizzie made acid remarks about people taking others for granted.

'You'll have a houseful when my baby comes, and I expect Clare will want her turn, too,' she said.

'Babies have never been a bother to me,' Jane said. 'I'll find room for them all.'

'You couldn't find room for Alan and me when we had no home,' Clare pouted.

'We made a very comfortable home for you the day you arrived,' Emily said sternly. The twins stared at their usually quiet sister as she went on, 'You are lucky to have a nice home and babies on the way, but you both do nothing but grumble.' She put away the crochet and took the last piece of cake. 'As I made the cake I might as well have one piece. I made this for tea with Mrs Barnes tomorrow and you might at least have the politeness to ask before you take everything there is to eat from our larder!'

'I don't think we'll stay for supper,' Lizzie said, her face scarlet. 'I know where I'm not wanted. If you're not careful, you'll end up as dry as Annie Cooper.'

'As for my baby, you can have it as soon as it's born,' said Clare. 'I never wanted it and I'll be glad to be rid of it.'

'Stop it!' Jane rose to her feet. 'I won't have that wicked talk here. If you can't get on it's better you stay away until you are invited. I like to see you both but you do treat this place as your own and I've earned a little consideration! Come to tea next Sunday and bring your husbands, but don't expect it every week. Get here at three and we'll discuss Annie's funeral arrangements.'

Lizzie looked abashed but Clare tossed her head and

gathered her coat and bag ready to leave as soon as Alan called for her. Jane suggested to Emily that she could take Vikki along to feed the horses in the field by the stream and the twins were left alone to await collection. Janey took one look at their sour faces and joined her mother in the kitchen.

'Clive is in the North Sea and they'll take him off in a smaller boat to get into port while the submarines go to Scotland for repainting. He writes longer letters now and I treasure every word he sends. He hopes to be home in about three weeks' time.' Jane felt herself relax. 'I look at his picture to remind me of how he is, Mother. Isn't it funny? I can never visualize the faces of people I really love yet I remember every wart of strangers I see only once. I'll have to take a really close look at Clive when he comes home!'

'I wish the others knew how lucky they are,' Jane said. 'They'll miss so much if they think everything is unfair.' She laughed. 'I can't begin to think what to send Sidney for a wedding present. They have everything over there and he said that most people even have an ice-box now! Can you imagine one in every kitchen keeping things nice and cold? Perhaps I'll wait until nearer the day. I wish they were getting married sooner. I hate long engagements.' A wedding ring on Lucy's hand would mean the end to old Mrs Lee and her tealeaves for once and for all.

Vikki rushed in. 'One horse kicked higher than my horse,' she sulked.

'I'll give her her supper and put her to bed,' Emily said rather wearily, and Jane left her with Vikki until after Clare and Lizzie had gone home. Janey stayed until George woke up and took him home too, leaving Emily and Jane to cook their fish for supper.

'I'll just pop up and check that Vikki is asleep,' Emily said later. 'We can close the door and listen to the gramophone while we eat.' She ran down again, quickly. 'She isn't in her room!' Emily called but there was no answer. She went into each room and searched, suspecting that the child was hiding but there was complete silence. 'Do you think she slipped out when Janey left?'

'She wouldn't go out in her nightie,' Jane said, and put a hand to her mouth. 'Did you lock the playroom door?' She stared at the key in the lock.

'I put the key away but I think Vikki saw where it was,' Emily said, growing pale. 'She did promise never to go in there alone.'

Jane flung open the door and felt the room go round as she clutched at the table for support. Emily gave a low cry and sank to the floor, gathering the small child into her arms.

'She's still breathing,' Emily said. 'Leave her as she is, Mother, but cover her warmly while I go for the doctor.'

Vikki opened her eyes and looked puzzled. 'I don't like my horse any more. I wanted him to kick as high as the one in the field, and he tossed me.' Her face crumpled into tears. 'I hurt, Gran. My back hurts and I can't feel my legs.'

Chapter 14

'We should have watched her,' Jane tormented herself.

'All the time she sleeps?' Dr Barnes sat in the drawing room of the house on the Mall and eyed her quizzically. 'Nobody is to blame. She has your son's wilfulness and Nellie's energy and that makes a heady mixture. Time heals young bones and I doubt if she will have lasting damage but she'll need care for a while.'

'What a terrible week. First Annie dying, then Bert telling me about Maudie.' He nodded and she knew that Bert had informed him. 'Then Vikki lying like something dead on the floor! And Annie's funeral, with Bert almost smiling and me having to say to people that it was sheer relief that she no longer suffered!'

'And what of you, Mrs Darwen?' he asked kindly. 'I thought you were taking life easier, but you seem to gather other people's troubles in the same old way. We are all getting older,' he added gently. 'I was talking to Archie and he feels that time is passing far too quickly.'

'I know,' Jane said, her face clouding. 'Dear man that he is, he helps me in all sorts of ways but I must stay here to look after Emily and Vikki and to have George when Janey goes away. And now with the babies coming...' She smiled. 'Your Alex will be home soon, too, and he's welcome as one of my own. I know he may be lonely, so do make sure he comes to us whenever he wants company. With Clive home too we shall be a large happy family again. In many ways we seem to have been here for ages. I try not to pass the old shop too often, as I still expect to see Walter in the doorway.'

Emily brought coffee and cream and a small dish of thin almond biscuits. She looked anxious and Dr Barnes hastened to reassure her. 'The specialist said that there is a hairline fracture in the spine with bruising of a nerve but all this will heal in time. It would help if you rub her back gently each day with oil to keep the blood flow normal and the brace may come off in six weeks or so.'

'Thank you, Doctor,' Emily said, with tears in her eyes. She picked up her cup and retired to the window seat and her crochet.

'I shall take on a girl to help,' Jane said. 'I need someone here when Emily and I go out for a break.' She glanced at her daughter and the doctor nodded. He had seen how pale Emily was and how much the accident had affected her.

'Very wise,' he approved. 'It's good for Vikki to have a change from you and good for you to get out. In fact, my wife asked me to invite you both to tea on Thursday if that's convenient.'

'That will be an opportunity to tell her all the American news,' Jane said, blushing with pleasure. 'The wedding isn't fixed yet but they are making plans. The inauguration of the President comes this year and it seems to take over everything, much more than our elections do. Sidney wants a big wedding, and as it might be lost among the accounts of the elections, they may wait for even longer.'

She shrugged. 'It's a puzzle to me but they all seem to have voted for someone called Warren Harding – so I expect he's a great man. Bert maintains that it's all rigged and that gangsters are the ones who rule America, but I can't believe that! We read about crime and those terrible murders and drugs and drink, but surely if they are violent they shouldn't be allowed to carry guns?'

'Don't believe all that the papers say, my dear. They like to shock us but there is an element of risk as I believe that Mr Hearst can stop anything he dislikes from being printed in the papers he owns, so perhaps we never get the true picture. I hope you haven't stocks in the American market?'

'No. I told Bert I wanted to invest in safe British stock. I've set up a small workshop for three dressmakers who had no permanent workplace. It might be a little moneyspinner and a nest egg for Emily. The other girls know nothing about it and Bert can be a closed oyster when he likes, so I can stay in the background.'

'Well, I must be off. I have another patient to see,' Dr Barnes announced. 'When you go over to Alice next, do tell her to keep to the diet. It really does help diabetics and I hope that soon we may have a drug to help her even more.' He frowned. 'I have to be careful as some silly women get to hear of this diet and use it to get slim. In fact it's quite fashionable to go "Banting", which is named after the man who created the diet and is working on the cure with two other men, Mcleod and Best. They have found a way for humans to replace insulin that the body no longer secretes and take up the excess sugar. Schafer isolated the substance in 1909 but they haven't been able until now to use it successfully. One of my colleagues, Dr Lawrence, will probably die of the disease unless this new drug can be used. He's much worse than Alice and so has offered to take the drug on trial as an experiment. I pray for him to survive and be cured. He's a fine man and a good doctor.'

Jane went to visit her ailing daughter-in-law and came back encouraged. Alice had a new neighbour who kept a close eye on what she ate, and Alice even offered to knit a vest for each of the two babies when they arrived. Edward was happier too and looked more like Walter had done in his youth but without the forceful virility and temper that had made life difficult. Jane walked back from Newport station deep in thought and found Archie in the house.

'You are early,' he said. 'I was coming to meet the next train.' He saw her glance at the door of the playroom. 'The horse has gone,' he said quietly. 'I watched the man load it on to the waggon and I told him to sell it. Was that right? I also told him to make it safe on a base before he sold it or there would be trouble.'

'Vikki loved it so,' Jane said sadly. 'In spite of her toys and treats she doesn't have such a good time as mine had, with so many others to play with in the house.'

'She loves the farm,' Archie said. 'It's waiting for you, Jane. Bring her and Emily and all of them! I have a manager now and take things easy and I've made a lot of improvements.'

Jane kissed him tenderly. 'Some day,' she said gently. 'Not now when I have Vikki to care for and the babies are coming. You are the dearest of men and I love you but I can't leave just yet.'

'And after that? They will walk and go to school and I'll be in my grave!' He shook her gently then held her close. 'I love you and I know we could be happy.'

'Would you give up everything to come here?' she asked sadly. 'No animals and just a patch of garden?'

'I would for you, Jane.'

'And put that burden on me? No, Archie, come whenever you want to and I'll come to you, but I have to stay until my girls are settled with families.' She touched his face, smoothing away the frown. 'Do you know that Walter never once said he loved me, not in those words, even when he was most loving?' She held him tightly in her arms and felt his strength and safety and the grief of not being able to take him to bed. 'One day,' she said, and released him.

'I put two chairs in the room where the horse was,' Emily announced, entering. 'Vikki heard it go and shed a tear or two but I said she could go down to the farm when that nasty cage is off.' She smiled at Archie. 'I rub her back and legs as the doctor told me and she said just now that I tickled, so she must have the feeling coming again. Oh, Mother, someone said they saw Maudie Dove getting on the ferry to Portsmouth.'

'Alone?'

'Yes, but carrying a large suitcase as if she's going away for a while.'

'Why are you two smiling like that?' Archie wanted to know.

'She may be establishing residence as they say, for three weeks of banns before the wedding.'

'You think that Bert will marry her?' Archie looked astounded.

'He deserves a bit of warmth after a lifetime of Annie,' Jane said firmly, 'and if he wants Maudie then why shouldn't he marry her?' She told Archie to say nothing but that Maudie was pregnant.

'Is she far gone?'

'No, but she refuses to see Dr Barnes yet and I think wants to hurry things along before Bert changes his mind!' Emily said. 'She knew that Annie was dying and I think brought this on herself to make sure of Bert before he looked out for another wife! I wonder if she *is* really pregnant.'

'Imagine two virtuous women thinking like that!' Archie said, laughing. 'I didn't know that Maudie had that much sense.'

'Do we give them a wedding present?' asked Emily. 'It will be a nine days' wonder, and people will have forgotten the dates by the time she shows.'

'I wonder what Bert will tell people?' Archie mused. 'Everyone knows about their love nest and will wonder why the rush now.'

Bert came back from a quiet wedding in Portsmouth a few weeks later and announced rather defensively that Annie had helped him with business problems and he needed a wife now to do the same, and to comfort him in his sorrow.

'I almost believed him,' Clare said, 'but I can't think why he wants to *marry* her.'

Jane sat with Vikki and read to her one day when the leaves sent dry reminders that summer was over, and lay thick and crisp under the chestnut tree. It was a time of harvest and waiting, Jane thought as Vikki picked at the woollen hair that Emily had replaced three times on her favourite rag doll. The two sticks that were all she needed now to help her walk lay by her chair and would soon be unnecessary. Lizzie was well and happy but Clare ignored her pregnancy and did everything that was risky, like reaching up to high rails to dust and carrying her heavy shopping even after Alan had forbidden her to do so; however, she remained blooming and pregnant.

And Janey. It was early days for her but she had come back from seeing Clive off to Scotland again, ready to wait peacefully with George for the birth of her second child, content and with a new maturity.

Alex had gone back too, but to another destination. 'I can't tell you what this leave has meant to me, Mrs Darwen,' he'd said as he left. 'This is the only place where I feel I belong. If I had a wife and family, I'd buy myself out of the navy and open a hotel here. I'm not a born sailor like Clive but I may stay in the service for a year or so yet to pass the time, and then come back here.'

'Where would you have your hotel?' Jane enquired, interested.

'My parents suggested that I could take over Old Manor Farm, which belongs to my mother's family.' Alex sighed. 'That's thinking too far ahead to a partnership, though. Who can tell what the future holds?' He laughed. 'Read my palm!'

'I don't hold with fortune-telling,' Jane said abruptly, but sent him away with little presents and a parcel of food.

Bert seemed to think the dolphin door-knocker was made for demolition and Emily hurried to let him in. 'You look all hot and bothered,' she said.

'How is the second Mrs Cooper?' asked Jane. 'I half-expected you to bring her calling on us.'

'Not until you say, Jane. If you can't meet Maudie then she stays out at West Wight!'

'*Bert!* Maudie is your wife whatever the reason for it. You know I don't want her here – how could I? – but the fact remains you married her, she is going to have your child and you are my friend. If Maudie can bear to come, bring her to afternoon tea this Sunday. I'm willing to do it to make people know I support you, but you needn't stay long!'

'You are a real friend, Jane,' Bert said with emotion. 'I've heard some nasty things being said about Maudie and me. The old harpies who gossip respect you and will do as you do, and if we're invited here I'll be able to hold up my head again.' Emily filled his sherry glass for the third time and he sat as if waiting for something more.

'What is it?' Jane asked.

'I'm all mixed up, Jane,' he blurted out. 'Maudie now says she isn't expecting – that it was a false alarm.' He mopped his face with a large handkerchief to hide his emotion. 'I wanted that child, Jane. I didn't know how much until Maudie said it wasn't to be. You've no idea of the hunger I felt for it. I wouldn't have believed it myself a year ago.'

'I do understand,' Jane said sympathetically. 'I wanted every one of mine. Poor Bert – poor Maudie.'

'Poor Maudie? Can't you see she tricked me?'

'You wanted her and you used her, Bert! Before this you had grown very fond of her and now she is your wife and still young enough to give you a child. Be firm but love her. Maudie is warm and good-looking and will make you an excellent wife if you give her the chance.' She laughed. 'Think how the old biddies will tot up the months and find you married her for love and not because you had to! Only a few trusted people know about the false alarm and so it shall stay until we have something better to report.'

She watched him go, knowing from the determined set of his head and a certain jauntiness that Maudie must now fulfil her marital obligations with a vengeance. 'We'll invite some friends and Clare and Lizzie and their husbands, so that I have no need to sit and chat to Maudie,' Jane said when Bert had gone.

'I'll make a fruit cake and scones but I don't see why we should have to give them all high tea,' Emily said. 'If Clare wants more she can bring her own sandwiches!' But when Sunday came there were four kinds of cake, sandwiches and thin bread and butter, and Janey asked if there were a hundred invited.

Maudie looked pretty and well-dressed. Her shoes were well-polished and her lace petticoat which showed briefly when she sat down, was spotless. 'She's come a long way from Sea Street,' Janey murmured when she met Jane in the kitchen. 'Uncle Bert seems happy, too.'

Jane sat with her guest for a few minutes while Bert was in the garden with the others. 'Bert wants to sell up and move from the old address but I don't mind staying if he gives me a free hand to have the house painted,' Maudie said. 'I have to decide quickly where to live as he wants a family.' Jane listened politely and nodded, as if that was only natural. 'It's a long time since I had Lucy,' Maudie went on, 'but I suppose it gets easier after the first. I hate the idea but I always did know which side my bread was buttered and now I can have jam on it.'

'You'll lack nothing with Bert,' Jane said, and Maudie seemed to find her quiet dignity subduing. She picked up her bag and went to find her husband.

He came in to say goodbye to Jane, grinning. 'Thank you for today,' he said. 'I'll walk her along the Mall where the curtains can twitch all they like, and then we'll be on our way. You needn't invite my wife again but I'll be over regular with the papers and to see you about repairs to that cottage.' He coughed and made sure that Maudie hadn't followed him. 'I have left a bundle of papers next door and would like you to take care of them for the present. I want to keep some things private. Annie never did understand business but Maudie might pry and I'll wait until I see I've value for money before I give away any more!'

'You're a hard man, Bert, but it makes sense. I have kept the old bureau that Walter used. Lock it and take the key and nobody need know what's inside.' Her eyes twinkled. 'Keep her on a loose rein Bert and she'll be fine, just fine.'

Maudie came up and pulled at his sleeve. 'Right, gal? I feel like a walk. We'll stroll up to the crossroads and back and pick up the car here.'

'It's blowy and cold!' Maudie objected.

'Pin your hat on then, and put on your gloves. You are on parade, my dear. Come on, Mrs Cooper, best foot forward.'

Chapter 15

'I'm sorry to drag you away from your beau, Lucy, but we have a three week engagement in Palm Beach and Sidney has to go for screen tests.'

'Hollywood isn't far away,' Sidney said and kissed Lucy briefly on the lips to make her smile. 'Cheer up. I am the one to worry as they might not like my voice enough for the talkies.'

'They'll love you,' Nellie said with conviction. 'Your voice is good and who wants to hear "I love you" said in the heavy Bronx accent that some of the silent stars have? In any case you have two contracts for silent films and can't take on much more at present.'

'Yes, two big contracts,' Sidney said with wonder. He hugged Lucy. 'It's all due to you, you dear funny girl. Do you know just what you have done for me?'

Nellie fitted a cork-tipped cigarette into a long amber holder and drew in the smoke, then regarded Sidney through half-closed eyes as she exhaled. 'You aren't married yet and the talkies contracts aren't signed. Don't leave it too long or your sponsor may get restive.'

Lucy looked at him adoringly. 'Sidney won't hear of me leaving you before the year is over. Go and get packed, darling.' She sighed and blushed.

'Well, it's Bradley's Beach Club for the next few weeks and we'll keep a room for you there, Sidney,' Nellie offered. 'It's a good thing that Monty has stopped gambling now, as the casino there is really grand and the stakes high.' She stubbed out her cigarette. 'I'll leave you two to say goodbye,' she said tactfully. 'I'll be in the car in ten minutes.'

'Goodbye, darling,' Sidney said and kissed Lucy with closed lips.

'Kiss me again, properly,' she begged. She took his hand

and placed it over her breast. 'Feel my heart beating, just for you,' she whispered.

'We mustn't, not yet,' he said, but kissed her with greater warmth as she flung herself into his arms, bending her over one arm as he did to his film sweethearts on camera. 'Better?' he asked.

'Better,' she said shyly, 'but I know girls who go a lot further once they are engaged. Perhaps we'll be alone more at Palm Beach?'

'Yes, when we are at Palm Beach,' he said. 'Run now or Nellie will be waiting.'

Lucy giggled and went out to Nellie who was surrounded as usual by admirers. 'Did you wonder what we were doing?' Lucy asked coyly.

'No!' said Nellie. 'Driver, we are ready to leave now. My husband will join us at the station.'

Lucy twisted her engagement ring. 'Some girls say they feel almost married once they are engaged,' she said. Nellie smiled faintly, looking beautiful and very worldly-wise. 'I mean,' began Lucy.

'I know what you mean. They keep their men at bay but let them feel around a little, so to speak! Don't worry, dear. Sidney won't go too far. He lacks a certain . . . curiosity. He had a lot of loving sisters. Just take it easy and let him make the pace.'

'That's the trouble.' Lucy looked sulky. 'He's always too correct and never passionate even though he is very sweet and kind to me. Do you think he'll be better once we're married? I want him so badly that I could eat him!'

'Please don't! His fans would kill you if he appeared even slightly chewed and it would scare him away for ever.' Nellie laughed and waved to Monty who was waiting with the tickets for the reserved compartment.

'Said goodbye?' he asked. Nellie nodded and Lucy went into the compartment. 'Everything hunky-dory?' he asked quietly.

'Lover isn't exactly a Tony Moreno,' she whispered, 'but some British take a long time to warm up and if he doesn't, there are plenty ready to step into his shoes. Lucy has it in all the right places.'

Monty saw that Lucy was near to tears and Nellie was still surprisingly upset over the news of Vikki's accident. I could have two very damp ladies on my hands if they don't cheer up, he thought. 'You can go to your first casino, Lucy,' he suggested. 'I'll stake you for a modest amount but don't go over that as it's a dangerous game.'

'We have the rest of the day to ourselves and I plan to sleep,' Nellie announced. 'I need several things so you'll have to go shopping when we arrive, Lucy.' She was almost curt, and Lucy knew that Nellie liked to be left alone if she was in a mood, so she leaned back in the carriage and closed her eyes to think her own private thoughts and worries.

By the pool at *Vizcaya*, she had seen couples who were not even wearing engagement rings, touching and kissing in a way that showed they were more than good friends. She had envied the caressing glances, and even more caressing hands and the stolen kisses in dark corners under the fragrant romantic nights, but Sidney seemed almost repulsed by anything but cool kisses. She touched her own lips, full and warm and soft and eager for love whenever he was near. She had expected the stars to explode when they finally kissed but nothing had happened, apart from her feeling that a wonderful dish had been removed before she had tasted a morsel.

It's not my fault, she thought. Men admire me and I've been asked out by at least seven in the past week. I wish I'd gone now, she decided bitterly. At least I'd know what was wrong with me! She dozed and Nellie watched her, wishing that the girl was less innocent and vulnerable, and far less attractive.

As soon as they had settled in comfortable rooms, Lucy went off to find the local shops to buy hairgrips, shampoo, a sponge and some white handkerchiefs for Nellie. A voice hailed her; it was low and intimate and Lucy turned, startled. 'Hello, remember me?'

'Yes! I mean no.' Lucy turned away.

‘I can’t think why you avoid me,’ Frank Garsey said. ‘I hoped that we could be friends.’

‘I don’t know you,’ she replied stiffly and went to the counter to ask for the special soap that Nellie preferred as it had no perfume and no harsh ingredients.

‘I’m sorry, we don’t stock that one,’ the girl said.

‘I think there’s a bigger store down the road. This is a two-bit place,’ Frank Garsey said. He smiled at the girl and asked for a bag for the other small purchases and held it while he piloted Lucy to the door. His hand on her elbow was caring and he guided her across the busy junction as if she was a precious child. ‘There it is,’ he said and pointed, then left her alone to continue shopping, but watched her until she disappeared into the store. Lucy was aware of him there but when she came out with the soap, he had gone and she experienced a pang of disappointment.

Nellie was still recovering from a bout of late nights and rich food; she told Monty to take Lucy to dinner and the casino, and to leave her alone with a jug of fresh orange juice. ‘Make sure the management know what I want and see that there are enough hangers in my dressing room. There never are,’ she grumbled. Monty grinned and made his escape.

‘Our Nellie is a bit liverish and best left well alone,’ he said. ‘Come on, Lucy, we can eat at the casino and you can watch the gambling but maybe not have a flutter tonight. First let’s see what is needed in madam’s dressing room.’

The gold star on the pale blue door made Monty smile with pride and Lucy quickly inspected the room. ‘Nellie is right, we do need more hangers and a few more bulbs over the dressing mirror. Could you test the iron, Uncle Monty? The last one fused before we used it, and I have a lot of costumes to press when I unpack the main trunks tomorrow.’

At last they had finished. ‘I don’t know what we’d do without you, Lucy,’ Monty said gratefully.

‘You don’t have to,’ she began then looked sad. ‘Oh, Uncle Monty, I hate the thought of leaving you. Can I come back, sometimes?’

'You're family to us, my dear.' He hugged her and she smiled wistfully. 'If ever you need us, just come and don't bother to let us know. We'll always look after you.'

'Perhaps I'm not ready for marriage,' Lucy said, feeling more cherished than she did with Sidney.

'I just hope that your young man knows how lucky he is! There are dozens of wolves out there just waiting for you to come their way!' He watched Lucy fold a dress with skill, padding the puffed sleeves with tissue paper. 'Even if you didn't work for us, you could always be a dresser with a star as you are so good. I just hope you aren't wasting yourself,' he said abruptly.

'That's silly – you know how the girls flock after Sidney. I get quite jealous at times, but he treats them all the same. Men like him, too. You do like him, don't you?'

'He's fun and amusing and adds to any of our little parties,' Monty said.

'That's not what I mean.'

Monty looked uncomfortable but saw that she wanted a real answer. He pulled his wide brimmed fur-felt hat over his face to hide his expression. 'Come on, I need a steak. Sidney isn't what I call a ladies' man, is he? But then he isn't exactly a man's man, either. He likes people, but there are men who have a low libido through no fault of their own and they can't do anything about it. If anyone can make him spark, you can, Lucy. He's very fond of you.'

'Fond?' She slipped back into her long silky cardigan that came almost to the hem of her short skirt. 'I want him to love me, not to be fond of me as if I was a pet kitten!'

'You need some good red meat and tonight you must drink a little wine to put the colour back in your cheeks.' He hailed a cab and they went to the casino restaurant. 'We'll take in the show as well so that I am not likely to disturb Nellie when we go back.' He laughed. 'They'll wonder why I'm here, as I turned down a good offer for Nellie to appear. They show some cheap trash, with girls taking off most of their clothes and that's not our style, however much they pay.'

'I'll have grilled salmon,' Lucy ordered. 'Salad, but no potatoes.'

'That's what you always have, except for the time on the *Mauretania* when you *did* have potatoes with it at every meal.' Four men in dark suits passed the table, their hooded eyes taking in the scene. Monty turned to watch them. 'They are professional gamblers,' he said. 'They go round a circuit of casinos and make a killing.' He lowered his voice. 'A killing in more ways than one at times, if rumours can be believed.'

Lucy sensed their sheer animal magnetism, a fleeting sensation she had had when Frank Garsey took her arm. It was not so much attraction, rather a kind of stimulation and an awareness of their potential. The girls on stage danced, dipping tall ostrich feathers on diamanté headbands. They smiled as if afraid to appear tired but the lights, ever changing, filtered through pastel blue to deep purple and pale pink to old rose and ochre, flattering the powdered skin. 'We could use that lighting sometimes,' Monty murmured. He saw that the four men sat looking at the audience and not at the dancers and told Lucy it was time to go to the casino. He didn't like the way one man eyed her, and he walked Lucy past their table quickly. Lucy seemed unaware of the glances following her from others as well as the four men and Monty was relieved to be in the bright lights of the gaming rooms.

'You can have ten dollars in small chips,' he said. 'It's only a little and you needn't come again if it bores you.'

'That's quite a lot,' Lucy said and sounded worried. 'I'd hate to lose your money.'

'You needn't lose more, and I'll charge it up to publicity as it's good to be seen in these places.' A flash made Lucy start. 'See what I mean? You are with Nellie and are engaged to Sidney Darwen so you are interesting now. It's secondhand fame but useful to a point. Be careful, though, Lucy. These reporters can ask you questions that tie you in knots.'

'What could they ask me?' Lucy laughed. 'I'm always careful to ignore questions about Nellie, Uncle Monty.'

The journalist came closer, encouraged by her smile. 'Will you let me have one of the pictures?' she asked.

'To be sure! It's a pleasure to have a pretty face in our paper.'

'Is it one of the Hearst papers?'

He began to look cagey. 'No, we are an independent, fairly new journal but our circulation is rising all the time as we print the truth.' He mentioned the name and Monty tried to push past him. 'Come on, Mr Morris, give me a break! I know you spent some time in *Vizcaya* and my readers want to know all about it.' He tried to look pious. 'It's their right to know what goes on there and the Hearst papers hush up everything they want swept under the carpet.'

'If you print a lie that we gave you an interview, I'll sue your paper and report you to the Senate!' Monty was furious and half-scared.

'Miss Dove! You could give me the low-down. You must have seen the illegal drinking and snorting and the hectic nightlife? Is Miss Davies in love with her new leading man and do the guests swim naked in that fabulous pool? You've got to give me something,' he pleaded.

'Come on, Lucy.' Monty gripped her arm firmly. 'Never speak to scum like that and always ask what paper they represent before you let them take a picture.'

'I can't tell him anything bad if that's what he wants. Everyone was very nice to me, or nearly everybody,' she added.

'That's the bit you keep under your hat!' growled Monty. The reporter followed them. 'We'll watch the roulette in here,' Monty said. 'Later, we can play the pinballs and watch the poker in another room but the blackjack room where they play for high stakes is no place for a lady.'

'When's the wedding?' The reporter tossed a chip on to number seventeen and eyed Lucy in a friendly way.

'Soon,' she said, and Monty smiled.

'How soon? May I quote you on a date? Or is this just a stunt to show the world what a straight guy Sidney Darwen is?'

Lucy clenched her hand over the chips and sent two flying on to the numbers just as the croupier called '*Rien ne va plus*'. She bent to pick up the others and so did the reporter. He whispered, 'Where does Ivor fit in with your plans?'

'Ivor?' Lucy said but heard Monty give a shout of triumph and the croupier pushed a pile of chips over to her. 'I didn't place a bet!' she said.

'Maybe it was by accident, but you won! Give me the winnings to look after and keep your original stake. That way you never really lose more than the ten dollars you started with. Now choose again.' Lucy was excited and a large man pushed the reporter aside and took his place, hoping that the girl had a lucky streak that might rub off on him.

'Eleven won and that's Sidney's birthday, so I'll play that again,' she said. Monty saw her win three times more and then lose the ten dollars. 'That's enough,' he said as she turned to ask for some of her winnings. 'We haven't time to play the pinballs and Nellie will wonder where we are.' He noticed her over-bright eyes and wished they had gone to a movie, but she followed obediently.

'Who is Ivor?' she asked. They were drinking coffee in the suite and spoke quietly so as not to disturb Nellie, who was asleep in the next room. Monty choked on a biscuit. 'The reporter mentioned him just as I won and then he was pushed out of the way and didn't get near me again. A man of that name answered the phone once when I rang Sidney. He sounded very grumpy.'

'I didn't know he was still in the picture. Sidney had a row with him and they parted. Ivor Sinclair was Sidney's manager at one time but did nothing for his career.' Monty wondered what Lucy really thought.

'So he's English, too? Sidney came out with a boy called Herbie Walters. What happened to him?'

'Oh, he married and has a family out west where he runs a small hotel. Sidney apparently visits them from time to time. Sinclair became his manager when Herbie left.' Monty set his jaw. 'His real name is Snitzler, but as German names were unfashionable he changed it. If a reporter asks about Sidney and Ivor Sinclair just clam up: just as you must about Nellie and me,' he added hastily.

'I have this feeling that everyone knows something that I don't know, and yet I can't imagine Sidney ever having a row with anyone. He's sweet and kind and I know he'll look after me well. I am sure that I can make him love me as much as I love him.'

'I'm awake and feel fine now,' Nellie said, popping her head round the door. 'Before you undress, would you go down and fetch some spa water for me, Lucy? I can't get room service but the bar will have it. I've drunk pints of water and fruit juice and I know I'll want some in the morning.'

Lucy went down to the bar and brought the bottle back. She put a hand to tap on the half-open door of their bedroom then paused, her attention caught by the words she overheard. 'That little heel means trouble,' Monty was saying. 'If the Press begin to whisper it they'll think there's no smoke without fire.'

'What does it matter so long as Sidney isn't meeting Sinclair any longer?' Nellie asked.

'If it was that easy! Creatures like Sinclair are similar to jealous wives – they never let up.'

'Who means trouble?' Lucy asked, walking in. 'That reporter, or the man called Ivor Sinclair?'

'Both,' said Nellie and Monty left it to her. 'Sinclair is jealous because since he left, Sidney is getting better and better parts and he loses the ten percent he had as his agent. Don't worry about him, Lucy. You'll soon be married and need never see the man.'

Lucy relaxed. 'He sounds nasty. I think I'll go to bed now. I suppose Sidney does need a manger or an agent. He's not as good as you at money and contracts, Uncle Monty.'

'I'll help him – keep it all in the family. You don't want a strange man travelling with you everywhere, do you?'

'You are so good to me,' Lucy said and blew a kiss from the doorway.

'Oh dear,' Nellie said when the door closed. 'It was fine at *Vizcaya* but now Sidney is in the open and alone. Hollywood isn't as fussy as his Bible-punching sponsor and the mid-west! Thank heaven he has two contracts firmly signed.'

'It might be as well to push the wedding forward,' Monty said in a low voice. 'He's very fond of her, he's very ambitious and it might work but don't forget – hell hath no fury like a woman scorned and that Ivor is a bitch!'

Lucy sat on her bed and sipped orange juice. She felt excited about winning and recalled her mother after a successful flutter on the horses. I hope I'm not getting like her, she thought. The telephone rang discreetly under the frilled Dresden shepherdess cover. 'Miss Morris is not to be disturbed,' Lucy said.

'Call for Miss Dove.'

'Sidney! Where are you? I've missed you so much!'

'I'm still in Hollywood and I want you to come over for half a day if Nellie can spare you. They want pictures of us for two newspapers.'

'I can't come tomorrow, but the day after I'm sure I can.'

'That's marvellous, darling.' His voice seemed to change. 'I had dinner with my sponsor and he suggested it. He's here now and would like to speak to you.'

'Hello, Miss Dove,' said the gravelly formal voice. 'Sidney tells me you are about to name the day and I suggest we do just that before the cameras. It's as well to get the record straight before the press print a lot of lies. That does no good to my pictures!'

'It can't be soon enough for me, Mr Gunnar, but I promised to stay with Miss Morris for a year when they brought me to America.'

'I applaud your honesty in sticking to a promise, but you can get married and stay with her while Sidney goes on location and is far too busy for a honeymoon as such.'

'Does that mean you really do want him in your talking pictures?' she asked breathlessly.

'I signed him up today but we'll keep it for the Press until you get here.' The telephone changed hands.

'Sidney? Isn't it wonderful!'

'I can't believe it. They like my voice and my face and want to get started right away.'

'Mr Gunnar seems in a hurry to get us married. I think under the crusty surface he likes me.'

'He does, Lucy. Who couldn't like you? I love you, and want you to be happy, but I . . . have things on my mind and you may find me boring.' His voice broke. 'So many people are pulling at me in all directions, and I never ever want you to be hurt.'

'Meet the noon train from here the day after tomorrow,' she said. 'Goodnight, my darling.'

Smiling, she slid out of her satin cami-knickers and pulled the sheet over her naked body. It pained Sidney to admit he loved her and he was shy about marriage but that would all come right later. She slept lightly, hoping to dream of his face but the face that intruded was dark and intense and had the fascinating undercurrent of violence that she had sensed in the four men and in Frank Garsey. She shivered and found the bedclothes on the floor. Lights from the street were too bright and she went to close the curtains securely. The casino was still humming with business, and her two chips lay on the dressing table. I'll have to go back some time; I can't waste them, she thought with a sudden sense of daring and anticipation.

Chapter 16

'That's enough!' The publicity man waved his clipboard and stood between Lucy and the cameras. 'Be nice, fellas. Miss Dove has been very patient.'

'One more? Show a bit more leg, Miss Dove!'

Lucy smiled politely but shook her head. She had been pictured sitting, standing, looking pensive and gazing into Sidney's eyes. There were two shots of them kissing and Lucy wondered if she would always have to be kissed in front of cameras if he was to show passion.

'That's real good,' Mr Gunnar said. 'I've ordered English tea and muffins for you to eat in private. Lucy my dear, you are an asset to us all – the perfect picture of modesty. The public will love you! I might even give you a test for the movies, but that must wait. Just turn up in eight weeks' time for the wedding, and all the world will see you.'

'It all sounds very public for a wedding,' Lucy ventured.

'In Hollywood everything is public. We'll see to your dress, the food and the place and you can choose the music,' he conceded. 'Not too much, and not too sad but a hymn that everyone can sing.'

'I hate fuss and I want to slip away for a few days after it with Sidney,' she insisted.

'It's written into my contract that I can go away for two days.' Sidney was apologetic. 'We can go for a longer holiday after the first film is made.'

'Have they finished with us?' Lucy said. The trolley of tea things was ready and they were finally alone.

'I feel ten feet tall,' Sidney said, and hugged her tightly.

'Because you love me and I love you?' she whispered. He kissed her tenderly. 'Eight weeks more and then we'll be together for always,' she said. 'Why should we wait, Sidney? Take me now, my darling, and we can remember this when we are apart.' She threw down her jacket and kicked off her shoes. The bed on which they sat moved across the floor as she flung herself into his arms, and her body fell across his lap. She pulled him down to rest his head on her breast and for a moment he tensed but then held her close and kissed her lips with more passion than he'd ever shown.

She saw that his eyes were tightly shut. He was pale, and the emotion with which he held her owed more to desperation than lust. 'It isn't wicked,' she reassured him. 'We needn't go all the way until we are married, you dear old-fashioned man!' His hand was cold on her breast and he was trembling. Lucy drew away, ashamed. 'You think I'm a forward huzzy. I'm sorry.'

'It isn't that. I just don't deserve you, Lucy. I can never be everything you want.'

Lucy saw the door open slowly and went to the bathroom to tidy her blouse. Mr Gunnar stood by a waiter with a fresh supply of muffins. 'I thought I'd join you,' he said, and Sidney welcomed him with effusion.

Lucy felt vaguely resentful and very deflated, but ate two muffins and made bright conversation nevertheless. 'I have to get my train,' she said at last.

'My chauffeur will take you to the station. I want to talk to Sidney,' Mr Gunnar said. Sidney kissed her again and Lucy hardly noticed the journey back to Nellie and Monty and the warmth of their love.

'Sidney should have come back with you,' Nellie frowned. 'Monty and I have to go out tonight and you'll be alone. It's too bad. I know how restless I feel after a camera session. You need company, but we can't get out of this date.'

'I'm very tired and may go to bed early,' Lucy said.

'We'll creep in and not disturb you,' Nellie promised. 'Eat down in the restaurant. André will look after you and it might be more interesting than food on a tray.'

Lucy took a hot bath and turned out clothes that she had not worn for some time. Some needed discarding but she was so busy with Nellie's wardrobe that she neglected her own. She found the slender silk dress she had worn on the *Mauretania*, her first gift of love and care from Nellie. She put it on and found the beaded jacket that went with it, feeling again the pleasure she had experienced on that first occasion. The restaurant was half-empty and André sat her by a palm where she could watch the talented black pianist who would appear later, and yet be private.

Should she have her usual grilled salmon? She smiled. Tonight she would do everything in a different way so she ordered clam chowder and veal in a creamy sauce. Lucy looked up when the waiter brought her soup and saw that Frank Garsey sat a few feet away at the next table. He smiled and she half-smiled back then bent over her soup. The waiter brought a scribbled note and Lucy hesitated then nodded. It seemed silly to sit apart in a very safe public place when at least he was someone to talk to. Garsey came and sat with his back to the room, making an oasis of privacy while the waiter laid a place for him. 'I drink water,' she said when the waiter brought a bottle of sparkling wine.

'This champagne is sweet and light,' Garsey shrugged. Lucy sipped the wine, thirsty after the salty clams. 'You are wearing the dress you wore on the *Mauretania*,' he commented. 'It's beautiful – but not as lovely as you.' His eyes took in the curve of the soft breasts and slender arms and Lucy blushed to think he remembered. She drank more champagne and then water as she was suddenly afraid, but Frank Garsey chatted quietly on about people she had seen, places he thought might interest her and amused her until the raspberries and cream had given place to cheese and coffee. By then, Lucy was wondering why she had ever mistrusted this charming man.

'I must go,' she said at last. 'Nellie might be back and needing me.'

'Surely not,' he said smoothly. 'Nobody goes to bed at this hour and I sleep badly, so you must take pity on me and walk for a while and come back here for a nightcap.'

Lucy opened her bag to find her handkerchief, and the two gambling chips fell out. 'A gambler?' Garsey said in mock horror.

'I've been there only once with Uncle Monty,' Lucy explained.

'You ought to cash them in,' he said. 'We'll walk over and cash them or put them on a number.' Lucy followed him slowly, half-hoping that Nellie would appear to rescue her. 'I feel lucky,' Garsey said. He flipped a coin. 'There! It came up heads. That means I have to place a bet or two. You must let me stake you for a small sum,' he suggested.

'No. I have money,' said Lucy firmly. 'I shall use my own and not go over a certain amount.' She walked more quickly, aware that she felt excited.

'You are right, of course.' Garsey shrugged. 'It is very moral and very boring but I understand that a good woman can turn a man away from sin.' She laughed. 'There have been so many rumours about the stars, but one picture in the newspapers of a face as innocent as yours dispels all evil and unworthy suspicion.'

She tore away from the hand that held her arm as they entered the casino. 'Are you making some kind of sneering remark about Sidney?'

'Not me, but many do,' he replied calmly. 'I'm only jealous. I bought a couple of papers and it breaks my heart to have you look at him that way and not at me. I fell for you when I first saw you on board.'

'I want to go back to the hotel,' Lucy said, but he led her firmly into the bright lights.

'He will have you for the rest of his life. Give me just one evening with you, Lucy, and afterwards, if you say so, I'll go away and never trouble you again.'

Somehow she found herself sitting at the table with a pile of different coloured chips in front of her. She pushed them to one side as she knew they weren't hers and brought out her two discs. 'Sidney,' she whispered. 'Bring me luck.' She put them on eleven and won. She bet again and Frank Garsey put piles of chips at random on the board. He laughed as his were raked in and Lucy won again then held her hand as if he shared her excitement, and she felt a thrill of danger and attraction. She gathered up her winnings. 'I do very well on my own,' she said smiling, 'but now I've had enough. Sweet champagne gives me a headache and I'm thirsty.'

Reluctantly, he picked up the chips he had tried to make her accept. 'I hoped to have you in my debt,' he said and she knew that he wasn't joking. At the kiosk, she was surprised at how much she had won, and gasped when she saw the value of the chips that Garsey had pressed on her. If I'd taken them and lost I'd have owed him hundreds of dollars, she realized.

She glanced at the expressionless face, the smooth skin and the mouth that promised sensual pleasure at which she could only guess. Her hand, tucked into the fold of his arm tingled with awareness and he captured the other hand and smoothed the palm and made tracings over her wrist. The small coffee shop by the lobby was empty but Lucy insisted on ordering coffee and refused to go to the bar. 'Has Miss Morris come in yet?' she asked the waiter.

'An hour ago. She left word not to be disturbed until nine tomorrow morning.'

'You'll have to go in quietly,' Garsey said.

'It's lucky that here the rooms are quite separate and I have my own door to the corridor,' Lucy said, then bit her lip.

'We could have coffee there,' he suggested but she shook her head vehemently.

She drank two cups of coffee and smiled. 'I've enjoyed this evening, Frank,' she said.

'And now I have to give you up to Sidney Darwen!'

'We are to be married,' she reminded him.

'Wait a few more minutes while I finish my coffee,' he said, and took out a silver snuffbox. 'I suffer from catarrh.' He took white powder and sniffed it discreetly from the dimple by his thumb. 'Have some? It will clear your headache and make you sleep.' He placed a large pinch of the powder on her hand. 'Sniff it all at once and then breathe deeply,' he said.

'What is it?' Lucy sniffed and breathed in. She thought she would choke and then her head began to reel. Frank Garsey pulled her to her feet and walked her to the elevator. Lucy was walking on a cloud of feathers and the walls dissolved as they went into her room and he laid her gently on the bed, her hands hanging limply over the edges. He kissed her lips and his hands smoothed her hair and throat. He kissed her ears and closed eyes and she dreamed that she was watching this happen from a great height. He smelled good and her arms came up to hold him close. His kisses made all other kisses seem as mild as the touch of flower petals and his hands undressed her with relentless gentle purpose.

Colours throbbed through the room and her skin felt cool, with breasts taut and fit for fondling by the gods. She couldn't open her eyes but imagined she was with Sidney and he was doing everything that she had longed for but with this compelling expertise. 'That is good?' he said softly, as she moaned and moved under him. He pressed down and there was pain and a great feeling of release and explosive satisfaction. Her body arched and her fingernails tore bloody tramlines down the smooth skin of his back.

It was over and Lucy felt wet and ill. She began to cry slowly with shuddering breaths and felt sick. Her teeth were chattering and he covered her with a sheet. 'Listen to me,' he whispered harshly. 'You wanted me! You wanted me and I was the first! You have to come to me now, Lucy. I want you more than any woman in my life. You haven't a hope if you live with that queer!' He began to dress and eyed her with apprehension. 'I was the first and there'd be hell to pay if this got out! You must never tell anyone about tonight but we must be together soon for ever, to enjoy each other as we did now.' He kissed her and she clung to him. 'Your Sidney has a male lover,' he whispered. 'He can never rouse you as I did tonight!' He laughed softly. 'Believe me, my darling, you are dynamite. There'll be no need of coke the next time.'

'Where are you going?' she groaned.

'I have to be in Hollywood tomorrow. Forget me if you can, and make believe he really loves you, at least until you are married. I can wait until you find out what he's really like.'

When he had gone, Lucy felt along the walls to the bathroom and sank into a cool bath, then washed the sheet and hung it to dry by the window. Her dreams were strange and her eyes seemed to bulge outwards.

Nellie tapped on the door early and Lucy blinked and shook herself back to sensibility. 'You look terrible,' Nellie commented.

Lucy dabbed her runny nose. 'I may have a cold starting,' she said.

'Stay in bed! You have done everything to the dressing room and I can manage now but for heaven's sake stay away from me!' Nellie was terrified of colds. 'I'll send the maid with some breakfast.'

To her surprise, Lucy could eat scrambled eggs and toast. She drank cup after cup of strong coffee. Her nose was still sore but eventually she felt better although very depressed. She passed the time by ironing everything that needed it, then put the dress she had worn the night before out for cleaning. The telephone rang and she answered it, holding the receiver as if it might attack her. 'Lucy? I wanted to tell you I love you. In one way I'm sorry about last night but in another way I wouldn't have changed the smallest moment.' The voice was as soft and seductive as she recalled.

'I think I hate you,' she said clearly, and hung up.

The telephone rang again and she said her name listlessly, thinking it was Garsey again. 'Lucy? Have you seen the papers? The news of our wedding is everywhere and you came over so beautifully.' Sidney went on to tell her how impressed Mr Gunnar was with the film rushes and she listened to the warm brotherly enthusiasm.

'I hoped that you rang to tell me you loved me and that you would never have a lover,' she said, the tears flowing down her cheeks.

'Lucy! We are to be married and I promise I'll never look at another woman! You must know how much I owe to you and I'd never hurt you.'

'What about other men?' she blurted out, past caring.

He gasped. 'Don't listen to people who are jealous of me and hope to ruin my career. We are going to be married and we'll make a success of it.' He paused. 'I'll be with you soon, my darling, and we'll show the world that we are meant for each other.'

Lucy put down the receiver. He'd said those words in the film test. 'If I acted with him I'd have more passion,' she decided – and knew that something had died.

'I left Nellie in rehearsal,' Monty said, coming in and sitting heavily on the bed. 'Her new leading man is tall and strong and makes a good foil for her.'

'Are you sure that they can be trusted?' Lucy was only half-joking.

'Nellie has a way with men that they can't resist, but I can trust her. We have our spats at times but that's only natural, and it adds something to our real feelings. Believe me, Lucy, we do love each other.'

'Sidney never argues,' Lucy said. She sat on the bed and swung her legs like a child in her short linen dress. 'Sidney never kisses me unless I make him do it. He never cares for touching and yet he's so sweet and gentle.'

'Snap out of it, Lucy! You sound as if you're coming up from a snort! It isn't like you to be depressed.'

'What do you mean?' she asked sharply.

'You must know. Some people use cocaine in a white powder that they sniff up to make them bright and happy but it doesn't last. After a while it's a habit they can't shake off and it ruins lives.'

'It sounds horrid,' Lucy shuddered. 'I met Frank Garsey in the restaurant last night, by the way. We went to the casino to cash a few chips I found I had left.' It was as well to tell Monty a little as someone must have seen them together. 'He tried to lend me money for chips but I refused and did as you told me. Even then I made quite a lot of money. I feel better now after a nap and I don't think I'm having a cold after all.'

'I don't like to think of you with Garsey,' Monty said uneasily. 'He's a bad lot, Lucy, and a menace to women.'

'At least he notices them,' Lucy said bitterly. 'Don't worry, he's going away and I shan't see him again.'

'That's fine. Now Nellie was talking to Mr Gunnar on the phone and he agreed to let her choose your wedding dress and not to doll you up in something you'd hate. You are a celebrity now and it's good for all of us.' He showed her a headline: LUCY, THE GIRL WHO MAKES EVEN THE MOST HARDENED NEWSMAN WISH HE HAD A DAUGHTER LIKE HER. There was a whole article on how Lucy had come over on the *Mauretania* to see Sidney Darwen, and how they'd been childhood sweethearts. Monty saw her disbelief. 'You'll get used to it. The studio gave them this information and Sidney filled in the background. Nellie answered any questions that didn't hurt you. You see, Gunnar wants to present you two as the perfect married couple, above reproach. He's willing to spend thousands to exploit that fact and get you launched.' He laughed. 'There are always men who will back a pretty face if it pays them, but this way it is safe for you.'

'What ways aren't safe?'

'They say that Garsey has a very exclusive little cathouse in New York – that's *his* way of exploiting women! And Marion Davies is a star only because Hearst backs her.'

'I need some air,' Lucy said suddenly. 'The casino was stuffy and I drank some sweet champagne. Do you need anything in the drugstore?'

Monty regarded her with a worried frown. 'If you feel you can't go through with all this, then say so now, Lucy. We'll back you whatever you decide. You aren't tied to him yet.'

'To Sidney?' She smiled. 'I know how he feels and I know that I shall never mean as much to him as his work does, or be first in his heart, but I love him and you mustn't worry, Uncle Monty.'

He left her alone, passing her a note that had been pushed under her door. Unsigned, it just said that Sidney Darwen was staying at a certain motel with his lover Ivor Sinclair if she wanted to check on him. 'Goodbye, my darling,' she said, and tore the note into shreds.

She pulled on a pretty hat trimmed with cornflowers and poppies, and carried a long thin cardigan that matched her pale pink dress. The foyer was busy and no one saw her leave. By the sea along the boulevard she breathed in the warm humid air and saw everything as in a dream again. Couples laughed and held hands, a boy kissed his girl by an ice cream stand but she had no partner and no place in the scene. Was death like this, looking down on others in an impersonal way without pain?

A man pulled at his wife's sleeve and said something. The pile of newspapers showed Sidney kissing her with all the passion that a bridegroom was expected to show and she smiled modestly from the pages. More people recognised her and she felt threatened. Lucy hastened towards the busy shopping complex to escape into the crowds. Would it be like this after marriage? Sidney showing the public how much he was in love with his young wife, and then . . . nothing?

The lights at the crossing blinked brightly and she saw the shop she needed on the other side of the busy street. She stepped out and heard a scream as a racing noise exploded inside her head. It's not peaceful, she thought as she lost consciousness.

Chapter 17

'She may die and then Sidney will never marry,' Jane Darwen said. Her hand shook as she read the letter again.

'You keep on saying that,' Emily objected, puzzled. 'I pray that Lucy may get better but if she doesn't, Sidney can take his pick of pretty girls. It may not be as bad as it sounds. She is young and healthy and may recover even if she can't walk.' Emily's voice trailed away. How could anyone recover from such terrible injuries? After six weeks, it was still uncertain if Lucy would live.

Jane stared at the newspapers that Nellie had sent rather than write a letter to explain, and she wondered how anyone could be so insensitive as to publish pictures of the girl lying in the hospital bed like a dead thing. Sidney's long letter told her that once Lucy regained consciousness, he would marry her and care for her even if she was an invalid. The papers painted a picture of a frantic and sad lover who swore eternal fidelity and had to be comforted by his sponsor Mr Gunnar and his manager Mr Ivor Sinclair, who hardly ever left his side.

Jane told nobody that she had gone to the Catholic Church on the other side of the Island to light candles for Lucy's recovery, but Emily sensed that her feelings were more complex than she admitted. 'We must get on with life here, Mother,' she said firmly. 'With three new babies coming there won't be time to worry about Sidney, however sad he might be, and Vikki needs us as much as ever.' She smiled. 'Clare is so big she can't travel in the sidecar now and gets very cross. She's due in February and Lizzie in March and Janey after that, but far enough ahead to give us a breathing space.' She put down her crochet. 'I think I'll make another little jacket for Lizzie. This gets so heavy now. I'll put it away until after the babies are born.'

Jane folded away the papers and made tea. 'I'll write

today and tell Sidney to buy flowers for Lucy from us instead of sending us ridiculous presents like that large print. We must write to Lucy and have him read the letters to her. They say that even in a coma people do hear a lot, and we must make sure she knows we love her.'

Emily laughed. 'We certainly don't want another picture.' They had gone all over the house to find a dark spot where the colours of the last one could be hidden.

Mrs Barnes had stared at it and chuckled. 'It's very fashionable,' she said. 'I have read about the artist, Maxfield Parrish. His *Daybreak*, with all that purple and rose and castles in the sky is really quite pretty, I suppose. It sold a million copies, apparently. Alex has one by Duchamp that he keeps in his room and I believe that Janey has a print that can't be hung in the hall in case the vicar sees it! *Nude Descending a Staircase* is very rude, in my opinion!'

'Is Alex coming home soon?' Jane asked Emily. 'I wish that Clive would consider leaving the navy but he's as keen as mustard.'

'Yes, Alex is leaving for good, soon.'

Jane watched Emily start the delicate knitting for the matinée coat. 'I wish you were doing that for your own baby, Emmy,' she fretted.

'I'm content, Mother, and I'll never marry. Lots of people need my help and the babies will be a joy. I can help Alex, too, a little if he wants my advice but don't ever think I'll set my cap at him! He never looks at a girl now, except of course Janey, and we would never get on in that way.'

'He's a brother to you all,' Jane agreed, but Emily only smiled. They sat by the fire in the morning room and added fresh coal to the blaze in the open grate by the side of the new red-tiled Yorkist range. It was as near to the old black one that Jane could buy but far more convenient, and like the old one never went out, winter or summer, while the new gas cooker in the kitchen remained fresh and rarely used.

'Why do you worry about Clive now, Mother? You used to be so calm about him as if he was protected from danger. The North Sea is nearly free of mines by now and he'll be home just after Christmas and again in May when the new baby comes.'

'You're right, Emily.' Once more Jane shook off her superstitious fears.

Bert Cooper seemed to be thriving these days, she mused, her thoughts wandering to their recent encounter.

'You look like a cat with a saucer of cream,' she had said when he visited the house on the Mall. 'Some people make money by touching it!'

'I do all right,' he admitted with a grin, 'but it isn't that. This time, Maudie really is expecting. The doctor says so!'

'Oh, Bert! I'm so happy for you. There's nothing to compare with holding your first baby in your arms!' She chuckled. 'You managed that well, and I never thought Maudie would buckle down to running your home so efficiently. You look well-fed and contented.'

'She wasn't pleased at first but after hearing about Lucy she seemed shocked and now she's written to Sidney. After you had her to your house, she found people far more friendly and now enjoys handing out cups of tea to all and sundry! They can't say she *had* to get married, either.'

'Everyone is having babies,' Clare moaned when she was next with Janey in the car. 'I'm sick of people asking how I am and talking about births.'

'Well, you have a very nice home for yours when it comes,' Janey said. She was amused that Clare had slavishly copied the crimson flocked wallpaper of the house on the Mall, the deep blue stair carpet with brass stair rods and the white painted banister rails, but knew that the outer warmth hid an inner chill that even the coming baby didn't warm.

'I wish that Christmas was over,' Jane said. 'We wait and wait for the babies and the days are dark and short and depressing.' Clive came home and brightened the two houses with his humour and affection but Jane hated the newspaper cuttings from America. Sidney appeared in dark suits as if he was already in mourning and Lucy remained in a coma.

Janey saw Clive off on a biting day in January and then

brought George over for the afternoon. She paced the house and Jane let her roam, worrying at the thought of Clive under all that grey cold water. Emily played the piano for her and it seemed to help and when Janey set off for home, Emily insisted on going with her to stay the night. It was the first time she had offered and Jane was glad to see that Janey accepted readily.

George had supper at the Lodge and the girl who helped put him to bed while the two sisters played cards until bedtime. Janey slept soundly and put out a hand to where Clive should be as she felt the child stir inside. She woke and recalled that by now her husband would have been ferried out to his submarine from the frigate that took the relief crews back to port. She turned over and went to sleep again and Emily left her to rest while she got up, gave Daisy orders for the day and made breakfast. She saw the rain lashing the windows and wondered if her duty was with Janey or with her mother, as Janey wasn't alone in the house, but when she was dressed, Janey seemed pale and fretful. 'I hated to see Clive go this time,' she admitted. 'It was so grey and miserable and I think I may have a cold starting.'

'Go back to bed and I'll stay for a while,' Emily promised. 'The rain is easing off and Daisy can take a message to Mother and bring the groceries on her bicycle.' Janey dozed and looked hot but not really ill and Emily waited to see how she would be later.

The evening news came crackling over the wireless set that Clive had bought before he left and Emily listened, fascinated by the voices from the air. Storms had swept the east coast, apparently, and two fishing boats had been lost. Emily bit off a thread and began a fresh side to the drawn thread-worked table napkin.

'Mines have been sighted in the Channel. A minesweeper that the authorities thought might go back into dry dock as it wasn't needed is now on its way to clear the area,' an announcer stated. Emily hesitated. Clive had said that the set should not be used all the time as the accumulator battery might give out before the next one was charged.

Also, she didn't want to alarm Janey so she switched the set off. Clive would be back in that horrid slug of a boat now, safe and deep under the waves.

Janey was still hot later on and complained of a headache. Emily suggested telephoning Dr Barnes. Janey smiled weakly and said she'd do so as Emily was scared of using the instrument. Alex answered the phone. 'I thought you'd gone back?' Janey said, surprised.

'My ship is still in dock,' he replied. 'I can stay here but report to Portsmouth each day for orders.' He promised to pass on a message to his father and Janey staggered back to bed, knowing that she had caught a chill on that last cold day with Clive, walking in the West Wight. 'I'll come if you need anything,' Alex added, but Emily spoke on the phone too and told him firmly to keep away until she rang again, in case Janey had the 'flu.

The next day, Janey felt much better and asked for lots of water and fruit juice to drink. 'Why not ask Alex to come and play cards this evening?' she suggested.

'Not until you are downstairs and dressed.' Emily saw the loose hair and feminine curves lightly hidden under the thin robe and thought that Alex would have more peace of mind if he only spoke to Janey on the telephone.

A pale sun formed a square on the wall and Janey made up her bedroom fire and sat dreaming. The doorbell rang and Emily spoke urgently to the maid. 'You are not to disturb her, Daisy. Give that to me!'

'But it *is* for the missus and I hates them buff envelopes,' said Daisy obstinately. From the landing Janey saw Emily rip the envelope open and put a hand over her mouth and look up to her sister.

'Clive?' Janey swayed and clutched at the banister rail and Emily ran up to save her but Janey fell heavily, knocking Emily sideways.

'Don't just stand there, Daisy! Run for Dr Barnes and say we need an ambulance urgently.' Emily sat on the floor and lifted Janey's head on to her lap. She was still trembling with shock and the words of the wire ran through her mind. '*We regret . . .*' A stray mine, wallowing on the surface, had touched the naval launch transferring crew to the submarine, and destroyed it.

'Clive?' Janey stared at her.

'A mine destroyed their boat,' Emily sobbed, knowing there was no way of lessening the impact of the news. Within an hour, Janey was tucked up in bed in Ryde Infirmary and Jane and Emily shivered in the draughty corridor while the doctors did what they could.

'Holy Mary, is there no end to this?' Jane mourned. The news had hardly been a surprise, but Janey and the baby were her concern. Dr Barnes had hinted that the baby might not live but Janey was well enough.

'Go home, Mrs Darwen,' the Sister said kindly. 'We'll keep you informed.' Alex came to take them home and George was already transferred to his room on the Mall with Daisy to look after him. Alex had locked up the Lodge and turned off the water in case of frost and Jane hugged him as she would her own sons.

They sat and waited for morning, unable to think of going to bed and Emily prepared an early breakfast. 'Clare is coming over today, Mother. She and Alan don't know about the accident yet. Shall I send a card by first post to put her off?'

'There isn't time! Alan has the day off and has borrowed a car from a friend to bring Clare here for dinner. It will have to be mutton stew and bread and butter pudding.' It was soothing to do homely things in the kitchen but Jane dreaded having to tell the others that Janey would lose her baby.

'Mutton stew?' Alan Dewar walked into the kitchen and rubbed his hands together. 'We came early,' he said. Emily glanced up: it was only eleven o'clock. 'I expect Clare would like a cup of cocoa and I wouldn't say no,' he added.

'Well, haven't you seen enough of the rich and famous,' Clare said, riffling through the new magazines. 'They are lucky! Some of the men at Cowes don't know where the next wage is coming from.'

'You are lucky, too, Clare.' Emily was pale. 'Sit down

and listen.' She told them the news and Alan blew his nose hard. Clare only picked at her glove and tossed her head.

'She should never have started that baby,' she said. Outwardly, for the next few hours they were a family and even laughed at things that George did and said, but Emily spent as much time as she could away from them all in the kitchen. Alan played with George and offered to take him out the next week, spoiling his offer immediately by saying that he knew they would do the same when his baby was born.

'Janey will need a lot of help,' Emily pointed out.

'What about me?' Clare followed her into the kitchen. 'I shall be ill but I haven't heard you offer to have me here to look after me.'

'You have everything settled with the midwife and Dr Barnes, and you are strong and healthy,' Emily said. She felt near to tears again, and still in a state of shock.

'It's afterwards I shall hate, but when I suggested to the midwife that I wanted to put the baby on the bottle straight away, she was quite rude.'

'You might enjoy breast feeding, and Alan will certainly love being a father,' Emily said as George laughed, playing bears with his unclc.

'I'm not a cow! And I shan't let Alan have much to do with it as he'd spoil any child. I'd be glad if you'd help me with the baby, Em. I really don't like children.' Clare's laugh was harsh. 'I'll call it after you if it's a girl – Emily. No, Emma is more genteel. That's right, it will be Emma and you can be aunt and godmother and have her for all I care!'

Emily hid her delight. 'You'll change your mind, Clare,' she replied as if it meant nothing to her. She tipped away the washing up water.

Alex arrived with flowers for Janey and asked if he could see her. 'Not for a few days,' Jane said firmly. 'She is well over the miscarriage and it isn't good for her to brood. She needs young George to make her do things for him and make her tired out!' She saw his disapproval. 'Janey has lost a baby but is still healthy,' she pointed out gently. 'She is grieving and that will take a long time to heal, but she will be home within another week.'

'That's too soon,' Clare said. 'When I have my baby, I am going to stay in bed for at least three weeks, the nurse said I could!'

'Janey can go to bed here and get up when she feels like it but George will have her on her feet soon enough!' Jane saw that Clare meant to stay for supper so she sent Alex to buy meat pies and asked him to stay, too. He talked well and even made them laugh at things that Clive had said.

'I hope you talk to Janey like that,' Jane said to him later, in private. 'It will do her much more good than to sit with a long face. She'll need the broad shoulder of a man who knew Clive so well.' She eyed Alex with speculation. 'You will be here for a few more days before your ship sails, Alex. I know that you are very fond of my daughter, but don't tell her so yet. After this, go away for a while. She may want you, she may not, but give it time.'

'I'll wait for ever, if necessary,' he said with absolute determination.

Jane shivered. Archie had said those words and she had not had the courage to marry him, but Janey and Alex were young and Janey needed a father for George. She smiled sadly. I turn to Archie each time I need him, she thought, and Janey will do that with Alex. Annie Cooper would have accused me of matchmaking and must be turning in her grave to see the bright paint and pretty curtains flung back from her windows, but life must go on.

By the end of the week, Janey could speak of Clive without weeping and George was delighted to have his mother back again. Alex left for Gibraltar and Janey clung to his hand before he left the house in the Mall, her face thinner and very beautiful. 'Did he talk to you about his plans for a hotel?' asked Jane.

'A little, but it's only in the planning stage as yet,' Janey said.

'I might have to lend him Emily,' Jane said cheerfully.

'Emily?' Janey looked confused. 'I suppose so. I couldn't go there, could I?' She took a tuck in another skirt to make it fit and looked pensive. 'I'll go home soon, Mother. I must know how I feel in the Lodge. As yet it seems that Clive is simply away and will walk in through the doorway, smiling.'

Jane gulped. 'That's how I felt when your father was away. It never leaves you, but dulls in time. Does it worry you that Clive has never been found?'

'No. The sea was where he was happiest and I couldn't bear to follow his coffin and see it sink into the ground. I can look across the water now and think he is out there, somewhere. I loved him so much and I know I can never really lose him.' She picked up a small scuffed shoe. 'I wanted a daughter for our family to be complete.' Janey burst into tears and the two women sobbed for an hour, tears that embraced Clive and Lucy and the dead baby and Jane's own dead children, but Walter was far away.

When Archie arrived, it was no surprise. 'Jane my dear,' he said, and gathered her into his arms. 'I heard today and came as soon as I could but there was a new calf.'

For one heavenly minute, Jane relaxed in the luxury of the strong masculine embrace and then, as she did each time, moved away gently. It put everything into perspective. 'I'm glad you spared the time now,' she said, smiling.

Chapter 18

Emily smiled when the telephone rang, as it did every day now if Archie was too busy to visit them. 'He's fine,' Jane said. 'It's turkeys he's raising now, the dear man! He wants us to go down next week and see the chicks.'

'You go today, Mother. Now that Janey is better and is playing golf with Mrs Barnes we have more time, but next week, we may be busy if Clare has her baby.' Emily looked annoyed. 'She hasn't given up the idea of having the baby here, even though the midwife has all the rubber sheets and linen there, and Alan has made a nice cot for the baby. I'll take George to look for sticklebacks. It may be too early in the year but he'll be happy getting wet with a net! I like to leave Janey free to do something different as George is a very demanding boy now, and she needs a few treats.'

Winter boots felt heavy now that the sun shone with more confidence and Archie had made his yards mud-free, so Jane put on stout shoes and wrapped up well, eager to see the farm again. 'I didn't expect you!' Archie said. He hugged her and kissed her on the lips.

'I'll go away if I'm unwelcome,' she said, laughing.

'Never that! Come and see what we've done.' He went before her with the enthusiasm of a boy and Jane followed more slowly, noting the well-painted wicket fence and the general air of good husbandry and prosperity. The new turkey shed reeked of pine and pitch and the windows were wide open to let it dry out. 'I want no disease here,' Archie said. 'In three years I aim to have the best breeding stock in the south of England. Next week when the new chicks come I'll put oil stoves in this small enclosure where they'll live for a while until they harden off, and I've fenced in a big plot for them to be in the fresh air later.'

'It's long-term planning,' Jane said.

'That's farming and life, Jane. I can't sit around biting my nails, waiting for you to leave the Mall and come here to me.'

'We both have responsibilities, Archie. Until they are safely delivered and can manage, I have the girls. Vikki is less of a care now as she stays with Janey quite often and loves George. She wants to go there for a few weeks while Clare has her baby. I think she's afraid she might have to look after it! She's right, and I refuse to let her be a slave to Clare and Lizzie. The walk from the school to the Lodge is good for her legs and she is really quite strong now.'

'Good! At last you sound as if you are clearing decks for action. Bring Emily and hide here until it is all over.' Archie looked at Jane in such a way that she had to pick up a handful of straw and hide her own emotion.

'I'll not shirk my duty any more than you did, Archie. I miss the horses but I'm glad you took them, and the gaps get filled.' The memory of so much hung between them.

'Come inside, Jane. There are no ghosts left if that's what stops you from marrying me.' The farmhouse door no longer stuck at the top and let in draughts at the bottom. The main room was covered with fresh linoleum and a carpet square, and thick rugs lay by the fire. Jane glanced around but could not see the tiny room where Rose had died of tuberculosis. 'I had it blocked off,' Archie explained, 'and use the room where we stayed to be near Rose as a store now. I have moved upstairs in comfort.'

'I'll come here more often now,' Jane said. They walked in the yard. 'It certainly smells better in here!'

'I got rid of the pigs except for one to eat the swill and give us a bit of bacon. The cows went before the last frost and I've only a couple of calves left for market. From now on, it's poultry and flowers for Emily if she still wants to make bouquets and decorate churches for weddings.'

'It sounds grand, just grand!'

'It could be better,' he said and kissed her so tenderly that she almost said she'd marry him. A distant train whistle brought her back to reality and she fixed the pin to her hat and buttoned up her coat.

'I said I'd be on this train and Janey is meeting me with the car at the station on her way back from the golf links,' she said.

'Take some eggs if that's all I can give you.'

'You give me more than that, you dear man.' She reached up to kiss him 'I'll bring George down to see the chicks.'

Janey was waiting and asked about Archie. 'He's trying to impress you, Mother,' she joked when Jane told her about the improvements. 'He thinks you might marry the turkeys even if you don't want him! Why don't you?' Her tone was brittle and despite the joke, she looked unhappy.

'I might, one day.'

'You must do as you want to do, Mother – just as you did when you gave up the shop. You deserve it but you are lucky, too. You have me and George and the others with their babies. I shall never have another child and when Clive died all that died, too.'

'You've been so brave,' Jane said. 'I don't talk about it but I admire you and love you more each time I see you.' She glanced at the pale face. 'You have so much love around you, Janey.'

'That kind of love, yes.' Her expression softened and she made no attempt to open the car doors when they reached the Mall. 'Am I wicked, Mother? I cry out for Clive in the night and want him there to make love to me and fill me with another child. It's not just in my mind, it's physical.'

'I know that, too,' Jane said softly. 'I felt it when your father was away for two years, and it was even worse when he was here, long before that . . . when it wasn't safe to have another baby.'

'Was it as bad as that? Oh, what must you think – Clive has been gone for such a short time and I talk like this to you!'

'Walter came back, that's the difference. You need love just as I did and you'll marry again. You must. You can't go through life as you are. Just let the tide take you and find its own time.' She thought of the letters that came from Alex every few days. Janey read them eagerly. It wasn't in her mind yet but it would come if she felt no guilt. 'George needs a father,' Jane said definitely. 'He is a big boy and getting naughty. By the time he goes to school he'll need a firm hand and a slipper to his little bottom if I'm not mistaken!'

'I won't come in, Mother.' Janey kissed her cheek. 'Thank you, Jane Darwen,' she said softly. 'You make life easier to bear.'

Jane's eyes were misty when she reached the front door. It was open and Emily was waiting for her, looking very disturbed. There were voices from an upper room and Jane tore the pin from her hat and shed her coat quickly. 'What's wrong?' she asked.

'It's Clare.' Emily's face was red. 'She walked all the way here and sits there refusing to go home.'

'She often does that!'

'Having labour pains?' Emily took away the telephone receiver. 'It's too late to ask Janey to take her home. Clare saw to that. She was having pains every fifteen minutes when she started from home and there isn't time to move her now!'

'Does Dr Barnes know? And the midwife?'

'They are both here. Clare sent a message to the midwife that she was having the baby here and also left a message for Dr Barnes.'

Jane sat on the stairs. 'We'll just have to put up with it then, Emmy. In a way it's better than having to be at her beck and call at Shide. I shall send her home after a few days for the nurse to cope with her.'

'Don't go up. The midwife said she'd call when she needs something. Alan came with all the sheets and rubbers and it looked as if they'd planned this for some time. There was even a neatly packed bundle of first clothes and binders! We need a strong cup of tea!' She saw her mother's reluctance. 'Come on, there are plenty up there to see to her. Remember the tea we had on the hob all day at Coppins Bridge? It tasted better than from a silver pot just warmed.' She led the way to the morning room and the old brown teapot that now purred on the top of the range. 'We are going to need gallons of this,' Emily said firmly. She poured out the brown liquid and added a generous tot of whiskey and sugar.

'Glory be! It's wonderful,' Jane said, laughing. The clatter of feet made her go to the door. Behind her the kettle sang and the bowl of instruments and string sat ready for the midwife who now took it but refused offers of help.

'You sit there and try not to worry,' she said. Jane nodded and took a second cup of tea.

'Dr Barnes will enjoy a cup. He's had enough of them in the past,' Jane said when they were alone again.

Emily giggled. 'I feel quite tipsy, but we must try not to worry, the midwife said! There's nothing for you to do, Mother. I cleaned the tiny bath and put it in Vikki's room and lit the fire. The cot is ready and well aired.'

'It's not just the Irish tea, is it, Emmy? You are excited!'

'I'm going to love this child as my own,' Emily said. 'Clare will never love it properly so I shall, but I shall never let on to Clare.'

Screams from upstairs and a frantic knocking at the front door coincided. 'She timed that well,' Emily said dryly. 'That will be Alan back again!'

'You can't go up,' Jane told him. 'Have a cup of tea instead. I think that Emily put a drop of something in it for our nerves. Drink it and thank heaven you've got a healthy wife.'

Alan sat down thankfully. 'I'm not much good at times like this,' he said apologetically.

'Men aren't,' Jane said, and wished she liked her son-in-law better. 'You can do more once she's home in a few days but you'll still have the nurse in each day.'

'Clare says she's staying here for three weeks. She knows very little about babies.'

'She'll go home as soon as the doctor says she can,' Jane said firmly. 'She'll never learn about babies if she has it all done for her, and she *does* know about babies. There were enough in our family, and she helped out with the neighbours for a few coppers when she was saving up for a bicycle!'

A cry from the newborn baby shattered the tension. 'Well, one of them is in fine voice,' Emily said. Her eyes sparkled and she tried to hide her impatience.

The midwife put her head round the door. 'It's a girl and they are both fine,' she grinned broadly.

'May I go up?' asked Alan jubilantly.

'Just for five minutes, and then leave her to sleep. Your wife told me she had to walk all this way, having labour pains,' the midwife added reproachfully.

'She was lucky to find anyone here! We didn't expect her as she was having the baby at home,' Jane said sternly, looking at Alan.

'But last week you said, Mr Dewar, that . . .' The midwife fled, followed by a very embarrassed new father.

'So it *was* all planned,' Emily said. She looked angry. 'I might have gone to the farm with you, and little Emma would have been born in the gutter!'

Upstairs, Jane bent over her own child and smoothed the damp hair from her face. 'I'm sorry, Mother,' Clare said, and picked at the broken nail on her finger. 'Is she all right? She hasn't this, has she?'

'That was an accident, not a family thing to be passed on as well you know, Clare. If you felt you had to come here, then you had to come but this is a precious time that you must have with Alan and the baby. I took a peep and she's lovely. He's bringing her in now.' Clare touched the tiny cheek and Jane breathed a sigh of relief that the child wouldn't be rejected.

'Is everything all right?' Jane asked Dr Barnes as he packed his bag.

'Your daughter has a lovely child with all the good looks of your family. You fey Irish might say that she has the look of someone who has been on this earth before. Let's hope that Lizzie is as fortunate.'

Jane sent Alan back to work and said he ought to keep his free time for when Clare went home. He had the grace to blush and apologise, but Jane's goodbye lacked her usual warmth. Emily held the baby when nobody was looking, savouring the smell and the soft snuffling to get at a breast. She put the child in the cot and went to find her crochet. It was very heavy now, but very beautiful. Clare doesn't want it, she thought. I'll save it for you, Emma. You can have it when you get married. She wrapped it in black tissue paper to keep it white and put it away carefully to finish when she knew that Emma was ready to get married. The knitting was lighter and grew fast, and she finished another small bonnet before bedtime.

Alan drove to Cowes to tell Lizzie the news and she put a hand to her side as if she felt labour pains, too, but it was another month before she herself emerged from labour, startled at the force of birth and vowing that she was far too delicate to have any more children. She looked down at the infant Henry, who had none of the Darwen features, but Lizzie told everyone that he was the image of his famous Uncle Sidney. 'He'll be so good-looking and not a nasty rough boy. I can see it now,' she added as she wiped away a dribble and tried not to be disappointed that he wasn't a girl to dress in frilly things.

Bert brought gifts for Clare while she stayed with Jane and neighbours visited. Clare made the most of her two weeks in the house on the Mall before going home to tell her neighbours about her trials and to lord it over Lizzie.

'I miss Vikki but we need a little time to ourselves now, Emily,' Jane said. 'Clare would stay for ever if I had let her, but she's fine and the baby is no trouble at all.'

'I'd have the baby any time she wants to leave her but I daren't suggest it as Clare is a dog in a manger and would rather keep Emma away if she thought I might be fond of her. Even Alan isn't allowed much contact so no wonder he's joined the working men's club at Cowes with Harry.' Emily smiled. 'That doesn't suit Clare as she thinks she's a cut above that.'

'We'll go and see Alice next week. Dr Barnes informs me that his friend who was so ill and went abroad to die is now better, thanks to the new drug, insulin. He has some in stock for Alice.'

'Let's wait until the sea is calm,' Emily suggested. 'I want to go to the Great Exhibition in London as well, Mother. We can buy the latest records there and I said I'd try to get *Sonny Boy* for Lizzie. It's a pity that Henry is so plain but Lizzie will see him as Sonny Boy and enjoy weeping over him!'

Janey collected her mother for the day saying they both needed a change, despite the threatening weather and high wind. 'Vikki picked a lot of primroses and we can take some over for Lizzie. If I drive you there it saves the walk from the train. Vikki has a piano lesson and George can play with Daisy and then pretend to have a lesson when the teacher has gone.'

The sea at Cowes by the Royal Yacht Squadron was wild and grey beyond the line of small cannon pointing out to sea ready to fire signals to racing yachts and visiting royalty. Many small boats moored at the river mouth were swamped and Janey looked out to the line of spray of a force nine gale where sky met sea the same colour, then she turned back. 'I'm cured, Mother,' she said. 'I saw the primroses and remembered when you were so ill and the flowers helped. You recovered and so shall I.'

They had tea in a café by the shore and went home as the evening darkened. Winds howled over the river and the car swayed like a leaf. Janey put on the headlights. 'I thought the floating bridge would sink on the way over and I'm glad we aren't going back that way,' she said, laughing nervously. They went down Snook's Hill and Janey braked sharply. Water streamed across the road from a gap in the parapet overlooking the river. The wall of a house hung away and dropped as they looked, fascinated and astounded, and the huddled woman who had lived there was taken in by neighbours.

'It's all going,' Bert Cooper bellowed as he waded ankle-deep in water to reach them. 'Water seeped through the Sheaths' cellars and flooded into the shops. They say the whole row will have to be rebuilt. Pity you didn't ever sell.' Jane looked up at the open devastation that was *Darwen's* and saw that the tenants had never changed the wallpaper

Sidney had had in his attic room. A brass bedstead with a chamberpot under it was exposed and undignified, and she turned away, her head bent.

'It's over, Jane,' Bert said gruffly. 'Leave it all to me.'

Chapter 19

'You're both soaking.' Emily stirred the fire into a blaze. 'What on earth happened?'

'Telephone Daisy and say I can't get home tonight,' Janey said, her teeth chattering. 'She'll be glad to stay as it's not safe out on a night like this.'

Emily saw their shocked faces and ran to put the kettle on to boil. She used the telephone and then brought warm slippers for the two women. Janey sat breathing in the fumes of the strong tea and spirits and closed her eyes.

'The shop went in the flood,' Jane said simply. 'I never knew just how much I disliked the wallpaper in Sidney's room until I saw it exposed, and someone had left a dressing gown on a brass bedpost as if they had just got into bed. It made me feel undressed.' Her teeth began to chatter again.

'It's no longer our home,' Emily said soothingly. 'I'm glad it's gone! Now they can build the wall they have wanted there for ages, and have no shops on the bridge. This is where we live now and I hated seeing the old place in other hands.' Her forthright words were like balm.

'You're right, Em,' Jane sighed. 'We shall all grieve for what it meant to us in so many ways, but now I'm glad it's all over.'

Emily watched the colour return and the faint smile of relief on her mother's face. 'I've a hotpot I made for tomorrow but we'll have it now,' she said. 'They say it's good to talk of old times at a wake and you both look shrammed but not all that tired.'

'A wake? Yes, I suppose it is a wake – and this will be the last time we may have together, just we three, to share memories in the right way, without Lizzie and Clare to spoil it,' Janey said.

'We used to do this in Ireland,' Jane said. 'It's good to be able to laugh as well as cry over the past.' She helped herself to more tea and felt a great peace forming in her mind. The talk flowed and the firelight and the laced tea made them all warm and relaxed. They remembered things long forgotten, joys and hidden sadness that until now they had never confided, and were shriven of the past. Even Janey who had been so raw with sorrow and guilt, laughed gently and felt better.

'It all came true,' Jane said at last, gazing at the tealeaves clinging to the sides of her cup. 'Walter forgot his green thread and had to borrow when he went away to the war, Clare and Lizzie married the men she saw, and Sidney will never marry.'

'Who is the she that saw all this, Mother?' Janey interrupted. 'I know you are fey but not that fey.'

'Old Mrs Lee read my cup, but I felt that she did not need the tealeaves. She told me about Clive, my love, and about Jack leaving home, but you see, when I heard that Sidney was going to marry Lucy I hoped desperately that Clive would be spared, that the spell was over – but she was right after all.'

Jane unfolded the letter that Nellie had written to her telling of Lucy's death and the awful vulgarity of the funeral. Photographers had climbed over other graves to get the best shots of the mourners. '*Sidney looked very handsome and distraught as if it was all his fault and not that of the driver who ran into the poor girl. He swears he'll never marry now and had to be helped from the graveside by his sponsor and his manager Ivor Sinclair,*' Nellie wrote. '*Lucy was very dear to Monty and me and I tried to keep things as dignified as I could, Mother, but she's dead now and life has to go on. I have dropped a note to Maudie but I may not write for a long time but hope you keep well,*' she ended formally.

'And Sidney will never come home again,' Janey said wisely. 'His life is out there with the film stars.' She wondered if her mother knew the truth about her own son and was glad that he was far away. 'But you will see Sidney again, Mother. I kept it a secret but his first talkie is coming to Portsmouth soon and I have tickets for you and me and

Emily. Not a word to Clare who would love to go! There were only four spare tickets and we need them!'

'Four?'

Janey blushed. 'Alex reserved them for us. He is coming home to do a desk job in Portsmouth for a while before he gets his discharge and sets up the hotel. He'll be on the Naval Reserve, though, and if war comes again he'd have to go back. If the hotel fails then he might apply for a shore posting in the navy again later, but I know we can make it work.'

Emily smiled. 'Has he asked you to marry him?' she said simply.

'Am I wicked? I love Clive with all my heart and yet he seems to be there in Alex now as if they were one. I can think of Clive with great tenderness and see his face when I look at George, but Alex needs me and I need him.'

'Mrs Lee said that you would find happiness after a great loss,' Jane said to ease Janey's misgivings, and mentally she asked the Holy Mother to forgive the lie.

'Did she really? And what about Emily?' Janey asked eagerly, her eyes shining with new confidence.

'Emily has her own inner happiness,' Jane replied and knew that this was true with no need to glance at the future.

'Emma will fill my life if I'm careful and never let Clare know how much I love her.' Emily laughed. 'Maybe there's a bit of an actress in me, too.'

'What did Mrs Lee tell you, Mother?'

'She said I'd never want, Janey, and that should be enough for a woman of my age!'

'She told you more than that.' Janey eyed her with curiosity.

'A lot more that I've forgotten,' Jane said firmly. 'I prefer to make my own destiny.'

'With Archie?'

'And what would I be doing with another man after so many years?' Jane asked blushing.

'What all married women do,' Janey said dryly.

'There'd be bed and underwear and I'd be embarrassed,'

she said frankly, and when the telephone rang they were all spluttering with laughter.

'*Archie*!' the two girls said and pushed Jane towards the door.

'I know it's late but I've only just heard.' Archie's voice came over the line, anxiously.

'You're a dear man to call me, so you are, and I'm fine if that's what's bothering you. It's a relief to know it's all over.'

'That sounds very final, and yet you sound happier than you have done for ages.'

'I am happy. All the bad things have come and now I can feel free.'

'Free to marry me, Jane?' She smiled at the eager, almost boyish voice.

'Let's say we can have a long courtship and allow the gossips to have a good time. All my ghosts are gone but you need the farm and I need people. I love you better than any man after Walter and I shall come to the farm to stay from time to time if that suits you, if I can bring Emily, too.'

'Bring the whole bang shoot of them if that means you come to me,' he said, his voice shaky with emotion. 'Just to see your face across my table and to feel you close will be enough for a start.'

'Have you bought the new rabbits? You promised one to George and Alex has made a big hutch for it,' she said to make him come down to earth.

'I'm investing in more sheds for birds and making a deep pond by the orchard for ducks,' he began, and Jane listened for five minutes, smiling as Archie told her of his plans. The dear man, she thought. He's wrapped up in his beasts and crops and the flowers for Emily and he doesn't need me there, any more than he'd fit in on the Mall doing nothing. She only half-listened, dreaming of Janey's wedding and knowing that again she would hold a child of hers. With five grandchildren how can I bother with ducks, she thought.

'Archie,' she said at last. 'The girls need their cocoa and

I have to get to bed. Bring the rabbit for Georgie when you come to Sunday dinner and we'll walk up the Mall and back again and make all the curtains twitch.'

'Now, who could that have been?' Janey asked with mock innocence.

'It was himself, telling me all about his ducks,' Jane said. 'I'm going down to Wootton to stay for Whitsun and you can take that silly smile off your faces.'